the tears of *hope*

BOOK ONE OF THE TRILOGY

PETER A. HUBBARD

ISBN 979-8-88945-000-9 (softcover)
ISBN 979-8-88945-001-6 (ebook)

Printed in the United States of America.

Brilliant Books Literary
137 Forest Park Lane Thomasville
North Carolina 27360 USA

THE MENTOR

"We had a plan, a good plan, but like all plans, once we war-gamed it, we discovered it would not have survived the first few minutes of battle. So now we have created several plans and strategies; you might call them one for each force element. You will be self-tasked on your timetable under your command and control. You will have just one primary target, with a secondary only if the primary becomes compromised. You will be expected to work from our data and fit into our overall timing schedule. Still, the logistics, personnel, weapons, delivery systems, and exit strategy are for you to create. And only for you to know. It's your backside, and we trust you to keep it in one piece out of self-preservation if nothing else." The two people, one at the penultimate stage of a brilliant career, the other still radiating the bloom of the fast-tracked youth, sat opposite each other, the late afternoon sun creating exciting shadows across their faces.

"Imagine you committed an atrocity—an act of terrorism so vile that literally, half the world would be trying to either kill you on sight or incarcerate you forever in a deep hole, you would never see natural light again. Imagine that others, like you, committed this heinous act in parallel to you another five or even six times in the same seventy-two-hour period. Thousands, possibly tens of thousands, dead or worse, broken, maimed, or damaged and mentally scarred for the rest of their lives. Predominantly collateral damage, civilians, real innocents of the finest type, with a small mix of real targets, but sadly in the minority. Where would you hide, for the rest of your days, assuming that you were still alive at the end of it all. Where?" The general's piercing green eyes bored into the young woman, looking for the faintest sign of discomfort. The woman smiled back, completely at ease, confident and comfortable with the concepts being discussed. After all, war was just politics and the projection of power by other means, however and wherever politicians might apply it.

Their cause was possibly the most just cause ever underpinning a warlike action.

And the woman was a warrior.

Trained from an early age to instinctively follow the Code of the Warrior to the point of death.

"Sir, the only place that would be safe."

"And where would that be?" the general asked, somewhat amused by the sense of calm that seemed to exist between the two of them, given the nature of the discussion and the difference in their experience, rank, and age. The woman smiled again, twisting a small gold band over and over between one thumb and forefinger.

"Sir, the only place where people like us could survive. In plain sight."

CHAPTER 1

The solemn Conclave of Cardinals moved in rustling procession, two by two, into the bowels of the Sistine Chapel, to start the laborious process of electing a new Pope. By Apostil Law, revised as recently as 2005, only a strictly controlled number of ordained cardinals could enter this most revered sanctuary of the Catholic Church, while any cardinals over eighty years of age either waited outside or lingered in their beds, ignorant and uninformed, just like any other Catholic.

Thus, so it was on the tenth day after the sudden and unexpected death of Pope Pious IX.

The Conclave cast its first collective vote at exactly eleven hundred hours, following a moving celebration to rival any Mass ever held anywhere in the world. One hundred and twenty old men, dressed in flowing dresses and capes, rich in texture and embroidery, more so in history and pomp and circumstance, made their way one by one to the golden chalice and dropped in their most secret wish.

Although due to the natural politicking that surrounded any event related to a shift in power, not really much of a secret as you might expect.

Eleven cardinals waited patiently outside, ministered to by acolytes trained for the task since early childhood, protected by one of the finest private military forces on the planet. The extensive staff of the Conclave members mulled about in the central courtyard, well aware that in just a few hours, some of their members would be instantly elevated beyond the level of any Rock groupie by virtue of the fact that their "man" had been elected to the highest office of the world's richest and, arguably, most influential political entity in the world.

Outside the Vatican, just three cardinals remained, too old to qualify for voting, too frail to travel to the heart of the Church and stand to watch outside the doors of the Chapel with their peers.

And on this most important of days, the Vatican Museums were closed to the public, all outside doors and access points shut and bolted, and guarded at street level by City Police wearing black bandanas, with their caps reversed as a mark of respect.

Thousands of people flooded the public spaces, watching the proceedings as they were on large video screens strategically positioned all over Rome, anxious to discover who the church's new leader was and, therefore, the titular head of the Holy See would be.

One TV camera was fixated on the small smokestack, which would announce either success or failure of the voting process, and one camera was permanently focused on the balcony high above Saint Peter's square, where the new Pope would acknowledge both his victory and his new flock with his first official public appearance.

When the mushroom cloud suddenly erupted from the heart of the Vatican, sending out a massive pulse of light and wind, every screen went blank, electronic noise replacing the talking heads and static camera views. It took just a split second for the rolling thunder of the enormous air burst to break free of the twelve-hundred-year-old Vatican walls and wash over Rome, following a shock wave so powerful, it flattened everything not built out of solid rock or stone, all the way out to the De Vinci International Airport, where massive jumbo jets and smaller aircraft were suddenly flipped on their backs or simply crushed against the terminals, caus ing passengers to spill out onto the tarmac like spaghetti out of a tin can.

Those lucky enough to be far enough away from the epicenter of the blast were given the most magnificent view of a majestic climbing mushroom cloud, with a burning sun at its core, the previously blue sky now streaked with white and sooty grey contrails, supported by a cast of thousands of spot fires, smoke bellowing up into the atmosphere like a canvas from Dante's Inferno.

And while the less informed somehow construed all this as an act of God, their inability to make the connection between what their senses were telling them and reality could not change the fact that a critical component of the history of mankind had just been evaporated and turned in the blink of an eye into the fourth state of matter, right down to the subterranean core of the hidden tunnels and caves below the Vatican that had held the vast majority of the secrets and treasures upon which the very myth of the Church had been established for the last two thousand years.

It was as if the perpetual commercialized sham of Christmas and Easter had suddenly, irrevocably, been given back to the pagans. And as if to accentuate this point, the magnificent bronze sculpture "Sphere Within Sphere," created by Arnaldo Pomodoro, measuring four meters in diameter and weighing several thousand kilos, was found some time later wedged into the reconstructed floor of the Coliseum, one and a half kilometers away from where it had previously resided in the heart of the lawns in the center of the Vatican Museums, bruised, dented, and now resembling a caricature of its former self.

CHAPTER 2

On the outside, he looked younger than his true age. On the inside, a vastly different story. Several serious arguments between the unyielding ground and the aircraft he was flying during his early years had left their scars, even creating the need for some major replacement surgery as time wore on. Not that they were all his fault, as he was quick to say, claiming that at least three were due to extremely unfriendly people shooting at him for reasons never explained. But he never let any of this show, his slow smile hiding any discomfort, his deep blue eyes daring you to look elsewhere. He carried no wallet, folding any bills in half on the rare occasion he had any, stuffing them in a back pocket. He wore no watch but had the uncanny knack of knowing the exact time anywhere in the world, night and day. His shirts were all of one type—loud, multi-colored oversized Hawaiian, and his shorts, faded to the point where the casual onlooker would fear he was naked, only ever changed their length, from above the knee to just below. And right now, he appeared to be fast asleep on a sun lounge, on the edge of the Great Barrier Reef, off the eastern coast of Australia.

I watched his chest's rhythmic rise and fall, a small forest of light grey hair puffing out along the midline of his unbuttoned shirt. Deep down, I loved this man to bits; his vast intellect, quick wit, and exceptional ability to cut straight to the heart of the worst imaginable situation. Still, at the same time, he was the single most difficult person in the world to work with, and on the many occasions when I got stuck with him, he had never let me forget that I was not only his junior in every aspect but also beholden to him for my position in Interpol. He was never nasty about it, but clearly, it was payback for my sins, of which I was well and truly aware. But we made an effective team, having solved some of the most notorious cases together in the last few years, and I know he respected both my opinion and my skills.

"Colonel, are you awake?" the officer with me asked, impatient to get on with the business of delivering us both to the waiting helicopter I had arrived in once I had managed to find out where my devious Boss was hiding this time. As the policeman leaned forward to shake him, a scratched, dirty, grey Sig-Saur P226 suddenly appeared in a meaty fist, pushed right into the face of the cop.

"ID, now, and get on your knees." The policeman literally pissed himself, the stain spreading down his kakis with a flourish as he bounced back away from the sunbed.

"Colonel, enough!" I barked in my best parade ground voice. He turned his head slightly, looking at me from the corner of his eyes.

"And who the fuck are you?"

"Captain Riley, Interpol, sent here to specifically collect your sorry arse for reasons as yet unknown. Sir." I stared him down, daring him to embarrass me even more in front of the already apoplectic cop, but all I got for my trouble was a grunt as he sat up, tucking his favorite brute of a pistol back into the waist of his shorts. "Well, why didn't you say that in the first place?" he asked in the most innocent voice I had ever heard. If you knew my Boss like I did, then you knew what a bullshitting act he was putting on for the hired help, but at least he seemed to be with the program momentarily in that he sprung to his feet, slipped on a pair of decrepit sandals, and gestured to me to set the pace.

"Lead on, dear Captain, lead on!" he mocked, smiling evilly at the poor embarrassed police officer. I turned on my heel and headed for the grass clearing, knowing he would follow me without further issue. He was like that. Create an instant storm in a teacup, get everyone offside, and then conform as politely as the best-behaved person you have ever met. But woe betides the person that took him for a fool, or for granted, they could count the remaining seconds of their self-mage—and sometimes even their life—on the fingers of one hand. I had seen him, literally, destroy princes and presidents with no more than a few well-chosen words, the odd thing being that the angrier he got, the quieter he became, and in that state, a more dangerous man I had yet to meet.

Or shoot.

I jumped up into the open door of the Navy Seahawk, helped in by the gunner, who then reached out to pull my Boss in. The gunner, hiding behind his glare shield, gave no indication that the casual beach costume was an issue, my first clue that there was more going on here than I knew about. As if to prove the point, the gunner handed him a "go" bag, a long military green sausage made out of Kevlar, which looked like it had a life of its own, judging by its sleek surface reflected the inside of the Seahawk. Obviously, the chopper team had been briefed, a detail that my head office in faraway Lyon in France had failed to mention.

"Don't look." And with that, my mentor and tormentor stripped to his jockey shorts and pulled on a soft blue-grey military style-flying suit, complete with socks and flying boots. Last but not least, he slipped on a lightweight armored vest, shoulder holster rig, and flight jacket, all faded and slightly crumpled, giving me my second clue. He was expected, or he was known to this crew or the people who had sent this ride and me, and they had provisioned it specifically for his benefit.

Why wasn't I surprised? I worked with this man in the field sometimes for months at a time, but I had still not worked out how he was connected to the various military forces around the world that often provided backup for us, sometimes to the point where it seemed that he owned them.

Intriguing, but not out of character for one of the smartest men on the planet. He had been involved in some of the most violent actions imaginable in the last thirty years. I know because I once read about some of them, which had been declassified and used as case studies for law enforcement agencies around worldwide. He was a pilot who had flown many different aircraft under combat conditions, crashed a few times, survived, and then been recruited into a branch of the military that didn't have a name, let alone an address. Then he became a lead investigator within Interpol with amazing political, legal, and military authority, a technical expert in weapons and tactics, a counter-terrorist activist, and a strategic thinker. And he took off and hid from the world at every opportunity.

And he didn't seem to have a direct report, other than the occasional vague reference to "the general." But which one? A military general somewhere, the head of Interpol, or the secretary general of the UN?

Dressed and now sucking on a can of soft drink sprawled against the bulkhead, feet up on the canvas seats, he looked as if he didn't have a care in the world.

He motioned me to put on my headset, which I did, more to keep the brain-scrambling noise from the chopper out than to obey him.

"Okay, sweetheart, what's up?" he asked, his voice distorted by the aircraft intercom system. "And we're private, just us two, so let's get down to it, shall we?" His evil grin did nothing but remind me how much I loved him and how much I hated him. I shook my head to clear my thinking. Having a crush on your Boss was one thing; letting him get away with politically incorrect behavior in public is quite another.

"Sir, less than fourteen hours ago, unknown forces bombed the Vatican. Thousands are dead, massive infrastructure damage, and it seems the entire head of the Catholic Church has been assassinated." When my Boss was working, he demanded respect and all the formalities that went with rank. Claimed it made it easier to manage people like me. He was probably correct. That's why I addressed him as "sir," something he picked up on instantly with the smallest nod of his head, undetectable to anyone but the person looking straight at him. Playtime was over; time to get down and dirty. Again.

"Why me?" has asked, looking at the miniature computer screen I had handed him. The photos were the usual crime screen blood and guts, broken bodies, stray limbs, and fused objects, everything you expected after a massive explosion in a small residential area. He scrolled through the images with practiced ease and then grunted.

"Okay, I got it. Two bombs, at least a ground penetrator and an airburst, probably a MOAB (Mother of All Bombs). By whom, and how delivered?" I sat in awe at my Boss's quick assessment of the situation, just from looking at a few grainy photos mostly taken with phone cameras by civilian witnesses literally scared out of their minds. It had taken a room full of experts looking at copious video footage and listening to eyewitness accounts over three hours to come to the same conclusion.

"Unknown, and it would appear at this time that the delivery mechanism was a UN Hercules L-100 on an approved over-flight out of Serbia."

"Crew?"

"Jumped out of the plane somewhere over the Med, left the aircraft on auto-pilot, it was eventually shot down over the sea just short of Barcelona. The chase pilots only got to the aircraft after the crew had jumped, and as you can imagine, an extensive sea and air search were done to find them."

"No sign of a fast boat along their flight path?"

"Several. All stopped and searched, over a thousand sailors and crew were taken into custody by the Italian and Spanish navies; we have a team working them all now. But my gut tells me they are not in the net. Yet." He looked at me as if trying to divine why I didn't think the terrorists had been captured. He nodded, answering some deep question from within himself.

"You're right. Too much preparation, too much planning, too much horsepower." I nodded my agreement; it was the same conclusion I had come to. After working with this genius for the last few years, I had picked up some exacting processes from which the logic of an attack could be extrapolated, "walking the cat backwards" was the expression we used behind closed doors. Simple, really, put yourself in the terrorist's shoes, go back to a starting point, and plan the attack as you planned it would unfold. Make an initial assessment of the resources, material, manpower, money, and timing involved and the risk management required, and suddenly, you could often turn a mystery into a series of deductions that took you some way towards solving the crime.

Look for the sources of finance, hardware, and resources, the downstream supply chains, the vested interests,and the choke points. For example, one of his first questions was about the crew of the unknown aircraft—they had to have come from somewhere, and they had to have gone somewhere, and that provided two potential choke—or "data" points, in the new language—where a shrewd investigator might pick up the scent. Crew manifests, initiating airports, aircraft owners/operators, flight plans, flight licenses, all the usual stuff that supposedly made our skies safe. The fundamental thought here, apparently!

Terrorism was a political act of aggression, some called it outright asymmetric warfare, but to us at Interpol, the world's largest international police organization with 194 member countries, it was just another form of crime, albeit one that always came with a lot of broken bodies and screaming, posturing politicians attached. But because our Constitution expressly prohibited any intervention or activities of a political, military, religious, or racial nature, our tactical group was formally constituted as Section Five and funded in turn by three different governments on loan to the host organization, which was Interpol. We were family, but we were different, which our commissioners never failed to point out every time we got into trouble.

And with my Boss at the helm, this was just about every time we got involved in some countries' backyards. Politically astute he was not, but connected he was, and safely ensconced within his overly large shadow, I had been introduced to some of the heaviest hitters in the police and military systems everywhere in the world. Make that "underworld" as well, because my Boss was never slow to call on some creepy, deeply distrustful soul in the dark of night if the purpose suited him.

The one real advantage we had over everyone else was that we could cross borders rapidly and with the total support of the host country concerned because it was understood that we had no vested or military interest other than solving the crime and bringing the perpetrators before the world court if they were in any recognizable shape after we caught up to them. The other real advantage we had was that we could call on some of the most sophisticated assistance imaginable to make our arrests; so far, in all the years I had worked for the agency, the survival rate of the bad guys was almost zero. So not many actual arrests. Not my fault they always seemed to want to shoot or bomb their way out of captivity!
"What does Lyon think?" he asked, referring to the headquarters of our secretariat. It was here that eighty nations worked side by side to make the world a better place. But mostly, the secretary general delegated to specialists, and in this case, because of the massive political and religious ramifications of the case, they had reached out to the United Nations and requested a neutral agency to take the lead.

The UN responded by calling us, and completing the daisy chain. Here we were, in the rank bowels of a screaming military helicopter, heading away from paradise to the mountainous and somewhat inhospitable surroundings that made landing at Cairns International Airport such a thrill in the middle of a cyclone.

"No comment. They flicked it to the UN, who flicked it to us at the speed of light. That computer pad was given to me by a courier out of the back of a USAF Blackbird, and I respectfully suggest that you will be its next passenger." He nodded, acknowledging what I had said but not necessarily accepting it. He seemed to be mulling something over. He switched the intercom back to inter-plane communication and called the pilot.

"Captain, can you contact your Command and Control (C-an-C) please?"

"Sir." The pilot did something on his panel, and a new voice introduced itself. "Tindal, how can we help?"

"Colonel Anthony, to whom am I speaking?"

"Group Captain Roberts, Colonel, duty officer."

"Group Captain, can you authorize fast jets to pick up two POBs ASAP, and get them to Rome? Priority zero-fife."

"Wait, one." My headphones utterly silent, indicating that the digital signal had been "boxed." I loved it when the Colonel talked dirty; in this case, one of the POBs he was referring to was me. I briefly wondered who the second body would be.

"Colonel, your eta Cairns is fifteen minutes; your bravo-bravo is refueled and waiting. I take it you have other interests?"

"Affirmative. I'll take the bee-bee, but need two others to travel."

"Two seats available in forty minutes, allowing fifteen for turnaround; they will be around six hours behind you at the other end." Of course, we would. The SR-71 Blackbird was still the fastest jet in the sky, able to fly at around two thousand nautical miles an hour. By contrast, the Super Hornets that would carry me and the yet unknown second passenger could only manage a mere 1,200 knots— downhill, with a tail wind!

"Thank you, Group Captain." My Boss clicked off, looked at me with hooded eyes, and then clicked through to the front cockpit again.

"Captain, secure line, please."

"Sir." Leaning over slightly, my Boss half turned his shoulders, effectively creating a physical barrier between himself and the gunner.

"Black Pete, Cairns International, thirty minutes, look for Captain Riley." And he clicked off again.

Black Pete. We were preparing for a confrontation with the worst of the worst. Black Pete was the nick for one of the more subterranean agents we sometimes employed, an ex-US Navy SEAL who, rumor had it, had been kicked out of the teams for insubordination. The problem is, when Special Forces personnel are publicly flogged and removed from the service, it is usually just the start of a varied and colorful career!

In this case, to my knowledge, Black Pete had successfully tracked and, with the help of my Boss, eliminated a vast number of creepy types in some of the worst locations you could imagine around the world. When I asked why he had been discharged from the teams, he laughed and swigged another beer! Black Pete could sail any vessel, navigate anywhere on land or sea without a map, and kill you with either hand or any weapon someone was stupid enough to give him. Or even with a simple pencil. But under his somewhat harsh exterior, he was a lovely man, partnered with a barefoot cellist of international repute, whom he absolutely adored. The striking contrast between his personal and professional lives never ceased to amaze me. Just another bizarre marker in my daily life when on the job! I wondered what the Boss had deduced from the small amount of information I had given him that had created the need for Black Pete. And how he had even managed to contact him without my fore-knowledge.

I didn't get a chance to pursue this thought before the Seahawk slammed down onto the tarmac at the military end of Cairns International Airport, where a gaggle of black-suited ninjas were jealously guarding the sleek grey-black SR-71. My Boss looked me in the eye as if mentally sending me a message, which, in a sense, he was, then jumped out of the helicopter and sprinted to the side of the Blackbird, where he was pressure packed into one of the yellow-silver space suits you needed to ride in to survive at the extreme altitudes it flew at. A smart-looking Air Force officer dressed in snappy but creased camos suddenly filled my doorway.

"Captain, this way, please." I followed his broad back to a small, air-conditioned trailer, and the cooling breeze as we entered made me suddenly realize how hot and humid it was up here in the tropics. Or was it down here?

"Captain, we have a coded message for you from Venice. It's on that laptop," the officer said, pointing to a sweet little black thing that was dwarfed by the huge flat screen monitors lined one entire trailer wall. I sat down at the laptop, booted it up, brought up the URL for our so-called home office, and entered my access code. A short paragraph flicked into existence, and as I read it, I realized with a cold shudder that the world I lived in would never quite be the same again.

CHAPTER 3

I think at this point, to help you make some sense of what happened next, I need to give you a little background on myself. I was an average student at an average college when I had a bad experience—a very, very bad experience. You know the type. Beach-tanned, blond-haired hunk, alcohol, drugs, fast cars, more alcohol, more drugs, stunningly concluded by a crushing accident in the early hours of the morning that killed five of the six of us in the car.

When I came to three days later, in plaster up to the neck, the first person I saw was a cop. A highway patrol officer, to be exact, and he only had one question for me. Hovering in the background was my mom, anxiety written all over her face, still wearing her apron from the truck stop where she worked as a waitress. A bunch of supermarket flowers was clutched between her soaked hankie and her fake alligator-skin purse, which she was so proud of. She was literally shaking with fear – I was soon to learn why.

"Miss Riley," the cop asked, pen poised over his flipbook, still wearing his Ray Bans, "can you hear me?" I looked at him and saw the reflection of my bandaged head in his dark lenses and wondered just how badly I was broken. I couldn't feel my legs, my arms were suspended in front of me in some sort of sling arrangement, and I could see a myriad of tubes and wires heading in under the sheet that covered me from the waist down to all sorts of interesting places.

"Yes." It wasn't my voice, and I sighed with relief; this was just an awful dream, and I'd wake up sometime soon to find myself—where? I suddenly realized I not only didn't know where I was—hospital screamed into my brain, but that was part of the dream, surely? But I couldn't remember much of anything to tell the truth.

"Good. Who was driving the vehicle?" Car? What car? I wasn't in a car; I was in a bad dream! I screwed my eyes shut, and the next thing I was aware of was a lovely male all dressed in white smiling at me.

"Hello Jessica, welcome back," he said, offering me a plastic drinking cup. I bent forward as far as I could, once again aware that my neck seemed to be locked into something – I had an image of a plaster cast from somewhere, but frankly, for the life of me, right now, with a bucket and a shovel, I couldn't dig up any memories that made any sense.

"Take it easy, you've been banged up pretty good, but you're getting better by the minute!" he said, his enthusiasm almost infectious, but I had a vague recollection of someone else telling me something good, but it didn't feel right. He wiped my forehead with a moist towel, obviously a caring soul, but where the hell was I?

"Where am I?" I croaked, a vague recollection swimming around like a drunken frog at the very far reaches of my mind, that I had had this very same thought just a while ago, but bugger me for a blind man, I couldn't remember when or why. My white angel just smiled, standing there like he was my great protector.

"You're in the Sisters of Mercy Hospital, Chicago, and you've been in a bad accident," he said. I did my best to process that information but got nowhere. Sisters of Mercy? Chicago? Wow! Had he been smoking something?

"I don't live in Chicago," I croaked, "and what accident was I in?" He just smiled and wiped my face again with his lovely, soft, cool cloth. I could get used to this pampering. I knew I lived in—well, I was pretty sure I lived in—my mind was a complete blank, so I shook my head to clear the cobwebs and the incredible pain that suddenly jolted all the way down from the back of my head to the base of my butt almost made me pass out.

"Take it easy, take it easy," the nurse said, moving in so close to me I thought he was going to give me a hug. He tightened up some contraption just above my head that suddenly made it literally impossible to move anything but my eyeballs. "Now, I think you need a little peace and calm. Your lovely mum is outside; would you like to see her? I tried to nod; that failed. I could feel, then see, the tears streaming out of my eyes and down my face, so I just grunted, hoping he spoke unhappy patient!

"Jessie, Jessie, how are you feeling, my love?" my mom asked, suddenly materializing between the privacy curtains. Now I really started to cry, and she joined in, so the nurse slipped away on silent feet, probably to get a mop and bucket.

"What happened?" I mumbled, "and where am I?" The flood of tears made it hard for me to see my mum's face, and her crying made it hard for me to hear her, but bit by bit, the shocking truth rolled across the counterpane like a tornado, and I mentally resolved to never ask a question I didn't want the answer to ever again.

I had been in a car accident. Five of my friends had been killed. The police pathologists revealed that all five had massive amounts of alcohol and drugs in their system. I was the only survivor. I had massive amounts of alcohol and drugs in my system when I was brought into the hospital's emergency room. I was lucky to be alive. And the police believed that I had been driving the car and had a warrant for my immediate arrest for multiple counts of driving while under the influence, using class-three drugs, and culpable homicide.

Depending on your point of view, it all went downhill from there. I eventually recovered, was arrested and incarcerated, and my mom, having only one job as a waitress in a truck diner, couldn't raise bail, so I stayed behind bars for seven long months until I finally faced a judge.

He was short, sharp, and to the point.

The prosecutor could not prove that I was driving. I couldn't prove that I wasn't. It was a tragedy of monumental proportions, so he offered me a deal. Go to a public trial and risk ten to fifteen years without parole for five counts of murder two, or volunteer for a minimum of seven years of military service, starting now, after which time he would order my records sealed because I was a minor, still under eighteen years of age, even as I stood before him.

I joined the navy. Within six months, I was back at college, studying law and working nights and weekends as a trainee naval criminal investigative agent. The irony never left me as I sweated and swotted my way through the next four and a half years, gaining my commission as a first lieutenant one day after my twenty-first birthday.

The next three years saw me posted overseas to Europe, where I got my first taste of culturally different. Applied for and got a seat in the Joint Services Language School and mastered French, German, Russian, Spanish, Italian, a little Greek, a little Mandarin and Cantonese. Seemed I had an ear for languages, a latent talent brought to the surface by being immersed in different countries and having to survive.

Then one windy, bleak day in October, a registered package arrived, and when I opened it, the past suddenly rushed back and swamped me. It was a folder declaring that the police and court records of one Miss Jessica Riley, previously held under the seal of Judge Beckinsworth, First Circuit, State of Milwaukee, had been officially destroyed.

I was free. Sort of. Until the package arrived, I had not given my future any particular thought, happy to be absorbed in banging the heads of wayward sailors and studying the various courses available to me through the NCIS Professional Development program. Advanced weapons training, ballistics, forensics, psychology, communication, more languages, computer technology, and international law, just the sort of stuff that any girl my age eagerly chased after if ghosts constantly pursued her. I had re-upped for another five more years to run on my commission, now as a full lieutenant in command of my own agents, in a nice little place called Souda Bay in Crete, with responsibilities that ranged all around the Mediterranean, wherever the US of A anchored its ships.

The next day was October 12, and my life changed significantly for the second time. I met the Colonel. Under challenging circumstances.

And, of course, him being who he is, and me being who I am, and what I had been training for, I shot him.

You might remember that on October 12 of that year, seventeen American sailors were killed in a terrorist suicide bomb attack on the USS Maryland in the Yemeni port of Aden. We got the flash warning about twenty minutes after it happened, and I placed the base on an immediate lockdown, no one in, no one out, weapons free, shoot first and ask questions eventually. We were very tense and excited, as you can imagine, our first real live emergency, and to describe us as hyped to the eyeballs on adrenaline would be to understate our condition by a million percent. We were a mixed bunch of sailors and soldiers, with only one Marine on attachment, a liaison officer to our CO who oversaw all the movements and logistics for the navy from the east coast of Britain all the way to Turkey.

Right through that night, we walked the grid in teams of three, covering every inch of the fence line, infrared and low light scanners protecting every approach, desperately waiting for hard news from Aden. We knew a ship had been hit, people killed, but not by whom at that time or even how they had made their attack. The rumor mill was working overtime, as it always does under these circumstances, so we had to cover every eventuality with our limited resources, from the sea, air, and land.

At exactly oh-four-oh-one—I remember the time because the next minute, oh-four-oh-two, I will relive every day for the rest of my life—five unidentified figures were detected approaching from a group of small brick and adobe buildings that ran down one side of the base. As luck would have it, I was in my Humvee ten seconds away, so I ordered my driver to coast to a stop, and we lit up the night gear that scanned into a small flatscreen built into my side of the vehicle. Sure enough, four fluorescent images were worming their way across the gravel, heading towards one of our enormous tubular gates. Without warning, someone on our left turned on a spotlight, and about a thousand rounds instantly reached out from inside our perimeter; red and blue tracers created a beautiful display, chewing the four images into little pieces. Then, again, before I could even stop to think about what had just happened, a fifth figure suddenly rose up just in front of the gate on my side of the Humvee.

Instinctively, I pushed my Car-15 out the open window and fired two three-round bursts, just as we had been trained to do, right into the center of the mass. The figure dropped like a stone. I bolted out of the Humvee, followed by what felt like a hundred soldiers, but was probably no more than five or six, and stuck my head through the huge bars, carbine pointed at the body, hands shaking like I was holding a concrete jackhammer in full flight. Three sailors climbed through the gate, two running over to where the first four bodies lay and one to the black suit I had topped. "Ma'am, this one's still alive!" he shouted. I climbed through the gate and joined him, and sure enough, the body was twitching, and I thought of shooting him in the head and was about to take aim when my common sense took over as suddenly as if I had been doused by a cold shower, and I regained my calm and composure.

"Cuff him, get him to the medevac area, hold him for questioning," I barked in my best parade ground command voice, trying to hide my anxiety while I walked over to where the other bodies were. No survivors here, just body parts, blood and gore, gunk and guts. They had been hit by a fifty caliber, more than once by the look of it, and a fifty could chew up a tank. "Okay, get a squad out here, clean these guys up, set a perimeter ten meters outside this area, get some fifties on the corners, expect more uninvited callers."

I walked back to my Humvee, this time through the open gate, quite pleased with myself. I had been baptized and was still standing, something everyone who carried a gun for a living worried about all the time.

Nothing else happened that night, and three platoons of Marines arrived by chopper at first light to relieve us and take formal charge of the base's defense. I was about to hit the sack when I got a call on my beeper. The commanding officer wanted to see me ASAP. I got my driver to take me to the base operations office, mindful that I looked like crap and smelled twice as bad. But I had been in action; I had defended the base from an attack, as yet not officially described as other than by "intruders," mainly because the medics were having some difficulty putting the puzzle pieces together in any sort of shape that made sense. Trust me, a fifty caliber will do that to you every time!

"Sir, Lieutenant Riley reporting as ordered, sir!" The captain was in his starched whites, dripping ribbons, medals and badges, which was always a bad sign. He looked perplexed, holding a sheaf of papers in one hand, a coffee mug with C-in-C-PAC (Commander in Chief, Pacific) in bold blue letters lined with gold in the other. Didn't know that abbreviation, probably part of the secret navy boys' club. I held my salute for a fraction longer, then released it, sensing something was up but getting no clues from the crusty captain.

"Lieutenant, I've just read your after-action report; is there anything you'd like to add?" he asked, slipping a pair of reading glasses up over his equine nose and not losing eye contact with me while he did it. I ran the pictures from our engagement through, my mind locking onto the guy I had shot, his camouflaged face when I was debating whether or not to finish him off, the high fives my team had swapped after we had calmed down, and the bloody mess the fifty caliber had made of the other four "intruders."

I couldn't see anything I had missed; I had read and reread my short action report before transmitting it over the net, even letting my master chief check it for the correct military diction. I think we got it right, and to be frank, I was so tired that I couldn't really think of anything we might have missed.

"No, sir." He slipped his glasses off, both hands came down to his sides in unison, as if he was standing at parade attention, and he tilted his head to one side. "Well, I have to say your team did extremely well, but we have a slight problem with the intruder you shot." He looked at me as if I could divine what he was alluding to; that didn't work, so I took the direct approach.

"Sir, as reported, said intruder popped up in front of my vehicle, outside the gate, between us and four identified targets, whom we had just been in action with. I can't imagine what the problem might be," I said as calmly as I could. He nodded and seemed unsure what to say.

"Well, Lieutenant, I suggest you go over to the medevac area and see for yourself."

"Sir, yes, sir!" I saluted again, turned on my heel, and strode back out to the Humvee.

"Medevac."

"Ma'am."

Two minutes later, I demounted again, this time into a darkened tent lit by red lamps designed to preserve your night vision. But it was well and truly daylight now, so the effect was no more than spooky, bordering on Parisian night alfresco. I walked in behind the blast door to find three green-garbed medicos attending a well-built male who was all but naked, with massive bruising over his stomach area and upper chest. Underneath the gurney was a pile of sodden black clothing that I assumed was the patient's, a Sig-Saur P226 in a shoulder rig, a K-Bar combat knife, and an MP-5 silenced submachine gun, and what looked like a shattered Kevlar vest. Slowly, ever so slowly, it dawned on me. At least six times, I had shot one of our special forces at very close range.

But what the hell was he doing outside my perimeter? And why didn't I know of his deployment? I was temporarily in charge of the base's defense; I was supposed to know all the resources we could apply to prevent another attack on US property. Maryland had a hole in it the size of a truck; we were on high alert; what the hell was going on? Something was way out of whack, and suddenly I wondered just how much trouble I was in.

I didn't know then that this was probably the least amount of trouble I was would experience for the foreseeable future! A pair of deep, resonating blue eyes under thick eyebrows, a small scar running down one cheek, and a two-day old stubble that made him look slightly Italian. Well-muscled, no tats, other scars on his shoulder and chest, old by the look of them, and a long-running red welt cresting from thigh to ankle on his left leg. One of the things you learn quickly on this job is how to size a person up, part instinct, part training, and my gut was telling me this was a heavy hitter, a survivor of battles won and lost at the personal level, but unquestionably one of the good guys.

"Is this the intruder from last night?" I asked the nearest orderly, holding my carbine lightly in one hand, my fist clenching and unclenching in the other. The patient sat up, more like an athletic move a cat would make, stared at me for a full ten seconds, then smiled, revealing a set of near perfect teeth.

"So, you're the agent who shot me?" he asked, voice calm, as if this was an everyday occurrence. I sized him up again, seeking some hint of whom he might be, what his line of attack would be. Strangely, I sensed nothing in him but weariness, and regret.

"My team was responsible for the engagement," I offered, admitting nothing just like any well-trained prisoner. He just smiled again, rubbing the deep purple and blue bruises on his upper chest.

"Well, please thank your squad for me, tell them I am extremely relieved that they are so well trained." This took me aback; I was expecting to have a new bum-hole ripped, and here he was congratulating me.

"How so?"

"Six shots, center of mass, nice, tight grouping, it's the only reason I'm still alive." I thought about telling him I had nearly put a burst through his head but decided not to spoil his day—just yet.

"Why were you outside our perimeter, unidentified?" I asked in my best cop voice. He stared back at me with an intensity I almost felt.

"Not your fault. I was out of touch when the Maryland got hit, decided to come in only to find a bunch of crazies marching around sounding off, so I decided on a quiet approach, when you started shooting the crap out of the neighborhood. The terrorists you killed must have spotted me and been following me to the gate." I thought about his statement for a minute, considered the millions of holes in everything he said, and knew intuitively I was being fed BS of the highest caliber.

"No comms?" I asked, my suspicions heightened by his calmness.

"No. Completely out of contact." Boy, could he sell a lie. I decided to end the charade there and then.

"Master Chief, re-cuff him, dress him, and take him to room three." My second-in-command muttered a near silent "Ma'am" under his breath and moved to comply. His instincts were also on high alert, as we had worked together long enough to feed of each other. As my anxiety increased, so too did his. I turned and walked back out of the tent, wondering what I'd find out during the interrogation. But first, a shower, then another shower, some food, and about a gallon of coffee, all made in my office in a lovely stainless-steel espresso machine I had commandeered from a wayward smuggler some months ago.

By the time I had repaired my self-image, climbed into a pair of blue-green Italian jeans and a nifty leather jacket, which covered my holstered pistol while still making me look stylish, the sun had reached the top of the buildings, and another brilliant sunny day was getting underway in the Mediterranean. As overseas postings went, this had to be one of the best places in the world to be sent to, that is, when the bad guys weren't trying to carve your heart out, or just blow you up. Mug in hand, I entered the interrogation room to find our "intruder" sitting comfortably at one end of the table, dressed in camos, right down to polished boots, drinking coffee and reading a report.

My after-action report. That observation got my juices flowing, and the sheepish look on my master chief's face told me all I needed to know.

"Rank?"

"Colonel."

"Detachment?"

"Loose, but at this very moment, TDY (Temporary Duty) your establishment." I thought about that, the utter calm and confidence in his voice underlining a strength and position of power I didn't doubt, and I still did not feel threatened, even by him suddenly being on my org chart, and at the very top of it, at that.

"I still want to know why you were outside my perimeter unannounced."

"Can't tell you that here." Mentally, I recoiled from his flat statement; then it dawned on me. If he was a spook, and I was definitely starting to get that vibe off him, he would never say anything meaningful while being videoed and taped in an interrogation room.

"Walk with me," I said in a tone of voice that left him in no doubt as to what I expected. He was a Colonel, or so he claimed, outranking me by at least three paygrades, but he had said he was TDY to my attachment, which, technically, left me still in charge. Plus, I had my master chief all riled up and carrying guns to back me up.

He stood, flexed his not inconsiderable shoulders, and walked to the door. I mouthed the word "spook" silently to my master chief; he nodded, scratching the back of his close-shaved head. I followed the Colonel out into the corridor and then out into the sunshine.

He reached into a top pocket and found a pair of Ray Bans reminiscent of what military pilots had made famous back in the last century. Curiouser and curiouser, as the white rabbit said. Where had he gotten all his equipment? He had everything but a weapon—no, wait one, the tell-tale bulge in the small of his back. Bugger me, what was going on here, and how come I was the only one who didn't know the answers?

"Lieutenant, before you implode, let me tell you a story." And he did.

And what a story it was.

RESURRECTION

To a Jew, Jerusalem is *Ir Ha-Kodesh*—the Holy City, the Biblical Zion, the City of David, the site of King Solomon's Temple, and the eternal capital of the Israelite nation. To a Christian, it is where the young Jesus spoke to the sages at the Jewish temple, spent the last days of his ministry, and where they believe the Last Supper, the Crucifixion, and the Resurrection took place. To a Muslim, it is where the prophet Muhammad ascended into heaven. To the unidentified pilot sitting in an underground air-conditioned bungalow six and a half thousand miles away, circling the UAV high above the dome on top of Mount Moriah, it was the perfect target. The sun was heating up the golden dome to the point where her four heat-seeking tank-killer missiles had a steady lock, so she fired the four Hellfires simultaneously, waited just long enough to confirm four perfect lock-ons, then pressed the self-destruct button, shredding the UAV into a million pieces.

She watched the explosions silently, neither cheering nor wincing at the incredible destruction, slowly sipping from a stained coffee mug. In a way, she felt sad for what she had caused to happen, then, with a deep sigh, shrugged her shoulders, shut the command center down, locked the control room, and walked off down the tunnel.

For the many and varied worshippers on the ground below in that most scared and venerated forecourt, at first, all they saw was a massive fireball high in the sky, then four streaks of flame arcing away over their heads, slowly turning into a huge circle, leaving smoky contrails in the shape of a corkscrew. Eleven seconds later, the missiles impacted the dome, turning the building and the dome over the most famous rock in all of history into sparkling plasma and dust. *Bethel*, the Gate House to Heaven, was no more.

CHAPTER 4

The Boss was in his Blackbird, flying faster than a speeding bullet, while Black Pete and I were strapped like so much rolled steak into the back seats of two screaming FA-18 Super Hornets, crashing through the sky like demented demons in perfect formation, just inches apart. It wasn't exactly unpleasant, but then again, it wasn't exactly comfortable either.

"How are you going back there?" a cheery voice asked, the inevitable hiss of the oxygen mask dulling the vowels. My pilot was long-legged, female, bright, and bushy-tailed, as only a fighter jock can be before they grow up and join the real world. At the ripe old age of thirty one, I think I was becoming a bit of a cynic!

I grunted a reply and pretended to be trying to sleep. Just as my head started to roll to the side for real, a huge grey fuselage surged over the top of us, and I mentally tried to pull my head in. It was the first of the aerial tankers we'd need to cross the Indian Ocean, the horn of Africa, then up into the Mediterranean before we could land in Italy. Ah, now there was a country with style!

My intrepid jock plugged into the swirling refueling basket on her first attempt with a 'thunk,' and I noticed from the digital gauges on the cockpit panel in front of me that the fuel load suddenly started to increase. Nothing for it but to try to sleep for real.

In the SR-71, the Colonel had an entirely different experience, flying at eighty thousand feet, faster than your average rifle bullet as it leaves the barrel. The middle seat of the Blackbird had no forward vision, just two small triangular windows on either side, not that you could see anything out of them. A micro military laptop sat on the Colonel's lap, uplinked to Interpol's command and control center in Bonn. The news was not good. Over a thousand pilgrims were killed in Jerusalem, and the world leaders were stunned and seemingly powerless in the wake of the two attacks on two of the most revered and important religious sites in the world. Trouble was, it wasn't just the one point five billion or so Catholics around the world baying for someone's blood; now, it was the Jews and Muslims, estranged bedfellows at the best of times.

No one yet had a clue.

The Colonel decided to make a few connections, so dialing up the URL for a secure military website, he plugged into the world's most sophisticated and secured online chatroom.

"Online, emperor, maggot, fish 'n' chips, brush-cut, black bear, who calls?" He looked up his code page and discovered that the head of the CIA, Naval Intelligence, British MI5, Jordanian Secret Police, and the Russian Special Forces were available. He typed as fast as he could with his two highly trained forefingers, bulked out as they were by his pressure gloves.

"Snowman, rq info on rc and tbe, advs." The cursor blinked steadily, waiting for something to do. On the screen, three chat boxes expanded into existence. In the first, "no itl" appeared. In the second, "nada," and in the third, "wlk cat bk on hwre." The Colonel nodded to himself inside his yellow space suit. He agreed with his Russian counterpart. If they could backtrack the hardware, they would eventually find the sponsors of the terror attacks. If they found the money trail, they'd find everyone connected in any way. His gloved fingers flew over keys, hitting the delete key more times than any other as he pecked out his response.

"Agd. Cntctl with ICC?" The screens remained blank for a few seconds; all three repeated the same message.

"lol"

Indeed, he thought to himself, he would need a huge quantum of luck because of the sheer number of potential distractions in this case. He hit the keys again.

"A1 wknaglsyt?"

"ys"

"who?"

"evbdy!" He grumped into his helmet, snapping the chatroom closed. After entering the encrypted access code, he dialed up his direct link to his secure server and got his workspace. He selected "Current 60 minutes" and scanned the graphic descriptions of the carnage he was about to land into the middle of.

While the images of blood and gore and broken bodies were strewn about like so much trash revolted him, all his senses were screaming at him that this terrorist activity was different from any the world had experienced so far. Put him up against a brick wall and hold a gun to his head, and he couldn't tell you why he felt so strongly about this, but his conviction was as solid as a rock.

Back to the French's first attack on American soil in 1812, it had always been about politics and power, or religion and power, or money and power. All by itself, the USA had invaded over one hundred countries in the last one hundred and fifty years. Politics, money, power. But where was the potential gain in enraging over one-half of the world's population at the same time by attacking the icons of their strongest religious beliefs? Perhaps it was an effort to unite some group or other? But who was left?

Interpol's real strength was in rapidly crossing international with the support and respect of local governments and authorities, mostly on the European continent. Interpol didn't take the credit for a bust. If the criminal ended up before the World Court, he or she was represented there by military or police forces from his or her own country. In fact, Interpol as a physical organization was minuscule in size compared to even the smallest of its member countries' police forces.

When the Vatican had been bombed just hours ago, it had seemed logical to form a task force led by Interpol. But now, he was not so sure. The Americans would more than likely claim their right to lead, given their past history of "you're either our friend, or we bomb you back to the Stone Age" philosophy, and there were now two confirmed attacks using high-tech weaponry previously thought beyond the reach of the ordinary everyday jihadist. And of all the intelligence forces on the planet, the

Americans had every toy in the playbook, and thanks to recent economic events, good relationships with many of the world's intelligence forces.

He punched up his chatroom window again, requested an address that only three people in the world had, and watched the blinking cursor.

"Yes." No shorthand or code with this contact; although he was as two-fingered on a keyboard as the Colonel, he refused to reduce any conversation to codes or cipher.

"Why?" the Colonel typed in. His mentor, in faraway Boston, had been at the forefront of commercial "think tanks" for nearly sixty years and was one of the most information-connected people in the world. If anyone had any idea, speculative or not, about the motive for the current attacks, it would be him.

"Think about the assets."

"I am. UN aircraft, the US or Russian bombs, Israeli UAV, US or Israeli missiles, on approved flight plans, in full view in daylight, being flown by security-cleared military crews, all of whom are now missing. All faithfully recorded by a hundred spy satellites."

"Good start. But you're missing the point." *Of course, I am,* the Colonel thought to himself, itching in his crotch area but unable to do anything about it, protected as he was by his yellow space suit. *That's why I called you!*

"Which is?"

"How would you mount such an attack?"

"Working on it."

"Send me the summary."

"Thank you." *For nothing,* the Colonel thought; he was already "walking the cat back" with his team. Bonn would let him know the second they had mapped out all the variables, and then perhaps he would have something to work with. He tried to peer out the minute side window of the speeding Blackbird, getting nothing but his reflection for his trouble. It didn't feel right. Nothing about this case felt right. Way too professional and high-tech, too well planned, and so far, at least, implemented to perfection. He rolled the cursor over to another icon using his gloved thumb on the little square pressure pad, then clicked the mouse button with his finger.

A series of videos floated up to his screen, each one imploring him to click on it and put it out of its paused misery. He selected one, tapped it, and watched as the images dissolved up to fill the screen. At the back of his mind, the words "State-sponsored" kept rattling around like marbles in a soggy bag. What had happened reeked of massive resources, infrastructure, and planning, something the more traditional Islamic terrorists really did not have. But if you thought about the targets—the literal center of the Catholic universe, the heart of Islam, Jewish belief, and Christian dogma-it looked like some sort of pogrom against the world's dominant religions.

But by whom? And why?

He dialed up another video, his mind swirling with questions, but, as yet, with no answers.

I woke suddenly, the green glow of the cockpit creating a strange feeling. Outside, the night was black as pitch, as the saying goes, and if squid ink was any more smothering and light absorbing, I would be very surprised. The beep-beep-beep of my computer pad is what had shocked me out of a wonderful dream, which, of course, now I couldn't remember the details of. It had involved an empty beach, cold champagne, and a hunk of Italian maleness and somewhere very, very remote, but the details were gone. Probably a good thing as I scanned the message from the Boss.

"Ck dod naval mnts med." The Boss's shorthand was sometimes hard to decipher, sometimes easy, like this time. He wanted me to check out the US Department of Defense for naval movements through the Mediterranean Sea around the time of the attack on Rome. I had the connections; I had once been in the US Navy, still had a few good contacts from my NCIS time, and as a field agent for Interpol, my request would be processed quickly. But I knew the Boss. If he wanted to find out something badly enough, he would call up his little chatroom of spooks from all over the world and ask one of them.

So, this had to be a "play," where he set something in motion deliberately by asking a specific target a question designed to promote an involuntary response. And if he was asking me to make the enquiry, then he was prepared for the major security forces around the world to listen in on the conversation, as they most surely would try to do, electronic spying having scaled such technologically fantastic heights lately. I thought some more, and then I got it. The Boss thought this was an attack supported by a client State, not a rag-tag bunch from some fundamentalist terrorist group. Now I started to think about who could possibly gain something out of pissing off half the world at the one time and struggled to find an answer.

No one obvious, that was for sure, which was why the Boss was prepared to stir the pot. I dialed up the DoD chatroom, entered my Interpol code, and got a sweet-looking captain staring into my screen. I'd lost track of time, so I had no idea if I was looking at the night shift or not.

"Yes, ma'am, how can I help you?"

"Zero-fife level request, all movements for seventy-two hours pre and post-GZ (Ground Zero) Rome, please, ASAP."

"Ma'am, we have that data transmitting now."

"Thank you." I clicked off, watching a huge stream of compressed and encrypted data flow across my comms link, straight to our processing center hidden away in a little warehouse in gorgeous Italy, as well as to as many security agencies as had managed to tap into the brief conversation, and I had absolutely no doubt it would be everyone with any technological capability more sophisticated than an Xbox!

In fact, I fully expected to see the entire download on BoobTube by the time we landed!

The cat was amongst the pigeons, and I wondered what the outcome might be. Just as I started to work that thought, my screen rippled with an interrupt icon, and a flash message appeared.

Dear God, not again!

DESERT STORM.

The Muttawa, the Arabian religious police, ruled by the baton and the boot. Taking great pleasure in having yet another hapless target for their wrath, the three policemen wasted no time reducing the vagrant to a crying, bleeding, rag-covered shell of a man now begging for his very life. To them, it was an affront to their one God and their very self-image as men to allow such behavior in Mecca, the heart of the Muslim empire. As the Red Crescent ambulance pulled up to the front entrance of Masjid al-Haram, the largest and most revered Mosque in the world, one of the policemen turned, checking out the driver. His bushy black moustache twitching with derision, he immediately ran over and poked his bloody baton into the open window, demanding identification and documents. There was no driver, just a permit stapled to the seat.

He looked at the work order, noticing that the emir himself had signed the authority, so he reluctantly waved the ambulance into the courtyard and radioed for the gatekeeper to let the ambulance in. One of the many sheikhs who served the great mosque appeared ill, requiring immediate transportation to the Al Noor Specialist Hospital. He watched the back of the ambulance until it disappeared into the thousand-year-old façade, then walked back to the bundle of misery that was still being kicked mercilessly by his companions. A thin smile formed on his protruding lips as he raised his baton for a mighty hit, and just as he was about to swing with all his force, he suddenly felt a hot flush, then nothing.

The shockwave rippled out, taking thirty percent of the ancient Mosque with it, the fireball reaching up out of the ground and into the sky like the proverbial hand of Satan. The sheer force of the explosion was enough to knock a helicopter flying two kilometers away out of the air. The marble pavement that curved from the entrance buckled and melted until it looked like a glassy snake lost in the desert.

Of the old beggar, all that remained was the crude wooden bowel he had been proffering for alms, vibrating on a single remaining tile as if it had a life of its own.

CHAPTER 5

Usually, like any smart cop, my Boss liked to physically work the scene of the crime, but now that we had three separate events, with multiple police and military forces running wild all over the place, not to mention the literally thousands of politicians flapping their gums on prime time TV, and the millions of civilian bloggers, email photos, iReports, and all the other amateur stuff that now erupted every time something happened anywhere around the world, he had decided to go to the ground where we could best assess the situation and develop a strategy to try and work our way through the mess.

The City of London

Starting from RAF Base West Ruislip, a brutal hour in traffic from where we had secure quarters in the COMNAVACTUK (Commander Naval Activity United Kingdom) facility in the navy headquarters building in Audley Street.

Black Pete and I got there eight hours after the Boss, as a helicopter had whisked him into town; the hired help—us—had been battered and bruised in the back of a black military four-wheel drive that seemed to hit every cobblestone and brick edge as it screamed around the back streets of inner London.

"I need you in thinking mode, not stinking mode" were the first words out of the Boss's mouth, so Pete and I headed for the showers, left no choice but by the door to the secured conference room shutting in our face. So much for the warm welcome, but frankly, I was tired, and a hot shower and a scrub would cheer me up to no end.

I also knew from past experience the Boss worked longer and harder than anyone on his staff and was using my sweat-stained flight suit as an excuse to give us time to collect our thoughts.

Twenty minutes later, we were back at the door, to a much warmer welcome. Around the conference table sat the heads of Scotland Yard, MI5, MI6, Bexley House, army, navy, RAF, SAS, Sûreté Nationale, Compagnies Républicaines de Sécurité, Direction Générale de la Sécurité Extérieure (DGSE), Direction de la surveillance du territoire (DST), the Minister for Defense and Terrorism, and the prime minister's representative. I knew them all by sight, so apart from a few heads nodding in my direction, that was it for the formalities, but I wondered how and why the French were all here in force.

Soon answered.

"The French are here because, by coincidence, they were attending a conference on international cooperation just up the road at the Dorchester. In front of you is a summary of everything we know, and the US DoD report on Mediterranean vessel movements you requested is included. Only two issues," my Boss said, leaning back in his chair, revealing a pair of matching sweaty armpits. Maybe he should have stopped for a shower as well! "The first is obvious—how the hell do we coordinate this investigation, given the targets and vested interests, and what the hell is really happening here?"

"*Monsieur*, to a certain extent, why must it interest us? Surely the Italians, Israelis, and the Arabians have it under control?" offered the head of the DST. Right then and then, I should have twigged, but it would take me two agonizing weeks and a change of government to remember this comment and understand it in context. The DST was the French equivalent of the CIA and MI5, only much slipperier. Positively Teflon coated, in fact. The CIA often paid them the compliment of labeling them as the most difficult security intelligence group to work with in all of history! And then there was the GIGN—*Groupe d'Intervention de la Gendarmerie Nationale.* Don't get me started!

"We agree, up to a point," offered the representative of Bexley House. They were in the business of signals and electronic snooping, similar to the NSA in the US but more focused on European intelligence gathering on behalf of the British and NATO. This was another clue I missed because it was the first time I had heard anyone from Bexley House say anything more profound than "please pass the tea."

"It's quite clear from the data at present that all three ground-zero countries have amassed quite large forces to deal with these terrorist attacks."

"Well," my Boss said, suddenly sitting forward, "Interpol cannot work without a mandate, so unless someone here wants us to get involved, we will leave it all to you." Several balding, grey-fringed heads nodded in agreement; my Boss looked to his left, and right, saw no possibility of engagement, and stood up. "Thank you all. You have our number; I hope you run the bastards down as fast as you can." He walked from the room, Black Pete and me trailing like anxious bridesmaids at a bad wedding, then waited until the door had been closed behind by the guards before turning on his heel and getting in our faces.

"My turn for a wash and polish. Join you in the cafeteria in ten." Pete and I nodded silently and then moved off in the opposite direction to the Boss. *Game on*, I thought to myself, but what was the game, who were the players, and what, exactly, were the rules?

The evil grin on Pete's face led me to believe either he was salivating at the thought of some hot food or he already knew more than I did about the game and the rules. How, I didn't know; he'd been squished into the back seat of a fast jet for as long as I had, all the way from Cairns, near the northern tip of Australia, on our dash across half the world at supersonic speed.

"You know, I just love it when the Boss does that," Pete said, almost dribbling with joy. "He has just put every one of those pompous bastards on notice, and they haven't got a clue."

"Neither have I," I said, pushing the swing doors to the cafeteria open. "I haven't really digested that Med data yet, but we now have three separate and unattributed terrorist attacks, half the world in an uproar, the other half scared out of their wits, and just hours ago, all I had to do was find the Boss and get him back to Venice!" Black Pete smiled, an evil grin splitting his pockmarked face like a stiletto cutting moldy, crumbling cheese.

"That's what I like about you," he said, leering at me, "always so positive and in the loop!"

CHAPTER 6

The priest was razor thin, almost emancipated in appearance, nearly two meters tall, and immaculately dressed, if you didn't look too closely at him and from a distance. Around his neck hung a miniature stone cross with a tiny hole in the center. The thin leather thong it hung from was aged with sweat and physical wear, creating an unusual aroma. His lined face spoke of harsh times and harder wear and tear, suggesting deprivation of the highest order. Only the dirty soft leather climbing boots proudly standing out from the hem of his cassock gave any hint of the steel that ran up and down his backbone or the intensity with which he focused on any task.

Right now, he was listening to a group of anxious mountain people who had literally climbed down several thousand meters through rainforest and jungle so dense no white man had ever tried to penetrate it to bring him their story.

And what a story it was.

Late one evening, two days ago, a huge aircraft had flown to the top of their mountain, right to where the stone markers had been so carefully laid in honor of the forest spirits and landed straight down, the downwash from its huge propellers blowing everything off the peak. Strange, heavily armed men had jumped out, all dressed in black, with hoods and goggles, and run down the dirt track straight to their village. There, the men had taken two young boys prisoner, putting bags over their heads, tying their hands behind their backs, then frog marching them back up the track to the top of the mountain and into the strange aircraft.

As the aircraft rose back up into the sky, a body had been thrown out of the back, and when the tribe had recovered it, they found that it was the remains of an old woman who had every bone in her body broken and most of her skin cut or shredded. At this point of the story, the villages had unwrapped the body they had carried down from their village. It had been washed out of respect for the dead and rolled in large palm leaves, as was their custom.

The priest made the sign of the cross, muttered under his breath in Latin, then bent his long frame to look at the corpse. His already well-worn face creased to the point where it took on a ghoulish appearance, and the intensity of his grey eyes was like a laser. Again, he made the sign of the cross, kissed his fingers, then made the sign of the cross on the corpse's forehead. Unfolding from his cramped position, he drew himself up to his full height, looked around at the expectant faces of the tribe, then strode purposefully through them to the small mud and grass hut he lived in. One minute later he emerged, an ancient leather bag strapped across his back and a mahogany walking stick in one hand, a broad-brimmed black priest's hat in the other.

Without a word or a backward glance, he strode off down the jungle track, so intent on his quest that, for him, at least, the very world he had helped shape for so long at the ends of the earth no longer existed.

The jungle soon removed all traces of his passage, and the tribe did what it had always done, collecting the body and chanting as they prepared for their celebration of death after life. The strange behavior of the tall white man passed unnoticed, just another curiosity in an already event-filled day.

RED, WHITE AND BLOOD.

What makes the West Point Academy on the banks of the Hudson River, just forty miles north of New York, so remarkable is that through its hallowed halls have passed some of the greatest leaders, civilian and military, in all of American history. It is the oldest continuously occupied military post in the country and covers an area of some 1,600 acres, comfortably large enough to host its own ski slope and an artillery range. Its grounds are littered with great monuments with names like Patton, MacArthur, Eisenhower, and Washington, while its buildings, some as old as the Civil War, some new, reek with the spirit of military domination and world control. One of the four military hearts of the most aggressive nation on the planet, West Point stands as a reminder to any evil empire that not only is America prepared to come and kick its front door in, but it is training the next generation of future warriors in the long Grey Line every day of the week, rain, hail or snow, to do exactly the same thing in times to come.

The preferred Pentagon strategy to neutralize such a large area is to use "denial" weapons, which America had developed and perfected to the extent that in three Gulf wars and another dozen smaller incursions, just one single-seat jet aircraft could now drop over five thousand "bomblets" the size of baseballs in one pass. With each bomblet having a kill radius of some thirty meters, it doesn't take much imagination to visualize the incredible damage caused by such an attack.

The A-10 "Warthog" that lifted off from Andrews Airforce Base in Washington was scheduled to fly up to Boston on a navigational exercise to trial some new software for the ground-mapping computer that had recently found favor with the Air Force. The aircraft successfully tanked from a KC-135 just outside the Westchester border, then continued on track straight over the military academy at a recorded twenty-five thousand feet. The last bomb hit the hallowed grass of the parade ground fifty-six seconds after the first impact on the top of Grant Hall.

Unlike the other three terrorist attacks worldwide, only a few hundred cadets and staff were killed in the initial strike. But these bomblets had become world famous for a reason, never more apparent than when the general evacuation of the entire campus commenced, and the delayed action fuses suddenly came to life.

In the second "strike," as it was to become known in the frenzied media, somewhere between three and five thousand staff, cadets, and visitors were killed, buildings going back to the Civil War were destroyed, and the campus was made virtually redundant for the next ten years.

By the time the command and control center inside the Pentagon could make any sense of the attack, seeing no unauthorized aircraft anywhere near New York, the A-10 had disappeared off the radar screens as if it had never existed.

The mightiest country on earth, by its own measure, had been struck a blow that would reverberate around the world for the next century, by one of its own aircraft, and possibly by one of its own pilots, in the most devastating "blue on blue" attack ever recorded.

CHAPTER 7

The Boss had set his small laptop up on one corner of the table, his burger-with-the-lot taking center stage. Black Pete was killing a cheesy-tomato-stew thing, and I was picking listlessly at a salad. In between mouthfuls, the Boss was summing up everything we knew so far.

"DOD(Department of Defense) has three subs, four frigates, one hundred other commercial ships of different types, and that's before we count the speed-boats, cruisers, and yachts in the Med. However," he said, stopping briefly to chomp another quarter of his burger down, "our brainiacs have overlaid the radar track of the C-One Thirty for us, and as you can see, this reduces the field down to one sub, one frigate, six speedboats, and two yachts along the flight path."

"And if you factor in the timeline from when the Hercules was intercepted, you cut that down even further." Black Pete looked at me with an amused smile and nodded his agreement.

"Yes, and if you allow the two military boats to be NATO members and Client States, that only leaves the civilian craft."

"Which we intercepted and searched," I added, just to be thorough. "Which we intercepted and searched," the Boss echoed.

"Then what are we missing?" asked Pete, wiping grease off his mouth with the back of one meaty hand. The Boss looked at him, frozen in the time honored and universal halfway pose of "man lifting burger" to mouth.

"Boats that were there but not tracked, or something else altogether." The Boss nodded, finishing his move, chomping the last of the burger in one swift bite. He chewed for a minute, looking at me all the time as if he were willing me to read his mind. I finally got it and smiled myself.

"The Hercules was a UAV," I said. The Boss nodded. Pete looked confused, then shook his head.

"No way. I like the unidentified boat option." The Boss smiled again, wiping his face with a moist cloth. As he ran it around the back of his thick neck, he said, "Pete, you might be right, but when you look carefully at the hits so far—the Vatican with two bombs, a penetrator, and a fuel-air-burst requiring heavy lifting not precision delivery, four Hellfire's from a UAV in Israel, an ambulance with one and a half tons of HEP-4, and now a high-level bombing run from a USAF Hog, and you are looking at super high-tech armaments and delivery systems, high-level security access, high-level compromise, not to mention state-of-the-art training and planning. This is no terrorist organization we are familiar with, no group we have ever looked at before, and quite frankly, I'm not even sure we have access to all the data yet."

"What makes you say that?" I asked, finally surrendering any attempt to eat my salad.

"The Brits and the frogs were too closed mouth. They either know something or suspect something, and they are scared of both the information and sharing it," Black Pete said, leaning back in his chair. He seemed to be thinking about something, his brow furrowed somewhat. "You know, back there in the room, I had the distinct feeling they knew squat." Both the Boss and I looked at Pete, precariously balanced on the back of his chair.

"Same feeling I got. I think they are scared of not knowing anything." The Boss wiped his hands, turned the little laptop towards us, and pressed a few keys. "Look here, the Hog that bombed West Point disappeared off the radar one minute after it hit, completely and utterly, was seen by no one, reported by no one, went nowhere if you believe the data. How is that possible?" he asked.

"Well, turning off his IFF (Identification, Friend or Foe) transponder would make him invisible to airways radar, but I can't believe another aircraft didn't see him," I offered. "That airspace around New York has hundreds and hundreds of aircraft flying through it every hour. How could no one see him, or for that matter, with his transponder turned off? How come he didn't literally hit someone else?"

"The weather was cloudy with full cover at ten thousand feet, five octas at fifteen thousand, some cumulonimbus at twenty thousand, with a few showers passing through. The bombing run was from under the lower cloud layer; it would have been simple for him to drift back into it and turn out towards the ocean. No one would have seen him in all that crud."

"Why do we assume he headed out to sea?" I asked.

"Why do we assume it's a 'him'?" Pete asked somewhat whimsically.

"As I said, we don't have all the data. Imagine the sheer embarrassment in Washington and the Pentagon when they discovered that one of their aircraft had maliciously and deliberately bombed the most hallowed military establishment in American history. How do you spin that on the six o'clock news?" The Boss looked happy, something I had gotten used to over the years because when he was pleased, his giant intellect was at its best, mixed up in the quagmire of politics, bombs, carnage, and duplicity. And I knew no one better to penetrate all the bullshit than him, which is why I harbored such strong unrequited feelings for him, bastard, though he was.

"We need to get to a source inside each country, get the skinny on everything they know and don't know, and look for the patterns. As I said before, this is all new. No one we have ever looked at before is anywhere near this level of sophistication; we have a new kid on the block."

"And he—or she—is a homicidal maniac of the worst type, on a worldwide stage, and I wonder if they are done yet?" Pete asked, raising the spectra of more havoc to come.

"Trouble is," the Boss answered, snapping his laptop shut, "if you don't know why they are doing what they are doing, it's impossible to predict what might be next." He stood up, and we joined him; he walked out down the long corridor, and we followed like little sheep, the mood heavy with concern and ignorance. As we exited the centuries-old building that had survived rape, pillage, and world wars only to be structurally challenged by the massive strands of creeping poison ivy that covered almost every square inch, I wondered what we would do next. Hitting a brick wall so early in an investigation was not a new thing for us, but hitting one where we were patiently not wanted was something we never enjoyed, whatever the reason.

A grey-black Humvee was waiting for us, driven by a Special Operations (SpecOps) team, dressed out in the very latest urban camouflage pattern generated by a computer run by a five-year-old, quite the contrast with the white-shirted, immaculately dressed London bobby standing outside the door, who actually saluted the Colonel.

We climbed inside.

The Humvee raced off, one massive front wheel running up and over the curb, making the cab crash back into the gutter, causing a mild smile and a shake of the head from the bobby as if to say, "Those bloody Americans, driving like bloody idiots!" We got that response a lot these days.

"Where are we headed?" Pete asked, checking out the myriad of electronic equipment housed in the back of the Humvee.

"We're cops, not soldiers; we need to solve these crimes, so we are going off-campus where we can concentrate on the data and work out what is going on."

"Too many cooks," I said. He just nodded. Interpol worked well across most European borders because we were seen as completely neutral, working with the local authorities, not against them. Our now more-than-frequent rubbing of shoulders with the various security and military forces was due only to the steep rise in terrorist activities in so many different countries. We provided a facilitative hub, someone who could assemble information and look for patterns in all sorts of places where competing nations either couldn't go or weren't allowed to go—their neighbors' backyards. We also often crossed the more difficult but physically invisible barriers created by culture and religion. Again, because we had no particular persuasion other than catching the bad guys and handing them over to the appropriate authorities, we were often welcomed to work where no other agency dared to tread.

This job looked like the worst possible combination of interests—cultural, historical, religious, national pride, political, and emotional, all elements that would make finding the bad guys behind the attacks extremely difficult, if not out-right impossible.

The miracle of modern travel revealed itself this time as a rapid flight in an RAF helicopter to a small airport on the coast of France, then a slightly bigger jet to Venice, followed by a lunatic driving a cigarette boat at low tide from the airport to the island of San Michele, located in the lagoon close to Venice. This stunning pink brick-walled edifice looked somewhat incongruent from the Venice side of the lagoon, but it has been the city's *cimitero*—cemetery—since the early nineteenth century.

Divided into untidy sections, it was really easy to get lost in it, making it the perfect place to have a remote working headquarters for Interpol. It is entirely staffed by members of the Italian Carabinieri (*Armadei Carabinieri*), a Gendarmerie-like military corps with police duties who also serve as the Italian military police. The two things I could always count on when we worked out of Venice were buckets of hormone-charged charm and the quiet, efficient provision of all the necessities of life—like a good cup of Italian espresso!

I'd managed to sleep most of the way; the Boss having immersed himself in his laptop in between snoozing and staring out of the window. Black Pete had simply curled up and fallen asleep until we hit the water when he came to life as the exhaust note increased on the twin Vee 8s that pushed the knife-shaped boat across the lagoon at close to one hundred kilometers an hour. The flashing blue light mounted high up on the radar mast cast a strange pall across the boat, but it served its purpose because we hit nothing, and everyone else in gondolas, speed-boats, and ferries gave us a wide berth.

"You know," the Boss suddenly said, cutting into my thoughts like a razor, "the one thing that worries me the most is the timing of the attacks."

"How so?" I asked. I'd had similar thoughts but not managed to reach any conclusion.

"If you really wanted to make a statement in Mecca, why not wait until the Hajj? Then you get literally millions of innocents as collateral damage."

"Same story in Jerusalem. One month later, and the place would have been packed with pilgrims," I said, having worked around this in my mind several times. The Boss looked off into space as if seeking divine guidance. Black Pete stepped back into the small, covered area behind the maniac driver, holding onto the stainless-steel center post as the boat tried to get airborne every time it hit someone else's wake.

"How about what happens next?" he asked, a crooked, lopsided grin made all the eerier by the rotating light.

"Yes, Pete, it worries me as well. We have a swath of religious targets, followed by a war college. Where's the pattern? Who does this make sense to? What I can't get my mind around is that, if anything, these attacks will unify the different religious factions, not get them at each other's throats. If you wanted to start a religious war on a global scale, why attack all the major religions at virtually the same time?"

"Well, I'm not here for my brains, but to my simple way of thinking, if this was me at work, I'm setting you up for a huge ask, and I'm going to hit you where it really hurts during any conversation to keep you off balance and be focused on what I want you to give me."

"A big ask, and more attacks to up the ante?" the Boss asked. "Yes."

"I agree," I said, just as the cigarette boat lost way and slid into the dock in front of the beautiful old renaissance archway that led into the cemetery proper. "I think we will get hit again, probably sooner rather than later."

CHAPTER 8

The president of the United States (code name POTUS) sat, as was her right, at the head of the long table that neatly divided the war room deep under the White House, now made famous by a television series, two movies, and the sheer number of times people of power had been photographed in it. Around the table sat the chiefs of the Army, Marine Corps, National Guard, Coast Guard, CIA, NSA, FBI, Secret Service, and Homeland Security. Ominously, the seat usually occupied by the chief of the navy was empty, as were the three seats immediately behind it usually occupied by his personal staff.

"Before we start this meeting formally, I would like to pay tribute to Admiral Jones, who, as we all know, was killed earlier today while a guest of the commandant of West Point. We still don't know all the facts other than his detail. He ran into a bomblet that exploded as he got into his vehicle. Admiral Jones will be missed, and his deputy will fill in for him once she arrives from Indianapolis. Now," the president intoned her gravelly voice reflecting the emotions she was fighting to suppress, "we need to understand the nature of this attack and our response. Half the country thinks we've been hit by Al Qaeda or ISIS, the other half by homegrown terrorists or rogue Air Force pilots. Which is it?" she asked, looking deep into the eyes of every man and woman around the table. Laptops and flatscreens built into the top of the table flickered and buzzed, creating patterns across intent faces, and as was the pattern in the information age, the data was immense, but the facts were minimal.

"Madam President, as far as we can determine, from all sources, including Air Traffic Control tapes, first-person witness reports, a film from the West Point campus, mobile phone pictures, and satellite tracking data, the aircraft was an A-10 Warthog on a training mission out of Andrews Airforce Base. It was scheduled to fly to Boston on a navigational exercise to trial some new software for the ground-mapping computer we have been progressively installing across the fleet. The aircraft was tanked by a KC-135 en route, part of a training mission for the Air National Guard out of Byrd Field. The KC reports regular contact, and immaculate procedures, and the film from the aircraft shows a totally normal mid-air refueling. The pilot had the necessary security codes, the aircraft number checked out, and the pilot's history has been checked all the way back to the briefing at Andrews."

"Who was the pilot?" asked the head of the Marine Corps, his tone indicating his total lack of respect for said person and their actions.

"That's where this whole thing gets squirrely," replied the general. "She was a contractor test pilot attached to the program by the vendor, ex-navy pilot, and excellent credentials, decorated in the Gulf, well respected by our people."

"Do you have a positive ID on her?" someone down the back of the room asked.

"Yes. Look at this film," he answered, turning the digital projector on. Once the grand blue-and-silver seal of the Air Force faded away, a series of images taken by security cameras filled the big screen and the flatscreens around the table.

"Here, you see her entering the hangar, where she completes a thorough walkaround, gets the test card from the flight engineer, signs for the aircraft, then goes back inside the facility. Here you see the Hog being towed to the flight line, and while the images from this point are small, we've blown them up for you, and they are a bit fuzzy at times—but here you can clearly see the seven GIB-71s being loaded onto the wings, and one on either side of the centerline, and here you can see the armorer loading the fifty-caliber cannon—four hundred fifty rounds in total."

"Why was a test article carrying live ammunition?" asked the National Guard chief.

"Sir, since 9/11, it has been Standard Operating Procedure for all active aircraft over the continental United States to be armed, and in this case, the GIBs were supposed to be inert, carried for load and balance reasons as part of the flight-test dynamics."

"Inert how?"

"Sir, the pods each have an arming pin that has to be pulled before flight, and an electronic attachment has to be made to the aircraft's weapons system from each pod. According to the aircraft log and the flight engineer's inspection prior to the flight and the pilot signed acceptance sheet, the pins were not pulled, and the connections were not made."

"Well, they were, weren't they?" A flat statement that instantly shut everyone else in the room up while the poor-quality security camera images continued to roll on all the screens. The distinctive figure of the pilot carrying a flight bag as she made her way out to the flight line, the blurry figures of the three linemen, hidden momentarily as the pilot climbed up the little yellow steps on the blind side, a dark figure bending as it rose into the cockpit. Eventually, the canopy closed, and to the ground staff's extended finger and hand music, the two massive turbofan engines started, and after a final salute, the aircraft taxied away, out of the fixed range of the camera.

"We have secured the pilot's workspace, quarters, and vehicle, and tracking down all known associates and family, and a forensic team looking at every single detail of her life." The head of the FBI was sincere in his delivery, but these days, everyone in the room had been made immune to the language of the FBI by numerous TV shows that always had miraculous scientific outcomes in less than sixty minutes, sometimes as quick as sixty seconds, while in real life learning anything important in less than a day or two unless they were lucky was the norm.

"Do we have any footage of anyone pulling the pins on those bombs?"

"No, sir. If the pins were pulled, then it was done between the time the armorers fitted the ordnance, and the pilot taxied out to the active runway."

"Cameras can be fooled, vision loops substituted; you see the bad guys do that all the time on the TV," someone said far enough away from the president to not be consumed by her glare.

"People, we have a serious issue here; in twenty minutes, I have to go on national TV and tell America that they are safe, this is a one-off, isolated attack by a crazed pilot, and everything will be okay in the morning." The room went pin-dropping quiet again. The silence was finally broken by the click of a mouse. Every head turned towards the perpetrator, a young man with a severe military brush cut sitting immediately behind the general responsible for the Marine Corps.

"Madam President, sirs, there are a number of anomalies in the data that we have. I wonder if anyone is running them down?" he asked, with the confidence that only a well-pressed uniform sitting in the shadow of a general staff officer could provide. The director of the CIA answered, a thin smile etched into his face, the certainty that he and his organization would be hung out dry like they had been after 9/11 hanging over him like a pall.

"We have a forensic team working every element, including everything we just saw here. For example, the ATC tapes show the A-10 at twenty-five thousand feet at the time of the bombing run over the Point. We have other data that clearly shows the aircraft made its bombing run from just eight thousand feet AMSL (above mean sea level). Obviously, what we have here is a very sophisticated event, the likes of which we have not seen before in this country."

"Have you seen this type of attack somewhere else?" asked the president. "Sir, early reports indicate that the attack on Israel and the Vatican also involved aircraft, military in origin, supposedly military crews, and ATC data that does not agree with other observations about the attacks.

"For example, a TV crew shot images of the Hercules overflying the Vatican just before the bombs fell, and our analysts tell us that the aircraft was at fifteen thousand feet, while the ATC tell us that on their radar, it was painting at twenty-seven thousand feet. We are trying to get inside the Italian and Israeli information processing channels, but so far, they have rebuffed us quite strongly. We believe it has something to do with the origin of the aircraft and the weapon systems. There is a strong suspicion in Europe that we are behind, or at least supporting, these attacks if not providing the equipment and hardware."

"Have you identified who was flying the UAV?" the president asked, mindful that in just six minutes, she would have to face the nation and tell them—what? She still did not understand what type of attack they were under, and it was becoming increasingly obvious that no one in the room really had any idea who was behind the attack on West Point or what exactly was going on over the other side of the world.

"Well, ma'am, again, we have conflicting data. Our satellites tell us the signals directing the UAV were coming from our station in Afghanistan, but our people there tell us that they haven't flown a UAV for several days due to extreme weather keeping everything on the ground. If I had to draw one single conclusion from everything we have so far, it would be that we are under some sort of cyberattack as well as a physical attack. But by whom, and why, I have no idea."

"Why do you think it is a cyberattack?" asked the head of Homeland Security. Information communication and technology security were one of his responsibilities, at least as far as preventing an attack on US commercial and government systems was concerned.

"Sir, to fool ATC systems, you have to be either inside them or transmitting false data, suggesting high-level penetration of the information, communications, and technology sphere here in the United States and Europe."

"Surely it must be easy to fool radar?"

"Not anymore, sir. We now use radar data supplemented by DGPS (differential global positioning system) and satellite information; you would really have to know your way around the intricate electronics of the airways system to be able to fool it so completely."

"Well, what do we have here exactly?" the president asked, standing to leave the room to face the nation. She had never felt so under-prepared in her life! Her stress levels were not helped when all the people in the room turned towards her with the same bland, noncommittal look.

"Sir, it's not Al Qaeda."

"Or ISIS."

"Are you absolutely sure about that?" asked the president, seeing a slight chance to offer some positive hope to her expectant TV audience.

"Well, no, sir, we're not. But we're pretty sure!"

ROMAN CANDLE

"It's a sign from God!" the young cleric yelled, running through the dark corridors of the hospice. He collided with a frock priest carrying an armful of bandages, sending them flying all over the floor.

"*Señor Presidente, discúlpeme por favor, mis disculpas,* I'm sorry, I'm sorry, but God has put the life back into Father Francois!" the young cleric babbled, scrabbling to pick up the bandages, which all seemed to have a mind of their own, rolling around like toilet paper streamers in a strong wind.

"*Cálmate, mi hijo, que aún,* calm now, what do you mean?"

"Father Francois is awake and asking for you, *Señor Presidente.*"

"I see. *Gracias, mi hijo.* I will see him now. Take these bandages to Sister, please. *Gracias, vaya con Dios.*" The frocked priest walked back the way he had come, into the rectory, which bulged off the corridor like the top of a dumb-bell. He collected a long-printed email he had received from his lifelong mentor, a Sedevacantist priest in Paris, quickly scanned it, then found his way down the dimly lit corridor to the room in which, until just now, Father Francois had been quietly passing on into the next life. He made the sign of the cross, kissed his fingers, and suddenly, the shock at seeing the eighty-three-year-old priest sitting up and looking like he had shed thirty years caused him to almost stumble into the bed.

"*Querido Dios, es realmente un milagro*! Brother Francois, it is a miracle!" The old priest nodded, his mouth too dry to speak. He gestured for the small water container and sipped greedily at the raised lip, water spilling from the corners of his mouth.

"*Si, si,* a miracle. *Dios trabaja en formasmisteriosas, y la voluntad de Dios por hacer.* What has been happening while I have been sleeping?" he croaked. The priest furrowed his brow in thought; sleeping was hardly what he would have called a morphine-induced coma lasting the better part of two weeks, but the proof of God's will was before him, in the form of a seemingly rejuvenated bishop who, for all intents and purposes, had been next to death just minutes ago.

"Brother Francois, the world is in turmoil. Terrorists have attacked the Holy See, and the Conclave of Cardinals have been massacred. The terrorists also attacked the sacred site at Mount Moriah. The Catholic world is in turmoil." The old priest's eyes boggled, opening so far that his eyelids appeared to have disappeared into his face.

"*Dios tenga misericordia*! When did this happen?" he asked, his voice a thin shell of its former choirboy glory.

"Just two days ago. An aircraft of some type dropped bombs on the Holy See while the Cardinals were in conclave for the first vote. All their staff and those of the Vatican council and all the invited bishops, priests, dignitaries, and nuns were killed, along with several thousand worshippers waiting outside."

"Were the catacombs damaged?"

"*Si*, it appears that what was not destroyed directly by the bombs, the fires, or the rubble from the explosions was ruined by the waters from the Tiber that flooded in through the subterranean vault walls when they collapsed. The assessment from the curator from Paris is that we have lost most of our history and most treasured icons, other than those in museums around the world."

"*Dios en el cielo*! Who did this terrible thing?" the old priest asked, suddenly looking all his eighty-plus years again. As the conversation had progressed, his skin had taken on a grey pallor, and his eyes had visibly sunk back into his skull.

"Brother, we do not know. But if you are recovered, God's will must be done, and done this day." The old priest slumped in his bed, looking more than frail as if his body was only just managing to hold his spirit back from ascending to a better place.

"*Dios en el cielo*, what could you possibly want from a dying old man?" he croaked, sliding further down the bed. The priest made the sign of the cross, kissed his fingers, then read from the email he had been holding by his side.

"Obispo Monseñor André François Lyon, Monsignor Bishop Andre` Lyons Francois, as the most senior surviving member of the Holy Roman Catholic Church of our Lord Jesus Christ, you are petitioned by the surviving ordained clergy of brothers, priests, and bishops to assume the mantle of our Holy Father and travel to the second city of the Holy See and reestablish the seat of Peter." The old man rolled his eyes once, sighed deeply, and died, his heart shocked into submission. His spirit had been trying as hard as it could to get out of the retched and wasted body to start its ethereal journey for over a month, finally fled upwards towards the stars at the speed of light, wondering what all the fuss was about, delighted to be free at last!

CHAPTER 9

The Interpol control room hidden beneath the murky waters of the lagoon that lapped against the northern side of Venice was a wonderful place to work. Murano glass of museum quality filled every empty space, exotic coffee machines hissed and puffed in every corner, and the most magnificent Turkish scatter rugs covered the polished timber floor, suspended as it was over a huge, cavernous area that was filled with the most sophisticated computer processing equipment outside the National Security Agency (*Puzzle Palace*) in the USA. Funded entirely by the European Union (EU) and built mainly by the Swiss and the Germans, but manned exclusively by members of the Italian Carabinieri (*Ar- madei Carabinieri*), a Gendarmerie-like military corps with police duties who served as backup to Interpol field agents when required; the soundproofed walls reverberated to the music of a dozen different languages, not to mention the eclectic choices of multi-genre digital radio streams.

But unusually for anything Italian, this particular space worked as smoothly as the best-engineered Swiss watch and had gained a worldwide reputation for being a center of excellence when it came to identifying and causing the incarceration or immediate removal from the planet of international thugs from all walks of life—white-collar crime Bosses, drug lords, pedophiles, murderers, gun runners, people smugglers, serial killers, and the odd dictator or two caught with their fingers in their countries' cookie jars.

Today, it was Lt. Colonel Indigo Kashasini who was the duty officer and, as such, responsible for making sure our rag-tag team didn't dent the furniture or steal the silver. A booming man of just five feet six inches, he was a qualified paratrooper, counter-insurgency specialist, and master sniper, and his blue-black trooper uniform with its red-and-gold trim was an incongruent decoration on such a hard man. His eyes glittered as if they were permanently attached to a power point, and his smile was infectious. I had once seen him run down a fit young killer without even working up a sweat, so I had no illusions about his combat ability. But he did make a great espresso, and I couldn't help but smile as he handed one to me with a little bow.

"*Signorina*, your usual?" he asked in his gravelly voice, completely ignoring the Boss and Pete.

"Thank you, Colonel, very kind of you."

"No trouble at all," he said, painting the Boss and Pete with a frosty look. "Not that I can say the same for your two companions."

"Hey, Indigo, you can't still be pissed because of your little boat," Pete asked, lightly punching the Colonel on the arm.

"Indeed, I am," he replied, the chills in his voice enough to petrify most human beings. "That boat cost the Italian Navy three million euros, and it deserved better than to be rammed up the backside of a dubious Greek fishing vessel," he huffed, obviously upset. I found it a little strange because at the time Pete had been doing the ramming, little Indigo had been belting away with a Barrett fifty-caliber sniper rifle and was successfully shooting great chunks off said Greek fishing vessel with gay abandon. Then I got it!

"Actually, Indigo, I completely understand how angry you are at Pete."

"You do?" asked Indigo, his normal gravelly voice going up an octave in surprise. "Absolutely. You're upset because he sank the boat before you could finish shooting it to bits." The room suddenly erupted with laughter as Indigo got the joke, and everyone on duty responded. Another thing I loved about the Italians was that they were extraordinarily proud and macho, but loved a huge joke, so long as it was at someone else's expense!

"Got you, Mister Pete, got you," Indigo shouted, slapping poor Pete on the back so hard he nearly fell over. "Come, let us begin the brief." We followed him over to a massive, computerized conference space, relaxed back into the Natuzzi patent leather armchairs, and tried to relax for the first time in perhaps thirty or forty hours. We were home, or at least amongst friends, far away from the raging insanity that seemed to be consuming the modern world outside.

"Colonel, as you asked, I have all the known data for every incident so far, organized by timeline, with a technical and forensic analysis where available. While we have excellent material on the attack on Rome, we are not so fortunate with the Israelis, Arabians, and Americans, who, quite frankly, do not want to share with us at this time. It seems they suspect everyone, including each other."

"Indigo, if you were put on the spot by your president to summarize in less than two minutes exactly what we are seeing here, what would you say?" the Boss asked. Indigo literally grew centimeters in height as he physically preened at the compliment. But while he often exhibited the macho physicality of his native country, he was also one of the smartest policemen we had even come across. This is why he ran our Italian office and de facto headquarters with such efficiency and pride.

"Colonel, I have been giving this a great deal of thought since the first attack on our beautiful Roma. Once I cleared my tears, I started thinking about who could profit from such a monstrosity of an attack. And then the terrorists bombed the scared Rock in Jerusalem, and everything I had constructed to that point disappeared in a puff!" he said, snapping his fingers theatrically.

"At first, I thought it was terrorists of Muslim persuasion, then I changed my mind completely. When they struck Mecca, I got even more confused. But when your West Point was bombed, it all became clear to me." He looked expectantly at us as if we were going to guess his insight. The Boss sat calmly, giving Indigo his head. "Simply put, in two minutes or less, either the Chinese or the Russians, or the Russians or the Chinese, are making a bid for world domination by getting the major religions completely offside and in chaos and the populations of major countries scared out of their wits. This ties up all our resources, creates multiple possible bad guys for us to go off and chase while they slip in and take over everything."

"Yes, I started to think that way too. But then, after looking at the methodology of the attacks, I started to wonder. The Russians and the Chinese both have the technology and the technical skills to mount these attacks, but neither government is stupid enough to think we would not put them in the frame and prosecute a case against them as hard as we could in the world court. No, Indigo, I think we have someone else entirely different here, someone we haven't ever heard from before." Indigo looked thoughtful for a moment, then, as if the air had been sucked out of him, he visibly seemed to shrink in size, rubbing his forehead with one meaty hand.

"Then who, Colonel, has tried to kill my country, tried to kill my Church, and tried to kill my spirit?"

"I don't know. And so far, we're not even invited to the party." Indigo looked at the Boss, a huge smile splitting his chubby face, the life pumping back into him as if from some hidden battery.

"Colonel, but of course. On behalf of my country, may I officially request Interpol to take the lead as the agency of note in the investigation of the atrocity enacted at the Vatican by persons unknown, and I will have government documents to that effect within the hour!" he exclaimed, jumping up from his chair. "Ah ha! Now we are in business, yes?" he asked.

"Yes. We are in business," answered the Boss, "and now all we need is for the other players to realize it as well."

BLACK GOLD

The incredible oil field at Shaybah sits around forty kilometers from the northern edge of Rub' Al-Khali, the "Empty Quarter," as the Arabs call it, in Arabia. It is just 10 kilometers south of the border with Abu Dhabi and is noted for the hundreds of kilometers of massive white pipeline that winds its way around and across the desert like a gigantic lost snake all the way to Abqaiq. Its reserves have been estimated at fourteen billion oil barrels and twenty-five trillion cubic feet of natural gas. But the extreme temperature range from minus ten to forty degrees Celsius drove most of the people who worked there to drink. The oil field, albeit a massive one, appeared to be relatively small on the surface, located by an imposing tall white pressure tower that looked a lot like a lighthouse looking for an ocean.

One of the well-documented features of this oil field was that there had been small deposits detected that were inconsistent with the main field, in that while the quality of the major supply was a golden-colored light crude, the quality of the subsidiary find was of the heavy variety more expected further north in Iran, Iraq, and Kuwait. Geologists and engineers had long speculated that the vast underground reserves throughout the desert were interconnected at many geological levels, and they had proved their point to a limited extent on some occasions by pumping water back down into a well that had been exhausted, only to have it spew back up again thousands of meters away from a different borehole.

The seven hundred people that lived and worked at Shaybah lived in a series of air-conditioned metal huts, all set in rows like a chicken farm and surrounded by a five-meter-high razor wire fence. Huge valves with wheels as big as a tractor littered the landscape, and the bitumen road that linked everything together tended to slope from left to right where it had softened and melted in the extreme heat.

The pump truck made its way warily along the thin road, rocking anxiously from side to side, finally jerking to a stop opposite valve number six. The two workers, covered from head to toe in oil-stained caftans and burkes, highlighted by their bright orange-and-yellow safety vests, worked slowly, attaching the dimpled aluminum filter tank to the bleed line, being very careful not to jam their exposed fingers between the massive collar and the seal. The crane mounted on the back of their truck strained with the effort, made all the more difficult by the twenty-degree tilt of the road.

Once completely happy, the two struggled for about a full minute to get the massive wheel to crack, the pressure in the pipes such that everything metal tended to resist unlocking. When it gave, it rotated so fast that one of the two workers was thrown to the ground, letting fly a colorful curse. His companion just laughed, spinning the massive wheel to its stops. Flicking a lever on the now securely attached tank, the two waited until the noise of the pressure equalization died away, gave the tank a symbolic bang as if to thank it for a job well done, waited another minute or so, then rewound the wheel to its original position. As they walked slowly back to their truck, the relentless sun bounced and shimmered off the sides of the tall tank, creating a light show that was largely ignored by the surrounding workers, intent as they were on getting their jobs done before they literally boiled alive in the intense heat. No one noticed the truck depart, and when the Arabian Al Mabaahith Al Jena'eyah (Arabian Secret Service), Al Mukhabarat Al A'amah (Arabian General Intelligence Directorate), and commandos from the Lightning Force (Qowwat Al-Sa'eqah) arrived to investigate a supposed nuclear explosion ten hours later, there were, literally, no witnesses, the only indication that something might be amiss being the blistered, charred, and broken bodies carelessly strewn around the site and the incredible amount of twisted radioactive glasslike material that poked up out of the desert floor like dead roses in a spring garden.

What really put the world on edge was that within a day, there were reports of radioactive oil coming out of the ground three thousand kilometers away, for no apparent reason, and people dropping from radiation poisoning as far away as Turkey.

CHAPTER 10

We had been pouring over the details of the attack on the Vatican that Indigo had provided when we learned of the new attack on Shaybah, and our entire world seemed to stand still. In one small moment, the world lost access to more than seventy percent of its oil reserves for perhaps thousands of years, and the economic chaos that would follow would be catastrophic and might make World War II look like a kindergarten tea party with plastic cups. Within seconds of the news hitting the World Wide Web, stock markets in every country crashed to their lowest point in one hundred years, and countries involved in the supply of petroleum products out of the Middle East went into receivership. It was pure fear that triggered the tsunami of economic destruction, as oil workers around the world downed tools and fled for their lives as soon as news of the radiation poisoning spread throughout the industry. It might have been an irrational reaction in many countries, but the purely human instinct for survival effectively shut down more than half the mobility and production capacity of the twenty-first century in just a few hours.

Someone had managed to blast a tank full of Strontium-90 pellets, with a half-life of 29 years, into a wellhead that polluted the underground oil field at Shaybah and irradiated the oil-rich substrate for thousands of kilometers in every direction. The Pan-Arab oil business was no more, and as military law was mandated country by country, mainly to control the mobs who were desperately seeking fuel for cars and busses from any source, bicycles, horses, and solar-powered hybrids became the order of the day.

And those countries that did have oil that was unpolluted setup barriers to entry that could only end in invasion and outright war. The Arab oil-producing nations that one minute were controlling the world's economies suddenly had no customers, and no customers meant no revenue, and no revenue meant that playtime was suddenly over. Black Pete was the first to break the silence, the truth being that this attack's sheer scale and audaciousness had beggared the mind.

"Well, I said we'd get hit again, but bugger me dead. I never thought it would be on this scale. Now, all we have to do is wait for the 'ask.'" Indigo had slumped into one of the beautiful leather armchairs and was visibly distressed. But his prodigious mind must have been working overtime because he looked up at Pete's words and seemed to grow twice his size.

"No, no, we will not get any 'ask,' as you say. No, now I think I understand exactly what is happening." The Boss gave him an opened-handed sign, both palms held upwards, encouraging him to go on. "What we have just witnessed is so monstrous that no sane or even insane government could ever expect to survive the repercussions. Even though it was only an oil field, and only seven or eight hundred people were killed in the initial attack, the world will still see this as using weapons of mass destruction. And not even China or Russia could stand up against this type of world condemnation without going to war and risking their ultimate annihilation. No, my friends, I do not believe we will get the 'ask' you refer to; I think it will go remarkably quiet for some time to come. And I think now for certain it is not either Russia or China doing these terrible things."

"Then who is behind this? What, exactly, is happening?" Pete asked, voicing the questions we all had on our lips.

"I think we have a—how do you say it—new kid on the block, as the Colonel said earlier. I think we have a client state somewhere bankrolling an independent group of terrorists, all military trained and, in many cases, I believe homegrown. I also think there is a religious—or more specifically, anti-religious—aspect here we can't see yet, but the primary attacks are politically motivated, of that I am sure." The Boss and I looked at Indigo in amazement, not having the faintest idea how he had come to these conclusions. The client state aspect had been dancing around in our minds for a while, but largely because the money and logistics involved in planning, implementing, and financing attacks of this magnitude would have been considerable. Possibly in the billions of dollars or hundreds of millions, that was for sure.

And you don't just wake up one morning and decide you will walk onto a heavily guarded military base, strap yourself into a modern-day jet fighter, and fly off on a hazardous mission on a whim.

"Take just one aspect of this latest attack," Indigo said, stopping to sip at a delicate blue-green glass coffee cup with a handle that looked like the F-shaped bow of a gondola. "How long and from what source do you obtain many kilos of Strontium-90 pellets, one of the most secure and guarded radioactive substances anywhere in the world? The terrorists must have taken years to collect what they used, or someone, somewhere, would have posted an alert that they were missing such a quantity. This did not happen, so exactly where did this infernal material come from?" The Boss looked grim, wiping his forehead with his right hand, his broken and misshaped little finger sticking up into the air as if seeking permission to leave the room.

"Indigo, I'm starting to form an opinion about that, and quite frankly, I don't like the shape of it one bit. Who is our resident database management expert?" Indigo thought for a minute.

"Luigi Antoinette is our absolute best. He is in Milano; we can call him if you wish."

"I wish." Indigo waved a hand at one of his assistants, who immediately brought up the image of the Interpol logo on the big screen; then, seconds later, a swarthy face covered in paint filled the arena.

"*Ciao ci*", Indigo said. "Luigi, please meet my associates Colonel Anthony, Captain Riley, and Master Chief Pete, all of Interpol. The Colonel would like to engage your expertise."

"*Ciao*, Colonel, but first I wash this off if you please, then perhaps we can chat!" he said, stripping his shirt off and dipping his head into a porcelain bowl. The camera must have had auto tracking because we then got a perfect series of pictures as we watched him scrub the paint off a well-toned and muscular torso, flick his long black hair back, smooth it, then pull on a red football jersey as he moved rapidly around the room, a well-fitted studio by the looks of it, with large canvasses and equally large plasma screens littering the background.

"Okay, Colonel, how can I be of service?" he asked, finally sitting at a huge wooden desk, lit by the soft light of the afternoon, which streamed in through a beautiful glass mosaic window at one end of the elongated room. The effect was somewhat surreal; high-tech meets Tullio Crali in the middle of a worldwide crisis!

"Mister Antoinette, I want you to steal a kilo of Strontium-90 from anywhere you choose, but you can leave no tracks," the Boss said, instantly creating a stir in the control center. We were in the business of catching the crooks, not mounting the crimes, but suddenly I started to see where the Boss was going, and a whole lot of what had happened over the past two or three days suddenly started to make more sense.

"From my attic, here in Milano, you want me to steal some Strontium-90?" Luigi asked, astonished at the request. The look he gave the camera was one of doubt and mistrust.

"Luigi, the Colonel, is the finest agent Interpol has, and I assure you, if he aks of you this impossible task, then there is good reason for this, and you will be protected and supported at every step." Indigo had drawn himself up to his full height while staring down the barrel of the camera lens as if the sheer physicality of his personality would lend credibility to his statements.

"Well, now, who said it is impossible?" Luigi asked, a wan smile forming from one corner of his mouth.

"You say that as if you have done this before?" the Boss asked, a humorous inflection in his voice.

"No, not actually done it before, but many, many times I have thought about this when we have played our little war games. Unfortunately, I think it might be much easier than you believe it to be."

"Please show us," the Boss asked, this time in a tone that was shy of a direct order. He was like that, good cop, bad cop, all in the one crusty body!

"Well, to do this, I have to hack into a number of different databases, send some commands to different agencies, create some delicate paperwork, then have a destination for the material that does not raise any eyebrows," Luigi said, clicking away at his keyboard. "Here, you see, already I have found seven kilos of Pu-239 waiting to be disposed of at the Henley Nuclear Power Station in the UK. It has been sealed as required, transport has been commissioned, and it will be collected within a day by the licensing authority responsible for its waste management."

"What would you have to do to physically get possession of this material?" the Boss asked.

"From this point, all we would have to do is replace the transport agency, because all the hard work has already been done for us. The waste is in a containment capsule; it is certified safe to transport, and the documents required by the AEC— the Atomic Energy Commission, the people who control this all over the world— have been created, checked for authenticity, and filed electronically with all the relevant parties, ready for us to use."

"What would you need?" the Boss asked, his voice so low I had to lean forward to hear him. Luigi seemed to be considering his options on the other side of the cameras.

"Many, many possibilities, but the easiest one that comes to mind is canceling the transport request with the handling company, something that is done all the time, then providing my own secured pickup service as a replacement, collect the material, then simply drive off to a predestined location where I could move the shipment onto a different form of transport and make my getaway."

"But I need to you leave no trace, and I need no one to suspect that the delivery has not gone off as normal, and aren't the shipments all electronically tagged?" the Boss asked, letting a little excitement creep into his voice.

"Yes, with radio frequency identification tags (RFID) and GPS (global positioning system) trackers, both easily fooled and, funnily enough, monitored by Interpol when the shipment is to cross international borders."

"But what about the original destination for the nuclear waste? Why would they not kick up a fuss when the material does not arrive as scheduled?" the Boss asked. His intensity was starting to put everyone in the room on edge. He was now leaning forward in his seat, as if to get in the face of our computer genius to put additional pressure on him to be very clear with his answers.

"Colonel, to make the system work for you, you have to know intimately how the system works." The Boss sat back, a smile forming where just a second ago a scowl had been cemented in place.

"Explain."

"Colonel, everything these days is done online, by certified and monitored contractors, all responsible for their little bit of the drama, but only three agencies actually follow the process, and then only one from end to end. The AEC take a high-level, strategic position, ensuring all processes are conformal and safe; they are the auditors, so to speak. As I said before, if nuclear waste is to cross international borders, then Interpol has a watching brief to manage any potential border or political issues, but Interpol's remit starts and ends with the borders."

"And the third agency?"

"A company by the name of BRETQA makes its business by counting all the radioactive material in the world and making sure it always adds up," Luigi said, suddenly chewing on the end of a pencil. "Ah, I see what you are getting at; how do you hide the totals if you are siphoning off nuclear waste over a long period of time?"

"Yes, how do you do that?" the Boss asked, suddenly impressed with the quick intelligence of the Italian computer specialist. Luigi broke into a huge smile at the other end of the cameras.

"Actually, Colonel, that may be the easiest part of the whole exercise!" I suddenly had a question pop into my mind, and I quickly looked at the Boss to see if it was okay for me to butt in. Without looking directly at me, he nodded silently, totally aware of every person in the room and their body language, a trick he claimed to have learned from a hot, young card shark on the World Poker Tour.

"Luigi, excuse me for interrupting, but if there is an agency that actually counts all the radioactive material on the planet, where do they get their source information from?" Luigi's entire face lit up, and he seemed to be bouncing up and down on his chair.

"*Signorina*, that is just such a wonderful question!" he exclaimed, seemingly internally vibrating with happiness. "If you can control the starting figure, you have control over the finishing figure," he said and then suddenly looked quite somber, "unfortunately, this is not what I would do to steal someone's processed nuclear fuel, no, not really. What I had in mind was to keep all the sums adding up and all the deliveries on schedule, although I might change the schedule here and there of a truck or two. No, *signorina*, the secret to this mission is the old "shell game" and having an intimate knowledge of how the materials are handled, checked, and stored." He said all this in such a manner that there was absolutely no way I could take offense at being corrected, one of the reasons I just loved the Italians!

"It's the sealed containers!" exclaimed Black Pete. "It's the bloody containers! I remember them from a trip I did once on a nuke sub. Every container is color coded, and if you pull a rod at sea, you slip it into a container within a container that is hermetically and physically sealed. On board the ship, the containers stay in the pool area until they can be recovered landside. I bet you anything you like that the civilians have a similar system." Luigi nodded in agreement, suddenly happy again.

"Yes, you are correct. If you can obtain the exact containers that are to be transshipped, prepare them properly for inspection, then exchange them en route, the quantity numbers don't change, and you can manage all the electronic processes in such a manner that no one will ever know what happened or, more importantly, ever be suspicious about what might have happened and think about checking that something might be wrong."

"But how do you hide radioactive waste?" Pete asked. Luigi broke out into raw laughter, turning to face the camera.

"In plain sight, Master Chief Pete, in plain sight!"

"Okay, Luigi," the Boss said, "let's get down to business. How much Strontium-90 was in that container, and how do we steal it?"

"Well, Colonel, this particular radioactive substance is used in medicine all over the world, as well as being a byproduct of the normal processes in a nuclear power plant; in one form, it is relatively harmless; in another, it is quite lethal to human physiology. So I can create for you different scenarios where you obtain a lot very quickly or a little very slowly, but the baseline here would have to be the time frame from the first collection to the last because storing and transporting a large quantity over a long period of time would make you susceptible to discovery, even if only by accident." The entire room went quiet as if everyone was suddenly absorbed, trying to work out the answer. The Boss suddenly stood up, rolling his shoulders to loosen them, taking his time to look everyone in the eyes.

"We need answers, and not just to this question. What was the container they used to mount the attack? How did it work? How did it get to the wellhead undetected? Where did the crew go after they fitted the container to the valve? How come security let them in, then let them out, and why can't we find them now? For that matter, where is the truck? Satellite images of the area don't show it anywhere on the access road, going in or out. Luigi, can anyone hack into military satellites and change the images?" He turned around again, looking everyone directly in the eyes, then back to the camera that transmitted his image to the Italian computer genius. "Luigi, please, as fast as you can, find us the answers to these questions. You have the full authority of Interpol behind you, but we need to know how these attacks were mounted, and we need to know now!"

CHAPTER 11

As the tired and sooty A-330 landed just as dawn was breaking over Miami-Dade Airport, the gateway to Florida and some of world's most expensive beach real estate, the priest stared out the small window, seeing only his quest. As the aircraft started the long taxi to the terminal, the landing gear bumping and thumping across the many fractures and splits in the concrete caused by too much sun and too much tropical rain, he silently prayed to his God that he would have the strength to get his message through to the one person that could perhaps stop the carnage that had gripped the world. The onboard newscast played out on the little TV screen built into the back of the seat in front of him during the long trip had told a grim tale of death and destruction across three continents and of the impending economic doom that would saturate the entire world in the coming months and, perhaps, for even years.

As the aircraft finally shuddered to a halt at the gateway, he steeled himself for what was to come, as all too often in the past, civilizations had literally shot or butchered the messenger who had brought them the bad news. After waiting patiently for nearly twenty minutes, he politely allowed an old Spanish lady to hobble down the aisle in front of him and finally exited the aircraft into the fetid humidity of the aerobridge.

The Customs and Immigration gates queue was ordered into long, sweeping rows that filled the hall, and as he joined the back of the line, he realized it would take at least an hour or two before he reached a processing point.

Then, he mused to himself, the real fun would start. He wondered what jail he would end up in and how long it would take him to find the person he most needed to talk to. Americans were funny people, sometimes impossibly gracious and kind, more often closed and selfish. When he looked closely at the immigration control officers seated in the raised booths, he only saw Hispanic and African American faces, a sign that he may find a sympathetic ear.

The line lurched forward the width of two people, and he mentally relaxed. It would take time and time he did not have, but if he was to save the world from itself, he also had no option but to wait his turn.

CHAPTER 12

The sign on the door was unambiguous—ءيراوطلاتاوق—which for the visitors from the GIGN (French *Groupe d'Intervention de la Gendarmerie Nationale*) was not only in Arabic but instructive, as it simply said, "The Emergency Force," which, given what this elite unit did for a living, was the understatement of a lifetime. Working mainly as a special operations counter-terrorism unit of Arabia General Security, out of some thirteen centers around the Kingdom, the SEFC's main mission was to combat terrorism. As the six French Special Forces staff made their way into the command and control room, they were very much aware that they were in the presence of a military force second to none, with an international reputation for being much, much more than just a deadly force.

The GIGN were no slouches when it came to fighting terrorism and putting hard men and women into body bags, making this tactical briefing all the more poignant. The Arabians had been quite specific in requesting the meeting and made their intentions clear to the French government. Back in 1979, GIGN commandos were instrumental in regaining control during the seizure of the Grand Mosque in Mecca, and now, both Mecca and the oil field at Shaybah have been viciously attacked by terrorists, and Arabian oil production was literally brought to a halt, and the Arabians had not hesitated in calling on those they believed to be the best in the world at what they did to attempt a fast resolution.

Besides, for many years, the French had enjoyed a privileged status as far as the guaranteed supply of well-priced Arabian oil was concerned, and the Kingdom, in many ways, felt that the French owed them. So, the call had been made, king to the president, and within hours, six of the three hundred and eighty members of the elite GIGN entered the command and control room built into the bowels of one of the most famous mosques in the world.

"Allah Akbar," coursed the waiting general and his staff, all bowing from the waist in unison. Indeed, God would have to be great in this time of national crisis. The space on either side of the commander of the SEFC was occupied by two massive bodyguards dressed in traditional Arabian costume, white robes flowing freely to the ankles and headdresses held in place by red-and-white bandanas. The illusion of desert warrior was enhanced by the silenced MP-5s slung around their necks and the evil black-eyed stare they greeted the Frenchmen with. In their belts, ceremonial jambyas glistened in gold-and-silver scabbards. It was no secret that the hard men of the desert held no real love for the French, who over the various centuries had invaded and pillaged the Kingdom just like everyone else, from the Moors and the Romans to the Americans and the British.

"Welcome, my friends. Please come and sit with me while we discuss your mission," the general said, leading the French into a seating area in full view of the massive screens forming a horseshoe around the room. A servant served traditional coffee in silver fluted-shaped cups as a large soldier dressed in street camos entered the seating area. In his hand was a huge mobile computing tablet, which he held up to the assembled soldiers. The image on his screen was duplicated on all but two of the larger screens around the room, creating the illusion that he was the center of the electronic universe.

"Gentlemen, as you know, when the Al Mabaahith Al Jena'eyah, Al Mukhabarat Al A'amah, and commandos from the Lightning Force arrived to investigate the nuclear explosion, there were no witnesses left alive, and the site had sustained considerable damage to the infrastructure. Our forensic experts were able to piece together a story, mainly from satellite imaging and security film, which were taken on the access road into Shaybah. Because the field is so close to Abu Dhabi, they also sent in their special forces under our command. They were able to contribute digital imaging taken from their cameras that monitor the border where the highway runs parallel for some kilometers." The leader of the French contingent held his hand up as if asking permission to leave the room.

"*Monsieur*, with respect, how is this germane to us being here at this time?" he asked.

"Sir, I have been instructed to give you every detail of the attack on Shaybah so that you may see for yourself the coincidences between this attack and the one on Masjid al-Haram in Mecca."

"But, *monsieur*, again, with respect, we are aware that the attack was made by trucks driven by disguised persons and that all the paperwork, authorizations, travel documents, security passes, and access permits were legitimate and correct in every detail. As were the reasons for the presence of both vehicles at their destinations both legitimate and expected."

"Sir, that is true, and that is also why I have been instructed to give you all this detail." He snapped a pen out of the side of the tablet, tapped at the icons on the screen, and brought up a satellite image of an eighteen-wheeler moving swiftly down a road, surrounded on both sides by a featureless desert. The Pantech had the name of a well-known aid agency plastered down the side and was the only vehicle on the road in any direction. The soldier clicked at his screen again, and another truck appeared, this time weaving its way through a huge flock of sheep, which seemed to flow around the vehicle like angry floodwaters.

"As you can see, both trucks are identified as belonging to the same agency, and both were the only vehicles in the vicinity of the two attacks other than smaller vehicles, all of which have been accounted for. Do you notice anything unusual about these two trucks?" he asked, now dividing the screen into two halves so that the two massive trucks seemed to be racing away from each other.

"Apart from the obvious, no, please explain." The soldier tapped his screen again, this time making the camera appear to zoom into the driver's side door area. The high oblique angle of the satellite image made it hard to see through the window, and the dark fuzzy area where the drivers would have been sitting was so indistinct that it could have been a dog driving, and you could not have proven otherwise.

"We believe that from these images, we can backtrack the source and destination of the vehicles and that they were involved in the attacks."

"Why do you say that? They are just two trucks of the same type, run by the same aid agency."

"Well, sir, we have some interesting questions then. Where did the two attack terrorist trucks come from? We have no footage of them further away from their targets than ten kilometers. And the truck that delivered the contaminated filter literally disappeared almost that same distance from the wellhead. The paramedics that drove their truck through the Gates to Heaven disappeared as if by magic just meters away from the explosion, yet their remains have not yet been identified. How would you suggest they performed this miracle trick?" The soldier stared at the Frenchmen, looking each one in the eye, oblivious to the hard stares he was getting in return. Suddenly the room got distinctly colder, and the staff working the screens and data terminals all stopped what they had been doing, sensing a tension between their leaders and the visitors.

"*Monsieur*, I am at a loss as to why you would ask us this question. We were invited here by your king, but what I sense I am hearing is some form of accusation, *non*?" If anything, the Arabian stood even taller under the glare of the French Special Forces officer.

"Well, sir, if you hear an accusation, that is probably exactly what I meant to imply. By the way, your coffee has been drugged, and if you move even just a centimeter, you will be shot to death where you sit."

CHAPTER 13

In contrast to the earlier meeting with the president, only three people and their staffs were present this time. And the luxurious setting of the White House situation room was replaced by the bland, electronically impenetrable concrete, steel, and lead walls of the "vault," the ultra-secure control room deep below "Puzzle Palace," or the headquarters of the National Security Agency (NSA). Regarded as one of the most secure places to hold a conversation in the world, the NSA "vault" had been the host to a myriad of high-level military and political people over the years, but none more intent than the current group.

They had a problem—a serious, real cut-your-balls-off-if-you-are-wrong type of problem. And Julius Bronstein, the head of the CIA, was only too aware that his agency was yet again in the gun over poor intelligence. The consequences this time were dire, as he was about to point out to the other two directors—of the NSA and the FBI.

"Gentlemen, since 2002, the FBI and the CIA have been jointly tasked with the global audit of all military hardware on behalf of the US military and its agencies. We all know what a pain in the arse the audit process has been; we have both had nothing but complaints from the get-go about the process, the time and resources required, and the so-called interruptions to normal military activity. But, gentlemen, trust me, the pain of the past will seem like a caress by a lovely woman compared to the shit storm we are now facing. And frankly, the CIA is not going down alone."

"Julius, calm down. What could you possibly know that we don't that has your knickers in such a twist?" Frank Reynolds asked, nicely decked out in an Armani suit, looking more like a mafia hitman than the head of the NSA. At just forty-four years of age, he was considered a genius with electronics, computers, and encryption and had multiple degrees to prove it. Definitely not a "company" man, with an independent fortune sitting in the background multiplying by a few million dollars every month, he liked to think of himself as above the normal cut and thrust of the Washington set, whom he saw as no more than crude men and women running around killing people in and out of uniform in the name of economic freedom.

"Frank, you smug son of a bitch, your agency is supposed to be able to tell us where every bomb and bullet is, twenty-four seven fifty-two. You fucked up!" The head of the NSA laughed, lifting a pale blue Wedgewood china cup delicately to his lips to gently sip at his chamomile tea.

"Julius, we just record where everything is based on the GPS and/or RFID signals sent to us by the individual weapons or weapons systems. It's your responsibility to ensure the weapons are tagged correctly."

"You prick! You mean that nowhere in this overpriced electronic playpen you swill around in every day, you can't tell the bloody difference between a true signal and a fake?" The young NSA director crossed his legs elegantly, pulling the bottoms of his trousers up a fraction to prevent creasing. He calmly put his cup and saucer on the low table that filled the area between the couches.

"Julius, if you would stop thinking with your dick for five minutes and listen carefully to what I said, you would have recognized the one critical fact in all of this drama that causes us here at the NSA real concern." He leaned forward, holding his silk tie in place with one hand, and picked up a slim red folder with the other off the table.

"Marshall, as I read from the list, can you check the identification file and compare the data, please?" he asked over his shoulder to one of the highly trained acolytes he maintained on his personal staff. He ran his finger down a long list of numbers, compared another data sheet, and then leaned back into his seat. "Item one, attack number one, the Vatican. One by GBU-43/B twenty-one thousand pounds GPS/JDAM guided munition."

"Sir, identification via GPS chipset #33-345H-46352_876662. The location of all active and inactive munitions known by that designation was verified by a physical audit in the last twelve hours. Full complement accounted for, sir!"

"Thank you, Marshall, now for item two, attack number one, the Vatican. One by BLU-82 Daisy Cutter, fifteen thousand FAE GPS guided munition."

"Sir, identification via GPS chipset #24-465J-48576_098790. The location of all active and inactive munitions is known and verified by physical audit in the last twelve hours. Full complement accounted for, sir!"

"Marshall, thank you. Julius, Roger, can you now see our problem?" The two directors looked at the relaxed head of the most powerful information-gathering agency in the world with ill-disguised contempt. "Okay, then, let me spell it out for you. According to our electronic data, provided to us by your systems, reports, and field agents via securitized data channels, not only are the munitions not missing, but they have also never been missing, and we can theoretically, at least by your provided data, assume that they are safely stored somewhere in a climate-controlled bunker. Like to explain that to the president?"

"Okay, smart arse, I have a question for you. How come we have visual confirmation that both those munitions were dropped onto the top of the bloody Vatican, and to make matters worse, one of our own aircraft dropped about ten thousand bombs onto West Point? How do you account for that?" asked the FBI director. He was so furious he literally spits the last words out, thumping the table with his fist.

"Roger, that is exactly my point. We have other disturbing data from all the events of the last few days that would indicate that someone is manipulating our most secure data channels from the inside. The Air Traffic Control in Rome had the wrong track and altitude of the Hercules and, in fact, had two tracks, where we now know that only one aircraft was flying in that area. The Dome of the Rock episode has a double question mark over it—the altitude and track of the UAV were incorrect, and the control signals were supposedly emanating from inside one of our own control rooms in Afghanistan. Add to that the blank spots in the digital video of the launch of the Hog, its subsequent incorrect flight path details, altitude, and track, and what we see here at the NSA is a massive breach in security somewhere in our electronic arsenal, and possibly over a long period of time. That's the real issue, not some nonexistent missing bombs."

"But you're in the bloody business of sorting all this electronic stuff out!" shouted Roger, standing so suddenly the briefing papers on the tabletop flew everywhere.

"We can only work with the data we intercept or receive directly. That's our mandate, not to guess or idly speculate. Your job," Julius said calmly, "is to prove and then provide the data for us. Now, if you have been doing your job as you say you have, then the only reasonable explanation is that someone is able to direct and control our data from the inside. That's what I believe you have to focus on." Julius stood up, smoothed out his jacket lapels, and picked up the slim red "Top Secret—Magneto" folder. He idly flicked the corners of it, making a "burrrrrrr" sound, then turned to look at his fellow directors. "You know, if I were you, I'd go look for someone who has enormous credibility, cannot in any way be tainted with this or by this, is outside both your organizations and chain of command, and can't be got at, and won't want to take any of the credit at the endgame. Someone who can move freely around the world and has the smarts and the organization to be able to unravel this mess in double-quick time. Think about it." He nodded slightly to the two directors and then left the room trailed by his acolytes.

The head of the CIA looked at the head of the FBI in astonishment, completely flummoxed by the NSA director's suggestion. "Where the fuck do you get someone like that in this day and age?" he raged, sweeping his papers across the table with the back of his hand. Frank thought for a moment, smiled, and began to laugh.

"Actually, I think I know just the guy. You'll just love him!"

CHAPTER 14

I had never seen the Boss so despondent. Not only had the young Italian computer genius Luigi Antoinette been able to obtain some Strontium-90 pellets within just three and a half hours, but he had also successfully managed to get over five kilos of the volatile nuclear waste onto special trucks supplied by Interpol. And it wasn't as if he did it the easy way. He took some from France, Germany, and England, and then, just to prove how simple it really was (or perhaps how smart he was!), he took half a kilo from the nuclear power plant just outside Milan, where he operated from. And there wasn't a single trace anywhere in cyberspace to indicate that anything unusual had taken place because every time he located a source and arranged delivery, Indigo called Interpol's HQ in Lyon and organized both visual and electronic surveillance of each site by the local enforcement authorities as the deliveries took place. By not using our agencies' people to do the work, he had effectively established an independent and objective overwatch to ensure the continued security of the nuclear material now that we had taken it away from its usual owners.

To cap a tense few hours off, we had just been notified by the Arabian Secret Police that two charred bodies had been found in an abandoned burnt-out hulk of a truck that matched the satellite images of the vehicle used in the attack on the oil field at Shaybah. DNA samples were on their way to Interpol and all other centralized police and military databases for comparison matching and identification. And then the phone had rung, and the Boss was handed a handset with an encryption device attached to the side.

"Go for Blue Bird."

"Hello, PJ. Nice to hear your voice."

"I'd love to say the same about yours, but then I'd be bullshitting," the Boss snapped back.

"Now, now, no hard feelings. You can't win them all." The Boss tossed the handset across the table as if it were a cobra about to strike. The encrypted, disemboweled voice of the director of the FBI, Roger Winslow, crackled with laughter from the speaker mounted in the center of the table. "Listen, if it makes you feel any better, I personally apologize for the mess we made." The Boss and I looked at the pain of the last operation we had tried to bring to a successful conclusion, still fresh in our minds.

Over several months we had successfully tracked a group of people-smugglers out of Egypt who sold the young, fresh, and most healthy bodies they kidnapped out of the refugee camps to a large Chinese corporation that turned out to be a body-parts farm operating all over the Pacific Rim. When we had captured the main offenders, literally in the act of handing over their latest organ crop to the merchants of death, Winslow's men had moved in, forced us to the sidelines, made the arrest in front of the TV cameras, claimed full credit for the bust, and then had the thrill of trying to explain to their Congress and other interested parties why six of the captured people smugglers had been handed over to the Chinese government, who had promptly put on a show trial and then shot all six men in full view of their version of the six o'clock news.

Interpol liked to work in the dark—we left the PR to the countries who had a vested interest in the outcome, and it had taken us a long time to understand why the American FBI had bothered itself with what was essentially a North African and Asian activity. Then we found out that the number seven smuggler was a deep-cover FBI agent, and it all started to make sense.

Sort of.

"You're on the clock, Roger. What do you want?"

"Physical meeting, eight hours' time, at Marco Polo Airport, Military VIP section."

"And how do you intend to be present? Developed some beam-me-up-Scottie stuff lately?" the Boss asked sarcastically. "And how did you find me here?"

"Finding you was easy, took maybe three seconds, thanks to the efficiency of your HQ, and I'm calling you from Airforce Two, smart-arse. See you on the tarmac." The snap of the digital line disconnecting was like a rifle shot. Indigo, who had made a quiet tactical withdrawal during the heated conversation, returned with a tray of fresh coffee. For a tough ex-paratrooper and the head of the Italian arm of Interpol, he sure made for a good caterer!

"I wonder what Frank's up to now?" the Boss mused, taking a steaming mug from Indigo's tray. Everyone else used the exquisite Murano glass cups, a point not lost on the Italian contingent in the control room.

"I suspect I can guess," Indigo said, settling back into his chair. "The ease with which we just obtained the Strontium-90, and the fact that we could do it so quickly, would suggest that the wonderful electronic systems we rely on so heavily may not be all they are cracked up to be." He turned to a small monitor, which was still connected to Luigi Antoinette's office in Milan. "Pronto, Luigi, can you connect, please?"

"Colonel, what can I do for you this time?" the young computer expert asked, seemingly quite relaxed about having just hijacked some of the world's most guarded material without having even raised a sweat in the process.

"Luigi, can you tell if someone else is tapping into your system or could be following what you were doing when you were hacking just now?"

"*Sì*, Colonel, every good hacker has tracking software to alert them to being discovered. In this case, I can positively say that no one has the slightest idea of what we just did and even less interest."

"*Grazie*, Luigi, could I suggest you get ready to travel? I believe that we will need you here quite soon."

"*Certamente*, Colonel." His screen faded, and Indigo turned to face the Boss. "Colonel, I may be presumptuous, but I think having our young man at your disposal may be greatly beneficial." The Boss smiled, reached forward, and patted Indigo on the arm.

"Indigo, spot on, and I think we will need a few extras off the books before this case is closed. Pete," the Boss said, turning to face his long-suffering friend, "how about you go with Indigo and recruit a few hard bodies for us, all the usual stuff, plus languages and covert training? Half a dozen should be fine." The Boss hesitated, thinking through something, then turned back to Indigo. "Indigo, if the data we have been working from is corrupted in some manner, how can we establish a baseline to work from?" he asked. "What I'm thinking is that we are outside all the investigations except your own, and we have no way to check on the accuracy of what we are being told by the other countries."

"I agree, Colonel. It is a problem that has been taxing my limited capacity for some time. But I believe I have a solution if you can be a little flexible?" The Boss raised his eyebrows, not so much at the question but surprised Indigo felt the need to ask. "Some friends of mine, over on the Island, have a huge computing capacity that is only known to few outside a very tight group of people. They maintain their independence with a fierce disposition towards interference by government or party politics and have the best information retrieval and filtering system I have ever seen. Perhaps they could be engaged in providing us with a private network that no one, not even the Americans, could penetrate?" The Boss smiled, rolling his shoulders. It had been a tense day all around.

"Excellent. I think I need a quick catnap, shower, shave, and a change of clothes before we meet our American friends. Captain, I suggest the same for you, and Pete, take the hint!" We all laughed at the joke and stood up. "Indigo, if you can arrange for us to call on your friends before we go to Marco Polo, that would be just great!"

SILENT SERVICE

Temple Abbot, or the "A" of the "A-B-C" temples as it was sometimes irreverently called, is a small, unpretentious building at the end of Kenworthy Lane, just off the M63 Sale Eastern and Northenden Bypass in Manchester. Only three and a half stories tall and made of an undistinguished grey brick, it looked exactly as its owners wanted.

Nothing serious, nothing to get worked up over, just another nondescript building full of dull people, none of whom seemed to live in the neighborhood, coming and going in ordinary cars and the occasional taxicab.

In reality, it was one of the three cornerstones that the 340-year-old Lloyd's insurance empire was now totally dependent on. Staffed twenty-four hours a day, the three small floors hummed and whirred to the monotonous sounds of high-speed cooling fans and ultra-high-speed electronic processors, all jammed into two impressive-looking CRAY-9 supercomputers and all their attendant bits and pieces. Temple Abbot was the home for billions and billions of bytes of data and information, all faithfully transferred at the speed of light from the spectacular green glass-and-steel Lloyd's building in the heart of the City of London in Lime Street. As every deal was agreed to, almost before the ink was dry on the "Slip" anywhere in the world, the data found itself sucked into an electronic vortex that ended in one of the three temples, so called because of their seemingly monastic, cloistered occupants and their dull, almost reverent facade.

Temple Abbot held every known piece of information on every insurance claim ever recorded by Lloyd's. Temple Cottesloe, in faraway Bristol, held all the data on premium income rates, debtors and creditors, and billions of bytes of financial analysis. And Temple Blackfriar, buried in full view of the airport just outside Norwich, stored everything Lloyd's had learned on every company, business, and person the massive trading floor had ever dealt with for as long as they could remember. And in some cases, that went back centuries.

When the sensational, architecturally stunning new Lloyd's building was completed in June of 1986, the real task had begun. For the next seven years, two hundred programmers and over a thousand clerical staff, supported by the largest companies in the computer world, labored to digitally enter three hundred years' worth of knowledge and hard-won experience. First, they got it safely into a series of complex machines, recently installed in the bowels of the new building, and then they duplicated it and fired it off to the three remote sites that would later become known as the "A-B-C" Abbeys.

Then they emptied the complex machines and, for good measure, had them crushed, incinerated, and the ashes placed in a huge brass jar that sat under glass in the main foyer. A small handwritten note lay at a slight angle to the jar and, with a touch of irony for which Lloyd's was not known for, simply said, "Here in this ash is everything we once were."

The philosophy behind the gigantic effort required to digitize Lloyd's world was simple—after three centuries of doing everything by hand, and mostly with real ink on real paper, the massive worldwide conglomerate of some twenty-five thousand "Names" would never allow itself to be held to ransom by an electronic breakdown, or a sudden attack of the technology burps.

Thus, the three independent, sophisticated computer centers, linked only to their Lime Street masters by independent fiberoptic cable and satellite dishes were created, changing how business was done and recorded at Lloyd's for centuries to come.

"Gentlemen, if I may have your attention, please." The three programmers/clerks on the second floor stopped in their tracks and looked up at the small TV monitor that linked every nook and cranny in Temple Abbot. Not only was it unusual for the system to be used as a public address system, the code at the bottom of the small color screen indicated that all three temples were being linked in real-time and online simultaneously with the Lime Street headquarters of Lloyd's. Every single person in the Lloyd's empire was seeing exactly the same image at exactly the same time. The face of the ex-Scotland Yard detective inspector who ran the security organization for Lloyd's swam up into focus.

"I'm sorry to disturb you, but I have an announcement of some serious importance." The bland face looked down at a hidden, off-camera object, then stared back into the lens of the camera, creating the impression that he was looking at every individual staff member watching the TVs in the eye, one on one. "We have received confirmation of a claim from our intelligence center concerning one of our own people. At this early stage, I'm unable to report the exact status, but there seems to be a solid foundation of fact in it. Sufficient to say, Sir James Benson, our immediate past chairman and one of our greatest syndicate leaders, is missing, believed dead, in a tragic boating accident in the North Sea. As you all know, Sir James was responsible for the creation of the temples and was a well-known and much-respected figure around our hallowed halls. I will keep you posted, and we are notifying all off-duty members as a matter of course. Because of the nature of your sensitive work, there will be a public reaction, which you must avoid at all costs. Thank you for your attention."

The stunned silence that greeted this news took nearly five minutes to break down, and trading momentarily stopped in midsentence for the first time since the second Great War. As the Lutine Bell rang hollowly through the hushed tiers of the trading floors, each person came to grips with the thought that their inspiration, their mentor, a man they had all looked up to for advice and motivation, was now no more than a series of clicks on one of their keyboards.

And as if to underline the tragedy of their loss, every computer went down at exactly the same second. Forever.

CHAPTER 15

Miami-Dade Airport is a large, sprawling facility in a large, sprawling tropical state, as well known for its infamous drug and smuggling propensity as for its fabulous beaches and weather. Conversely, Florida is also where spaceships and rockets boom off into the stratosphere and beyond on a regular basis, and children of all ages ride to Mars in surreal simulators. A state of contrasts, huge ethnic diversity, and paranoid security forces. The proximity to Cuba and South America makes Florida the automatic landfall for a veritable flood of refugees and asylum seekers every day of the year, and as such, the local authorities deal with these issues with practiced ease, if not a slightly heavy hand on occasions.

Hence the priest from South America found himself in a holding cell in a purpose-built building just off the concourse from the main terminal. It was clean, and he was treated with respect, but it became obvious early in his forced incarceration that it would take considerable time before he would sit in front of someone high enough up the food chain to get him the hearing he so desperately needed. While his English was passable, his Spanish, Italian, French, German, and Russian were first class, but so far, even his most earnest appeals in any language had been met by bemused disinterested smiles and polite "Not now, Father, wait, please, until we can get to you in turn."

He had tried to enter the United States with a passport twenty years out of date, no visa, and no current identification other than his name inscribed inside his Bible. He had explained that where he had worked as a missionary for the last twenty years demanded none of the modern requirements for proof of identity, and that all his personal papers were safely stored in a little warehouse maintained by the Jesuits in Salt Lake City, where he had started his most recent odyssey from over a quarter of a century ago.

No one was interested. Post 9/11, no identification meant that you were automatically suspected of being anything from a full-blown member of Al-Qaeda or ISIS to a people smuggler working for the Cubans. Arriving from South America automatically meant that you were probably a secret member of the cartels, sent to America to seduce little children to smoke dope and do drugs. Starting from a baseline of suspicion so deep in probable causes tended to fill up the detention centers very fast, with a processing speed resembling that of a Florida swamp slug slithering out of boyos for take-away.

The priest slept, prayed, ate, relieved himself as modestly as he could given the three high-mounted security cameras that covered every inch of his accommodation, and asked at every contact opportunity to see "*l'uomo in carica per favore, perché ho un messaggio molto importante per il Presidente degli Stati Uniti*—the man in charge please because I have a very important message for the president of the United States."

This one statement was enough to create paranoia in the security staff that the priest ran the risk of never seeing the light of day ever again. Still, as these things tend to unfold, by a pure stroke of luck, another priest was in the same facility but, this time, free and unencumbered by the need to provide his identity, giving the last rites to three boat people who had simply died from years of neglect and exhaustion and from the panic of trying to escape across the ocean from Cuba. One of the guards casually mentioned that "another dude claiming to be a priest, dressed in a tattered cassock and climbing boots," was in a holding cell somewhere, and the priest, as was his right, requested an interview. What he saw when he was finally taken to the cell was a shock, to say the least. The man from the mountains was wafer thin, looking like an emancipated cancer patient, dressed in a torn and many times patched cassock over a faded and torn pair of very old jeans and a pair of mountain climbing boots that looked as if they had been on his feet for centuries.

"Brother, my name is Father Ronald. How can I be of assistance?" the priest asked, making the sign of the cross and bowing at the same time as a mark of respect. For he recognized this most famous of all the Jesuits, a man about whom legends had been created for his amazing work with the hidden and primitive tribes of lower Central America. The Jesuit bowed back, placing one bony hand on the arm of the Priest.

"Brother Ronald, I need your urgent help. I have a message for the president of the United States, which I must deliver as a matter of the gravest urgency." The priest was taken aback by this, spoken as it was in a mixture of English and Spanish. The idea was preposterous, of course; what could a common Jesuit missionary from the wilds of South America possibly know that was so important he had to speak to the president of the United States personally? Even the cardinal of New York only saw the president twice a year; what hope would a mere priest have? He smiled to take the edge off his next words, mindful that the authorities controlling this facility were deeply concerned about the security implications of the Jesuit's arrival in Miami and were recording and observing every second of this strange encounter.

"Brother, I will personally speak to the commandant and seek his help. In the meantime, is there anything I can do for you personally?" The old Jesuit looked deep into the eyes of the priest and realized intuitively that what he was seeing was the manifestation of someone who was not necessarily telling a lie but perhaps also was not really telling the truth. He shook his head, patted the arm of the priest, and sat down on the metal-framed bunk.

"The fate of the world could well hang in the balance," the Jesuit whispered, "but I trust God to decide how and when I can deliver my message."

CHAPTER 16

The same lunatic coxswain ran us across to the Grand Canal in his bright red cigarette boat, lights flashing, siren going full out until he surfed to a stop and drop us off at the dock at the foot of the beautiful Santa Maria dells Salute. The church, which was currently undergoing severe restoration, was literally swathed in metal cross bars and scaffolding, leaving the magnificent three-hundred-and-thirty-odd-year-old dome peeking out like a child stealing a look from behind her mother's skirt. Designed by Baldassare Longhena, the basilica was dedicated to the Virgin Mary after Venice was delivered from the plague in the early eighteen hundreds, which had indiscriminately killed one third of the population. I had always loved visiting this particular church, as it always seemed to have fewer tourists than many others in and around Venice, and the peace and quiet that ghosted through its massive stone and baroque façade were spiritually powerful, whatever your religious persuasion might or might not be.

This time, however, Indigo led us to a small doorway opposite the Guggenheim Gallery that took us down a rank and smelly, dimly lit alleyway, which suddenly curled in on itself, ending in a series of stone steps covered in slimy green and black algae. We didn't scramble down the steps. We did walk through a solid stone wall that had the thickest doorway I had ever experienced, straight into an electronic security zone.

Indigo opened his hands and physically shrunk, his shoulders rounding, almost in supplication, obviously embarrassed at what was coming.

"Colonel, Captain, my apologies, but from this point, you must dispose of all weapons, cell phones, GPS systems, tracking devices, RFID patches, watches, pens, smart pads, and anything metallic. This microwave security system will not let you proceed with any modern electronic article; in fact, you may well be seriously injured by the defensive mechanisms should you miss something." Now I understood Indigo's embarrassment. Pete, the Boss, Indigo, and I started to shed the accouchements of our daily life while the four young officers of the Italian Special Forces who Indigo had quickly recruited and had come with us turned around and walked back outside, probably to smoke their young lungs to death. When we were metal-free and electronic device-free, Indigo pressed a big red button, and another door opened, this time into a purple-lit anteroom, where we were washed by ultraviolet and low-frequency microwave scanners. An orange, rotating beacon created an ethereal feeling as the microwave tickled my insides.

"This way, presto," Indigo finally said once the beacon had stopped rotating. We followed him through yet another armored door, which finally led to a long, dark subterranean room that was lined from floor to ceiling with books, real live old, musty analogue books! We walked through this wonderful arena following a twisting route, then passed several corridors leading to more and more books. At the far end of the walkway, a small cubicle radiated pulsing light, and as we approached it, we could see that there were three people, all dressed in white smocks, sitting at large computer screens. A fourth person was leaning against a glass partition with his back to us. As we approached, he turned, revealing a welcoming smile crucified by fire-ravaged skin. The hand he offered Indigo had only three fingers, all twisted and fused together. They shook hands, hugged and kissed the Italian way, then Indigo turned and introduced him to us.

"Colonel, may I introduce my brother, Stefarino, the curator of this hidden treasure," he said, "Stefarino, this is Colonel Anthony, Captain Riley, and Master Chief Pete, all of Interpol and also my most trusted friends."

"Welcome to my humble abode," offered Stefarino, leading us into an even smaller alcove with straight-backed wooden chairs and what looked a lot like my old wooden kitchen table. "Can I offer you refreshments of any kind? I'm sorry, all we have here is coffee, tea, and a few dry biscuits."

"*Grazie*, Stefarino, we have to meet a plane at Marco Polo in an hour. Could we please just let the Colonel explain what he needs to us?"

"Come *desidera*, Indigo, as you wish. How may I be of assistance?"

"Well, I'm not sure what you do here, and I really don't need to know, but we have come to a conclusion regarding the events of the last few days, and your brother believes you may be able to help us," the Boss said, looking extremely relaxed in spite of being in someone else's space without his trusty Sig Sauer 9 mm. "We believe that someone has penetrated the Air Traffic Control system in Europe, as well as other systems used by military and police agencies, and we'd like to try and find and track whomever it is, preferably without them ever knowing we have done so."

"And you want us to do this for you because?" Stefarino asked, somewhat puzzled by the request. He was a humble librarian entrusted to catalogue and preserve some of the most treasured printed material ever collected. Opposite him sat one of the most powerful policemen in the world, with the ability to summon military and police forces on a vast scale, not to mention the technology that simply boggled the mind of most people. The Boss stared at him for about a full minute, judging what was really behind the question. Did I mention that my Boss was one of the smartest people I had ever met? He smiled, nodded, and then said just one word.

"Okay." He pulled a sheet of paper from his jacket pocket, unfolded it, and passed it to Stefarino. The curator looked closely at the list, pushing his glasses up his nose several times as he read the data.

"So, my Colonel, you want me to start at these data points, work backward from the timeline, penetrate the government, police, and military systems connected to each without being detected, and find out how they were hacked and by whom, is that all?"

"Yes." The Boss was smiling so broadly now his face was lit up. "Again, my original question. Why us?"

"Because your brother knows what I know, and he believes you can help us in a manner that no one else can."

"I see. And what if I politely declined your offer?"

"Then I'd ask for that paper back and leave as we arrived, with no hard feelings, and preserve your secret." Stefarino looked at his brother, brow furrowed in concentration.

"Do you believe this to be so important that we might risk being discovered?" he asked Indigo.

"*Assolutamentesì*, brother, this could set the whole world on fire, and we need to prevent that from happening at any cost." Stefarino looked at his brother with a wan smile, his disfigured face creating a most unpleasant look. He slowly nodded his acceptance and then turned slightly and looked at the Boss.

"Colonel, just so you know, this library has been one of the best-kept secrets in the world for seven hundred years, and now we risk this for you. Personally. Please keep us in your hearts and minds as you work on this case, and we will do all that we can to help. As you leave, you will be given small mini laptop computers that only I can send messages to. Whomever you entrust this device to will literally hold our future in their hands, as will you."

"I understand. Thank you, there is no proper way to express our gratitude at this time; your secret is safe with us. We, all three, will take it to our graves if that is what it takes to protect you. You have my word." If Pete was shocked that the Boss had just enjoined him into a potential suicide pact, he showed no sign, but inside, my guts churned; even though I did not yet fully understand the importance of this particular library, having someone tell me to take its location and existence to the grave was quite a serious request!

"*Andate in pace*, my friends, and may you succeed in your mission." We hugged and kissed all round, got all gooey, then followed Indigo out back through the three massive doors, collected our weapons, phones, computers, PDAs, watches, bugs, and everything else metal and electronic, and emerged like butterflies back into the daylight, which was now just a wan glimpse of its earlier glory. The Boss was deep in reflection, walking alongside Indigo. To see the two of them side by side was almost comical, both dressed in anonymous street suits but more unlike each other physically as you could get. Adonis versus the dwarf! Armani versus K-Mart. Height versus width. Just as I was starting to develop these analogies in my mind, we bumped into our Italian escort, who promptly formed up around us as we headed for the dock.

Lunatic and his red cigarette boat waited, bobbing up and down in the late afternoon swell, an evil grin splitting his face in two. I was looking forward to this next trip with the same sweaty anticipation that builds up before you visit a dentist!

CHAPTER 17

The general sat relaxed, legs crossed behind him, arms crossed on his chest, and as was his way, he was bowed deeply from the waist, head touching the ground in front. To an observer, he may well have been at prayer. To those who knew him, this was a flexibility exercise he had practiced a hundred times a day, every day, for nearly eighty years. When he finished his last repetition, he uncrossed everything, then lay flat on his back. He stretched like a cat, wriggling his toes, rolling his wrists and flexing his shoulders.

He had come full circle.

His life had started in the desert, and it would finish here, at a time of his own choosing. His children had performed wonders, gone out into the world and virtually conquered it, each in their own special way. He smiled at the thought of the little innocent faces he remembered from their childhood and how they had glowed as he read to them of the battles and conquests of the past.

He had no regrets.

Well, perhaps just the one. The Devil he had recruited for the second part of his plan had turned out to be a wildcard. Perhaps he should have chosen more carefully. But that was in the past, and he wanted to enjoy the time he had left.

To the best of his knowledge, he owed no man favor or kind, had no debts other than to his God, Allah be praised, and his heart and mind were pure, secure in the knowledge that what a man achieved in his life was more important than what he may or may not be remembered for.

He hoped that someone would speak for him when he passed but smiled at the thought, knowing that it would make no real difference to him because he would be in Heaven.

He stood, walked out to the edge of the tent, and looked towards the massive dunes that rose majestically up into a clear blue sky. Not a grain of sand moved and not a sound could be heard.

He imagined that this might be a lot like Heaven, so pure and wonderful was the vista before him.

He would be sad to leave this world for the next but understood at the subliminal level that the inevitability of the end of his life was no more than a focusing mechanism for getting things done, not a death sentence.

He looked up into the sky, where a thin white contrail carved itself across the horizon.

He smiled and waved, pretending that the aircraft could see him. "يئاقدصأهلإلاعمباهذلا and enjoy it while you can!"

CHAPTER 18

Bishop O'Neil led the group in Grace, twenty-one ordained priests and seven monks in total, served by ten novices, traditionally ranked around the long table, sharing an evening meal before spreading out into the community for evening Mass and prayers. Father Ronald was on his immediate right, being one of the senior clergies in the parish. At the far end of the table, a monk with his head bent in supplication muttered the words in a strange tongue, slightly unsettling to the common ear. As the Grace finished and the collected gathering made the sign of the cross, the monk raised his head and addressed the head of the table.

"Your Grace," he asked in heavily accented English, "is it true that one of our brotherhood is incarcerated by the immigration authorities at this time?" The bishop looked up from his meal, a fruity vegetable gruel with a hint of New Orleans spice.

"Brother Andretti, sadly, it is true. Father Ronald visited him only today." The monk looked directly at Father Ronald, midway through breaking a loaf of bread in half.

"Father Ronald, how was he, and how did he get put into jail?" The monk's accent was so broad that those around the table now paying attention to the conversation could barely understand the questions. Father Ronald put his bread down and turned his head to see the questioning monk better. Feeling quite superior as the deputy to the bishop, he tended to look down on the wandering brethren who worked at the bottom end of the food chain, preferring the slums and squats to preach their ministry in rather than the mansions and beach-side condominiums that most of the priests around the table preferred.

"Brother, he was well, though quite gaunt, but I am told that this is his usual demeanor. And he spoke some nonsense about a message for the president of the United States, which no one is taking any notice of, of course." The monk looked ashen and suddenly stood up.

"Your Grace, with your permission, I will visit my brother in jail immediately." Both the bishop and Father Ronald shared a glance, and the bishop shrugged his prodigious shoulders.

"Of course, brother, go with our blessings." As he made the sign of the cross, emulated by all those sitting around the table, the monk turned on his heel and rushed out of the dining room. In a matter of seconds, everyone else was settled back into their dinner, only mildly interested in the exchange and in no way concerned about the outcome.

CHAPTER 19

The cigarette boat pulled into the docks at the back of Marco Polo International Airport like a Ferrari crossing the finishing line at Monte Carlo. Indigo's young Italian Special Forces men had arranged for an open-top four-wheel drive to take us to the military VIP area; so stuffed into the back like so many crates of tomatoes, we jolted and bounced around the perimeter of the airport, skirting the wetlands that bordered Laguna Veneta. I had changed my mind about the boat driver; he wasn't a maniac or even lunatic; he was just plain out-of-his-mind stark raving mad.

"Okay, here's how we'll play this. Indigo, you and the boys stay outside, form a loose perimeter, and pretend you are guarding us. Pete, stay with Indigo and roam around as if you are checking up on the security of things. They will have their own security, and they will be as paranoid as a fly stuck to honey and twitchy because you can bet the arrogant bastards won't have anyone who speaks Italian, and everything will have been arranged at the last minute by the local CIA, who, at best, couldn't make cupcakes for a Sunday stall."

"Are you wired?" I asked, interested in how the Boss viewed his old acquaintances negatively and with such skepticism and suspicion.

"Yes, they may scan me. You never know with these bastards; they tend to judge everyone by what they would do under the same circumstances!" We all laughed, the effort nearly sending my teeth shooting out the side of the truck as it hit a monstrous hole in the track, and I bit my tongue. And, of course, the driver, being Italian, was literally driving flat out as if he were late for his lunch break.

"Don't forget you are Interpol, and you now represent the interests of the Italian government," shouted Indigo, "and make sure they understand we can lock up their backsides if we want to!" We all laughed again, the second light moment in a very stressful few days. The four-wheel truck coasted to a stop, right up to the outstretched hand of a soldier, whose MP-5, while slung around his neck as was the fashion these days, still managed to point it straight at the head of our driver. Indigo leaned over the top of the cab and shouted at the guard.

"*Colonnello* Indigo Kashasini, Italiano Interpol, *ci sonoattesi*!" The guard saluted, lowered the machine pistol, and waved us to the gate. We dismounted, and the Special Forces guards and Indigo, followed by Pete looking like a ruffian with evil intent, fanned out to form a circle around us as if we were the principals. It was a nice feeling that was short-lived as we ran straight into a group of Secret Service agents, their guns not drawn but clearly in evidence under the sides of their jackets, all talking into their wrist microphones at the same time. The two armed groups faced each other off, the Italians bouncing up and down on the balls of their feet, itching for a fight. This was the last thing we wanted, so I pushed ahead of Indigo, faced the first agent I came to, held up my Interpol credentials, and looked around at his team as if inspecting them.

"Agent, we are here at the invitation of the director of the FBI; behind me is the head of Interpol Division Five. Move your men out of the way, please." If he felt affronted by being challenged by a woman dressed in a black pants suit but obviously carrying a firearm as well as a big pair of balls under her armpits, he didn't show it. He muttered into his wrist mic, signaled to his men, and casually waved us on. The Boss and I walked up to the bottom of the airstairs that had been placed against the massive side of the 747, Airforce Two. As we walked up the stairs, a shadowy figure filled the doorway.

"PJ, nice to see you again." The Boss looked up and kept climbing, an evil grin splitting his face.

"Must be a pure bitch to have you so available," he said, finally reaching the doorway. Roger Winslow offered a hand; the Boss ignored it, standing so close to him that the FBI director was forced to move back into the aircraft, finally getting the hint and heading for the stateroom usually reserved for the vice president.

"Nice set of wheels you have here. Why not the Gulfstream?" the Boss asked as we entered the plush conference room from where you could literally control the world. We all sat, joining a group of hard-faced individuals all looking as if they had not slept since they had left Washington.

"PJ, I've already apologized for the bust, so stop breaking my balls and sit down. Can I offer you any refreshments? We have already ordered a meal, and it would be nice to think you'll stay long enough to share it with us." The Boss looked around the room, searching for any "tell" that would indicate a hidden agenda or an outright lie. Or that it might all be some elaborate trap. He literally radiated menace, like a caged tiger caught in a net.

"Roger, you just plain fucked with us last time; we have no interest in any of your bullshit; let's just get down to the reason for your panic call, shall we?" The temperature in the room dropped about twenty degrees Celsius in a split second, and several of the suits around the table stiffened as if to draw their weapons. To his credit, Roger Winslow just sighed, a clear sign to the rest of the room that he was choosing to take no offence at the Boss's harsh but accurate words.

"Okay, okay, PJ, said it once, say it again, sorry, now can we concentrate on why we are here, please?" The Boss waved his acceptance, and a large data panel came to life on the bulkhead wall.

"PJ, this is a tactical summary of the attack on West Point; on the left-hand side, you will see what was recorded in real-time by satellite, ground corrected DGPS, the Air Traffic Control system, security cameras on military bases, and raw radar tracks from some defense sites in and around Manhattan and the surrounding districts. On the right is an animated version of what we have learned actually took place from intelligence sources, real-time observation, and data projected from the actual event. John over here," and he pointed to one of the young suits sitting at a data console, "will provide a running commentary. You okay with this?" The Boss waved his acceptance again, and the screen split into two images, the one on the left grainy and surreal, the one on the right clear and sharp and with a linear definition you can only achieve with digital animation.

"The aircraft, an A-10 Warthog, on TDY with the Armaments Group based at Andrews Airforce Base, cleared the tarmac with live ammunition. As you can see here, we have since modeled the only possible way it could have been done." The grainy security camera footage on the screen showed the pilot pre-flighting the aircraft, the aircraft taxing out, then talking off in the distance. On the right-hand side of the screen, the animation showed a small vehicle about the size of an open-top Jeep parked abeam the aircraft in a holding bay, then an indistinct figure pulling little red flags off the aircraft from under the wings, then holding them up for the pilot to see just before it launched.

"So, your cameras didn't see the bombs being armed, but someone else did?" the Boss asked.

"Yes, sir, a controller who was watching the flight launch thinks she remembers seeing the aircraft arming adjacent the pit, as it was supposed to do on any normal 'live' flight. However, her view was mostly obscured by a hangar, so we can't be sure."

"But your report said that this aircraft was supposedly on a test and training run to prove a new ground mapping Lidar (laser radar), so why was it armed in the first place, and why were the armaments live?" the Boss asked. Suddenly the room was full of very embarrassed people, none of whom would look the Boss in the eye. The director tapped one fingernail on the polished surface of the oval table, gritting his teeth.

"Sir, the facts are that the aircraft was carrying the weapons as part of the test; we still do not know how, why, or by whom the weapons were armed," answered an Air Force captain, his face as grey as his camos.

"You don't."

"No, sir."

"The person in the Jeep?"

"No record of them, sir, we can't find the vehicle, and according to the guard house, it is still on the base; however, an extensive physical search has turned up nothing."

"You backtracked the pilot?" the Boss asked, really getting into the swing of things, prodding with little questions so that when he started in hard, he had a baseline to judge the amount of bullshit he was so professionally fed.

"Yes, sir, FBI forensics investigated every bit of her file, life, home, and history." The Boss smiled, smelling a monster snow job.

"Okay, stop the dog-and-pony show, and let's move on. Your report says that ATC had the HOG at twenty-five thousand feet when the actual attack—again, according to your report, was from eight thousand feet. How come?"

"Sir, we believe the ATC computers were hacked into, and the flight data indicators changed."

"Why would someone bother to do that?" the Boss asked. "If the bastards wanted to bomb West Point, what the hell difference would it make to know they were several thousand feet off their assigned altitude?"

"Well, sir, just after the attack, the ATC lost track of the A-10 completely."

"It just disappeared?" the Boss asked, incredulous.

"Yes, sir. No transponder signal, IFF, radar trace, and, as far as we can tell at this time, no visual trace whatsoever." The room went deadly quiet, the only noise the almost imperceptible rumble of the massive diesel generators attached to the nose of the 747 that was providing power for the aircraft and the air conditioning, and Roger Winslow's constant tapping. Being one of the best interrogators I had ever seen, the Boss said nothing, an old policeman's trick. The first person to break the silence loses, and this time it was the director of the FBI.

"PJ, we've been compromised at the highest levels, military or security doesn't matter which, but the bastards are inside our IT systems, and while we will find them eventually, I have a very angry president and a Congress wanting to go to war with someone. Can Interpol help us with this one?" The Boss stared right through the director, lost in deep thought.

"Mister Director," I said, drawing every head in the room to my seat. Up until this point, I had been completely ignored. If there was one thing the supposedly powerful men in the world hated more than being challenged face to face, in my experience, it was being publicly challenged by a woman. "Interpol will take the lead, but this time, we will control all media, no debate, and at the first sign of any chicanery, we will publicly denounce you to the world press as somehow complicit in the events of the last few days."

"Captain, don't get your balls in a knot; we know the stakes better than you do."

"That's good, Mister Director because I need your expressed permission to cross borders, question any national, foreign or domestic, and work with any agency, military, security, or political with total immunity, on your letterhead, now. And that includes the right to bear arms, make arrests, and ask really, really sensitive questions of everyone and anyone we get in our sights, right across the United States of America if that is what it takes." Roger Winslow looked at me so hard I expected bullets to fly out of his eyes, but after just a few seconds, he nodded, and a really sad look crossed his face.

"Captain, the stakes are so high on this one I can tolerate your arrogance, but don't fuck up because if you do, I'll bury you right alongside the worst bitch of a dog I can find while you are still alive." He threw down a small manilla envelope, which slid across the table. I opened it and quickly read what was on the state department letterhead, addressed to the secretary general of Interpol. It was a carte blanche commission to act for and on behalf of the United States in any country in the world, for the foreseeable duration, until a successful conclusion (not specified) had been reached. In short, an open invitation from the most powerful country in the world to hunt down and secure the terrorists responsible for the gravest attacks in recorded history.

With hundreds of thousands dead with more to come from radiation poisoning, more than half the world's oil supply contaminated, the entire ruling cadre of the Catholic Church assassinated, and three of the world's most prestigious religious sites violated beyond belief. The premier war college in the world bombed out of existence, the world had been stood on its collective head, and to date, no one had a single real clue as to the who, how, or why the terrorists had attacked in the first place.

But things were looking up because we now had the power to act for the Italians, and now the USA, with only the Jews, Palestinians, and Arabs yet to come onboard.

That I should live so long!

CHAPTER 20

The discussion between the ragtag priest from the mountainous jungles of South America and Father Andretti began as they knelt in prayer, heads bowed, facing each other in humility. It had taken the monk almost six hours to walk and bus from the rectory to the Miami-Dade immigration facility, and it was now well after midnight. Not only were the guards reluctant to let him through, and he had also been forced to call the bishop to add weight to his visit. After each making the sign of the cross, both priests hugged each other in the European manner, something the guards found mildly amusing.

Like all holding facilities where the possibility of incarcerating terrorists was a reality, the cell was monitored 24/7 by both video and audio. Every feed from every cell was monitored in real-time by a bank of language experts, mostly university and college students studying languages up and down the peninsula. The pay was reasonable, the hours suited study time, and the work was classed as "light" in that they were required to do was listen for keywords and identify any tape that may be of interest to a more senior agent.

Most of them never even bothered to look at the visual images anymore, preferring the depersonalization of a hollow anomalous voice coming in through their headphones, interspersed with the latest rap tracks off their iPods.

When the words "Middle Eastern" and "terrorists" followed by "latest attacks" floated into the consciousness of young Dieter Gregory, he nearly dropped his physics book in surprise. Quickly punching the time/date/location code onto the tape, he pushed each interpreter's little red button on his console and waited in mild panic. Had he really heard the words, or did he imagine them? Within seconds, it didn't matter because a gruff voice demanded that he transfer the digital signal through to the secure line that, he believed, went all the way to FBI headquarters in Washington.

At the other end of the line, an agent in charge listened to the conversation between the two priests, clapped his hands with joy, shouted, woke the other three agents pulling night duty, and grabbed a phone.

"Get me the director, stat!" he shouted, glad to have something break into the eternal boredom of the night shift. The world might well be going to Hell in a handbasket, but it was happening everywhere else but here. "Don't care where he is. Connect me, priority one!"

Back in the cell, Father Andretti started to plan his next journey all the way to Washington, a mighty feat at night, particularly for a monk with no money. However, God's work would be done, and the message he had to convey was so important that he left the cell in haste, which was commented on by the guards. They speculated it was something to do with the smell, late for a date, laughed another, neither realizing that the little monk now held the key to a series of crimes pushing the world to the brink of insanity.

CHAPTER 21

Back in the Interpol control room under San Michele, the Boss was doing what the Boss does best. Issuing orders to all and sundry and creating independent self-managed teams of people all tasked with specific objectives. This was police work at its best, and we had access to all of the best cops on the planet, just for the asking. The FBI would take the lead in the US, passing everything to us through our newest best friends under the Santa Maria dells Salute. The FBI didn't know this, of course; even the NSA would not be able to source how we were moving the information around. All the Americans had left with was a simple mini laptop with what looked like a satellite phone attached to pass the data through. We didn't really care who else knew what we knew, in bits and pieces, but we did care that the data, once it was centralized, stayed within a very small group of select minds.

Ours.

And the data that the Boss was after was very different from anything else all the other military and security forces were searching for.

"Indigo, I want you to coordinate all the teams, please, and here are the critical elements we are looking for." The Boss lit up one of the big screens and started drawing squiggles and boxes on it with a data pen. Using wireless technology, the data would also appear on our PDAs and laptops, saving us the trouble of duplicating it. "We know that the Euro Control air traffic system was hacked, the US system was hacked, and we now know that the US military-air-to-space system was also hacked out of Afghanistan. All these events have a common thread—no electronic fingerprints, no way of establishing who did what, but in each case, there is a very specific timeline, and that's how we will find whoever did this."

"What do you mean?" Pete asked, feeling a little left out of it due to the fact that he was more muscle than brain and usually only came in at the end of a case when we needed boots on the ground to make an arrest or stop someone from getting shot unless the shooting was done by Pete and his cronies. Having said that, you would be very unwise to underestimate his intelligence because, as a rule of thumb, Interpol attracted the most intelligent people in every discipline for one very good reason—they could work anywhere, with anyone, at any time, across any border, and the only thing anyone cared about was a righteous result. A very rare capacity in any political system.

"Well, if you are going to control an unmanned air vehicle, as someone did in the Israeli hit, you have to have a ground station with all the gear. Now, we know the Americans did not run that UAV out of Afghanistan, but we also know that the signals were made to look as if they came from there. So, we have a control point somewhere, and then we have radiated signals from somewhere else. The real question is..."

"Did the signals that supposedly came from Afghanistan actually exist, or were they just a data point that someone entered into the system?" Pete said, finishing the sentence for the Boss. We all looked at Pete with renewed respect.

"Exactly. If you are inside a system, there is no real need to actually generate anything. All you have to do is record it as if it had happened. The US military satellites that are used for this type of activity are geostationary and linked, so if you can get inside one, you are inside them all."

"Smoke and mirrors," Pete said, "smoke and mirrors. And if I remember the briefing properly, the air traffic control system in Europe and the US relies upon satellite-to-satellite communication as well."

"Yes," Indigo added, "now I see what you are driving at, Colonel. To create all the misleading data we have been given, all you need to do is to be able to get into one system and feed in the data you want everyone to find. You do not necessarily have to create the signals in real-time."

"Correct. Thanks to our young hacker here," the Boss said, pointing to Luigi Antoinette, who had joined us from Milan, "we know how easy it is to create false documentation, event lines, data points, and even waybills and ecurity clearances. Once again, you don't actually have to do something, just create the data as if something was actually done."

"Virtual warfare," I added, thinking to myself just how easy it had been for us to steal five kilos of Strontium-90 just hours ago. "Create the illusion of an event, based on the fact that people will see the data believe it, because it is data from their supposedly secure systems, and act on it."

"Yes. What makes it worse, in this case, is that the bad guys did it so well, that no one challenged the data until well after each event. So, the path I want us to go down is as follows. Indigo," the Boss said, handing a small green data USB to him, "take young Luigi and work out how to hack into a command-and-control satellite, what it would look like, and what you can do once you are inside. What I am looking for are the commands and time chokepoints related to each event. When you get some traction, link up with your book club friends over at the Grand Canal to keep everything off the net. Okay with you?"

"Colonel, with pleasure, what else are you going to do?"

"Well, for starters, I'm going to take the captain here and Pete, and we are going to fly, drive, and motor over every inch of each attack, and that's going to take us about four days, assuming the Arabians and the Israelis will let us into their party."

"You are looking for anomalies?" Indigo asked. "From the inside?"

"Yes, we have found that retracing the path of a crime sometimes gives us insights into the planning, as if we were committing the crime ourselves."

"What about the money trail?" I asked. This aspect had been worrying me for a long time now, as Interpol had enabled several high-profile arrests by tracking down the source of finance for several acts of terror and major crimes in the last few years.

"Well, now, I'm starting to develop a theory about that. Let me ask you all a question." The Boss looked around the room, making sure everyone was included in his scan and that they understood that they were being included in the process. "Take the bombing of the mosque, one truck with HEP-4, two people, both of whom have completely disappeared, only to turn up three days later as the charred remains of whom we now know to be two of the missing team of the French Special Forces. Do we have one event or several events made to look like one event? Either way, we know the French sent their team into Arabia after the bombing and after a direct request from the king. Or that is what the data tell us; who the hell knows what really happened?"

"Well, the mosque was bombed, it was HEP-4, and there were two people driving the truck." I thought I was sure of at least those facts!

"Yes, but why did the Arabians try to implicate the French? Was it to misdirect? Payback? Something else? Do they actually know who bombed their precious mosque? And were there two people driving the truck?"

"Sir, if I may ask a question?" a young Lieutenant working one of the data stations asked. The Boss nodded.

"Certainly. We need everyone's input on this; we are a long way from understanding the usual tools of our trade, means, method, opportunity, and motive. We can clearly see what was done and we think we know how, but everything else at this time is pure speculation. Ask away."

"Sir, the HEP-4 is traceable. Every block has an RFID chip that can be tracked worldwide. Also, the chemical signature from the site can be identified back to a batch/process delivery time, ex-factory." The Boss waited for a second, allowing everyone in the room to absorb what the young Lieutenant had just said.

"Lieutenant, excellent point. I had dismissed the RFID trace because we know someone has penetrated the military computers and can pretty much hide anything they like. I forgot about the chemsig (chemical signature). Well done. Pete, you might like to get on that before we fly out of here." The chances of the Boss having forgotten any detail about this case had about that same chance that you would have trying to fly to the moon and back next week, but this was his inimitable style and why I loved working with him so much. He made everyone feel special, needed and rewarded their every effort with recognition before their peers. Perhaps encouraged by the success of his fellow technician, another hand shot up.

"Sir, *mi scusi*, we know that the bombs dropped on our holy city were made in America, and that no one can account for their loss, even by physical inspection. But if the number of bombs is correct, then perhaps someone is playing a shell game with us, no?" The Boss looked extremely impressed this time and broke out into a huge smile.

"Spot on! Even the FBI hadn't worked that out. Excellent. Pete, while you are tracing the chemsig, contact the FBI about opening and looking inside the casings, please." The Boss looked around the room again, seeking any further spontaneous contributions from the staff of the Interpol control room. "Okay, then could you all put your minds to this problem—while a lot of the equipment used in these attacks has obviously been stolen—literally—from under the noses of the military in at least four countries, probably more, the terrorists still had to have money behind them, either to make their escape with or to bribe key people to do the wrong things at the right time. We need to find the money trail, please, and we need to find it now." A chorus of "*sì*'s" and "*pronto*'s" rippled around the room as everyone bent back to their workstations. The Boss grabbed his go-bag, Pete already had his on his shoulder, and Indigo handed me mine with a hug and a kiss on both cheeks.

"Stay safe, please, just for me," he whispered in my ear. I smiled, nodded, and followed the Boss back out into the moonlight, where our four-man guard had been lounging around smoking smelly tobacco. The red cigarette boat bobbed up and down as if it was a greyhound itching to chase a hare, looking quite grey in the moonlight, and I swallowed. This job had its perks, but traveling with insane boat drivers at high speed within the tight confines of the canals of Venice in the dark of night was definitely not one of them!

CHAPTER 22

"We've lost just over half of our oil supply, the world's religions are going nuts, and we can't even keep track of our own bloody bombs," exploded Julius Bronstein, the director of the CIA. Running on a treadmill deep in the basement of Langley, his partner in crime, the director of the NSA, Frank Reynolds, just huffed and puffed, not having the breath to argue with the dapper director. Even here in the CIA gymnasium, the director managed to look as if he had just stepped out of a fashion magazine. He rewound the speed of his treadmill back to a slow jog, a monogrammed towel around his neck, which he used delicately to wipe the sweat from his forehead. "The real problem is that we have too many questions and not enough answers."

"Gas prices have gone through the roof; our strategic reserve is just that, strategic; we need a long-term fix, and we need it now," huffed Frank. "To make matters worse, our own systems seem to be working against us. More and more data is turning up to be false, and the time it takes to prove the good bits is really killing us."

"How the fuck did they get inside your machines?" Julius asked, stopping his treadmill. He wiped his face, suddenly having a flash of insight. "Frank, I've just thought of something. What do all these events have in common?" The director of the NSA looked baffled, they had been searching for patterns for days, and apart from the inside use of the cyber network and the fact that every single person involved in the attacks had completely disappeared, there seemed little to go on. The data corruption and real-time hacking that had taken place around every terrorist attack was definitely a "signature" event, but all attempts to track the hackers had met with, literally, nothing. And this was the single biggest issue the NSA was working on because up until these attacks, it was a commonly held belief that any hacker left some electronic trail somewhere and that a smart investigator could backtrack that trail to the hacker.

"Apart from the obvious?" Frank asked.

"Yes. Think about it for a second. Every attack has one clear similarity, and I only just worked it out." Frank looked mystified; he had spent every waking moment for the last few days studying every report, every bit and byte of data, every satellite photo, intelligence report, eyewitness report, everything the mighty intelligence agencies of the world could produce. He finally shook his head in frustration, his mind muddled by what he couldn't work out.

"Okay, follow this for me." Julius held up one finger. "Rome, bombed by a Hercules. What happened to the aircraft?"

"Shot down by the Italian Air Force."

"Correct. Dome of the Rock was attacked by a Predator UAV. What happened to the UAV?"

"Blown up, we assume by the self-destruct charge that every UAV has fitted to it."

"Two for two, keep it up, Frank!" Julius asked, almost gleefully, holding four fingers up, "what happened to the truck that delivered the nuclear material to the oil field and to the truck that delivered the bomb to the mosque?"

"One destroyed by, we assume, the drivers, and one destroyed in the explosion."

"Four for four, Frank, you're on a roll. Now, for a ten-dollar lunch, what happened to the Hog that bombed West Point?" The only sound in the gym was the ticking of the wall clock as the director of the NSA rolled the question around in his mind.

"Disappeared. We have no trace of it."

"Exactly, it disappeared, camouflaged by whoever was hacking into our ATC and satellite systems. But it wasn't blown up; at least we did not detect any explosion on any system, and believe me, after 9/11, exploding aircraft tend to get noticed around New York. So where is it?"

"The Air Force said they had three fighters in that airspace, as they always do now, flying a high-level combat air patrol. None of these aircraft picked up the Hog on their radar, and one F16 was over West Point within seventy seconds of the attack being reported. It never saw anything; I've read the pilot's report."

"Frank, I don't know how much you know about aircraft radar, but those fighters are tuned to see air threats. What if the Hog descended down to ground level and flew out to sea?"

"Someone would have seen or heard it."

"Yes. And we have zero reports of a low-flying aircraft. So where did it go?" Frank looked blankly at the CIA director, working through the problem as he had trained to do for thirty years. He slowly started to nod, suddenly seeing a possibility they had completely ignored.

"It flew right on out of New York controlled airspace disguised as another legitimate aircraft."

"Yes. They hacked the system, entered false data to disguise the attack, and then flew on a legitimate flight plan that aroused no suspicion. We've been looking in all the wrong places. Where could you land a Hog and have no one take any notice?" Frank looked quizzically at the director, thinking through the question. He shook his head.

"On that particular day?"

"No, Julius, wrong question. Where did all the legitimate aircraft go on that day? Unless we have another aircraft suddenly disappearing, and we might, he probably just landed at a base somewhere that was expecting him because of data put into the system by the terrorists. Remember, we didn't know what the attack aircraft was until we interrogated the ATC system nearly fifty minutes after the attack. We were all too busy looking for the terrorist aircraft, which, if you remember, had disappeared. No one thought to look at all the legitimate flights at that time. The airspace was closed, aircraft scrambled, and a visual ID was made of everything within a one-hundred-mile radius. An A-10 Hog can make around four hundred knots at altitude for around eight hundred miles. We know it refueled just outside the New York ADIZ (Air Defense Identification Zone) prior to the attack, so we need to check every airport within that radius. The Air Force can do it visually; that way, we will know that what we see is what we see."

"Do you actually think we will find the aircraft?" Frank asked. Julius nodded and then broke out into a deep smile.

"Of course, going on past performances, you can expect it to be trashed beyond recognition, but yes, I expect we will. Somewhere."

CHAPTER 23

The Boss was flying the UN L100 Lockheed Hercules, and I had co-pilot duties. Pete was sitting in the jump seat between us, and a real pilot on loan from the UN was sitting in the flight engineer's position. We were flying the exact same route the terrorist aircraft had flown, even to the point where we duplicated a holding pattern just outside the Serbian border while we waited for airways clearance. The Boss had the lumbering trash hauler on autopilot and was just adjusting our heading and altitude with the control buttons. The NSA was tracking us via satellite, and we were getting an overlay of our route on a laptop wired into the navigation system, the earlier track of the terrorist aircraft in red and our "mirror" flight in blue. We were tracking over Sarajevo to Split in Croatia, across the Mediterranean to make landfall in Italy midway between Ancona and Pescara on the east coast, then onto Rome, and then back out across the Mediterranean until we reached the point where our predecessor had been shot down just before they made landfall at Barcelona. The Boss was extremely relaxed with his feet up on the control panel coming and was using the dead time en route to Rome to build a framework from within, which he hoped that would be able to identify some elements of a pattern that would help us catch the terrorists.

"Okay, Pete, you are in charge of planning this attack, so start from the beginning; how do you go about it?" Below us, the rolling but scarred hills from years and years of secular fighting passed by, giving our flight a somewhat surreal feeling.

"Need an airplane. Need a crew. Need the bombs. Need handling equipment wherever I load the bombs on board. Need aircrew scheduling, airways clearances, food, water, and fuel. And I would need time. The biggest question for me has always been where the bombs came from? They were both highly specialized, not made in large numbers, but both required very specialized equipment to transport, store, and load. Someone, somewhere, must have seen them being placed on board. And one other thing that I just can't get away from."

"What's that?" I asked. Pete was surprising me more and more every day, as previously I had only worked with him as hired muscle, expert boat driver, and laconic killer. He leaned forward and tapped the "Ramp Up/Down" switch on the overhead console.

"Getting rid of those two bombs would have taken quite a bit of skill, so at least one person in the crew knew how to operate a mid-air extraction."

"Good thinking, but I have another question for you," the Boss said, turning the little heading bug on the horizontal situation indicator (HSI) to change our course a fraction. Probably a crosswind was pushing us slightly off course. "Both bombs were GPS navigated, so the extraction could have been preset, and the ground penetrator was a glide-bomb, good for three to four miles of horizontal distance if dropped from the correct height and speed. Let's assume they got that bit right, but the daisy cutter was a direct aim-and-drop; how did they do that so accurately?"

"That particular daisy cutter was course steerable for at least a mile if dropped from twenty-five thousand feet," I said, referring to the top-secret notes that had been supplied by the USAF earlier that day. "It has little fins on it that can be manipulated in flight."

"Okay," the Boss said, smiling as he flew, "just for the sake of argument, can either of those bombs be fitted with laser detectors?" I flicked through the perfectly normal and, therefore, incredibly complex military specifications for both bombs, and sure enough, right at end of the "Aiming and Control—delivery phase" was the answer to the Boss's question.

"Yes, both types of munitions have been modified for dual GPS/ laser target designation just four years ago, according to this."

"Okay, so look at a picture of the Vatican, there's a satellite pic in there somewhere, and tell me what you would aim at if you were flying the attack." Pete held the high-resolution color satellite picture of the Vatican between the Boss and I so that all three of us could look at it at the same time. There was no doubt, even from three thousand feet (virtual), that the answer leaped out at us like a signpost. The magnificent dome of Saint Peter's attached to the bicycle wheel of Piazza San Pietro made for an unmistakable aiming point, you could not miss it, and of course, the terrorists hadn't.

"The limit of most military laser designation equipment, in daylight, is around six thousand meters. The higher up you are, the better you can paint the target. Remembering the force of the explosions, the man on the ground would need robust cover to survive so close to ground zero. Got any chutes in this thing?" Pete asked. The Boss smiled, nodded, looked out to see the coast of Italy approaching under the nose, tweaked the heading bug again, then pointed back behind us to the cargo compartment.

"Two types of rig, HALO and counter insurgent, take your pick, I'll drop you off at eight thousand feet, and I'll have a helicopter waiting on the ground. Find us where they lit the dome from; I'll get Indigo to have some forensic people available."

"You know, laser light can be seen in daylight if you've got the right filters,"

I said, thinking back to a technical article I had read some time ago. "There was a lot of footage being shot by TV crews and tourists, and I know the Italians gathered most of it up at the time of the bombing." The rolling hills that ran down the spine of the Italian "boot" were passing under us, and the unmistakable building-scape that was Rome was starting to emerge out of the haze.

"Good thinking. Use your phone and text Indigo to run all the footage through again and see if you can get a landmark for Pete." The Boss made little adjustments to the knobs on the glare shield, motioned for us to put on our oxygen masks, which hung over our heads like dead chooks hung by their feet in a slaughterhouse, waited for the thumbs up, opened the rear cargo door, and started to duplicate the terrorist's bombing run on the Vatican. He pulled the throttles back, slowing us to one hundred and eighty knots indicated, so Pete could jump out and not be killed by the slipstream, then accelerated back up to our previous airspeed. It got cold, drafty, and very noisy all of a sudden, and not for the first time, I wondered why perfectly normal people chose to jump out of perfectly functioning aircraft of their own volition!

The little laptop went into a countdown, and at the first "zero," the Boss called "first bomb gone," twenty seconds later, "second bomb gone," and he adjusted the heading bug to align our track with the red line on the screen. I noticed that we had been joined by a flock of angry-looking fighter aircraft, all with their noses pointed up high to stay level with us as we trundled along at a stately two hundred and forty knots. The noise and the draft continued, and I looked over at the Boss expecting him to raise the rear ramp, but he did not move. I looked back down at the briefing notes supplied by Indigo and quickly found the description of the L100 the Italian Air Force had intercepted after the bombing.

Twenty-five thousand feet, two hundred and forty knots airspeed, no response from the cockpit, and the rear ramp down, streaming the tale tail canvas rip cords used to pull open parachutes as the cargo pallets or parachutes were dropped out into the slipstream. The Boss suddenly sat up, switched frequencies, and started babbling.

"Captain, exactly where was the first point of interception by the Italian fighters?" he asked, his voice sounding tinny through the interphone wired into our oxygen masks. I looked through my notes, found the relevant page, and put my finger on the number.

"Thirty-seven nautical miles from the point of the attack."

"Six or seven minutes from ground zero."

"Yes, sir, assuming they held their airspeed."

"Why do you say that?"

"Because you slowed to one eighty indicated for Pete's jump."

"Yes, I did, didn't I? Does the report say anything about any airspeed variations?"

"No, but the flight data was incorrect, as far as we can ascertain, because the heights varied between the visual sightings and the ATC radar reports."

"Assuming that they did descend for the second bomb drop, they could easily have climbed back up to twenty-five thousand feet by the time the fighters found them."

"Yes, sir, and your point is?" The Boss had the most annoying habit of grinning like a Cheshire cat whenever he thought he had outmaneuvered me, and right now, his face was lit up like a Halloween pumpkin.

"They never left the aircraft."

"They what?" I exclaimed, picturing the fiery destruction of the terrorist's air-craft as it was shot out of the sky by a formation of very angry Italian pilots armed with all manner of missiles and cannons, hauntingly similar to the aircraft that currently flew just off our wingtips.

"They never left the aircraft. And I can prove it."

CHAPTER 24

It took seventeen hours, made up of three truck rides, four hours of walking in the dark, and finally a car ride provided by a bunch of Australian tourists off to see the White House, the Mall, and "all those great statutes and things, mate!" No amount of prayer could thank his last hosts enough, as they had literally picked him up off the side of the road three hundred miles from his destination, so unlucky had he been with his earlier hitchhiking efforts.

Now he stood outside the White House, behind the concrete posts designed to stop a tank, thinking about how he was going to get in to see the president. By coincidence, at the same time as Father Andretti was pondering his next move, the massive 747 Airforce Two was touching down at Andrews Air Force Base, and a blacked-out FBI sedan was speeding away from the detention center at Dade County Airport. Its occupant now wore bright orange overalls, had a black bag over his head and was shackled at the feet, waist, wrists, and further restrained by a thick chain that ended at a bolt head on the floor of the car.

The White House was regarded by most terrorists as the juiciest target on the planet, and more than one well-known aspirant for the FBI's "Ten Most Wanted" list had lost sleep plotting and planning a way to attack it. Equally, the entire American military-industrial complex had invested thousands of hours and millions of dollars working out how to protect it from every imaginable type of attack. Snipers and

Marines carrying MANPADS (man-portable anti-missile defense system) patrolled the roof, six different types of radar monitored every movement in the air-space for a hundred miles around, Secret Service, the FBI, and Capitol Police patrolled the grounds in constant physical and electronic contact with each other, and three separate perimeters had been established. The first was a series of ram raids and tank traps outside the fence line, then the fence line itself, which was loaded with every kind of motion sensor imaginable, and finally, the area of the entire ground was scanned by motion sensors and CCTV cameras, monitored in real-time twenty-four hours a day.

But it was an off-duty Washington police officer that saved the situation and prevented the Jesuit priest from praying the White House gates open. He had noticed the priest, who by now was somewhat shabbily dressed from his extraordinary trip from Miami in the dead of night, pacing back and forth in front of the tank traps, and decided to find out what was aggravating the obviously distressed monk.

"Can I help you, Father?" he asked, then seeing the confusion on the priest's face, switched to Spanish. "*¿Puedoayudarle, Padre?*"

"*Sí, tengo que ir a hablar con el Presidente.*" The officer considered his options, sensing no immediate danger from the priest. While he looked ragged and sleep deprived, and was obviously tense and stressed about something, he didn't radiate any kind of threat. The officer pointed to his car parked back along the road, where emergency and police vehicles could stay for extended periods while their occupants rested between patrols or ate their traditional fare of doughnuts and hot dogs.

"*Ven conmigo a mi coche, y voy a llamar a la Casa Blanca para usted y ver lo que puedohacer.*" The officer gently took the priest by the arm and walked him towards his parked vehicle, wondering whom to call. The White House was out of the question; he was off duty, so the Police station was a poor option; then, he decided that there was one solid way to find out what was worrying the ruffled priest.

"*Padre, vamosair a mi Iglesia, y hablar de la Casa Blanca existe.*" They got in the car, and the officer used his mobile phone to call his local priest, Father Jacobson. He handed the phone to the priest.

"*Si?*"

"Father Andretti, how can I help you?"

"Ah, my English nota so gooda, *¿hablas español*?"

"Sorry, no, I have a little but not enough to pretend I could understand you. Can you tell me what you need to do, please?" The priest held the handset away from his ear and looked over the seat at the officer who was watching him intently but with kind eyes. He nodded to himself.

"*Si*, I trya. My brothera, he locked up in Miami jail, they think he *allegado inmigrantes*. But hea has mosta importanta message for president of America. Very importanta he get thisa messagea to him, *rápidamente*. It from a man who attacks alla world religions, bombs Holy City. Mutsa get this *mensaje* toa him *rapidísimo*." The officer suddenly screwed up his eyes in concentration at the mention of the bomb attack on the Vatican. What on earth had he walked into? And on his day off?

"Where did your brother come by this important message?" Father Jacobson asked, wondering what this was all about in the name of God.

"*Hace mucho sañoshea* was a—how you say—*misionero*—in a smalla campamento *de refugia dos* calleda Gouraud, en Baalbek, Lebon. Hea takea thea Holy Worda to poor peoples, hea very good Jesuit." The officer quickly typed in what he heard, "Gouraud, Baalbek, Lebon," getting the gist of the one-sided conversation. Within seconds, his computer screen that sat on the console between the two front seats came back with a tightly worded paragraph—a refugee camp in Lebanon closed twenty years ago, famous for the highest number of child deaths in the camps at that time, and for the fact that the Catholic Church had successfully run a small school there for some ten years before the camp was demolished, and the Catholics were kicked out of the camps by secular Muslims. The officer looked at the priest, pointing to the screen.

"Was your brother a teacher at the Catholic school?" he asked. "*Suhermanofue un maestro en la escuela*?" The priest looked at him blankly for a second, then started to nod.

"*Si, si, hea enseñar la palabra de Dios* to thea childs, *si*!" he exclaimed. "Do you know the name of the man your brother met in the camp?" the officer asked, completely amazed at the way the conversation was shaping up. The priest stared at him blankly, shaking his head from side to side.

"*Alofue un maestro, pero no jesuita*. Hea come from the *desierto*."

"From the desert, and was also a teacher?"

"*Si, si.* Mya brother and him worka junto, *tres años.*"

"Three years?"

"*Si, tres años.*"

"What was the message?" asked Father Jacobson, lost in translation.

"No, no *sólo puedo de cirle al Presidente*!" suddenly, the priest was agitated again, bouncing up and down on his seat. "My brother very *específico.* Only *al Presidente*!" The officer looked bemused, took the handset back, thanked his priest, and hung up.

"No *sécómotodavía, mi amigo, peroyote el presidente. De alguna forma.*" As he made the promise, he hoped he could make good on his word. In truth, right at this very moment, he hadn't the faintest idea how to reach the president, let alone get the Jesuit before him, as he had just said that he would.

It was turned out to be an interesting day!

CHAPTER 25

The Directorate of Al Mabaahith Al Jena'eyah, Al Mukhabarat Al A'amah, and the Lightning Force, representing the very best and the very worst of the Arabian security forces, sat around a huge glass table on which were several hundred excellent satellite photos of both Shaybah and Masjid al-Haram in Mecca. The images represented sixty minutes on either side of the two events that had changed Middle Eastern politics, influence, and power forever, and the images that had the target vehicles in them had massive red marker pen circles drawn on them as if to underline the amount of innocent blood spilled at each site. The mood in the room was upbeat, in contrast to the horrendous devastation and death the images recorded. In fact, to a casual observer, you could be forgiven for thinking that a celebration was in progress.

Which, in a sense, it was.

Two of the three men in the room were drinking expensive French champagne. It was obviously not a day to observe their religious faith's strict "no alcohol" rule.

The odd man was sipping soda water out of respect for his liver and kidneys, which were all but dead by any medical standard.

"The other bodies will turn up later today, which, in spite of official French protests, will clearly upset the balance within the European Union and with any luck will energize the Jews and every crazy religious group with a grudge."

"But the king will also be entrapped, as he was the reason the French sent their people here."

"So be it. God is great, and his vengeance will be swift and final. Let the king and his bastard sons reap what he has sown."

"Do you really think it will be that easy?" the soda water drinker asked. A limp cigarette hung carelessly from stained fingers, and his whole demeanor was that of someone who had lost all interest in life but hadn't found the right box to lie down in yet. Another cork was popped, frothy champagne overflowing the neck at the rate of forty dollars a second. The clink of the bottleneck on the edge of glass rang through the room, creating its own expectation.

"Yes, I do. By the will and grace of Allah, His Name Be Praised, someone has chosen to attack the greatest symbols of our faith. They have created a level of political and religious fervor and tension in the world that we have not seen since the Second World War. Taking advantage of this God-made situation is the logical thing to do." The third man, the youngest and therefore the one most likely to benefit from the trio's deception and malice, raised his glass to his companions. "Then let the hellfire rain down on the infidels; may all their children be still-born, and their women wither and die!" For a moment, the room was dead silent.

Then the soda man smiled and raised his glass.

"You're an evil bastard, Abdul, but you're my evil bastard!"

CHAPTER 26

ה669 דיחי was painted in light blue along the side of the Augusta 109 medevac helicopter in such large letters it could be seen from miles away. For the last few days, the crews had flown in and out of Jerusalem, ferrying the dead and injured Israelis from the vicious attack on the Dome of The Rock on top of Mount Moriah. A unit of the Israeli Air Force, it was renowned for flying in under all conditions, day and night, including into the maw of shelling and mortar attacks by Hamas to bring back the bodies of fallen or injured Jews. *Ir Ha-Kodesh*—the Holy City, the Biblical Zion, the City of David, the site of King Solomon's Temple, and the eternal capital of the Israelite nation, was rocking back on its metaphorical heels.

A second agency was intimately involved in the recovery effort, הלצהויוהיז - יתימאדסח (Identification and Rescue - True Kindness). ZAKA is made up of mostly volunteer Haredi Jews who assumed the duty of collecting human remains to provide a proper Jewish burial, known as *Chesed Shel Emet*, or "True Virtue." And right now, they were working overtime because, as with most devastating explosions that come into contact with flimsy people, there were more torn and shattered remains than whole identifiable bodies. Their work was bloody and painstaking and induced such grief in some of the workers that they had to be taken away in ambulances originally called in to spirit away the dead.

Watching this gruesome effort on remote monitor screens, a group of grimfaced men and women also showing all the signs of induced fatigue caused by sleepless nights and too much coffee worked slavishly to identify the terrorists. Their country was demanding a response, and just this past day, the Knesset had unanimously agreed on all sides of the political fence to mount a massive, conclusive attack on whoever was responsible. And in this case, conclusive meant that the Israeli Parliament had secretly sanctioned the use of nuclear weapons if the IDF (Israeli Defense Forces) decided that they could minimize the inevitable collateral damage.

All they needed was a provable target.

The three principal organizations of the Israeli intelligence community, Mossad, Shabak, and Aman, were for once working side by side in a furious effort to backtrack the terrorists. The satellite footage clearly showed that the unmanned air vehicle was a Condor 656 in Israeli Air Force markings, and the Hellfire missiles had been identified by their chemical residue signatures as having come from the secured weapons store at Palmachim, which was the biggest IAF/DF helicopter base in the country.

The Americans had first denied and then been able to prove that the UAV had not been remotely piloted from Afghanistan, which created an even bigger mystery, because looking at the video of the flight, it was clear that the pilot was an expert, so professional and accurate had the attack been mounted.

Unfortunately, the popularity of drones being flown by every Tom, Dick and Harry, created a significantly large pool of talented pilots to sift through, literally from all over the world.

And they now knew with certainty that someone had successfully hacked into the American military satellite system and was able to manipulate data at will. In one simple act, eighty percent of the available intelligence available became suspect, once again demonstrating how hard it was for anyone to move their minds and thinking processes backwards when the technical or digital electronic world failed.

Three-second attention span. Three clicks for any answer to any question. Except, in this case, it really didn't matter how many clicks were hammered into keyboards; nothing worthwhile emerged from the electronic detritus.

The control room was an excellent example of controlled chaos, as uniformed officers mixed and merged with suited and casually dressed spies. On one wall, a huge countdown clock, usually formatted to bring everything to a head at the launch point of an attack, was counting backwards, showing the time elapsed since the attack. On smaller screens to one side, digital readouts showed how long it had been since the other four attacks had taken place, superimposed over the image of the location of each terrorist attack. Larger screens with concise summaries of the little that was actually established as fact sat under, looking forlorn in spite of their 4D brilliant displays. Staring intently at these smaller screens was Arie Rosenberg, at seventy-nine years of age, probably the oldest person in the room. As the former head of Shin Bet (*Shabak*), he had been invited to sit on the sidelines by the incumbent director in the hope that he would see something that they had all missed. As a former "boots and doorknob" policeman, he had never taken to computers and data files, still maintaining that the old-fashioned and now almost impossible to get eight-inch-by-six-inch filing card was the perfect repository for most information. And yet, when Israel had formed the NSA's electronic equivalent, Arie was appointed its director, unchallenged.

Arie used the remote controller to fast forward the footage they had obtained at great cost, in this case, the lives of three young agents who had been caught by the Arabian Secret Police just after they had uploaded the images to a satellite phone. The three had been working undercover as "sleepers" for some years in the Arabian security apparatus, gathering invaluable information that had literally prevented thousands of deaths around the world.

And sad though Arie was to have lost such valuable human intelligence— "HUMINT"—assets, the product they had obtained was first class and provided a unique aspect to the investigation. And it was this very uniqueness that had spiked his interest.

"Shami, lend an old man a minute if you will." The young Colonel responsible for all the data management in the control center sat down with relish, having been on his feet for what felt like three days on the trot. He looked over at the screen and focused on the UAV's top-down image as it approached Mount Moriah. The screen suddenly cut to what appeared to be a mobile phone or home video footage of the truck exploding, flaming debris raining down, then tilting up at the burning sky as the blast wave knocked down whoever the unlucky videographer had been. The next shots were more professional, taken from a helicopter with a gyro-stabilized mount, and showed the damage to the Masjid al-Haram Mosque in great detail. The camera started at the massive spires at one end, carefully panned around the perimeter, the staging area, then back towards the spites, passing over the three black domes that dominated the center area at the peak of the Hajj that could hold thousands of pilgrims.

"Do you see what I see, Shami?" the old general asked. The young Colonel respectfully dipped his head at his mentor and took the video controller off him.

He fast-forwarded the images, stopping occasionally, then reversed it in places, then spun it up again, replaying the sections that showed where the Imams had their billets and held their meetings. Then he wound through the side shots again until he was back at the epicenter of the explosion. He paused the image, looked around the room at the frantic activity, furrowed his brow, and then handed the controller back to Arie.

"Sir, with respect, I think you have to take this information somewhere neutral." He stared at the general, almost with a pleading look. The general smiled, a thin movement of his lips, and he nodded just once.

"Thank you, Shami. You make an old man proud!" The Colonel stood, nodded, then re-entered the fray, heading for his station behind a huge bank of computers. The old man stared at the second screen, on which was a series of images taken from supposedly secure sources in Arabia. Again, he moved the images forwards and backwards until he once again nodded to himself. The third screen was showing detailed photos from inside the shattered golden dome that once had so proudly covered the most treasured rock on earth. Once again, his interest was piqued, to the point where he froze one photo in particular and stared at it for what seemed like five minutes.

He switched the screens off, leaving the event clock ticking its ominous message. Like all good cops the world over, he intuitively believed in the "rule of 48"—if you hadn't managed a major break in a criminal case in the first forty-eight hours, you were unlikely to ever solve the crime successfully.

He stood up, slowly unbending a frame that had endured a hard life and was paying him back for it day by arthritic day. He moved over to a computer station near one of the analysts, where a row of encrypted satellite phones sat in their desktop charges. Taking one, he headed for a small alcove where someone had placed an ornate desk and chair against a magnificent mural painted by Shopie Ryngold, one of the bright and upcoming Sabra artists making their mark on the world of modern impressionists. He sat as slowly as he had risen just a minute before, wondering for the first time in his very long and productive life what this particular phone call would unleash.

At least he was too old to be tried and shot for treason!

CHAPTER 27

With the enigmatic statement from the Boss still hanging in the air "that the crew had not jumped out of the aircraft," we returned to retrace our path back across Italy. The Boss had the L-100—a stretched version of the venerable C-130 Hercules that had served so many nations so well for over fifty-five years— on autopilot and still with his feet up on the cockpit panel. For all intents and purposes, we looked like just a few guys out having fun flying for the day. The shrill of a satellite phone shattered the quiet, and the Boss reached into his flight suit and pulled the offending item out. The conversation was short, to the point of three grunted words—"yes, okay, fine." The Boss turned to look at me, then looked back over his shoulder at the UN pilot sitting in the engineer's seat.

"We have to divert, sorry, it might be a while before you get home again." The UN pilot just shrugged his shoulders as if this was an everyday occurrence. The plane banked sharply to the right, or to starboard as the aircraft nuts liked to say, and within ten minutes, the Italian F-16s that had been escorting us were replaced by a brace of Israeli F-16s, bristling with air-to-air missiles and obvious hostility. Same aircraft as the Italians, but you could just tell that the pilots were a cut above everybody else. The Italians had held a loose formation around twenty meters off our wingtips, whereas the Israelis practically pushed their missile-tipped wingtips through the cockpit window.

"UN special zero-zero-one, maintain formation, you will be landing at Tel Nof, runway one-fife left. Do not move off track, or we will shoot you down. Do not change frequency, or we will shoot you down. Follow my lead!" suddenly, we had an F-16 exhaust in the middle of our windscreen, leading us across the Mediterranean to Israel.

"What's their ICAO ident?" I asked the Boss.

"LLEK," he answered as if he had memorized the entire database of airports around the world. I punched in "LLEK" into my airport directory on my laptop and got a vanilla satellite shot of one of the three most important Israeli military airbases known. The photo was heavily degraded for security reasons, but it looked like it had two parallel runways of around three thousand meters, and one oblique runway around two-thirds as long. The area around was a collection of dense buildings or dirty brown agriculture, like most of that area surrounding Negev near Rehovot. Occasionally a green patch stood out, obviously irrigated, as water was a scarce as the proverbial hen's tooth.

We started a high-speed drift-down, the F-16 suddenly pulling away slightly to give us a clear view of the ground. In a little less than seven minutes, we were slowing to one hundred and twenty knots, dropping the landing gear, and then progressively the flaps as we followed the Israeli pilot. At a thousand feet, he suddenly shot up and disappeared into the clear blue sky so fast he must have been using his after-burner, and three minutes later, we were on the ground, slowing down with reverse pitch, wondering where to taxi to and park the aircraft. Not for long. "UN special, taxi to Romeo Tango three, follow the vehicle." The Boss turned us off onto the designated taxiway, where a Humvee armed to the teeth waited for us, with a yellow "Follow Me" sign in six languages mounted on its stern. We did what we were told, and eventually we bumped and ground our way to a parking area in front of a brace of Russian Migs, all with the distinctive blue double Star of David on their tails. No telling where they came from, or what they were for, but I did know that Tel Nof was the home of 601 squadron, which conducted flight testing and evaluation of foreign aircraft and weapons systems. No doubt they had been wrung out at some stage to give the Air Force the advantage in air-to-air combat, as a number of the nations that opposed the State of Israel used the Russian supplied Migs as their primary airborne platform.

"Captain, come with me please; Johan, this is again your aircraft. I will get you approved to depart and return home; will you need fuel?" the Boss asked. The UN pilot glanced at the row of gauges on the sidewall he was sitting in front of and shook his head.

"No, sir, plenty left to get home on." The Boss and I unbuckled our harnesses, and I followed him down the stairs to the loading door portside, which by the time I got to it was up and open, revealing a squad of Israeli soldiers dressed to kill, forming a narrow corridor that led to the open door of yet another Humvee, this one as black as the ace of spades and with the windows blacked out. I closed and locked the door, patting it twice as was the custom, then making sure I didn't inadvertently walk into the spinning propellers ducked my way into the vehicle. Door closed, no introductions, just a heavy-set grunt pointing an overly large weapon at me, trying to smile and frown at the same time. Without waiting to be asked, I handed him my pistol, my combat knife I kept down my leg, and fold-up emergency flick knife I kept in my pocket. After all, a girl still had to have some secrets in this day and age!

We drove for exactly fifteen minutes in relative silence, relative in that the Humvee was obviously well worn, and the driver seemed to love over-revving it at every gear change, leading to a somewhat explosive series of sounds coming from the exhaust, which I figured I was sitting on top of. We drove down into a tunnel guarded by tanks and machine gun nests, turned around several times in the dark, then stopped. The door opened, and another group of Israeli soldiers greeted us, swarming us into a small alcove where we were invited to strip off our flight suits, socks, and boots and dress in a lovely blue number that was obviously made of plasticized paper and was as far away from haute couture as you could get and still call it clothing. Our Interpol ID folders, passports, and minicomputers were handed back to us, and without hesitation, both the Boss and I flipped open our IDs and slipped the hard leather back into the top pocket of our jumpsuits, to give us some measure of authority. Strangely, our smartphones, keys, and some minor personal items were withheld. I couldn't help but smile as I imagined the look on the face of the soldier who would eventually have to bring me back my little black packet of tampons!

"Colonel, I trust you had a good flight?" an old man asked in broken English. The Boss reached forward, clasping the old man with both hands; it was obviously someone whom he respected a great deal, because the Boss never gushed and, in my presence at least, rarely showed any emotion except when he was yelling at someone. More often than not, me.

"Arie, Arie, how are you?" he asked, also something I had never heard him say before to anyone. The old man beamed, his thin lips creasing his face, which I realized had either been severely burned sometime in the past or reconstructed for some other reason.

"I'm fine, PJ, and who is this lovely lady you have with you?"

"Arie, this is my second-in-command, Captain Riley, but you can call her Jessica." The old man let go of the Boss and reached for my hand, which he held in the European manner and lightly kissed.

"Shalom, Jessica, welcome to Israel, I am Arie, as you heard; how did you get mixed up with this ruffian?" The Boss laughed, giving me a sort of affectionate look, another surprise, then shrugged his shoulders.

"Actually, I got hooked up with her, Arie, when she tried to kill me one night." The old man led us into an anteroom, leaving the IDF soldiers behind, eventually stopping at a small, ornate desk. He sat on the far side, allowing the Boss and I to sit facing the huge control room, where utter chaos was in full swing, with around two hundred people in all sorts of uniforms racing around white-coated technicians and young people in jeans and T-shirts.

It wasn't that much of a surprise, as at the major Interpol command and control centers, we tended to have the same eclectic mix of people, with the jeans and T-shirt brigade firmly in control of the electronic agenda, as they were the only ones who could SMS, play with a PDA or game controller, listen to iPods, and watch television at the same time!

"PJ, without compromising your position of independence and political neutrality, can I show you some evidence we have collected? I cannot tell you the source, but I can guarantee the providence. I also can't give you any direct information other than confirming or denying anything that you may deduce for yourself at this time. Is that okay with you?" The Boss gave Arie his patented "don't dare fuck with me" stare, then looked at me. I nodded; this was territory we often got to visit when an outraged nation needed help from Interpol but was scared to tell anyone anything in case it inadvertently helped the very people they were trying to bring to book. Paranoia is okay when they really are after you! And in the case of Israel, everyone always seemed to be after them and had been for a couple of thousand years, and the Israelis had taken paranoia to a new and exalted level!

"Arie, I must caution you, Interpol has been commissioned by both the Italians and the Americans so far to work on this case, so anything you show us or say to us can and will be used in the prosecution of our case and may be shared with both countries at some level." The old man looked at the Boss for a full minute, then slowly nodded.

"Okay, this you can do, but can you not attribute the source of any information you might pick up here without calling me first?" he asked, watching the Boss closely.

"So long as we do not have to seek your permission for any action we may decide to take, anywhere this case takes us, I can guarantee confidentiality on source material."

"So be it. Look at these videos and tell me what you see."

So, we did, and we slowly we came to the same conclusion the old man had, and the minutes passed with a speed that was bewildering. I wish I could tell you that I was the wiser or even closer to working out why it had happened or who made it happen, but now we clearly knew exactly what had happened in Jerusalem and Arabia.

CHAPTER 28

The Israeli gunboat was driven by a cloned twin of the maniac who constantly tried to kill us in the Venetian cigarette boat. Apart from smashing into every wave at fifty knots, leaping into the air like a demented flying fish, then smashing back down so hard my teeth rattled, it rocked and rolled from side to side as well with furious white water roaring in from every direction. Of course, the boys loved it; faces lit up like kids under a Christmas tree. I didn't have my last meal, pride alone stalled the acidic juices in my throat, but I did make a silent promise to kill the Boss at the first opportunity once we got on dry land.

As the beautiful Church of Santa Maria dells Salute came into sight as the gunboat powered around the red and green marker buoys that led up the Grand Canal, it seemed to twinkle in the moonlight, an optical trick, of course, because the magnificent structure right up to the very top of the dome was covered by a massive latticework of scaffolding. The Israeli coxswain made a perfect arrival at the dock, and waiting there to greet us were four Italians, dressed to the hilt in beautiful suits and silk ties, all smiles, such a contrast to the sour-faced Israelis. What a difference a stretch of water could make. On one side bitter hatred and the threat of annihilation on a daily basis, on the other a twenty-four-hour never-ending fashion parade of style and moxie!

As we entered the underground library, once again removing anything metallic or electronic at the entrance to the vault, the smell of coffee beans wafted through the air conditioning making my taste buds go crazy. Someone had installed an espresso machine since our last visit!

"*Il colonnello, il capitano, si famished, sì*?" Indigo asked, plonking a platter down onto a low table and pulling the plastic wrap off with a flourish that would have made a Vegas magician proud. On it was what could only be described as a huge selection of antipasti, French bread, open sandwiches, fruits, and pickled vegetables. He handed us beautiful glass plates, in the center of which was a small impression of a mailed fist holding a feather. I had seen that somewhere before, but my innate hunger got the better of me, and I loaded up my plate and found a seat. "Indigo, thanks, that's very thoughtful of you. Where are we up to?" the Boss asked, mimicking my poor behavior with the delicious food.

"Well, my Colonel, a little bit of the good news and a little bit of the bad." Indigo settled himself opposite us. "The good news is that Mister Pete will be here shortly. I have a helicopter about to drop him off at Plaza Stefforee, five minutes from here. He has some very interesting news for us."

"And the bad?" I asked between mouthfuls of the best food I had had in days. Indigo looked a little uncomfortable and wriggled around in his seat as if he were shaking ants out of his trouser legs.

"Well, I am embarrassed to say this, but I can tell you what has been reported, but I cannot give you the facts." We both stopped eating at the same split second, caught with food on our forks and our mouths open. We were Interpol. We dealt with international court-worthy hard evidence, just the facts, ma'am, just the facts. And for the head of Interpol's Italian branch of the world's most respected international police force to make a statement like this was seriously uncomfortable.

"What's up?" the Boss asked, putting his plate down on the table. Mine made a little "clink" sound as it joined his. Now Indigo looked embarrassed as well as uncomfortable, and we intuitively knew something really bad was about the surface. "Well, my brother here has remarkable talents as far as secure communication is concerned, and as well as working on the problem we gave him about tracking how the terrorists had successfully hacked into the systems and hidden their tracks so well, he decided to expand his efforts a little, and through this, we have learned of something quite frightening." Indigo put his hands up as if he were surrendering. "But we cannot prove anything of what I will tell you, and I fear that our inability to provide you this evidence will make trouble for you." He looked crestfallen as if he was personally responsible for whatever had happened.

"Indigo, we've worked with you long enough to know that you are utterly focused on our task, and I don't care what the bad news is; the worst thing I will do to you is let the good captain here tickle you to death and dispose of your body in the canal!" It took a second, then the room erupted into laughter, completely dispelling the gloom that had settled around the group.

"*Il miocolonnello, la ringrazio, la ringrazio*, but it might be worth it to get tickled by this pretty lady you know." The Boss gave me a smirk, looked at Indigo, shook his head, then opened his hands impatiently. He was strictly a one-joke kind of guy, and now he was all business again.

"Okay, Colonel, I take my chances. We have learned that the Arabian king requested that the GIGN send some special operatives to a meeting with the SEFC. Supposedly, it was to help the Arabian security forces track down the terrorists that drove the truck that bombed the Grand Mosque. If you remember, once before, in nineteen seventy-nine, I think, the GIGN assisted the Arabians when terrorists actually occupied the Grand Mosque, so they have a history."

"I remember, massive gunfight, hundreds killed, only one or two of them terrorists, mostly innocent civilians who had come to pray. The French claimed all the credit, the Arabians proclaimed them heroes so they wouldn't lose face, and the bodies were quietly removed and buried."

"*Precisamente.* Well, my brother, he intercepted the request to the French Direttore Generale and managed to track six agents as they left France in a French Special Forces Falcon, which landed at Hafar Al-Batin Domestic Airport at King Khalid Military City. Then the agents disappeared. The Falcon returned as per its original flight plan." The Boss was by now sitting forward in his chair, leaning towards Indigo. It was his way of both showing interest and apportioning seriousness. This was yet another reason I loved to work with the Boss; he managed to make everyone around him feel important, whereas I had just hacked back into the food on my plate and tuned in with one ear, not really picking up on anything yet.

"When you say 'disappeared,' do you mean in the electronic sense or physical sense?" the Boss asked. Indigo raised one eyelid, a comical look for someone with such bushy and busy eyebrows.

"*Sì*! Both. Even their personal RFID tags became invisible." Indigo started to fidget, something he only ever did when he was nervous. With a mighty shrug of his bulky shoulders, he seemed to have reached an internal agreement with himself and visibly relaxed. "*Colonnello*, this is where the bad is. The next day we are informed officially through our HQ in Lyon by the Arabian government that their security agencies have tracked down and killed two of the terrorists, supposedly the ones who drove the truck that bombed the oil field, and that they are clearly identified as French." That got through to me, and I nosily put my plate back down again on the table. The Boss sat back in his seat, folding his hands behind his head, and rolled his eyes up to look at the roof.

"French?"

"*Si*. Now, just as I am adjusting my mind to this, HQ contacts us again, to tell us that the Arabians have again called, this time about finding and kill ing the two terrorists who drove the ambulance bomb into the Grand Mosque. They wish us well with the rest of our investigations, but clearly, from their perspective, their cases are now closed."

"The identity of the second pair of terrorists wouldn't by any chance have been French, would it?" I asked, astonished at this turn of events.

"*Si*. Again, it seems the terrorists were of French origin." The sudden quiet in the room was palpable as we wrestled with this amazing turn of events. We had been on the case for nearly four days straight, linked to every military, police, and security forces in the world, and yet we had never even gotten a whiff of this at any point. A clicking sound broke the silence, and I turned to find the Boss tapping his fingernail on his teeth.

"Let me guess," he said, smiling so broadly his face nearly split into two. "All this information was distributed via normal channels, which we know to be compromised, and there's a full-court press by the French to hush it up until they can work out what is going on."

"Well, *il miocolonnello*, that may be, but it is the effect these reports have had on some of the fanatics we chase from time to time that is of most concern to us. We are getting many, many indications that several terrorist groups of a particular religious persuasion are getting ready to attack French targets of opportunity at any moment."

"Muslim Brotherhood, Al Qaida, ISIS, Hezbollah, Wahhabis, Al Jamia, just to name a few?" the Boss asked. Indigo nodded, his body deflating, obviously distressed at this turn of events.

"Well, let's get to the facts then, and now I see your quandary—did the French send in the GIGN to help cover up what the Arabians claim to have found, or is something else going on? And is the timing of these so-called discoveries relevant to the attack, or is this the start of a new game?"

"New game or same game," I said, suddenly feeling very tired. This could be a monumental breakthrough, a red herring, or an overt attempt to derail us. My mind flashed back to the group of English, and French spies we had briefly encountered in London and their somewhat frosty attitude exhibited that day, and I started to wonder.

"Stefarino, these little computer pads you gave us, are they completely secure?" the Boss asked. The curator nodded, pulling out his own from the folds of his robe.

"*Si, il miocolonnello*, they send their encrypted signals through our private network; not even the Americans, pardon me, I mean no offence, have ever been able to track us, let alone find us. This is the world's only secure communication system with God's blessing." The Boss nodded several times.

"So as long as we restrict what we communicate to these devices, no one else will know what we are doing?" The curator looked at the Boss with a tight face, obviously thinking deeply about both the question and its consequences. He was, after all, lending his secure communications net to an outsider, albeit one championed by his own brother.

"*Si, il miocolonnello*, but you must be aware that you are being constantly tracked and monitored in plain sight?" he asked. He was referring to the network of security cameras that now numbered in the hundreds of millions around the world, in streets, banks, buildings, ATMs, bus stops, airports, train terminals, along roads, in fact, just about everywhere that no one ever took any notice of, unless you were trying to find, track, or trace someone and you had the official providence to do so. Or you knew how to hack the system, I reminded myself, which an ungodly number of people now seemed to be able to do at will.

"Indigo, are you saying something else?" I asked. He looked at me with a shrewd look in his eyes.

"*Il mio capitano, sì*, indeed, I am. This is the "bad" I was referring to earlier. My brother found hard evidence that everything you do, everywhere you go, is being monitored by at least three different parties. One, of course, is the American NSA, which we would expect. But when I queried Lyon as to whether they had been formally advised that you were persons of interest, they became highly agitated, and the Direttore Generale herself contacted me in the clear to deny any such thing. This gave me pause to think. What if the terrorists are tracking us as we would try to track them?" My pulse started to race as Indigo developed his argument. If the bad guys were, in fact, tracking us, it meant that either they were afraid of what we could or might do with the investigation, or they were waiting for us to get to some unknown point in the case before launching another attack. Either way, they involved us—and that meant prior knowledge of our resources, personnel, systems, and procedures. And that gave us something to work with and something to think about. The Boss, as usual, was there hours ahead of me because he suddenly leaped up and hugged Indigo.

"Indigo, my friend, you not only make the best antipasti and expresso in the world but also bring good news on an otherwise disappointing day. Well done!" Indigo almost recoiled from the Boss's hugs, but being Italian, it only took him a minute to return it with interest, and suddenly, we had a six-foot-three bear romping uncontrollably with a five-foot-six bear threatening the longevity of everything in the room!

"Er, if you boys are finished," I said, trying to keep the laughter out of my voice, "I think we actually have some thinking to do." They both finished up on the floor, the Boss with tears in his eyes. If the Interpol top brass could see this, they would have had a heart attack at the very least, if not a stroke! Their top anti-terrorist operative, most senior field agent, and the head of Interpol in Italy rolling around on the floor like two kids in a kindergarten sandpit. I had to admit, though, that it did break the tension. The Boss rolled onto his back, looking completely at ease. Indigo made a fuss about standing up and straightening his usually immaculate Armani suit. He couldn't hide his smile; however, it was obvious he felt deeply about not being able to give the Boss hard facts to support his observations and those of his brother. The curator had been sitting stoically while all this was going on, pretending to be above it all. The slight smile that creased his tight face gave him away, so I decided to get us all back into the groove through him.

"Sir, where did you get to with our brief on backtracking the terrorists and their hacking into the ATC (Air Traffic Control) and security systems?" I asked, pointedly ignoring the two men still on the floor. He looked down at his brother, shrugged his shoulders as if to say, "boys will be boys," then handed me a small data disc.

"*Capitano, mi exscuse*, I was distracted for a moment," he said, pointing to the mess on the floor. "We have been a little lucky, I think; on this disc, you will find how they are hacking into your systems and a timeline of sorts."

"Of sorts?"

"*Sì, come si dice,* one of the tracking programs shows an intruder from two years ago, while another shows more recent activity. I am no analyst, but to a humble librarian, it looks as if the European air traffic system was first penetrated via a backdoor established when the system was first set up, and then the terrorists simply reconnected to the pathways they established when they needed to. It is obvious that they are working from the inside, and I doubt that any other Security Agency in the world would be able to find out how they did it."

"Why not?"

"They would be blind to the simplicity of what the terrorists have done. They would be looking for exotic and complex attacks, as it is the way they are used to working and thinking. Simple people such as our brotherhood only have limited means, so we have to have very simple systems that provide us the pathways we need to exercise our sworn duty to God." I decided to let that comment go because I absolutely did not have to know what Indigo's brother did or whom he did it for. It was enough to have their obviously expert assistance and the temporary sanctuary they provided.

"Do you think they are inside Interpol's systems?" I asked, already suspecting the answer.

"*Certamente.* Without a doubt. And this is the problem that worried Indigo so much, the one we can't prove with facts, but to us, it appears that the terrorists have been inside every major security system in the world for a very long time."

"Well, thanks to you, Stefarino, we now have a secure means of communication between our field agents and obviously a home base to work from if we need it," the Boss said, looking pointedly at the data disc in my hand. I was about to answer when there was a slight disruption at the entrance, which resolved itself by Pete entering the room. The disruption had been him trying to get his little laptop back from the guards, who were still resisting, politely but forcibly, about to break both Pete's arms, or so it seemed.

"Boss, you need to see what's on this; can you call the boys off, please?" he asked, both arms pulled up behind his back and with one guard almost sitting on his shoulders. True to form, he hadn't actually hurt anybody—yet—but his enormous core strength was obvious as he was still moving into the room with all four guards now hanging off him in different directions.

"*Attenzione—siprega di lasciarlopassare*," called the curator. The result was immediate, if not a little comical. The guard on Pete's back slid to the floor with a resounding "thump," and the other three let him go as if he had suddenly caught fire. Pete just ignored the fuss and moved straight to the antipasti platter, which I had only managed to half finish. With a casual flip, he threw me his mini laptop and proceeded to load up a plate with enough food to feed a regiment.

"Nice to see you too, Pete," the Boss said somewhat sarcastically. He took the laptop off me, turning it over in his hands as if looking for a secret entrance, then gave it back. "What did you find?" Pete looked at the Boss a little guiltily, chewing frantically to empty his mouth.

"Lots. Let me get a coffee, and I'll run you through it," Pete answered. I passed the laptop to the curator, who walked it over to a console and enabled the wireless link. Up on the big central screen, the images of the bombed Vatican appeared, and for the first time, we could see the horrific damage in detail. It looked as if the penetrator had caused a massive cave-in that had literally sucked the ground down for kilometers in every direction. The view pulled back, and the camera panned around the horizon, overlaid with a compass, and as the picture revealed buildings in the distance, a red marker appeared in the frame. Pete had obviously taken this from a helicopter and was marking buildings of interest by looking back from the blast site towards the surrounding infrastructure.

"Okay, what you will see next is a filtered view of the footage taken by TV cameras on the day, supplemented by security camera footage and private citizen iReport footage seized by the police. The local stuff is a bit fuzzy because a lot of it came from phones, but we really don't need to see the detail. The filter will show you any light at less than one thousand nanometers, where most lasers operate." And sure enough, running through some of the footage was a fickle beam of coherent light that could only be from a laser-targeting designator.

"Now, this gave us a direction, and so we walked around the precincts in a helicopter, looking for any buildings high enough to give a clear line of sight to ground zero that matched the target line of the laser. Incidentally, thanks to Indigo's clout, the assistance we got was nothing less than fantastic." Pete dug into the food again, wiping the back of his hand across his mouth. "Guess what we found?" This time we were presented with a crystal-clear image from a stabilized helicopter mount, which tracked around the horizon until it settled on one specific building.

As it steadied, two black figures could be seen walking across the roof, then the picture moved in a sweeping, panning movement and zoomed into the Vatican. It had obviously been taken before the terrorist attack, possibly the day before or perhaps even earlier than the day the conclave had started, as there were several empty areas where people in their thousands were still to congregate and what looked like police setting up traffic control barriers.

"These stills I took with my phone are a bit grainy, but you will get the picture if you forgive the pun," Pete said, pointing at the big screen. He was on a roof somewhere, up very high, and his shadow ran off at an angle that suggested late afternoon. The next shot showed a series of holes in the concrete at his feet, then a close-up of one of the holes, and it became apparent that someone had fired a bolt into the roof, then pulled it out when they had finished whatever it was that they had come to do. The next shot showed the relationship of the holes, which formed a perfect triangle, and the next shot was taken almost from rooftop level, looking out across the landscape. Then the same shot was repeated, but this time from waist height, and in the far distance, you could just see the carnage that had once been the most significant modern icon of the Catholic faith, the Holy See.

"Now, back to the newsreel footage taken two days before the conclave. The men you see were with TVI; they were contractors, and their job was a seemingly simple one." As Pete spoke, the TV camera images came back, and we could see the two men setting up an apparatus that looked like a huge binocular mounted on a tripod. The picture froze and zoomed in step by step until the stenciled words on the top of the tube could be seen. "Digital sonic laser device - *Direzione del suonorivelatoredispositivo* laser – DO NOT LOOK AT DIRECTLY (*NON GUAR- DARE IN DIRETTA*)". And then, to our utter amazement, the helicopter positioned itself in such a way that we could clearly see the line the laser device was focused on. The dome of St. Peter's!

"What did they think they were setting up?" Indigo asked.

"A laser device that could 'read' vibrations of the dome, in the hope that the TV network could get the jump on the announcement of the new Pope."

"You're joking!" I exclaimed. Intelligence Agencies used these types of devices to eavesdrop on conversations all the time, but the idea of a common civilian TV news crew using one offended my sensibilities.

"Absolutely not. They even had a permit from the city to fire the laser over the heads of everyone, on the pretense that it was a micro link for the TV crews."

"Did you talk to the TV people?" the Boss asked. "Yes."

"Did you find the device?" I asked.

"Yes. Looked exactly like the photos, but the techs that Indigo's people provided pulled it apart, and it was, in fact, a MilSpec Laser Designator, dressed up to look like a sonic detector."

"Do we know where it came from?" Indigo asked. The comments about how his people had been so helpful were having their effect because he was starting to look like his normal Italian macho self again, all strutting five foot six of him.

"No. According to the TV people, they hired the device about a month ago, when the last Pope died, from a technology company in Milan that supplies all sorts of electronic equipment to the media industry. Indigo's people are checking them out now, but the really strange thing is that the city people picked out the building for the TV crew. There were considerable fees involved, but it all seems to be legitimate. On the surface, anyway."

"What was the building?" the Boss asked. A new photo popped up, this time a high-rise around eighty meters high.

"Palazzo En, built in nineteen sixty-two, five point two kilometers from the Vatican, clear line of sight, and absolutely full of people all week celebrating the papal election. Couldn't have picked a more populated or busy location if they tried. And don't forget that this installation was sanctioned by the city officially."

"Checked out the ownership?" I asked, knowing the answer. Pete was muscle but smart muscle, and the reason why the Boss tended to involve him early in a case was because of his ability to look outside the square.

"Yes. Old money, legitimate as far as we can tell, but Indigo's people are chasing that down to be sure." I nodded, expecting the answer, but around the Boss, you leaned to ask the obvious questions as well as the tough ones.

"What now?" The Boss smiled that little alligator smirk he reserved for really evil occasions. He took his time to look around the room as if considering all his options, but we all knew he had worked this out ages ago.

"Captain Riley, I would very much like you to go to Afghanistan and replay the flight of the UAV that attacked the Dome of the Rock. I'm going to visit our friends in the US and retrace the flight of the A-10 that attacked West Point. Pete, I think you and Indigo have some field work to do, looking for the movers and shakers who organized the Vatican attack. For the first time, we have some solid leads. The laser designator came from somewhere; someone anticipated what the TV news crew would do, and we know the terrorists have penetrated the Interpol network and those of other security agencies. We now have something to track back to a source, and let's not forget the excellent work young Luigi

Antoinette has done for us in showing how easy it is to steal radioactive materials. Which reminds me, Indigo, can you use Luigi here in this facility to work through what your brother has so kindly found for us on the security breaches?"

Indigo looked over at his brother, who nodded.

"*Si*, this we can do, *il miocolonnello*." I promptly threw the data disk Frisbee style to Indigo, who made a huge bow in return. The Boss waited until Indigo had finished, smiled at the byplay, then continued.

"Use your c-pads so kindly provided by Stefarino here, and only your c-pads, no phones, no chat by any other means. Let's plan on being back here in forty-eight hours to compare notes. Is that okay with everyone?" The Boss looked at us one by one, seeking the slightest sign of hesitation. All he saw were tired, grinning faces, hungry for results. I smiled my best "see you later" smile and started on the process of getting to Afghanistan and back in quick double time.

CHAPTER 29

The office of the director of the FBI is impressive, to say the least. The FBI crest made famous by seventy years of TV shows and movies is woven into the carpet so that it dominates the room. The logo also sits proudly on a flag, displayed right next to "Old Glory," an original US flag with only forty-eight stars on it, proudly stolen from Fort Mead in 1942 by an ambitious young agent who was subsequently fired for his trouble. The director of the day had kept the flag. The desk that the current Director Roger Winslow sat behind had once hosted the now infamous J. Edgar Hoover. The chairs provided for guests boasted crooked legs and were lower than normal, giving the occupants a sense of being physically dominated by the person on the other side of the desk, as well as an extremely uncomfortable sitting angle, something that J. Edgar had well used to his former advantage.

Arranged around the table this day was an eclectic group of people, summoned at short notice by the director to create a battle plan. The problem was no one had been able to identify the enemy as yet. Despite billions of dollars worth of surveillance equipment, billions of dollars worth of the biggest, fastest, smartest computers in the world, and the greatest intelligence apparatus ever assembled, no one could identify the enemy.

The FBI reacted similarly to Interpol when they learned of the supposed French involvement in the Arabian attacks. Too obvious, too late, and why would a nation State that depended heavily on the Arabians for their oil supply put that very supply out of action? There was something going on, but it was seven thousand miles away and of absolutely no interest to the FBI unless it helped shed some light on their own internal situation.

And to make matters worse, the director now had no less than two Catholic priests on their way here to supposedly reveal the identity of the mastermind behind the terrorist attacks! Outrageous! For about the hundredth time, Roger Winslow read the "Flash – Priority" email he had received from an off-duty Washington cop via the police link to the "Common Security Communication Channel" (CSCC) set up by Homeland Security after 9/11. This electronic network allowed anyone in the military, police, government, or police forces to send what they believed to be critical information to a central registry without fear or favor or recriminations of any kind if the data proved to be useless.

And according to this specific flash message, the key perpetrator in this gigantic mess was a teacher at some Catholic school at a refugee camp in Lebanon thirty years ago! His staff had quickly run down everything that was known about Gouraud, en Baalbek, Lebanon, the keywords first searched by the policeman from his car.

Not a pretty story. A refugee camp where during its lifetime, the highest number of children in any camp at any one time under the age of ten years had died. A camp where thirty percent of the surviving children then went on to die from malnutrition or preventable diseases before they turned twenty-one. And a camp where, in the face of great opposition from several Middle Eastern fanatical religious organizations, the Catholic Church had established the very first school in the refugee camps with great success.

And, apparently, one of the teachers who had been there at the start was the mastermind behind the worst terrorist attacks in recorded history. The FBI director scanned the list of workers in the camp again, not being able to make head nor tail of the data, as there was so little of it. The camp had been closed years ago, and the survivors moved into one of the sixteen camps now run by UNRWA. None of the information at the time had found its way into a computer; his staff had been chasing a thirty-year-old paper trail across six countries and nine languages by phone and email for five hours now and were getting very little return for their efforts. The most obvious source of data, the Catholic Church, was in meltdown as they tried to bring the surviving members of their senior clergy to some point where a new Pope could be anointed, so their help had been less than enthusiastic. In fact, they doubted that anything other than a journal—handwritten by one of their missionaries—would even exist at this time, and no one in the Washington diocese could tell the FBI where such a journal might be stored if it had, by some miracle, survived.

Try Lebanon. Try the United Nations. Try anyone but please stop bugging us, because right now we have enough problems of our own! May God be with you.

"This Brother Andretti, he checks out?" the director finally asked.

"Sir, we have contacted the bishop in Miami and Brother Ronald from the same diocese. Apparently, Andretti visited a Jesuit monk who was being held in the Miami-Dade detention center on suspicion of trying to crash our borders. Arrived with an out-of-date passport and a confusing story, and precious little else. From South America." All the heads in the room nodded solemnly; any one of these three reasons earned jail time, but all three? Find me a brick wall and a spare bullet! The agent paused, turned the page of his notes, checked something in the margin, then continued. "The story goes that a priest doing the rounds of the detention center came across him and was told some wild story about having to contact the president about meeting someone in Lebanon when he had been a missionary. The priest thought it was the ramblings of a disturbed person, thought nothing of it, until later that day another Jesuit, this Andretti, sought permission from the bishop to visit the priest in the detention center." He turned his notes again, then looked the director in the eye.

"Sir, as far as we can tell, what happened next just a few hours later was a detailed conversation between the two Jesuits in the cell, which was recorded and flagged; you have a copy of the transcription. The trigger words were 'Middle Eastern, terrorists, and latest attacks.' While we have had the tape reviewed by language experts, there are whole sections that are literally indecipherable, as the two men were talking head to head, on their knees, almost at floor level."

"But there is no doubt that the priest in the cell passed a message to the other Jesuit?" asked the director.

"Yes, sir."

"And the details are consistent with what this Andretti is saying now?"

"Yes, sir, it would appear so." The director thought for a moment, then looked at the men in the room with him.

"Where is the Jesuit from the Miami detention center?" he asked.

"On his way to Washington, headed for our interrogation center at Westchester."

"And this Andretti person?"

"Currently being soft-detained by our off-duty cop here in Washington." The director stood, straightened his jacket, then looked at his watch. He had a funeral to go to.

"Okay, get me speakers in every language these two might talk in, get me both of them here, and then get everybody to the ComTac (Communications Tactical) room, and leave the rest to me." Several heads nodded in unison, and they all got up to leave the room.

"And make sure everyone is clean and well dressed, with no orange suits or hoods. I want two presentable monks or priests or whatever you call them on their own two feet, looking like they know what they are doing, dressed and handled appropriately as if they were on a mission from the Pope. Oh, and bring that cop in, have him standing by somewhere in case I want to talk to him. I'll be back in three hours, be ready."

CHAPTER 30

From the air, Arlington National Cemetery, just off the Potomac River in Washington, looks like a huge field planted with white crosses, almost three hundred thousand of them, spread over some two hundred acres divided neatly by rows of trees, manicured narrow roads, and fields of green. Buildings appear out of the shadows in various places, discrete in their design and location. But from dawn to dusk, five days a week, solemn processions of bereaved family and friends stand by gravesides as the death of their loved ones is celebrated as only the military can. Honor guards, buglers, riflemen, pomp and pageant, rigid precision in the midst of high emotions and precisely folded flags.

The burial of Admiral David Anthony Jones, killed by one of the bomblets dropped from the A-10 Warthog when it attacked West Point, was everything the funeral of a warrior should be. Long columns of unformed sailors, soldiers, Marines, Cost Guard, and airmen representing every branch of the armed services lined the road on either side, forming an honor guard one mile long. The coffin arrived on top of a flag-draped gun carriage, and rows and rows of spectators from all over the world came to pay their last respects to someone who had not only had a long and distinguished military career but a varied and successful political impact on all four major continents. Out of the setting sun, the Navy-Blue Angels demonstration team, flying immaculate blue-and-gold FA-18s, roared overhead and performed the "Missing Man" formation exactly as the rifle platoon fired their first shocking volley. As they reloaded, the jet representing the missing aviator roared on twin afterburners straight up into the heavens, leaving a vertical flaming smoky trail for as high as the eye could see.

Looking at it from the gravesite, the president of the United States, supposedly the most powerful woman on earth, stood helplessly, tears rolling down her cheeks. David had been a close friend and mentor right since grade school, and the president was going to miss his sharp wit and dry humor. She made a silent promise to get the bastards responsible, then looked over the grave to where an entire regiment of admirals and generals stood at attention, saluting, backs straight, chests festooned with medals and ribbons.

The president could not but feel tiny, insignificant, and almost irrelevant next to this overt display of militarism, but she was, after all, their commander-in-chief.

And had a reputation that matched any of her steely-eyed generals. The first woman of color to be elected to the White House.

But what good was a chief who couldn't point her Indians at a target and shout "charge"? Her thoughts were interrupted by a Marine Colonel who marched up to her, saluted, and handed her the folded flag from the coffin with stilted reverence. The president turned, tears now cascading down her cheeks, as she bowed down to the level of the grieving widow and handed her the flag.

"I'm sorry, Julie, really sorry," she said in a whisper. Her sister looked back up at her, her eyes red and swollen from days of unrelenting grief, for she had truly loved her husband for over thirty years as he had loved her. She took the flag and looked vacantly across the gravesite.

"It's okay, Robbie, it's okay. You'll get them, make an example of them for all the world to see, and then David can rest in peace." The president nodded in total agreement with her grieving sister. There was just one little thing she had to find out first. And then she would act with a force and a power more deadly than any president had used since the end of the Second World War with Japan.

The very minute she found out just who the hell was responsible for turning the world upside down!

CHAPTER 31

The Communications and Tactical (ComTac) room at the FBI looked like any high-order commercial high-tech environment—benches, screens, technicians, theater seats, and a massive wall screen that could hold up to one hundred images at a time. The only real difference to most other government-secured communication facilities is that in the second row, the theater chairs had inbuilt restraints, cleverly designed so that viewers on the other end of the cameras could not tell that the occupants were being physically restrained and held in place.

Leaving the front row vacant, the director's personal assistant had arranged the seating in such a manner that the two Jesuit monks were sitting side by side but one seat apart from each other, flanked by interpreters in Spanish, Russian, Italian, Urdu, Farsi, and Arabic. The director sat to one side, and his station heads behind, ready to provide detail on the meagre historical data they had been able to locate so far from what they already knew. Experts from the CIA's Arabian, Middle Eastern, Israeli, and North African desks were strategically positioned at workstations, and a full Colonel from Military Intelligence paced back and forth at the back of the seats, wired into a headset and personal TV system that he carried in his hands like a leaking hot dog.

Sitting next to Father Andretti was the off-duty Washington cop, still dressed in his Hawaiian shirt and loafers. He was under no illusion as to the position he filled—the curt manner in which he had been brought here and subsequently treated said it all—guilty by association, and there was to be no presumption of innocence. He had been relieved of his sidearm, phone, the backup gun strapped to his left leg, his badge and credentials, stripped, body searched, then allowed to redress minus his belt and socks. The only good news from his point of view was that he was not strapped to his seat, as were the two Jesuit priests.

"Gentlemen, are we ready?" asked the operator, sitting at his console, which housed forty different screens, each showing a different picture. On one, the presidential seal could be seen, and as the director gave his assent by waving his hand, the seal swam up on the wall-sized screen that dominated the ComTac center. Seconds later, the face of the president sitting behind her desk came into focus just as a technician finished adjusting an earplug.

"Mister Director," the president said, staring straight into the camera.

"Madam President, sorry to bother you, ma'am, particularly at this time, but we have come into some information we believe you need to hear direct from the source."

"I've been briefed by my staff. Let's get to it."

"Sir, may I introduce Father Andretti and Brother Fernández Gómez of the sacred Order of the Jesuits. Brother Gómez has a message for you from someone he met in a refugee camp in Lebanon in the nineteen eighties or nineties. Father Andretti also has the same message, which was passed to him by the good brother in a holding cell in Miami, or so he claims, but English is not their first language, so we have arranged for interpreters to provide a clear text on the bottom of your screen and an audio feed in real-time." The director waved his hand again and turned to look at the two Jesuits. What no one had anticipated was the effect such high-tech equipment would have on a lowly monk who had not been in a civilized area for over twenty years, and it took some minutes before either of them could get a coherent sentence out without stuttering. The fact that they were secured in their seats within an inch of their lives also added to their general discomfort.

"*Señora Presidente, Dios estará con usted, gracias por escuchar mi mensaje*" magically turned into "Madam President, God be with you, and thank you for hearing my message" in the president's ear and in bold letters across the bottom of the viewing screens. "I have been instructed to bring you this message some thirty years ago, from when I worked in the camp known as Gouraud in Baalbeck, Lebanon. My friend, he was a teacher from the desert and cared very much for the poor children in the camp. We lost many, many children during the years we worked together, but slowly, we see the bright return to their eyes. Then, one night, after we have celebrated prayers together, he turns to me and says that his God cannot look down upon what is happening in the camps without crying tears of blood."

As the interpreters produced their script, the analysts in the room were frantically typing in every "key" word in the hope that they could produce a data stream of information to add to the briefing for the president. As the words "tears of blood" went into one of the keyboards, multiple screens started to flash red, and a small siren went off. Everyone in the room froze, uncertain as to what to do next.

"Ident hit, terrorist organization identified, Hussein Blasck, details to follow!" yelled one of the analysts. The director looked furious at the interruption, the president had a look on her face that plainly said, "duh!" and the pacing Colonel snapped the master switch, killing both the noise of the analysts and the image simultaneously.

"Can we PLEASE get back to the story?" the director shouted, standing and balling his fists. The room sunk into embarrassed silence. Nothing happened for about forty seconds, then the cop whispered into the ear of the Jesuit. He nodded, a shameful look on his face, but for the love of God, he did not understand the fuss that these strange people had made of his simple words.

"Then, for a while, all went well until we had a very bad time when many, many children dies all at the same time. It was influenza, and we begged the aid agencies for help, but at that time, there was tension around the camps, and soldiers stopped everybody from helping us. Every day we buried these little babies and children, and soon even the mothers were dying. Every night we said our prayers together; we prayed that things would get better, but they got worse. My friend, he disappeared for days at a time, then sneaked back in with medicines he said he stole from the troops. He had done this for a long time. Our school is very small, but the children love to come, and our Holy Church managed to get us some supplies and books that come to us from the Red Crescent people. Then one day, my friend told me one of his children is being very good at counting, and he thinks she could go to university somewhere. He was very sad that night, but after prayers, he tells me he has had an idea." The translators paused while the Jesuit drank from a plastic water bottle sitting on the arm of his chair. As he had been restrained above the elbows, the lifting movement of his arm looked somewhat strained and jerky, and he had to fold his head down on his chest to be able to sip at the straw.

"For all of the next year, we struggle to keep the school open, and the Red Crescent manages to bring us books and food, and for a while, it looks like our children will get better. Then we are told that another two thousand people will be joining us in the camp because there has been another war with the Jews, and when the people arrive, we have no room, and our little school is given to them for them to sleep in, and very soon, I am asked to leave the camp, because they are thinking of closing it. So, I pray for guidance, and one day my friend takes me aside and tells me this." The Jesuit stopped again, this time, because the cop had been handed a piece of paper and was whispering in his ear. The Jesuit nodded, then looked up at the image of the president on the wall screen.

"*Señora Presidente, los motivosexcusadivagaciones de un anciano*, I am sorry to be taking up your time. My friend sits with me after prayers, and he tells me this. My brother, Fernández, says our children are very bright, and one day they will be the power on this earth. I have decided to take them away from here and help them on their quest. Do this for me as your brother before your God. One day, many years from now, when you receive the broken body of an infidel woman, go and tell the president of all the world that the children of God have spoken. Do this for me, and for all the little children we have buried together and prayed for all these years." Around the room, a buzz slowly developed as the data screens filled with thousands of references for the words "Children of God." One commercial data search engine showed 35,300,000 hits! Everything from the title of books to the description of different families, but no data presented itself about any terrorist organization.

"Brother Gómez," asked the president, "when did you receive this woman of whom you spoke, and where were you at the time?" The

Jesuit waited while the cop whispered in his ear, then nodded vigorously. He made the sign of the cross, crossed himself, kissed his fingers, and muttered a short prayer.

"*Sí, he recibidoestamujer, y se toman dos de los niños de la aldea*" turned into "Yes, I received this woman, and they took two of the little children from the village, for why I do not know. I have been working there these twenty years, bringing Christ to the tribes. It is what God told me to do when I asked him." The president looked momentarily confused, then pulled the earpiece out and dropped it onto the desktop.

"Mister Director, perhaps you can take it from here?" she said, standing up and buttoning her jacket.

"Yes, ma'am, of course." The director moved to the front of the room as the big screen faded back to the presidential seal, and the lights suddenly came on full strength, causing many to shield their eyes. In the room immediately adjacent to the ComTac, the actor who had been hired to impersonate the president removed her suit and wig and then pulled the latex face off, revealing pockmarked skin desperately in need of some maintenance.

"That went well," she said offhandedly to the assistants. They nodded, little smirks saying silently what they really thought.

In the ComTac room, the two Jesuits and the cop were being escorted under heavy guard to the basement detention cells, where a more thorough debriefing would now take place.

The director of the FBI stood in one corner with the Colonel, now devoid of his headgear and TV setup. "Who do we share this with, and what exactly do we say?" the Colonel asked. The director shook his head; that was the sixty-four-dollar question. Perhaps in the next few hours, the Jesuits could be persuaded to part with the real information they required.

CHAPTER 32

As locations go, for an airport, Bagram would have to be one of the most picturesque. Situated some six thousand feet up between massive snowcapped mountains on three sides, the ten-thousand-foot runway, which is big enough to handle a jumbo, cuts a straight line across some of the most terribly harsh landscapes in the world. Built by the Russians in 1976, just three years before they invaded Afghanistan, the base is around fifty kilometers north of Kabul. Thanks to an Italian jet jockey, probably related to our cigarette boat driver, it had only taken me three hours to fly from Venice, which included a thrilling mid-air-refueling link every six hundred nautical miles. The way the pilot seemed to challenge the huge tanker aircraft reminded me of Spanish bullfighters warming up the crowd for the kill.

The base was a hodgepodge of contradictions. Outside the gates, barricaded by Humvees armed to the teeth in front of huge sandbag emplacements, the locals ran stalls selling everything from Chinese-made AK-47s and hand grenades left over from the Russian invasion to locally made Afghan pakol hats and MREs (meals ready to eat) stolen from the base. Inside the wire, British Special Forces played soccer on a flayed minefield as if it were the World Cup, and US soldiers jogged up and down Disney Drive, the main street through the base. My destination was two long, air-conditioned trailers linked to massive generators that chuffed black smoke up into the sky, off to the side of a rusted-out

Russian MIL-9 helicopter, which had definitely seen better days. Behind it sat three ubiquitous "instant" hangars, in which sat three Predator UAVs resting in the shade.

"Captain Riley," I announced, saluting the major who greeted me at the door of the first trailer.

"Captain, welcome. We've been briefed; your bird is already in the air, waiting for you." I followed his broad back down the narrow corridor, on either side of which were massive banks of electronic equipment. We reached the command-and-control suite, where a young man dressed in jeans and a faded tee shirt was watching an aerial view on a large monitor while eating a burrito. I couldn't help but notice that some beef and red chili had leaked out onto his shirt. "If you sit here, I'll plug into the Israeli Air Traffic Control and get us cleared in." He pulled a really comfortable-looking armchair out for me, ever the gentleman, and I slid behind the duplicated controls that allowed an armchair pilot sitting at home to fly a deadly remote mission halfway around the world in air-conditioned comfort.

The screen in front of me was an aerial view from twenty-five thousand feet, showing latitude and longitude equivalent to the southwestern border of Jerusalem. The UAV had been flown out of Baghdad and was duplicating the known flight path of the UAV that had attacked the Dome of the Rock. In the far distance, the now calm waters of the Mediterranean shimmered and flared in the early morning sun, and it looked anything but like a war zone, although long columns of dirty grey smoke could be seen heading up into the stratosphere from different places around the border between Israel and the now infamous Gaza Strip.

"Shalom, Rudi, are we cleared to fly?" the major asked, sitting behind us on a raised chair so that he could see both control positions clearly.

"Hello David, you are cleared to fly and maintain one hundred knots. We have a CAP (combat air patrol) that will follow you in and out, so don't be alarmed if you see them over."

"Roger that, Rudi, thank you, ingress starts now." The major hit a small remote, and a large clock started to count the time as it elapsed. The kid next to me still munched at his burrito, oblivious to the unfolding drama. No one touched anything, the computers did it all, and suddenly I saw what the Boss had been alluding to inside the Hercules over Rome.

"Can we change the view to ground mapping, please?" I asked, wanting to see the run into the target area. The kid finally did something; a small flick with one cheese-stained finger, and the view slued down to about a seventy-five-degree angle, looking forward to the UAV's flight path.

"What altitude did it attack from?" I asked, knowing the answer but wanting to establish some relationship with this crew. The major looked at me as if he knew what I was up to, and a small smile creased his lips fleetingly.

"According to the AWAC's (Airborne early warning and control), it came in at twenty-five thousand, then ten miles out, descended to eight thousand, then one mile out started a shallow dive eventually self-destructing at six thousand five hundred feet after firing all its missiles."

"Can we do all that minus the blowing up a bit?" I asked.

"Sure. My instructions are to let you control the bird if you want to; we are as keen to get this off our plate as you are." No wonder, for almost two full days, the world was convinced that the UAV that had attacked the Dome of the Rock had been flown out of this very caravan. I watched as the ground below slowly changed to built-up areas, adobe houses, small buildings, roads, and tracks diving off in every direction. There was no doubt in my mind that a skilled operator could fly just about any profile they wanted to with the right aircraft, never having to actually touch the controls. So, I gently moved back into cop mode and started in on what I was really here to find out from the experts.

"Major, for the sake of argument, how far away can you be and still control that UAV?" I asked. He looked at me with a focused look, thinking through the security ramifications of what I was asking. But he had his orders, and I had my clearance from so high up his chain of command that his hesitation lasted only a split second. And in military equivalence terms, I outranked him by two levels.

"Wondering when we would get to this. Okay, full briefing, Top Secret, no notes, no recording, agreed?" he asked, his voice crisp and commanding.

"Agreed." Why fight city hall? Easier to let him think he was in control; I would get more information that way.

"The unrefueled range of the UAV that mounted the attack was six hundred miles, so that gives you the combat radius. It was not located by the AWACS until it entered Israeli airspace on a previously submitted flight plan and turned on its transponder. It did exactly what everyone expected it to do. No one was looking for it until its window became current. And here's the thing that baffles us." I turned to look at the major, whose voice had taken on a distinct edge. "As you know, we only launch and recover the UAVs here; once airborne, we hand control over to Nellis Air Force Base in Nevada, where they fly the mission. But the AWACS, the Israelis, and even our own monitors told us that we had flown that mission out of here. All the electronic data pointed straight back to us. I have a copy of the tape if you would like to see it."

"How did you prove that you didn't?" I asked, already knowing the answer from the report the Boss had given us after he had returned from Israel. And we had already seen the tape, thanks to our newest and greatest friend this week, the FBI.

"Sheer fluke. We were weathered in, five thousand witnesses; even the Special Forces Chinooks didn't fly for two days. It gets like that sometimes, and this time we got lucky."

"So, we have a rogue UAV with a six-hundred-mile range and an unknown control center that could, literally, be anywhere in the world." He looked at me with a fixed stare and slowly shook his head.

"Sadly, yes. All you need to be able to do is pass the control signals through a satellite network, and you could be anywhere and control anything."

"In absolute terms, how much of all this equipment do you really need to fly one of these things?" I asked, pointing to the picture coming in from the UAV as it started its attack run. On one side of the monitor, the altitude readout was dropping quite quickly, the airspeed was increasing, and the shattered buildings that had once housed the most precious piece of stone on the planet were starting to fill the entire screen. The collapsed "Wailing Wall," thought to have been built by the Romans back in BC sometime, looked like any brick structure blasted by modern explosives—a total wreck.

And from the images, it was obvious that one of the missiles had been targeted at the largest area of the Western Wall, as the Jews call it, which really did start to add a religious flavor to the whole attack. I held my hand up to stop the major from answering my question for a minute while I leaned forward to study the images. Right dead center was the shattered remains of the golden dome and the remains of the buildings that had been erected around the sacred rock over the centuries. But the Boss had been right about this attack as well; I could see clearly now what his friend Arie was on about.

"Okay, bring the bird back; now, where were we?" I asked. The image suddenly shifted back to the "look-ahead" mode used for navigation and broad-scan observation, and the sky filled the screen as the UAV started to climb back up to altitude. The major smiled again, this time, I think because I had not so subtly taken charge of his pet toy!

"Well, as you have just seen, it doesn't take a lot; we pre-programmed the aircraft before you arrived, and apart from steering it on the ground, it has been totally autonomous since it got airborne. As well as that fact, every aircraft is programmed to find its way home in the event of a total signal loss situation, using onboard GPS and ground-mapping software." I looked at the kid, now chewing his nails to the quick, seemingly not interested in anything we were talking about.

"If you were the terrorists, how would you do it?" I asked. He turned his head to look at me as if I was from the Moon or somewhere. Shrugged his shoulders, picked his nose with his thumb and forefinger, then collapsed his hands into his lap as if he had no more energy.

"Well, let's say I managed to steal a bird with its weapons and hid it in a shed somewhere. Any dummy with a laptop and the program codes could pretty much get it to do anything you wanted it to do. Especially if you didn't care too much about collateral damage at the target end." That got my juices flowing, because suddenly we had a "chokepoint" to run down. Program codes. Stolen UAV. Six-hundred-mile radius. Then I had another thought.

"How much of the onboard equipment could you do away with if you were just focused on flying and hitting the one specific target?" I asked. The kid looked at the major, who turned and looked at me in amazement.

"Why on earth would you want to deliberately degrade the potential of the UAV?" he asked, astonished that the question had been asked. And by a ground pounder. And a female one at that. I smiled to show him I meant no harm.

"To get more fuel on board, extend the range. I know these things can stay up for twelve or thirteen hours in surveillance mode, and I'm wondering if all you need to do is take off, fly a predetermined route, then fire your missiles at a big fat juicy static target to have all the satellite stuff and communication gear on board, and not much else."

"Well, actually, if you put it that way, you could probably rip out a few hundred pounds of gear. Take out the sensor package, computers, optics, and all that sort of thing. That might get you another three to four hundred miles."

"So suddenly, our radius is a thousand miles." He thought about that, then said something I had suspected but not had the guts to voice.

"You know, if it was the diesel version, and it was stripped out, you could fly that thing at forty knots for thirty-plus hours. And another thing," he said, standing. "If you knew exactly how to fool all the air traffic computers, the AWACS, and all the radar stations that populate that part of the world, you could have literally come from anywhere."

I took that ugly thought back to Venice with me, and for all the two thousand eight hundred and eighty-seven nautical miles of the return trip, I used the onboard radar repeater in the mapping mode to try to work out where the hell the UAV could have started from, given that we were now looking at a combat radius in excess of twelve hundred nautical miles!

CHAPTER 33

While I was enjoying joyriding around the Middle East with an Italian stud and his Tornado, the Boss was back in his Blackbird doing Mach 3 at eighty thousand feet, chewing up the distance between Venice and Andrews Air Force Base in Maryland, Virginia, at the rate of forty nautical miles every minute, making the four-thousand-mile trip in about half the time it took me to fly half the distance across the Mediterranean!

Because Andrews is where the presidential flights launch from, the security was intense, to say the least, and as the Boss deplaned onto the tarmac, stepping quickly to avoid the corrosive fuel leaking out of the red-hot airframe, a veritable phalanx of camouflaged guards surrounded him, led by a very intense first sergeant.

"Sir, you are Colonel Anthony, confirm?" he shouted, his MP5 machine pistol strapped across his chest. His salute said Marine Corps, but his rig said Special Forces, and there wasn't a single item on him that wasn't slightly worn, suggesting a seriously experienced solider and his well-used tools of the trade. The Boss snapped a salute back, dressed as he was in a regulation Special Forces flying suit, dull grey with Velcro patches but nothing stuck on them to identify him. His cover was a sweat-stained baseball cap with a blacked-out full Colonel's bird on it, the only way anyone could identify his rank. If the Top was impressed by his guest arriving in the fastest aircraft in the sky and wearing a shoulder rig in full view, he didn't show it. He studied the Boss's credentials intently, finally handing them back with a quick snap of his wrist.

"Fuck, sir, you've gone pussy on me!" he exclaimed, reaching out to shake the Boss's hand.

"Don't fuck me, Top. I notice you're on kindergarten duty, so who's gone pussy on whom?" the Boss snapped back, holding in a huge laugh to see what the reaction of the guards would be. Confusion reigned supreme on their faces, but to their credit, not one broke their stern posture, waiting to see what happened next. "Gentlemen, may I introduce Colonel P.J. Anthony to you, once a real man on the teams but obviously now promoted beyond his ultimate level of competency. Colonel, sir, this is Team Seven, and where you go, we go." The Boss smiled and looked at all the keen faces, sucking in the intensity and the focus. He had worked for Interpol for some time now, but his military roots were never far below the surface, and he instinctively braced himself, growing half an inch taller.

"Top, first off, we have to walk the path the Hog took, and I want to sit on the roof of the Humvee while we do it. Two-way comms to the Tower, which I want to visit after we do the backtrack. I may need you to move the Humvee around quite a bit, and if it doesn't work out, we may need to borrow a Hog from someone. I also need to see the contractor's hangar where the Hog was prepared."

"PJ, all organized, we have the cut-out you ordered, laser sighting equipment, the Tower has been stood down except for the crew on duty that day, and the CO has closed the base until you are finished. Security is tight, no one knows what you intend to do, and the FBI has been isolated in the VIP-ready rooms without comms until you are ready. I understand you have a security issue with them?"

"Yes, Tom, not their fault, but everything other than the link we sent you has been compromised by the Tangos, and we still have no real idea who they are or what they are up to. You and the boys will need to keep what you see and hear of the net for the foreseeable future."

"Unlike you to be so slow, PJ," the sergeant said, walking away to the line of Humvees that had encircled the still smoking Blackbird. "And the one thing I can guarantee is that this bunch will be as tight as the proverbial fish's arse hole." The Boss slapped him on the back, instinctively agreeing with the nuggetty Marine who had saved his life at least three times that he could remember in the not-too-distant past.

The second Humvee had a massive sunroof opened, where the gunner usually sat behind a fifty-caliber machine gun. This time a plywood arm had been mounted in the hole, with a laser sight mounted at the same height as the pilot's eye level when he sat inside an A-10 Warthog. A digital camera was mounted on either end of the arm, providing a live view along the axis of the laser sight. The Boss and the Top climbed into the Humvee, waited until the rest of the guard had mounted up, then drove off in a puff of smoke to the flight line.

Starting at the hangar where the Hog had departed from the day of the attack, they followed the white center line down the taxiway towards the end of the main runway. The Humvee stopped in the arming bay, and the Boss climbed out onto the roof. On the left-hand side of the bay was a deep bunker surrounded by sandbags with a thick metal blast deflector. The theory was that if the bombs or rockets slung beneath the wings and the fuselage of the aircraft suddenly went "hot" during the arming process, the pilot, crew if any, and the armorer could all jump into the pit and be saved. So far, no one has tested the system in real life successfully.

To one side of the bunker, a small access road led to a massive double security gate, wide enough to handle two fire trucks side by side. A person-sized access was located on each side, covered in razor wire. The Boss took all this in, then sat back in his seat, thinking.

"Top, leave this Humvee here, exactly where it is, and take me to the tower, please, ASAP."

"Sir!" The Sergeant dismounted and signaled to the number-three vehicle, which emptied except for the driver, allowing him and the Boss to climb into the back. The guards fanned out, taking a relaxed but watchful stance around the parked vehicles. They didn't know much about what was going on, but they did know enough to keep their guard up, their professional motto being "when there is doubt, there is absolutely no doubt!"

When the Humvee reached the tower, the Boss literally ran up the stairwell, five stories high, emerging into the lower control room where the area operators usually sat. Today there was just one controller keeping a watchful eye on the airspace around Andrews, making sure no wandering aircraft encroached on the closed airspace. The Boss continued up to the main room, where a three-sixty-degree view of the base drifted in through the smoked glass of the tower. Three men and one woman waited anxiously, their supervisor pacing between the rows of empty seats.

"Ma'am, gentlemen, I'm PJ Anthony. Thank you for your time today. Could you please take the positions you were in on the day of the attack?" the Boss asked, smiling to relieve the pressure. These good people had spent days second-guessing themselves and everything that had happened and been brutally and impersonally questioned by military police, the CIA, FBI, and finally, Homeland Security. Now they faced yet another inquisition by a comparative stranger who had arrived in one of the only two remaining airworthy SR-71s, which alone indicated a very heavy hitter from somewhere well connected up the food chain. The Boss, sensing the tension, tried again to put the tower crew in a more relaxed frame of mind.

"People, I'm with Interpol, I know none of you did anything wrong, and I know that none of you could have anticipated what happened at West Point. What I need for you to do is to focus, please, on your actions that day, and to help you, I am going to read the incident report you all contributed to. When I hit each action point, I want you to announce your name and describe for me exactly what you did and then mime it for me exactly the way you did it on the day. Any questions?" The Boss looked around the room, and the only smiling face was Top's, now sitting comfortably against one angled window, admiring the view, his MP-5 pointing loosely into the center of the room, coincidentally covering the entire tower crew.

The Boss started reading, and the crew started acting, and within ten minutes, the Boss had the answer to the first part of the puzzle.

It only took six extra minutes inside the contractor's hangar for him to find the second part, and slipping a data disc into the top pocket of his flight suit was all it took to for him to take possession of thousands of pages of technical information regarding the setup of the A-10 Warthog that had made the attack.

As he climbed back up into the waiting Blackbird that had been refueled while he was playing policeman, he looked hard at his friend and mentor.

"Tom, the shit is going to hit the fan well and truly on this one, and I'm going to need a squad to work with Black Pete, probably in a few days. Can you get your people to Italy under the radar, and I'll arrange for you to be collected. Strictly civilian appearance, but have all your toys shipped to our hangar in Milan. Spread the arrivals over a couple of days at different points of origin. I suggest you work from somewhere like Milan, and I don't want the freebies or any other service other than yours getting wind of anything."

"Can do, Boss; we can disappear with the best of them. You'll clear this at the top?"

"Yes. Come prepared, I don't think we are up against a large organization this time, but I do suspect that they will not go quietly into the night. And I know that they are well armed and very dangerous, and probably well connected politically. And take this minicomputer, and only use to talk to us. Keep it very secure." The top slipped it into his pants pocket, nodded.

"Transport?"

"We'll have what we need onsite. See you in a few." And with a hiss, the canopy closed on the Boss, leaving the Top standing on the access ladder. As he climbed down, he grinned, welcoming the chance to work with his friend again. Young he might be, crossed to the dark side he may have, but dull he was not!

CHAPTER 34

The small farmhouse had been on the ten-thousand-acre plot for as long as the locals could remember, and even though successive generations of occupiers had tried their best to modernize it from time to time by adding a room here, plumbing there, and, more recently, the latest in satellite TV, it still looked exactly like a wooden shack built out of stern timber and fading cinder wood block, with a slight lean that seemed to increase slightly from year to year.

And the roof still leaked, exactly as it had since the day it had been finished one hundred and forty years earlier, in spite of successive layers of mud, tar, plastic, and, more recently, metal sheets. The only thing that had really changed for the better over the years was the style of the bucket that collected the annoying drips on those rare days it actually managed to rain.

Outside the wooden paling fence, which had once been a sparkling whitewash but was now a dirty grey color, a dust cloud formed on the horizon, building to a small orange and brown storm following a dull black helicopter flying so close to the ground its skids practically cut the top off the untidy weeds. With a sonic whisper, it settled nose up outside the farmhouse, then bumped down on the ground, with twigs, leaves, and dirt swirling up and around as if a tornado had just arrived. With a shriek and a whine, the rotor started to slow, and the popping and cracking of the hot exhaust cut through the air like rifle shots.

The pilot deplaned, a black flash shield lowered from a black helmet, creating the appearance of a moon-headed alien. Sixteen quick steps later, the long black figure was being hugged to within an inch of its life by a woman dressed only in cut-offs and a tank top. The pilot flipped up the shield, snapped off the helmet strap, and shook out a shimmering mane of silver-white hair. The two women kissed passionately, hugged again, then walked inside the depilated farmhouse. What furniture there was looked like overstuffed sausages, with springs clearly visible through the worn fabric. Broken light fittings hung carelessly from the roof, and forty years of dust and neglect covered every inch of the floor.

The two women, arm in arm and head to head, walked into what looked like a broom closet but, in fact, led to a wide stairway. As they went down the stairs, the door closed silently behind them with a faint hiss. Hundreds and hundreds of grainy black-and-white photos were blue-tacked along the wall that supported one side of the stairs, some so old they had started to turn yellow and crack. As the wall turned the corner, the photos seemed to flood the room; the only relief was a long bench with rows and rows of modern electronic equipment and flat screens.

Above the bench, a row of security screens showed three-hundred-and sixty-degree views of the exterior, completely empty and barren except for now dusty and silent helicopter, which was slowly sinking into the ground, being swallowed up as if by a sinkhole.

A single bird flew through the images, lonely and forlorn, looking for its mate. The area it flew over was so vast and empty of anything edible; even the ants had moved out. All in all, the perfect location if you don't particularly want to be bothered with the humdrum of normal everyday living. A small sign lay rusted and broken against a deserted well, dirt, and fungus doing their best to consume it. On the rare occasions when the wind blew sufficiently, you could just make out some illegible characters, which most in the area would mistake for Chinese or maybe even Russian. In fact, the inscription was written in Hebrew, "לוכיהתאשןמזבתאזתונהל," and, loosely translated, meant "Enjoy it while you can." If there was one single thing the two women in the old farmhouse believed in, it was exactly that.

CHAPTER 35

Luigi Antoinette and Stefarino sat side by side, six massive computer screens surrounding them. Black Pete looked on in awe; his world was one of the hot bodies and hotter weapons, not the esoteric one of bits and bytes. He marveled at the way the two seemed to mesh, one starting a sentence, the other finishing it. Their hands flew over the keyboards, and the occasional "ah!" and "*maledizione*!" flew around the otherwise quiet library. On the big screen, a series of lines and boxes of data started to appear, adding to the element of mystery. Indigo finished his coffee with a flourish and noticed that Pete's plate was empty for the first time since he had arrived so dramatically just a few hours ago.

"Pete, *il mioamico*, I think it is time that you and I do some old-fashioned police work."

"Couldn't agree more, mate. I was thinking that these brainiacs will be at it all day, and they really don't need our help. I'd like to start working on where the bastards got their hardware from and how they managed to hide it so well." The head of Interpol Italy nodded in agreement, shifting his somewhat stout frame over to a workstation where one of his squad had been working almost unnoticed.

"Pete, *il mioamico*, Bruno here has been working on this for some time. Our early work back at HQ has probably been compromised, so he has been rebuilding the list from scratch within the confines of this establishment. Bruno, where are you up to?"

"*Sì, colonnello, ho l'elenco per voi,*" Bruno said, punching up his data to the big screen, where for a few seconds, it fought with the information put up there by Luigi and Stefarino. When the new data settled down, victorious, Pete could see that Bruno had produced a list based on the timeline detailing the attacks from the information that had been provided to Interpol by the countries involved.

Data boxes listed "L200 Hercules/UN/Vatican – UAV (UID)/ Dome of the Rock – Van/Red Crescent/Mecca – A-10 Warthog/USAF/ West Point – Service vehicle/(UID)/ Arabia," and under each box was a detailed construct of what was known about each attack. Under the first box, the munitions that had been used were listed, as far as they were able to be, without confirmation from the countries concerned. Data that had been proved by multiple independent observations were in blue, and data that had not been proven were in red. At first glance, the red data outweighed the blue data by a ratio of around one hundred to one!

"The issue is that so much of the information has come to us via our own computers or from those in America and Europe, and we know the terrorists have changed data streams for some time now. So, we are checking visual reports, iReports, TV footage, and reports from policemen and military personnel. The second issue is that the terrorists have had as long as they like to change all the data sets everywhere to hide what they have done and try to confuse us." Black Pete chewed on an apple, looking at the big screen and its story. He knew the Boss had a theory about the Hercules crew, and Pete was now waiting on his insights from the A-10 Warthog attack on West Point. Captain Riley was sussing out the procedure for flying remote unmanned vehicles, and Pete himself had found out how the terrorists had successfully targeted the Vatican. So it wasn't as if they didn't have some hard facts to work with; the problem seemed to be that because the terrorists were literally inside most of the security and military computer systems around the world, they could change, add, delete, or obscure data whenever they felt like it. Looking at the screen, he suddenly had a thought.

"Indigo, from what you know of Interpol's computer system, what is the sort of stuff that couldn't have been changed without someone noticing?" The Italian visually sat straighter in his chair, surprised and delighted that he had been asked such an important question.

"Pete, my friend, such a good question. I have been thinking about this all the days since our lovely Roma was so brutally attacked. Remember, I am a policeman at heart, and if I put myself in the shoes of a local *agente di polizia,* I would have to say there are three things I would always be able to check for, how you say it, *autenticità*. The first," he said, hitting one of the computer keys, "is the fingerprints of a fugitive." A fingerprint card with all ten impressions came up on the screen, with coded data blocks. Pete looked at it critically, then shook his head.

"No good, mate, the terrorists could have got into the system and changed them, and you'd never know." Indigo looked crestfallen, then suddenly brightened up.

"But what about a DNA report, *sì*!?" Pete shook his head again. Indigo deflated again, then suddenly puffed up for the third time.

"But what about major crime reports? How would you change that, eh!?" Pete patted Indigo on the shoulder, grimacing at the news he was about to deliver.

"Indigo, my friend, if you can get into the computers and make a few specialized weapons disappear, then changing reports would be chicken feed to these guys. No, mate, sorry, I'm looking for something before the electronic age, something on old-fashioned paper, something that was faxed or, at the very worst, scanned into the system, so there's still a paper trail somewhere." Indigo screwed up his face in concentration.

"Ar, *sì, sì, un percorso carta potremmoconfrontare le electgronicdati*."

"Exactly. Something we can compare from then to now, to see where the terrorists have been or maybe even how they got into the systems in the first place, or maybe just when they took them over."

The two men looked at the big screen as if seeking inspiration from it, looking at the boxes and all the red data. Overlaid on one corner, the images from Rome created a fuzzy image, as if the provider was trying to eliminate the evidence of their very existence. And it gave Pete an idea.

CHAPTER 36

The walled city of Avignon is located in the Department of Gard, in the Region of Provence Alpes Cote d'Azur. Avignon's history dates back to Celtic times, and it was one of the most flourishing cities under Roman rule and the first transalpine province of the Roman Empire. Avignon lies on the east bank of the Rhône River, 125 miles south of Lyon, 50 miles northwest of Marseille, and 51 miles northeast of Montpellier. It is located to the east of Autoroute A9, at the juncture of Route National 580, 100, 570, and 7. In a sense, if you wanted to mount a modern-day style of attack on the city, it could not have been better situated in terms of easy, free-flowing access by road.

In its three-and-a-half-thousand-year checked history, it had been built, sacked, rebuilt, sacked again, then rebuilt, burnt to the ground, and then rebuilt yet again, and had even been the seat for seven Popes from 1309 until 1377. It remained the papal seat until the French Revolution in 1778, when, after sufficient heads had rolled, it reverted back to the newly declared republic of France. Avignon is such a rich story in the context of the history of Europe that the city center has been granted historical relevance by UNESCO. So it came as no surprise when the Bishop of Avignon, previously retired to a monastery in the south of Spain, suddenly emerged from his seclusion and claimed the right to establish the Holy See in the old Popes' Palace. Built between 1335 and 1352, under the pontificates of Benedict XII and Clement VI, the Pope's

Palace is the largest gothic palace in the world and is considered by many to be, without a doubt, the most elegant and beautiful ever constructed.

This latent claim to fame by the aspiring retired bishop may have gone unnoticed by most of the non-Catholic world who were still trying to deal with a massive fuel shortage that had grounded two-thirds of the world's air and road traffic, created by worldwide terrorism on an unprecedented scale, and no indication that any country involved had any idea who to attack in retribution to "make things right again." Unfortunately for the prospective Pope and his hoard of hangers-on who recognized a seat of power when they saw one, his ascension to the highest and holiest of orders was not to be.

At exactly sunset, it appeared that fifty highly motivated individuals spread around the city in bread vans shouted "Allah Akbar!" and pushed little red buttons on the top of cheap Bakelite detonator switches and blew sixty percent of the city to bits, seemingly including themselves, the Pope-to-be, his entourage, and approximately eleven thousand bystanders whose only crime had been living in or visiting a city someone else wanted to destroy, for no particular reason other than "payback." At least that's what the Jihad Al'Alkalemia claimed in a world wide web posting one minute before the bombs went off, pointing out that the French had been clearly implicated in the atrocities involving Mecca and the Arabian oil fields, and it was only "just" and "God's will" that the French should be taught a lesson never to "take Allah's name in vain" or attack the Kingdom ever again.

Predictably, this atrocity had the exact opposite effect, galvanizing the French in a way that would have seemed impossible if you knew them well. Within seconds of the posting on the web and the subsequent destruction of Avignon, the French president had issued an edict to the Arabian king, in clear twenty languages so there could be no excuses or misunderstanding, "to make full restitution without delay" or "face consequences so dire that your very survival as a nation will be in doubt!"

To back this extraordinary communication, a full squadron of the Rafael next-generation multipurpose fighter/bombers from the French Force de Dissuasion (Deterrent Force), each carrying a range-enhanced "ASMP Plus" missile (*Air-Sol Moyenne Portee*), suddenly found themselves in a holding pattern in international airspace, just outside the Turkish border, with the Kingdom clearly in sight just over the horizon. To say that the twenty elite pilots were a little surprised at this turn of events would be to make the understatement of the century!

When the Arabian king was made aware of both forms of French communication and the murderous suicide attack on Avignon, he was bewildered. His aids had told him of the earlier request from the French for information about their elite GIGN troops who had mysteriously gone missing after landing in the Kingdom, supposedly at the king's request.

He had made no such request. No one on his staff had made such a request, so he had dismissed it as just another one of the numerous irrelevancies he suffered every day.

And now he was being threatened by the president of France for something he knew nothing about and being threatened physically and visibly for the entire world to see by nuclear-armed aircraft, as well as being blamed for mounting a devastating attack on a French city he hadn't even known existed!

He did the only thing he could under the circumstances: he called for four of his most favorite wives to attend, called for a hooker, and instructed his principal aid to immediately call the heads of Al Mabaahith Al Jena'eyah, Al Mukhabarat Al A'amah, and the Lightning Force and have them come to the palace immediately, from wherever they were, irrespective of anything they may be doing, on pain of instant and immediate death!

CHAPTER 37

The "exclusive" gentleman's club, which was not only hard to find but really was exclusive, was just off the beltway south of Washington, known as the Adenvista Country Club. The real "exclusive" bit was an area removed from the public eye three stories above the car park, an enticing rotunda that was not only glassed in but was protected by the best security devices known to man, including a full pack of Alsatian dogs that just loved to chew on human flesh and bones should they find any wandering through the grounds. Tonight, six people sat around a casino-sized card table, looking at each other as if the end of the world had come, while, downstairs, around forty support staff, drank fizzy water and then sweated it back out again. The head of the CIA, Julius Bronstein, and the heads of the NSA and FBI were interspaced with the chiefs of staff for the army, Air Force, and navy. Thick cigar smoke filled the roof spaces, and expensive Cognac bottles littered the card table. The mood in the room was as heavy as the smoke, and even the overly large plasma screen that had a Hooters contest running on it failed to lift the spirits of the six heavy hitters who were responsible for the safety of the United States and the people within.

"Roger, your man Anthony seems to have gone off the reservation," remarked Frank Reynolds. As the head of the NSA, he was used to being able to find out everything about everybody, which is what the NSA did by listening into every phone conversation and ripping off the WWW in every email, chat, and blog. Massive supercomputers manned by legions of plastic-pocket-protected technicians beavered away day and night in the bowels of the NSA building, perfecting the art of the high-tech peeping Tom, always careful to never cross the line and violate the civil liberties of the common folk. Unless they had to. Which, of course, was always easy to justify after the event. If they got caught, which they rarely did. So, they did it all the time.

"Well, we have visuals on him in Israel, and he just left Andrews for Venice. One of his team parachuted into Rome, and the woman he worked with was on her way back from Afghanistan. But you're correct; he is now using a secure comms link we can't find access to."

"Do you still trust him?" Julius Bronstein asked. Personally, he never trusted anyone unless he could exercise total control over everything they did.

"Yes. PJ is on our side, I have no doubt about that, but we all have to realize that Interpol is forbidden by its charter to intervene militarily or politically. They are the cops, not the Marines, so when he turns something up, more than likely we will have to deal with it if it isn't a simple arrest scenario."

"I thought Section Five had a different mandate?"

"They do, but let's wait and see what he turns up before we worry about that."

"No terrorist arrest is ever simple!" said Julius, almost smiling at the thought. "Do you have any idea what he might have found out at Andrews?" Frank asked.

"Well, we have eyewitness accounts that he drove all over the place in a modified Humvee shooting video and then interviewed the tower people. They said he had them play-act what they did on the day. He had a long conversation with the Top that provided his escort, and that was about it."

"How is he getting around in that SR-71? I thought we had mothballed them."

"We did. But we kept two on the active roster with NASA for research purposes. When we first got the call from Interpol for assistance in recovering him from Australia, we sent the Blackbird. As a sign of good faith, we let him keep it in case he needed it, and as it turned out, he did." The chief of the Airforce grimaced, filling his shot glass in the process.

"It's a bugger of a thing to keep active. We have to ship its fuel around the world, as well as its ground crew. Then we have to tank it en route wherever it goes. Not a cheap exercise, by any means."

"Sam, right now, you can have any amount of money you want. If we don't turn up a credible bad guy to go and blow off the face of the earth in the next few days, the country will go bananas."

"Like those crazies just did in France?" asked the chief of the navy, newly appointed to replace Admiral Jones, who had been killed at West Point.

"Well, here's the thing," drawled Frank, putting on his best Texan accent, "came out of the blue. No back chatter, none of the usual build-ups in the background; if it was Al-Qaeda, ISIS, or Islamic Jihad, then it was a cell not connected to anyone we monitor, and if it was any of the other crazies, then the same thing applies. You want my opinion? We have another new boy on the block, hiding in the shadows of all the other bastard organizations."

"Jihad Al'Alkalemia was the name used in the web broadcast."

"Yes, but that means about as much as my little finger. Never heard of them before, doubt if we ever will again."

"Another terrorist group?" asked the chief of the army. "Another one."

"Why do you say that?"

"Well, our analysts believe that the first series of attacks, Rome, Jerusalem, Mecca, Arabia, and here, was carried out by five separate cells, loosely coordinated. We are starting to develop the theory that the timing of the attacks was proximate. We also believe that there are very few involved in these attacks, but there are enough similarities between each attack to suggest a master planner somewhere, with a big budget, that they spent over a lot of years setting everything up in their own good time."

"Why a lot of years?" asked the Admiral.

"Well, if you just take the weaponry, the two bombs used on the Vatican could only have been obtained around two thousand one, or maybe two thousand two at the very latest. The Hellfire missiles used in Jerusalem could only have been acquired after two thousand six. And the key explosive used in the Mecca attack was only invented by the Australians in two thousand seven."

"What gives you the timeline on the bombs?" asked the chief of the Air Force. His people were unable to trace where the two massive bombs had been taken from, and while a total physical search was now underway, so far, every container had the right armament in it.

"In two thousand two, every bomb over five hundred pounds was given a security lock that could only be opened by two independent armorers. This lock prevented fusing the weapons, was the best-kept secret in the military, and has had a one hundred percent success rating in every audit carried out since then."

"So, the daisy cutter and the ground penetrator were taken before that?"

"Yes. This we know with certainty, as the whole lock process was non-electronic, never entered into the computer systems and was managed locally at every base by round-the-clock security teams. In fact, we made the audit process so anal people would lose their keys before they would admit to making a mistake."

"So, we are looking for someone who thinks long term?" asked Julius.

"Or someone who is an opportunist," added the Admiral. Frank shook his head. "No, we think this is definitely a long-term deal. If you create a battle plan that uses the death of a Pope as its trigger, you are thinking years out of the event. Our best people think this is a fifteen-to-twenty-year plan, which was triggered by the papal election, and the other four attacks synchronized around it but not necessarily timed to it by the minute in terms of implementation."

"Why do you say that?"

"The other attacks took place half a day or so later; from start to finish, four days elapsed in total, even allowing for the time difference between Europe and here. What makes sense to us is five separate groups of highly trained people, all equipped and waiting, with a time window of a few days to mount their attack once the first strike has been made. Now the kicker is the old Pope took ill five months ago, so they had their own early warning system. And we think we have the key to one of the attacks."

"Which one?"

"West Point."

"How so?"

"Think about it. You can't steal a fully armed Hog from just anywhere, anytime you like. We checked that the contractors scheduled the test flight two weeks in advance. Then a strange thing happened. The date of the conclave was announced, and on the same day, the contractor's schedule was changed by ten days. No one will admit to the change, and no one can find who made the change, but the Andrews staff and the contractor's staff were in complete accord. Someone added ten days to the test date."

"From the inside?"

"From the inside."

"Is that unusual?" asked the Admiral.

"Happens all the time. Test flying is just that. Sometimes things don't come together as planned, and something doesn't work as advertised, but in this case, the equipment was good to go on the original date, when a high-speed taxi run was performed, but then the aircraft sat in the hangar for ten days longer than necessary to meet the new schedule. When we spoke to everyone involved, they all thought the other side had made the call."

"The contractor thought Andrews had moved the date, and Andrews thought the contractor had moved the date."

"Yes."

"What about the mid-air refueling?" asked the Admiral.

"Tasked out of Andrews, normal request, excellent training for the National Guard pilots and crew; they received a twenty-four-hour heads-up, then flew the mission as part of several they had scheduled that day. They always have a tanker or two in the air nowadays because we are flying so many CAPs over the cities."

"Thank you, 9/11."

"Yes."

"So, what you are saying is that we have a planner working in tens of years and an attack schedule in days. This doesn't strike me as one of the crazies."

"Agreed. This is well thought out, deliberate, and flawlessly executed."

"Then who blew up Avignon?"

"Oh, that will turn out to be a bunch of Middle Eastern or Arab crazies, no doubt about that. Why they did it is a mystery, Avignon is not exactly the center of the world for anyone these days. But it has all the hallmarks of a traditional suicide bomber attack, except for the scale and the precision."

"Precision? Scale?"

"Those vans were placed exactly where they would do the most damage, all exploded at the same time, and were placed so that their footprint overlapped to the point where the absolute maximum value in blast terms was achieved. Again, this was world-class expert planning, make no mistake, by someone who knows their blast dynamics."

"What will the French do?" asked the admiral. He looked through his crystal-cut shot glass as if seeking inspiration.

"Who knows. I doubt they will use their nukes, too much international downside; besides, they still get most of their oil from the Arabians, so it will be interesting to see what happens next." By now, the admiral had finally worked out the secret message in the bottom of his shot glass and refilled it from the bottle at his elbow. He looked at the chief of the Air Force, someone with whom he had clashed frequently in the past in other lives on his way up the greasy power pole.

"Did we ever find out what happened to that damn Hog?" he asked, mindful of the fact that all five men were now looking at him as if he were the enemy.

"We put over three hundred helicopters and low-flying observation aircraft in the air, worked the unrefueled range plus two hundred, using the Eastern Seaboard as the limit, from Florida to the top of the Canadian border. The Canucks put their own aircraft up, and between us, we had eyes on every square mile out to the edge of Texas. Not a single sign of its presence." The admiral grimaced, liking what he was about to do but sensing it was the wrong thing at the right time.

"Well, on a hunch, we had three attack subs, and a bunch of destroyers and escort boats run their sonar and lidar over the seabed, out to four hundred nautical miles. Guess what we found?" The silence in the room was electric, every hand poised in mid-air.

"What?" the question fired across the room like a cannon shot.

"A lot of junk and wrecks, as you can imagine, and this." He pulled a creased facsimile out of his pocket, a grey-and-black-smudged affair that would take a fortune-teller to interpret it. The facsimile sat where it had landed, no one choosing to be the first to pick it up in case it bit or exploded in their hands.

"What is it?" Frank finally asked, voicing the question on everyone's lips. "Our experts tell me it is the outline of an A-10 Warthog, sitting fair and square in seventeen hundred feet of water, intact, looking for all the world as good as the day it was made."

"Canopy intact?" asked Roger.

"Can't tell. But the aircraft looks pristine; whoever landed it there knew exactly what they were doing because it appears to have suffered no real external damage at all."

"Well, in a way, that is to be expected," the chief of the Air Force said, suddenly claiming rights over the abandoned aircraft that his own force had been unable to locate. "The Hog was designed to be able to land wheels up, its main wheels sit proud of the wheel canopies, its engines are mounted high above the main wing position, and its belly is relatively flat. Right airspeed, right angle of attack, favorable sea state, and it would probably just float on the surface for hours."

"Are you pulling it out?" asked Frank. The admiral nodded.

"Got a recovery rig on the way. It's down deep, but not that deep; we should have it up in two or three days tops, weather permitting."

"Well, won't that be interesting?"

The admiral smiled to himself, knowing something else that would become apparent in a few days or so to everyone else. Because he had deliberately misled everyone about the canopy. From a photo taken with a digital camera on the sail of one of the nuclear subs that had eventually found the aircraft, it appeared that the canopy was smashed and shattered and had been removed by the impact, and the pilot was crushed by either the impact or the depth. The idea of a locally grown terrorist was not something he relished floating amongst all the present gloom, doom, and despair, but clearly, the image of a dead pilot still sitting in their harness in the ejector seat would be hard to argue!

CHAPTER 38

As we landed back at Marco Polo, the tower let us know that the Blackbird was less than an hour out, so after thanking my Italian stud of a pilot, I decided to walk around the waterside boundary of the airport to waste a little time and get some exercise and fresh air. It also gave me a chance to reflect on everything I had learned, suspected, worked out, dismissed, and been confused by from the get-go. The moonlight beat a path across the water all the way to the outskirts of Venice; it was calm and warm, and I could almost imagine myself in a gondola, sipping champagne, being wooed by a tall, dark, handsome stranger.

That's where the Boss came in because keeping up with his crippling schedule all over the world chasing crooks and terrorists is what had effectively stalled what little I had of a love life before I joined Interpol. Thinking about that massive transition from naval criminal investigator to Interpol sleuth made me smile in spite of my dark thoughts. The bloody Boss again. I can still hear him talking to me in a whisper as we walked the boundary of Souda Bay, having met a few hours earlier over the smoking barrel of my Armalite rifle.

We had killed four terrorists that night whom we thought had been following up the attack on Maryland the day before, and somehow the Colonel had popped up right in the line of fire. His story at the time that the terrorists had been following him had seemed a little thin, but as his story unfolded as we walked, trailed by my master chief, I started to believe him in spite of my instincts. The Boss—a special operations Colonel as he presented himself then, was again carrying a cut-down AR-15 and had regained his Sig Sauer P226 and K-bar knife in spite of my protests to the contrary back at the medevac tent.

It seems that he had been "in the wind" for a week or so, trying to track a bunch of crazies out of Iran who had loudly boasted in a small town as they passed through that they were "about to wreak havoc on the Great Satan, and all the bastard offal that passed for Americans in Europe," which had been duly noted by one or two American tourists, who had promptly phoned their embassy and passed on the glad tidings from the Ayatollah. The Special Forces team the Colonel was a part of had split up, with each member covering a different base, or more correctly, the prime chokepoint that gave access to the base, in the hope that the less than culturally sensitive terrorists turned up.

Which they had.

But you already know the rest of that story.

Back to the Boss. It seems that he had done many things in the first sixteen years of his working life, mostly in the military, and all at top speed. Having left college at fifteen with a double degree in aeronautical science and international law, he was rudely told he was too young to join up, so he promptly took flying lessons and, in the space of two years, graduated top of his class and successfully finished up at a privately run test pilot school run out of Mojave. While slogging through the desert one day after crashing an old Beech 18, he had been picked up by a SAR (search and rescue) helicopter out of Edwards Air Force Base, the home of real military test pilots and trainee astronauts.

After being checked out by the base medical staff, he hitched a ride back to Mojave with a sergeant who just happened to be cross-training as a SAR jumper, working with the SEALS. The Boss had taken his details and, three days later, appeared back at Edwards, this time under his own steam. After a short conversation with his new best friend, he flew to Santiago and joined the navy.

In the next five years, he won his commission, qualified as a pilot, trained as a strategist and mission planner, then went to the Army Special Forces school at Fort Bragg. Then on to SEAL training and then, strange as it may seem, was seconded for eighteen months to the FBI training facility at Quantico, where he taught the Feebies how to think and act like terrorists. They liked him so much they tried to recruit him, so the navy responded by promoting him to bird Colonel and posting him off to a hot zone for a live-fire experience.

He never told me much about that, but I had seen the scars and bullet holes on his body back at the medevac tent and a couple of times later in more private encounters, so I imagined he got what they sent him to get—live fire experience! The next day he was gone, until just seven months later, when he arrived on my doorstep again, but this time to recruit me for an elite unit, he was established under the Interpol banner to combat terrorism predominately throughout Europe. A substantial raise in pay and rank rose with the commission, along with the promise of lots of freedom to study, chase bad guys, and make a difference.

Well, I got the rise and the rank, but so far, the study had been centered around all the latest tricks and devious little behaviors the bad guys were adopting to try to fool their way into our hearts and minds. I had kept up my languages, actually getting to immerse myself in lots of local dialects in the process, and I was getting a bit of a reputation for understanding the locals wherever we went. And Interpol was blessed with a relatively clean reputation as far as most of the countries in Europe were concerned, being seen to be truly independent and interested only in solving the crime, not taking the credit or making a political statement at any countries' expense, so I always got lots of local help in learning the language and customs.

And now we had a global meltdown of monumental proportions threatening our very existence as we knew it, and not a single clue as to who the bad guys were! Well, actually, as I considered that thought, I suddenly became aware that we now had a lot of facts to work from, and the possibility of walking the cat backwards was becoming a viable option. The trick would be to bring all the facts together and make some kind of sense of them. Just as this thought started to percolate, the roar of the Blackbird landing cut through the calm and tranquility of the night, snapping me back into Tonto mode, as I had privately started to call it. Him Lone Ranger, me sidekick! Now, where did I leave my horse?

"*Il mio capitano, ben tornato, abbiamopersovoi*," a voice said out of the dark. I froze, wondering who thought I was their captain and had missed me so much they wanted to scare the pants off me.

"*Chi è là*?" I asked, slowly drawing my Beretta. I wasn't really concerned; this was a secured airport, and I was on the track used by the police vehicles during their rounds, and the tower—and therefore everyone else in authority—knew where I was and where I was going because I had told them before setting out in the dark.

"*Il mio capitano, mi scuso per startling voi, il colonnello mi ha mandato a casa una scorta di*," the voice answered. Then, out of the dark, one of the four guards that usually stood in proximity to the secret library dungeon emerged, followed by my personal nightmare.

"*Signora, è in barca vi aspetta*!" I just bet it did because it was becoming very obvious to me that the red cigarette boat and its driver were going to be my personal cross to bear for as long as we were in Venice. I briefly considered shooting him by "mistake," but just as this alarming but beautiful thought started to take shape, a massive four-wheel drift caught my attention, and a dusty Lancia rudely pulled alongside.

"Hop in." I did.

"Good trip?" the Colonel asked, looking entirely relaxed in spite of having flown to the United States and back in a little under ten hours.

"Perfect, thank you," I replied, smiling in the dark. His demeanor reminded me for the millionth time that this was not a game for pussies, and in a strange way, it felt right to be so out of control but in such high gear. I think it's called the "zone." We slid to another dusty stop at the boat ramp, climbed into the red terror, were not in any way disappointed by the extreme sport of crossing the waterway on one chine all the way to the jetty outside the church, disembarked with what small measure of calm remained, then sank back into the bowels of Venice for the umpteenth time in as many days.

More excellent food, more superb coffee, another quick shower, and then Indigo, his super smart hacker Luigi, Stefarino the curator, and Pete and the Boss and I sat facing each other over the tops of our secured little laptops, eyeing each other off. The excitement on Indigo's and Pete's faces was unmistakable, and even the little curator seemed juiced. I wondered what they had found out. The Boss had noticed it too and, true to form, put his people first.

"Pete, Indigo, what can you tell us?" he asked, scanning the room to see where everyone was. As before, all the technicians and real librarians seemed to be engrossed in their work, which looked like an around-the-clock activity. I idly wondered what the real purpose of the library was. Strange how you can be working somewhere under pressure, and the actual surroundings take on a bland reflection, and you only really see what you specifically look for.

"Well, Boss, our mate here, Luigi, is a bloody genius. He and I are going into business when this is over; I reckon we can rip off any computer system in the world and get away with it!" Pete exclaimed, as worked up as I had ever seen him. Everyone laughed, realizing that Pete was more paying the computer guy a compliment than establishing the baseline for a future business plan! "We had an idea," Pete continued, clicking on the big screen. We turned our heads to look at it and saw some paper forms in stacks and a series of computer data screen replications. "We decided to try to find out how long the terrorists have been in the computer systems." He flicked up another image, this one with a dateline running across it, from 1995 to the current date. A red starburst sat on top of 1999/2000, and a little atomic bomb symbol sat on top of 2002. An even bigger bomb symbol sat on top of 2006.

"What we can prove, using Interpol's physical records, backed up with data from seven other sources, which, unfortunately, we can't attribute"—and here he gave a little evil grin and a huge wink to Luigi—"proves conclusively that the bad guys slipped in their backdoor worms during the workup to Y2K, tested it on several systems in two thousand two, then went 'live' as it were, in two thousand six."

"What did they attack?" asked the Boss.

"Nothing. All they did was follow and mirror several activities. They were learning how things were done, what the steps were, and how the documents and authorizations were managed. And I bet you can't guess what they tracked."

"Aircraft movements, European Air Traffic Control procedures, response times, that sort of thing?" I said, stating the obvious. Pete shook his head.

"Nothing so simple. No, they linked into a specific nuclear power plant and followed everything they did for around two years. Then they moved in, took control of the dispatch and monitoring systems and lifted, by our best guess, around ten kilos of the material they used in the bomb in Arabia."

"What else?"

"They followed the UN flights in and out of every European country for around the same time, then they 'acquired' their aircraft, covered their trail, and pretty much left the ATC system alone until the day before the attack on Rome." The Boss suddenly leaned forward, holding one hand up in a universal sign for "stop."

"Hang on a minute, they took a Herc out of the system undetected?" he asked.

Pete nodded this time.

"Yes. An L200 that was going to be scrapped, literally out of hours and only useful for spares. They purchased it legitimately, got a once-use permit to fly it to Athens for disposal, then disappeared it completely."

"And no one followed up because the aircraft was off the register?"

"Correct. It never got to Athens; the bad guys were well and truly inside the ATC system by then. It just disappeared."

"This was when?"

"We think in August of two thousand eight. September at the very latest because we can find no trace of them after that time until the day before the first attack."

"Outstanding. Now, just to tickle everyone's fancy, I've got something to add to the Hercules story." We all looked at the Boss, now sitting back very relaxed, with a Cheshire cat-like smile lighting up his face.

"Jessica and I discovered something quite amazing when we retraced the flight path of the Hercules. And I want to challenge you all to project what this means in terms of the overall strategy of the terrorists." He had us at "amazing," but we all played the game and sat forward like young, attentive college students.

"There was no crew in the Hercules." Everyone but me looked astonished because I kind of had worked that out for myself in a quiet moment back at Marco Polo. The Boss's reaction over Rome had been the first clue, plus the logic bomb that was underneath us on the day we flew the mirror flight. The ocean was literally covered in boats of all sizes, as far as the eye could see, and it was logical to think that the picture would be the same or even worse on the day of the Pope's election.

If a crew had parachuted out of the Hercules into the Mediterranean before the Italian Air Force shot it down, someone would have seen them, and it would have been on the airwaves. For that matter, the Italian fighter jets had made visual contact with the Hercules literally minutes after the attack, so they should have seen the crew exiting the aircraft.

"Correct, Jessica. No crew; it was modified to be a UAV, probably flown from the same control point as the UAV that hit Jerusalem. What did you find out about that, by the way?" he asked. I thought for a minute, mentally sorting out what I was going to say. This was a very bright group of people, and they tended to only hear the good stuff, and they liked it fast and condensed. In a sense, they mirrored the very best and worst of the "modern" generation. Three-second attention spans, three clicks, and dot points!

"Well, three things come to mind. The first, the UAV could have been controlled from anywhere with the right equipment, literally from anywhere in the world." Everyone nodded; they had already read my Digi pad notes that I had sent while airborne on the way back from Afghanistan. "Secondly, the UAV was probably stripped out, with a full fuel load plus extra tanks, giving it a probable one-way range around twelve hundred nautical miles. This means it could have been launched from anywhere from Libya to Greece or Bulgaria to Iran. But where it came from, I think, is not as important as what it did." I felt every head turn toward me questioningly.

"It bombed the Dome, not the rock. The evidence is quite clear. The superstructure around the rock had been destroyed, but the rock was untouched. In contrast, one of the missiles hit the Wailing Wall at its biggest point, creating a massive shock wave, completely destroying it for hundreds of meters in both directions."

"How accurate can the operators be firing missiles from the UAVs?" Pete asked.

"Deadly. The guys I talked to in Afghanistan showed me how the optical and targeting systems are integrated; believe me, they really can fly a missile through a window while sitting in their armchairs. But in this attack, the terrorists used the natural energy being reflected off the dome as their primary aiming point, and the Israelis suspect that a micro-transmitter was placed on the Wailing Wall to enhance the accuracy of that particular hit."

"Are you convinced that the UAV was not controlled by the Americans in Afghanistan?" Indigo asked.

"Totally. What I didn't know before is that all they do locally is launch and retrieve the UAV. Once airborne, they hand over control to a team in Nevada, who actually 'fly' every mission. In spite of the data stream that was detected coming from the US system, I believe that they had nothing to do with the attack. And I am positive that the UAV did not come from Afghanistan."

"Okay, so to summarize so far, the Hercules was obtained years in advance, then converted to fly as a UAV. The FBI has given us hard evidence that the bombs used in the Vatican attack were obtained around or before two thousand two. We know the hellfire missiles used by the UAV that attacked the dome were obtained after two thousand six, but we don't know where or how. And we know that the attack on the dome was specific to infrastructure, leaving the rock unscathed. What does this all suggest to us?" the Boss asked, playing the role of facilitator as usual. Another reason I was smitten with him. He never seemed to dominate his team unless he was busy saving their lives!

"*Il miocolonnello è molto vedendochequestiattacchihanno una forte polariz-zazione religiosa?*" asked Luigi, surprising everyone.

"Yes, definitely a religious bias," I replied, interpreting for Pete's benefit and pleased that the computer genius felt comfortable enough in this high-powered group to contribute. "But all the way back from Afghanistan, I have been trying to figure out which religious group benefits the most from destroying the Vatican, the heart of the Catholic Church, wrecking the buildings surrounding the rock in Jerusalem but leaving the rock untouched, and taking out the Wailing Wall completely. Anti-Catholic and anti-Semitic is a strange combination, even in this day and age. Then add in the attack on the Grand Mosque in Mecca, which makes it anti-Muslim, then the attack on the Arabians, there goes the Muslims again, and somehow work in an attack on the US via West Point, no religious affiliation to speak of, and where does that leave you?"

"Perhaps if we look at the genesis of the importance of Jerusalem in religious history, we will get a better perspective," suggested Stefarino. He opened a huge creased, leather-bound book and placed it on the table. "It's the only place in the world where Jews, Christians, and Muslims celebrate their origins. Each for their own very special historical reasons but goes to the very core of their beliefs. Perhaps the question we have to ask is, which of the three benefits most by the destruction of the physical infrastructure surrounding the rock?" The room fell silent; we had all shared the background briefing prepared by Stefarino when we had first come into contact with him, and frankly, I had been blown away by the sheer complexity of the story.

A city at least five thousand years old, associated with names, places, and events that sounded like the definitive role of the backbone of religious history—Solomon's Temple, the Crucifixion, Resurrection, and the Last Supper, and the prophet Muhammad. The Temple Mount, David, the founder of Israel and Judah, the Ark of the Covenant, and, of course, Mount Moriah, which all by itself was a highly sacred site, largely because of an ancient Semitic tradition that said that the bare rock atop the mount was held in the mouth of the serpent Tahum and that this place was the intersection of the underworld and the upper world.

And then you have Abraham and the sacrifice of his son to God and the infamous plundering of the holy relics by Nebuchadnezzar. All in all, if only a small part of this was actually true, there was enough religious history here to focus anyone's attention.

But whose?

I couldn't quite get my mind around it, but a blurry idea was starting to form. "What about the West Point attack? And Mecca, and let's not forget losing half the world's oil supply? Where do all these attacks fit in?" I asked again.

"And while you are on the subject, what about the last attack on Avignon?" asked Pete. The Boss smiled, held up his stop sign again, paused, and then blew us away with what he said next.

"Let's just keep examining the attacks one by one for a minute. I think we are developing a picture here; not particularly clear yet, but an image is starting to take shape. I've got more detail on the West Point attack, and somehow I think it is the key to everything else." We all looked at him expectantly. He craftily built the tension by reaching forward and hitting the keys on his little laptop, throwing an image up on the big screen. Five movies started up, each in their own little box, showing a control tower, a sandbagged revetment, a massive gate in a security fence with little gates on either side, a long tarmac going off into the distance, and a wide view of an airport obviously taken from somewhere high up, probably the control tower in the first video.

"Now, this is Andrews, where the A-10 Warthog took off from. I can talk you through each of the videos or just give you my summary."

"Summary," I said quickly, then looked at everyone else to see if I had over-ridden their desires in my haste to get to the guts of the story. Indigo smiled, Pete shrugged his shoulders, and the curator gently nodded his head. I was forgiven!

"Okay, remember, I can give you the detailed chapter and verse any time you need it, but here goes." He turned the screen off, sat back, interlaced his long fingers, and for a split second, I thought we were going to get a sermon. "The pilot of the A-10 did the pre-flight in the contractor's hangar, about two hours before the planned departure time. That turned out to be SOP—standard operating procedure. They allow two hours in case the pilot sees something they don't like, and then they have time to fix it if it's minor."

"Are all the weapons on the aircraft during the pre-flight?" I asked.

"Yes, but not fused or armed. In this respect, they are like the navy on a carrier; the fusing and arming are done when the aircraft is ready to launch—in this case, at the sandbagged revetment you saw in one of the videos. An armorer clears the aircraft, pulls the safety pins, connects the wiring if required, fuses any bombs, then waves the pilot off when it's all done."

"How far from the revetment to the take-off point?" Pete asked.

"Wrong question," the Boss replied, smiling to make it clear he was not dissing Pete in any way. "The question is why was an armorer needed in the first place, as this was a test flight to see how a new low-level ground-mapping navigation system worked, and allegedly the only reason the bomb canisters were on the aircraft is because a test is not a test unless the aircraft is configured the way it may be for a real attack. When the A-10 left the hangar, the canisters were not wired into the aircrafts' weapons system, and the safety pins were secured in the weapons pods. We have proof of that."

"So an armorer pulled the pins and connected the wiring at the revetment?" Pete asked.

"No."

"No?"

"No. And now we enter territory that I think will be revealed because we have got physical evidence to work with post-attack for the first time. I've already made the FBI aware of my thinking, and they have their best people on it as we speak."

"Well then, speak!" Pete said, throwing a sandwich at the Boss. He caught it without effort and ate it, to the amazement of all.

"Okay, I take the hint. The butler did it."

"What?" I laughed, desperately trying to figure out where the Boss was taking us.

"The butler. You know, in every good who-dunnit, the butler did it." The Boss wiped his mouth, laughed, then looked around at all of us as if seeing us for the first time. "I believe that the pilot dismounted from the A-10, armed the canisters, plugged them into the weapons system, then drove off the base in a military vehicle."

"Then who flew it to West Point?" Pete asked.

"The same team that flew the UAV and the Hercules." Silence descended on the room like a blanket. The cop in me saw all sorts of possibilities, and this time I smiled.

"Okay, that means we have a contractor's hangar, mechanics, electronic engineers, instrument specialists, and lots of different people all playing with the airframe. We have inventory lists, spares lists, work orders, paper trails, any one of which could show us who was involved." The Boss shrugged his shoulders as if to say "maybe," but then he left us in no doubt.

"No. Remember, these people have been inside the computer systems for years. I had a technician look at the data, and there is absolutely nothing to show anything out of the ordinary. Yes, the terrorists did have people in that hangar modifying the aircraft, but they did it so cleverly that no one detected it, and their trail is as cold as ice."

"Bugger!"

"Yes, indeed. But we still have physical evidence to work on. We have a picture of the vehicle that was parked at the revetment, and we have a video of the female pilot. Now, while all her records have vanished, as you would expect, the FBI is building a case file from interviews with people who worked with her or knew her and trust me on this, they will be very, very thorough. They will follow her back to the cradle." I thought about the process involved in getting out of an aircraft, closing it up, arming it, then driving away while someone else far, far away in a caravan or bunker took control and flew it away remotely, and a sudden thought occurred to me.

"Why didn't the tower see what was going on?"

"Simple. Firstly, all the tower knew was that it was a test flight. Secondly, you cannot see the arming revetment clearly from the tower."

"Okay, next question. The A-10 was refueled midair, yes?" I asked, tongue in cheek because I was sure I had the Boss nailed on this one.

"Yes. The aircraft was tanked by a KC-135 en route, part of a training mission for the Air National Guard out of Byrd Field."

"Then they saw a pilot in that aircraft, probably talked to him or her."

"Correct again, Jess, and how do you think the bad guys managed that?"

"You are certain they turned it into a UAV?" I asked, a little more sharply than I meant to.

"Yes." If the Boss was fazed by my tone of voice, he didn't show it. A tickle started somewhere at the back of my brain, and then I got it.

"Have they found the aircraft yet?" I asked.

"Yes, the navy found it in deep water around two hundred and fifty nautical miles off the coast, sitting on the bottom, as pretty as a peach. We only know that because we have access to their military summaries as we are now the lead agency of the investigation on the attack. The navy expects to have the aircraft recovered in about a week to ten days, depending on the weather."

"Does the US know everything that we know?"

"Not yet. I intend to share it when we have talked it through here. They still leak like a sieve, and they know it. What's your line of thinking?"

"The pilot. Was a switch made, was it really a UAV, and how did they make the refueling work if it was? The boom operator looks right into the cockpit; I've seen a video of it; if there wasn't a pilot, then they would have seen that."

"Trust me, the standard training video taken by the KC-135 clearly shows a pilot in that cockpit, helmet on, flash shield down, oxygen mask on, exactly as you would expect."

"Just like a store dummy," Pete offered, somewhat derisively. Being a boatie and ground pounder from way back, the Air Force and everyone in it came off as pussies in his eyes, something he never let us forget.

"Exactly. Just like a store dummy," the Boss said, smiling.

"You're not serious?" I asked, amazed at the thought of a store dummy flying a multi-million dollar killing machine. And then I finally got it. Sometimes the human brain is very stubborn, and mine more so than most. Talk about being limited by what you think you know! "Okay, sorry, having a moment here, I got it, sorry, my bad, must be all the coffee!" Everyone laughed, easing my intense feeling of stupidity.

"*Il miocolonnello, come sonointelligentiquestiterroristi? Io non ho maisenti-toparlare di taliattività di programmazione e di strategia*," Indigo said, shaking his head in amazement.

"Yes, Indigo, I agree. This is the highest level of planning and strategy we have ever seen outside perhaps, the major powers. This was a military exercise carried out around the world with scary precision and on a scale that boggles the mind. Just for a minute, think about all the people you would have to involve and how you would have to maintain the tightest security for a period of years. Even the US and Israel have trouble achieving that." The Boss shook his head, emphasizing how deeply these terrorist attacks had affected him.

"Well, you know, I think you might not be so right on one aspect of these attacks," I said.

"Which one?"

"A large number of people." He looked at me, a puzzled frown forming. "Explain." Like a rifle shot fired across the table at me.

"Well, I think we actually have a very small team of people involved here, and I would be very surprised if it were more than a dozen or so."

"*Benedici anima mia, solo twelveterroristi*?" exclaimed Indigo.

"*Il colonnello, signore, sonod'accordo con il bel capitano. Essa non avreb-bemoltepersone preparate per montarequestotipo di attacchi.*" Luigi was as emphatic as I had been because, as a tech-head, he could probably imagine just how easy it was these days to run things using computers, cameras, robotics, and AI. He also had the advantage of having been inside the minds of the terrorists because he had successfully cracked their access points into the system and seen what they had been able to achieve firsthand.

"Lay it out for me," the Boss asked, enjoying the interplay. I looked at Luigi, and he nodded, ready to support my deductions.

"Okay, one master planner, four drivers, and one, perhaps two, to run the remote-control point."

"*Inoltre il pilota di sessofemminile, e forse uno o due esperti computer hacker*," added Luigi.

"Yes, a couple of hackers would round it out nicely, and the female pilot is a given."

"So, ten to twelve people in all, and does that include the people who got the bombs from the US, and the Hellfires from wherever, and the explosives from Australia? Does it include the people who obtained the Hercules, the UAV, and set up the trucks?" the Boss asked, putting the pressure on. The two Italians recoiled slightly from the Boss's tone of voice, but I knew exactly what he was doing; he was forcing me to justify my deductions. Across from me, Pete just sat and grinned, happy for me to be the focus of the Boss's intensity for a change. To borrow a term the Boss had just used, this was "SOP" for him.

"Okay. I'll grant you teams spread around the globe to provide the infrastructure, but I stick with my deduction on the size of the attacking team. I think we have five or six very tight cells here, each tasked with a cradle-to-grave strategy, totally responsible for their aspect of the attacks, isolated from each other, and only concerned with the specifics of what they had to achieve. If you follow that logic, the pilot plus someone, maybe two to three of the terrorists on the outside, probably got the bombs, the Hercules, the Hellfires, and the UAV. Your computer hackers set everything up electronically, wiped out all the forensic data, created the documents and security clearances, and provided the information database. One or two running the remote-control point, no need for physical contact with anyone else, all they had to do was obtain the necessary equipment, and that could have been done exactly the same way as the bombs were lifted. The only real human intervention, physically, is that someone collected the radioactive material and packaged it so that it would do its job. But that could have been one of the four people in the two trucks if you look at them as players, not just drivers. To me, less is more, and I think we are dealing with the brightest, cleverest, most highly motivated terrorists we have ever come across, with a brilliant strategist providing the game plan and probably the money."

"Okay, then, we need to concentrate on motive, means, and opportunity. We need to find the money trail, and we need to track this female pilot and find out where she came from. We need a top-down strategy—how many people in the world can fly remotely piloted UAVs, how many of them have experience in bomb runs, and don't forget, they were flying three entirely different types of aircraft that do not have similar flight characteristics. That funnel should produce someone of interest."

"*Mi scusi, il miocolonnello, che non puòessere il caso del tutto*," Luigi said, looking a tiny bit scared of how the Colonel might react.

"*Va bene*, Luigi," I said, "the Colonel will hear you out; we are a team." He immediately looked relieved, although I was not sure how much English he really had. "*Il mio capitano, forsesipuòspiegare il colonnello come è facile preogram-l'UAV, a presentareiloroattacchi*?" Luigi asked. I looked at the Boss and shook my head. I knew he spoke Italian as well as a local, so he was playing the dumb game for a reason.

"Boss, Luigi wants to know if you understand how easy it is to program a UAV to make those attacks," I said, watching for his response. No tells that I could detect, but then this was a man that had been shot several times and lived to face another gun another day.

"No, I don't. That's what I thought I sent you to Afghanistan for," he replied. I smiled at the implied insult, finally understanding what the Boss was doing. He wasn't sure Indigo, Stefarino, or Pete understood the technical aspects of what we were trying to make sense of, and he didn't want to embarrass them by asking. So he wanted it spelled out in clear and precise terms that everyone could understand.

"Boss, if you take each attack and break it down, assuming you have inside control of the ATC and radar environments, each attack was, in a sense, quite broad."

"What do you mean?"

"Rome was a carpet-bombing exercise run by altitude, time, and DGPS coordinates, using a laser designator for fine-tuning the point of impact. All computer controlled, all predictable, and manageable remotely if not by preprogramming on the ground."

"I see. And Jerusalem?"

"Different, but the same; the bad guys used the sun reflecting off the dome as their primary target; the Hellfires had infrared seekers and used an electronic locator to home in on and bring down the wall. Again, simple programming in this day and age, and well within the capabilities of most computer gamers."

"Uh-huh. And West Point?"

"The easiest of the lot. Canisters full of bomblets, designed for area denial, just line up on the centerline of your target area and program the drop. The only really difficult part of this attack was the mid-air refueling. I didn't know computers or remote operators could do that."

"Well, now, it would seem that my funnel will be a waste of time," the Boss said somewhat reflectively, but I wasn't falling for that trap, been around him too long.

"Actually, your funnel idea will work; all you have to do is refine it a little and apply it to each of the technologies." He looked at me as if to ask what I was waiting for, but I cut across him, the nagging thought at the back of my mind finally forcing its way to the front.

"Boss, if you don't mind, can you share with us what you learned from the meeting with Arie Rosenberg?" I asked, putting on my best and most charming face. Suddenly, amusement creased his lined face, and I knew I had scored a minor victory; he thought I had forgotten the meeting with the Israeli Intelligence expert a day ago. Or was it two? So much had happened that I had lost track of time.

"Arie showed me some video; he had made the same deduction about the attack on the dome you just illustrated for us. Plus, he showed me how the attack on the Grand Mosque went down and the outcome of that attack."

"And?"

"The attack was tightly controlled, taking out great chunks of towers, walls, and gates, but the main part of the mosque, the prayer areas, the central stage, and the Imam quarters were untouched."

It was my turn to say, "I see." I didn't but added to the targeting data from the attack on the dome, a picture was forming, just like the Boss had said it would.

"What next?" I asked. "We seem to be at an informational brick wall if you'll excuse the pun."

"Maybe we are, but like bad guys all over the world, they have made mistakes, and we will find those mistakes and track them down." The Boss looked around the room. "That's what we do, people, that's what we do."

CHAPTER 39

"*Monsieur le Président, vousprésenterimmédiatement à nous la direction de votregroupeterroristeconnu sous le nom de Jihad Al'Alkalemia, ou je vais commander mes bombardiers à effacer vosvilles. Vousavez dix heures.*"

"He says, 'if the Arabians don't hand over the leadership of Jihad Al'Alkalemia in ten hours, they will bomb cities in the Kingdom,'" the interpreter said. Every person in the room was frozen in place, not daring to breathe. World War Three was just hours away, and the entire staff of the NSA wanted to get home to their families and drive up into the hills or out into the desert, anywhere but be in Washington, which they were convinced would be attacked by the terrorists at any time.

"! موجهالنحن ، داهجلاAl'Alkalemiaهذهبطقاوعمسيملنحن ، سيئرلايديس"

"The king denies knowing the terrorists and swears they did not attack France."

"*Monsieur le Président, encore unefois, je l'État, la main sur les chefs terroristes pour nous dans un délai de dix de nosvôtre bombes pleuvent sur vous, comme la colère de Dieu!*"

"The French President is promising the rain of God, ten hours, or it's all over for the Arabians."

"Shit and damnation, that drags us into a nuclear war with the bloody French! Get me the White House!" screamed the duty officer, just one heartbeat away from a stroke.

نحنو!عيظفلا ءيشلا كلذ لعفن مل اننأل ،كيلإ لسوتأ انأ ،سيئرلا يديس" مل اننإ
،رخأ ةرم لوقأو ،ناطيشلا ءانبأ لبق نم ةقيرط عشبأب انمجوه دق انسفنأ !"مجاهن

"Now the king is saying that they have been attacked and swears that the Arabians did not attack France." There was a palpable pause in the eavesdropped transmissions, and being digital, not even a crackle or pop could be heard. Then a sound like someone taking a huge breath filtered through the speakers, and the French president spoke once again.

"*VotreAltesse, je vaisretenirnos bombardiers, maisvousdevez nous donner unepreuveirréfutable, la preuve que jepeux prendre à la population de la France avec conficence total, que vousn'avez pas sponsor, ou le soutien de toute manière, cette terrible attaquecontre le République.*"

"He says he will hold the bombers off for now, but the king has to prove that the Arabians had nothing to do with the attack and prove it now to the satisfaction of the world court."

"And how, exactly, are the bloody Arabians going to be able to do that?"

"Not our problem. Get this transcript to the FBI, CIA, Homeland Security, and to Interpol, ASAP, and where is the White House?" screamed the duty officer again, suddenly grabbing at his side as his face seemed to melt into itself. He slowly collapsed to the floor, shaking and vibrating as if he had been electrocuted. Drool started to leak out of his twisted mouth, and the interpreters looked down at him in shock and awe.

By the time the medics arrived, the duty officer was well on the way to becoming a vegetable, and the room was in an uproar, with analysts and interpreters running all over the place trying to work out what to do next.

Off the coast of North Africa, the French bombers slowly turned back towards their base in France, while in the Kingdom, the king did the only thing possible under the circumstances by directing his staff to call all the heads of every internal security agency together immediately to find the proof the French president had demanded. As he watched his staff bow and scrape their way out of his chambers, he wondered, not for the first time, why life had to be so hard.

He missed the desert, and the peace and tranquility he had enjoyed until his father's death had propelled him center stage. And he just knew that his brothers we constantly plotting to kill him so that they could rule the Kingdom the way they thought it should be done.

He sucked deeply on his hooker and idly fondled one of his wives, totally miserable and completely out of his depth.

CHAPTER 40

Jason Roberts stood alone in the sea of noise on the crowded and littered floor of the New York Stock Exchange, tears flowing down his face, his hands clenched, body bent. In the last thirty minutes, he had gone through Hell, as the value of the portfolios he managed had literally disappeared before his eyes. The rumor that had gone around the world at the speed of a Jedi's lightsaber was that Lloyd's of London, the biggest industrial insurer in the world, had gone bankrupt, potentially defrauding millions of companies billions of dollars in claims and premiums.

Nearly every aircraft, ship, or major industrial facility in the world was either insured directly by Lloyd's or underwritten by a syndicate of "names" from Lloyd's. Without any notice or preamble, the news loop featured on so many cable TV shows on the bottom of the screen simply flickered the message "....at ten past midday Universal Standard Time, Lloyd's of London regrets to announce that all trading will cease for the foreseeable future. While we regret any inconvenience, we believe that the situation will be rectified shortly. Please stand by for further details."

From Jason's perspective, what had happened then was still a blur, but as the NYSE opened to this news, trading was initially not halted because no one actually believed the news ticker, thinking it was a practical joke from the IT department. It took the directors thirty-six minutes to get confirmation that Lloyd's was no longer booking insurance at any level, a time during which the rumors simply overwhelmed the market, and panic set in. Any stock that had an insurance risk associated with it was sold off in a heartbeat, prices plummeting so fast and so far that the directors had no choice but to shut the most famous Exchange in the world down. The NYSE traced its origins all the way back to 1792 when twenty-four New York City stockbrokers and merchants signed the Buttonwood Agreement. Originally called the "curb market" because its brokers traded outdoors in the street, right now, Jason wished more than anything else in the world that that's where he could be, right now, this very minute, out on the street, and not dreading the possibility of facing his syndicate management on whose behalf he had just lost a few billion dollars in as many minutes.

High up on the balcony, sitting in one of the visitor booths, a rather large gentleman, dressed to the hilt in a starched shirt, pin-striped suit, and immaculate brogues, all of which spoke of volumes of money beyond the reach of the average person, slowly stood, reflecting on the carnage playing out below him. He checked his rolled gold Rolex, shot his emerald-encrusted cufflinks, looked left, then right, as if acknowledging the other visitors in the booth, then quickly stepped forward and threw himself over the rail.

The floor trader he landed on after his three-story fall crumpled into a heap, leg bones protruding through his kneecaps, his head lolling from side to side like a bobbing monkey on a car dashboard. While this interaction took some of the stings out of the inevitable collision with the ground, the gentleman had rather unluckily fallen in such a manner that his neck and head hit the floor unimpeded, reducing his spine to a series of chips and fractures, and his head to a bloody pulp. He had traveled all the way from Wisconsin the day before to personally witness the listing of his new company, one he had put his entire life into, as well as the stolen funds from several trust accounts he supposedly managed in isolation from his normal financial duties.

Unknowingly, thousands of normal families went about their daily routine, or as routine as it could be given the current state of the world, totally unaware that their life savings, mortgages, retirement funds, and 401-K's had literally hit the deck, never to be seen again.

CHAPTER 41

Three of the four special agents who sat in front of the director of the FBI were nervous to a fault, realizing that not only in this case might the messenger be shot but also hung, drawn, and quartered just for good measure. The forty-odd support staff sitting behind them on fold-up chairs were just as uncomfortable. The mood of the country was bleak, to say the least, with all commercial air travel suspended and the use of motor vehicles limited to emergency use only. Public transport was stretched to the limit, and fully half of the American workers simply could not get to their jobs, further adding to the economic chaos created by the failure of Lloyd's and the terrorist attacks. Adding to the chaos was an untypical snowstorm that had literally submerged the Midwest, and every newspaper, TV, and radio station, backed up by massive public outcry on the World Wide Web, was screaming for vengeance without delay. "Let's go kill the m'f'ers, NOW!" was the consensus; the trouble was, of course, that no one actually knew yet whom to go and bomb back to the Stone Age or beyond.

One thing that had gone "right," if you were an extreme optimist, thought Roger Winslow was that Interpol's Colonel Anthony had been able to provide a secure method of communication and data swapping from some unknown source. And that connectivity had provided both the FBI and Interpol with the benefit of exchanging and comparing data in real-time and making some small headway in identifying the perpetrators. And if the director was brutally honest, that was the only reason he now had three nervous agents sitting in front of him waiting to tell him their stories. His instinct to contact the head of Interpol's anti-terrorist Section five, and being open and honest with him, had proven to be a good one. "You first," he barked, pointing at one of his most senior field agents, Thomas Robertson, a long, thin man of African American heritage with huge eyes and a flawless reputation for detail. His hair was so short it looked like he had painted it on his head, and his long, thin face looked a little taught as if he had plastic surgery just before the meeting.

"Sir, we have over three hundred agents manually following the trail of the female pilot and the weapons that were used in the attacks both here and overseas, and we now have some of her histories as far back as nineteen eighty-nine."

"Manually following?" the director asked, mildly amused at the terminology. "Yes, sir. As you know, there are absolutely no electronic records available on any database we have access to, and I believe we have access to all. So, over the past two days, we have followed a physical trail by interviewing everyone who had ever worked with her, met her, gone to college wither her, that sort of thing. Of course, once we had her name confirmed, we were able to speed up the process somewhat by making direct enquiries as well.

"But I am confident we have an accurate story on her at this time." The director looked down at the thick report that he had read earlier, tapping it with one finger.

"You don't speculate on her whereabouts prior to nineteen eighty-nine. Why is that?" the director asked. He had found the report interesting for what it didn't say as much as for what it did.

"Sir, we have not been able to trace her parents at all, other than by word of mouth. No DMV, social security, paper, or electronic data of any type. We do have good physical descriptions, which we included in the report, but for all intents and purposes, they have never existed officially and have completely disappeared as well."

"But a few years earlier than the pilot?" the director asked.

"Yes, sir, they seem to have fallen off the face of the earth around two thousand two."

"Around the time Interpol believed that the terrorists started to actively hack into our computers?"

"Yes, sir."

"And we don't know where they came from or when?"

"No, sir. They could be indigenous or immigrants; we simply have no records, but from the descriptions, it is logical to assume that they were immigrants of some type."

"What about the Interpol idea of tracking back to pre-computer times, to find physical documents that preceded the switch to electronic data entry?" the director asked. He already knew the answer to this; the NSA had successfully established the transition point for him using the data supplied by Interpol, but he wanted to see how thorough his lead agent had been.

"We did that, sir; we physically searched every file from nineteen sixty up to the point where we went electronic. We picked that date because we believe the age of the pilot puts anyone surrounding her outside that date range." The director tapped the report a little harder, starting to feel the frustration starting to build inside him again.

"Your conclusion?" he asked, snapping at the agent like an angry Rottweiler.

"Sir, we believe the parents were illegal immigrants, furnished with fake social security numbers and other personal data, living in the community as normal people. In fact, the profile is amazingly similar to the Russian "sleepers" we have encountered in years past." The director suddenly looked up; this was new, and he had not heard anything like this from the analysts working in the background, checking every single detail that the agents had been uncovering. "Russians?"

"Yes, sir, although we are not prepared to say that they were Russian 'sleepers,' we are prepared to say that the methodology is very similar."

"Clients of the Russians?" he asked.

"Quite possibly." The director reached for the phone, holding his other hand up in the time-honored "halt" position.

"Mable, get me my counterpart at the Russian Embassy, please." He fiddled with the cord, then pushed the speakerphone button, replaced the handset, and leaned back in his orthopedically designed chair.

“Роджермойдруг, привет!” boomed out through the desk speaker as every head in the director’s office turned towards it.

“Hello, Sergei. I need your help on something, please.”

“Certainly, my friend, in these treacherous times, friends must always provide whatever help they can, eh?” The director nodded, remembering an old Russian adage about keeping your enemies close and your friends even closer!

“Sergei, we have reason to believe that the female pilot that bombed West Point may have been a ‘sleeper,’ or part of a ‘sleeper’ family, and the best information we have is that her family was styled or managed along the same lines as all those families of yours that gave us so much entertainment over the years during the Cold War. What I’m interested in is if you were training any particular country in those techniques back in the sixties and seventies.”

“Roger, please, my friend, I’m shocked to think we ever behaved that way towards our old and greatest ally, the United States!” The director smiled, wiping his hand across his face. He was tired. He was disturbed. He was short on humor. Particularly of the Russian variety.

“Sergei, forget it. I just want to know who your client states were at that time and who you were running through USAville. Names would be great, but if all you can manage is the identification of participating countries, that would also be greatly appreciated.”

“I will call Moscow immediately, my friend. I take it you need to know this urgently?” The director hooded his eyes with his hands, tiredness washing over him like a tidal wave.

“Yes. Please. Thank you.” He looked at the agents sitting on the other side of the table, wondering how long the Russians would take. Even if he got an honest answer, which, as far as the Russians were concerned, was always doubtful, he wasn’t sure where it might take the investigation. He turned his attention back to the agent sitting uncomfortably in front of his desk. “Where were we?” he asked. “Sir, our pilot worked for a contractor for the last two years and nine months at Andrews. She was recruited from the Air Force, where her final posting had been working as a test pilot based at Mojave Airport. She was responsible for testing the QF-4 Phantoms that were converted into military target drones. We believe that's where she gained the skills to convert the A-10 into an RPV."

"And before that?"

"Exemplary record in the Air Force for ten years graduated top of her class from the Academy, got her pick of assignments, chose fighters, started on F-16s, was selected for test pilot school, topped her class, went to an F-22 Raptor squadron, became an instructor, then moved into the Phantom program at the request of the Weapons Research Establishment (WRE) when the opportunity came up." The director tapped the thick file again, his agitation finally starting to show.

"Did she ever fly anywhere in Europe?" he asked.

"Yes, sir, posted to Turkey for eighteen months, spent ten of those flying with the Israelis helping out their conversion to the F-16AF. She was rated as the best American pilot we ever lent them."

"What specifically did she work on with the Israelis?" the director asked. "All the preand post-test flying and training for the installation of the Mark-71 missile system and an integrated navigation and electronics package. It's where she earned her credentials in that sort of work, and it was the same contractor on the Israeli program that was doing the work on the A-10s at Andrews."

"You've checked them out?" the director asked, already knowing the answer. About ten seconds after the attack, Homeland Security, the CIA, and the FBI placed every person, company, and organization that might have been marginally involved under the most intrusive and intense scrutiny, applying the full force of Homeland Security and the Anti-terrorist Act in the process. In fact, over a thousand people incarcerated at the time for questioning were still locked up somewhere in the system, waiting for some sort of outcome, their only crime being that they turned up for work that day.

"Yes, sir. They seem clean. They have produced everything we have asked for, provided hundreds of people for interviews, and have been very open from the get-go. Their computer systems were compromised, as were ours, with only one slight difference. They seem to have been penetrated in two thousand nineteen, long after the terrorists slipped into our systems."

"But that's it?" the director asked.

"Yes, sir, on the surface, they appear to be a legitimate contractor with all the necessary defense security clearances." The director wiped his forehead again as if purging his mind. The pilot was still a mystery, to some extent, but not the aircraft, because the navy had it in its gun sights. Or so they said.

"Johan, what have we found out about the A-10?" he asked. The second young special agent suddenly sat a little straighter in his seat, feeling the eyes of everyone in the room suddenly swing towards him.

"Sir, the A-10 was modified with the new LanMap-SatAttackPac (LM-SAP) as part of the block number three upgrade planned for the whole fleet. The aircraft was being tested under virtual combat conditions as part of the final acceptance trials before large-scale implementation."

"How did the terrorists turn it into a remotely piloted vehicle?" the director asked. The special agent looked embarrassed as if he were personally responsible for the misuse of the aircraft.

"Sir, as part of the upgrade, the control system was modified to the latest digital standard, which allows for control from the ground in an emergency situation.

"Unfortunately, it also allows for direct control by a suitably equipped RPV control center. Swapping out the command codes and security locks is relatively simple, given that they are designed to be used on the battlefield, under assumed stressful conditions."

"So, taking the plane and then piloting it remotely was a relatively simple exercise?"

"Sadly, yes, Director."

"Okay, that leaves you, Agent Richardson; what have you learned?" The third special agent suddenly sat straighter in his chair and opened a folder with a massive red band around it. The fact that the director had called him by his surname and not his first name as he had with the other two agents was not lost on him.

"Sir, our technology division has followed up on the weapons data supplied by Interpol, and we have now physically searched every weapons store, and we have positive identification on the weapons used in Rome. Sometime between two thousand one and two thousand three, the bombs were removed from the factory and the records substituted. Without computer records or physical evidence, we can't be any more definite than that. But we can say they both came from the same location because the forensic evidence is identical in each case."

"How does someone switch out a twenty-five-thousand-pound bomb?" the young special agent named Johan asked, risking a stare from the director. Agent Richardson almost smiled but caught himself just in time.

"We asked the armorers that very question and ran a simulation using the war room at the Pentagon; six teams from different bases, it took them three days to agree on the method, but once they had, we went in and ran a full-scale test, right up to the point where we loaded a bomb into a Special Forces C-130J. It really was simple." Every head in the room turned to look at the special agent, some with disbelief embedded in their eyes. The idea of stealing a twenty-five-thousand-pound anything was hard to get their minds around, let alone a highly classified bomb with the destructive power of a small nuclear weapon from a highly secured military base in the heart of America.

"Sir, the terrorists had control of the computers, from the supply side to the delivery and receipt side. Bombs are normally delivered in batches, but the really big ones like the FABs (Fuel air burst) and daisy cutters are too large to send in batch lots, so they are usually trucked and flown to their destination one at a time. What happens here turned out to be really, really simple. The bombs left the factory as planned, went onto a transport as planned, then disappeared, sending the receiving station a delay-of-delivery message. Then three days later, a second bomb is delivered, with the ID and paperwork matching the first bomb. It goes into the records, is stored, then gets used or remains stored for its useful service life. A few days after the deliveries, the terrorists go back into the computer records and remove an item from the batch processing data at the factory, and by the time of the first physical audit, everything adds up."

"But someone took the two bombs, in aircraft, from the loading point to somewhere else, with a lot of hardware and people involved. Twice."

"Yes, sir, but again the war gamers were able to demonstrate how easy that would have been. The aircrew was briefed by system documents generated by their headquarters or one of the field commands—Weapons and Targets, Airlift, or Transport, all of which generate 'orders' that are coordinated in turn by one of the area commands. The aircrews know they have to fly to destination "A," load materiel "X," and transport it to destination "B," where it is unloaded. Weapons are shipped unarmed, inert, and largely unidentified, so apart from local curiosity, if you controlled the scheduling process, you could literally move anything from anywhere to anywhere you had logistical command and control support, no questions asked, all safely within the system."

"And these weapons were highly classified, so moving them secretly fits in perfectly with the requirements of the terrorists. So you are saying that these bombs left the factory and then were airlifted by the Air Force straight to their destination, in plain sight, and no one asked a single question about the process?"

"Yes, sir. Our war gamers believe the bombs were delivered to either Turkey or one of our other bases in that theater as a normal uplift, in total secrecy as required, and then repositioned by the terrorists in their own time. Needless to say, the security at a forward base is nothing like what we maintain here in the States, and if you were on the receiving end of a shipment of very large weapons and all the paperwork was in order, you would be expecting it to be used by someone equipped for the job. All they would need is the right tasking orders from the correct command."

"So, when an aircraft with the right marking arrives in the middle of the night, with the correct paperwork, and collects the weapons, it's business as usual."

"Yes, sir." The director wiped his face for the umpteenth time, now looking as weary as he felt.

"From the start, we have believed that the terrorists penetrated our IT systems globally back in nineteen ninety-nine or thereabouts, just before the Y2K debacle. What have we learned on that front?" All four special agents froze in their seats, not wanting to be the messenger. Down the back of the room, a lone figure stood up, a wan smile creasing a tiny face that looked like it had suffered a stroke. A cascade of blond hair that had escaped the regulation length for a month flopped around his head, creating the impression he was nervous.

He was, but not about the data he was about to share. "Sir, I think I can help in that area."

"And you are?" the director asked, flicking through his c-pad to match the face to his ID database.

"Malcolm Tannery, sir, from the NSA." The director looked up in surprise, suddenly realizing that this was one of Frank Reynolds' "stars" over at the National Security Agency, the organization most impacted by the terrorists so far, as computers, technology, and security were their stock-in-trade, and they hated the thought that they had been outsmarted for two or more decades by a bunch of terrorists—no matter how smart or clever they were!

"Speak, Malcolm."

"Sir, using the baseline data provided to us by Interpol, we were able to track and trace the penetration of our systems back to nineteen ninety-nine. We have successfully identified all the code, backdoors, programs, and spoofs the terrorists implanted and backtracked two of their activities to identifiable sites." The room seemed to freeze; was this the first major breakthrough in the case? People turned in their chairs, some almost twisting themselves in half, trying to see the diminutive analyst from the NSA.

"Identifiable sites as in…?

"As in two distinct geographical areas, in one case around three hundred square miles in area, and in the other about four thousand square miles." You could have dropped a hand grenade in the room, and no one would have noticed, so focused was everyone on the NSA analyst. He slowly stood and walked with an uneven gait to the director's desk and placed a colored map under the digital projector. A split screen image swam into focus, one side showing a desert area identified as "Terrorist site #0001," and on the other, a rural farming mountainous area identified as "Terrorist site #0002."

"And these would be where?" the director asked, doing his best to hold his temper in check.

"Montana on the right, and Libya on the left," the analyst answered. "Montana?"

"Montana. Exactly where we don't know yet, hence the rather large area we have indicated."

"Holy mother of God," muttered one of the support staff. No one in the room had expected genuine American nationals to be involved in the terrorist attacks.

"What are we doing to isolate a more precise target?" the director asked, wondering for what seemed to be the millionth time why the NSA continually played their cards so close to their collective chests! This was time-critical data that should have been shared across the security agencies at the speed of light. And then, the director suddenly remembered that only the FBI had a securitized communication system for the time being, and he calmed down a little.

"Sir, we have keyhole satellites sitting over the epicenter of each location twenty-four seven, so any radiation in the observable spectrum will be detected. We also will have teams on the ground supported by helicopters equipped with detection gear working in Montana. Libya is a little harder asset-wise, and we are hoping you can help us out there." The director listened with one ear, already trying to scope what assets he could put on the ground to expedite the detection of the terrorist cell in the US. As for the keyhole satellites, they had a finite over-the-target time dictated by their orbits, and he knew from past experience that there would be inevitable gaps in their real-time coverage.

"What are you looking for in Libya?" he asked.

"Sir, it would be nice if you could arrange for one of our carrier groups to be in place to provide side-scan coverage because the area we have identified is not all that large, and a couple of aircraft flying the right pattern could provide pinpoint accuracy when the terrorists broadcast again."

"I'll organize something through navy, but it might take a little time because we can't use electronic communications yet." The director thought for a second, then looked the NSA analyst square in the eyes. "Or can we?"

"Sir, as I said, we believe that we have traced every source of the terrorist's intrusion, and there is no evidence that they have been tampering with encrypted military communications, just the so-called securitized data files. Which, by the way, are all being re-encrypted in our latest one-zero-five-six bit code as we speak." The director smiled to himself, excellent after-the-disaster action as usual! The single terrorist event that worried him the most was Interpol's report about how easy it had been for them to take kilos of nuclear material out of the system undetected in broad daylight. So far, the terrorists had only used the material they had stolen to pollute the Arabian oil fields. But what if they had more material hidden away, waiting to be used on another soft target?

"Okay, to prioritize, you want eyes and ears on Libya. Our mystery pilot is still a mystery, is that it?" he asked, looking around the room. No one moved, all too aware that the director's boiling point was not too far away. "Okay then, Senior Special Agent Bernstein, what have you learned about the priest that started all this?" he asked, looking at the last agent in the seats sitting before his desk. An older woman, dressed immaculately in a dark pants suit with a muted scarf around her neck, could have been anyone's mother, let alone one of the best detectives in the FBI. Having survived the hugely difficult climb up through the sectarian boys' club that the FBI was for nearly fifty years, she was not only tough but hardened to the inevitable verbal backscatter that continually swirled around her like a dust storm.

"Mister Director, as you know, the Jesuit priest Brother Fernández Gómez received a message from one Al Hemish al-bin Mohammad Karesish while they were both working as teachers in a refugee camp in Lebanon, formally known as Gouraud, in Baalbeck. This camp was subsequently closed by UNRWA in the early nineties. The message was simple and, we now believe, literal. The message was in two parts—'His God cannot look down upon what is happening in the camps without crying tears of blood,' and 'The children of God have spoken.' If you want the fuller version, his statement to Brother Gómez was, 'Our children are very bright, and one day they will be the power on this earth. I have decided to take them away from here and help them on their quest. Do this for me, as your brother before your God. One day, many years from now, when you receive the broken body of an infidel woman, go and tell the president of all the world that the children of God have spoken. Do this for me, and for all the little children we have buried together and prayed for all these years.'"

"How did we find out his name?" the director asked.

"The UN had good paper records for all the camps that the French were supporting from nineteen sixty-seven to nineteen ninety-five. Al Hemish al-bin Mohammad Karesish was registered with them as a teacher and a doctor; he was, at one time, only seventh removed from the Arabian throne."

"What do we know of him?"

"Rich as Croesus, studied in France at le Sorbonne, in the UK at Manchester and London, then at Wharton in the US. Top of his class, highly respected, and a bit of an intellectual according to his peers, but he is always passionate about the refugee situation in Sudan and North Africa. Some of his relatives ended up in camps because of where they grew up, and his youngest brother died in one camp while his big brother was studying overseas. As you know, the Arabian money tree is not necessarily organized along traditional family lines, and blood relatives somewhat removed from the mainstream are often left to their own resources."

"What got him involved in Lebanon?"

"When he came back from the US, it seems that his family was on the out with the then-king, and he was sent to work as a doctor with the Muslim refugees who were emerging all over the Middle East because of the war with Israel, and then the war with Egypt. Camps were springing up all over Lebanon, Syria, Jordan, and northern Iraq as thousands and thousands of people were displaced. By all accounts, he became very involved at that time with the terrorist organization identified as "Hussein Blasck," or "The Tears of Blood." This group was largely passive until nineteen eighty-six when they bombed the American Embassy in Cairo."

"How did he move around the various countries he studied in?" the director asked.

"We've tracked British and French passports; he had dual nationality, and we believe he has several other passports in different identities. Once we knew what to look for, we pulled up entry and exit photos from Customs and Border Security that shows he has been here in the US several times, always under a different name, and sometimes even leaving under a different name, right up to two thousand four, when we introduced biometric identification. We have no trace of him from that time."

"So, what did he do in the camps?"

"Initially worked as a doctor, then when the camps started to get more organized with French and UN help, started a series of schools, some of which lasted for nearly twenty years. This is where he recruited his cell members from."

"The schools?"

"Yes. Picked out the brightest of the bright and then paid for them to attend a proper school in either the UK, France, Spain, Italy, Israel, or the US. Lodged them with families that were sympathetic to his cause, then as the children graduated high school, he moved them on to who knows where."

"What do you mean?"

"When they leave high school, they literally disappear. We have no trace of the children from that point."

"Photos, friends, something from the families they boarded with?"

"Nothing. It seems that our terrorist friend went into a lot of trouble to make sure that any documentation with useful information was either destroyed or compromised. Even a school yearbook that had photos of one of the children completely disappeared through a combination of accidents and, we now suspect, arson. He must have had huge resources because, by our best estimate, he moved some thirty children out of the system during a ten-year period, and there is not a single trace of them that we can find. Even the descriptions we have obtained from some of the families with whom they originally stayed are vague, bordering on useless. Too much time gone, and we got onto this far, far too late."

"What's your best guess?" asked the director. Anyone else would have begged off answering on the basis of a lack of clear evidence, but Anna Bernstein had learned long ago to trust her gut, so without hesitation, she placed a thin purple folder on the desk in front of the director.

"I believe the children were moved into families that were what we used to call 'sleepers,' as discussed earlier, and positioned in different countries where the children continued their education, then entered the workforce in different disciplines. Disciplines, which I might add, were probably chosen for them by our master terrorist."

"What do you base this assessment on?" the director asked, moving the "guess" to "good" intelligence with his question.

"By backwards modeling the story of our female pilot, it becomes obvious to me that she was no accident, and if you go all the way back to where she came from, I think you see the basics of a pattern."

"Explain."

"Well, we know nothing about her until she enters the Air Force Academy, as Agent Robertson mentioned in his report. Her whole family eventually disappears, so her history as we know it starts and finishes with a mystery."

"Where did she come from, and where did she go to?"

"Yes, sir. Her clearance level was so high that she had to have been backgrounded by the FBI several times and the Air Force at least three times. Yet she passed these checks with flying colors, if you'll forgive the pun, and worked at the highest level inside the military for many years."

"Have you reviewed her service record?"

"Yes, sir, those bits that still remain in the system. The computer people are still trying to rebuild most of it, but my assumption is made on what we don't have more than what we do have." The director rubbed his eyes again, the tiredness breaking through in spite of his best efforts to disguise it. "For example, we now know, thanks to Interpol, that the A-10 was remotely piloted. As was the UAV which attacked Jerusalem. Interpol believes that the L-200 Hercules that bombed Rome was also remotely piloted. One thing you can't hide is the specific mix of electronic waves that make up guidance and control inputs, and as you know, the NSA captures everything transmitted in real-time. We have been able to isolate the specific signals that were used to manage all three remotely piloted vehicles." At this, the director sat upright in his chair as if he suddenly had a new lease on life.

"We have?"

"Yes, sir. The bursts were encrypted, but there is no doubt they were steering signals and time-stamps for the RPVs."

"Where did they come from?"

"That, sir, is the big question. We know where they went and how they got there, but we cannot locate a source." The director thought for a minute, then scanned the faces of the four special agents.

"Okay, explain the how."

"Sir, the terrorists used the French Landsat satellite mapping network for the carriage and delivery of all RPV signals."

"The bloody French again!" the director muttered under his breath. "How did the signals get up to the satellites?"

"No idea, sir. It's as if they were already up there, just waiting to be used." The director thought this piece of data over for a minute, then waved to the NSA agent Malcolm Tannery.

"Mister Tannery, a moment, please. Everyone else, well done, please go and find me these terrorists as fast as you can." As everyone stood to leave the director's office, Anna Bernstein fiddled with her briefcase, just long enough to make sure the director and the NSA analyst were the only people left in the office.

"Sir, if I may, I would like to make a suggestion," she said, subtly positioning herself between the NSA analyst and the director's desk. Malcolm Tannery looked a little bemused, the director a little taken aback. "There is a consistent pattern here, one that I believe we are missing in the main."

"And that is?" the director asked, curious in spite of his immediate personal agenda being hijacked.

"Sir, we tend to look at the very high end of the data stream, and I think we have overlooked a lot of information that might help us if we could only focus on it a little lower down, as it were."

"Give me an example," the director demanded, a little more forcibly than he meant to.

"Sir, these attacks are all about people and icons. Why attack West Point? It's a soft target at best. When you think about it, killing the navy chief was a fluke, collateral damage at best. What was the message they were trying to send?" The director looked bemused; this aspect had cost him a lot of sleep over the past few days, and as yet, he had no firm idea to offer.

"What are you getting at?"

"Sir, I believe that if the terrorists were really trying to send us a message, they would have hit a higher value target. Taking the attack literally, symbolically, I believe that this was to punish us by killing some of our 'children'—the cadets— to remind us of the disaster of the camps.

I don't think this was a terrorist attack in the sense that we have gotten used to." The director paused; this was an aspect he had not considered. He nodded slowly, suddenly realizing that the female instinct to nurture and preserve was constantly overlooked in situations like this, where male egos tended to dominate, seeking answers to justify hitting back at the unseen enemy. He motioned with his hand.

"Go on."

"When you look at the targets clinically, you see a definite pattern emerging, and while I know we are mainly concerned with what happened here, the European attacks seem to have the same sort of pattern."

"Which is?"

"Punishment."

"Punishment?" the director asked.

"Punishment. I've talked this through with some of my people in our behavioral unit, and we think there is a clear message being sent here that is aimed at three, possibly four, different audiences. Very strong, unmistakable messages." The director looked astonished; none of the hundreds of analysts that had been pouring over the data for nearly a full week had come up with anything like this. He wondered for a brief second if his lead agent was suffering some kind of mental breakdown, then dismissed the thought just as quickly. Anna Bernstein was many things, but mentally challenged was not one of them.

"Talk to me."

"Well, start with the attack on Rome. Who had the most to lose when you eliminate the collateral damage to commercial buildings and loss of civilian life?"

"The Roman Catholic Church. Almost all their leaders worldwide were killed in that one attack. It's thrown them into chaos for the first time that anyone can remember."

"Yes, sir, plus they lost thousands of years of religious artifacts, the very icons upon which they have based many of their beliefs and rituals."

"So they are being punished, as you put it, because…?"

"Throughout documented history, the Roman Catholic Church or its agents sponsored or directly instigated more religious pogroms throughout Europe and the rest of the world than any other political or religious body. Just for starters, two thousand years of bloody murder, persecution, and political and religious dominance. If you were one of the 'lesser' religions, wouldn't an attack like this at the very seat of Catholic power light your fire?" The director smiled at Anna's use of modern idiomatic language, something he didn't hear very often. "Now, the telling point for me was the data from Interpol that suggest that in the attack on the Dome of the Rock, perhaps the most sacred religious site in the world, the buildings, and surrounding infrastructure were specifically targeted, but the Rock left unscratched."

"Meaning what?" he asked.

"Meaning that the terrorists, in this case, were sending another message, probably to the Jews and the Christians—hands off our Rock, or some such."

"Anna, you're Jewish?"

"Yes, sir."

"What does the Rock mean to you?"

"Well, to be truthful, not a lot, but in our culture, to the Jewish people, it is Ir Ha-Kodesh (the Holy City), the Biblical Zion, the City of David, the site of Solomon's Temple, and the eternal capital of the Israelite nation. There's an awful lot of religious history associated with Mount Moriah, and let's face it, the Wailing Wall, or Western Wall as it is called now, is the most visited religious site by Jews in all of Jerusalem."

"Maybe not so much now," the director said, reflecting on the fact that the terrorists had also deliberately targeted the Wall, smashing it into a million fragments.

"No, sir."

"Who gains with the destruction of the infrastructure around the Rock and the Wall?"

"Well, sir, the Jews lose with the Wall coming down, and the Christians lose with the buildings being shredded. The Muslins win big time because they have always claimed the Rock as theirs, going back as far as the ninth Caliph, Abd al-Malik, who built the great Dome of the Rock between six eighty-seven and six ninety-one. Also, you have the significance the Muslims attach to Mount Moriah itself, where they believe Mohammad arrived on his mystic night journey escorted by the Archangel Gabriel. Riding on a winged steed called El Burak, they landed at Temple Mount and encountered Abraham, Moses, Jesus, and other prophets. As legend has it, Muhammad supposedly led them all in prayers. Right there, you have a dominant motivation to work with."

"You obviously know your Middle Eastern history."

"Sir, being a Jew, living in the Midwest, and being female, you didn't really have much of a choice if you wanted to keep up with the boys!" Anna said, smiling for the first time since she had entered the director's office.

"Anna, let's say for the moment we go with this punishment theme of yours; where do the attacks on the Arabian oil field and the Grand Mosque fit in?"

"Well, sir, given that our terrorist friend Mohammad Karesish is an Arabian and is in line for the throne, albeit at a bit of a distance, I think he is punishing the Kingdom for what he perceives as their greed and reliance on oil and its westernization—moving away from the true tenets of Islam." The director nodded, having arrived at a similar conclusion.

"And the attack on the Grand Mosque?"

"A message to the Imams: keep the faith and don't despoil the Koran and the fundamentals of Islamic beliefs by supporting some of the terrorist activities. If you remember, sir, the areas that are the most sacred to the pilgrims, as well as the Imam quarters, were untouched by the truck bomb."

"Yes."

"And one other thing about that attack—the symbology of using a truck bomb, which would have normally been a suicide attack, should not go unnoticed."

"I see. Our terrorist doesn't mind blowing things up, but not his people. Okay, Anna, I get all that, but how do you explain the attack on Avignon?"

"Can't explain that one, sir, except to hypothesize that as the second seat of the Holy See—you might recall that the Pope was situated there back in the fourteen hundreds—it was attacked to limit the options of the Catholic Church in their rebuilding efforts."

"Doesn't really fit."

"No, sir, if you want our opinion, we believe it may be someone else using the primary terrorist attacks as an excuse to get their own chop in."

"Based on what?" the director asked, knowing that his analysts had actually arrived at this conclusion as well.

"The apparent use of suicide bombers, for starters; our terrorist friend has gone to great pains to keep his 'children' alive throughout all the other attacks, plus the fact that several vans were used, parked strategically, then exploded simultaneously, whereas every other attack has been a single precision strike at a defined target."

"Well, we agree with you on that one, Anna; how does Lloyd's crash fit into your punishment scenario?" Anna smiled again, thinking about the late-night session just completed with her team trying to understand the message contained in this massive, financially motivated worldwide precision strike that involved no weapons other than the ability to destroy electronic data.

"Well, sir, we have the terrorists penetrating our computer network as far back as nineteen ninety-nine. They obviously have some very talented hackers— most likely technical geniuses, working in the system somewhere, completely at ease because no one will ever suspect their involvement. Getting the electronic bombs into Lloyd's system would have been a massive effort, but we think it is quite achievable given their level of demonstrated expertise. Especially as they had, literally, all the time in the world. Or, at the very least, two decades or so to work with."

"Who are they punishing?" the director asked, already suspecting Anna's probable answer.

"Everyone who stood by all those years when the camps were filling up and shipping their dead onto funeral pyres because no one really did anything to help or stop the disaster from unfolding—and in point of fact, we still sit by while refugee camps in Africa and the Middle East continue to fill up. My people have interviewed families who are third- and fourth-generation refugees, the camps being the only life they have known for as long as they can remember. He's financially punishing us, everyone, and hitting us in the pocket, where it really hurts personally, for continuing to turn a blind eye to the plight in the camps."

"Okay, Anna, be that as it may, we still have to catch the bastard and all his so-called children. How do you suggest we go about that?"

"I'd like all our notes and data sent to Interpol, and I'd like a team to help me to backtrack our lady pilot more thoroughly. I understand the navy was a little embarrassed when the pictures taken from the sub appeared on the Net?" The director smiled, remembering the conversation with the joint chiefs when it had been learned that the navy had tried to keep the fact that it appeared as if the pilot was still inside the submerged aircraft. When the photos were leaked onto the World Wide Web, they had to quickly deny any such assumption on the basis that the images were too blurred to be certain. The rest of the intelligence community had roundly condemned the navy for their secrecy, knowing only too well that they would have probably done exactly the same under similar circumstances.

"That they were, that they were. Okay, I suggest you get to Andrews, and I'll arrange for you to be flown to Europe to hook up with the lead Interpol Agents working the case over there. Don't know where they are, but I will by the time you are airborne."

"Why send me to Europe?" Anna asked, unable to hide the shock in her voice. "Because you need some specialized help, and the team I am sending you to can give it to you better than anyone I know. Leave the pilot and her history to me. Now go."

DRONE

The McDonald Douglas F4 Phantom, tail number 2-3347, had a long and checkered a history as the companies whose name it still bore. Both McDonald's and the Douglas Aircraft Corporation had long gone, sucked up by fitter, larger, hungry companies who in the 1980s were hellbent on consuming every aerospace company they could get their hands on. First Douglas by McDonald, then McDonald by yet a bigger, hungrier company.

Tail 2-3347 had been accepted at Patuxent River Naval Air Station, situated at the mouth of the Patuxent River overlooking the picturesque Chesapeake Bay, sixty-five miles southeast of Washington, in 1969. It had passed its acceptance trials with flying colors and promptly been assigned to fly aboard the USS Constellation as part of the eighty-four other jets that made up its combat wings.

In 1970, flying with five separate crews, it flew 169 sorties out of the Tonkin Gulf, never so much as getting a flat tire.

In 1971, as part of a land-based experiment for the USMC, it was transferred to Ubon, in Thailand, where it flew another 122 sorties over the next two years, again surviving both inexperienced pilots and the guns of the enemy unscratched. It was repainted three times as the Marines tried out different camouflage schemes, each one patiently over-painted by the locals with little regard for aerodynamic flow, durability, or weight. Consequently, by the time it was due to be flown back onboard a carrier, it looked like a moth-eaten sheepdog with rabies, earning the nickname "Mutt."

Its arrival back on a flight deck coincided with the need for major maintenance, so it sat out the trip back to the States in the hanger, waiting for someone to fall in love with it again. And because it wasn't on the flying roster, it was quickly cannibalized for parts, so on arrival back at Santiago, it not only looked like a moth-eaten sheep dog with rabies, it looked like a broken down skeleton of one as well, earning the new nick of "Mutt-the-hack."

Mutt-the-hack was craned off the boat onto a flatbed and unceremoniously trucked to the nearest maintenance facility, where it sat for a whole year while the system made up its mind what to do with the carcass. Someone somewhere finally looked casually over the paperwork and stamped "retire to storage" on the front of the folder. Some months later, Mutt-the-hack was in four parts, wings and tail section having been separated from the mottled fuselage, and inside a C-130 Hercules cargo aircraft on its way to the Military Aircraft Storage and Disposition Centre (MASDC) at Davis-Monthan AFB in Arizona.

When it arrived, it was given a close scrutiny, and the tech sergeant who did the inspection noticed that the airframe under the atrocious paint scheme was in pristine condition, had relatively low flying hours, and ordered the aircraft to be rebuilt from the thousands of spares that the MASDC handled on a daily basis. At the very least, once qualified for flight again, it could be used for training somewhere.

This took seven months when a retired captain now working for the civilian contractor responsible for flight-testing finally took Mutt-the-hack back up back into the clear blue sky, where she really belonged. This time she was professionally painted all-over matte grey, having been stripped back to bare metal, and resembled what she truly was—a frontline fighter aircraft of considerable power. Once signed off, she was mothballed and stored in the dry desert air until 1989, when the white plastic covers were pulled off, and the preservative gunk was washed out of her systems, once again revealing a sleek, ready-for-war fighter plane. After a short proving flight, this time at the hands of a pilot just two years older than her, she was flown to a private contractor in the Mojave Desert in California, where she was stripped of all her twenty-year-old instrumentation and fitted with all the latest gadgetry required to convert her into an F-4G "Wild Weasel."

On the 15th of August 1990, she was mobilized to Shaikh Isa Air Base, Bahrain, for Operation Desert Storm, where she participated in cutting the head off Saddam's ground defenses and just creating merry hell with his radar-based electronic systems. At the end of the "hundred-day war," missions were few and far between, so she found herself back on the deck of a Marine supply ship and headed back to the USA and an uncertain future.

One boneyard retirement and resurrection later, she was again back in the air on the way to Mojave, where yet again, she was attacked with a paintbrush. This time a stinky red hi-glow concoction was applied to her wing tips, tail feathers, and underbelly. Fitted with a digital control system, GPS, and with her radar disabled and radios unplugged, she was given the designation of "QF-4" target drone and flown to join the 82nd ATRS, based at Tyndall, as part of the 53rd Weapons Evaluation Group. For the next three years, she did great service over the desert of New Mexico, fulfilling her role of "hit me if you can" fast-jet aerial target, encouraging young pilots from all walks of life to shoot at her with guns and missiles, in all weather, day and night.

Then, on the 14th of September 2009, coincidentally, thirty years exactly to the day she was "born" at Pax River NAS, she was taxied out to the end of the active runway under the blazing desert sun. She felt different. Something was missing, but she was not fitted with the sensors required for her to make an accurate assessment. Afterburners lit, she accelerated down the strip, rotating up into the air with gusto and all the grace of a powerful animal, climbing on maximum thrust to thirty thousand feet. She flew the traditional racetrack pattern for twenty minutes, then lit her burners again, broke the sound barrier effortlessly, and streaked towards the horizon at 1,200 knots, just a fraction under her maximum speed, like a stallion in heat.

Nine minutes later, she erupted into a massive spinning ball of flame and debris, temporarily blinding the young pilot ten years her junior as he flew through the fireball, pulling up into a massive hammerhead, yelling and punching his fist as the wreckage fluttered down to the desert floor. It took just scant minutes for the wreckage of the magnificent F4 to impact, the debris field around ten square miles in size. One engine managed to spear head-on into a small depression in the desert floor and promptly buried itself down to its afterburners, leaving a soot-covered exhaust pointing uselessly up at the clear blue sky. Compressor stators still rotating from the force of the air as the engine had plummeted down from thirty thousand feet made a noticeable clicking sound, the only noise for hundreds of miles in any direction.

As the smoke rose into the still air, the F15 Eagle screamed across the crash site, rolling around its longitudinal axis, finally pulling up into a vertical climb that soon took it out of sight.

Later that day, the young pilot's logbook would show a simple entry—"live fire ex, Fox-two, one AIM12 fired, one hit, target destroyed."

CHAPTER 42

Sitting in my corner deep in the murky bowels of one of the oldest churches in Italy, it was hard to imagine a world gone completely mad. But that is what I was seeing on the digital screen that dominated one wall of the library. Tuned into the European equivalent of CNN, the screen was filled with the blood and gore of hundreds of thousands of civilian protesters as they lost the fight with some of the best-trained police shock troops in the world. The demonstration had started off peaceful enough, just a lot of very concerned people trying to make their point about the utter chaos that reigned across Europe after the terrorist attacks. But it was obvious the authorities were as stressed out as their people because neither side seemed to want to go home peacefully. It was as if they all needed to vent their anger and fury at someone, and anyone under the circumstances would do.

"Captain, there is a visitor for us arriving by boat in ten minutes; would you like to go and collect them, please?" asked the Boss, being so polite I was shocked into silence. Sweetness and honey were definitely not his styles, and while my hackles started to rise, my curiosity rose faster, wondering what this might be about— given that the mood in the room had decidedly taken a sharp turn for the worst once we started looking at the international reaction to the protesters. Part of me was glad for the distraction, whoever it might turn out to be; the other part worried that we still had very little real intelligence to act on. We now knew a lot about the how but very little about the why. Maybe that would change soon, but like all detectives everywhere, I was firm of the opinion that you had a definite time window from the initiation of a crime to solve it before the momentum moved back to the bad guys.

I walked up the twisty, dank stone steps, the Italian guards suddenly standing and nodding their recognition as I passed. Sitting on little canvas chairs, each anchored to small alcoves cut into the centuries-old stone walls, their black combat suits blended perfectly with the mottled green and dark stained walls, but there was no hiding their enthusiasm and focus. They were here to help, and all I had to do was ask. I smiled at each one, looking into dark, shiny, intelligent eyes, very proud to be part of this elite, multinational team.

The dreaded red cigarette boat, and its maniacal driver, was screaming in from the direction of the airport, leaving a wake that shot up tens of meters into the air, the ocean cut by twin slipstreams as straight as a die. For once, the water traffic around the small islands that made up a large proportion of Venice proper was very light, just a small powerboat here and there, as if everyone had gone home for the holidays.

The maniac sloughed to a perfect stop alongside the wooden jetty, water from the overspray flicking past my face with a vengeance, and on seeing me, he stood up behind the wheel, all five and a half feet of him, and waved and shouted over the now muted engines. I couldn't help but smile and wave back. Three of the commando guards secured the boat, and a solid-built female form, well wrapped in a navy overcoat, was helped off the boat. She paused, looked around at her surroundings, and took in the guards, who now formed a loose cordon around us in the shape of a "U," fronting onto the side of the boat. Her focus was unmistakable, as was her seemingly relaxed posture. She was coiled like a spring, obviously waiting for a clue as to the next exciting adventure in her life, having just survived what had probably been one of the most furious rides in a boat she was ever likely to experience.

I stepped forward, holding out my hand, and smiled to break the ice. "Welcome, I'm Jessica Riley, Interpol, and you are?" I asked in my friendliest voice. She fixed on me with her penetrating green eyes, nodded slightly, turned, and took my hand. A firm handshake, not forced, confident, neither male nor female, and before I had time to develop this thought, a little grim smile split her lips, but her eyes remained on mine and, if anything, bored even deeper into my soul.

"Anna Bernstein, SSA, FBI. Where am I, who was that maniac of a boat driver, and what the hell is this all about?" she asked, her tonality anything but warm, frosty even, but having survived the Italian's "need for speed" a couple of times myself just recently, I understood her reaction. I gently motioned for her to join me, the guards forming up around us, and led her across the jetty to the waiting steps.

"This is a restricted secret intelligence site we—that's Interpol—are using for the duration due to the penetration of the technological world by the terrorists. Why are you here?" I asked, mildly confused, as I had not received any briefing on a senior supervising agent of the Federal Bureau of Investigation joining us. She seemed to take into consideration my dress, which was definitely not Italian "chic," but nonetheless immensely practical given where I had been and how I had got there in the last forty-eight hours or so and shook her head ever so slightly as if she didn't believe what she was seeing. A dark slimline Armani-designed pants suit topped by a shoulder holster and a thin utility belt holding phones and other necessities, all covered by a warm peach-colored loose-fitting jacket, sleeves rolled up to just below the elbows, and one wrist decorated by a large electronic watch, the other by a pair of bracelets, one featuring miniature diamonds looped into a platinum chain, the other a simple string holding a brace of Buddha beads.

Both were gifts, but from very different people and very different times.

As we walked down the dark stairway, I told the solid FBI agent where the church was, who ran it, and just before all her phones, guns, and electronic equipment were stripped off her and put into safekeeping, the Boss arrived, a huge smile lighting up his face.

"Anna, long time no see!" he shouted, hugging her so hard she visibly winched as he picked her up off the stone floor, swinging her around like a Spaniard at a tango festival.

"PJ put me down!" the FBI agent shouted, a hint of real anger at the edges of her demand. The Boss did what the Boss always did. He ignored the instruction and promptly spun the FBI agent around one more time, then gently placed her back on the stone floor, finally placing a huge, wet, sloppy kiss on her forehead.

"Anna, you're a gift from Roger, and I accept!" he said, taking her hand and almost pulling her down into the control room. "Everyone, this is Anna, and she is one of us," the Boss shouted, startling the monks. He quickly led her to our couch, deposited her with a bow, then stood looking at her with his hands on his hips. "What have you got to trade?" he asked, so softly only the three of us could hear him. The FBI agent looked at him, a smile just behind her eyes, as she rolled her shoulders and settled into the couch.

"Well, a good strong cup of coffee would not go astray, and then maybe we can talk." Indigo, who had stayed off to one side while the FBI agent had been swung around like a plaything, practically tripped over his own feet, rushing to the massive coffee maker now hidden behind a brace of computer screens.

"And, Anna, that little guy trying to be invisible is our great friend Indigo, head of the Italian branch of Interpol, and his geek Luigi, who just stole a few kilos of radioactive material for us. I see you have met the good captain," he said, bending over to one of the overstuffed couches. Indigo arrived with a beautiful, monogrammed cup and saucer, which he placed almost reverently down in front of the FBI agent.

"*Mi scusi, per favore, gentile signora, miocattivemaniere di non presentar*mi." He bowed from the waist, the genuine look of pain on his face one for the record. "*Indaco, non c'èbisogno di scusarsi, il nostro amico qui PJ è ben noto per la suamancanza di buonemaniere – tra le moltealtrecose*!" Anna responded, in perfect Italian, bringing a genuine frown to my Boss's face.

"Okay, if we are finished with the language lessons, why don't you tell us why you have flown halfway around the world just to join our little party," he asked, the tone in his voice letting everyone know he was suddenly serious.

"My pleasure. From the hard data you were able to send us, we were able to make an assessment using the behavioral analysis unit, and I'm reasonably sure we understand the motive behind the primary attacks now."

"You discount the event at Avignon as we do?" I asked.

"Yes. Different setup entirely, someone piggybacking on the main attacks. Wouldn't be surprised if it were our friends at ISIS or some offshoot. But not the main players. Plus, I have some intelligence we haven't yet shared with you." You could drop a pin in the room and hear it fall through the air; the silence was so absolute. The Boss looked puzzled; the FBI agent sitting here with us was not congruent with the concept of the FBI withholding information from Interpol. So, he opened his hands in a form of supplication, smiled that crocodile smile of his, and turned the full force of his deep blue eyes on Anna.

"Why don't you bring us up to date, then?" he asked, so softly I actually leaned forward to hear him.

And in less than twenty minutes, she developed her theory about the attacks and the role of the Jesuit brothers and introduced the team to the key suspect, Al Hemish al-bin Mohammad Karesish.

"The problem is, we don't know how many of the children he actually took, what he did with them, what countries they ended up in, and how they worked their way through the various systems to enable them to achieve what has been the most significant terrorist attacks in the last thousand years. And we can't find a single mention of him anywhere after two thousand four; he just fell off the face of the earth, as it were."

The Boss's brow furrowed in that way of his, making him look almost scholarly. "Maybe we can help with that," he said, turning to look at our resident computer genius. "Luigi, can you help, please?"

The little hacker smiled, bobbed his head twice, smiled like any good digital predator, and scooted off to his console, humming.

The Boss rubbed his face, a sure sign his mind was in overdrive. "What you're saying, in effect, is that an unknown number of refugee children—specifically girls—were taken from the camps over a period of years, placed with families all over the world, and trained to be 'homegrown' terrorists. Do we have any knowledge of how many of these terrorists we are dealing with?" he asked, spearing the FBI agent with a very pointed stare.

"No. As I just said, we don't know the actual number. We don't know how many are working together or working solo. But the priest did say one thing that might help."

"And that is?"

"He believes that the girls were only taken for three or four years, and in the first year, he only took five children. So, possibly, we are only dealing with maybe twenty or so."

"Maybe."

"Yes, maybe."

"Anna, can your people do some digging and find out more about the identified incidents where we have some identification? Develop some sort of pattern we might be able to work from? For example, you have a solid ID on the A-10 Warthog pilot, even if she magically disappeared and turned into a store dummy at the bottom of the ocean."

"We're doing that, deep background on every incident, every bomb, rocket, aircraft, nut, and bolt; all that data will be made available to you progressively thorough secured military couriers, who will stop at the airport, so your location isn't compromised. We're also deep diving into the family backgrounds where possible; remember, so far, we have only had one single identification with the A-10 pilot."

"Not a lot to work with." The Boss looked reflective, his whole body seeming to shrink in on itself. He shook his head from side to side, then looked up, straight into the hazel eyes of the FBI agent. "But there is one thing we can track—how the hell did they compromise our communication systems? How far back does that go?" Anna nodded, a wan smile creasing her face.

"We thought of that, and we have the geek squad working on that twenty-four seven. Frankly, it's a little scary just how far they have penetrated. Just accepting that they were in our munitions stockpile over twenty years ago is mind-blowing." All three of us nodded, accepting the fact that the penetration of the world's supposedly secure military and government nets was compromised.

"*Senorita*, perhaps there is one thing that we are finding that we can work with?" asked Indigo, bowing almost in half as he addressed Anna. It was hard to know if the bow was out of respect, servitude, or anticipation!

"What would that be, Indigo?" she asked, smiling to take the tension out of the conversation.

"Well, *senorita*, we know that many of the attacks were delivered remotely, with the exception of the attack in London. Plus, we have the intelligence community penetrated by a master hacker—or two—why don't we try to find out where they came from? Your data shows the girls' ages approximately at the time they were taken out of the camps—between eight and twelve years old, just like how you estimated. Now, allowing for the fact that up until that time, they would have had very little formal education, even though they were selected for their innate intelligence—they would still need to have gone to school somewhere, graduated, then onto university to gain the skills they have so amply demonstrated to date. Give that we are speculating that only twenty or so girls are involved and working backwards from today, by tracking when we think things were compromised, we should be able to track at least some of them going through the formal process of getting educated."

The Boss looked at Anna, Anna looked at Indigo with new respect for his astute reasoning, and I looked at everyone in the room as they suddenly became energized, realizing that we actually had the first hook to build our case on.

SHOOTING STAR

The F4F Phantom rose majestically into the upper atmosphere, like a bullet fired out of some sort of exotic gun. Still bearing its dull grey and bright orange paint denoting it as a remotely piloted target vehicle (RPTV) in military-speak, the only difference an external viewer would see from that of a standard RPTV was that there wasn't the soft-edged shape of a pilot in the cockpit, there were two massive underwing fuel tanks dominating the sleek shape of the fighter, and a massive missile slung along the centerline protruding from both the front and rear of the fuselage, creating the illusion that the fighter was riding on top of it, like a massive jet-assisted take-off rocket.

The aircraft topped out of its bounce "dive" at one hundred and eleven thousand feet, almost a height record for a fighter, and just as the laws of physics and the inevitable pull of gravity reclaimed the ungainly mass of the jet, flame erupted from the tail of the centerline pod, and in a split second, it dropped off its rail and shot out from under the falling aircraft, zooming up into the empty sky.

The Phantom fell awkwardly, the laws of aerodynamics having been violated too severely, and entered a shallow inverted spin, a maneuver only the most skilled of pilots could recover from. Just as one wing dipped, threatening to pull the aircraft out of thin air and into a vertical death dive, the massive tanks under each wing flew free, tumbling end over end, almost in a perfect formation with the tumbling aircraft.

Above them, the fiery streak of the exhaust of the massive missile laced the black sky like a plasma torch, leaving just the faintest vapor trail as it arced up into space. As every aeronautical engineer and space cadet will tell you, it was not the height that got something into orbit but velocity.

The missile soon faded from vision; its bright plume diminished as it reached up into the heavens, hunting its target like a cat readying itself to pounce on a mouse. Through a fluke in circumstances, the International Space Station was only manned by two Russians and an Italian cosmonaut—two men and a woman. The rocket bringing four Americans up to serve their six months rotation had been delayed by a fault in the service module, which threatened to hold the launch up for three to four days. As it turned out, on this specific occasion, it was the absolute best thing that could have happened for the astronauts—and their families.

The ISS floated in its usual orbit, some four hundred kilometers above the surface of the Earth, racing around space at 17,500 miles every hour—one complete rotation of the Earth every ninety minutes. It was fitted with the very latest in detection equipment designed to seek out the smallest speeding particle that could impact the station, and an automatic system drove small ion thrusters strategically positioned around the massive superstructure so it could be moved out of the way of any errant meteorite or space junk. The whole system was predicted on the assumption that the potential intruder was smaller than the first joint of the average man's thumb. Anything bigger was supposed to be detected by the satellite observation network linked to Earth-side electronic telescopes, usually able to locate threatening objects well before they became a real threat.

The protection system worked, up to a point, in that as the missile arced up directly into the path of the speeding station, an alarm ran throughout the modules, a shrill screech irritating enough to wake the dead. However, the computers could not predict the potential impact point because the missile came from the right along the blind spot, and the computers were programmed to calculate closing speeds and angles for foreign objects that were in the same relative orbital plane as the space station.

The missile slammed into the exact middle of the Harmony Module, causing it to implode and effectively drag the modules on either side together in a silent crash. What had taken over fifty years, one hundred billion dollars, and tens of flights by the space shuttle and Russian Soyuz to build, was a sagging heap of space junk in less than eleven minutes as inertia and mass fought gravity and momentum and lost.

The massive solar sails broke free, spinning and rotating slowly like snowflakes caught in a burst of strong wind.

The irony was that the total destruction of the space station could still be seen from Earth for the next few days as it gracefully spiraled into the atmosphere to burn up in fiery balls of exotic metals and plasma. Some of the bigger bits, capsule attachment rings, mass storage batteries, and other technological wonders crashed willingly into the land and oceans around the world, barely noticed due to the civil upheaval promoted by the terrorist attacks.

But before that even occurred, and almost directly under the path of the attack, located on a small side road half a kilometer from the most prestigious football stadium in London, a "B-double" truck pulled up. Wembley Stadium is known around the world for the fabulous FA Cup matches played there and the storied teams who had graced its hallowed turf. It could easily fit ninety thousand screaming fans in, many of whom had, over the years, enjoyed the experience so much that their memories couldn't cope with all the alcohol they had drunk on the way home!

Harrow Road runs almost parallel to the motorway, and the truck, being as large as it was, drew the attention of the locals. Without any fanfare, the tarpaulin sides rolled up, and a barrage of rockets ejected a swarm of UAVs into the air with a belch and roar that damaged eardrums. The spent shells fell away, and the UAVs formed up into flights one-hundred-wide and climbed up rapidly to get over the stadium walls.

The next thing the startled onlookers heard was a mighty roll of explosions as the drones impacted the seats, shooting massive fireballs up into the overcast sky, so much so that the very oxygen was sucked out of the entire stadium in one huge final insult.

Not a single seat survived, and the thirteen groundskeepers who had been huddling deep in the maintenance rooms' bowels with a non-approved "smoke" emerged to find such carnage and destruction that they were unable to give the police any coherent details of the brutal attack.

As the CCTV footage from the adjacent service rest stop would clearly show, the launch of the drones was a well-rehearsed and visually stunning exercise. Once all the images had been collected and stabilized, cleaned up, and had their pixels "scrubbed," whatever that entailed, the image of the massive truck and the weird launching tubes on the side of the truck stop stood out like an invitation to a swarm of bees looking for a home. Rows and rows of black tubes, ranged in lots of one hundred, poked out of the side of the main vehicle and its trailer, numbering some fourteen sets, making for 1,400 firing slots.

The head of Scotland Yard, the highest-ranking police officer in the UK, sipped his tea silently. Beside him sat the military liaison for the Special Air Service, a crusty Colonel dressed in camouflage, his posture anything but relaxed. Three other very senior public officials sat opposite them, all held by the incredible action on the screen. "Gentlemen, what do you see?" he asked, his gruff tobacco-stained voice sounding like a frog seeking a mate on a lily pad. "Or should I say," he continued, looking around at his compatriots, "what don't you see?" The men stared at the screen intently, wondering what the cop was seeing that they weren't.

"No driver." Every head snapped around to see where the comment had come from. A shadow emerged from the wall and revealed itself to be a very smartly dressed woman, a trench coat hung loosely over her shoulders.

"Gentlemen, you all know Fay Sailing, head of our security services. Fay, when did you become involved again?"

"About an hour ago, the space station was blown out of the sky. We went to full alert, and our satellites picked up the Wembley attack at the same time as one on Nürburgring. It can hold one hundred fifty thousand people, and we have no casualty figures from the Germans yet; they are all still in shock. But I'd be prepared to bet that their outcome will be the exact same as ours."

"Zero killed."

"Yes, sir, no one KIA. This was a magnificently timed attack in every respect. The space station was running an evacuation drill; all three astronauts were in the Mir evacuation module, which ejected just after the impact by the missile. I'm told they are all alive and on their way back to Earth due to splash down in about three hours. Wembley was empty, apart from the ground crew, who were taking their morning meal break down in the basement somewhere. These three attacks were well timed, exquisitely coordinated, and flawlessly executed. And in every case, no pilots, no drivers, no discernible human involvement."

"What about the space station attack? The aircraft that fired the missile?" asked the SAS Colonel.

"Augured into the ground out of control, no body found in the wreckage."

"So, this is what a robot war would look like," muttered one of the public servants, who just coincidentally happened to control the R&D Department that worked on robotic weapons for all of the UK. "Good to know."

"Yes," replied the UK's most senior policeman, "good to know. But what I want to know is why. What are these bastards trying to achieve?"

CHAPTER 43

The room was so quiet that I could hear people breathe. The Boss wore his "I'm thinking" face, Indigo just looked shocked, Anna was slumped in a beautiful leather chair that was probably seven hundred years old, and Black Pete held his head in his hands, his long blond hair falling over his tanned face like a waterfall.

We watched the data stream across the screen, looking from report to report to get a sense of the carnage that was being tallied by the talking heads from every network around the globe.

"If anything," I said, filling my coffee mug up from the espresso machine, which, in the totally silent room, sounded like a steam train starting off on a long journey, "we now have some proof that our hypothesis is correct. Somewhere in the data, we will find the minds that made all this happen. Look at it this way," I said, stopping to sip and think. It was a simple problem but a highly complex solution. Just track thirty unknown people over thirty years in every major education facility on the planet and then isolate those that fit our profile. What profile? Females, less than forty years old, possibly of Eurasian or Middle European descent. But we could refine it down to one group, the tech-heads.

"Anna, can you start looking in the US—I'll get my buddies to look in the UK and the EU, specifically for anyone who looks like a genius with IT and computers. At the heart of these attacks is some very crafty tech. Someone created it, made and tested it, fitted it to aircraft and trucks, and then programmed them with pinpoint accuracy. Aircraft and trucks—that shouldn't be so hard, should it?" the Boss asked, stealing my lines, and not for the first time. I smiled; one of the advantages of working with such a difficult personality was the way we were so often in sync. My thoughts finally clarified, and I raised one hand, finger extended, to stop anyone from breaking my train of thought.

"One extra point—with additive manufacturing as advanced as it is, perhaps we should also be looking at workshops and factories that specialize in making exotic devices?" I suggested, looking around the room. Black Pete was the first to respond, nodding his big head up and down, causing this hair to flick up and down as if in a storm. "And on the tech front, right now, who has the most advanced guidance system for getting things up and down from space with pinpoint accuracy?"

"The rocketeers!" exclaimed Anna, "last year, I watched a live landing of twin boosters at the Cape, and it literally took my breath away."

"So, what you are both saying is don't necessarily just focus on the stolen hardware—the planes, UAV, trucks, and munitions, but look for who could design, build, and program all this with such finesse?" Pete asked, shaking his head from side to side this time, probably in disbelief.

"Yes. Exactly." I looked at my compatriots, and to my surprise, Shami, our purloined computer geek, had his hand up as if asking permission to leave the room. He was a full Colonel in the Israeli Intelligence Service, so he had the seniority to ask any question he liked of anyone in the room. "Shami, you don't need to put your hand up," I said, smiling. "You're a critical part of this team. What do you want to add?"

"*Secusi, senoria*, but if youa looking for special people in computers and software, there'sa one place theya sure to have been some time."

"Where?" demanded the Boss, standing up with such suddenness even I was a little startled.

"Wea geeks have a private chat room to swapa theories and stories. Some time or other, these girl people woulda havea been ina there. For sure."

"Well, Luigi, my friend, let's go and find them!" the Boss exclaimed, moving over to slap the diminutive programmer on the shoulder. "Let's go find these bastards."

Anna and I just shook our heads and left the men to go play with the computers. "Anna, when do you think the navy will retrieve the A-10?" She looked at me with a slightly skeptical frown, then her face relaxed as she remembered whom she was talking to.

"Sorry, only a very small group of people know about that, and I forgot for a moment you were in the loop. As I was leaving, I heard that the navy had a ship over the top and had sent down a submersible, so add in my flight time, and you could guess in another hour or two. Looking for anything specific?"

"Yes. The ubiquitous black box—but, in this case, not the flight recorder but the control head they attached to the aircraft systems to handle the complex programming needed to pull this off."

"Why is it complex?" she asked, following my lead at the magnificent espresso machine. We drew our coffees too much chuffing and steaming, then returned to the massive leather chair, which was really almost a couch, and sat facing each other, separated only by the wafting fumes of our coffees.

"Well, let's take the Hog—from the time the pilot left the cockpit, the aircraft had to taxi, obey ground control, take off, obey area control, fly a designated track, hook up with a tanker, tank, breakoff as per refueling protocol, navigate to the target, change altitude, make its bombing run, climb back up, and then disappear out to sea." Anna bent her head over the rim of her coffee cup. She rolled her eyes up, looking directly at me.

"I hadn't thought that through. If you take in wind, temperature, navigation drift, and all the things that affect an aircraft in flight in real life, you couldn't just have it on autopilot. It would have to have either some sort of real-time feedback loop to a controller or a sophisticated software program and onboard computer capable of working all that stuff out."

"And sensors," I added. "I know GPS, satellite, and inertial navigation platforms are both sophisticated and accurate, but they can't think for themselves. And as far as I know, the only automated tanking system at this point is UAV to UAV— and smallish ones at that."

"You mention the word 'think.'" I nodded, putting my cup aside and pulling out my secure minicomputer pad that the priests had given me. I dialed up a search engine, entered the words "Lex Silverman," and then handed the pad to Anna.

"AI. Wow! This investigation just took on a whole new level of WTF. AI. As in, artificial intelligence capable of thinking and acting like a pilot."

"Or a truck driver."

"Or a truck driver. I'll say it again. Wow!"

"Yes, wow. I think we should spoil the boys' fun, don't you?" I asked, getting up. Anna simply grinned from ear to ear and nodded.

"Teach them to dismiss us girlies!" she said, striding over the bank of computers.

CHAPTER 44

The two women sat opposite each other, the ever-changing images on the wall of screens creating the illusion of a flickering sunset. The only light that penetrated the natural gloom of the underground bunker was artificial and well-filtered. The air was held at an exact sixty-five degrees, and massive HEPA filters at the head of the pressurized airway, some sixteen kilometers from the farmhouse, filtered out everything up to sub-microbial size. The system could handle anything short of a direct hit by a nuke.

And amazingly, that's exactly what the infrastructure had originally been designed for. Holding off a nuke. The underground facility had been built as the support center for a Minute Man missile complex, long since decommissioned and, as far as anyone was concerned, not on any database anywhere in the world.

"They seem to have found our electronic backdoors and have changed their encryption and coding progressively," the blonde engineer said, swinging her chair around to point at one of the screens that showed a work-in-progress chart designated by Homeland Security as totally electronically sealed and "safe." Little red bars slowly expanded against datasets on charts, and to the uninformed eye would look like great progress was being made at something, even if the observer didn't know the circumstances of the work.

"Yes, we anticipated this," the pilot replied, shaking her hair out of the net she habitually wore under her flight helmet. She ran her fingers through her hair, reveling in the feeling of freedom. "They have a long way to go before we need to change tactics. What we need to do now is initiate phase three, and once we do, all their hard work in uncovering us will be for nothing. How are we going with the preparation?"

"Well. Everyone and everything is prepositioned, and apart from Avignon, the collateral damage numbers are where we thought they would be. It's a real shame we can't get rid of the crazies at the same time." She smiled; the irony of her statement was not lost on her. Here they were reshaping the geopolitics of the world, and no doubt the majority of the governments involved would think they were the craziest of all!

"What's the latest on Coxes Bazar?" The pilot looked down at her dust-covered flight boots, her shoulders sagging as she sighed.

"Worse than we thought. The daily count is now in the hundreds, and while we've got as much aid and support into that area as we can, the politics are still killing us. Bangladesh is such a shitty country to start with; their government is inept, their infrastructure frigid, and there hasn't been a single individual at any level of the hierarchy who will actually do what they are paid to do."

"Okay, then let's leave that for now; dial Helen up, and we'll start the day with a bang!" The pilot laughed, but her heart wasn't really in it, and her partner accepted the lack of enthusiasm for what it was. They were both totally motivated by their cause, but the constant suffering of the people they were trying to free dug deep into their souls every minute of every day.

The pilot tapped out a code on a small keyboard, negotiated the security levels, then smiled with a little more energy as Helen's face swam into view, the background a bewildering cacophony of color and shapes.

"Hi from the deep south," she said, waving her partner over into the range of the camera embedded in the screen. "Got someone here who wants to say hi!"

"Go, girls, how are you both?" With the slightly worried look on Helen's face betraying her observation, her two friends looked a little peaked.

"We're fine," the pilot answered, "just a little tired of skulking around. How goes it at your end?"

"Well, as you anticipated, Interpol have been brought into the fray, and they are, as usual, being very busy backtracking the attacks, interviewing all sorts of intelligent people, but they've gone to ground somewhere in Venice. We have also lost them on the military nets, and we are now only getting partial data from the US intelligence groups, suggesting they are starting to catch up to us."

"Yes, we are seeing that as well. Do you think Interpol will be an obstacle to our implementation?" The bunker went very quiet, and the two women swapped looks, tension replacing the smiles around their eyes.

"We gamed this, remember, and it was a less than thirty-four percent chance of them interfering. I can't see it being a factor."

"Do we know who they have assigned?"

"Before we lost track of them, we had identified Colonel Anthony, his offsider Captain Riley, and an unknown Special Services type they picked up in Australia. They have US military backing, an SR-71 Blackbird, and pretty much everything else they need. They were all over the place for a day or two, Italy, the Mediterranean, Israel, even the US, but they have now gone to ground."

"Isn't Interpol's HQ in Italy in Venice?"

"Yes. But they haven't been seen anywhere near there for a day or two. An unidentified woman did arrive sometime last evening our time, but she has disappeared as well.

"Are they in Venice?"

"We think so."

"But we don't know?"

"No."

"How good is Anthony?"

"Very. He led the investigation into that child smuggling racket out of Turkey last fall, taking out the entire cadre in five countries without so much as a ripple of negative comment from the press or the politicians."

"They were all too busy hiding their involvement and getting their money socked away."

"Okay, well, we just concentrate on our plan, keep the pressure on before the game becomes apparent, let them chase their own tails for a while. We strike again in an hour; you two take it easy, get some sleep. You've got a full day before we need you in the field again. Is your location secure?"

"We have moved into base number two; it's sixteen clicks from the farmhouse, and there is no apparent connection between where we are now and where we were. So yes, we think so."

"Okay, then. God bless!" And as these words echoed around the cavern, her face dissolved, the cacophony of colors and shapes in the background buzzing around the screen for a second or two before dissolving.

"Well then," the pilot said, getting up and stretching, "shower, bed." Her companion looked at her and nodded in agreement. "And some food!"

CHAPTER 45

Luigi literally vibrated in his oversized chair in front of myriad screens. He bounced up and down like a two-year-old on a sugar rush. The Boss and Indigo, and the head monk stood behind him, nodding to themselves. Before we had a chance to tell them what our conclusion was regarding how to filter out the search for the missing children, Pete suddenly exploded into laughter.

"Bloody hell, Indigo, where did you get this dude, and can I have him when we finish?" he yelled, slapping the skinny computer expert so hard on the back that the little Italian shot forward, nearly biting his keyboard.

"What's all the excitement about?" I asked.

"Luigi has traced the Al Hemish al-bin Mohammad Karesish dude from Gouraud. He changed his name when he went dark but forgot to close out one of his bank accounts, and Luigi here managed to get into the bank's data and find his non-d-bloody-plume. Bloody exciting, I tell you, we could make a fortune with this guy!" We all laughed; the idea of one of the top cadres of Interpol using a computer geek to line their own pockets was so out there as to be humorous. And the idea of the special forces master chief we knew as Black Pete being patient enough to rob a bank that way caused me to shake my head in wonder. He'd be happier blowing it up, shooting all before him, then setting the remnants on fire to make his point!

"What's his new handle?" Anna asked.

"Mohammad bin Azaria, now an upstanding citizen of Egypt, by way of Arabia." Anna fiddled with her minicomputer and flicked through a series of pages, all bearing either the seal of the FBI or ICE—the Immigration and Customs Enforcement Agency. She muttered to herself, tapped furiously some more, then relaxed and addressed the room.

"Anyone interested in how many times he entered the United States? Or Israel? Or Arabia? Or the UK, Ireland, France, Spain, or Italy?" she asked. The Boss looked directly at her, seemed to reflect for a minute, then, turning towards where we stood, asked the obvious question. "Why did you two crash our party?"

"We have an idea for the filter we can use to find our missing girls."

"Hold that thought. Anna, get all that data into our system here; Indigo, get our analysts on it pronto. I want patterns, touchpoints, and a virtual map by a timeline so we can overlay our hunting expedition. Captain, what do you have for us?"

"Anna and I have worked out where our girls might have gone, what they might have done, and when you match it to your map," I said, pointing to the gathering storm of data spreading over the wall screens. "We think we might be able to identify some of them."

RADIO DAH DAH

Montana and Libya had been identified by the NSA as potential locations for the transmitting of the data required to manage the drone attack on Israel; they also believed that the commands for the L-100 Hercules that bombed the Vatican had emanated from somewhere in those two regions. Subsequently, the USA had dispatched ships from the 5th Fleet, airborne electronic detection aircraft, helicopters, and ground support for the monitoring of Libya; Montana proved to be a whole lot easier logistically to manage, given it is located in the northwest of the United States, bordered by Idaho, Wyoming, North Dakota, and South Dakota, and the Canadian provinces of British Columbia, Alberta, and Saskatchewan.

However, at over 145,552 square miles in area and the third least populous state in America, finding a needle in a haystack was no easy matter. Let alone finding the haystack in the first place. But a burst encrypted signal was detected near Deadman's Falls; it lasted just one point one second, was triangulated by at least seven monitors, and within a few minutes, helicopters from the 165th Airborne Ranges were feet-up, the furthest away being just 155 minutes from the target.

Margaret Westhead was a typical millennial, living in the virtual world almost every day, even working at Shorts Cuts on Broadway, New York. A long, shapely woman with skin the color of coffee light, long black hair that flowed almost to her waist, she usually radiated happiness the way some people could. It was exactly 1647 East Coast Time when her world, as she knew it, ended. She was midway between serving an annoying customer and listening to the most fabulous podcast on the subject of hair coloring and styles while talking to her closest girlfriend on her second phone when, without any ceremony, both her phones went dead.

Not even static.

Just absolute silence, broken only by the forceful demands being made by her customer, now at the top of her Hoboken-born voice.

Margie-J, as she was known to her friends and possibly to all 345,000 of her most intimate Twitter followers, went into an immediate meltdown, screeching at the top of her voice about the fact that both her phones were dead as she rapped both against the side of the wash tub her now scared customer had previously had her head and hair resting in.

She was not alone.

Sometime later, that mystical powers-that-be who also controlled the world's telecommunications estimated that their approximately 5.9 billion customers worldwide had also lost all connectivity, seemingly at the same time.

While potentially annoying from a commercial point of view, what was perhaps even more worrying was that no one anywhere, in any country, could use their Wi-Fi. And in fact, in very short order, reports came in about mini-computers, portables, and electronic pads failing, their screens defaulting to total black.

The anxiety in the younger population was palpable; their screams of angst and fury could be heard right around the world. The anxiety in government circles was tangible. The anxiety in military circles was on the brink of visible panic until it was remembered that the old landlines between bases and strategic sites still worked, and in a heartbeat, the handset from the century before became the most precious object outside of a museum.

What had been left of the stock markets after the earlier attacks crashed within a heartbeat like a series of dominoes, forcing exchanges around the world to close. Possibly for a long, long time.

Panic was the new "normal," and with only local live-to-air TV and radio available, providing the technology relied on valves and not computer chips, the transmission of news slowed down to a crawl, further adding to the confusion and fear among ordinary people who had for decades been used to immediate gratification by the worst the modern world had to offer.

The only collateral damage that was officially recorded against the event, which became known as "The Black Out," was a teenage boy riding a dirt bike tuned into his favorite podcast, who crashed in a fury of anxiety when his earbuds went suddenly silent.

The obvious question was what had happened to the often-vaunted satellite communication systems that billionaires around the world had funded, and it took around an hour or so for people to realize that they, too, had gone quiet, although no one in any country had the faintest idea how that had been managed. As their anger grew, so did their unrest, not having their normal social media channels to spew their vitriol down.

"Target location visual, no apparent movement. Going in," called the lead helicopter, flaring to land just outside the high fence guarding the Rural Fire Service Observation Tower on top of a hill literally surrounded by massive pine trees. Three helicopters raced around overhead, providing cover from any potential ground attack. A fifth helicopter flared just to the left of the first, and before the skids hit the ground, three Rangers armed to the teeth jumped down, fanned out, and approached the tall gate.

"Breach the gate," snapped the lead Ranger. On his order, a long grey tube was placed against one side of the gate; the three crouched down, and as the Ranger yelled "Fire in the hole," the tube blew, the gate fell, and the three Rangers sprinted inside.

To find a burnt-out shell inside the wooden building and a slag heap where the satellite uplink had stood. Both still smoldered, indicating that the event had been recent. But the Rangers noticed the strange behavior of the fumes and smoke—they seemed to be being sucked laterally into the giant maw of radically looking device, which, on closer examination, turned out to be an old mechanical wood cutter, rigged to act as a temporary chimney. The Rangers shut it down, took photos, kicked at the machine to vent their frustration, then marched back to their helicopter. With no means of communication this far away from their base, this information didn't get back to Command HQ for another hour and a half.

What further confused the issue was that everything electronic in the helicopters that relied on a computer chip went dark, killing not only the communications but the navigation and automated control systems stone motherless dead.

Libya was a different story. There, several signals were tracked simultaneously and traced, and in every case when a physical inspection was able to be made, in some cases hours after the event, often after a firefight that cost hundreds of lives on all sides, the only evidence that was found was sand-covered piles of molten junk, which may or may not have been some sort of transmission device. The wreckage was tagged, bagged, and flown back to the aircraft carrier, where the commanding admiral and her staff waited impatiently. Amid mild panic. Because everything electronic with a chip in it had also failed instantaneously, killing around eighty percent of everything on the carrier from radar, gun systems, navigation, and communication to simple things like toasters and refrigerators. The "internet of everything," which had proved such a boon to both manufacturers and consumers alike, now became the kiss of death, as across the world, ordinary people had their ordinary, but connected lives totally disrupted in a manner never before experienced in human history.

When the helicopters finally landed back on the carrier, the first question the pilots were asked by the flight director was, "How did you find us?" To which they answered, "We used our maps and compass, dead reckoning, old school, you know, looking out the window. Besides, we could see the fleet from fifty miles away, and you really can't hide a carrier effectively in daylight."

The effect of the World Wide Web and Wi-Fi hack rippled around the world, grounding airlines, crashing banking, elevators, food service, transportation, and digital equipment, and historians, sometime later, would estimate that around six million souls were lost in the first ten hours after the attack due to collateral damage from the unintended consequences of shutting down anything with a chip worldwide. The exception seemed to be anything connected to emergency services, but it took days for that to be established.

Anything mechanical, human-powered, hand-cranked, or just wind-blown still worked. It was like being thrown involuntarily back to the middle of the last century, and the shock and horror reflected in the face of the simplest person said it all. What have you done to my life, and why have you done this to me?

CHAPTER 46

By the end of the first day, every screen on every networked system—video, television, diagnostic equipment, billboards, and effectively anything linked to a distributed network system, had stopped working, as if the world had been infected by a mighty virus, which, of course, was exactly what had happened. Except for one single communication network, the heart of which was buried deep beneath a thousand-year-old church in Venice, the world was effectively electronically castrated.

And the only reason why the monks' secret network didn't go down was that it was never linked to any external network system known to anyone outside of the monks' order. It was, in effect, the perfectly air-gapped system.

Something the Boss was able to take advantage of very quickly.

"Roger, Arie, we have our team here in Venice. What do you know?" he demanded, giving no one time to dither or grieve. Having all three ends of the conversation on one of the monks' securitized laptops, he was confident that no one else would be a party to what was discussed.

"Colonel, no more than you have already concluded. The Lloyd's attack was an anomaly and, following on from the viscousness of the other attacks, caught everyone by surprise. The attacks on the football fields in London and Germany were likewise surprising, in that, again, there were no casualties, and the timing of the attack on the space station was simply remarkable."

"The astronauts were practicing an evacuation drill?" I asked, concerned by the wan and tired looks on the faces of two of the most powerful, Intelligent specialists in the world.

"Yes. The timing was not public knowledge but was published on NASA Net the day before, so we can assume that it was hacked as well. However, what has given us pause for thought, is that the time for the evacuation was indicated as a time block, not a fixed time. The missile hit exactly twenty minutes after the drill had started…"

"…Which suggests inside information or, at the very least, a hack of the space station's systems," finished the Boss.

"Yes." If the head of the vaunted FBI was put out by the Boss cutting him off mid-sentence, he was too tired to let it show.

"So, you wonder why there were no casualties in the last four attacks?" I asked. The Boss fixed it with his "careful what you say" look, so I immediately changed my mind and zipped it.

"We are concerned about that, of course, but the most recent attacks on the telecommunications networks threaten to close us all down for some time. The reports indicate millions of deaths worldwide, and every supply chain for every industry, literally, has been shuttered. We are very concerned about the fallout of this latest attack. That's the biggest fear we have over here; how about you, Arie?" The nuggety but diminutive Israeli intelligence Boss had a face that only a mother could love, and right now, it was creased around his eyes and mouth, almost like he had a massive headache. Which he probably did, given the attack on the Dome of the Rock, one of the great icons of the Jewish faith.

"We are, to some extent, a little luckier than you in that we have embedded landlines between all major or sensitive locations, and our aircraft have never been on any network other than radio-based air traffic control, so they are relatively unscathed. Of course, their control centers are a different matter. What really concerns us is the seeming impunity with which these terrorists are operating. You have to admit, they have attacked now some ten times; the attack on Rome, the Dome of the Rock, your West Point Academy, the oil wells in the Middle East, the Great Mosque, the Wembley Stadium in London, and Nürburgring in Germany, the space station, Lloyd's, and now a worldwide attack on electronic networks that is proving to be extremely damaging."

"And we are no closer to knowing who they are or how to stop them."

"Yes. Frank has shared the information from the two Jesuit priests, and we have done our own background on that data, but we're no closer than you appear to be."

"Okay, I need you both to stand by for an hour. We were just developing some leads when all this went down. I want to finish this work before we chat again. Venice out." And the Boss closed the link, sending the wall screen that held the American and Israeli images blank. He turned to look at me again. "You and Anna were cooking something up just before all this went down. Care to share?"

"No. You first. What had you, boys, all so excited?" I asked. The Boss looked at me with somewhat of an icy stare, but I had survived worse than him and with him, so I held my ground and waited him out.

"You drive a hard bargain. Okay, when Pete and I replicated the route of the Hercules, it was apparent that at the very start, they had to have had a launching point with people and equipment. I can buy automatics or AI starting up and taxiing, then flying a pre-programmed route, and all that other jazzy technology stuff, but not the ground refueling, the loading and setting up of the bombs, that took real human beings, albeit not a lot, we figure it could have been done with just two well-trained people.

"But where did the Hercules start from? We need Arie or someone in that area to find their base. If we take the Americans seriously, that bunker buster was stolen way back in the early two thousand's; where was it hidden all that time? How was it maintained? Armed?"

"You're thinking Libya somewhere." The Boss smiled and nodded, but his smile was just a grim slit across his face.

"The NSA located two sources for transmissions; Libya was one, so it makes sense. We need to locate that base."

"Okay, that's fine, but you and Indigo were worked up about more than just the bombing of the Vatican." He looked at me out of the corner of his eyes, the smile widened a little, and he nodded to himself. Just a little minute bob of the head, but enough to know I was on target.

"Thanks to Luigi and Stefarino here," he said, pointing to the Italian hacker and the head monk, who was obviously on a par with Luigi when it came to computer chops, "we have found the footsteps of Mohammad bin Azaria, formally known as Fernández, and whose real name appears to have been Al Hemish al-bin Mohammad Karesish back in the days he worked in the camps."

"Fantastic. But that only gives you the money, man—and maybe the planner. We need the troops on the ground, the control points; we need to be able to stop any further attacks from happening."

"Is that so?"

"Yes. History is fine, data is fine, information is excellent, but in the now— that is right now—there are a number of unknown women or persons waging war on us with total impunity. Look what they have managed to achieve in just one week—first, they took out the heads of the Catholic Church, effectively neutering it, a two-thousand-year-old institution that has been a cornerstone of our history since biblical times. Not to mention the loss of the centuries of artifacts that the Vatican had hoarded over the years. Strike one against an estimated one point six billion followers, who now have the head cut off their beliefs and their seat of power destroyed." Every head in the room had turned to watch me; all tapping, page-turning, and other activities had stopped. It must have been the passion in my voice because I realized I was getting just a little worked up with my summary.

Anna, Pete, and the Boss looked at me, nodding to themselves as if absorbing the analysis for the first time. Or wondering if I was having a meltdown.

"*Si, Capitano*, we Italians feel this loss personally; it is not something we can quite comprehend yet. It is a brutal blow to our beliefs." I nodded to Indigo, never wanting to hug him more than right now.

"I know, Indigo. I'm not a Catholic, but I feel your loss. And what about the Israelis? The Dome of the Rock goes all the way back to the Second Jewish Temple. Suddenly you have two of the strongest faiths in the world shaken to their very roots."

"And then you have the attack on the oil fields."

"Yes, striking at the very economic heart of the Arab states, you might as well have bombed them back to the Stone Age given that their wealth has suddenly become worthless for around twenty-five years or so. Think about Arabia—was that a subtle attack on them? But we know that both the attack on the Dome and the oil fields was specific—just like the bombing of the Great Mosque. Lots of smoke and damage, but the Muslim side of things was barely touched. We know that the priests reported that Al Hemish al-bin Mohammad Karesish was both a member of Arabian Royalty, albeit somewhat removed, and also a staunch Muslim. But it is not the Muslims necessarily behind these attacks. I think they are being punished too. I feel it in my bones."

"That's why the damage to the Dome and the Great Mosque was so minimal on the Muslim side," suggested Anna. I clapped her on the back.

"Yes. Absolutely. But I feel you had that under consideration before you arrived here."

"Yes, I did. When you look at the after-action photos, it is quite clear that both attacks were tightly directed and targeted."

"And that brings us to the attack on West Point. What better way to make the point about children than to obliterate the most storied military academy in the Western world?"

"They killed the senior leadership of the navy," interjected Pete. "It wasn't just the cadets."

"Collateral damage. You have already told us that you have determined that the trigger for these attacks was the election of a new Pope. They are not interested in the military hierarchy, just making their point with very specific images." The room was deadly quiet. I looked around quickly to see if I was offending anyone but only saw curiosity and empathy being reflected back at me. I sucked in a breath.

"And now we have the non-casualty attacks—Lloyd's of London data centers, which effectively takes out all known information regarding transportation and insurance for hundreds of years, not to mention the effect it had on stock exchanges around the world."

"Do you hold that the death of their retired chairman was coincidental?" Anna asked question she had been carrying around in her mind for some time.

"Maybe, maybe not. The attack didn't depend on anything the temples were doing after his death. But the point is, they were able to bring down the most secure data centers ever designed." Again, everyone nodded in agreement, but I could see actual pain reflected on the faces of Luigi and Stefarino, our two geek brainiacs. To them, any attack on technology was a personal insult!

"Which takes us to the space station and the network denial attacks."

"Yes, again, but not bloodless, but devastating to the psyche of many countries and most people over the age of two. Look, I don't think the space station was all that important to them, other than as a symbol of their skills and ability to reach anywhere. I also suggest it was a way to get us to look up at a time we should have been looking down."

"Taking out the telecommunication networks," the Boss chimed in, breaking the tension in the room by walking over to the espresso machine and making a visible fuss about drawing a coffee. He took it black, so the performance was all about us; he must have sensed something I had missed. I paused to let him continue if he wanted to. He did.

"Jessica, what you've just done is crystalize what has happened. Anna's theory as to the 'why' is that they—whoever they are, our mysterious highly-trained women warriors—are seeking restitution for the tragic management of the refugee camps and the children in them." He looked at Anna, and she nodded, then he turned his laser-like eyes on me.

"So, Captain, we have the 'what' and the 'why'—we know the form and the shape of the 'who' but not the detail; we know the money man and possibly the planner, and given time, we will track him down, I have no doubt of that—but the question remains: how do we find these seriously talented women who have managed to bring the world as we know it to its collective knees?" I looked him straight back without blinking or flinching. His tone had been sharp, but I expected that; it was part of who he was, and I knew from first hand experience that his aggression was not aimed at me but at the terrible situation we were doing our best to solve.

"Anna and I did some thinking, and we came up with a series of filters that might help us to track them down. Mind you, we worked all this out before the network attack happened, so some of our methodologies might now be flawed. But the logic remains the same. Anna?" I said, turning to the FBI agent, who by now had managed to secure yet another excellent expresso from Indigo. It appeared that she had become his personal focus, something I was grateful for. We were a tight-knit team, she was the interloper, and anything that made her more comfortable around us was very much okay with me.

"Thanks, Jessica. Our thinking goes like this," she said as she moved to a huge blank screen and fired it up as a whiteboard. "Just take one girl—age approximately ten years,"—and she drew a stick figure Black Pete would have been proud of. "She leaves the camp for one of the first world countries"—she drew a dotted line, with three question marks at the end—"and then studies for the next ten or twelve years. In this case, let's just say she learned all about computers." She drew a squiggly keyboard after the question marks, then arrows pointing down. "Can you name the best schools anywhere for teaching computer science?" she asked, looking around the room.

"Look at it this way—these women are heavy hitters in the STEM world— they are not just average hackers but high-level programmers and technologists. Someone taught them their skills, and some school somewhere provided the environment, equipment, tutors, and support for them to excel at their chosen skill set. Now, where could they have been placed to learn?" The Boss looked amused, Anna had a concentrated frown on her face, and Indigo was a study in confusion. Then his eyes popped open to twice their usual size, and he clapped his hands as if celebrating something.

"*Capitano*, one moment, please. These little bambinos first have to have homes, yes? And then go to grade school? Getting into university, what you call college, is no easy matter. It takes a lot of money and good grades. But just trying to find thirty women from twenty over the years ago might now be impossible with the attack on all our networks!" Anna shook her head.

"No, Indigo, not impossible. According to my boss, the data is still in the machines somewhere; it seems that it's the connectivity that is fatally damaged. We just can't get it online at the moment. He believes that they will have a system up and running in the next hour that will enable us to interrogate the computers of the various institutions that might have trained these women. We may have to do it manually, onsite, and using very old technology, but there is something else we can do first. Luigi and Stephano believe they have tracked our money man—Mohammad bin Azaria—in and out of several countries. Can we look at his movements closely and see who he was traveling with? With any luck, this might give us a starting point."

"Okay, team, well done. Here's what we will do. Let's get Aire and Roger back online and plan it out. Luigi set up the tracking data; Anna brief the travel data idea based on Stefarino and Luigi's work. Jessica, you brief me on the education data. I'll cover off the Libya idea, and that should do it. Any questions?" No one spoke up, as the Boss had effectively condensed hours of discussion and hypothesis down to four dot points.

And you ask why I loved him so much? Unrequited, but nevertheless, I could only hope!

CHAPTER 47

Arie Rosenberg sat in his worn and tiny office, almost as depressed as the appearance of his battered furniture. He had supposedly retired as the former head of Shin Bet (*Shabak*) some time ago, but having been called in by the current director once the Dome had been attacked, he had no choice but to stay the distance and provide what little help and guidance he could. The small laptop given to him by his long-time nemesis gave a polite shrill, then beeped until he opened the screen. The room under the church in Venice swam into view, to be replaced by a group shot of the Interpol team.

"Hi Arie, hang on a sec while we get Roger back." The image jittered around some, then two boxes opened up, one holding the Interpol team, the other the tired faces of Julius Bronstein, the director of the CIA; the director of the NSA, Frank Reynolds; and the director of the FBI, Roger Winslow. The faces were tiny on the small laptop screen, but the weariness in the eyes of everyone on the call still managed to make its presence felt.

"Roger, thanks for lining up your team. Don't want to know how you did it. Just remember the laptop I gave you is the only one secured enough to get around the terrorists."

"It's okay, PJ. They're here with me in our basement. What have you got for us?"

"Hold one. Arie, can you get your computer genius, Shami? I think it was, in with you, please?" the Boss asked. Arie nodded and disappeared from the screen, which showed a stained wall with a Hamesh Hand painted on it larger than life.

Traditionally, the Hamesh, or Hamsa Hand, is reputed to protect the wearer or user from the "evil eye," a strong belief in the Jewish community.

"Here is Shami," Arie called, squeezing into the frame by leaning in against the computer genius.

"Thanks. Okay, everyone, we need a coordinated effort here, no politics, no bullshitting around. We have what we believe is a method for identifying the women terrorists, and if we all pull our collective fingers out, we should be able to have results in twenty-four hours or less. Roger, I'll let Anna brief you after we brief Arie. Shami, shalom, good to see you again. We need you to work your magic, and I'll get our nerd squad to brief you in a minute. Arie, who do you know in Libya?"

The diminutive Israeli intelligence specialist smiled a wan smile, more from tiredness than anything else. "Rumor has it you just had boots on the ground stomping all over the place. More bodies piled up than from an outbreak of Ebola, and the palace and everyone in it is screaming bloody murder. What could you possibly want now?" he asked, closing his eyes and taking a deep breath, a relaxation technique he used more often than he cared to think about. "Let me guess. You want a HUMINT to follow up to the slag heap you flew out to sea." At the other end of the screen, one set of faces frowned, mostly from their professional feelings of pride being dented by the casual way Arie dismissed the huge military exercise required to actually get the slag heap in the first place, an effort that had cost twenty American lives, not to mention the hundreds killed on the opposing side; at the other end of the screen big grins because Arie was so astute.

"Spot on, Arie, our esteemed captain has divined a theory she would like you to test for us. Same for you, Frank, maybe Rodger, you'll have to work it out between the two of you. Jessica, your turn," he said, pushing me into the center frame. Indigo kindly moved to the side, affording a little more space for me, his natural instinct to be polite coming to the fore.

"Gentlemen, our theory is that the slag heaps you know about were connected to some infrastructure controlled by the terrorists. Maybe by dark fiber. Can you think of a way to track back from the slag sites without necessarily tipping your hand?"

"You think we will find some terrorists lurking at the end of the cable like little fish?"

I smiled, Arie was in fine form, and I—make that we—needed his support to yet again invade a sovereign nation, albeit one that harbored the worst kind of terrorists known to man and had one of the worst records for human rights on the planet. "Yes. We think the slag heaps were the remains of satellite transmission uplinks, power sources, and communication interfaces. If we're correct, the commands and instructions came from another location, which none of us were able to detect at the time."

"Landline linked transmissions deep underground via fiberoptic cable," Arie summarized, nodding silently to himself. "Of course. We do exactly the same thing here and have done so for decades. But I'm not familiar with the technology you need to detect them?" he said somewhat disingenuously, looking straight down the axis of the sight line of the small camera embedded in the top of the laptop.

"Arie, Frank here. We can help you with that. I'll have the necessary technology for you within twelve hours. It's a neat package of ground penetrating radar and lidar, and naturally, it's top secret, so try to keep it out of harm's way, please." This time Arie smiled and rolled his eyes, not in the least offended by the implied insult. Israel had a long history with the US and technology, and not all of it was above board.

"Frank, thank you, we already have our own version of the GPRaL; we borrowed the design from the Russians." Laughter broke the tension, and everyone relaxed just a little.

"Okay, that's step one. Now for number two. Captain, if you will?" the Boss said, setting me up for the second time in as many minutes.

"Mr. Winslow, sir, this is perhaps more up your alley, although having the Israelis look into it in their part of the world would not go astray. We believe we have a way to profile the women and perhaps identify them to enable us to track them down. But if I may, I'll let Agent

Bernstein speak to this." Anna looked at me, nodded, and then took my place in front of the tiny camera.

"Sir, Mr. Rosenberg, Luigi, Stefarino, Shami, this is where you come in. The women had to have been educated somewhere, in first-class institutions, and those records will still be held by the various schools, colleges, and universities. As far as we can ascertain, the recent attacks on our telecommunications did not take out previously stored data, just the local and remote connectivity that provided access to it. We need both electronic, and HUMINT detective works to locate where they were educated. Now," she said, getting into the meat of the briefing, "we don't necessarily need to find them all."

"Just the super technology geeks and the super pilots," Luigi offered, his tiny face on the screen jammed between Indigo and Black Pete's shoulders. To the viewers on the other end of the communication, he looked like a doll's head cut off at the neck!

"Yes, thank you, Luigi, just the—I supposed we could call them the superstars of the terrorist team, although after what they have done, it is very hard to have any respect or sympathy for them. Be that as it may if we look for a couple of first-class pilots with a strong background in programming and electronics, one of whom we have already identified, and then the geeks, as you call them, who are going to have had backgrounds in both the open and dark-web underground computer worlds, we might just be able to work back and dig out more of the group."

"Well," Black Pete offered, to the surprise of everyone, "your key places to start looking at are going to be MIT, Stanford, Colombia, and maybe Caltech in the US, Tsinghua University in Beijing, Nanyang Technology University in Singapore, the University of Cambridge in the UK, and perhaps even ETH in Zurich."

"How on earth do you know that?" exploded the Boss, encapsulating what no doubt everyone on the call had also thought about Black Pete's casual summary of the best senior and possibly most well-known STEM education institutions in the world. He was muscular, highly trained, and experienced, and the thought that he could name some of the top advanced science, technology, engineering, and mathematics facilities off the top of his head was a little unsettling. Black Pete just smiled, reminding me of an alligator just before it snapped its lunch off a meat hook.

"Ran penetration drills against them all at one time or another, you know, the typical televised terrorist takeover of the infrastructure, posturing for the cameras, cutting off a few heads to prove their dedication to whatever crazy cause was popular that day, then they make impossible demands and get blown to kingdom come by the likes of us."

"Interesting. But an accurate assessment," said Arie, smiling for the first time as if he meant it. "We will get on all of this as soon as we finish this call."

"Thanks, Arie, appreciated. Frank, one for you. Has the FBI successfully unpicking the background of the pilot of the Hog?" the Boss asked.

"PJ, we have all her records going back to her days at the Air Force Academy, but nothing before that. Even the background checks that are done as a matter of course on any applicant for the Academy have been wiped. And as Jessica surmised, she was a star pupil, graduated top of her class, did a double degree in aeronautical engineering and computers, topped her class in both, and was offered multiple positions in Doctoral programs, she refused them all, but while she flew on squadron duty, she continued her education, gaining a masters in both computers and nano-electronics. The Air Force rated her as one of their best, slated for high command, but she resigned at the end of her ten-year indentured service period and accepted a role with a development and test company, working on AI and nanotechnology as it applied to airframes and UAVs. Once again, she was rated as the best engineer/test pilot by the Air Force, so Jessica's theory about the best of the best appears to be, at least, in this case, spot on."

"Why can't you find her records before she joined the Academy?" I asked, already knowing the answer.

"Wiped, not a single byte of data on her anywhere. Even her purported family doesn't exist, so who she visited on her various leaves and vacations is as much a mystery as her background."

"Have you found the Hog yet?" the Boss asked.

"Yes. We will have floated the hull by now. Why do you ask?" My turn again. "We believe that you will find a box of tricks in the airframe somewhere, unique to the mission, and if we can unpick the technology, we might get a better understanding of how they operate. The only attacks that may have had a human hand on the wheel were the trucks used in the attack on the oil fields and the Grand Mosque. And they were unquestionably male drivers, according to the eyewitnesses, although we don't know the nationality or sex of the drivers of the trucks that collected the terrorists after each attack. If, in fact, there were drivers."

"Why do you say they were males?" The Boss asked. Arie also looked skeptical. "That's what the witnesses said—male drivers at the oil pipeline, unsure of the sex or details of the driver at the mosque."

"No, I'll bet my next paycheck they were women in disguise. Not hard to do given that they were wearing headdresses and thaubs. Okay, onto other things. Jessica, do you have anything else?"

"No, I think we have covered it all. Anna?" I asked, and the FBI agent shook her head.

"We'll let the nerds take over the call then; thanks, gentlemen, a pleasure to be working with you all again." The Boss signaled to Anna, Pete, and me to move away and led us into a small alcove that was decorated as some kind of shrine, with a stained fresco in the shape of a crying Christ reaching up to the ceiling, reminding us all of the holy nature of the place in which we now worked. If there was a God, and I sincerely hoped there was, I just hoped she was looking down on us now and thinking about really helping us solve the dilemma we found ourselves in.

"I have a question for you all. Have they finished?" I looked at Anna, she looked at Pete, and we all looked back at the Boss.

"No," I said, "not finished. If they are true to their cause, it has to do with releasing or at least providing some form of restitution for the children in the refugee camps. There are a lot of camps. There are a huge number of children. No one had been able to come up with a suitable solution in over seventy years."

"An awful lot of children," added Anna, "from figures I saw back home before I flew here, approximately fifty-six percent of all refugees are under the age of sixteen years. The real tragedy is that in some camps, we now have third and fourth-generation children who have known no other life. In many ways, I can sympathize with their cause, but I just can't condone the method of these attacks."

"Do you have any idea of the economic chaos these attacks have caused? Let alone the fracturing of the religious sphere in a way we haven't ever seen before. Yes, I understand your instinct to support the cause, but the outcome of these attacks will likely not move the bar an inch—the anger is palpable, and you would be lucky to find anyone sympathetic to what is going on. Too many people were killed. Too much infrastructure damaged or wiped out." The Boss had his "cross" look on, but I wasn't fooled for a second. I knew he felt as torn as we were about the issues at hand. Interpol had played a major role in rounding up and arresting hundreds of people traffickers and had whole divisions dedicated to detecting and preventing child slavery and the worst kind of abuse imaginable. The Boss and I had worked with some of these divisions in just the last two years, so the images of naked, starved, violated, and undernourished children were fresh in our minds.

"With the sheer economic disruption to transport, food supply, and everything necessary for a normal, well-lived life, where will the passion and empathy come from to address such an existential issue? Especially as the majority of the camps are all far away from civilization in third-and fourth-world countries?"

"Out of sight, out of mind," I said softly, but my feelings for the refugees were extremely strong, and I worried if this might cause me to miss something in our complex and continually expanding investigation. When the Boss and the team we had recruited stopped the child trafficking ring in Turkey, it took me months to find my balance again, so bad were the conditions of the youngsters—some only just two or three years old. And the Boss had disappeared for over two months after that operation, so I wasn't the only one to feel the effects of the raw brutality. "I wonder what their end game is?" I muttered, thinking out loud. Pete turned to look at me, a wan smile on his well-worn face.

"You can bet it won't be a simple 'give me the money' gambit," he said, walking over to the overworked espresso machine, which was taking a beating by anyone's measure. He looked down at the cup he was filling, shook his head at some internal discussion, then turned and faced us all again. "There are literally millions of refugees in camps all over the place, and that means millions of kids. How in the name of Hell do we do anything meaningful about that?" he asked, looking extremely pissed.

The Boss stepped in and took control of the room, where the emotional temperature had risen considerably. "Well, we are Interpol, not Social Services, and quite frankly, those types of questions are well above our pay grades. Let's get on with what we are good at—finding the bad guys and putting them behind bars."

"Or in the ground."

Everyone nodded silently but in a way that clearly signaled that while we were accepting what we had just heard, we were not necessarily accepting the finality of the Boss's argument.

COLD WAR

The penultimate attack was as breathtaking as it was effective, not actually being discovered until some days after it had been implemented. Heihe, in northeastern China, on the border of Russia, had a sister city just across the Amur River called Blagoveshchensk, which had an approximately ten times larger population than the smaller Chinese town. What made them of any interest to anyone outside of either town was that just recently, they had been linked to another Russian town known as Svobodny, also on the Amur River, which in turn had been linked further east to Khabarovsk, which then had been linked to Vladivostok in the south, and with Sakhalin in the north.

What enjoined these six mostly unknown towns, with perhaps the exception of Vladivostok, was the little matter of a seventy-five-billion-dollar gas pipeline, which had been decades in the making but now provided Russian gas to China. The confluence of the so-called "Power of Siberia," "Sakhalin-Khabarovsk-Vladivostok" pipeline and the "Heihe-Shanghai" pipeline was the town of Blagoveshchensk, and it was there that the Russians and the Chinese finally found evidence of how their pride and joy had been effectively killed motherless stone dead. It took decades to design, argue about, finance, and then eventually build the seven-thousand-kilometer pipeline, only to have it totally destroyed in what was thought to be just a day or two.

The evidence was a tiny glass capsule hidden in a pile of refuse, in which was a slithering mass that looked like minute jellyfish wrapped in a mercury bath. It would take both Russian and Chinese scientists weeks to establish exactly what the solution was, as the moment it was exposed to air, it evaporated, so neither country could effectively backwards model it, reproduce it, or clone it.

It was nanotechnology at its finest, though no one anywhere was celebrating the incredible feat of physics and engineering. And the only reason the West got to hear about it at all was that one of the workmen involved in digging up the pit told his wife, who told her friend, who told her husband, who told the shopkeeper when he went into town to collect his rice allowance.

The shopkeeper just happened to be in the employ of a French intelligence agency, the DGSE—*Direction Générale de la Sécurité Extérieure*—who had then accidentally shared the intelligence with their American counterparts, the CIA. Thank you, NSA signals division!

All the Russians and the Chinese could do was document the fact that the entire gas line, as far as it reached in any direction, no longer flowed, effectively choked with billions and billions of liters of solid mass, which dissolved into the air with a sour, rotten egg smell when exposed.

The politicians postured, shouted, drank themselves into many sleepless nights, ranted and raved, all to no avail.

Every centimeter of the pipelines, every valve, pumping station, connection, wellhead, and filter was useless, and what finally pushed China off the edge of the reason was the downstream pipelines to Harbin and Jilin were equally sabotaged. The world was down to less than thirty percent of its oil reserves. And the single biggest exporter of natural gas was now a hundred percent out of business.

Russia, China, and most of the rest of the world were angry—very, very angry, particularly as they had no one to point the finger at. And most of all, they were scared.

One thing that had not been shared with the Russians or the Chinese was the information brought to the USA by the two priests.

Some thirty years ago, a disenchanted Muslim teacher started taking girls out of refugee camps, rehoming them, and then having them educated and trained by the best minds on the planet.

The economies of most countries threatened to collapse, and major energy providers were shuttering their businesses. The media, which usually managed to pour gasoline onto any story with incendiary possibilities, was stymied by the worldwide blackout on anything networked. So they were relying on landlines, old-style fax machines, and real live reporters, most of whom were so wet behind the ears that they missed the essence of the story in their blind enthusiasm to get the word out "NOW!"

After all, they had all been brought up in a world where instant gratification and three clicks solved everything!

The world was being brought to its knees by a band of highly intelligent, highly motivated, superbly trained, and dedicated ex-refugee women. Not a country—not a nation-state—just thirty or so previously stateless and now anonymous women working alone but somehow well connected.

Or so the world thought.

And their reach had been proven to be four-dimensional—worldwide and into space itself.

CHAPTER 48

"We can't keep the lid on this any longer. With the Russian/Chinese pipeline attack, there are now so many competitive political interests screaming for justice. It's a wonder we're not at war."

"We are. You just don't know how to locate the other side," Julius Bronstein said, settling in his chair and reaching for the scotch bottle. He looked at the fourstar general sitting directly opposite and held the scotch up; the general nodded, and Julius added two fingers to another glass.

"Easy for you to say, I've got the White House screaming at me, the Joint Chiefs running around like chooks with their heads cut off, and absolutely no idea who we are fighting and how to stop them.

"Bridget, we have an invisible enemy who has had thirty-plus years to prepare and a group of terrorists who have been inside our infrastructure and systems for at least twenty-five of those years, maybe longer, and as you well know, a homegrown terrorist is the hardest to find at any time."

"Okay, I buy that. But why can't we pin down the Hog pilot? We have her fingerprints, DNA, photos, military history, and civilian history; for Christ's sake, we even know her shoe size. How the bloody hell can she mount a daylight attack on West Point and just disappear?"

"Good question, and one we have asked ourselves several times over the past few days. But the simple problem is they are—or were—well inside our IT technology and communications—at every level—and everything they don't want us to know has been wiped so completely there is literally no record of any of the data. Not even the holes or gaps you would usually see when someone removes metadata. Yes, we have the paper records of the transfer of the ammunition back in two thousand one, but that only helps us understand how they managed the switch. We tracked that to the point of destination, where they have effectively shuffled around so much became invisible. And, at a guess, the team we are fighting now isn't the team that stole the hardware, the aircraft, the drones, the missiles; all that has the ring of a completely different set of actors. They may be part of the same group, but they are certainly not the same people who are attacking us now."

"So, you're saying we have nothing."

"No, not nothing. I believe Interpol has the best handle on this; after all, they are working all ends of the problem."

"Your famous Colonel PJ Anthony." Roger Wilson, the head of the FBI, drank from his glass, smiling over the rim at the four-star general. Like most of the military of her ilk, action spoke louder than words, and terms like "battlespace," "prosecute," and "terminal force projection" got thrown around like rice at a wedding. In his experience, the military had very little understanding of detective work, police work, or the finer and detailed things any great investigator would hold as their bible.

"Yes, Bridget, PJ. One of the best soldiers I have ever had the pleasure to serve with. And if he hadn't gone over to the dark side by joining Interpol, he'd be sitting right where you are now."

"He's that good?" she asked, eyebrows raising and gesturing with her nowempty glass at the director of the CIA.

"Yes, he is. And the team he has assembled is first class, and the team of hitters he has hidden away somewhere in Italy is simply the best of the best."

"What do they know that we don't?" she asked, accepting her refilled glass with a wan smile. Her untidy close-cut blond hair hardly moved when she bobbed her head in thanks. As the head of the most important arm of the military services- in that she provided direct interface with the joint chiefs of staff and the president- she had learned long ago that short hair saved time and energy and was an efficiency point for the daily grind of high-risk environments.

"PJ has shared everything Interpol has discovered with us. If the truth is known, he is, in effect, driving Israeli intelligence, the Italians, and probably us. His reach into the intelligence and military communities in the EU countries is something we can only dream of because Interpol is still seen as an untarnished badge by the Europeans and the rest of the world. Truly apolitical and independent of any nation-state." She nodded again, looking down at the dregs in the bottom of her glass.

"Better stop drinking, or you'll all tell stories about me." She looked up, held the eyes of the three powerful men around the table with her, then placed her glass upside down in front of her. "But one thing you may not have thought about is that you are unlikely to be able to find deep-seated dark fiber with any technology unless there is a signal being carried by it. We invented the bloody stuff so it couldn't be detected when it was quiet, for very specific reasons," she said, leaning back in her chair, wiping one hand through her hair.

"Arie will have thought of that. You can count on it. The bigger question is what we do if we find the cable?" said Julius Bronstein. As the head of the CIA, this unfolding worldwide catastrophe was the stuff of nightmares. Not one single byte of information had been detected prior to the first attack, and nothing since, making the CIA look not only old-fashioned and useless but a deterrent to finding the answers needed to shut down the terrorists.

His gloomy thoughts were interrupted by the buzz of Frank Reynolds' miniature laptop, provided by the Interpol team as the only known secure means of transmitting data around the world under the current circumstances.

"Yes, Indigo, isn't it? How can I help?" Frank asked. The small screen showed the wall of screens inside the cavern, deep under the foundations of the centuries-old church in Venice, and the faces of Indigo and an as yet unidentified person leaning on his shoulder.

"Sir, Mister PJ asks you to holda for onea minutea if you pleasea," Indigo said, moving out of the frame. The Colonel's face replaced it, and one large hand blocked the screen, then managed to pull back and point to the unknown person. "Frank, apologies, I forgot to introduce you to a very smart person; more to come, and if you repeat any of this out loud, I'll come over and kill you." Frank moved the screen so that only he could see it and plugged in a small headset.

"Okay, PJ, I am secure."

"Frank, meet Brother Stefarino, he's one of the very good guys, and I need you to listen to what he has to tell you. Okay?" The line went dead quiet. Frank furrowed his brow in concentration, knowing that the other three people in the room were now looking at him to the exclusion of everything else. He finally nodded, stood up, snapped the laptop closed, and walked out of the room.

"Well now," said Julius, "that's interesting. I wonder what's up in the land of fine dining and glassware?"

"We'll soon know. Perhaps we should adjourn for half an hour until Frank can come back to us?"

"Yes. Good move." And with that, the three stood up, stretched, looked as uncomfortable as it was possible to do and still maintain their dignity, and left the conference room.

In a dark alcove just off the same space, Frank listened intently to the monk, wondering, and not for the first time, why he placed so much reliance on PJ, someone with whom he had gone into the trenches with but was, in the very best of times, impossibly difficult to deal with and as unpredictable as the weather.

"Sir, we are a humble order. Our quest is simple: we gather up all the known published history of our Christ and add it to our digital library so that it may be preserved throughout all time. We are funded by a conglomerate of independent sources whose only objective is to see that we achieve our mission. They do not interfere. They do not question. They only provide what we need when we need it to be successful."

"Okay, Brother Stefarino, I understand that. How can I help you?" At the other end of the transmission, Stefarino looked at the Colonel, who nodded his permission. Trust was hard-earned, but the monk trusted his own brother Indigo implicitly, who in turn absolutely trusted this strange man who he had brought into the most secret sanctuary of the brotherhood, so he nodded, then turned to face the camera.

"Signore, this is difficult for me, but I am encouraged by the integrity of the people my brother has brought to me. You have a traitor in your midst, perhaps many, but we can help you find the perpetrators of this calamity if you choose to allow us." The monk looked serious, his creased face a study in concentration. He did not know the person to whom he was talking. But in the very short time, he had been in the company of the tall Colonel and his people, he had come to trust their almost fierce dedication to each other and to track down the terrorists. And to be perfectly honest, a world in disorder did nothing for his order, which was almost totally reliant on the generosity of believers to survive.

"When you say a traitor in our midst, do you mean the women who have penetrated our systems and networks?" asked Frank, holding the Monk's eyes.

"No, *signore,* although without a doubt, some of these refugees will still be inside your networks as we speak. It has not been necessary for them all to reveal themselves at this point, as I am sure you have worked out for yourself. No, *signore,* I mean that you have a traitor in your very ranks at the highest level of government. This we know without fail." The monk's words hit Frank like a sledgehammer, reinforcing something that had been tickling away at the back of his mind for some time. It was inconceivable that the damage to the worldwide infrastructure could have been successfully achieved without top-level political cover somewhere. After all, the terrorists had stolen two massive bombs, aircraft, Strontium-90, and missiles and then had developed such sophisticated nanotechnology that he, as the head of the FBI, had never heard of. Neither had the NSA, the CIA, nor any of the thousands of geeks they kept on staff between the three agencies for just that purpose.

"How do you know this? And do you know who it is?" Frank asked.

"*Si, certo, signore*, that we do. It is the head of your refugee department; I think you call it your Department of State. She has been corresponding with the man you have identified as the potential head of the terrorist organization, Mohammad bin Azaria. We came across this by accident when we were looking at a disaster at one of the camps in Turkey some time last year. At first, we did not know what it was or what it meant. But when your Colonel here briefed us on this man, we went back to the conversations we had recorded, and this is our conclusion now."

"You're saying the Secretary of State is one of the terrorists?" Frank asked, disbelief written all over his face.

"*Si, signore*, she has been corresponding with this man for over a year, and possibly longer. We can provide you with the tapes if you wish, but their size will be too big for the little unit we provided to you. Perhaps we can send it by courier to you?" Frank nodded his mind a blur of confusion and hope. If this was true, and if he could get to the Secretary without tipping his hand, they could perhaps get to the terrorists before they struck again.

"Brother Stefarino, can you please put Anna back online, and thank you for your information. I assure you; we will use it in a way that never can or will be attributed to you or your organization." As he finished, the image of Anna replaced that of the monk on the small screen.

"Sir, you called?"

"Did you hear what the monk said?"

"Yes, sir, he told us about this earlier today; it was one of the reasons the Colonel wanted to talk to you."

"Okay, get yourself to DaVinci ASAP. I'll commandeer the Colonel's SR-71 and get you back here pronto. Put PJ on, please."

"Frank."

"PJ. You heard all that?"

"Yes. And I want to suggest something to you that will not sit well." Frank's face went from bemused to confused in a split second. *Working with PJ did that to you*, he thought to himself.

"What?"

"Do nothing about the Secretary. Absolutely nothing."

"You're joking?"

"No, deadly serious. She is our direct link to Mohammad bin Azaria and may also be in contact with the terrorists. Though how she is managing this given that we have lost all our networks is beyond me, perhaps she has her own monk on tap." Frank thought for a minute, working through the possibilities. "No, my advice is to let her run. We can set up covert surveillance and try to track and trace her communications; let's see where finding the dark fiber gets us. We may find we have more to bargain with than we realize."

"We've got a team in the field in Montana as we speak. Do you have a view on this as well?"

"Yes, I do. Same thing I said to Arie. Use the weakest signal you can use to get a lock on the fiber, then go dark. Track it back to its point of origin, but don't go anywhere near the locus. When you get a location, let us know, and we'll have another chat."

"You seem very sure of yourself."

"Frank, this group has brought the word to its knees in less than ten full days. Don't underestimate them, don't tip them off. I have a feeling about this, and if I am correct, there may or may not be another attack, but I'm betting on not at this point."

"PJ, I know you. I trust you implicitly, but how do you come to this conclusion after all that has happened?"

"Two of the last three attacks have been bloodless. The network outage wasn't, but the damage was collateral, not direct. It was also very specific – as if someone ringfenced anything really important to keeping people alive. The space station and the gas pipeline had no casualties—and the really clever move with the network attack is that every local node was left working; in so much as hook a new screen or laptop up to the local database, and you have access to all your stored data. Problem is, the chips were fried, according to our geeks, so replacing all of them may take years. And only very limited damage was done to medical equipment, elevators, traffic management systems, airport systems, or transport systems. Even aircraft that didn't have manual reversion or backup flight controls only lost their navigation and information management systems. That takes considerable skill and a huge amount of knowledge and forethought—and what it says to my team and me here is that they are getting ready to negotiate. There's a reason we're walking the cat backward from the transmission sources; and a reason we now know the Secretary of State is somehow involved. These are not errors or mistakes." Frank took all this in and, not for the first time, wished he was anywhere else but in the middle of this worldwide disaster. He nodded silently to himself, the old adage of "If you have a dog, don't bark yourself" came to mind, and with PJ, he had the finest investigator he had ever known.

"Okay, you win. We'll hold off on the Secretary and go very slow and careful with the dark fiber. Keep me informed, please." He cut the connection, wondering how he would break the news to his compatriots, probably waiting for impatiently by now, and wondered how he would get them to agree with his plan of essentially "do nothing, slowly." Well, he got paid the medium bucks for something, so he straightened his shoulders and walked back into the room.

He'd give it his best shot!

Back in Venice, Anna was on her way to the airport, a small briefcase with data disks under lock and key, the computer geeks were back at their screens, and the Boss, Pete, Indigo, and I were sitting around the low glass table, which having been made in Murano had little tiny, colored fish inside it, creating the impression that we were putting our well-used coffee cups and mugs down on top of an aquarium.

"We can trust Arie to manage his end. Frank will get his troops in line. If you look at this from an investigative point of view, we know who did it—even if we can't identify individuals; we know who the money man is—or was; we don't actually know his status; we think we know where the command, control, and communication centers might be, and we know the motive—or at least part of it, in so much as the historical context we got from the priests."

"The question is," I added to the Boss's summary, "we don't know what they want now. But I think we can hypothesize." The Boss looked directly at me, a curious look on his weather-beaten face. He raised an eye as if to say, "Well, spill it," so I did. "With over twenty-seven million refugees in the world and half that many again who are stateless, I'm willing to bet they want to force us to do something about changing their status in some way. And before you ask, I haven't the faintest idea how that could be done. But I think we need to find out."

"Do we?"

"Yes."

"Then take Indigo and start working on that." The Boss stood up and signaled to Pete. "Pete, let's go for a walk." They moved out of the room towards the musty cave-like tunnel that provided entrance to this ancient basement as Indigo, and I moved more into the room, thinking about our approach.

How did you manage to repatriate millions of refugees of multiple nationalities, all ages and religions, all shapes, and sizes? For that matter, by comparison, the State of New York held—what—nineteen, twenty million people? I knew the whole Australian continent only had a population approaching twenty-six million. Maybe we could set them up there?

RECOVERY

The USS *Ulysses* was one of the finest deep-diving support vessels ever put into service, equipped as it was with the best deep-diving equipment on the planet. Originally designed to support stranded nuclear subs sitting uncomfortably on the bottom of the ocean somewhere, usually, in very deep and unwelcoming water, the *Ulysses* and her crew had fined down their skills to the point where they not only thought they were the best, they actually were.

On the deck sat two bright yellow diving bells, a super high-tech remote-piloted miniature submarine, and in her deep well usually sat a fully manned submersible that had already set the record for the deepest recorded and filmed dive in history, some 36,690 feet down into the Mariana Trench, which was some 690 feet deeper than that achieved by a well-known filmmaker. The fact that it had taken two full months to find the 690-foot crevice in the murky bottom of the trench to set the record went largely unreported!

At the moment, the "Blue Belle," as she was called, sat on top of the wrecked A-10 Warthog, delicately lifting the cracked and warped canopy off the airframe. The blow-up doll pilot had been speared by part of the instrument panel and now lay like a wrinkled, lifeless skin, its helmeted head lying at such an angle as to defy gravity. With the canopy removed, pincer-like arms extended and grappled the bent airframe behind and in front of the wing attachment points. Within minutes, the sub moved away, giving the signal to start lifting the wreck topside.

As the depth was 3,450 feet, and not 700 as originally reported, the lift took thirteen hours when the airframe, gushing water from every orifice and impact hole, finally emerged into the sunlight. Within another half hour, the airframe was secured on the deck, and the real work started. A member of the crew dressed in a nondescript bodysuit, complete with helmet and mask, approached with a Giger counter. He ran the instrument over the nose, into the cockpit, then under the fuselage where the wheels would have been had they survived the crash. He looked up towards the bridge and shook his head.

Thirteen crewmen, including five females dressed in bright blue overalls and carrying a myriad of electronic devices, descended on the airframe like a swarm of ants. Silently, they worked in harmony and, within minutes, had the extraneous contents of the cockpit stripped out, laying on a canvas sheet. Bits and pieces of the internal electronics soon joined the cockpit debris until a second sheet had to be laid out to accommodate the plethora of bits and pieces. With its hard-shell helmet, oxygen mask, and visor, the deflated blow-up pilot made an interesting con trast to the electronics.

A photographer and a video technician recorded every action, sending the data stream up to the bridge, where it was secured on old-fashioned silver DVD disks and USB pens. An armed courier took the mechanical data stored in a small leather pouch, saluted the captain, then left for the flight deck at the bow of the *Ulysses*. Within another ten minutes, the Coast Guard helicopter was on its way to the aircraft carrier *Ronald Reagan*, where a fast jet would ferry the material back to Washington. Meanwhile, back on the *Ulysses*, technical experts pulled every electronic component apart, laying out the component bits and pieces with ordered precision. One of the blue suits found the extraneous control box, signaled to the photographers, then gingerly eased the top off. The insides were fused together in one mass, so much so that the individual component parts could only be identified by their smudged color coding. She shook her head. No one was getting any intelligence from the wreckage, no matter how hard they tried. She recognized plasma fusing when she saw it and smiled to herself. Whoever was creating all these problems for the world knew their job. And had very high tech at their disposal.

The southeastern region of Libya is both vast and mostly empty. If you travelled along the Coffa-Jalu-Ajdablya until it terminated in an unnamed village behind which sat a modern airport, then jumped up to a thousand feet or so into the air, you saw what appeared to be green crop circles. This was not the work of aliens but rather the work of industrious farmers who used water sprinklers on massive wheels to create a green oasis of rich crops. It was through these very crops that a small group of camouflaged insurgents crawled so slowly that they were invisible to the naked eye—which mostly reacted to movement, as well as light.

And there presently wasn't any, the night being literally pitch black and moonless. The column paused, then the point man flattened out to allow the technician behind him to come alongside. They both froze for a minute, then, sure that they were still undetected, fed a small probe into the rich earth, millimeter by millimeter. A third insurgent looked at the heads-up display inside his helmet, tracking the progress of the probe. When it got to the optimum depth, calculated by the science geeks back in Tel Aviv, he tapped the second man on the leg.

The probe stopped. The watcher pressed a small button on a hand controller and watched the pattern of the electromagnetic pulse ripple out from the probe in concentric circles, which bent slightly just off to their left. He pinged the probe a second time, watched the same pattern emerge, then reached out and tapped the point man three times on his leg.

The point man raised his off hand, bending from the waist, and started a delicate crawl off in the direction the watcher had indicated. The probe man retracted the micro cable, then followed the point man, who had stopped ten meters from their previous position.

The probe went into the ground again, two pings radiated silently some five meters below the bellies of the insurgents, and the whole process was repeated again five meters further away. After the twelfth probe, the leader of the insurgents formed an opinion and, with a series of leg taps, redirected his column and then withdrew back in the direction of their pickup point. Once they had cleared the irrigated crop circle, they were able to stand and make good time. Their stealth helicopter stood ready and, within minutes of their arrival, had risen to a safe thirty meters above the desert floor and headed back out the way they had come.

The team huddled around their leader, helmeted head to helmeted head. "דפטעקמןדןקדשנקי"

"Huh! Who would have thought!"

In Montana, it was a different outcome; the same team of commandos as had discovered the molten satellite dish flew into the Ranger station again, then probed the ground, firing up minute electronic pulses, creating an electronic map of the cable that lay buried beneath the forest floor. Once they had a visual, they then used their LIDAR to track the direction, all the way back to a dusty plain, where a rather ramshackle hut sat in splendid isolation, standing out on the long-distance radar like a beacon. Their instructions had been clear and unambiguous. Don't get detected. Don't annoy anyone. Just get the intelligence and come home.

However, unbeknown to anyone on the helicopter, their electronic signature had been detected by a remote sensor that was part of a hidden ring surrounding the farmhouse three kilometers out, not that it particularly mattered.

CHAPTER 49

Pete and the Boss walked up the moldy stairs and out into a beautiful starfilled night. The protective detail fell in around them silently, ghosts that faded in an out of sight as they passed through the inky-black shadows. There were only four protection staff at this time, as two of their cohort had escorted Anna to the airport.

"Pete, there's something we have to consider and something we have to do with some haste." The Boss walked towards a bollard on the edge of the canal, gesturing for Pete to join him on an adjacent rusted metal protrusion, which may or may not have been a bollard a hundred years ago.

"You always get the best seat!" Pete said, squatting uncomfortably on the wet and slippery surface. He wiped his meaty hands on the side of his pants, leaving long, green-and-black trails of seaweed and fungus.

"Rank hath its privileges," the Boss replied, turning to face his long-time friend. They had taken bullets together, bled together, and even had a few drinks together, but they had never lost respect for each other.

"First off, I sense that our captain and perhaps even our stalwart FBI special agent might become a little emotional once we close in on our female contagionists. That's not a bad thing on its own, but given the emotional and political temperature that currently exists, we need to be ready for any sign that we might lose them to the investigation." He waved his hand as if swatting that ugly thought away. "That's not the real issue. Pete, if I asked you to find someone, how would you go about it?"

"Using all possible resources?"

"Yes."

"Even off-book?" Pete asked, referring to the darkest and most illegal depths of the internet and electronic record keeping.

"Yes." Pete sat perfectly still for a minute, turned his head to the side, looked down at the dark water of the canal, then looked up and smiled. Which on his ugly, scarred face looked like a first-class sneer.

"Well, step one, establish nationality. Then look for personal IDs such as social security, medical identification, library cards, driver's licenses, bank cards and accounts, and police histories, then attack social media, and find their electronic trail. Then you get serious. If you have their face and a location, root through all the CCTV footage until your eyes bleed and build up a profile. Find their cell phone, locate their Mac address, track their GPS data, mapping data, and app use. I imagine the monks and our tame geeks could do this in a heartbeat." The Boss looked impressed and, not for the first time, was reminded that his "muscle" had a brain—and a very good one at that.

"Yes, they probably could. And we have the face and body type, coloring, height, and weight of at least one of them, our missing pilot from the A-10. But that's not really the problem."

"No. You're worried about what they are going to ask for and the reaction of the countries most impacted by the attacks. Discounting the football field, the racetrack, and maybe even the space station, you have some very upset religious groups with long histories of open warfare, and then you have all the countries that have been impacted by the oil and gas attacks. No one is going to be in the mood to talk, let alone negotiate, and if it comes to that, what could the terrorists possibly offer to get any of the injured parties across the line? They have wiped out sixty to seventy percent of the world's energy supply, crashed economies all across the globe, scared the general population shitless, and wiped out the greatest toy anyone could ever have—the bloody internet!" The Boss smiled at this, not for one minute interested in such trivial things as people playing games or looking up porn. He had far bigger issues to address.

"According to our head monk, the internet attack took out every node, router, Wi-Fi hub, and computer or device connected to the net at that time. Stefarino believes that all the cloud and hardwired data storage is still intact and can be accessed via local area networks—albeit constructed from scratch. And if that is the case, then we should be able to find a lot of what we are looking for."

"But we know they wiped the records going back to two thousand two—or at least any that included data on any of the perpetrators. I think what we will be looking for are black holes in the data."

"Yes. Remember, Interpol is charged with remaining neutral and independent of politics and religion, and with one hundred ninety-four members, we represent a truly global police force. Emphasis on the word 'police.' We are also independent of the UN. But these attacks have affected every single one of our members, and while Israel, Italy, and the United States have actually engaged us, we are honor-bound to act in the best interests of all members. And that might put us in direct conflict with one of our three current sponsors down the road." He went into his thoughtful pose for a minute, then turned to look directly at Pete. "You know, if you look at the hacking, it's either brilliantly simple or as complex as hell. I wonder which?" he mused. "They have effectively thrown us back to the nineteen sixties."

"Boss, you are always telling us to concentrate on the 'now'—work forward, even when we are walking the cat backwards. What's the real issue that's worrying you?" Pete asked, standing to wipe some more slime off the back of his combat pants."

"The Secretary of State. She is a very big stone on our path, and while we can count on Frank and his friends to manage that situation, she suggests a level of penetration into our system of government at the very highest level. And if they can get one person into such a position of power and influence, the chances of them getting others into similar positions in other countries is very high. Remember, we don't know the nationalities of these women, we don't know what countries they were embedded in, and we don't know how they have been managed all this time. Twenty to thirty years is a very long period to maintain control over an individual, let alone twenty or thirty of them from differing cultures and beliefs. We can't assume anything about them at all. But I have had one thought on that."

"And that is?" Pete asked, sitting back down on the rusty bollard. He wiped his grimy hands down the sides of his pants again, with exactly the same result as the previous two attempts to clean his hands, then turned them palm up to inspect his work. "I'm going to have to decontaminate when we finish here. I can feel the bugs crawling all over me." The Boss smiled, warmed by the attempt of humor by the weathered special forces operative.

"Surely the people in the camps would know who was taken. We ask enough questions in enough camps, and we will get at least five or six names and descriptions—and okay, they may be years older now, but we have to start somewhere. I like your idea about the education facilities, and we'll run that down, but I would really like to get someone into the camps to start asking questions." Pete looked at the Boss, his eyebrows crinkling up in concentration.

"What about the rescue teams we used last year, cleaning up that kiddie trafficking gang? They had a lot of very experienced and skilled medically trained staff, multilingual, and could probably put thirty or forty in the field in quick double time."

"And they know their way around the camps."

"Yes, probably as well as anyone." The Boss looked up at the sky, which was starting to fill up with stars, reminding him that no matter how deep the problem they faced may be, the world still turned on its axis, the sun rose every day, and the stars came out every night to play.

"Okay, Pete, make that happen. Take a couple of secure e-pads with you. I'll speak to Lyon and the general and get you the money, resources, and transport. Manage the whole exercise as if our lives depended on it because I suspect that unless we start learning more about our female terrorists, what little of the world we have left might just get squished under their highly talented young feet!"

CHAPTER 50

The room was both spacious and luxurious, and the lightly colored pink-and-cream silk curtains flowed in each doorway on the light air, fluttering silently in a hypnotic dance. The distinctive odor of hashish permeated the entire area, and while the scarce furnishings were distinctly rich in their heritage and appearance, they paled into insignificance when compared to the magnificent costume of the king, Freok Bib Mohammad Al Sin wore, putting the sixteen members of his harem to shame. The jewelry he wore on his fingers alone was worth well over seven million US dollars, and the jewels woven cleverly into his headdress probably gave that number a sincere push. He lay indolently on one hip, hooker pipe to one side of his mouth, his deep black eyes currently staring holes in the head of the Al Mabaahith Al Jena'eyah, one of the three security forces that supposedly protected the expectations of the king and the kingdom.

"You assured us the issue was finished with. You assured us that the terrorists who attacked our oil field and the Grand Mosque were discovered and removed. You assured us that it was the French who did this to us and that you would take the appropriate action. On your advice, I requested a French team to discuss the issue with us, and now I find you have not only not solved our problem, but you have murdered the entire French contingent and lay the blame for the attacks at their feet." The king paused and sucked on his pipe stem, causing a stream of bubbles to rise in the hooker. Smoke limped out of his generous mouth, and spittle ran down his meaty chin. He seemed to shrink in on himself for a second, then puffed out to his full size, causing his colorful robes to ripple and flow as if attacked by a small tornado.

"Your Majesty, we did your bidding. To the letter. No more, no less." The king screwed up his eyes as if trying to focus on the uniformed man standing at attention, then sucked on the hooker again. He shook his head from side to side, pulled the stained mouthpiece out, and shook it at the intelligence officer. Bits of spit flew out, hitting the soldier in the chest and staining his shirt.

"No, you did not. You did not solve the issue; you did not kill the right people, and now I have Interpol sticking its nose into my business again. Take him away!" he said to the three guards who stood, if it were possible, even more rigidly at attention, Kalashnikovs strapped across their chests. They each reached forward to grab a piece of the unfortunate intelligence officer, who suddenly sprang away, drawing his side-arm, and as he dove towards the back of the king's reclining throne, fired five shots, one into the middle of each of the guards and two into the head of the king.

The screams and shouts of the harem almost drowned out the sounds of the shots, and the guards posted at the doors hesitated for just a split second, which gave the members of the Al Mukhabarat Al A'amah, the second arm of the triad of security forces, who had been patiently waiting outside, enough time to move in and kill them all. In less than a single minute, the kingdom had changed regime, hardly bloodless, but under the circumstances, with the palace guard and the king as the only casualties, it could be said to have been efficient, if not timely!

In what would later be seen as a coincidence of timing, sixteen indoor sports stadiums across the USA disappeared in a rain of drones fired from the same identical type of trucks that had launched the earlier attacks in the UK and Germany. However, this time there were casualties, mostly working staff who kept the stadiums in tip-top condition, and the trucks were all identified by corporate logos on the side, representing the biggest companies in the US. Local police were baffled by the empty cabs and the burnt-out chassis, making it almost impossible to work out if they had been manned or drones. The branding immediately led to an outrage so loud that the stores and companies identified on the trucks were the subjects of pop-up protests, mostly with armed activists, which turned a simple terrorist act into a massive, country-wide civil insurrection. The national news on old-style valve radios that night talked of troops in the streets, shooting and lootings, imposed curfews, and unrest on a scale never seen in the United States since the Tea Party two hundred years before.

And in faraway Venice, PJ shook his head when he heard the news. He had been wrong.

CHAPTER 51

Julius Bronstein, the director of the CIA, the director of the NSA, Frank Reynolds, and the head of the FBI, Roger Winslow, sat before the president of the United States and a veritable plethora of representatives from both Congress and the Senate. The military contingent, notable for their shining gold and colored ribbons and hats, sat off to both sides as if surrounding the main audience of the elected representatives of the country. The media, camera-less and recorder-less, notebooks balanced on their laps, filled the first row, their discomfort clear for all to see. They had been selected to attend on a "pool" basis from the White House Press Corps. The briefing room had been arranged like a college auditorium, with rows and rows of seats, all offset as they rose up and away from the stage. Julius felt like he was back in middle school, facing the class with his—as it had turned out—very poor presentation of how to grow a plant inside a soda bottle. The three men and the president were arranged so that they faced each other and the audience. A military guard stood rigidly at attention behind the president, who, while outwardly calm, was churning inside as much as anyone else "in the know." But she hadn't been elected just for her stunning looks, so she applied some of her legendary charm and whit and led off the conversation she was sure would resonate around the world in seconds, even though every cell phone, communication device, computer, and electronic watch had been forfeited as the price of admission. Not that any of them actually worked anymore!

"This is a pivotal moment in the history of the world, and any thoughts you may have about political advantage, bipartisan behavior, coalitions of rejection, or any other attempt at suborning this office or this country will be met with the harsh reality of enforced martial law. This is not negotiable. Martial law will be declared from noon Eastern time today, right across the fifty-one states. We are also closing our borders to all countries immediately, grounding all international and internal flights that are still in the air; in short, we are going into a complete lockdown for the foreseeable future." She paused, looking critically at her audience, and saw shock and horror on some faces, smirky joy on others, and bland acceptance on the rest. The military, as was their wont, sat stony-faced, giving nothing away. But she knew the internal temperature of her soldiers in arms, having briefed the chiefs of staff and their staff just prior to this defining meeting.

It had not been a pleasant experience.

They hated what was going to happen but accepted the necessity of it in the interests of maintaining a semblance of normality within the nation and getting America back on its feet. The critical issue for them would be balancing a police action with military strategies and tactics, something previous administrations had failed to do on numerous occasions.

"Any citizen caught overseas will have the support of our local embassies but will essentially be on their own. Any foreigners caught here by the border closures will be either allowed their freedom within the limits of all civil rights or incarcerated, depending on how they match up when questioned. Let me sum this up for us all. We are down to our tactical reserves of gas and oil. We have rioting and civilian warfare in thirty states. We have armed insurrection in sixteen states, and frankly, the National Guard and local police can't cope with the current rules of engagement. Our people have very little food, our hospitals are overrun, and we are having extreme difficulty maintaining any rule of law. People are panicking, desperate, scared, and rudderless.

“Then you add in the panic and chaos overseas, in literally every country of note, and you have an untenable situation on a planet-wide scale.

“Now, as the elected representatives of your respective states, you all have one job, as the elected officials supposedly representing the people of this great country, and one job only. Get out to your districts, get to your mayors and governors, your priests and teachers, and get them focused on calming things down. The faster you do this, the faster we can ship in food and medical supplies and get everyone at least partially catered for. We will come out of this, but only if you do your jobs.

“The priorities are simple—food, water, shelter. And it will be up to you individually to drive this conversation in your states. You might think you were elected to sit on your backside here in Washington. But the truth is, your electorates put you here to look after their interests. And right now, that single interest is survival.

“We have already informed every governor and mayor of what we intend to do and have told them that you, their representatives, will be connecting with them personally to help with their decision making, their communication with the federal agencies, and their implementation of any plans they make. Let me make this crystal clear—whatever happens, how bad it becomes, or how good, will be on you— and no one else.

“The uniformed people sitting on either side of you will do their jobs, as briefed, and will—in the parlance of the military—take no prisoners, of that you can be assured. The first priority at every level from now until we succeed is getting our nation back on its feet, calming everything down, and getting into a position where we can regain some sense of normalcy.

“So, a warning. Put your political differences aside and do your jobs. Any insurrection at any level by anyone, and that includes the very senior members of both Congress and the Senate will be put down with prejudice. This is not negotiable. This is no idle threat.

“If I have to, I will fill every jail, every cell with you, and let the locals take over. The very future of our country is at stake, and I will not go down as the president who let the country rip itself apart over ideological differences when we have the means to recover from the current situation.

"Now, to properly inform you of why I am taking this extreme approach, I'll hand you over to Mr. Bronstein, the director of the CIA. Julius?" the president gestured with a delicate hand movement and sat down. The CIA director stood, nodded to his president, then stepped to the rostrum. The silence in the auditorium was palpable.

"Ladies and gentlemen, members of the press, members of Congress, members of the Senate, members of the military, as you know, the CIA is forbidden to operate on US soil. Our bailiwick is what happens offshore, and anything that represents a threat to the United States or our allies outside our borders is our single focus. As you are aware, a series of attacks by as yet persons unknown have killed or maimed thousands, perhaps millions, of people both here and abroad. Seventy percent of the world's oil supply and sixty percent of our gas supply have now been denied to us by some sort of technology as yet unknown.

"Great religions of historical and international importance have been attacked at their very foundations, the International Space Station has been destroyed, and further attacks have been launched against sports arenas in the UK, Germany, and now here in the United States.

"The World Wide Web has been struck down, and a computer virus has destroyed every computer chip that was connected at the time of the attack. This means no internet, no Wi-Fi, no satellite TV, no cable, no smart home, no nothing unless it is local and old technology. Handphones and landlines still work, so fax machines will provide linked coverage as best as we are able.

"Like Israel, Italy, the United Kingdom, and various other EU countries, we have commissioned Interpol, who by their charter are apolitical and able to cross international borders in pursuit of criminals to work on our behalf in identifying the culprits and bring them to justice. However, our own FBI is also on the job, and I'll now ask Mr. Roger Wilson, who heads the FBI, to brief you on where they are up to. Roger." He sat down and was immediately replaced. Roger took his time to look around the room, taking in the shocked and almost catatonic faces, no doubt the threat of being shot or jailed by their very own military having made its point.

He imagined a thirty-year veteran of either party used to the comfort and status of Washington would be first incensed, then shocked, and then in denial about having to leave the cloistered walls of Congress or the Senate to actually go out and meet the very people who had elected them, in the middle of the worst civil insurection in modern history, with a message of "comply or go to jail!" or worse— "comply or be shot by your own National Guard or military. And by the way, if you don't do as you are told and do it now, I may well be shot or thrown in jail in your place!" He took a deep breath and straightened his shoulders.

"The situation is as follows. We have secured the remains of the aircraft that bombed West Point. We have a description of the pilot, and we are running down everything that is known about her. We have established where the aircraft that shot down the space station was stolen from, and we are working with the local military police to understand more about that attack. Our local FBI teams and Interpol counterparts have had success in tracing where the electronic signals came from that launched the attacks and are working on that case both here and in Libya. Interpol has had agents track and verify the flight path of both the UAV and the Hercules aircraft that attacked the Vatican and the Dome of the Rock. The French, Italians, Arabs, and British are tracking the history of the trucks that bombed the sports arenas, just as we are doing here. We have the best cyber experts working out how the internet cyber-denial attack took place, and we are building local area networks back up as fast as we can find the equipment we need to do so. To cover off that aspect, I'll hand it over to Mister Frank Reynolds." And he sat down, to be replaced by the tall and gangly director of the NSA, who ran his hand through his tangled hair as he approached the podium.

"Thank you, Roger. Ladies and gentlemen, I'm as stunned and shocked as you are by what has happened to us in the last few days. It should not have been possible, but it was. We now know that the terrorists embedded staff within the NSA and other intelligence agencies over twenty years ago as a deep cover operation. These people were ordinary Americans, just like you and I, with families and histories, and made no impact of any note until the attacks took us all offline and crashed our systems. We now know that there were at least five of them working in the highest echelons of government, with the highest of security clearances. I can't and won't apologize for their treachery; there was simply no way to detect them before they acted. They were the perfect 'sleepers.' And as we have now found out, there is almost no way to trace them now that they have acted." As the director finished his sentence, the crowd broke out into an uproar, with several members of the Congress and Senate standing and shouting over the rising crescendo. They wanted blood, and the tone of their shouts suggested they were not particularly interested in whose blood it might be. Frank thought he heard his name mentioned more than once and mentally ducked.

He stood still and let the uproar wash over him, having had a similar response from his own children when they discovered that suddenly all the devices that they desperately depended on for their social interactions no longer worked. He imagined what he was now facing was simply the grown-up version of the hissy fit his children had aimed at him, as if it was his personal fault. Which, in one sense, he felt maybe was the case. The NSA was charged not just with listening into every conversation around the globe as a matter of course but to protect America from any foreign electronic attack—which, on this occasion, had come from within his very own agency.

He held his hand up as if stopping a speeding truck on the freeway. "People, please settle down. I'll outline what we are doing to rectify this situation if you let me speak!" The noise in the room slowly died down until only a low grumble ran around the ranks, and Frank, sensing that this was possibly the best he would get, looked around the auditorium, trying to catch everyone's attention. "As director Bronstein said, we are rebuilding local area networks back up as fast as we can. Essential services such as fire, ambulance, police, civil support, and the military have priority, and the internet as you once knew it, will not be back online, possibly for months, maybe even a year or more. The Wi-Fi systems that were destroyed will be replaced progressively along with digital telephones, but again, there is a priority here for our essential services, so again, there will be long delays before the average household has the connectivity they are used to.

"There is the added complication of all the other countries involved in being able to stand up their own new infrastructure, so we could be looking at months or even years before we have a truly global service as we were used to. This is something you need to tell your constituents because there is simply no way we will get back to where we were before the denial attacks in the foreseeable future." The room broke up into an uproar, with the people in the center of the room standing and shouting, waving their hands around in anger. The military, who flanked them on either side, sat impassively, making the scene all the more macabre. The president walked to the podium, smiled at her NSA director, then tapped the microphone twice, sending a scratchy rumble around the room, which caught everyone's attention.

"Sit down, sit down now!" She looked around the auditorium as groups and individuals regained their composure, some shaking themselves as if to get rid of a bad case of fleas. "These are the facts. We, at the federal level, will do everything in our power to get things back to some sort of normal, and you carrying on like a rabid pack of spoiled school children will not help matters. We are under attack by an unknown enemy with great skill and even greater weapons. You now have just one single thing to do.

"Get back to your electorates and take control of the chaos; work with your governors and mayors and restore peace. One last thing—and think on this with all your political experience—if you fail to get control and your electorate disintegrates into a bloody shamble, who will lose the most?" She looked around the room and inwardly smiled as the importance of what she had said sunk in. If the electorates burned to the ground and people rioted and trashed their neighborhoods, there would be no process to reelect the esteemed and fine members of the Senate and the House. And with a full election due within fourteen months, she desperately hoped this point got through.

The three directors waited with the presidential detail until the room had cleared. Then as the last of the military contingent closed the massive doors behind them, the president let out an audible sight, looked to her left, then to her right, seeking the direct contact she believed was essential to every real conversation. "Well, now we will see what they are made of, and now I get to experience my very own form of mental anguish, but at least it's in relative private. Tell me about my secretary of state and your money man, Mohammad bin Azaria." The look she gave the director of the FBI would have leveled a less-experienced person, but Roger Winslow looked straight back at the president, swapping hard-edged look for hard-edged look.

"Madam President, I have a senior agent on the way back here from Venice. She will land within the next two hours, and if I may, I would like to brief you with her at that time. I think it will save us all a lot of grief and energy if we hear it from the horse's mouth, as it were." The president looked daggers at the head of the FBI, then slowly nodded.

"Your call. But you had better be very, very sure of your case, or I'll have your guts for the proverbial garters." With that, she stood forcefully and headed for the door at the end of the room, followed by her security detail and a flock of uniformed staff officers. The three men watched her leave, then looked at each other.

"Just when you thought it couldn't get any worse," Frank said, shaking his head. "Well, look at it from her perspective. She's known the Secretary for some thirty-five years, went to school with her, same college, same sorority, her brother married the Secretary's sister. You couldn't have two families more intertwined if you tried." Julius Bronstein shook his head in wonder, silently acknowledging to himself that this massive failure of the intelligence agencies would have repercussions far beyond their careers. "But look at it this way—if it does turn out the Secretary is connected—we will have our first first-person suspect that might give us the remaining terrorists. And from what you have said, it seems these monks of yours are inside their communications somehow, so we might have just got lucky."

"If you can call identifying a close personal friend of the president, the secretary of state, a traitor lucky!" added Frank, shaking his head. He wondered what it would be like to be suddenly unemployed and basically unemployable in the current economic climate.

CHAPTER 52

Black Pete had won his nickname in a hard-fought card game on the fringes of a raging battle that had threatened to overwhelm their small commando contingent. The reason Pete and his comrades were playing cards and not killing anything that moved was simple. They had been inserted deep into the South American jungle to find and then orchestrate a deadly firefight between two competing drug lords, both of whom could be counted on to do the wrong thing at the right time. It had taken over a month to track the gangs, then set up the scene that was now being played out. It had not taken much—a long-range sniper shot to the head of a senior member of one cartel, leaving evidence behind that the shot had been made by a member of the opposing cartel.

A short but deadly firefight at the crack of dawn persuaded the Morena cartel that they were under serious attack from their arch enemies. Within a day, they had marched across the jungle separating the two competing gangs with heavily armed specials and ex-drug enforcement helicopters dripping rockets and small fragmentation bombs.

Unfortunately for the Morena cartel and their air support, as they closed in on the enemy, a salvo of antiaircraft missiles roared out of the dense jungle killing the aircraft and their crews in a flaming explosion that reverberated across the countryside. The Fenestra cartel didn't stop to wonder about the air-to-air missiles and where they had miraculously come from; they were too busy fighting off the specials and their fifty-caliber Gatling guns that chewed through human flesh and jungle canopy with equal ease.

The body count was growing, and the odd stray bullet ricocheted over the heads of the card players. Pete—still Pete at that stage, pushed all in. His opponents, smothered in ammunition belts and camo paint, still smoking shoulder launch missile tubes stacked against their feet, gave him the gimlet eye, sensing he was either cheating or bluffing, and they couldn't decide which. Three folded their hands, leaving the comms man to take Pete head on. Pete sat back, stared at his protagonist, and shook his head dismissively. "Up to you, Roy boy, got the guts or got the nuts?" Roy boy, who was anything but a boy, being a twenty-five-year veteran of the special services and the DEA, and had the scars to prove it, looked daggers at Pete, sitting comfortably as if in a casino and not in the middle of a bloody battle to the death between competing drug cartels in the middle of the South American jungle.

"You're bluffing!"

"Then put your chips in and call me."

"You black bastard," Roy shouted, throwing his hand into the center of the ammunition crate being used as a poker table. He stood up so suddenly that the jungle canopy around them rippled back and forwards. Pete just smiled, which always managed to make his face look crooked due to a knife wound suffered some years before. He threw his cards onto the table and raked the pot back into his stack. One card flopped up, exposing a two of spades. The other sat tantalizing on its face, partially covering Roy's discards. Just then, an explosion ripped across the jungle canopy, collapsing a heft of vines and shredded tree bits all over them, which caused the inevitable cursing in three languages as the commandoes grabbed their weapons and packs and faded back into the foliage. But the name stuck, and from that time on, "Black Pete" was his moniker, even though the story had been lost in time, and Pete was, in fact, as white as a freshly baked loaf of bread.

On this occasion, he was meeting with the special forces team PJ had sequestered in Milan. As he approached the small alfresco sitting area outside the Shakerato Caffè on Piazza del Duomo, he was not surprised to see just one man sitting at a two-top, sipping delicately on an espresso. He looked around the area and spotted at least three men lounging insolently in varying poses; he picked them for what they were, members of the Guardia di Finanza, a militarized police force responsible for dealing with financial crime, smuggling, and illegal drug trade. In essence, they are the logical partners for Interpol because of their quick reaction capabilities and their specialist training in both protection and military tactics.

Pete wondered if Indigo had arranged their participation or if Tom and his Team Seven had attracted their interest in some way. He sat at the table and gestured to the waiter hovering at the door, "*Mi scusi, un espresso per favour.*"

"Didn't know you spoke the local language," Tom said out of the side of his mouth, the other occupied with a pink-colored cigarette. Thin wasps of blue smoke curled out of his nostrils like miniature snakes seeking somewhere to hide. His eyes were impenetrable behind his Ray Bans, and his well-weathered face gave nothing away.

"The minders yours?"

"No, locals picked us up yesterday; they are as curious about us as we are about them. Do you know who they are?" Tom asked.

"Yes. Guardia di Finanza. Wait for one, and I'll confirm." He reached into one of his prodigious cargo pockets in his pants and pulled out the minicomputer given to him by PJ before he had left Venice. "Boss, sorry to bother you, but can I speak to Indigo, please?"

"Wait, one."

"*Sì, signor Pete, come possoaiutarla?*"

"Indigo, did you sic the Guardia di Finanza on Tom and his team?" Pete held the little computer camera up to table height and casually scanned the three men. "*Sì, signor* Pete, the Colonel asked me to ensure their safety, so I spoke to my brother-in-law who heads the division in Milan. Isa therea problem?"

"No, thanks, Indigo, all good." And he snapped the computer shut, effectively cutting the conversation off abruptly. "The Boss was worried about you, probably thought you would get drunk and attack the locals." Tom grinned, stubbing his cigarette out in the crystal ashtray.

"Good of him to look after us. But why are they so obvious?" Tom asked.

It was Pete's turn to smile. "Keeps the locals away; you have to admit, they look like cops, and no one is going to bother you with them laying all over you. Interesting that the Boss thinks there could be a local threat." Pete took his espresso from the waiter, handed him some money, and nodded his appreciation, never taking his eyes off Tom. "Have you detected unusual interest since you arrived?" Tom shook his head, scanned the neighborhood slowly, and shook his head again.

"Apart from our three friends, no. Not a peep out of anyone. The boys have us well and truly covered, but you figured that. What's the Boss want?"

"It might be a soft job, or it could turn out to be our worst nightmare."

"Oh, one of those. Why didn't you say so?" Tom asked, throwing money on the table and standing up. He stretched, managing to scan the area again. Pete slurped down his coffee, joined the stumpy special forces soldier, and with one hand on his shoulder, followed him along the Piazza del Duomo. The three minders fanned out, covering the Piazza. The Milan Cathedral towered over them as they walked, casting a huge shadow, which was strangely comforting to the two operatives. Men born and trained in the shadows, neither really liked being out in the open, exposed and without their weapons, even though between them, they had concealed handguns, knives, a garrote, and even an old, rusty swiss army knife hidden about their persons!

"We need to establish if we can where these terrorists came from, and the Boss as an idea we would like you to run down. Do you remember those aid agency people we ran across last year when we pulled in that child-trafficking gang?"

"Yes. Hard to forget."

"Well, we need to make contact with them again, get their best people, and then you will need to provide two of your team for each nurse or doctor as a close protection detail and get them in and out of these refugee camps." Pete paused, handed one of the small computers to Tom, and tapped open a page on which was a list of twenty refugee camps in seven different countries.

"You will have Interpol documents, licenses, transport, funds, and any gear you require, and I have two more secure mini laptops for you to use for comms as well as this notepad. You have seven in your team, so three squads should do it, and maybe you go in where you think it might be necessary. This whole exercise is to be kept strictly within the team, and each agency on this list has already been contacted by our people in each country to get the necessary permissions. They don't know the details of what you want; how much you tell them will be up to you and your squad leaders. However."

"Yeah, Pete, however." Tom read the list that had been handed to him, shaking his head from side to side. "Every one of these camps is a powder keg just waiting for a match. What makes you think we won't be that match?" Pete looked as concerned as he was able to, feeling for Tom and his team. But the stakes in this game were so high that he had no choice but to send the team into a known high-risk, volatile situation and trust them to extract both the information and the teams with a minimum of fuss.

He hoped.

CHAPTER 53

Anna was met at Andrews Air Force Base by a blacked-out SUV and detail of hardbodies dressed in black suits with matching sunglasses. The way they surrounded her as she was helped out of the back seat of the SR-71 made her feel important, but the sweat stains under her arms and across her crutch made her feel dirty. As she reached the ground, she looked for the lead agent and quickly saw she was female, her close-cropped hair a shiny brunette, highlighting an intelligent face. Anna looked her straight in the eye and stood as tall as she was able, still harnessed into her flight gear and silver-yellow space suit.

"I'd appreciate a shower and a change of clothes if you don't mind before we see the director." The senior agent nodded, spoke into her cuff mike, and gestured to the other five suits, who formed up a shallow corridor to the waiting SUV. Minutes later, they were in the base officers' quarters, and Anna was led to a wide reception room where two Air Force specialists stood waiting to help her out of her suit. The protection detail dispersed, except for the lead agent, who hovered around the door like a mother waiting for her child to finish kindergarten. The space suit was tugged and pulled until Anna emerged like a butterfly out of a chrysalis, her heated and cooled undergarments stained from the flight across the Atlantic at twice the speed of sound.

"The head and showers are through there, ma'am, and we have a change of clothes for you." The airman looked impressed by Anna's space suit, which by this time was crumpled on the floor like a collapsed accordion. Anna nodded her thanks and waddled into the head. Fifteen minutes later, dressed in the typical black suit that the FBI had made its very own icon over the years, she rejoined the senior agent and followed her back out to the SUV. She settled into the back seat and gratefully accepted a cup of steaming coffee from a four-star general dressed in camos and wearing a sidearm in a shoulder holster.

"I'm Bridget Saunders, here on behalf of the president, and Frank Reynolds, who I'll take you to now. No need to say this is a very hot potato." She studied Anna over her own coffee and saw a beautiful, mature face slightly worn by her recent flight but eyes that held both intelligence and no surprise at being served coffee by a four-star in the back of a blacked-out SUV.

"Anna Bernstein, Senior Special Agent, currently on detachment to Interpol." Neither woman moved to shake hands; each seemed very comfortable in their own skins, and each seemed to be enjoying their coffee without any stress or strain. "Where are we meeting Frank?" she asked, noting that they were still on the base, albeit now at the far northern end.

She expected that Frank Reynolds, as the head of the NSA, would be involved sometime but was a little surprised that this general staff officer was taking her to an NSA meeting and not an FBI one.

"Frank and Roger are waiting for us at a secure location on the base. Julius will join us sometime; he had to clean up after a meeting with the president." Anna wondered what "clean up" meant but, under the current circumstances, decided to hold her counsel. Sometimes you learned a lot from other people's silences and their actions, and the number of agents that had been dispatched to get her to this meeting was a sign that it was being taken very seriously by everyone concerned. She decided to test the waters.

"As a senior agent, and especially on home soil, it's mandated that I be armed at all times. Do you have a weapon for me?" she asked, placing her cup into the holder built into the sidearm of her seat. The general reached into a mottled green bag at her side and handed Anna a weapon, holster, handcuffs, and three magazines. Anna checked the feel of each magazine, testing the load quantity and the condition of the feeder spring, and fed one into the grip of the slightly battered H&K USP9, which fit her hand perfectly. "Did your homework, I see," she said, fitting the pistol into the holster and sliding the holster onto her belt at her hip. The two spare magazines went into her coat pocket, and she wondered why she might need the twenty-eight additional rounds! The general just smiled and sat back in her seat.

"Call me Bridget, and yes, I did my homework on you; you are one of Roger's best, and you're going to need every tool at your disposal before we are finished. Welcome home!"

Five minutes later, the SUV pulled up outside a military barracks, guarded to within an inch of its life by what looked like a battalion of fully armed Marines, with serious mobile and antiair hardware parked at each end of the long building. Several Humvees and SUVs similar to the one she had arrived in were parked in a muddled fashion, suggesting that the occupants had been more concerned with getting here than displaying their parking skills. She noticed that her earlier detail had been trailing them in another SUV, which disgorged the agents like fire ants escaping a flooding mud hill. The general, with one hand on Anna's shoulder, led her inside to a thankfully airconditioned room, then down a flight of stairs, then down a longer corridor, another flight of stairs, until finally, they emerged into a well-lit conference room, with the requisite electronic screens and machinery that decorated every military base she had even been on.

At one end of the long table sat the director of the NSA, Frank Reynolds, her Boss Roger Winslow hovered over a huge coffee machine set on a bench nearby, and the director of the CIA, Julius Bronstein, paced up and down, speaking into a phone held between his ear and his shoulder.

She wondered about that, given that the cyber-attack had effectively killed all smartphone connections worldwide.

"Looks like Julius is finished cleaning up," Anna said, heading over to her Boss. The general joined the NSA chief, muttering softly in his ear for a second or two, then sat down next to him. Just as Anna started to make a move towards the coffee machine, the room literally vibrated with a thunderous roar as the air compressed to the point of pain. Anna ducked instinctively, turning to look back at the door to the corridor, seeking the source of the noise and the pressure wave, and just as she started to make a move towards the door, it stopped, so suddenly, the enveloping silence seemed out of place. A plethora of suited agents flooded in, spreading out along two walls, creating a funnel shape. A few seconds later, just as the cups stopped rattling on their saucers, the president of the United States entered, looked around the room, spotted the general, and headed straight towards her. The secret service closed up behind the president, closed the door, then stood mute, in a pose made famous by TV cameras and reporters for years and years.

"Bridget, good to see you," the president said, sitting to one side and gesturing a secret service agent towards the coffee machine. "You'd be Anna Bernstein, FBI?" the president queried, looking straight at Anna, who had suddenly lost her appetite for a coffee.

"Yes, Madam President. Senior Special Agent Anna Bernstein, at your service." Anna stood at attention, her gaze fixed on the president, keeping the general in sight out of the corner of one eye and her other on her Boss to better see their reactions.

"Sit down, get a coffee if you need one. Everyone lets lower the emotional temperature in here by a few degrees; we will not be disturbed by anyone in here until we are finished. I've had the Secret Service cut all communication links, and we are, for all intents and purposes, isolated and secure. Now, Anna, if I may call you that, I need the background on what you are bringing us, every little detail, no matter how insignificant it may seem to you, and then we will look or listen to the communications you have brought with you. Just to be clear, your Boss has told us everything he knows, so you are filling in the gaps. And I must point out, before you start, by way of full disclosure, that I have known the Secretary for some thirty-five years and consider her one of my best friends as well as a consummate professional in government service. I tell you this only so that you know how hard I will prosecute your information. Clear?"

Anna looked the president directly in the eyes, held her look while she slowly nodded, then relaxed back into her seat. She thought to herself that, not for the first time, something simple had turned out to be complicated by personal relationships. Still, she trusted Interpol and had intuitively trusted the monks who had provided the data.

She accepted the coffee handed to her by one of the secret service agents, sighed, then opened the little computer she had hoarded across the Atlantic as if her life depended on it. She looked at the blank screen, then snapped the lid shut, looked up, looked at her Boss, nodded to herself as if accepting something, then turned to look at the president again.

"Madam President, the facts are these. During the course of our investigation in concert with Interpol, we came across transmissions from the secretary of state to Al Hemish al-bin Mohammad Karesish, now known as Mohammad bin Azaria. This man is believed to be the banker and possibly the master planner of all the attacks we have endured this past week, with the exception of Avignon, which we believe was mounted by outliers taking advantage of the chaos the terrorists had created.

"Radio transmissions have been recorded between this man and the Secretary from as far back as early last year. I have only heard excerpts, a cut from a sample of transmissions, as informing you, the NSA, FBI, and CIA seemed to be more important in terms of timing. Colonel Anthony felt that, given the level that this penetration may be at, you be briefed personally." The president's face revealed nothing of her inner thoughts and feelings, making her a potentially deadly poker player, Anna thought to herself. She waited patiently; as a master interrogator, she knew the value of silence. The president held her look, then leaned slightly forward in her seat.

"You have irrefutable proof that the secretary of state has colluded with the perpetrators of these worldwide atrocities?" she asked, her voice so low Anna almost had to lean forward herself to hear her.

"No, Madam President. What we have are recordings of the Secretary conversing with Mohammad bin Azaria. These conversations were intercepted by a technical branch of Interpol over a period of years and only became prominent once the banker had been identified and the data reevaluated. I believe the recordings will need to be examined in detail before we can make any firm conclusion." The president looked at the director of the NSA, who looked a little uncomfortable. To his knowledge, his agency had not detected the transmissions, something that should have been almost an automatic occurrence, as the NSA literally scooped up every electronic transmission from anywhere in the world. And while it publicly denied snooping on US citizens, through its extensive satellite and ground station network, every byte of every transmission audio, video, or code was, in fact, collected, analyzed, and stored.

"Madam President, the NSA cannot confirm these transmissions at this time; we are investigating as we speak. I should have more information for you in the next hour."

"You didn't pick up these transmissions?" the president asked.

"I can't answer that, Madam President; there is an investigation underway as we speak, the results of which I will have very shortly." Anna smiled a wan smile, shook her head, and looked over at the director of the NSA. Prevarication obviously was not his strong point. And again, it looked very much as if the American intelligence services had failed in their duty.

"Sir, I believe you will find any and all records pertaining to the secretary of state deleted or deep-wiped; this seems to be a signature move by the terrorists." Frank Reynolds looked at the FBI agent, a grim look on his face.

"Anna, you are probably correct. I was talking to our audit people when you arrived, and they have already established that prime records have been hard deleted in a similar manner to those the military reported on concerning their weapons and asset management systems. It seems we have had the terrorists inside most, if not all, of our highly sensitive technology, possibly for decades." The president sat perfectly still, collecting her thoughts. Her problem suddenly got a lot deeper than just her best friend being accused of colluding with the terrorists.

"Okay, people, here's what we will do. Have the tapes examined and transcribed. I want copies on my desk by nightfall. Frank, compile a list of all the data we are missing as far back as you can. Cross-check it with the EU and the Israelis and make sure this Colonel Anthony is copied in. I assume you have secure communications with you?" she asked Anna.

"Yes, ma'am, the technical people at Interpol have given me this mini laptop, which connects to a secure network. I do not know the details, and I have been asked to keep the system secure at any cost."

"Even from us?" the president asked. Anna looked at her, noticed the stress and strain lines around her mouth and eyes, and could only imagine how she felt about her closest friend being tied to the terrorists.

"Yes, Madam President, especially from us. I'm sorry, but that is the instruction I received from Interpol, which my director supported before I left Italy."

"Can they do that, Julius?" The president asked, turning to look at the head of the CIA.

"Interpol is independent politically and legally, reports only to their own directorate, and the agency that Anthony runs is a separate and independent group outside any recognizable command structure. Roger here has a personal relationship with Anthony, and I can say with some confidence that on every occasion we have called on their unique investigative skill set, they have never let us down.

"You may remember that international child trafficking ring that was rounded up last year; that was a joint operation with Anthony and the FBI, the French, British, Swiss, Germans, and Italians, and then eventually Turkey, Iran, Iraq, and the UAE."

"There was a high body count during that operation if I remember my briefings," the president said, her dry tone emphasizing her distaste.

"Yes, saved us all a lot of time and effort trying to prosecute some of the bad guys in multiple jurisdictions. But as the FBI reported, the Interpol agency responded to the fire, never instigated it, and only used as much force as necessary to save the children. Over three thousand were returned to their various countries, and we judge that a great success." The president thought for a minute, then stood up, causing everyone in the room to join her on their feet and the Secret Service agents to move to attention.

"I'm going back to the White House. You know what you have to do; report to me in person when you are ready." And with that, she strode out, the Secret Service forming two rows around her as she moved up the long, dark corridor. Within another two minutes, the roar and pressure wave from the helicopters belted down into the room again, only fading as the trio of helicopters that formed the presidential flight winged their way back towards the Mall.

"We can't use anything that is not air-gapped," Frank said, heading to the coffee machine again.

"And we can't involve anyone outside this room," added Julius.

"Well then, let's get started," said Anna, joining the director of the NSA at the coffee machine. She watched as he fiddled and tried to generate a long black, then smiled when he threw up his hands in defeat. "Let me do that for you, sir," she said, smiling to break the tension. On the far wall, a screen came to life, and a bass ringing sound flooded the room. It soon turned into a vocal header, as someone introduced the first tape in Italian, which the machine automatically translated into English.

"*Nastrooen, data/ora* (Tape one, time/date stamp ......)"

Anna sat down, opened her little laptop, and sent a three-letter code to Italy. "WIP." She looked around the room, wondering what would happen next. They had several hours of tapes, all encoded and compressed, and she had no doubt that the NSA technicians would pull out all the information they needed as fast as they could. Nothing to do but wait, so she folded her hands and tried to visualize what was happening back in Venice.

CHAPTER 54

The Boss walked back into the underground dungeon, looked around, spotted me, and waved me over. Indigo turned his head at my departure, saw the Boss at the foot of the stairs, smiled, started to follow me, then stopped dead in his tracks when the Boss signaled him to wait.

"Jessica, while I was briefing Pete, I had an idea I wanted to run by you. You're at least a generation younger than I am, so you might understand the technicalities better than I can.

"I want you to facilitate a meeting of the minds as it were—we'll dial up Arie and Julius and get all the tech heads here involved, but I want to work out the best way to attack our systems to duplicate what the terrorists have done—I want to really know what they have accomplished, are still doing, so we can counter it. And I have a working theory I'd like to share with everyone." I nodded my assent, barely bristling at the ageism the Boss so readily practiced. I was no more than seven years his junior and walked over to Stefarino to get the room set up. Within five minutes, Stefarino had the Israeli intelligence specialists and Aire Rosenberg up on the screen sitting next to Julius Bronstein and Anna, who were sharing Anna's minicomputer. To maintain some semblance of security, they sat, heads huddled together, at the far end of the long table. Their screen showed PJ, Jessica, Luigi, Indigo, and Stefarino, all in little separate boxes.

"Thanks for joining us on short notice. I've got something I want to run by you all, but first, Arie, can you please link in Shami and Julius; can you get Malcolm Tannery up as well? This will be a geek fest, and the more, the merrier at this point," said PJ, wasting no time on pleasantries and cutting straight to the chase. The frame holding Arie went blank, as did the one holding the two Americans. Then the Americans swam back into the frame, joined by the NSA specialist, but this time the three sat side by side, obviously looking at a larger monitor. Aire's screen split into two, and both he and Shami swam into focus.

"Thanks, now, first things first. Julius, did the NSA pick up any of the chat between the Secretary and the paymaster?"

"No," Julius answered without hesitation. It burned in his throat, but he had learned the hard way that when the s-h-one-t hit the fan, the truth always won out. "I thought so. Okay, Arie, your turn to be uncomfortable. Did any of your intercepts give you any warning of the events of the past two weeks, and have you ever picked up any chatter between our secretary of state and Mohammad bin Azaria at any time?"

"No, Colonel, we have not. And I would tell you if we had; the situation at our end is so grave, you all deserve the truth. It is possible that our enemies will cross our borders before nightfall; we are on an active war footing, so I don't know how long I can continue working with you all, if at all." The stunned silence across three continents said it all.

"How bad is it, Arie?" asked Julius. "We have picked up the shelling and rocket attacks, but with our limited view with MilNet (Military Net) down, the attacks don't seem to be much more than you get every day."

"Far more than just our daily allotment; it's been going on for twenty hours now, and our intelligence is that both factions have massed troops and technical vehicles at major crossing points, and something new, we are under constant drone bombardment."

"You have anti-drone equipment?" Julius asked.

"Yes, of course, but when they swarm us, one hundred at a time, some get through, and they are doing a lot of damage to our morale. They look like toys and are, in fact, just converted civilian drones, but believe me when I say they pack a punch when they explode over our heads."

"Do you think this is related to the earlier terrorist attack on the Dome?"

"No. Just our perpetual enemies taking advantage of the chaos and confusion we are all enjoying at the moment. Do you want a report on the outcome of our track-and-trace of the dark fiber in Iran?"

"Yes, Arie, and we sympathize with your current situation." PJ cut across the NSA director, pulling the focus back to the war room in Venice.

"The cable goes into Egypt, so our team stopped at the border. They believe they were not detected, and there's no way to know how far it goes without violating Egypt's sovereignty. Perhaps Interpol can do something we cannot?" PJ looked across the room at me, and I shook my head to indicate the negative. One thing I was expected to be an expert on was the situation with respect to the international borders we—Interpol—could and could not cross at any one given time.

"Okay, Arie, we'll take it from here. Now, does anyone else have anything to add, or can I brief you on the reason for this call?" he asked, with just a tinge of command in his voice. No one spoke, so he took that as a consensual yes.

"I want you all to concentrate on the cyber-attacks. Malcolm has established that the terrorists penetrated us back in two thousand, taking advantage of the non-existent Y2K bug. Went live, as it were, in two thousand two, then six. He and his cohorts at the NSA have tracked all the backdoors, spoofs, and hacks they have used, and we are sure that we have identified and stopped any penetration by them using those methods.

"But I want us all to consider another possibility. And please, remember, I am not a geek, so I might have the technical details screwed up a little, in which case I expect you to straighten them out. Is that clear?" Again, silence reigned supreme across the three countries, at least as far as this call was concerned!

"As I understand it, when you wipe data off a hard drive, even overwriting it later, you still leave little 'echoes,' which can be untangled and reformatted back into the data that was wiped. Is that basically correct?" This time silence and frowns greeted him, and a quizzical glance or two.

"Well, yes, that is essentially correct. There's a bit more to it if you use a milspec wipe program; they go down a bit deeper, almost to the originating ones and zeros. But if you know the program that was used, you can reverse engineer it and get back to the shadows of the data and then rebuild it byte by byte. It's long and slow, but it can be done." Malcolm Tannery felt nervous giving this explanation to such an august audience. Still, his tonality was firm and positive. He had started life as a hacker, or "black hat" in geek parlance, before finding his way into the NSA. Wiping, disguising, coding, and retrieval were one of his specialties, hence his role in the current situation. The only drawback as far as working with him was his perchance for drifting off into dreamland in the middle of a meeting, which frustrated his superiors to the point of exasperation.

"Okay, I get that. But here's my question. How would you wipe the data once or while it was being transmitted but before it got stored on a hard drive?" PJ asked, watching the eyes widen towards shock and horror on the face of every geek.

Except for one.

"Aahhhh, Colonnello, *mi scusi, possorispondereallasuaeccellentedomanda*?" Luigi asked, a smile as wide as his face lighting up the screen. The Israeli geek, Shami, broke into the tail end of Luigi's question.

"דואמהלקהמישמתעביהוז ,לנולוק"!

"Colonel, if I may translate—the gentlemen from geek land are saying they want to provide you with an answer, and our Israeli friend is telling us it's a simple task." All the non-Italian and Hebrew speakers laughed, relieving the tension that had started to build around the conversation since Arie had mentioned the rocket and drone attacks on his home country. I sat back, feeling the tension go out of my shoulders. The Boss was not particularly technically literate at the best of times, and to have geek speak thrown at him in two different languages, neither of which was English, was just asking for trouble! But he seemed to have taken it well because his tonality didn't change as he continued.

"Okay, good, I take it that we might be on the correct track. My thinking is this—when we war-gamed scenarios where we wanted to hide aircraft from satellites, we came up with the 'black hole' concept. If you interfere with the radar signals, the enemy will know you are there.

If you falsify the signals, the enemy knows you are there. But if you create a black hole in their radar map big enough to disrupt all their signals, they know you are there, but they don't know where you are. And we can achieve that by catching their signals on the way back to their antennas, preventing them from painting on a radar scope. My question is, could a hacker do this to electronic transmissions, records, data transfers, whatever you want to call digital communication, so that they capture the content, the broadcast as it were, and prevent it from being written and stored somewhere?"

"Short answer, sir, is yes. It's not easy; it takes enormous systems on the level of a supercomputer or two and expert coders to write and run the program. In simple terms, you just duplicate the routers the data packets move through, create a false image, and divert the real data. I know of only two people in the business who have the talent to do it, and both work here at the NSA. But you are talking years of development and possibly years to test and implement—and that's just in America."

"We've got one of your brainiacs here as well," added Arie, "but she is currently locked up for the next forty years. Would you like to talk to her?" Both the Boss and I got a tingle; the very first we had experienced on this case, I could see it by the sudden set of his shoulders. But he gave nothing away, at least to the others on the video call, and just nodded.

"That might be helpful, Arie. What did she do?" the Boss asked. Arie smiled and looked at Shami, who seemed to share the private joke.

"Shami here busted her trying to blind our integrated forward protection systems, something she had nearly managed to do. Shami and his cohort tracked and traced her just as she was preparing to go live. We put her away because we didn't know what else to do with her. Interestingly, in her case, it wasn't just sabotaged; it was for ransom."

"What did she want?" I asked, no doubt voicing a question on everyone's lips. "Fifty million Euros for the code that would undo the damage she was setting up. We got the original code and the fix, and again, we don't know what to do with it at this point."

"How old is she? Nationality? Credentials?" I barked out, the tingle I had increasing to an inaudible buzz. Then I realized I had just shouted at the ex-head of Israeli intelligence and grimaced. "Sorry, Arie, that was rude of me." He just smiled, his weathered face and sparkling eyes leading me to believe he hadn't been insulted by my outburst.

"Interesting, we asked the same questions. She is a naturalized Israeli who came here as an orphan from the refugee camp at Gouraud in Baalbeck, Lebanon. She was sponsored by a branch of Red Crescent, who paid for her education and found her a foster home. She did outstandingly well at Technion University, getting her master's and later her doctorate in nanotechnology. She did amazing work on nanoparticle investigations and was also, from all accounts, a master coder. We wanted to recruit her, but she went to university in the US, then disappeared for a few years, and only surfaced to attack us with her denial program around six months ago." There was one very large elephant in the room in that we had not told Arie about the women we suspected were behind the terrorist attacks, and everyone on the call but Aire and Shami knew they had been excluded, and you could clearly see the guilt on their faces. Compartmentalization was de rigueur for security agencies, but we were supposed to be sharing everything we learned and deduced.

"Are you thinking what I'm thinking?" the Boss asked me, a gleam in his eye which told me he had the same buzz. I looked at him; he was literally ready to jump out of his skin. I motioned with my palm face down, telling him to calm down, and looked back at the screen that held Arie's image.

"Arie, firstly, I have to apologize for something you don't know and should have been told days ago. I am going to suggest something. Gentlemen, with your permission, can you get Anna back into the Blackbird and to Israel ASAP? Arie, will you clear the way for our boat to bring us back to you, and can you set it up so that Anna, Luigi, myself and perhaps yourself and Shami can meet with this woman? I'd like to suggest comfortable surroundings, not an interrogation room but one with remote viewing facilities and modern screen-based comms if you have any that work. If this is okay with you, of course." Arie smiled like a benevolent grandfather might at a young niece or nephew who had pleased him, and nodded.

"Certainly, Captain. When did you have in mind for this conversation?" I looked over at the Boss again, seeking his input. He scowled at me, no doubt to try and intimidate me into silence as payback for my hand gesture, so I just looked back at him with a shrug. It didn't pay to exhibit any form of weakness in front of the Boss; he would drive a veritable truck through you if you did. I factored in a probable return time for Anna, then added an hour for safety.

"Midday tomorrow, your time, Arie, with whomever we manage to get to you by that time."

"Excellent. I assume that your team will motor over early in the morning?" has asked.

"Yes. I'd like to brief you on what you need to know and our tactics and get your input."

"Colonel, Captain, gentlemen, see you all then." And Arie's face disappeared a fraction of a second before his computer geeks.

"Captain, what are you cooking up?" asked Julius Bronstein in the faraway USA. "Sir, firstly, the Israelis don't know about the girls that were taken by Al Hemish al-bin Mohammad Karesish. We've kept that to ourselves for the time being. As for the interrogation, we make it a female-on-female conversation, and we might just get something out of her we can work with. I want the computer experts to back me up in case she starts talking geek. And in any case, they are all working on the same task at present, running down the Colonel's 'black hole' idea.

"It just makes sense to keep them all together."

"I see. Actually, I don't. Perhaps the Colonel can fill us in on his idea?"

"Julius, just like we managed to get the Strontium-90 out of the system undetected, I have a theory about how the terrorists have managed to hide their data so well. I have our geek squad working on it as we speak. When I know more, you'll know more. Roger, I assume it's okay to have Anna back?"

"Yes, of course. We are running a scan on the tapes and already have her verbal report, so if you can, use her with our compliments. Do you have a comment on our current issue?" he asked, referring to the potential situation with the secretary of state. Something he didn't want to voice, even over the secure link he had from the monks.

"Anna and Captain Riley have an idea on that. I'll put her back on."

"Captain?"

"Leave it alone. No monitoring, no electronic surveillance, but have her Secret Service detail on high alert—possible attack, kidnapping, you have a lot of possible threats to choose from and make sure they know where she is every minute of every day. Then Anna and I will fly over once we finish in Israel, and we can negotiate a process with you. But for now, hands in your pockets." The director of the FBI nodded in agreement, the look on the president's face when she had declared her personal position still etched in his mind.

"Okay, good luck in Israel. Colonel, could we have one minute more of your time, please?" The multiple screens faded to black, leaving only the team in Washington and the Colonel in Venice facing each other.

"PJ, I know you are busy, but we have a few questions for you, as you seem to have assumed the leadership in this hunt for the terrorists."

"Ask away."

"Do you think there will be more attacks?" PJ looked thoughtful, then remembered his bold statement just prior to the sports arena attacks.

"I previously thought no, then they struck at your stadiums. I must admit that after the space station and attacks in England and Germany, which were essentially bloodless, I assumed they would take a rest. Truth is, we only have a thin idea of their motivation, and as yet, no idea of what they actually want. So, the short answer is I don't know." The FBI director looked at his companions, saw the same wan acceptance on their faces, and nodded to himself.

"Okay, PJ, good hunting. Keep us in the loop." And the screens went black.

In Venice, PJ looked at me, nodded, then sat backwards on a chair, folding his arms over the back. He rested his head on the back of his hands, creating the illusion of being relaxed.

"That was a good move to wrap everything up so fast. But what is your real plan?" he asked, accepting another mug of steaming coffee from Indigo. "Thanks," he said, mindful that his head of Interpol in Italy was running around the room, giving comfort to everyone.

"The geek squad needs to find your black hole; they need to work on that now and hard. Once we understand how they are blocking us, we might be able to tap into their system. We know the location of the dark fiber terminations, although I am willing to bet that the terrorists are nowhere near those terminations. We need a team to go into Egypt, but that is a separate conversation as to whether or not that's a covert operation or we go in with permission. Pete is chasing down the refugee camps, so he's effectively out of operation for the foreseeable future. That leaves this team here, Arie's boys, and anyone else we can draft from either his side or our side. Anna will be back inside the next fourteen hours, and the Americans will have reviewed the tapes by then, but frankly, I'm tired of smelling like yesterday's garbage, so I would like to take a shower, have a meal, and grab at least four hours sleep." The Boss nodded, finding it hard to keep his own eyes open.

"Sounds like a plan."

TUNDRA MACHINATIONS

What had cost the lives of thirty-two Alyeska Pipeline Service Company employees, and cost over eight billion dollars to build, ran eight hundred miles from Valdez in Alaska to Prudhoe Bay. At the time, it was considered one of the great engineering feats of the late twentieth century. It was responsible for providing some eighteen billion barrels of oil since its commissioning—oil that the USA had grown dependent on. It was considered a marvel because of the magnitude of ecological hurdles the engineers had to overcome to build the pipeline so that sensitive ecosystems like the permafrost and the tundra, which sat both under and over the pipeline in different places, had required one hundred and twenty-four thousand heaters be built into the system.

When the liquid petroleum that flowed with gusto through the pipeline suddenly turned to silver-colored gel, then solidified at the end of the terminal pump line, the initial reaction by the duty team was puzzlement, then astonishment, and then panic. Hands flew over controls, furrowed brows concentrated on valve diagrams looking for signs of a leak, a break or even swelling of the pipeline over its length. Every pump station reported the same story—every flow valve agreed, and every meter showed exactly the same data.

The line was full but static. There were no detectable leaks. There were no indications of swelling in the pipeline. In fact, there was no indication of anything. Just the clogging mass that choked every pump line around the Prudhoe Bay loading terminal. Phones and radios suddenly went mad as the tanker crews reported the same thing. The oil they had loaded or were still trying to tank had turned into the jelly-like clag. The shift supervisor's hand hovered over the alarm button, which would cause all work to cease immediately, emergency crews to be called out, and, worst of all, his direct supervisor, who was renowned for his lack of humor and rude and intolerant behavior at the best of times, to be woken from his bed.

Shrugging his shoulders, he pressed the alarm.

In what was not a coincidence in timing, the massive liquid gas loading terminal in faraway northern Australia clogged up at the exact same moment, and as the dials, bells, and whistles sounded throughout the $250-million-dollar terminal. People literally ran for their lives, and the world gave an invisible economic shudder as the oil and gas reserves were reduced to less than eighteen percent. For all intent and purposes, the modern world had been reduced to the most basic forms of transportation, communication, and survival.

Deep inside an abandoned missile silo in Montana, the two women responsible for launching the Alaskan and Australian attacks looked at their screens, confirmed the damage, then shut everything down. As the last screen dimmed to black, they both stood, picked up their "go" bags, and started the long haul to their transport, some fifteen kilometers underground. As they passed the hidden security cameras, little LEDs illuminated, confirming that the explosives that lined the tunnel were arming progressively as they moved to their destination.

It was unnecessary to mine the tunnel; even if someone got into the old, abandoned missile control room, the electronics had self-destructed, melting the computers and screens down to their chassis. But their briefing had been thorough, and as any good terrorist would tell you, make it hard for your enemy to determine your objective, make it painful and deadly for your enemy to approach you, and leave any base or camp created in a manner that caused your enemy to waste their time asking and answering unnecessary questions. If they lived long enough.

In Egypt, a similar scene was being carried out, as the team there, hidden in a deep abandoned well probably over a thousand years old, packed their bags and headed for their exit, a small tunnel cut into the side of a convenient mountain. For all intents and purposes, the attack phase of the terrorists' plan as they understood it had concluded, with zero casualties on their side but with millions of dead and total worldwide economic chaos on the other. In essence, the perfect terrorist plan, created over thirty years in the past, was based only on the hope that the future would offer solutions. And, of course, it did in the form of a group of ragtag refugees who, when given the opportunity of a rich and fulfilling life, excellent education, and loving home, had risen to the occasion in a way that could only have been dreamed of thirty years before. They had created a technological pandemic of biblical proportions, unleashed on the world by a cadre of highly intelligent and trained women who owed their allegiance to an old man of the desert, one some of them had not seen or heard from in over a decade.

But he had given them life, hope, and a vision of a future for their compatriots, who numbered in the millions spread all over the inhabited world in camps, tents, and sometimes with nothing more than a disused cardboard box for shelter. An underclass created by greed, power, lust, politics, and sheer selfishness of unimaginable proportions. But now, the homeless, stateless, discarded and largely ignored, and most denigrated people who lived and died and existed just under the threshold of visibility had, through the brilliance of their surrogates, struck back at an ignorant and uncaring world with a vengeance. And created an environment, not unlike the one they lived and died in by the thousands.

And the amazing thing was that not one single member of their worldwide scattered collective tribe was aware of the battle being fought on their behalf.

That would change, and in a way, that would change their lives and the lives of every refugee forever.

CHAPTER 55

Ethiopia had been the home of Somali refugees since May of 1988, when civil war threatened to decimate the indigenous population. Unfortunately for the refugees, the six camps that were established were located in the barren and remote region of eastern Ethiopia, and Hartishiek A, the biggest of the camps, was the first to receive the leftovers from the other camps closed by inter-tribal warfare and famine. While the UNHCR did its best to provide for the refugees, in most cases, there were just too many, and the resources available never meet the human demand. People did what they always did under these circumstances: they formed cliques and power groups, mostly led by established criminals, drug dealers, and people traffickers, who then prayed on the weak, the defenseless, and the young.

Religion and compassion came to their aid on occasions when the UNHCR allowed Red Crescent, various derivatives of the Catholic Church, and Médecins Sans Frontières to deliver food parcels and medical help. Such occasions were managed by the local Imams and brothers from various branches of the Franciscans, who kept some form of control simply because they were well known to the indigent refugees and respected for their work.

Two monks escorted the team of doctors and nurses that Black Pete had sent into the camp, and the two "minders" from Tom's SEAL team, wearing dirty thaubs, which easily concealed their automatic weapons, strolled along as if they didn't have a care on the world. Both spoke Arabic, one Farsi, and between them, they had a smattering of Oromo, Amharic, and Somali, and the only thing they were certain of was that, so far, they hadn't understood a single word that had been spoken around them.

"*As-Salam-u-Alaikum*," the doctor offered to the cleric, hands crossed over his chest and with a little bow.

"*Wa-Alaikumussalamwa-Rahmatullah*," replied the cleric, responding as if to a non-Muslim. But he smiled and let the three-medical staff to a small sitting area, where tea had been prepared. "We will speak English, please. I need to practice, and it will make for a fuller conversation." The doctor nodded his assent and bowed slightly again.

"Thank you. It is with great respect that we meet with you, for we have heard of your efforts for many months. It must be very difficult keeping your focus and your beliefs when you have so much to worry about." The cleric smiled, turning his head and shrugging his shoulders as if he agreed with the doctor, but had yet to accept the difficulty at the personal level.

"The times are hard; the camp keeps growing, yet we cannot serve those that were here before. But Allah, praise be to him, has sent us here to look after his people, and that we must do. Now, your note said that you are looking for specific people who may have passed through here some years ago. Is that correct? And if I may ask, what can you leave with us in return for any information we may be able to provide to you?" The doctor sipped at his tea, holding the small, delicate cup with both hands, giving the impression he was in deep thought.

"The two men you see over there, who are accompanying us as interpreters and aids, have two trucks loaded with the medical supplies you requested, and we have a further thousand bags of rice, flour, crates of eggs, and vegetables in a container being delivered to you later today. However, these gifts are for you and your people, irrespective of whether or not you can help us." The Imam looked at the doctor with an open quizzical look as if the offer was unexpected. He turned his head to one side and stroked his beard with one hand.

"I see. That is very gracious of you. Given what has happened in your modern world lately, I did not expect such generosity." The doctor placed his teacup back on the rattan table, willing himself to relax and not rush the cleric. Every fiber in his body was screaming at him to hurry up, get on with it, find the girls, and get the information back to Interpol. Still, from long experience working in the refugee camps over the years, he knew that rushing the conversation would be a mistake of monumental proportions.

"Our organization has worked in these camps for over eight decades, and we are all too familiar with what they lack. On this opportunity, we saw a way to give a little, hoping for a little in return." The Imam nodded to himself, satisfied with the doctor's answer. The doctor reached into a small satchel and pulled out a grainy photo of a bearded mullah.

"Do you remember this mullah from perhaps thirty years ago? He would have passed thorough here for a period and possibly taken some children with him when he left. His name then may have been Al Hemish al-bin Mohammad Karesish, or perhaps Mohammad bin Azaria." The Imam looked closely at the photo, the edges of memory stirring at the back of his mind as he remembered the exciting rhetoric and endless debates his brother had engaged him in all those years ago during the few short months he had been at the camp. While he had not necessarily agreed with him on every issue, the one thing that linked their minds was the plight of the poor children under their care.

And when his fierce and dedicated brother had requested the best and brightest children be given to him on the promise that they would be placed with caring families, educated, and offered lives beyond imagination, he had willingly worked through his flock, for that was how he saw them and picked out the eight cleverest young girls he could find.

Looking back, he could find no fault with what they had done. He was puzzled. Why was this doctor, whom he knew and respected for his unceasing work in the camps, suddenly interested in something that had happened over eighteen years ago?

"Sir, I am curious. Why would you want to know about a brother who was here—if my memory serves me correctly—some eighteen or nineteen years ago?" he asked, bending to fill the doctor's cup with fragrant tea. The doctor, who as well as a fully qualified medical technician was also trained in psychology, sensed he had before him someone who could provide information that could change the course of current events. He felt it in his bones. All his instincts told him that they had hit pay dirt, and all he had to do was dig the gold out of the ground without arousing his hosts' curiosity too much. Back at the initial briefing with Black Pete, the group had agreed on what they thought was a plausible story. To the best of their knowledge, no one outside a very tight group knew of the mullah and his girls, so they had agreed on a detailed reason for trying to track them at this time.

"As you know, Médecins Sans Frontières has been providing doctors and nurses in as many camps as we are able, remembering we are not funded by any government but rely on unrestricted funds from private donors. Most of the time, this keeps us free of politics and state issues." He paused to smile in response to the Imam's grin. "Yes, I know. Can you really ever be free of state issues? Or politics?" The Imam shook his head and looked sad.

"No, my friend, you cannot. Let alone get them to pay any real attention to the plight of our people here. It is a constant battle to stop them from bulldozing the camp away as if it was an irritant."

It was the doctor's turn to nod in agreement; he was only too aware of the frightening politics that swirled around this camp on any given day. Just getting permission to visit the camp had absorbed six people for two days. Then admittance had been granted only on the condition that they would be accompanied by Ethiopian security forces, who thankfully refused to come into the camp, preferring to wait at the very far limit of the boundary between the camp and a small village that had no name.

Not to mention the one hundred thousand USD cash "entrance and security fee."

"It is a simple matter. Mohammad bin Azaria, as we know him, rescued several other girls from different camps, and as it turns out, some of them have, in their later years, developed serious cancers. We want to track everyone if we can to try and isolate the source of this contagion and offer our support to every girl who may have been in contact with some of the infected. We have tracked several of them and are just trying to make sure we know all of the girls involved. As you would realize, they are now all women, many with families and children, who do not deserve to die prematurely if we can get to them in time." The cleric looked somber, dropped his head, closed his eyes, and sent a silent prayer to his

God, who he was sure was listening to this conversation. He looked up, nodded, and folded his hands across his ample chest.

"I will search our files and give you all that I can. You must understand that back then, we had only a very used Polaroid camera and paper and pens to record anything, and even then, we relied on friends to smuggle in the photo paper. But I remember Mohammad bin Azaria, and I remember his girls, and I also remember taking a photo of them all before they departed. Tell me one thing, did he keep his promise? Were the girls given homes, education, and hope? Are they living a better life than they would have if they had remained here?" The plea in his eyes turned the heart of the doctor, who nodded slowly, choosing his words carefully. He did not want to deceive this man who had dedicated his life to making the lives of others better. Still, he also couldn't tell him the truth—that these very same girls might have been responsible for bringing the world to its economic knees, creating chaos and despair on a scale not seen since the Dark Ages. And had been responsible for thousands, millions of deaths, some directed and others just collateral damage from the attacks. He looked the cleric straight in the eyes and smiled.

"I can assure you that your girls were well looked after and that some of them went on to make a name for themselves in many different disciplines. We just need to track them now and ensure that they and their families are, in fact, safe from the contagion that may threaten their lives."

CHAPTER 56

The president and her three senior directors sat at four corners of an oblong table deep in the bowels of the White House facing the general who used a laser pointer to highlight different boxes of data on a massive double-sided screen that ran the length of the table. Julius Bronstein, Frank Reynolds, and Roger Winslow each had an assistant taking notes sitting immediately behind them. General Bridget Saunders had three senior officers working the smaller screens that fed data onto the big screens. The data boxes were, at present, rearranging themselves into chronological columns, and keywords and phrases were being automatically highlighted as they appeared in fluorescent colors.

Twenty months of conversations had been dissected and analyzed and then grouped into timeline "episodes," with repeatedly highlighted keywords and sensitive phrases underscored. In this way, you could see the continuity of a line of conversation and thought across the timeline, as well as look at all the conversations in a specific period.

"There's no doubt that this is the secretary of state conversing with Al Hemish al-bin Mohammad Karesish person?" the president asked, the tone of her voice suggesting she badly wanted a negative answer. Frank Reynolds, as head of the CIA, had assumed command of the analysis of the data recordings intercepted by the monks and delivered earlier by the FBI SSA. He mentally took a deep breath and flicked up a black-and-white photo of the target onto the screens.

"We have voice-matched both parties, and we now know him as Mohammad bin Azaria, an identity he assumed sometime early in the two-thousands. This picture was taken by a reporter for *Time* magazine in the mid-nineteen nineties at one of the camps he was visiting. At the time, Mohammad bin Azaria was presented as a representative of an aid agency working with the UNHCR and was interviewed as part of the story *Time* was compiling on the plight of the refugees' post-Gulf War One."

"Do we have the story?" the president asked, her heart already heavy from the impact of discovering that her closest lifelong friend, someone she had danced with, cried with, shared babies with, and trusted more than many members of her own family might be in bed with the mastermind of the most atrocious terrorist attacks ever recorded.

"Yes, Madam President, we do. It is being analyzed as we speak. The FBI is trying to track down the reporter, and the magazine has released all the films and stories written and taken at that time. They, too, are being analyzed."

"What, exactly, are all these conversations about?" she asked, feeling for the first time that the position they were in was only going to get more and more complicated as they unraveled the details.

"Well, if we go back two years, they start off innocent enough. The Secretary asks for advice on how to handle a child smuggling ring that Border Control detected in Mexico, tracked back to Iran, then to India, and then back to the Middle East. Bin Azaria responds in kind and suggests a strategy that we know came from UNHCR. Then the conversation turns to a more specific area, where she asks how bin Azaria would relocate some of the refugee camps, and this they discuss for around seven months, as you can see from the timeline here.

"Then they seem to develop an overall plan on how to move multiple camps into local regions, and over the next six months, they develop a detailed plan on how to achieve this. We are talking about some twenty-six million refugees at this point, and they allocate around a million at a time to a long list of countries, all funded by something called 'Project Sandbag.' They even have plans drawn up of the types of housing and development they require, including the infrastructure and resources needed to move and rehouse such a large number of people. Towards the end of their conversations—which, I would point out, stopped just over a month ago, they had compiled quite a detailed list and timetable. The Secretary was obviously using resources of both State and Interior to help work all this out, and bin Azaria, at his end, was obviously working on the money end."

"What do you mean by that?"

"Well, from the tone of his conversation, he had no doubt that the money would be available for their plan as if it were a foregone conclusion. On the other hand, the Secretary never once intimated that money would be an issue. She was more concerned with the geopolitics of the different countries coming to the party in the relocation effort. Something bin Azaria assured her would, and I'm quoting here, 'take care of itself in time.' And one other thing." The room literally held its breath, every eye fixed on the NSA director.

"Everything she spoke about was recorded in her personal diary, and at different times, she involved hundreds of people from State, Border Security, Interior, local government, Treasury, in constant planning conversations based on a 'what if' case she was developing."

"There's no doubt that the Secretary is involved?" The general raised her hand slightly, seeking permission to add to the conversation. The president nodded her mind in turmoil, wondering how someone she knew so well could have betrayed everything they both held so dear.

"Madam President, if I could suggest, I don't necessarily see the Secretary as complicit in the terrorist activities. There is no doubt that she was working on a plan to relocate the refugees, but from my take, that's all she was doing—and I don't see any attempt to hide that fact. In fact, if you look at her personal diary, she is very open about it all. The only omission, as far as I can see, is she never once mentions bin Azaria by name. Just refers to him as a 'highly placed member' of Arabian royalty."

"Then how do you explain that we were unable to intercept any of her calls to bin Azaria?" Frank Reynolds asked, sitting back in his swing chair, seemingly relaxed. As the head of the NSA, it still grated on him that a bunch of monks, hidden away somewhere in a basement in Venice, had plucked these conversations out of the air. In contrast, his organization, with the most sophisticated electronic eavesdropping electronics on and off the planet, had not. The general, sitting perfectly still, hands clasped in front and resting on the table, turned to look at the director of the NSA.

"My read here is that our terrorists have penetrated your organization, or the Secretary's office, and have sucked up everything they wanted to protect. And in fact, I'd go so far as to say that if you can match these conversations with your own tapes and find the holes, we may well work out how they are doing it. I'm getting the distinct feeling that this is far bigger than just a handful of talented women making war on us all." Frank looked back at her, nodding his head. He turned to look back at the president.

"Madam President, it pains me to agree with Bridget, but I think she is correct. There is nothing in these conversations to indicate that the Secretary at any time was complicit in the terrorist activities. She seems to have been concerned with how to relocate the refugees and sought the advice of someone who had been presented to her as an expert on the subject, with the highest of recommendations— from the UN itself." The president nodded, not quite ready to accept the analysis. Somehow, she would have to test the waters herself. She stood up, looked around the gloomy room, straightened her shoulders, then looked around, catching everyone with her steely resolve.

"Gentlemen, general, thank you for all your hard work; please keep me informed of any developments and send a copy of these transcripts to my office." And with that, followed by her Secret Service detail, she walked back out of the briefing room and into a world in turmoil.

CHAPTER 57

The ex-orphan from the refugee camp in Baalbeck, Lebanon, sat with her hands folded, seemingly at peace with all around her, a can of soda leaking drops of condensation on the tabletop in front of her. Her long black hair framed a chiseled face, and her green almond eyes were clear and bright, suggesting an intelligence lurking somewhere behind them. She idly poked a finger the color of honey almond in the water and drew a little cloverleaf, filling in the leaves with the meniscus formed by the heavier droplets building up on the tabletop. She looked like a very young pretty girl sent to the headmaster's office for speaking out of turn.

"May I have your real name, please?" Arie asked in a soft tone, one that hinted at consideration and not aggression. On either side of Arie, Anna and I watched the girl—for that's what she looked like, even if she was around thirty years old— for any reaction. In the room behind the antechamber, the geek squad, as Jessica was starting to think of them, sat glued to big screens, watching the action in real-time as well as other screens tuned into different security and data networks. Amazingly, the Israelis had managed to keep some of their electronic equipment working, although so far, Arie had not been forthcoming as to how they had achieved this small miracle. Every word said in this room would be fact-checked, run-down, and examined for both content and accuracy. This was the first real lead Interpol had on the terrorists or at least a tiny part of their organization, and we did not intend to miss anything of value.

The girl looked up from her musing, turned her head to acknowledge the two women, then sat back in her chair. "My birth name is Amira; my parents died when I was very young, so I have no last name from my youth. The name my parents gave me when I came to Israel is Amira Abramowitz. I do not remember my original family, and I consider the Abramowitz family my own. They cared for me, sent me to school, then college, paid for my education, saw to my health and well-being, and asked for nothing in return other than unconditional love, which I am happy and proud to be able to give them. I ask that they be treated fairly, as they are not in any way to blame for my transgressions." Arie nodded, having run a deep background check on the family when Amira was first caught. Abramowitz Senior was ex-military, had fought with distinction on three borders, and was now retired to a small kibbutz in Ar Ram, where he farmed vegetables and goats. Amira had three siblings, all born after she had been adopted, and all of whom were leading perfectly normal lives, either in university in the United States or working on their parents' farm.

"Your parents will not be involved in any conversations we have concerning your—as you call it—transgressions—nor will anyone ever lay any blame at their door. On that, you have my word." Arie looked at the girl—because he, too, could see the youth under the frosty exterior—and wondered not for the first time why she hadn't accepted his department's invitation to work for Israeli intelligence at the time she had finished university in Israel.

"Thank you. I have already been debriefed by your people once; why am I here now?" she asked, exhibiting just a little of the frostiness she held as her outer shell. Not aggression, not arrogance, just a very positive stance suggesting she was his equal, at the very least. Arie decided to use her approach against her.

"You're here because we have found that you link back to a gentleman called Al Hemish al-bin Mohammad Karesish. We believe he was responsible for bringing you to Israel and placing you with your family some twenty years ago." Amira screwed up her eyes in concentration as if seeking deep memories. She looked quizzically at the two women as if seeking their help. I put a hand on Arie's arm. "You may not have been given his name. Can you recall how you got to Israel?" I asked, my tone encouraging and sympathetic. Arie remembered what PJ had told him some time ago: one of Jessica's great strengths was an innate ability to put a suspect at ease and use her ingrained empathy to get to the truth, which had gained her the reputation of being one of the sharpest interrogators in Interpol.

"Yes, vividly. In the camp, we were all starving. People were dying all around us. There was shelling going on somewhere close, you could hear the bangs, and the earth shook all the time. Then one evening, a man and a woman came to our tent, grabbed me and one other, put us in an ambulance, and drove us off to a shed. In the shed, we were fed the first meal we had in three days, given bedding, then allowed to sleep. The only person I ever saw after that was the woman who said she was an aid worker. To me, she was an angel, and the other girls all felt the same way."

I smiled, relaxing my posture to remove any visible sign of threat. Here was a young woman being asked to relive her memories of probably what had been the hardest and possibly the ugliest time of her life, and in spite of my own critical agenda, I felt genuine sympathy for the girl.

"What happened next?" I asked.

"We were loaded back into the ambulance and drove for about a day. We stopped twice for bathroom breaks, and we were offered simple food—rice and flatbread—to eat while in transit. Then we arrived at a village, I don't know its name, but we went into a hostel where we were put into rooms with other women and girls. We were able to bathe the first time for me in months, given clean clothes, offered a hot meal, then allowed to sleep again.

"The women looked after us until we were collected again. It was obvious that all the girls had been in distress and rescued from somewhere. No one spoke very much, but you could feel the kindness from the women." Amira paused as if reflecting on a hidden memory, smiled to herself, then continued. "The next day, a Red Crescent van picked me up, and we drove to a port, where I was put onto a small boat and brought here to Israel. The woman came with me, and my parents met us at the dock." She paused again, trapped in her memories, then tilted her head to one side. "It all happened so fast, and they were so welcoming and loving; I never stopped to ask why. I just accepted it as something that happened."

"Did you ever see the woman again?" Anna asked.

"Yes, on what was celebrated as my fifteenth birthday. I didn't know my birth date, and we assumed I was seven years old. We had to guess the date because I had no memory of it. She brought me a present, which I took with me to Technion University because, until that time, I had never seen a laptop computer." Anna's eyes glazed over, but she held herself in check. The tone of the conversation was anything but an interrogation, and Anna didn't want to spoil the flow.

"Didn't you have computers at school?" she asked, as softly as she could. "Yes, big clunky ones, in a computer lab, and you had to book time in the library if you wanted to use them out of school hours."

"I see. Where is the laptop now?" Anna asked, almost innocently. The girl smiled and nodded.

"It was confiscated when I was arrested. It's different from the first one I was given. I don't know where it is now."

"We know you went to university early—when you were fifteen. We know you excelled at coding and nanotechnology—in fact, some of your published work still stands as the benchmark in those disciplines. Arie said his agency tried to recruit you when you were just twenty after you finished your doctorate. Why did you not take them up on his offer?" For the first time, Amira looked smirky, as if she was hiding a joke. She shrugged her shoulders.

"I had a better offer," she said, the smile never leaving her sparkling eyes. Anna sat back, considering her options. She decided to keep it smooth and calm, sensing the girl would tell them everything they needed to know if she was not attacked.

"Who from?" Anna asked. The girl stiffened up and looked at Anna as if thinking about her response. She looked directly at Arie, making eye contact.

"Sir, you will keep your promise regarding keeping my family out of any trouble I might bring to them?" she asked, looking so hard at Arie he could feel the intensity.

"Yes. Your family will not be punished for anything you have done as long as you tell us the truth and we can prove that it is the truth." She sat back, considering the Israeli intelligence chief's words, looking for any hidden meaning. She had not enjoyed her time so far in the small room in which she had been imprisoned, with no outside contact and only two hours a day of exercise in a small walled-off area littered with dead grass. Maybe she could negotiate better quarters. It was worth a try.

"When I turned twenty, the same woman who had given me the first laptop met with me again. She said her name was Helen, and she worked for an organization that was vested with the responsibility of ensuring that people like me had all the things they needed to carry out their research. She gave me a new computer, a satellite phone, and access to a group of scientific and military databases that focused on the work I was doing. She introduced me to other women working in similar fields around the world, and she helped me format my thesis for my second doctorate. I was attached to a coding group and a nanotechnology group and given access to a huge laboratory at the university that I didn't know existed. All she wanted from me was my best work, and she promised me a role in a super lab at a different university when I finished my doctorate, with a stipend that would feed me and my family for life. She swore me to secrecy, and left a bag of shekels for incidental expenses—a bag, I might add, that held more than my parents earned in a year. At this time, I didn't see any real harm in it."

"You finished your second doctorate seven years ago. You hung around the campus for less than a month, then what happened?"

"You have my passport. The woman I knew as Helen came through. I went to the US on a post-doc scholarship to Harvey Mudd College. As you probably know, it is a world leader in STEM. I worked in the nano lab and also on coding for three wonderful years. I simply could not imagine life being any better." Arie, Anna, and I sat silently, considering what we were being told. For the first time, we all sensed that while this was a true story, there was an undercurrent to the narrative, and we weren't sure how to get to the root of our unease. I decided to break the nexus and, using my instincts, ask what I hoped would be a most unexpected question.

"Did you maintain contact with your parents?" I asked, signaling the uniformed soldier at the door for more coffee. I was suddenly in need of a caffeine boost, and I had a feeling that as the day went on, I would need all my energy. "Would you like another soda?" I asked Amira before she could answer her earlier question.

"Yes, please." The room descended into a muted hush as an aide poured coffee for Arie, Anna, and me and placed another soda can in front of the prisoner.

"You asked about my parents," Amira said, popping the soda can open. A little fizzle of bubbles spurted over the rim, which she caught in her generous mouth with a slurp before they could attack the tabletop. "Excuse me." She smiled and then, sensing the serious nature of the conversation, sobered up and regained her composure. "Yes, I spoke to them every week, sometimes twice a week. Why do you ask?"

"Arie, perhaps you would like to take this?" I asked, turning to look directly at Arie. I knew the answer, and so did Anna, but the tingle at the base of my spine told me that we were on the very tip of information that might crack open the entire case.

"Amira, we asked you this because we have been unable to find any trace of your communications with your parents since you left Israel. Can you suggest why that is?" he asked, pausing to sip at his coffee cup. He, too, had the "tingles," sensing the same thing as Anna and I did.

"I'll tell you, but before I do, I want to explain what happened at Harvey Mudd College." Arie looked at me, then at Anna, and, sensing that we were in accord, nodded his agreement.

"Having been brought up in Israel, I was used to a militaristic tension in ever thing we did in class. After all, we were being attacked almost every day from somewhere. After a while, you get used to it, but the constant threat and tension shape both your behavior and your performance. Then I get to the US, and it's as if I have entered a whole new world, no militarism, no overt censorship, no bombs going off, just wide-open fields of grass and smiling people and even smarter people doing very clever things.

"In the first year, I did more good work and advanced my thinking further than I had in the last five years at home. It was exhilarating. I was suddenly part of a loose cabal of thinkers able to run experiments with very little supervision and an awful lot of help." She paused as if remembering her time at the American university some considered to be the premium school for science, technology, engineering, and mathematics. A tiny smile creased her face before she managed to reign it in.

"It was heaven, as I told my parents every week. I even sent them progress reports, knowing that they would probably not understand half the language. But it was the happiest time of my life. I had several experiments running in three labs and a pile of people wanting to help or observe. Then the hand of God reached out and made me aware of my true purpose, the reasons for me being saved from the camp, the very reason I had been allowed to learn and prosper all this time." She sat quite still, the memory suddenly causing her to pause. Her hands started to tremble a little until she latched her fingers together and physically forced the tremors to stop.

"To say I was shocked is an understatement. Initially, I was horrified. Then they explained the background to me and asked me to think about it. No pressure. Just the thought of hundreds of children dying every day in camps all over the world made my skin run cold. And I had been one of those children before I had been saved and brought to my new family. I could be dead.

"They did not put any pressure on me at that time. But I felt it, ever so subtle, under the rhetoric, lying in wait for me to realize I had a debt to pay." Her hands started to shake again, and to the three investigators, she looked visibly upset. Anna reached over and put her hand on Amira's locked fists, calmly rubbing her hand in such a way as to suggest sympathy. The girl looked up at Anna and grimaced, which earned her an even bigger smile from the FBI SSA.

"You said 'the hand of God.' Did you mean that literally?" she asked in a quiet, calming voice, holding onto the girl's hands. They had stopped shaking, and Anna sensed that she was under control again, indicating a strength of character she could identify with. The girl looked up and around the room as if she had forgotten where she was.

"It was the woman who called herself Helen and a young cleric who identified himself as Mohammad bin Usha Rashad. He said he was representing the interests of my sponsor, a revered cleric who was now in self-isolation in the desert of his home, praying for our success. Bin Usha Rashad was direct and to the point. I owed my success, and my very life, to my sponsor, and I now had a duty to do his bidding. I asked what that bidding may be, and he told me that I would be briefed in detail in a day or two once I was able to commit unreservedly to their cause. They left me to consider my options, and I must admit, I yearned to tell my parents, but they had warned me that I couldn't contact anyone but them—and they gave me a cell phone with which to call them. They left, and I went back to my room."

"What did you do next?"

"I wrote a detailed summary of the conversation on my laptop, and then I spent all night using the university library to research the current refugee status. You no doubt know what that is today, but six years ago, it was bad enough. The UN estimated that a child was dying every eleven minutes in a camp somewhere, and I couldn't turn away from that. After all, I had been one of those children. I could have easily been one of the dead.

"I was working in very advanced nanotechnology and had two projects running on a new code algorithm, so at the time, I wasn't sure what they would want of me. I called them, and they set up a meeting the next day off campus in a little coffee shop. They were direct and to the point. I would work with a small group of hand-picked collaborators at the university and manage two projects— one to refine my nano work but specifically in the oil and gas field, and one in coding to create a means of filtering data off the internet and communications satellites undetected. Neither project looked threatening; the oil and gas work was for remediation of mass oil spills and gas eruptions from fracking operations, or so they said, and the data grab was supposed to enable the group to monitor some of the countries whom they judged to be the creators of the worst of the refugee problems without their knowledge. Again, given who some of those countries are, it seemed to be a reasonable request.

"I chose to believe them, thinking I could always pull back and withdraw my work. The next day I met my cohort and recognized three of the people from my own lab. There was one outlier, a brilliant Chinese post-doc from Tsinghua University who seemed to know everything that was going on and what we had achieved so far. She and I immediately formed a bond. I suspect it was because she had also been rescued from the camps, or so she said, so we had that in common. We started work, and in a very short time, we managed to produce a nano bug that would literally eat its way through the atomic structure of crude oil, leaving only a fine semi-carbon three dust. It passed every test on a small scale, and we sought and gained permission to try it on a large oil spill that had just been reported in the channel between Nova Scotia and New Brunswick. On the world scale of catastrophic environmental damage from oil pollution, it was quite small and had been mostly contained within floating barriers and the application of foam. "We were flown to Nova Scotia by the Coast Guard, provided every resource by the local technicians, and let loose. Our little bug worked, and within hours, the oil spill was a floating mass of little silver carbon three particles that bobbed around for a while, then sunk to the bottom of the bay to join their ancestors in the slime and muck of the seabed."

"I remember the incident, but I don't remember any report on the solution other than it was described as a new type of foaming reagent," Anna commented.

"It gained little attention."

"Yes, that was the PR that they put out at the time, as Michele, as we knew her, suggested that we needed to keep it quiet until we could file all the necessary patents and get approval from the university. As you know, anything developed at a university lab that goes on to be a commercial success automatically vests a twenty percent return in the IP back to the university. At the time, I thought we were doing the correct thing. And I must admit, I was more than just a little enamored with Michele." Arie gave a little smile, I tried my best not to look a little relieved, but Anna just looked a little bewildered.

"How far did your infatuation go?" Anna asked, not sure why she asked the question. Amira looked slightly bemused, then smiled, wiped her hair back behind one ear, and slowly shook her head.

"We had been very close for nearly two years, and then it just died on the vine, as it were, because the very next day, Michele had disappeared with copies of my notes, discs, reports, and samples, and we never saw or heard from her again." Anna nodded, in her mind at least, a good outcome for the young woman sitting in front of her, but not so much for the world in general.

"Did you keep backups anywhere?" she asked, and this time Amira's smile cut across her face and lit up the room.

"I may not have done everything right, but if I learned one thing working and learning here in Israel, it is to always keep a backup of your work somewhere and to keep the location to yourself. And no, it's not on my laptop. I think you will find that it has been compromised by Helen or someone from her organization. I suspect there is spyware on it, and I haven't used it since I left the university.

"There was a second major reason I disappeared for a while, then came back home. You see, my work on the code was also taken, but not by Michele. Helen came and got that herself. And that was the trigger for my going underground." Arie looked slightly confused, tilting his head to one side.

"What are you referring to?" he asked.

"The day after Michele disappeared, Helen turned up, asked for my laptop, worked on it for a while, then gave it back to me. Then she asked to be taken to the lab and asked for all the code we had generated, all the discs, and the backups, and then she wiped the entire system in the lab. Right after, she explained what she wanted me to do."

"And what was that?" I asked, thinking I already knew the answer. The girl— woman sitting in front of me was no doubt a genius, a master coder, and possibly a world expert on nanotechnology, but she just didn't fit the terrorist profile. Too soft, too introverted, and, in my expert opinion, too interested in discovering things rather than blowing things up. I had met quite a few people like her during my time in both the navy and Interpol and believed them to be a species both entertaining and irritating at the same time!

"She wanted me to go with her to Turkey to run what she called 'missions.' She pointed out how good everyone had been to me, how they had paid for everything I had achieved, and now they wanted my help righting some wrongs. She said I had to pay homage to the children who had gone before me, never having the chance of real life. To be fair, I had expected to be asked to do something from the very first time I had been approached."

"But you said no, and you ran?" asked Arie.

"I said okay, but I needed a day to clean up so the university wouldn't come after me for the damage she had done to the lab, and we arranged to meet up the next day at the airport. Then I ran." Arie nodded. The timing worked for him; his people had been keeping a "loose" eye on the talented woman since she had moved to America but had completely lost her four and a half years ago until she turned up in a kibbutz and was caught hacking into the military's most secret systems.

"Why did you decide to attack the country that had adopted you?" he asked, suspecting he also knew the answer to that question. She smiled again, more relaxed than she had been at the start of the interrogation, and opened her hands as if surrendering.

"It was the only way I knew to get your undivided attention, and then at the very top of the intelligence tree, with any vestige of credibility. I wanted to demonstrate what I was capable of so you would believe me. And I wanted a meeting just like this, so you could tell me what they have done, and I can tell you how to fix it."

"How much do you know of the events of the past four weeks?" Arie asked.

"Not much. I have been in a small, barred room for the past month or so, with no access to electronics, no visitors, just the scuttlebutt that passes between prisoners. If I have interpreted the gossip I picked up from the guards, you are all in a world of hurt. I can fix some of that." I smiled for the first time today, thinking we now had a chance if we could harness this undoubted genius to our side of the story. I wondered for a fleeting second if Arie would give her up or try to keep her for his own purposes. I looked at Anna, saw the smart brain working overtime behind her blue eyes, and nodded.

"Arie, what would you say to Interpol taking charge of your prisoner, with the guarantee that we will return her in the same condition she is in now, at any time you require it? I would like to get the boys in the back room on the fact-checking and follow-up, then get our contingent back to Venice—with young Amira here." Arie looked at Jessica, turned to look at Amira, then placed his hands face down on the tabletop.

"On two conditions. She wears a security bracelet, and you personally take responsibility for her security. Agreed?"

“Good at my end. Amira, are you willing to come with me to Venice and work with our people there to rectify some of the damage your work has done?” The young woman looked at Anna, then at me. Then gave Arie a hard stare.

“Providing your earlier promise about keeping my parents out of this is kept, I’m happy to swap a cell for a bracelet. And I’ve never been to Venice.”

CRACKS IN THE EARTH

The fracking site looked just like the thousands of similar sites around the world: lots of pipes, huge metal containers, rusted equipment, upright painted cylinders, and a massive tower that drilled and pumped fluid down into the subterranean substructure of the abandoned oil field.

The concept was to simply pump fluid down under pressure and literally force the remaining oil, gas, and methane out of the substrate and back up into the sunlight. The fact that many of these sites blew up during the process or remained mute as a ticking time bomb for some future environmental disaster was mostly ignored by the companies involved, in spite of the conservationists protesting to the contrary.

This particular field had been abandoned as a well-head three years ago, and the fracking had only started in earnest in the last year. Already a constant polluting plume of burning methane rose into the atmosphere from the overpressure pipe, and no amount of tree planting could hide the hideous eruptions in the topsoil that ran for miles in every direction. Time was money, and the men and women who manned the site twenty-four-seven had parked their guilt in the same pocket they slid their pay packets into every fortnight.

The food truck was not unexpected. It arrived every day at the same time, and in this relatively remote area was a welcome sight and provided a genuine social opportunity. Lines formed and then diminished as generous helpings of hot dogs, salads, sandwiches, hamburgers, and chips were carted off to the picnic tables trucked in specifically for that purpose. The chatter was lighthearted, mostly focused on the weather, which at the present time was hot and sunny, and no one enjoying their lunch particularly noticed the small utility van pull into the yard, almost at the end of where the wellhead still protruded several yards into the rich blue sky. It only stayed for a few minutes, then turned in its length and drove back onto the dirt road that provided access to the site. One of the engineers slurping at his cold drink would later remember that the logo of a plumbing company was on the side of the van and that the driver and the passenger looked "foreign".

A problem for the police who responded to the call out because, in this neck of the savanna, anyone who was not white, male, wearing a flannel shirt and bearded was considered to be "foreign". When the police arrived, apart from several extremely worked up engineers and a foreman whose chin dripped the results of a good wad of chewing tobacco which also stained his plaid shirt, the only thing they understood was that "someone had sabotaged our well, and we want them damn terrorist found and shot!" Further, when they were taken to the wellhead to see for themselves what the damage was all they saw was a slithering mass of silver beads running out of the ground, most of which soon dissolved into a thinner silver mass, then evaporated completely, leaving a slightly oily stain on the ground. The police didn't understand what they were seeing, and the workers didn't understand what had been done to the fracking site, but it would be a scene repeated all over the world during the next few days and would effectively contribute to the worlds' reserves of oil and gas dropping below twelve percent.

CHAPTER 58

"Stefarino, do you have another room where we can have, maybe, five or six people plus screens for five or six more?" the Boss asked, handing me what felt like my millionth cup of coffee since I had returned from the meeting with Arie and his people. To say I was invigorated was to understate my present condition because, on the boat trip back, Amira had opened up to both Anna and me with all the details of the software she had been developing. It was obvious that she would be able to help us with the Boss's "black hole" theory, and the two geeks who rode with us—Arie had lent us Shami for the duration—were literally vibrating with the thought of being able to crack the terrorists' codes. "I want the geeks to work here in your laboratory area while we get back to police work without any interruptions."

"*Sì, miocolonnello, certamente.* It will take us some time to set up the screens, *un momento*?" His mix of Italian and pidgin English underlying his uncertainty about what we were doing. Indigo had a personal style-perfect English equaled very serious; Italian equaled very, very happy; A mix indicated uncertainty or worry.

"Thanks. I'll leave Amira here with you; will you take responsibility for her, please?"

"*Sì, miocolonnello, con piacere.*" The Boss nodded and moved back into the middle of the room, looked at everyone, who, by this time, was either sitting and drinking coffee or standing and drinking coffee, creating the impression of a massive tasting event at some dingy espresso joint. "Okay, people, here's what we are going to do. Stefarino, Luigi, Shami, and Amira will stay here and crack the code the terrorists are using. Luigi, would you please take the lead on this, and Amira, would you please let Stefarino know if you need anything or need to leave the room for any reason? Indigo, Pete, Jessica, please come with me; we need to do some serious cop work."

The room broke up, with the geek squad moving to the massive computer screens while I watched as everyone else adjusted to the Boss's request. It was actually an order, but he had disguised it so that it just sounded like a gentle request. As Pete had only just arrived back, I pointed to him and looked at the Boss, who nodded silently.

"Pete, why don't you go have a shower and grab something to eat before you join us? Take your time; the Boss has asked the monks for a separate room with screens, and they need a little time to set it up."

"Thanks, Captain, will do. You've got my basic report, so I'll go and get cleaned up."

"Okay, Boss, let's do this." And I led the way further into the dungeon-like walkway into a huge auditorium carved out of the bedrock, and obviously well under the water line, as little spurts and drips came through the green fungus and moss on the walls. A bevy of monks was setting up big screens and workstations, and I wondered briefly what effect, if any, the moisture in the air would have on the electronics.

Not my problem.

We all sat in fairly straight-backed chairs, obviously made by a craftsman, as each had different carvings on the arms and back supports. Mine had two snakes eating each other's tails, making me feel like I was their next intended meal. I opened the conversation a little more sharply than I intended, but it had been a stress-filled couple of days, so I excused myself.

"Guys, Anna, there's something that's been niggling me at the back of my brain since we first received the heads-up from the US. Specifically, if this all started thirty-odd years ago, how did they know what areas of science would deliver their best opportunity to develop world-killing weapons, and how did they know the girls they moved into homes out of the camps would have the chops to be as good as they have turned out to be?" The only sound in the room was the constant dripping of the canal as it tried to flood us out of the cavern.

"And how did the planner or bank man know the girls would actually do his bidding when the time was right?" added Anna, looking at me with a smile on her face. "I'm with Jessica. This has been a constant question on my mind since the beginning; we all know what human behavior looks like from both the good and bad sides, and I'm having difficulty seeing thirty girls picked at random. Okay, they had the smarts supposedly, even at eight, nine, or ten years of age, but how do you control them to get what you want out of them fifteen to twenty-odd years later?"

"And that's an excellent question because if Amira is any indication, not everyone they plucked out of the refugee camps played ball the way they wanted them to." Again, the only sound you could hear in the room was the incessant drip, drip of the water trying to flood us out. Suddenly a motor started up, and a huge gushing sound ricocheted around the cavern like thunder, and I instinctively ducked my head. The cavern suddenly filled with laughter as Indigo sprang out of his chair and pointed to a black pump halfway up the cavern wall.

"*Nessunproblema, amici miei, è solo la pompacheabbiamo qui per tenere i piediasciutti*!" Indigo said, his laughter suddenly lightening up the mood. "Thisa pump, it willa run every so oftena, so no worries about having to swim out!" His laughter was infectious; even the Boss smiled and visibly relaxed.

"Okay, Indigo, thanks for that. Now back to Anna's point. How do you guarantee that someone will do your bidding twenty years in the future?" he asked, looking around at us all, seeking a response.

"Well, the tried and tested ways are blackmail—do this or I'll kill someone important to you; money, as in here's a million dollars, and there's more where that came from; fear, as in I'll kill you if you don't do what I want; fame, as in I'll make you a star in your own lunchtime; I could go on, but we have a real case study at hand, why not look at that first?" I asked, knowing that this was exactly what the Boss wanted us to get around to, but he wanted us to own the idea, a little trick I had learned from him some time ago. "Anna, would you like to comment?" Anna looked at me, then the Boss, and smiled to herself. She had intuited what was going on and was happy to play the game. She stood up and put her hands in her pockets, looking a little stooped-shouldered.

"During our little chat with her and Arie, and again on the way back from Israel, Amira opened up to us. She told us how she was plucked out of the camps, taken to Israel, and placed with a family. She was totally normal until her fifteenth birthday, which incidentally coincided with her going to Technion University. She was called on by a woman she called 'Helen,' who gave her a laptop computer. At that time, and at that place, Amira had never seen a laptop, so it was a valuable gift. Again, everything is normal, if you can call a young refugee girl earning her science degree, a master's, and a doctorate all before her twentieth birthday normal, until 'Helen' pops up again and makes her what she calls 'a better offer.'"

"A better offer than what?" asked Indigo in clear, unaccented English, a habit he had when he was concentrating or wanting to impress someone.

"Well, Arie's people had offered her a role in the intelligence community, to which she said no."

"Okay, go on."

"Helen offered her another laptop, more updated, a bag of money for her family, and access to several scientific and military sites not available to most people. She also offered technical support, introduced her to a group of very clever people in both coding and nanotechnology, gave her access to a super-lab at the university she didn't know existed and promised her access to a world-class lab in a US university when she finished what would be her second doctorate."

"She also gave Amira some funds, quite a lot from what she said, as well as a stipend to pass onto her family," I added.

"Yes, her family played into this at every level. In fact, the only thing she asked of Arie was that he excluded her family from any retribution or blame for anything she may have done," Anna added, "and then things got interesting."

"As in?" the Boss asked, sitting back as relaxed as I had ever seen him, which simply meant he was applying that huge mind of his to the problem, the story, and the consequences we had all suffered through so far.

"Harvey Mudd College, a world leader in STEM. She was sent there as a post-doc, given three labs to work in, a team of specialists, and for the first year, everything was, again, normal."

"Then what happened?" the Boss asked.

"The hand of God turned up and attempted to guilt-trip our young scientific superstar into working for their cause. Brought up in the refugee camps, her family, the support over all the years she had been learning, used every trick in the book. No real pressure, but clearly established that there a debt to be paid, and it was expected that it would be, in full, at some time in the future."

"Who was the hand of God?" Indigo asked.

"The woman Helen and a cleric called Mohammad bin Usha Rashad. We've run him through all our databases, can't find a single trace of him."

"So, what happened?" the Boss asked.

"After a day of thinking about it, she acquiesced and was provided a hand-picked group of collaborators and was asked to manage two projects—one to refine her nano work, specifically in the oil and gas fields, and one in coding to create a means of filtering data off the internet and communications satellites undetected. She believed at the time that neither project looked threatening; the oil and gas work was for remediation of mass oil spills and gas eruptions from fracking operations, or so they said, and the data grab was supposed to enable the group to monitor some of the countries whom they judged to be the creators of the worst of the refugee problems without their knowledge. Again, given who some of those countries are, it seemed to be a reasonable request."

"So, she went to work."

"Yes, with one caveat. She fell in love with one of the geniuses she was paired with, a Chinese woman named Michele, a brilliant post-doc from Tsinghua University. She was undoubtedly the ringleader who oversaw everything the cohort did. Not surprisingly, she claimed to also be a refugee from the camps, which no doubt helped the bonding process with Amira. That part may or may not be true. No way to check that now."

"Why do you make the assumption she was the head dog?" the Boss asked. "Some two years into the development project, they had a nanoparticle that could clean up an oil or gas spill. Don't push me on the science, but as Amira explained it to us, they ran a full-scale test in Nova Scotia, and it was wildly successful. Apparently, the nano bug produced something called carbon three particles out of the oil spill—and I would suggest that this-or a version-is what happened to the Russian/Chinese oil pipeline and in Australia and Alaska."

"Wow. How come we didn't hear anything about this at the time?" the Boss asked.

"The university PR machine dumbed down the scientific breakthrough, supposedly to get the IP issues sorted out before it became commercialized, but when we looked back at that, it's obvious the majority of the reporting was deleted by the same coding bug that took down the internet. And this Michele took off a week later with all the data, equipment, results, in fact, everything that would be needed to replicate the experiment. It broke Amira's heart; there's no pain like losing your first love; we all know that. But there was more. Helen then came and took everything to do with her coding work and propositioned Amira with an offer to join what was described as an exclusive group of genius scientists to run missions and pay back the debt she had accumulated since being rescued from the refugee camp."

"Did she go?" asked the Boss.

"No. She took a day to supposedly clean up at the university so they would not come after her, then did a runner. Four years, absolutely no idea where she went or what she did until she suddenly turns up in Israel threatening to subsume their most important military asset. Claims she did it to gain attention and credibility, and frankly, after spending two days with her, I believe her."

"I do as well if that carries any weight," I added. It was one thing Anna, and I agreed on absolutely; while Amira had created both the code and the nano bug, she had had nothing to do with their use in the terror attacks. "But we have bigger issues to untangle, and I'd like to start with that."

"What do you mean?"

"Amira backed up everything she did in a secure location no one could find. But she shared with us the location of the code she wrote, and that is being accessed as we speak by the geek squad next door. This might give us a window into their communications and solve your 'black hole' idea. What I'm interested in is nanotechnology. Amira seems to think that with the material she developed as a baseline, the process might be able to be reversed, and if that's so, then we need a very, very secure high-tech lab where we can develop the technology in total secret. Given America, Russia, Australia, and China have all lost significant strategic oil and gas reserves, just the idea of something that could undo the damage would be enough to start a war—and I mean a real mushroom cloud enhanced one, which, in my humble opinion, would be far worse than the position we currently find ourselves in." The Boss smiled, probably wondering when was the last time I had a humble opinion, but he chose to let it slide. I could see his mind was working at a million miles an hour behind the façade of his crinkled and scarred face. Even his head had started to nod slowly.

"You've got a point. However, we are an international police force, not a chemistry lab, and certainly not the provider of things to fix all the world's ills. I suggest we focus on the terrorists, cracking their communications, locating them, and stopping any more attacks." I was prepared for this from the Boss; one thing he never did was lose sight of the objective, and to be honest, I didn't really expect him to overtly support my suggestion. But Anna and I had discussed this issue on the wild ride across the Mediterranean, and we had a simple plan. I hit the group with it.

"Boss, I agree. I wasn't suggesting that we—Interpol—solve this issue. But I think we need to at least consider sponsoring it."

"What do you mean?"

"When the geek squad is finished with Amira, I suggest we take her back to Arie and let him work the problem. After all, the base work on this nanoparticle transformation was done at Technion University, and her first post-doc work was in the special lab that had restricted access at that university. Arie told us that this lab was plugged into the Israel security services, which is how Amira came to their attention in the first place."

"Send her back to Israel?"

"Yes, once we have broken into the terrorists' communications network." The Boss seemed to be thinking about what I had said, except for the suspicion I held that he had already thought of this solution. He was a sneaky bastard, and I always had to keep that in mind when dealing with him.

"I agree. But first, as I said earlier, we're policemen and women, and we need to get back on track with our overall investigation. Indigo, the room is yours; can you please bring us up to date?" Indigo smiled wide enough to light up the whole room and literally bounced over to the screens that had been set up just short of the dripping fungus-covered wall.

"My pleasure, Colonel, my pleasure. If you see here, screen one, I have a chronological list of every terrorist activity that we are aware of. Screen two has the method used for the attack, and screen three has all the data we have accumulated so far on each attack. Casualties are shown in the sidebar as of today. All in all, it is not so much the total of people killed or injured, or even who they may be, but the economic impact on the world as a whole that is the real concern. Add to that the attacks by other well-known terrorist groups taking advantage of the overall chaos the main attacks have created, and the world is in a whole lot of hurt." The picture was clear to see, and for the very first time, I realized that Indigo was absolutely correct—as severe as they were, the casualties did not matter. It was the utter destruction to the world's economy that was creating the majority of the pain and chaos—even the loss of the space station and the sports arenas didn't really add to anything other than the overall density of the terror and fear that was now palpable in every media report.

"So, what do we know about the perpetrators?" I asked, probably knowing a little more than Indigo at this time, having spent so much of it with Amira over the past two days. But I wanted Indigo's take; he was, in my humble opinion, one of the very best investigators I had ever worked with. And he made a killer of an expresso!

He looked at me and smiled, lighting up the dingy cavern again, reminding me of his amazing energy. "Captain, you ask a very good question, and I'll start by reading from your comrade Master Chief Pete's report. Here it is on screen four." Pete's scrawl was almost illegible, and in fact, some of the words were so badly formed that I couldn't read them. Indigo laughed, smacking his hand together. "Got you!" He laughed again, switched the data, and the screen filled with perfectly typed information, in perfectly formed paragraphs, with key points highlighted in red, yellow, and blue. It was only about three hundred words long, and I worried about that a little. With the resources of the team and the funding provided, Pete should have been able to generate a lot of intelligence.

"Firstly," Pete said, from the back of the cavern; he had crept back in unnoticed, a testament to his Special Forces training, I supposed, "we haven't got a lot more than we knew already. Only one camp had any real data; the others lacked anyone who had been around in a position of power thirty years ago. We struck gold at Hartishiek A, a refugee camp in eastern Ethiopia. Messy place, overcrowded, a blight on the landscape, but I feel for everyone there, and if the conditions were much the same thirty years ago, I completely understand why the girls that were given a chance to leave did so." He continued into the cavern to stand just under the screen on which his report scrolled, finally stopping at a grainy black-and-white photo of a group of girls, all wearing headscarves and tattered long skirts, and a well-dressed Arab in full turban and desert dress. His black waistcoat was a contrast to his long, flowing robes, and while the clothes the Arab wore were dirty, it was obvious that they were well made and possibly expensive.

"Meet our banker, planner, strategist, and from what I have learned recently, retired mastermind. Al Hemish al-bin Mohammad Karesish, or Mohammad bin Azaria, as we now know him, in the flesh." I put my hand up at the exact same time Anna did; she looked at me, smiled, then deferred with a nod of her head.

"Pete, can we get this photo to Roger; he has a pair of monks in custody, one of who may be able to confirm this identity." Pete smiled, or what passed for one on his damaged face, waved both his hands in the air as if to say, "been there, done that."

"Indigo sent it over hours ago, and Roger got confirmation while I was in the shower. It is him, no doubt, and once we have local LANs back up and connected, we'll run full facial recognition on him at every airport, train station, camel stop, you name it. The FBI will track him as best as they can, as soon as they can. We also sent the photo to Arie and the Colonel's friends in Russia, China, and a few other places he didn't name. However, the Imam I spoke to in the camp seems to think he is in the desert somewhere, and I'm leaning towards the central desert around here," he said, pointing to a vast barren area in central Arabia and a little dot on the map labelled Ash Sharqiyah.

"Why there?" the Boss asked, beating me to the question by a hair's breadth. "The Imam we meet with said that al-bin Mohammad Karesish raved on about this spot, called it the most quiet and safest place on earth, that it had been blessed by the One God himself, and that he hoped to return to there before he died. Putting two and two together, I figure the bastard is there now, given that he has supposedly 'retired.'" The Boss looked thoughtful, rubbing his face with one hand. He nodded to himself, accepting Pete's analysis. What they could—or should—do about it was still to be resolved, so he brought the room back to his central theme—what police action should they take, what should they really be thinking about. He stood up, a lean, tall man with a strong posture and a well-worn face, one that gave me confidence every time I looked at him.

"We need to put all the peripheral issues to one side for a moment—we need to go back to the start. The bombs. They were taken back in two thousand two. The oldest girl that we know of would have been twelve if that. So that action was planned well before the disaster we have now and managed by others. Who, what, how, where, when, why, all the normal questions—and we know some of the answers? Anna?" he said, sitting down and giving her the floor.

Anna rose slowly and looked around the room. She seemed to be thinking about something and put her coffee mug down on one of the small benches that had been moved into the cavern by the monks. "We know the two bombs were taken in two thousand two, each at a different time but essentially the same way. They were requestioned by a forward base commander, shipped on military transport to the destination, then supposedly stored in the weapons bunker on the forward base. What we subsequently learned is that the paperwork was a forgery, absolutely first class, passed every scrutiny, including a return telex check for authenticity, and once the missions were complete, they disappeared. Around the same time—we have no evidence of this, but it is the only thing that makes sense—dummy bombs were loaded into the safety containers the weapons were originally shipped in.

"For that reason, every year when the munitions stocks were audited, they were where they were supposed to be. We only uncovered this after the first attack, when the DOJ demanded a full physical audit of all stocks, both in the US and abroad. There is one more interesting fact that might contribute to the timing. The Air Force was working on electronically tagging all munitions with electronic chips so that they could be tracked from factory to target. This was scheduled to start in two thousand three and was widely published in military journals and a few newspapers that ran military news."

"So maybe our mastermind hadn't necessarily worked out where or when he was going to unleash them," I said, seeing for the first time just how loose this whole world-busting plan of the terrorists had been. Thirty or so refugee girls, with potential but not necessarily proven and possibly two decades before they would be of use; bombs that had specific uses but as yet no targets or delivery mechanisms; and twenty five years to plan, learn, plot, train, and fine-tune the events of the last three weeks. But there had to be more to this; just the science itself was world-class, mind-blowing, and bleeding edge, to say the least. I started to see a form in the shadow. My mind went straight back to the events of 2002.

"Boss, I think this was all planned less than five or six years ago. I don't think he had any of this in mind when the bombs were stolen, and Amira has told us she wasn't approached to participate in anything other than developing the nanotechnology and the software until just five years ago. I think our mastermind was waiting to see what his girls came up with before planning the attacks."

"That's all possible, but how do you explain the Hercules that bombed Rome, the UAV that destroyed the Dome of the Rock, the Hog that took out West Point, and the Phantom that took down the space station? All those attacks were hardcore physical military actions that required planning, resources, people, staging, support, and time." The Boss sat back in his chair. In his case, a pair of dragons spewing flames at each other, bending behind his neck.

"I'll give you that—but don't forget the trucks and explosives used in the attacks on the mosque and the sports arenas. By comparison, most of that hardware could have been sourced through Terrorists-R-Us or online. We know that stuff is in abundance throughout Europe and the Middle East."

"Yes, but the kicker is the nuclear material used in the first oil field bombing and then the nanotechnology used on the pipelines."

"And then we have the taking down of the World Wide Web, and the virus that took out every computer, phone, modem, router, and connector, and the whole issue of them being able to delete electronic material without a trace." The Boss stood up again, held up one hand, and looked around at all of us.

"You are all correct—and that's the tangle we have to unravel. It seems to me that we have three if not four, different attack styles and possibly just as many terrorist groups, perhaps working in harmony, perhaps simply feeding off each other. Jessica, can you please speak about the order of the attacks? We know—or surmise—that all the attacks were timed for the election of the new Pope. Is there any logic in the attack pattern?" he asked, sitting down again and accepting a refilled coffee mug from Indigo. I stood up, moved to the first screen, looked at it critically, then turned back to face everyone in the cavern.

"I want to start back in two thousand two. Before the girls were moved out of the camps, we had terrorists or vested interests shipping out major weapons from secured arsenals to stores we don't know where. Question one would be, who did that? Not the girls, but an established team with access to our military methodologies to understand how to pull the theft off seamlessly. Then the question I kept asking myself as these recent attacks unfolded was who was doing what and how? If you look at the aerial attacks, we have the Hercules flying as an unmanned aerial vehicle. That takes planning, resources, software coding, and all sorts of support infrastructure; just this one attack took extensive resources. The storage and arming of the weapons is not a trivial task by any means—specialized, trained staff is required at every step. The flight planning, meticulous, again skilled hands required, remember this flight crossed several borders, all with permissions granted, flew in commercial airspace, was tracked by several different radars, and up until the bombing event, the data seemed to be legitimate.

"And we know from Anna's people that the aircraft was purchased in two thousand seven from the Bone Yard in Arizona, restored to basic flight condition, then flow out of the country, supposedly on a UN flight plan. All track of the aircraft was lost once it left our borders. Then the attack—we find the height data spoofed, again, something only a skilled operator could implement. If you add all that up, you have a flight crew, possibly two different ones, munitions experts, flight engineers, a flight planner, a radar specialist, and a master software programmer. Plus, add in the odd activities like fueling, storage, hangarage, and aircraft maintenance, none of which we have been able to physically locate. This was a twenty-five-year plan, as far as the individual pieces are concerned, but executed in today's electronic environment without fear or favor.

"Then look at the second attack here," I said, pointing to Indigo's screen, "the UAV missile attack on the Dome of the Rock. Same radar specialist requirements, weapons and armaments specialists, and flight planning and software upload. They not only spoofed the flight details but convinced us that we were running the flight from one of our bases. And, again, we simply do not know where it originated. We know the broad area but not the specific airfield. For the sake of argument, let's suppose both aircraft used the same base. Not too much of a stretch, and it cuts down on the number of trained individuals needed to mount the attacks. What happens next?" I asked, knowing I now had everyone's attention, even the Boss's. I paused to catch my breath; I hadn't realized that I was getting a little worked up during my assessment.

"A truck—a simple, traceable truck, filled with explosives, takes out part of the Grand Mosque. And I say part because I believe that this attack was limited in its design and tightly targeted—as was the Dome of the Rock."

"Both targeted to maximize infrastructure damage to a point but manage to leave the most revered religious areas intact."

"Yes," I answered Pete's comment, knowing he and the rest of the team had come to the same conclusion days before. "The truck blew up, the driver and his or her passenger walked away and disappeared from sight less than five hundred meters from the point of impact. How do they do that? I'm going with the Boss's 'black hole' theory. Does anyone disagree?" Every head shook in the negative, reminding me of a set of dashboard dolls that bounced up and down with the bumps.

"Now, to the actual physical attack on West Point—an A-10 Hog on a test flight, the pilot identified, authorized, photographed, tracked back several years from her military files, takes the Hog out of the shed with armaments neutralized, inert, disconnected, stops at the arming pit, and magically, the armaments are enabled, wired into the aircraft, the pilot is replaced with a blow up doll, who then takes off, flies the flight plan to perfection, tanks at the appropriate time, communicates with the tanker aircraft as she was supposed to do, then flies on to West Point, disguised her altitude, bombs the college, then flies on out and invisible to radar and anyone looking for her. Not a bad day's work for a blowup doll." I was greeted with a gentle laugh, so I looked around the room and noticed every eye was on me and not the screen, and I felt a shiver run up my back. I had always hated the spotlight but working with these incredible people made up for that.

"Now, the Boss walked the cat back on this one, so I'll hand it over to him." I sat down, wriggled my fingers to loosen the stiffness, looked around for coffee, and before I could think about my next move, Indigo placed a steaming mug in my hands. This I could get used to!

"As the good captain said, this was one of the attacks Pete and I walked back. We drove the route the fighter took, checked the sight lines and the security, and later, the US Navy found the aircraft in the ocean. They dived deep and recovered a box of electronics, which the NSA and the FBI have all been over with relish, as you can imagine. The little black box—which in this case was little and black!—was a quantum computer the likes of which we have not seen before. It was interfaced to the aircraft's control system, a simple process, as this particular aircraft had already been converted to a pilotless attack profile in an earlier test of RSA—remote systems authority. This particular test that was supposed to be running was designed to use a remote navigation and targeting system that was going to be part of the autonomous flight profile the Air Force was experimenting with."

"So, you're saying this aircraft was already mostly capable of remote, pilotless operation?" Pete asked, the astonishment in his voice clearly evident.

"Yes. All the terrorist pilot had to do was plug in the box, close the cockpit, connect the weapons to their input sockets, and scram. The box did the rest."

"Who thinks up this stuff?" Pete asked in amazement. "Next, they'll be replacing me with a robot!" Laughter broke the solemn mood that had descended over the cavern during the Boss's explanation, a welcome relief from the specter of being killed remotely. But I felt Pete's despair because this series of attacks had demonstrated the ability of remote-controlled, autonomous, hands-off delivery of death on a massive technological scale, and once the genie was out of the bottle, so to speak, it wouldn't be long before the crazies in the world tried to copy the terrorists. From Arie's recent report, we already knew his enemy was using plain toy UAVs loaded with explosives to terrorize Israel.

"Do you think this is how the F-4 took out the space station?" Indigo asked in perfect English. The lack of accent was not lost on anybody in the cavern.

"Yes, I do. In that case, to skip forward a few attacks, the aircraft deliberately crashed into the ground at over sixteen hundred miles an hour. The wreckage was no more than bits and pieces buried in a mile-wide hole in the ground and with a ten-mile shatter zone. But the NSA analysts tell us the little black box recovered from the Hog could easily manage that attack from take-off to final impact. How that aircraft got into the terrorists' hands is another story, and I'll let Anna fill us in on that."

"Well, and this is still a closely guarded secret, so we have something to work with if we ever catch up with any of the terrorists. This specific F-4 was slated to be flown to the boneyard, having served as a remotely piloted drone target aircraft, and was collected by an authorized pilot who has been described as very similar to our Hog pilot. Different background but same physical features, and when we pulled her images off the security footage, we got a ninety-seven point six percent match with the images from Andrews.

"I might add, her credentials were impeccable, triple-checked, as you would expect, and passed every level. It appears she oversaw the refueling, did a thorough pre-flight check, then took off on the flight plan to the bone yard in Tucson, Arizona."

"Wasn't there a stink when it didn't arrive?" Pete asked.

"No. The 309th AMARG (Aerospace Maintenance and Regeneration Group) was not aware they were to get the F-4. So, no one went looking for it until the space station blew up, and the F-4 fell to Earth, just a few hours after each other. As it was, the only way they could identify the aircraft was from a photo taken by a French weather satellite that was scanning that particular patch of ground at that time."

"Pure fluke!" Pete said, his humor back.

"Yes, but one that works in our favor. So, I'll draw a long bow, based on these two attacks, and hypothesize that these attacks were carried out by the same team, one or more persons, plus a small support staff hidden somewhere in Montana again, somewhere they could hide the F-4 until they were ready, then refuel it, program it, arm it, then let it fly." The Boss made a good point, and I wondered where it would lead us.

"You would only need two people," Anna said, standing up and stretching out some kinks in her shoulders. The chairs the monks had provided us with were very artsy but also very uncomfortable! "One, this pilot we are familiar with and a support person, to manage the refueling, arming, etc. In the case of the F-4, they only used one missile, according to Space Force, who captured the whole attack on their long-range cameras, not to mention the imaging they got downloaded from the station itself before it blew up."

"So," I said as I also stood up and stretched, "you could also hypothesize that the Hercules and the UAV could have been managed by just two people with the right ground equipment. A pilot and support staff. If they used a similar box to the one pulled from the Hog, it could have been programmed anywhere, at any time. In fact, all the programming could just as easily be done off-site and shipped in over the internet, if it comes to that."

"Why a pilot?" asked Pete. I looked at him with a frown on my face. I almost said what I was thinking, in terms of it being a stupid question, but then I thought it through, and I realized he had a point. They didn't need a pilot, just someone who knew their way around a Hercules and a UAV. Technician, maybe, or even just an aeronautical engineer. I started to think about that, then looked at the Boss.

"Two people in the truck at the Grand Mosque, right?" he nodded. "Can't prove it, no bodies."

"Assume two people in the truck at the oil well head?" he nodded again. "So, two people in the Middle East, somewhere around Iran, Iraq, Turkey, yes?" third nod.

"And we're all comfortable with just the two people in the States running the attacks on West Point and the space station?" This time he just smiled, probably afraid his head would fall off if he nodded again!

"So, that leaves the attacks on the pipelines in Russia, China, Australia, and Alaska. Not to mention the technology hack that took down all the internet, Wi-Fi, computers, phones, etc., we'll just put that all in one basket for now. How many people needed to salt the pipelines with nanotechnology?"

"Let's say a team of two, based on what we know so far, but to be honest, I'm starting to get a picture from all your analysis that moves away from the refugee women as the perpetrators of everything that has happened. Including the trucks and their flying bombs that took out the stadia. In fact, those attacks scream out to me jihadi terrorism, not retribution."

The Boss looked up at the screens, scanned from one to the other, and shook his head with a grimace on his face. "The girls were used to develop the technology, the high-level weapons, and some, no doubt, were infiltrated into our highest levels of security—NSA for sure, Air Force, maybe FBI, but I don't think so, maybe CIA, that's more likely given the, what I'll call the overseas component. But your garden-variety terrorist could just as easily have been recruited and trained to deliver the truck bombs, the nanotechnology, or even locate the laser designator used in the Rome attack. It's not just about the refugee girls. What we have here is a self-contained ground force, localized to each area of operation and possibly independent of the women. Maybe."

"Yes, and if anything, Amira confirms that with her story. The terrorists made no effort to track her after she did a runner from Harvey Mudd. They took all her work but left her alone. That in itself is telling. No effort to clean up, hide what they had achieved, and were happy to wait—what—four or five years before using the technology in public. The feeling I get, and it's just a feeling at this point, is that our planner actually cared deeply about the girls he pulled out of the camps. Wait!" I said, suddenly having a thought that had been lurking at the back of my mind for an hour or two but, like most unformed thoughts, too grey and fuzzy to take any notice of. "Boss, get Arie on the line." The Boss lifted his little notebook, flicked it open, and dialed Arie, then fiddled with the keys and managed to transfer his image to one of the big screens.

"Arie, Jessica has something for you." He handed me the laptop, and I looked straight into the little green light of the camera.

"Arie, can you confirm something for us, please?" I asked. Arie nodded, which on the big screen looked like a forgiving grandfather overlooking the sins of a favored niece.

"Certainly. What do you need?"

"Can you check with Amira's family discretely and see if they are still getting the stipend the woman called Helen organized for Amira while she was at college?"

"No need. We already did that when we heard Amira's story. And yes, the family gets the equivalent of two thousand two hundred USD every month from a bank in the UAE. When we did a deep dive on the bank, we found it to be one of the paymasters for the United Middle East Finance Corporation, attached to the Pan Arabian Wealth Fund, which, in turn, is heavily linked to Arab royalty and, from our end at least, totally untouchable."

"Thanks, Arie, that is excellent. All we need for now." And I closed the screen on the little computer, letting this confirmation roll through my thoughts. The big screen went to black, a little white cursor winking in one corner.

"How does this change our approach, if at all?" asked Anna. I could see Pete had a perplexed look on his face, the Boss was smiling, and Indigo looked interested but not necessarily confused, so I floated my theory.

"We've been looking in all the wrong places, for all the wrong people. Yes, we need to track down the women who have been involved in the attacks—the pilots, engineers, armorers, and any others they may have used, but we really need to refocus on the terrorists, the jihadis, the supporting cast as it were because they will take us to the money man, the planner who set all this up." As I finished my statement, Stefarino walked into the cavern, a happy smile on his craggy face. He walked straight over to the Boss, bent to whisper something in his ear, bobbed a little bow, smiled at all of us, and left as he had come. Quietly, with just the faintest sound of a shuffle, as if he were sliding his feet across the floor.

"We've got some good news from the geeks, but before I get to that, does anyone have a comment on what Jessica has just put before us?"

"No, Boss, I agree with her. Let's go chase some crazies, much more fun!" Pete said, laughing to take any sting out of his comment. The Boss shrugged as if to say how could he argue with Pete's comment, stood, and led us out of the room. Behind us, the big screens still hold most of the story so far, and an ugly one at best, technologically challenging, but human devastation on a scale never seen before in the modern world. I wondered how any of us would ever recover our true balance, and not for the first time, even if we did identify and catch all the perpetrators, would it be enough to help the world get back on its feet?

CHAPTER 59

The president sat behind the Resolute Desk, a favorite of presidents for over one hundred and fifty years. The Oval Office had been redecorated some five years ago, and the then somber tones had been replaced with more bright colors creating air and a sense of space and freedom. The director of the FBI, Roger Winslow, sat on one side of an old French polished table next to general Bridget Saunders. Opposite them sat the secretary of state and the director of the NSA, Frank Reynolds. A silver coffee service sat squarely in the center of the table, and as yet, unused bright china coffee cups sat before each person. The president was sipping out of a go cup, contents unknown. Outside the huge windows that framed the president, sunlight floated across the trees and shrubs, creating shadows of mystery and fun as they danced to a silent tune.

"Thank you all for being available. I appreciate your time in this time of crisis. I know you are all very busy, so I won't keep you longer than I have to." She looked at her visitors, seeking any hint of discomfort, inwardly dreading the next few minutes, wishing for the best but preparing for the worst. "Frank, could you please start the conversation?"

"Madam President, thank you, happy to. As you know, we are tasked with the global monitoring and collection of intelligence from all and any source to prevent or at least anticipate any attack on the United States or its allies. During this current crisis," he continued, following the plan laid out earlier by Bridget and the president, "we have been collecting signals data from all over the globe, specifically looking for data regarding the terrorist cells we believe are behind the attacks."

"You have been doing that since nineteen fifty-four, so what's different now?" the president asked, knowing the answer, with her fingers crossed mentally as to the outcome of this conversation. She had known the secretary of state from early childhood, considered her one of her closest confidants and friends, and had enjoyed her smart mouth and smarter mind for close on twenty-five years. In fact, she probably owed her current position as president of the United States in some small way to her, something she hoped she was not going to regret.

"Before the web was crashed, we were tracking various terrorist groups around the world looking for any links to the current activity. We were able to identify the mastermind relatively early; do you all remember the priest who came to us with his story about the refugee children? He gave us a name, Al Hemish al-bin Mohammad Karesish, the location of the first conversation with respect to these children, Gouraud in Baalbeck, Lebanon. We followed up, chased every lead, and finally discovered he had changed his name to Mohammad bin Azaria."

As the director spoke, the president fixed her eyes on the Secretary, as did both the director of the FBI and the general. What they saw was puzzlement, creased brows, but no tightening of the body, no sense of being caught out, in fact, just a fairly normal response as if this was a curious thing but not really anything exceptional.

"I know that name," the Secretary said, sitting slightly forward in her seat and turning to look the president in the eyes. "Can't be the same person I know, but I do know that name." The room took on the feel of a tomb, the deeply soundproofed walls and windows adding to the silence. The president visibly relaxed, sitting slightly back in her chair. She sipped from her go cup again and gestured to her guests to use the coffee service. Frank Reynolds bent to pour the coffee, and after a little shuffling, the cream and sugar going the rounds, all five people in the room sat back, a silent consensus having been reached. They would hear the Secretary out without further interruption.

"Who is your Mohammad bin Azaria?" the president asked.

"He's the head of a refugee agency in the Sudan, someone my department and I have been talking to for a couple of years, trying to find solutions to the refugee problems they have over there and we have here." The president nodded, her gut unknotting for the first time since she had learned of the Secretary's conversations with the head of the terrorists. Still, one issue to be untangled, but she was feeling more confident by the minute. She nodded to Frank to continue.

"Madam Secretary, thanks for confirming that. We were in a bit of a blind, as the conversations you held were picked up by Interpol in Venice but not by our own signals directorate. And that caused us more than a little concern." Frank drank from his cup, his gaze never leaving the Secretary. If she was going to lie or prevaricate, now was the time. He was disappointed.

"Can't help you there, Frank, but every conversation I have had, or those my people have had with any aid agency, have been recorded by my department. I thought you knew that?" she asked. "Happy for you to have the records if that helps." Frank smiled, nodded, and put his cup down.

"Thanks, Madam Secretary, that will be very helpful." The president sat back, unsure what to do next. She was saved by Roger Wilson, who also put his cup back on the table.

"Madam Secretary, did you ever video with Mohammad bin Azaria?" he asked, almost as a throwaway. The Secretary looked a little puzzled by the question and titled her head to one side. Her long auburn hair fell away from her ear, revealing a trio of little diamond studs.

"No, he said way back, he didn't have the technology for video; we connected by phone. I'm not sure about my people, who may have spoken to others in his agency. I can check for you if that helps?"

"I'll leave the details to you all. Thanks for your time. General, if you could stay for a moment, please?" the president said, standing. She smiled as the others left the room and waited until the thick door closed behind them. She rolled her shoulders, shook her head, then sat back down. The general also sat, leaned back, and relaxed into the soft cushions of the couch.

"Looks like the Secretary is in the clear," she said, turning her head to better see the president.

“Maybe. I want you to follow up, get everything you can, prove absolutely the Secretary is in the clear, dot every ‘i’, cross every ‘t’, and make no mistakes; if she is implicated, it could bring us all down. Not that we don’t have enough problems to deal with as it is.”

“Well, don’t want to spoil your pity party, but we’ve just had a flash from Venice. They think they may have a solution to the ‘black hole’ that PJ described earlier. And if they do, we may be able to get into the terrorists’ networks without them knowing.” The president smiled, a thin, feral, bright-eyed smile that would leave no one in any doubt that she smelled blood, and not her own for once!

CHAPTER 60

The geek squad was in full flight. Hands scrolling screens, tapping keyboards, punching buttons, muttering in at least five different languages. Looking at all the movement from the back of the room could easily cause the casual observer to think that the chaos was pointless, confusing, and disruptive. In truth, it was anything but. In an hour or so since they had been let loose, they had successfully retrieved Amira's folder from the hidden and heavily encrypted cloud store, and the team was now trying to open it to get at the code to a test communication to either prove or disprove the Boss's black hole theory. I was astonished to see Amira hard at work on a keyboard and swiping at a large screen at the same time. She had obviously earned the trust of her companions beyond the respect that came with what she had already done by creating the original code. Not for the first time, I remembered that pressure made strange bedfellows, but my heart warmed with the prospect of being able to hit back at the terrorists, if only in a virtual way. And then I had a thought.

"Boss, are we sure this is the way to go?" I asked, causing both he and Pete to stop dead in their tracks. Indigo nearly ran into Pete, stopping himself by putting his arm out just in time.

"'Scusea me, Mister Pete, we seema to have run into a traffic jama!" he said in his best accented English/Italian, which simply meant he was being playful.

"What do you mean, Captain?" the Boss asked his use of my rank a sure sign he was anything but playful. He turned to face me, stepping slightly aside, so Indigo, he, and Pete ranged themselves in front of me. I looked at all three of them, knowing no matter how weird what I was about to say was, they would give it serious consideration.

"If we let the terrorists know we can crack their code and effectively track what they have done, and maybe even what they are about to do, we could lose an advantage." The Boss gave me one of his tight-eyed looks, narrowing his face almost to a point.

"Are you suggesting we keep this to ourselves?" he asked, his voice just a whisper.

"Yes, sir, I am." He continued to look at me, never blinking, staring me down as if challenging me to back off. Indigo started to say something, paused, then put his hand on the Boss's arm.

"Colonel, the captain has a valid point. If we can crack their code but keep it absolutely between ourselves—maybe letting our US friends and Arie in on the secret, maybe not—it will give us an enormous advantage in tracking them as individuals."

"And we already know at least two of the terrorists' names—we may even have their faces—this Helen character and Michele, Amira's Chinese lover," added Pete, once again showing his ability to think strategically. The Boss relaxed, Indigo took his hand off the Boss's arm, and I could see the tension flowing out of everyone as if I had pricked a balloon!

"You have a point, Jessica, but I want you to think through the opportunity – what do we most want to find out first?" I thought long and hard, my personal list was very long indeed, but I got the Boss's drift. He was going to prioritize what intelligence we went for in order of importance—at least to Interpol. I looked up and tried a thin smile but couldn't manage it for some reason. Maybe the sheer seriousness of the problem we faced sucked out any hope of feeling happy while we worked, or maybe I was just tired.

"Okay, data point number one, is there going to be another attack, where, when, how, etc. Happy?" I asked, throwing in the "happy" to see his reaction. He frosted me with another withering look, then burst out laughing.

"Got you!" he said, moving us all towards the deep-seated couch area which housed the massive and impressive coffee system. Just the smell started the salvia running behind my teeth, and I shook my head. Not for the first time, the Boss had thrown me under the bus in public to get everyone else involved in a way that allowed for mistakes and wrong comments. If you created an environment where you could survive your mistakes, you usually managed to move forward at a really fast clip, something we needed to do because so far, the terrorists had landed punch after punch, and we were not yet even in the ring. Indigo did his coffee service thing, and in just a matter of minutes, we were seated, steaming mugs of coffee in one hand, and warm croissants in the other.

"Okay, now that you've had your fun," I said, "what's your agenda here?" The Boss looked thoughtful while he finished a mouthful of warm French pastry. "I agree with your basic premise—if we crack their communications open, we keep it to ourselves. Except for maybe one of two other people."

"Who are you thinking of?" Indigo asked, looking back towards where Stefarino was overseeing the geek squad.

"Yes, Indigo, absolutely, we will be giving the good monk access. I see them playing a significant role in everything we do going forward for reasons I'll detail later. My thoughts are that we limit the access totally. And I do mean totally."

"Not even the NSA?" asked Anna, who until this time had almost been invisible. "Anna, with all due respect, we know the terrorists penetrated your highest level of intelligence and communications as far back as two thousand. For over twenty-five years, they have had free reign over everything we have said and done. Until I am absolutely positive they are no longer in our systems, I want to keep what we find to ourselves. We have let General Bridges know we have cracked the 'black hole' problem, but not to what extent. I'd like to keep it that way for now."

"What about Arie?" Anna asked, turning her head to one side as if seeking inspiration from the coffee machine. The tone of her voice left us in no doubt she was conflicted by what the Boss was saying. She was FBI first, USA second, then Red White and Blue, and the Americans had been very forward and open in their help so far, not to mention Anna's personal contribution.

"Anna, for the immediate future, no, not even Arie. I'll have a private conversation with him later, but I suspect he will agree in the short term at least. Don't forget that we are sending Amira back to him once we have the software sorted so she can try to reverse engineer the nano bug."

"Will I talk to Roger and tell him what we intend to do?" she asked, her voice warming slightly as she considered the merit in the Boss's stance.

"Yes. First call after this. And I have a plan to work out if the terrorists are still in our systems, and that is item number two on my list."

"And once you prove we are secure again, you'll share the software with them?"

"Arie and Roger, which, of course, means Julius and Frank, and probably the president, yes, we will give them full access. But not until I know with certainty that we are secure." Anna nodded her head, still lost in her thoughts, probably wondering how she could explain to her Boss why we hadn't shared the software the moment we knew it worked. But I could see she was working through the problem because the tension had gone out of her shoulders, and she had the fire back in her eyes. And then I saw something else.

"You're protecting Stefarino and his crew, aren't you?" she asked. The Boss nodded. He leaned back in his seat.

"Indigo's friends have given us everything we have to date—their secret network, their computers, even the information about the secretary of state. We couldn't have done what we have accomplished so far without their trust and support. However we manage the software, we must protect the Monks and their network. Anna, you'll have to keep all this to yourself because all Arie, Frank, and the others know is that we have a secure network that our little computers speak to that no one knows about. I assume they think it's some Interpol system, and I'm not going to disabuse them of that. I hope you don't mind?" the Boss asked. Anna shook her head, understanding that the Boss was not denying the US a tool in the fight against the terrorists but rather making sure we didn't give the terrorists another weapon. Something I totally agreed with!

"Okay, sure, I'll work out what to say to Frank. I can see where you are coming from and how this might work to our advantage."

"Great. Now, Jessica, what was your number two?" he asked, moving the focus back onto me. I held up two fingers.

"Sort out the attack profile, that's number one, as I said, then I'd like to backtrack satellite data in Montana and Libya and see what they have asset-wise, get a timeline on their coming and goings, then track and trace them as best as we can. Number three—possibly at the same time, depending on our technical resources, backtrack every attack, locate their physical bases, then plan how to take them out." The Boss smiled, but I just knew there was a crocodile in there somewhere, so I waited for the pushback.

"Good plan. Remember, we are a police force, not an army; any attack we support will have to be mounted by others, and we will need to give that careful consideration. If we really are only dealing with a few women, but potentially a lot of crazies, we might need to fight on different fronts with different tactics for each target."

"What do you mean?" Indigo asked.

"Well, capturing the women may not even be possible if they have gone to the ground and scrubbed their histories. Maybe the software fix will help us there, but we can't plan on it. Physical terrorists are another matter. And I suspect it's something we can do now, given we have come to that conclusion. However," he said, pausing to look at every one of us individually, "we have a couple of flies in that ointment."

"The attack on Avignon and the change of regime in Arabia?"

"Yes. Those two. I am referring to the fact that the Arab states have not yet asked Interpol to intercede on their behalf—officially—and the regime change came on the heels of the French delegation disappearing—and being blamed for the attack on the Grand Mosque. What I want to do is separate out what we can pursue as Interpol and what we can support via our military contacts. That keeps it clean from a political and policy point of view. But we need to move quickly because the terrorists that made the physical attacks will be in the wind by now, and tracking them might be problematic."

"But if you run through Jessica's second point," Anna said, rubbing the back of her neck to loosen the tension that had slowly built up there, "we might be able to identify the terrorists if we get clear enough images."

"Yes, my thoughts exactly. Remembering that we have very advanced satellite observation capability and that, as far as we know, anything stored before the cyber-attack will still be there, we only have to work out how to retrieve it without the bad guys getting wind and then get our military contacts the information, again, under the radar of the terrorists."

"You will have to tell Arie about the software, or at least we are working on the black hole theory if we send Amira back to him; he will have to know what we have achieved so far." Anna looked resolute as if she had made her mind up about something.

The Boss looked thoughtful, turning his head to one side as if listening to secret voices. Then he nodded to himself, stood up, looked around, then picked Stefarino out of the geeks swarming the keyboards and screens. He walked over.

"Stefarino, can you set up a secure video link to our American friends and Arie on a large monitor, so we can work out some intelligence stuff, please?" Stefarino looked at his geek squad, then around at us sitting in the conversation pit, looked thoughtful, then nodded.

"*Sì, Colonnello, possofarlo io per lei. Vuolemascharare la posizion, e non usare I mini portatilicheabbiamofornito in precedenza?*"

"Yes. I want to use the big screen as if we were in an Interpol office, and the minis make it hard to work with multiple people. We can go back down into the cavern if that suits." The monk nodded, turned to one of his geek acolytes, fired a stream of Italian at her, patted her on the shoulder, then turned back to the Boss and nodded as she literally ran out of the room.

"*Colonnello, la prego di tornarenellasuacaverna, le faròportare del caffè.*"

"Thanks, Stefarino. We are in your debt." The Boss signaled to us, and we all moved back the way we had come just a half hour or so before. This time, however, the cavern was well lit; there was a square boardroom-style table in the middle of the floor and a huge screen sitting on legs at one end, with a telltale video camera mounted underneath. I wondered where the monks stored all this furniture. The overall impression they had created was a high-class office. The Boss, Indigo, and I arranged us at the end of the table, with Anna and Pete sitting on the sides opposite each other, forming a hollow "U." The screen flickered, then broke up into squares, then faces formed, the squares grew in size until we had Arie in one corner and Frank, Roger, Julius, and, this time, General Bridget Saunders in the remaining area of the screen. No president.

"Gentlemen, General, hello from Venice again. I take it the president couldn't make this call?" the Boss asked. On the screen, Arie looked a little worn, and I worried about his health.

"Colonel, I'm deputizing for the president; she has a number of issues to manage at this time, and she felt I could get what she needs from you in her place." The Boss nodded, having no doubt worked that out for himself. I watched him do what he had done so often in the past, create an environment where hot, open, and honest communication could and would take place, removing the possibility of political spin or bullshit interfering with our agenda.

"General, may I call you Bridget? And I'm PJ—you know Arie, I assume, and Frank, Roger, and Julius. Can I ask you what your specific functional role is, please, just to set the scene, as it were? And can you tell us if you have been fully briefed?"

"Yes, to the last question, and my role is to assist the president in any way she sees fit as well as act as the physical interface between her and the chiefs of staff. I report to the president, and I take guidance from the chiefs. I take as many of her meetings as we can fit in, which gives her time to manage the country. That's the theory, and given the current circumstances, it seems to be working well."

"I can attest to that," added Julius, who, as the head of the CIA, would know if the general was a barrier or an enabler.

"Thanks, Julius, appreciated. Okay, people, listen up. But before we start, Arie, is all well?" the Boss asked, echoing my thoughts. Aire not only looked tired but had lost all the color in his face, aging him considerably since our last call.

"Well, if you count a state of war on three fronts as well as the previous crippling terrorist attacks as normal, then we are just fine. But we have had to employ some heavy weapons to stop the invaders, and we fear that the collateral damage and casualties will be high. But, please, let's concentrate on the bigger picture. You have news for us?" The room paused, and you could see that everyone on the call was taking a big breath because Israel being invaded on three fronts was no small matter and had the potential to completely destabilize the Middle East—given that it was already in turmoil from the terrorist attacks. The Boss looked around the screen, judged the mood, then got straight to the point.

"We believe we will have untangled the software problem in the next hour, will prove the black hole theory, and will then need secure access to all your satellite data for the last three months. We will want this data sent to us over a secured link which we will provide, and in thinking about it, we might need to go back a year or more." The room paused again; all we could hear was the incessant dripping of the water seeping into the cavern. I hoped the Americans couldn't hear it, or questions would be asked!

"No problems with that. But it sounds like you are going to do the processing yourselves and not share the software with us?' Julius asked, drawing the expected frowns from Roger, Frank, and Bridgett.

"Yes. We are going to set a trap for the terrorists, and once we work through that exercise and can prove we have them out of your systems, we'll share—but not before. Too much at stake. We have a geek squad here that is first class, fast, and willing to help as much as they can. Arie, you know the specific geeks we speak of, and we're planning on sending them back to you at some point, again, once we are sure the terrorists are not still in your systems as well. Then there's another issue." Again, the drip, drip, drip was the only sound in the cavern.

"And what might that be?" Bridget asked, just the faintest hint of sarcasm in her tone. Generals didn't get to be generals by carelessly delegating responsibility to lesser mortals, and it was obvious by her body language she didn't like being cut out of the information loop.

"Bridget, PJ is the most reliable and trustworthy investigator in Interpol. I— we, that's Julius and Frank and I—trust him and his team implicitly," offered Roger. His serious look underlined the emphasis he placed on his words. To him, the relationship between himself and PJ was non-negotiable, born out of hellfire and mass destruction and the mixing of blood, side by side, in the harshest of combat conditions.

"No offense, PJ. I guess I'm a little wired by recent events. What was your next point?" she asked, her tone now inquisitive and not in any way sarcastic. Again, generals didn't get to be generals by being pig-headed or by not listening with big ears! PJ just smiled, used to the attempts of generals and the heads of the different countries' police forces batting back at him specifically, and Interpol in general. Very few powerful people ever trusted anyone they couldn't directly control.

"None was taken, Bridget. In your position, I'd probably feel the same. My second point is that it may be possible to reverse engineer the nano bug that has taken out our oil and gas supplies. No guarantee, but it is a distinct possibility. Arie, we'll be looking to you to help with that, using that lab we are now familiar with."

"You know the lab where the nano bug was created?" interjected Frank, almost rising out of his chair.

"Yes, calm down, Frank; there's a lab in the US that was used as well. In fact, we believe the final work and testing of the bug was all done in the US, probably with government funds if you stop and think about it."

"Holy crap!" exploded Julius, shaking his head from side to side, slightly dislodging his swept-back hair. He shook his head, and his hair settled back down. "The bug was developed right under our noses. Are you kidding?"

"No, not for one second. And when we clear the black holes, we'll send you absolute proof that the FBI can act on locally to ensure there is no further secret development of country killing nano bugs. But that's not the issue."

"Then what is?" asked Roger, shaking his head in wonder. The events of the last few weeks had shaken his confidence in his country's ability to effectively manage these terrorist attacks, given that there had been no warning of anything even remotely like what had eventuated. In his experience, in over thirty years of law enforcement, there had always been some type of warning, some chatter somewhere, not necessarily taken notice of, as in the 9/11 attacks, but nevertheless, some chatter somewhere. This time around, and given the sheer scope of the attacks, there should have been some chatter somewhere.

But there hadn't been. And terrorists generally were not renowned for their discipline.

"The issue is whether or not we take the time to find a way to undo the damage or leave things as they are." For a heartbeat or two, I swear even the water stopped dripping, the silence on all ends of the video call so absolute. It drew on as everyone worked furiously to form a counterargument, but strangely, each of the five people remained silent, even though their faces showed that their minds were working overtime. The president's general was the first to break the silence.

"PJ, no matter how you look at it, having a solution and not applying it will never be accepted by the Arabs—not to mention the Russians and the Chinese. And I might add, my Boss will probably have a view on this that will undoubtedly be quite a strong one."

"Wait one—the Arabs are out of luck—they have a radioactivity problem, not easily solved, although I suspect that someone somewhere will develop a nano bug to fix that—but not now, and probably not in the foreseeable future. The Russians, the Chinese, and Australians all lost natural gas, not oil. And in all probability, you could raise a case for working on a solution for gas. But think about the oil production, where it sits, who has controlled it, and what it has fueled over the past fifty or sixty years. Take that out of the equation, and you could completely change the political scene in the Middle East."

"What about the Alaskan pipeline?" asked Roger.

"What about it? We have plenty of gas and alternative power and the will to develop and use renewables; it is, after all, the fastest-growing segment of the power industry, or at least was before the terrorist attacks."

"You're kidding us, aren't you? Interpol is supposed to be non-political and non-partisan. Have you gone over to the dark side?" demanded Julius, absolutely astonished at PJ's suggestion.

"Tell me, face to face, that the first thing any of you will do the moment you get the ability to reverse engineer the nano bug won't be to deny certain countries access to the solution." The Boss's voice had taken on a hard edge, and his face left no one in any doubt that he was both throwing down a challenge and making a point. At least Frank had the good grace to smile.

"You're probably correct. But that decision is up to others, not to us."

"Couldn't disagree with you more. Here's my reasoning. Right now, today, we have the face and names of two of the women terrorists. We have the face, history, name, and some good data on the mastermind or banker—he might be both; we just don't know. We may even know where he is hiding. We know the weapons and the delivery systems; we even have the locations of what we suspect are two of the terrorists' working headquarters.

"We are about to break through the communications hack that has virtually shut down the World Wide Web and most of the computers and phones linked to it. We have worldwide chaos on a scale never seen before, and that includes the two world wars of the last century. We are about to get our eyes and ears back, which will allow us to look back in time and work out how these buggers did what they did and where they did it from. Against all that, why would any political imperative take precedence? By what logic would you act like a God and give some players their assets back and deny others? Isn't it better to just maintain the status quo and drive for better energy solutions? Preferably ones that don't start or enable wars to be fought over them." For perhaps the fourth time, quiet reigned supreme across three continents, as they all considered the Boss's statement. It was Arie who broke the silence, and in the background, we could just hear the sounds of heavy gunfire, which caused us all to look hard at Arie's image, which was flickering from side to side as if someone was trying to pull it out of the frame.

"PJ, you make a good point, and of us all, we would benefit the most from the current situation with the radioactive oil coming out of the desert. But the reality is that we are still an oil-dependent economy, not to mention what we need to defend ourselves, which we are not doing a very good job of at present. I'm sorry, I will have to abandon this call; we are about to be overrun here at Khan Yunis."

"What are you doing down there?" I asked, mindful that just the day before, I had been working with Arie in Hebron.

"We moved into an old facility, the better to see first hand what we were facing. During the night, we got cut off, and now we are fighting on two fronts. It's local, no more than a few thousand insurgents, and not the first time they have attacked us here. Not to worry. I'll get back to all of you later in the day, perhaps?" and his image winked out, the screen segment going to black, with the title "Arie Rosenberg-Israel" sitting in the middle, as if commanding our attention.

"Poor Arie. Wish there was something we could do to help," Bridget said, voicing what was on most of our minds. Roger shook his head, Julius looked grim, and even Roger looked glum as the import of Arie's words sunk in. The Arab and Muslim factions were once again striking against Israel in an attempt to, as they stated, reclaim land that had been theirs for thousands of years. I'm sure I looked as despondent as I felt; a war in the Middle East was the last thing we needed at the moment, and I wondered how it might change our thinking about returning Amira back to Israel. And then I had a flash of inspiration, something I would look back on in years to come and think that we had reached a pivot in untangling the terrorist attacks.

"Roger, Julius, I have a suggestion. How about once we untangle the software issue and prove the Colonel's black hole theory, we bring our asset to the States, specifically to the college where the work on the nano bug was completed and tested? The work can be done as easily there as in Israel and, under the current circumstances, possibly in a safer environment." The Boss turned to look at me, his eyes narrowed, his face for once unreadable. Anna had also turned to watch the interplay between the Boss and myself, and even Pete turned to look at the Boss's reaction. In contrast, Indigo looked thoughtful, rocking his head softly from side to side.

"Colonel, the captain's idea is a good one, but as you say in English, once the genie is out of the bottle…" The Boss nodded, accepting the inevitability of what the head of Interpol in Italy wasn't saying but implying. If the Americans were in control of the reverse engineering of the nano bug, they could just as easily play God with it and use it to further their political interests throughout the world. The very thing the Boss was trying to prevent. For not the first time today, I wished I had kept my mouth shut.

"Good idea, but let's put it on the back burner for now and see if we can't hack the software used against us to shut us down. General, Frank Julius, Roger, thanks for your time. We'll update you later today." And the Boss made the cut-throat motion with his hand, signaling the monk that was managing the call for us to cut the feed, which he did without further ceremony. The Boss looked around at us, rolled his shoulders, then looked off towards the main room.

"How about a shower, a meal, then we meet back in the main room in half an hour?" he said, moving us all out with a sweep of his arms. He looked directly at me and nodded.

"Jessica, could you stay here for a minute, please?" I nodded. The others looked curious, but the thought of a shower and hot food overwhelmed any natural curiosity.

"That was not your best idea, and we'll leave it at that for the moment. I have a call to make, and I want you in on it." I nodded again, wondering what he was up to now. He pulled the minicomputer up towards him and dialed a number that I was unfamiliar with. The screen soon showed a worn, grizzled face of a woman I had only heard of just once, way back just after the Boss had recruited me into Interpol.

"General, I need your support for something."

"Speak."

"We may have the software issue sorted in a matter of hours, and when we do, I want to set a Trojan horse in an attempt to trap the terrorists."

"You don't need my help or that of this office to do that," she replied in a flat tone as if admonishing the Boss for even suggesting it.

"No, I don't, but now you know my strategy. One other thing." She raised one eyebrow; otherwise, her face was inscrutable. "I want your office to take control of the software used to create the nano bug and lose it somewhere deep and permanent. You won't be popular, you may even get shouted at by the Americans, but I believe it will be the best thing we can do under the circumstances." She looked at the Boss as hard as one can on an international encoded video call, then nodded to herself.

"You will brief me appropriately, won't you?" The Boss nodded, then cut the connection. He turned to look at me. "Jessica, this stays between the two of us. Understood?" It was my time to nod. Interpol was apolitical, and I understood that I used it to my advantage from time to time, but obviously, the Boss had a bigger agenda in mind, one he might or might not share with me sometime.

"Fine with me, but you will need to talk to Anna, and I suspect Amira at some point, and they may have a different view of us."

"Bound to, but we'll cover that ground when we get to it. Go make yourself presentable, and get a hot meal. I need you at the top of your game for when we tackle the terrorists and their comms." I nodded and moved off, not for the first time wondering just how much influence and power this strange little unit of Interpol really had and who actually had our back.

Time would, undoubtedly, tell!

CHAPTER 61

One of the many things the FBI was good at was closing the loop on an investigation. With the help of the Navy, the remains of the Hog had been recovered from the Atlantic Ocean, brought back to land, and reconstructed in a hangar that in a past life had housed blimps. Experts from the NTSB (National Transportation Safety Board) and the Air Force crawled over every bit, and the black box that had been recovered first had been examined down to the individual molecules. The FBI had been patient, letting the experts do their thing, simply making sure that nothing about the recovery got into the media.

A separate team overlooked the recovery of the hole in the ground that contained all the remaining pieces of the F-4 Phantom that had successfully shot down the space station. In this case, the biggest piece was around an inch long, bent on all sides, and unrecognizable, but with the aid of 3D modeling and the ability of the Air Force to provide an original aircraft in perfect condition as a reference, what was at first just metallic and plastic fragments soon became a wired-up fractured representation of an aircraft that had served its country in two major conflicts with distinction, and then served as a remote target for trainee top guns. Of the black box that had no doubt controlled the aircraft from take-off to attack and then the deliberate crash, the only evidence was an exotic plastic streamer fused into a mass of what would, after many hours, be identified as electronic parts.

The Italian Navy had also recovered the L-100 Hercules from the bottom of the Mediterranean Sea, which, given that it had been shot down by a pair of Italian Rafael fighters was surprisingly intact. It had been lifted and shipped back to the nearest Italian Air Force station, just south of Naples, and the US had provided a crash team from the NTSB and observers from the Air Force to assist in the reconstruction. The black box was intact and was immediately flown to the US, where it was set up next to its counterpart from the F-4 in a secret lab at the NSA. To say that it was examined was an understatement, as it was, again, literally, broken down to the molecular level.

What the boffins found astounded them, the science so advanced as to almost be unbelievable. What was totally unbelievable was that this advanced technology had been developed—and obviously tested—without any of the world's security agencies getting even the slightest whiff of what was happening right under their noses. This technology went beyond simple AI—it was deep-state learning at its highest level, quantum computing, and the application of the materials was indicative of world-class facilities—of which there were very, very few around the world with the machinery and human talent to create and manufacture the black boxes. The FBI felt, with reason, that this one point could help lead them to the terrorists.

Roger Wilson read the detailed report on his desk, making little notes with a blue-tipped pencil. Old-fashioned he may be, but he had always found the physical aspects of reading and notating a report somehow helped him to absorb the details and aid his thinking. The facilities that could make these black boxes did exist, but everyone, as far as he was aware, was under the auspices of a controlled government—in Israel, France, England, Japan, and the US. He reflected on the fact that the code writer, and creator of the nano bugs, had studied in both Israel and the US—but as far as he was aware, she had nothing to do beyond that point— essentially separating herself from the terrorist organization once the oil spill trial had been completed in Canada. Then he remembered her girlfriend—"Michele"— was Chinese and reached for his secured landline.

"Roger."

"Frank, quick question—do you have any data on Chinese development in exotic technology?" he asked the director of the NSA.

"You need to ask Julius that; as you know, we lost our ability to tap into their comms late last year when they went to laser-over-fiber. We will eventually crack their encryption but haven't quite got there yet."

"Okay, thanks. I'll ask Julius."

"Before you go, what do you think of the crash summaries?" Roger cupped the old-fashioned phone to his ear with his shoulder and reached for yet another antacid tab. His stomach was giving him a genuine bellyache.

"Scary. How in the name of hell did they get so far without us knowing what they were up to?" At the other end of the line, Frank scrolled through a mass of data on his main monitor, then tapped on a smaller screen to bring up additional information.

"State sponsorship—must be; this is way too big for a bunch of refugee women, no matter how smart and clever they are, to have done all this by themselves. Every project needs controls, management, milestones, benchmarks, and money management. I'll buy into the idea of a mastermind and financier, but somewhere there is a state involved here, and I have my suspicions probably just as you have."

"Has Bridgett cleared the secretary of state?"

"We have had access to all her office recordings, going back three years, and while we haven't captured any of her or her staff's calls directly, the recordings are exactly what you would expect to hear as she and her people negotiated different refugee issues in Europe and the Middle East. They have quite a detailed plan for the relocation of around twenty-five million refugees, not a small ask in any language."

"You didn't answer my question." Frank looked at his scrolling screens, noted the areas highlighted in red and yellow, and looked at his smaller screens as if comparing the data. In fact, he was looking inwards, seeking the correct answer for his long-suffering friend and sometimes mentor.

"I think so. But to be honest, until all this is resolved one way or another, I'm not prepared to let anyone off the hook." Roger considered his friend's words, respecting his inability to be certain. It left him wondering what exactly the president could or would do with respect to the Secretary's continuance. Not his problem; he had enough of his own.

"Okay, thanks. I'll call Julius." He pressed the U-shaped holder and pressed the little button for the CIA. The beauty of this system, apart from the fact that the technology was so old that it had not been affected by the cyber-attack, was that it went through several different physical switchboards, all manned by communications experts, so the person he dialed would be connected, no matter where he or she might be.

"Julius, got a minute?" he asked when he heard the unmistakable sound of the phone pickup.

"Yeah, for you, all the time in the world." Julius laughed, sending a melodious sound down the phone line, making Roger smile. It was a light moment in a furiously dark time.

"If I asked you how you would duplicate what these women and their terrorist friends have done, what would your answer be?"

"Do I have the same period of time?"

"We say ten years, just to keep it simple. I believe the people that broke into our systems back in two thousand were not these women but state-sponsored hackers. I believe that the planner/financier had state support somewhere and used that support to get his grand plan going. I credit the women with the software hack that brought our communication nets down and the development of the nano bugs. Maybe even the design and manufacturer of the black boxes we have both been reading about. But I don't see them for the truck attacks in the UK, Europe, or the US. Maybe their aviators were responsible for the Hercules, the UAV, the Hog, and the F-4, but the truck bombs and remote rocket attacks were not delivered by them."

"You're saying two different attack groups—one sophisticated, the women, and the other just plain terrorists?"

"Yes. If it interests you, Anthony has come to the same conclusion, and Arie supports his hypothesis. They are moving forward on the basis that old-fashioned terrorists have been in the mix from the get-go."

"Well, I don't want to steal your thunder, but over here at the puzzle palace, we have come to the same conclusion. And to further confuse the issue, we think the Avignon attack was part of their grand plan."

"You've read the interrogation of the Israeli woman, Amira Abramowitz?"

"Yes."

"Your conclusion?"

"I want to know where she disappeared to for nearly five years."

"Yes, that interests me too. As does the fact that she is now actively helping Interpol solve Anthony's 'black hole' theory."

"Interesting to see how that develops. But to answer your first question, I'd want around twenty billion dollars, in ready cash, and a support team if only to keep tabs on all the refugees, arrange for the families, etc. Remember, we're supposedly talking about thirty or so refugees, twenty-five plus years, and we can only guess at the number of countries, but let's say, for argument's sake, ten to fifteen around the world. I need interpreters or home-grown minders, and if we take what the Israeli said at face value, she had major contact only three of four times in twenty years. So, we have a management cabal, for want of a better description, let's call that five to ten people, one of whom was this 'Helen' person identified by Abramowitz, who she claims met her once when she landed in Israel, then eight years later when she gave her the laptop, then five years after that when she got another laptop and the offer to go to the States.

"Thereafter, her main contact was this Chinese 'Michele' she fell in love with, who worked with her for two years or so, oversaw the test of the nano bugs, then disappeared with all the data and files. The reason I'm spelling all this out is I have a theory—or my people do, and I'm just taking credit!" Laughter rang out over the phone line, bringing a wan smile to Roger's face in spite of his best efforts to remain serious.

"And your point is?"

"If we look at this clinically, how many Abramowitz's did this terrorist group develop?" Roger gave the question some thought; it was something he had not previously considered.

"You're saying there's a lot less in this than we originally thought?"

"Yes. Way less. If we peg Abramowitz and Michele as the two main techno assets and then allow a pair in the US and a pair in the Middle East to run the air attacks—and we know at least one of them was a woman pilot who was trained by us for nearly ten years—what you get is a huge underbody made up of old time terrorists, albeit perhaps a little smarter and patient that the usual, with a few seriously intelligent women on the top. Now, ask yourself this question: why did the terrorists let Abramowitz go? How come there was no hit squad ordered? How come she was allowed to return to Israel and launch her own attack on their military network?"

"Your first question is easy. They didn't want to draw attention to her or her work. Four-plus years before the main attacks, killing her back then might have seriously impacted their success. We would at least have been looking in the direction of a major software hack and nano developments simply because that was the focus of her work. By letting her go, no one was the wiser; the university was obviously compensated for their lost IP, but the software was probably not developed to the point it is now. In point of fact, now that I am thinking about it, the university was probably brought out of their IP in a perfectly normal commercial deal. With the new owner able to call the shots on future development and publicity. We can check that out."

"Yes. Good answer. What about her returning to Israel?" Roger scratched his head, he had to admit to himself that this was an excellent question, but on thinking it through, he found a possible answer.

"It was of no consequence. The attacks had been successfully planned and launched, and the damage had been done. No profit in hitting her at that point."

"Yes, that's what we suspect. However, here's another one to tease your brain. Isn't she now a weapon we can use against them?" Roger sat back, staring into space, his mind working at a million miles an hour.

"Yes, she is, particularly if we can reverse engineer the nano bug. They must have thought of that, surely?" he asked, genuinely confused at his own deductions. If they could overcome the communications hack and negate and reverse the nano bug, all the terrorists would have on their side was the chaos, death, and wanton destruction already wrought and would, in fact, lose some of their bargaining power.

"Maybe yes, maybe no. It's the end game that worries me."

"What end game?" Frank asked, genuinely curious.

"Exactly. What end game. We've been running scenarios here for the last few days, and while we have a certain level of confidence in our war gaming, I'm not at all certain we are even close to a real solution."

"Can we both agree that the oil in the Middle East is lost—at least until we develop a solution to the radioactivity?"

"Yes. With you on that."

"Then, if we can reopen the Alaskan oil line and free up the Russian/Chinese and Australian gas flow, we will have got back thirty to forty percent of our energy needs."

"Why do you think we can?" Julius asked, smiling into the phone as if he could see Frank's response.

"Isn't that what Interpol is trying to do now? Isn't that the plan with this Abramowitz woman?" Frankl asked, almost fearfully.

"Maybe. What if she is a Trojan horse?" Frank went dead silent, almost forgetting to breathe. The consequences of this being the case so dire he had trouble accommodating the concept.

"You're kidding."

"No, I'm not. It is just one of the options we have gamed, and of all the possibilities, it comes out the strongest with a probability in the high nineties." Frank was silent again as he processed this information, his mind working through all the really bad things that might happen if it were true.

"Interpol is breached—they not only are inside our communications and nets, now they are inside our physical response to the terrorist's attacks. Have you mentioned this to PJ?" Frank asked, shaking his head in doubt. It was one thing to war-game a scenario; it was quite another to actually put it in motion. If this was a betrayal, it would go down as the most successful penetration of any security agency in the history of espionage and make Mata Hari look like a kindergarten fairy tale in the process.

"Why don't we give him a call on his laptop?" Julius asked, dialing up the little encrypted and supposedly secured device that had been given to him by Anna. Frank mirrored the process, his screen initially blank. It took a few minutes, but finally, PJ's face swam into the screen, fuzzed up while the computers agreed to talk to each other, then finally sharpened up to hold the three images relatively stable.

"PJ, Julius has an idea he would like to run by you. Can you talk?" Frank asked, taking control of the conversation. At the Venice end, PJ moved away from the group, signaling Jessica to stay where she was. Indigo gave him a shrewd look as if trying to divine the content of the call.

"Go for it. I'm secure."

"Julius, over to you," Frank said.

"Hi, PJ, just something we war-gamed over here. I want your opinion on it."

"Shoot." Frank mentally held his head perfectly still, his face bland, his best poker face telling PJ that the matter was grave.

"What if we suggested that your Israeli refugee is setting us all up?" The three images pulled at the edges, stretching the faces into a comical replication of the worst cartoon character you could imagine as if the computers were insulted at the very thought that the enemy was now within their most secure connection. PJ was silent, turned to look at the geek squad, nodded to himself, then looked back into the micro camera.

"I'll send you both a text in just a minute." He disconnected from the link, walked over to Indigo and me, signaled to Pete, turned, and walked out and up into the twilight so fast the guards were caught sitting on their little wicket chairs smoking. They all bulleted up, flicking glowing butts into the canal, trying their hardest to look military.

"At ease, stay here, please. My team will be just a few meters away; we need a private chat." The senior NCO saluted and mumbled something that could have been "*Sì Colonello,*" but was lost in the light breeze.

"What's up, Boss?" Pete asked, forming one side of a loose square. He stuck his hands in his pockets, looking interested with his usual feral intensity.

"The feds think Amira is a plant, here to penetrate us from the very inside of our investigation." He let the accusation hang in the air, looking from face to face, and noticed Indigo nodding as if the news wasn't actually news to him at all.

"Indigo, you want to comment?" the Boss asked, his tonality leaving little doubt he was pissed.

"Colonel, I can only confirm what Stefarino has said to me. He mentioned just ten minutes ago that they have not been able to find the source code Amira developed, in spite of it being secured in an encrypted vault in the cloud-based somewhere in the EU. They have tried everything; they can get as far as the master file but no further. It seems we are locked out."

"I see. How is Amira handling it?" the Boss asked.

"She is getting more and more agitated as every try fails. I genuinely believe she believes she should be able to get to the files. This is just my opinion, Colonel, but I do not believe her to be trying to dupe us." The Boss looked at Indigo, remembering that as well as a seasoned special forces soldier, Indigo, as the head of Interpol in Italy, was a first-class investigator with a hard-won worldwide reputation. And he would take his opinion to the bank. He turned and looked at me. For once, I didn't feel any sizzle in his look; if anything, I thought he was looking a little worn around the edges. While Pete, Indigo, and I had luxuriated in a hot shower and a brief but delicious hot meal, the Boss had remained at the helm, as it were.

"Since I first met her in Israel, I haven't picked up any negative vibes. In fact, quite the opposite. When she was telling us her story, I picked up a couple of times where the passion and emotion in her story shook me to the core. I think she is a young, incredibly talented technology specialist who feels she has been betrayed by her workmates, betrayed by her lover, and if anything, a little lost. For what it's worth, I sensed that Arie shares a similar point of view." I looked at Pete; he now had a relaxed and calm demeanor, which at the best of times was deadly, and I wondered what was going through his mind.

"Boss, so far, we have established that at least eight other children—for that is what they were—were taken out of the camps. And frankly, I wouldn't let my dog live in one, not even if you paid me. This girl—woman—was taken out of a desperate situation in the refugee camp, with no parents, no relatives, and placed with a decent Israeli family, with whom she thrived. She did brilliantly at school, went to university at fifteen, did brilliantly again, won the admiration of her professors and her cohort, was then wooed by this Chinese creep, had all her work stolen, then managed to survive on her own for damn near four years. How would you manage that?" Pete asked, looking feral again. An impassioned statement from Pete was so out of character that both the

Boss and I had frozen still, not wanting to break the flow of his diatribe. But Pete was correct—Amira had had everything stacked against her at every turn, and I remembered my first impression being that she was very young for her years. But undoubtedly brilliant and, when we had first met, had a decidedly defensive chilly exterior. I put the frostiness down to nerves.

"What makes the boys back home think she is working against us?" I asked, noticing for the first time that our Italian guards had stealthily managed to surround us, albeit at a distance, and now stood guns facing out on alert. I looked up the canal and spotted the navigation lights of a fast mover, reminding me of my several stomach-churning voyages with the mad driver of the red cigarette boat. "Is that one of ours?" I asked, automatically flattening myself against the stained wall at my back. Pete had turned around and now had a flat black automatic pistol by his side. The Boss and Indigo joined me against the wall, and the Boss handed me a handgun, no idea where he had got it from or had it hidden on his person, and pulled his trusty Sig Saur out of his shoulder holster.

"Indigo, are we expecting visitors?" the Boss asked in a whisper. The Italians had now closed in on us, creating a human shield, something Pete was obviously not happy with. "Anyone got binocs?" One of the guards moved to the Boss and handed him a set of light-intensified binoculars. The Boss adjusted the focus and swore under his breath. "Back inside on the double! Move!" And he literally picked me up and forced marched me back down the steps and into the tunnel connecting the wharf to the cavern. The Italians formed a wedge behind us, then faded into the wall into carefully hidden hides. As I glimpsed back, just before my head was forced down by the Boss into the tunnel, the moonlight reflected off the barrels of two fifty-caliber machine guns, now pointed towards the fast-approaching speedboat.

Then the first RPG round impacted just short of the entrance, flinging rock and mold-covered stone after us, pinging off the walls and creating a singing sensation in my ears. The second and third rounds just blasted my confidence a little more, as now we were in the cavern protected by the bends in the corridor. The booming sound of the explosions rebounded around the room, bouncing off the walls like spilled ping-pong balls off a hard wooden floor. Everyone in the cavern had dropped flat on the floor, wherever they had been working, and I couldn't blame them. The next sound I heard was the unmistakable snap of the twin fifties, squirting off five-round bursts in a disciplined display of return fire. I wondered what, why, and who had attacked us. Then an explosion outside lit up the room, and the Boss was shouting at the geek squad, who were all now taking cover under their benches.

"Shut it down. Shut it down." Stefarino punched a small black knob, worked into his workstation, and the room went dark, every screen and computer shutting down in the blink of an eye. The Boss stood tall, holstered his weapon, looked around the room and shrugged his head from side to side.

"I apologize to you all for bringing this down on your head. The bad guys have traced us, probably using drones and watching for movements, of which we have made our fair share. We will move our people out as soon as we are secured and compensate you for any damage. If we retained your communicators, that would be of great help to us, but we will not endanger you any further." The head monk, Stefarino, bent his head towards us, smiling. Then, in perfect English, which we did not know he spoke, eased our concerns.

"Colonel, your mission is far more important than what we do here today; we will support you in any way we can for as long as we can. I have instructed Indigo, Shami, and Luigi on how to set up your own private network, and I have no fear that anyone will bother us further. God speed, and may bright blessings be upon you all." The Boss looked around and noticed that the head of the Italian detail had entered the cavern.

"*Colonnello, la barcastaaffondando, quindi ha deiroditori per noi*?" The Boss looked at Indigo, who fired back a string of Italian so fast I couldn't capture every word. The Boss nodded in agreement and stood with his hands on his hips as the guard ran out the way he had come in.

"Yes, Indigo, we want the bodies. And we want them fast." Then he looked around the room again and nodded to himself. "Okay, team, pack it up. Amira, you're with us; Indigo, we'll need transport to a secure base, I suggest somewhere around the airport, and we'll need decoys to get out of here in one piece. Odds are they have a drone, maybe more than one, and we will need to deal with them. Questions?" The room fell silent as the geeks who had taken cover slowly crawled back out into the open, nervously looking around in the dark, which suddenly disappeared as the red night lights came on, creating a macabre shadowed pall in the cavern.

"Pete, get Tom and the boys to obtain a secure location in Milan, anti-air, and ground weapons. I'll arrange transport to them, but I want them ready for us within four hours. Jessica, get all the equipment the monks can spare and any instructions we need to set up; in fact, see if one of the geek monks can come with us temporarily. Anna, let Roger know we are decamping to another location, don't let on where yet, and that we'll be out of contact for a few hours. Any questions?" Indigo looked at the Boss and nodded.

"Where do you want the bodies?" he asked.

"Lay them out on the dock, photograph them, get their fingerprints, draw blood, saliva, search them. I want to know everything about them back to the day they were born. If you can, strip the boat of its armaments and navigation equipment, and walk the cat back on that as fast as you can, that would be excellent. Will you stay here while all that is done or leave it to someone else and come with us?"

"I'll stay here, follow you over later. I've arranged for a small flotilla of boats; they'll be here in less than five minutes. They are equipped with drone killers, armed, and visually identical. However, rather than take you directly to the airport, may I suggest we get you all to Forte Marghera, put you into an innocuous van, then transfer you to the military side of the airport. Where will you set up?"

"Tom will sort that out, and I'll let you know as soon as we do. This is our big break. We identify the terrorists; we get closer to the bastards that wrought so much havoc on us all. Let's get going, people. Jessica, better let Arie know we are kidnapping Amira and the outline of our plans—no details yet." And with that, the Boss strode out into the tunnel that took him back to the shattered entrance, and just like that, our little adventure in Venice, at least for the time, was over!

CHAPTER 62

General Bridgett Saunders sat opposite the president in a small room originally designed for visiting dignitaries to mill around in, waiting for something grand to happen. Four Secret Service agents stood guard outside both doors, which were open, revealing the historical nature of the White House. On one wall that seemed to disappear into the distance, portraits of past presidents were framed, creating a solemn mood that was reflected in the anteroom. The other door opened to a huge ballroom space, with a dangling chandelier sparkling in the center, the flares and pulses of light reflecting off the highly polished wooden dancefloor. The workmen had been removed, and there wasn't a single person within one hundred yards of the meeting, with the exception of the Secret Service.

"The secretary of state, and her staff, have, over the past eighteen months, collaborated with our master terrorist and, I might add, bankers from the Pan Arabian Sovereign Wealth Fund to create a plan for moving some twenty-five million refugees out of their present camps and into permanent homes around the world. It is a stunningly bold plan and shows all the insight you would expect from a highly talented bureaucrat with the Secretary's experience. Remember, she spent her early years after graduating and before seeking a government role as an advisor to the UNHCR. Her knowledge of the plight of the refugees is firsthand, and it is likely that our terrorist mastermind met her somewhere in her travels, maybe even in one of the camps, because the tonality of the conversations between the two of them was always warm and personal."

"Do you think she had any idea of what this person would do?"

"We have no evidence to suggest she ever spoke about anything other than framing a solution to the problem, specifically the issue and tragedy of second and third generations of children being stuck in the camps."

"Is there any possibility she knew or was informed prior to the attacks of what was going to happen?"

"There is no evidence the Secretary was aware of anything other than the current statistics and condition of the camps and the overall problem in the Middle East concerning the ongoing wars and disputes that are displacing around ten thousand people every fortnight." The president leaned back in her chair, the tension in her shoulders evident by the way she twitched them. She looked like she had aged ten years in the last week, which, in some ways, was true, as she tried to deal with the ravaging of her country and the worldwide chaos the attacks had caused.

"Don't these bastards realize that they are making the situation worse, not better" she snapped, wiping her eyes with the back of her hand. She shook her head as if to clear her ears, then dropped her hands back down into her lap. "Sorry, Bridgett didn't mean to take it out on you. What do the chiefs think our response should be?" she asked, not changing the subject so much as seeking a small interlude to let her thoughts about the secretary of state settle.

"Well, as you would expect, they want us on a war footing, Defcon One, and bomb the crap out of anyone associated with the attacks, the countries that might be supporting the terrorists, and anyone who shows up on their radar. However, your instructions are being followed to the letter, our intelligence folks are working overtime, and the Defcon level is held at three awaiting your further instructions. We have dispatched our bomber fleet to their designated bases, all our ships have sailed, and we are as prepared as we can be under the circumstances to fight an enemy we can't see, don't know where they are, or even who they are." This oblique statement brought a smile to the president's face; she was only too aware of how totally unprepared they had been when the terrorists attacked. The country had just recovered from losing a president to a heart attack just more than a year after he had won a messy and hurtful election and bitterly contested inauguration from the previous president who had refused to admit electoral defeat. As the elected vice president, she had immediately filled the vacancy, to an outraged cry around the country from everyone who hated the outcome of the election, and just didn't like women of color. Which, unfortunately, was a very large slice of the country.

And then there had been the disaster of the pandemic, which had accounted for over ten million lives, and crippled the economies of countries big and small. The world was only just emerging from the shadow of all that and had suddenly found itself in terrorist hell.

"I've just received word that the Interpol team were attacked by a gunboat, no casualties other than the terrorists, and they have now decamped to a new location. They'll tell us where when they settle. But the interesting thing here is, as we were starting to suspect, identifiable terrorist cells are behind some of these attacks, and it does start to look like some form of state sponsorship is working in the background." The general continued, mindful that the president was obviously distracted by the blank look on her face from time to time.

"Okay, keep me abreast on that; how is our plan to put the Congress and the Senate into the line of fire locally working out?"

"About how you would think. We have around thirty senators and congressmen and women sitting on their fat backsides in various jails for refusing to take orders from the military. We actually had five suicides in the House before we even sent them out into their electorates. Only three have been killed on the streets so far, but that could change very quickly. A lot of the younger ones are doing really stupid things.

"But surprisingly, the overall situation is calming down somewhat. We had over three hundred thousand civilian casualties up until the time of the web being destroyed, but in the main, the army, the reserve, and the police are getting some semblance of order back.

"The biggest issue is the indiscriminate shooting into crowds orchestrated by the Homeboys Brigade and other civilian so-called militias, who really seem to be on suicide missions. But we are happy to pull their guns out of their dead hands and over their dead bodies, and with some vigor, as you might expect. Over one thousand have been shot and killed so far, but each one manages to kill or maim, on average, thirty to forty ordinary citizens before they are brought down, so their threat is real and palpable. The automatic weapons and arsenals of grenades and homemade bombs they have are staggering. In Texas, we even had a firefight on the main street of Austin between homemade specials built from Ford trucks and army personnel carriers. It was like nothing I had ever seen on the streets of America. To be honest, when I saw the film, I had a flashback about Afghanistan!

"That one engagement killed over five hundred people, and we lost sixty-three troops. What we are seeing is the very worst our country has to offer, and we are paying for the sins of the past, where we allowed rampant bad behavior to pass as normal and without consequences. You can blame your former president's predecessor for that; he really did run this country into the ground. And of course, he made fiction and lies the stable point of his presidency and made a personal fortune out of it to boot."

"Okay, so you didn't like my president's predecessor, I get that, and yes, we do have many systemic issues to grapple with, but since he and his entire cohort were literally thrown out of the White House by the voters and your troops, we have been trying to rectify the damage he did one issue at a time. It didn't make it any easier that the man elected to bring us all together died in office in the first year and a bit of his presidency. Now, how are we managing the looting and burning of homes and shopping centers?" the president asked, not for the first time finding herself in a position where she almost had to apologize for being president. As the vice president, it was her elected role to replace the president, but she still felt like she had gained office under false pretenses.

"As we have done for earlier disasters, we are using sports stadia both as gathering points and emergency hospitals. The biggest issue we have is across the Midwest; water is at a premium, and food is getting scarce. The civilian militias have been bombing dams, bridges, hospitals, schools, supermarkets, and literally any infrastructure or symbol of government they can reach, and we've been reactive at best, as we can't spare the manpower to try and anticipate them.

"We are setting traps, and we are prosecuting them on the basis of an open free-fire policy, which, as you can imagine, a lot of our troops are unhappy with. Shooting their own countrymen and women is not something they signed up for. And strangely, given the broadly embedded racism in the police force and all that led to the storming of the Capitol three years ago, they are doing a much better job than we anticipated. However, we will have to give up six or seven states until such time as we have enough control to move a serious force against the embedded militias and drive them out once and for all.

"But you know what would help—making the private possession of weapons illegal—and I know that flies in the face of the Constitution—but I cannot believe our forefathers could envision where an armed populace could go about indiscriminatingly killing everyone in their path simply because they can.

"The one good thing about the World Wide Web being taken down by the terrorists is that social media is dead, and flash mobs are harder to organize, so we are gaining control in the bigger states, albeit slowly. But if you want my honest assessment of the situation, we are in it deep, up to our armpits and rising, and it will not stop soon. And I am fearful that at the end when we are in a stable state and one that you can recognize, we are not going to like what we see." The president sparked at this, sitting upright and straightening her shoulders.

"Bridgett, of course, it will be a mess. This is chaos and destruction on the scale of a world war and on our home soil. We have never experienced anything like this since the Civil War, and that was over a hundred and forty years ago. But I believe the country will react to leadership, starting with the congressmen and women, and senators getting back in touch with their constituents and relearning what they are meant to stand for. We will win this fight; the alternative is too dark to even consider." She rolled her shoulders, flicked at her hair, then grasped her hands in her lap. "The former president that preceded our election brought this country to its knees, maimed our Constitution, destroyed the hope of many people across the country, and lied and prevaricated his way into a pandemic from which we still haven't managed to fully recover. The pandemic cost us over a million dead, with the worst unemployment we have seen since the depression, but look at what we have achieved in just eighteen months.

"We are—or were before the terrorists—on the way back. And with a vengeance. Now we stand to lose all those gains because of internal conflict created by unrest and uncertainty due to these attacks.

"We can prevail, and I am determined to provide the leadership this country needs to get back on its feet. It's what I signed up for when I agreed to partner the former president as his vice president." The general sat quite still, reflecting on the president's words. She liked the president at the personal and professional level, and trusted her instincts. But deep down, she wondered if she knew the sheer magnitude of the issues she would face putting the country back together.

"What would you like to do with the Secretary?" she asked, not changing the subject so much as coming back to their earlier conversation. The president looked up, her face creased in thought.

"There's only one real way to resolve this, have her meet me in the Oval Office in an hour. Get her here no matter what, use whatever resources you need to break through the rioters, but I want a face-to-face."

"Yes, Madam President. But could I suggest around three this afternoon, so we can get her here with a minimum of fuss?" The president nodded, having learned at her mother's side as a little girl that advice from smart, informed people usually made sense, and in this case, she intuited what the general wanted to do.

Smuggle the secretary of state in without creating a major military headache for the world to see played out on the streets in front of the White House.

She nodded her assent silently, wondering what her next drama might be. God knew she had a veritable plethora to choose from!

CHAPTER 63

The photos, body parts, blood, possessions, and skin and hair samples of the terrorists who had been on the boat sunk by the Italian guards ended up at an Interpol-sponsored forensics lab at the Ca' Foscari University in Venice, where their DNA was typed and their most-likely nationality established. The university staff, under Indigo's direction, immediately used his little secure laptop the monks had given him to transmit the results of everything they found to the FBI and Arie's main office in Israel. They also copied the data via fax to every member of Interpol as a matter of course. The question Indigo had asked was simple: "Do you know who these men are, their affiliation, anything at all about where they came from, and what group do they belong to?" Since 9/11, most modern countries have been building databases of terrorist organizations around the world and freely swapped intelligence. All that had come to a sudden stop with the terrorists bringing down the internet, but live human beings who remembered where the photos and data were stored soon proved the old adage "if you want something done properly, do it yourself," so a series of cranky, mid-level intelligence agents on both sides of the Atlantic were soon sending back data on the bodies, with "fuck you" smiles, as they passed the banks of useless computers on the way to the old-fashioned phone line connected fax machines.

Of course, the geeks were working overtime to try and establish local area networks without much success, as the chips that were integral to any technology actually working as designed had been completely destroyed by the terrorist hack. And the current estimate, given the level of civil unrest around the world, was months, if not years, before they could be remanufactured in sufficient quantities and replaced. So old school came to the fore again, and long streams of yellow and blue cables now snaked around the desks, across the floors, through the corridors, up and down elevator shafts, to emerge looking like lost snakes on a bush holiday. But the geeks had regained a minimum of connectivity, mostly to old-style brick computers and huge racks of humming boxes covered with flashing diodes, many of which no one knew how to operate. Byte by byte, some essential data was being accessed and transferred to smaller, more reliable desktop computers, dragged out of the bowels of buildings where they had previously been ignored by the current generation and had started to gather a serious covering of dust.

Indigo looked at the data that were flowing into the university library where he had set up a temporary headquarters guarded by the stalwart troops that had protected the monks' secret lair so effectively. And what he saw in the various reports, faxes, and laser-printed photos was something that gave him pause to think.

Al Bar al Shirak, a tiny terrorist group coming out of Arabia, known to hire mercenaries from all over the world but particularly in Africa; not known for any specific bombings or attacks but is frequently mentioned as a participant on behalf of other well-recognized groups like ISIS, would seem to be the genesis of the attack on Interpol. All of the five recovered bodies were identified as soldiers of Al Bar al Shirak, and three of the bodies had been foreigners—two French and one South African. The South African had international warrants outstanding for murder, rape, and cross-border smuggling of children and drugs. In a sense, just your typical terrorist. What was not so typical was the pedigree of the two Frenchmen— both ex-Foreign Legion, parachute trained, explosives experts, and one a long-gun shooter with a stunning record. If it hadn't been so typical, Indigo would have felt more revulsion for the good soldier turned bad, but in his line of work, this was a typical background for some of the worst atrocities conducted in the Middle East. Trained soldiers turning to the private sector and working for whoever had the biggest checkbook.

As he read the details of the terrorist group, he could see why they had been so successful in remaining hidden for the past month; it was a hallmark of their movement—strike and disappear, never claim credit, remains in the shadows. But not so much now, as one of the terrorists had had an electronic device secreted on his person that had not crashed from immersion in the murky canals of Venice and was now under the tutelage and skilled fingers of one of the university's geeks on loan to Interpol and, consequently, was dropping its guts all over the tabletop. And part of the guts was a map, with a latitude and longitude coordinate, with the route to the underground monastery clearly indicated by a little blue line.

He smiled to himself, knowing the pleasure this was going to give his team, who, to some extent, had all felt as if they had been beaten again by the terrorists by being forced to move their headquarters by the boat attack. He opened up the little laptop, dialed the Boss, and was surprised when the screen remained blank. He furrowed his brow as if physically willing the little machine to work, to no avail. It remained blank. Then he remembered his friend Stefarino's comments and briefing about how to set up a secure network that would engage with that of the monks and thought that perhaps the team had yet to accomplish this in their new headquarters. So, he composed a text message, entered it into the computer, and instructed it to send once contact had been established.

In the meantime, he had to look to his brother and secure their hidden headquarters. Once he had done that, he pondered how to get himself and his small team to Milan, over 260 kilometers away; then he remembered the Audi 8 the team had stowed away some months ago and smiled.

Perhaps a fast road trip would clear the cobwebs, and give him some thinking time, so he waved to his team to get their attention, told them what he was going to do, and, smiling, left the university with strict instructions on what they should do next.

CHAPTER 64

As the former head of Shin Bet (*Shabak*), the premier Israeli intelligence agency, Arie Rosenberg thought he had experienced every form of human depravation, deceit, and disgusting behavior imaginable in the field of combat. As he walked the burnt and bloody battlefield that had just a day ago been a shopping mall, he was forced to revise his opinion. The mall floor, previously a series of beautiful and highly polished black-and-white marble squares, was now a crated, smoking, blood-drenched repository for shredded body parts of women and children from all walks of life. Jew lay decomposing next to Muslims, their mingled blood sharing the same hole in the floor, with the mangled bodies of their children looking like shattered plastic dolls in broken pushchairs.

The attack had come just hours after the negotiated cease-fire when a platoon strength of religious fanatics drove into every door in heavy armored technicals and fired indiscriminately with rockets, mortars, machine guns, and grenades. Then, to add insult to injury, the vehicles had pushed as far into the structure as they were able, then detonated, bringing down the massive dome that had been the centerpiece of the mall.

On this occasion, Arie was accompanied by the Imam with whom he had negotiated the peace deal when the fighting had stalled the day before. Their security details merged around them like a flowing curtain, but from whom they were preparing to defend was a moot point, as nothing now lived within the walls of the mall, not even a stray mouse. The constant sound of dripping water from burst water mains added a calming background. The bottom of the Imam's robes was stained with blood, and his constant muttering as he prayed over the dead was the only human sound anyone could detect.

"Why?" asked Arie, English being the one common language for them both. He shook his head in anguish. He understood war, his country had virtually been at war his whole life, but he did not understand wonton carnage for the sake of it, never had, never would. The terrorists had only achieved the mass death of innocent civilians on a massive scale, and the destruction of a shopping mall that had been built with money from all sides of the conflict as a sign of the peace they all professed to seek just a few years ago. Then the worldwide terrorist attacks forced a new dimension in everyone's thinking, with the result that the three most virulent antagonists of the Jewish State had decided to take advantage of the chaos and launched coordinated attacks on three fronts along the border.

The sheer ferocity, speed, and depth of the Jewish response had crushed the attacks in just twenty hours, and the smoke from the bombings and rocket attacks reached all the way up to the troposphere for all the world to see. Israel had learned over the years that shock and awe were only valuable if it was delivered with a passion that left no doubt in the enemy's mind that their death was imminent. And the Israeli government had pulled out all the stops. Where once they would have sent in ten fighter bombers, this time they sent in thirty. This overwhelming force was utilized in every respect of the battle plan, as the attacks had been repulsed, with little or no regard for collateral damage on the "wrong" side of the borders. And this outcome had been made clear from the get-go with broadcasts on all civilian channels, leaflets dropped by drones, and massive trucks with loudspeakers fixed to their roofs racing up and down the lines. Arie had reached out to the Imam, whom he both knew and respected, seeking mediation, but in truth, neither had been able to do anything until the one-sided battle had almost run its course.

And now this.

"I cannot condone what you have done these past days, but I can sympathize with your position. And this tragedy," the Imam said hesitantly, pointing to the ruins of the mall, "serves no purpose I can see. I do not know the people who mounted this attack, and no one who serves on my council has been able to identify them. I cannot apologize, but I can join you in prayer for the dead and injured and hope that between us, we can contain or minimize any retribution your government may feel is now required." Arie looked at the Imam, who was obviously distressed at the attack and the aftermath. Inwardly, he wondered just what role the Imam had played in the earlier three-border attack but decided to put that question aside for the time being. The hard-edged animosity between the Jews and the Muslims went back thousands of years and would not be solved in a single conversation.

"I have spoken to my government, and in light of the attack being made on both our people, with what would seem to be a similar outcome, I have recommended we take no action except to heighten our state of readiness and add more protection to our public infrastructure along our common borders. I would ask that you do the same, and if you can help us identify the perpetrators of this nightmare, it will be appreciated." And with that, he turned and started to stride out the back into the flickering sunlight, trailed by his security detail. He suddenly stopped, causing his detail to concertina into each other, creating a brief moment of visual humor against a background of devastation. "Perhaps you can help me on something else—do you know of a group calling themselves Al Bar al Shirak?" he asked, watching the Imam's face for any sign of treachery.

"Yes, they presented themselves to us a year or so ago asking for a seat on the council, which, of course, was rejected; while they appeared to be well funded and well equipped, their allegiance was of concern to us, as was their past history." The Imam bowed and retreated in the opposite direction to Arie. Arie stood perfectly still, processing this new information. What in God's name could be so bad as to cause rejection by the most feared war council in the Middle East? And who was their sponsor that did not sit well with a council that had supported an ongoing war with Israel along its borders for the past sixty years? He opened the minicomputer given to him by his Interpol friends and reread the cryptic message left on it by Indigo. Mercenaries. Guns for hire. Not a new concept in the endless wars in the middle east, but certainly a new dimension to the current string of terrorist attacks. And pay-as-you-go killers rarely gave themselves up easily or enacted suicide missions. Where was the profit in not being able to spend your ill-gotten gains? He snapped the lid shut, signaled to his team, and walked out of the building, wondering what the next catastrophe might be and where it would eventuate. He felt old in every bone in his body; he had lasted a lot longer than he had expected, but he really didn't want too much more of this intense pressure just to get through another day of chaos.

CHAPTER 65

"As you would know from your staff, General Saunders and her staff have conducted a thorough review of all your correspondence with al-bin Mohammad Karesish. It has been established that he is the mastermind or, at the very least, the banker behind the terrorist attacks that have put us in the position we are currently in. However, it is also possible that the terrorists are working with the leadership of Al Bar al Shirak, who may well have carried out the ground attacks using the vans and the drones—and possibly even the poisoning of the oil and gas lines." The shocked face of the secretary of state said it all—shock, horror, guilt, fear, and confusion, the hallmarks of successful terrorism. She sat back in a chair positioned directly in front of the president, the backlit window behind her filled with falling leaves and waving trees, a sight the Secretary would normally revel in.

"Madam President," the Secretary started, responding formally, mostly from shock. This was someone she had known for all her adult life and a good portion of it before that. They were the closest thing to sisters, without sharing the same parents. "All my conversations and negotiations with this person were made in the very best interests of the refugees and America. He was introduced to me by the UNHCR as a moderate, vitally interested in the welfare of refugees around the globe, willing to do something positive, and concerned about their plight. I instructed my office to contact him and follow up, which they did. Then, over a series of internal meetings and audio calls, we helped formulate a basic plan that could be applied to the problem—how to rehouse more than twenty-five million refugees, half of whom were children."

"Who else did this plan involve?"

"We contacted three of the technology companies involved in off-planet exploration—mostly for habitat, water-from-air, waste management, power supply, and resource management. We contacted most of the big players in the electronics industry for advice and guidance on telecommunications, transportation, and infrastructure development. We involved most of the better-known universities to get a handle on multiculturism, language development, psychology, and medicine; we even went so far as to grant one university money to build a test site in Nevada on a very small scale."

"How come I am only learning of this now?" the president asked, slightly miffed at having so much work done on such an important subject without her or her office being kept in the loop.

"But you were informed—I wrote the briefing paper myself—and all the updates—starting last year back in October when we asked for funds for the university." The president looked stunned because the one thing she did every single day at five o'clock in the morning, rain, hail, or shine, was read her daily briefing papers, intelligence reports, and selected newspapers from around the world. Privately, she referred to it as her "smart" hour because she claimed she learned something new every single day. It was well known around the White House staff and, in fact, had been revealed in a TV interview a year or so before.

"When was the last time you wrote me a briefing note?" she asked, a sharp edge to her voice. The Secretary looked perplexed, not sure why the president, her friend, was so upset with her.

"When we signed off on the basic plan about three months ago, I think, let me check with my office." The president nodded, and the Secretary moved to a phone on the corner of the desk.

"State Offices, please, Helen Mirabal. This is the Secretary," she told the switchboard operator.

"Yes, ma'am, one minute, please." The Secretary wondered how long it would be before the normal communication between people using their secured smartphones resumed, listening to the clicks as the

White House switchboard, which had literally been reinstated from where it gathered dust in a back room of the National Archives Museum, provided the necessary contacts to reach the State Department.

"State, Mirabal speaking." The nonsense voice of the Secretary's personal assistant cut across her musing with a sharp reminder that this was a serious business, no matter how confusing it might be.

"Helen, when was the last time we briefed the president on Project Apollos?" she asked. She could hear her PA mentally running through the question, looking for landmines.

"One moment, Madam Secretary, I'll check our log." The line went dead; no elevator music had yet been implemented to fill the gaps, thank the Lord, she thought to herself, then the PA came back on the line. "According to the log, we submitted the summary of the final draft plan last October, on the fourteenth, in the daily briefing. We asked for a meeting later that month but were not offered one at that time. In fact, according to this log entry, we are still waiting on a response from the White House."

"Thank you." The secretary of state looked a little shocked. There were at least two discordant issues here, the first being that the president did not get the briefing and the second that her department had not followed up to pursue a meeting. She thought back to that time to try and peg why she had not pursued it herself, then remembered all the state visits, balls, and conferences that had been called between October and March, literally one every week, which would have kept her and her department extremely busy.

And distracted.

She looked at her friend with a very perplexed look on her face and wondered exactly what was happening here under the surface. A missing report should not have been a trigger for anything more major than an interdepartmental slap on the wrist. But she could see by the president's posture that this was much, much more than a wrist slap. On the other side of the two-hundred-year-old table, the president sucked in her breath, folding her chin on her chest. Then she looked up, having made her decision, and pressed a little red button on the phone.

"Send the general in and coffee for three, please." She looked up, sighed from the bottom of her toes, and tilted her head to one side.

"Let me tell you a story about two priests," she started as the door opened and Bridgett reentered, closely followed by the coffee on a silver tray carried by a brightly dressed Marine.

CHAPTER 66

"Indigo, that's excellent work. Thank you, please get here as fast as you can."

The Boss snapped the lid of the little microcomputer closed and looked around the warehouse that Tom and his team had secured, noticing for the first time there was no espresso machine, no wall of screens, in fact, not much of anything except for a few army cots slapped together in one corner, and piles of massive boxes and containers scattered everywhere.

"Captain, everything you can get please on a group known as Al Bar al Shirak. Some details are here in Indigo's report, but I want the lot. Tom, contact your buddies in the Pentagon. I want all they have as well. Pete, dig deep into your swamp buddies; someone there will have come across these guys at some point. Anna, contact Arie, see if he is still alive, and ask him the same. I want this group, and I want them now—crimes against the State should do it as a cover, use Italy for starters, terrorism across borders, murder, pick all or any, but I want these bastards either neutralized or in cages as soon as possible. Go!" the Boss said, shooing us away like schoolchildren. He turned to the geek squad, looking a little lost without their computers and electronic toys.

"Luigi, Shami, pick a wall. The boys will help you set up. I want to be able to talk to Stefarino in thirty minutes. And I want a conference call to the US, usual suspects, add in General Saunders, find her wherever she is. And I want the NSA's computer geek as well. Got all that?"

"*Sì, colonnello, possiamo fare tuttoquesto,*" Luigi answered, moving off towards a huge stack of silver boxes.

"Okay, Amira, that just leaves the three of us. Sorry about the accommodations and the lack of coffee, but we do what we can with what we've got. You and I need to have a little chat." He led Amira over to one corner of the massive warehouse, then flopped down against one wall, inviting her to slip down beside him. They both watched as the geeks and soldiers furiously unpacked the boxes, snapping frames, support structures, massive cables, and mysterious black boxes together like some giant Lego erector set.

"By now, you will have worked out I'm not a geek, don't speak geek, but love them just the same. I need you to tell me everything about your software, in layman's terms, please, and as much as you can about your nanotechnology. Let's start with why you can't access your stored data using the secured network the monks provided us with." He looked at Amira out of the corner of one eye, stretching his legs out as if pushing away a cramp and noticing not for the first time that in the dim light, she looked very, very young.

"Well, sir..."

"Call me PJ or Colonel."

"Colonel, before I left Harvey Mudd, I sent everything I had worked on up into the cloud, into a secured store I had set up when I was in Israel. I used my mother's maiden name, and as this was a commercial transaction with an annual fee, I prepaid for ten years in advance. The first month after I left the college, I connected to the store via a public internet café at an airport and checked that everything was accessible and intact. Since then, until this week, I have not tried to open the folders in the store. I had no reason to."

"You found your folders, but they were empty?"

"Yes, and no. We found the folders, but we could not open them. Their history file showed no activity from the time I last accessed them, the cloud store has not changed their rules, and while we tried everything we could think of, the folders would not open." The Boss dropped his chin onto his chest, a favorite pose of his when pretending to be a deep thinker.

"So, you found the folders, but you couldn't open them. Why did you keep the laptop Helen gave you?" he asked right out of leftfield, a well-known interrogation technique. "You must have suspected that it was infected or at least was tracking your movements?" He raised his head and turned to look at her full on.

"Colonel, the Israeli security forces that arrested me tore the laptop apart, broke it down into its component bits, and they found nothing suspicious. The only anomaly was that the battery had died sometime in the past, and they put that down to me not managing the computer properly. When the battery died, the power was eventually reduced to the point where the RAM and ROM discharged their contents back to the original factory settings—which, I might add, is normal. The truth is, I kept the laptop, but I never used it. My one thought was to become as invisible as possible and not get caught up in the grand plans Helen tried to entice me with. Looking back, I suspect I kept the laptop for sentimental reasons; as it was, I had very few possessions at that time." The Boss nodded, sensing he heard the truth. Then, to his surprise, two of the special forces team wobbled around, carting the biggest and shiniest brass and steel espresso machine he had ever seen. They got it to a hastily assembled table, where they dumped it without ceremony.

The next thing he knew, eight warriors tested in battles, too many to mention, were running around the place like demented souls in search of the Holy Grail. Then he saw what they were doing and smiled to himself. "Well, Amira, I think we are about to be spoiled again!" he said with a laugh as one of the soldiers unraveled a huge roll of power cord. Then, almost as an afterthought, he looked back at her and raised his eyebrows. "Where did you go to for nearly four years?" he asked, watching her closely for any prevarication or indication she was lying. To his surprise, she smiled as if remembering something that was warm to her heart.

"I went fruit picking, and looking back, it was the quietest and nicest time of my life. While at Harvey Mudd, I noticed an ad on the student notice board for fruit pickers and casual workers in Australia, guaranteed wages, board, transportation, and a worker's visa. Unbeknownst to anyone at the university, I contacted the embassy and made an application, and was accepted. The initial visa was only for six months, but then I was offered a five-year one if I signed on to work on farms all over the country as and when required. As I was by that time a double post-doc, I also qualified for immigrant status if I wanted it—but I put that back on the 'wait and see' list. I had never been out of Europe, and I had no idea if I would like Australia or not." The Boss looked amazed. There was a literal scientific and technology genius, still leading the world in her fields as far as he knew, confessing to picking fruit and working on farms as a casual, low-paid low-level worker for years!

And on the other side of the world!

"You did this for four years?" he asked, astonished. As a military-trained, task-orientated individual, the idea of cruising around the world picking apples was as foreign to him as flying to the moon. Although that was becoming a distinct possibility, he recalled, better pick a better metaphor.

"Mostly, but I managed to spend nearly a year in New Zealand, traveling with a bunch of backpackers from Italy and Spain. That was a fantastic experience, and I very nearly stayed there permanently."

"Why didn't you?" The wistful look on Amira's face betrayed her emotions, creating an uneasy feeling in the Boss's stomach. She looked up at him, tears forming in the corner of her eyes.

"I missed my family, and although I spoke with them almost every week, it was not the same as seeing them. And then I learned that Helen was planning an attack, so I came home to Israel, stayed with my parents for a while, then moved into a kibbutz where I could do my work untroubled by spectators." The Boss almost physically recoiled at Amira's statement about Helen, but years of training prevented him from showing any physical reaction. He paused, considered his options, then placed one hand gently on Amira's shoulder.

"Just hold on a minute, please." He looked across the warehouse floor, saw where I was working with one of the geeks, and called to me.

"Captain, here, please." He waited for me to respond, seeing that the use of my rank had alerted me to the importance of what happened next.

"Yes, Boss, how can I help?" I asked, squatting on the floor facing them. "Amira, how did you learn Helen was planning an attack?" he asked, looking for me to judge her reaction.

"Before I left the university, I set up a backdoor in the communications program we were using to talk between work sites."

"You did what?" the Boss asked, astonished.

"Nothing special. Coders do this all the time with programs they write—it allows fast access if there's a need to recode or correct bugs." The Boss shook his head in wonder but stayed very much focused on what Amira was saying. There was a possible solution to tracking and finding the terrorists.

"Can you still do this? Tap into the communications Helen, and her cohorts are using?" he asked, hoping against hope the answer would be yes.

"I can try. Give me your laptop." She held out her hand and looked expectantly at the Boss. To settle the issue and speed up the process, I reached over and gave her mine. She took it, acknowledged me with a nod of her head, once again throwing her hair over her face, which she wiped casually away with one hand. The other tapped on the keyboard at a maniac pace, and the look of concentration on her face was a sight to behold. This is what passion, dedication, and application looked like; really hard to see her as a terrorist.

"Here—these are the last fifty emails she has sent or received in the last few days. I can't plug in live as her computer will alert her to my presence. I can pull her voice comms as well, but that will take a little more time and computing power. Is this what you need?" she asked, a small smile forming on her young face as if she were seeking acceptance. The Boss looked at me, then at Amira, then over to where the beast of an espresso machine was puffing away to the chortles of the squad.

"Thank you, yes, this is a great start; why don't you go over with the boys and get yourself a coffee? Jessica and I will sit here for a while." Amira nodded her acceptance, stood up, handed me back my laptop, and walked slowly away. The Boss watched her go, a wan smile forming on his scared countenance in spite of his best efforts to suppress it. He was a hard arse; he walked the talk, he talked the talk, and he didn't like to loosen up in public and show his humanity.

Which he had just done by letting Amira go.

"Well, now, this changes everything. What did Arie have to report?" he asked, switching subjects so fast that if I hadn't been used to it, I would have been blind-sided.

"War is over, at least for today. They had a major incursion in a joint-built shopping mall, hundreds dead, the mall was trashed, and Arie got confirmation from our terrorist friends, who apparently mounted the attack. They are targeting Muslims as well as Christians and Jews; it doesn't seem to matter what you believe in, a target's a target, and they are bloody to the last. One strange aspect—if it is the same group, from what we know about them, they are mostly made up of mercenaries, who, as you well know, are never seen in the typical martyr-suicide garb blowing themselves up. Something very strange going on here." The Boss looked reflective for a minute, then called Black Pete and Tom over.

"Gentlemen, and yes, I am being sarcastic, the closest either of you has ever been to a gentleman is looking at a copy of *Marie Claire*. I have an idea for you. Just suppose, for a minute or two, I could give you definitive proof that a terrorist group, whom I can name, was behind the attacks carried out all over the world. Further, what if I could give you some specifics on where they have been recently, who their leadership might be, and where you might find them as well. Pete looked thoughtful, and Tom's face reflected amusement, both used to the Boss's little verbal games.

"Swell, Boss," Pete answered, "you keep reminding us we are Interpol, not Kill-Terrorists-r-Us, so we don't really know what we could do." The smile on his face betrayed his words. He very much knew what to do; he personally had led counter-terror operations all over the world with final outcomes.

"Har de har har. This is me laughing at you, not with you. Answer the question."

"Well, some details would be nice. Are they Muslims?"

"Some are bound to be."

"Christians?"

"Same answer. And a mix of anarchists, non-believers, and just generally fucked up in the head arseholes. Clear enough for you?" the Boss asked, using profanity in a way he rarely did, so something was really pissing him off, and I decided to find out what it might be once the troops had their brief. I think I knew what the Boss was doing, and if we could pull it off, it would literally smash the terrorist organization from the inside. And maybe reveal the location and identities of the women. Maybe.

"Okay, your all-around bad guys with guns. Nothing new there. What's your angle?" Tom asked, in a melodious deep base voice, which startled me, as he was narrow, skinny, and tall, not the usual body shape for a bass. But he was one of the most vicious killers I had ever met, so for what the Boss had in mind, the perfect profile. The Boss went quiet, looked down at his laptop, snapped the screen open, punched in the code for the underground cavern, and in just a few seconds, Stefarino's well-weathered face swam into focus.

"Colonel, what can I help you with?" his perfect English sang out, causing me a moment of regret that we had left the dignity and calm of the cloisters that he and his fellow monks had provided in Venice.

"Stefarino, we have the name and a prime location of the terrorist group who have been creating some of the chaos we are trying to neutralize. I am going to prosecute them country by country. I just wanted to give you a heads up in case they came after you again." The head of the oldest and most revered tribe of monks just smiled, and I could feel the heat of his passion coming through the little computer.

"Not to worry, Colonel, we have already taken measures to protect ourselves from future attacks; you might find it hard to locate us, but we are still here—as in Venice. If you need us, you only have to call. By the way, my brother, Indigo, is on his way to you with some materials you may find useful in your quest. May your God be with you, and bright blessings on you all." And the screen went blank, leaving a fuzzy white series of lines racing nowhere.

"Pete, Tom, I want you to prepare all your contacts around the world for a search-and-destroy mission. We will arrange funding through their governments, but I need you to prequalify everyone as willing to participate. You'll need contacts in the US, EU, Africa, and the Middle East. You can offer either a fixed amount or a per-head proof-of-death deal, whatever suits, but I want a seven-day deadline on it, and it can never be traced back to us. Clear?" Both Tom and Pete nodded their acceptance, stood, then moved off, muttering between themselves. The Boss turned to me.

"Put a package together, use whatever intel you need, but have it ready to go in four hours. Spell it out, get it translated, and use the fax. I don't mind what goes public, but make sure what you send is what we want others to read, not what we are going to do. When Indigo gets here, see if what he is carrying is of any help. Clear?" I, too, nodded my acceptance, thinking through what the Boss was going to do. It was a beautiful maneuverer, one that would turn the known terrorist organizations like ISIS, Hamas, Hezbollah, Gama'a al-Islamiyya, Hizballah, Palestine Liberation Front, PFLP-General Command, Shining Path, al-Qa'ida, Boko Haram, ISIL Sinai Province, Asa'ib Ahl al-Haq, and a multitude of others against the terrorists with a passion and ferocity that would be great to watch from the sidelines.

And just maybe, with a little luck, they would turn on each other at the same time.

CHAPTER 67

The Arabian king, Freok Bib Mohammad Al Sin, hadn't been in the ground one whole week before the next assassination occurred. The three prime movers of the original plan to overthrow the king, the directors of Al Mabaahith Al Jena'eyah, Al Mukhabarat Al A'amah, and the Lightning Force, were all gunned down within a day of each other and, not surprisingly, by their own personal guards. It was no accident that these assignations mirrored the exact same game plan that had removed the king. It had always been the old man's plan to throw the kingdom into chaos as punishment for what he saw as a betrayal of their faith and their one God. For decades, the kingdom had flaunted Shia Law, letting oil and wealth beyond imagination corrupt the very essence of their religious faith. What he had not foreseen was the incredible rise of his hand-picked mercenary warriors, who had taken the time to build a formidable structure around the assassination proven model of a dictatorship.

Now terrorism had a home, unlimited finance, and was on a roll. Led by a six-foot-six South African mercenary, known only as "Shetani," which meant devil in Swathi, the group now identified as Al Bar al Shirak had grown like an amoeba overdosing on a rich seabed. Recruiting dissatisfied soldiers from all over the world, they built a modern army with more traditional terrorist methods. Better yet, they had taken over one of the richest and biggest States in the Arab world and were now free to rape and pillage it to their hearts' content.

Which, he noted from the frequent bursts of gunfire and explosions on the horizon, they were obviously in the middle of.

He mentally listed the groups' achievements in just the last month—they had successfully bombed the Grand Mosque, blown up tens of infidel-ridden sports stadiums across Europe and in the land of The Great Satan, poisoned the oil and gas lines of three so-called major superpowers, and we're currently corrupting hundreds of fracking sites across Canada and the US, right under their noses. They had driven the pox-ridden Interpol non-believers out of Venice, possibly killing most of them in the process, and just yesterday, and certainly not the least or the last attack, they had blown up that abortion of a plague-ridden shopping mall that his very own brothers had paid for and helped build!

And when he said "brothers," it was only in the very loosest sense of the meaning of the word. He came from a long line of proud Afrikaans, his great grandfather had fought in the Boer War, and he himself had fought against the liberalization of South Africa until such time as the fight was lost to the black horde that rode in of the coattails of the lying, thieving, two-sided monster who had become president.

These Muslim heathens were not his brothers, just useful cannon fodder to be pointed at the enemy whenever and wherever he saw fit. He laughed to himself, the great joke being that the old man who had started him on this path actually believed that he would follow both the spirit and the intent of the old man's grand plan—to liberate the children from all the refugee camps around the world. In truth, if he were to be as successful as he believed he could be, the number of children thrown into refugee camps around the world would double!

In point of fact, he had followed the old man's plan, waiting patiently in the wings as it were for over ten months before the aerial attacks took place, as promised, before striking the targets he had been given. He had allowed the security forces to kill the French and frame them for the attack on the Mosque. He had even allowed the overthrow of the king and the subsequent overthrow of the very people who thought they now ran the country. He had waited patiently until events ran their course in the Arabian State, then struck without warning and taken over the country once and for all.

And in the process, he gained thousands of highly trained and equipped troops with which to continue his purge.

He was sitting pretty – millions of euros and American dollars in his bank account and mounting up at the rate of two million a mission. Yes, he had to pay his troops for each hit, but that only took less than a quarter of what he was banking.

And now he had the treasury of an entire country at his beck and call; it just didn't get any better than this!

He didn't care about the condemnation of the Arab countries surrounding him, the screams from the UN, and the protests that were breaking out all over the country. He ignored them all. If the people didn't like what he was doing, they could starve, or better still, fill the refugee camps that had started this ball rolling down a very slippery slope three decades before. He was untouchable; to get at him, you would first have to find him, then get through several layers of protection, and then personally face him down—something no one had managed to survive in forty years.

He smiled to himself, drank from a crystal-cut whisky glass, and saluted the waning moon, which he could just see out of his caravan window. Ironically, its crescent shape caused him to burst out into laughter as he wondered, not for the first time, why so many morons who believed in this symbol as the inspiration for their faith followed him, a true heathen to the very core!

CHAPTER 68

Indigo walked into the warehouse-like he owned it, all five foot ten inches of him, dressed in his best Italian Gendarme Blues, hat perched cheekily on his head on an angle. I hadn't ever seen Indigo in a formal dress before, and I wondered what the occasion was. He walked over to the Boss, saluted, then burst into laughter.

"*Colonnello, la suaespressione non ha prezzo! Devo vestirmi di nuovo presto, sì?*" His laughter was contagious because every Italian speaker in the warehouse joined in the joke. The Boss slapped at him playfully, letting the laughter break the tension that had slowly been forming since our hurried arrival. For once, he made the coffee and handed Indigo a very large mug.

"Here, Indigo, celebrate with this. Now, what did Stefarino give you to bring to us?" he asked, bending to the monster machine that was now spewing steam out of three different orifices. The Boss ducked, grabbed his mug, and retreated as if he was under live fire.

"Colonel, my men and I dressed formally the better to pass through the checkpoints along the road and also to get a gauge on how the general population is managing under the duress we are all experiencing. While the drive was only a little over two hours, we saw and learned a lot." He drank from the mug, a serious look replacing his laugh. "I would like to tell you that we are in good shape here in Italy, but that would be a lie. There are many people prostrating themselves day and night, mourning the loss of our Church, or at least the head of it, in such a bloody manner. We saw more temporary shrines and candle farms against the fences and roadsides than I ever imagined possible. My men are very sad, as am I, but I will let you cheer me up!" he said, leaping over to give me a tremendous hug! "Hello, my captain, how are you?" he asked, laughter shredding his sadness. "I'm fine, Indigo. Put me down, you maniac!" I laughed with him, happy he was getting his groove back. Not being particularly religious, I could not imagine the pain the Catholics, Jews, and other religions were feeling at the moment to have their most holy and precious sites taken away from them so brutally. Not to mention the elimination of almost one hundred percent of the cardinals that managed the church worldwide and the hundreds of Muslim clerics and Jewish rabbis killed in the attacks. "The Boss said you might have a package for me?" I asked as I was dropped none-too-gently as Indigo reached into a small satchel across his back.

"Yes, Captain, here are some documents and a Microdrive from my brother, Stefarino. He saysa this is very potent data, and please use it with respect." I deciphered Indigo's mixed message, as his brother wanted me to us to use the data judiciously and not reveal its source or any details that might blow back on the monks. Not hard to do, as I was so in awe of Indigo's brother and his monks. I would protect them with my life.

"Okay, let's look at this together," I said, opening my microcomputer – another gift from the monks. I fed the Microdrive into its slot and watched in awe as the screen filled with files and recordings, some dated two years ago. I decided to work backwards, but first, I had to get a bigger screen. I signaled to one of the geeks, pointed to the screen she was unpacking and waved her over. "Link us up to that screen, please, and give us a privacy curtain." She nodded and, in minutes, had us sitting in front of a massive screen with a little electronic disruptor at our feet, creating a barrier that prevented sound from flowing in or out. I smiled inwardly, remembering a TV show I had seen decades ago, Maxwell Smart, super-agent, who had a "Cone of silence," which was a plastic dome that encompassed the people talking. Science reflecting a comic!

I clicked open the first folder, dated three weeks ago. A choice of videos, audio files, and documents presented itself, so I hunkered down with Indigo and, using a small air-gapped computer, made myself a series of notes. Indigo was doing the same, and it would be interesting to see his take on what was being revealed.

Folder followed folder, and I was getting a cramp in my legs when the Boss appeared and handed us both mugs of coffee, the smell of which set my juices flowing. "Any chance of food?" I asked, standing up to stretch. The Boss nodded and pointed to a large table presently being mugged by all the security guys and the whole of the geek squad. I looked at the Boss; he nodded and took my chair, effectively providing the best security I could ask for, and, grabbing Indigo by the shoulder, marched over towards the food table. "Indigo, it's free for all. Consider yourself on a catch-and-kill mission!" I said and, very unladylike, ran for the table.

The food was first class, a hallmark of working anywhere within the Italian Interpol infrastructure, even in an abandoned warehouse. I don't know how they did it, and right now, I don't care. I loaded up a plate and, leaving Indigo to his own devices, walked back to the Boss. "There's a lot of stuff in here we have to talk about, but for now, look at these maps Stefarino has provided." I handed the Boss the maps, leaving a smeared trail on the edges of the salad dressing that had dripped on my fingers. I licked them to make the point, and we both shared a small laugh.

"Montana and Libya. Where we traced the fiberoptic cables."

"Yes. But look here," I said, pointing at a small mark on the map, around fifteen kilometers from the end of the comms cable—or at least, so these maps indicated. "In Montana, I figure they were using a decommissioned Minute Man site. You can see where it is here. Then if you follow this map, there is a second structure just here, and according to our satellite maps of the area, which, by the way, the monks were able to download, it is both above and below ground. Then here," I said, pointing to a third sheet, "is the deep dive the monks did from records going back to the sixties—and look what they found."

"An underground command structure. No doubt linked to the silo complex by a tunnel. We were very paranoid during the Cold War and had every right to be. Okay, so this is where our American team might be hiding; what's the story in Libya?" I handed the Boss a fourth sheet, this one, to my relief, unstained by my lunch.

"If you remember, the dark fiber cable started here in Libya, then crept into Egypt, and the team abandoned their track and trace rather than crash the border. But you can see here buildings hidden by a small mountain as if they had erupted out of the ground. The monks have pinpointed this as an ex-military bunker system originally set up by the Egyptian Army as a remote supply depot. Abandoned in nineteen ninety-seven and supposedly bulldozed into rubble. What's the bet the terrorists have dug out the area they need and have established their HQ in the Middle East there?"

"Possibly. The real issue to me is what is the relationship between these women and the more traditional terrorists?"

"I can help there. Both the monks and Arie agree that the group known as Al Bar al Shirak are responsible for most, if not all, of the land-based terror attacks, including Avignon. Which was not a red herring as we first thought. And before you tell me mercenaries rarely, if ever, strap on a bomb vest, let me remind you we are up against a really sophisticated group of females who excel at nanotechnology, artificial intelligence, and remote everything." The Boss looked at me with a cross look on his face, so I put the matter to bed once and for all. "The electronic devices we pulled from the aircraft have their own unique signature, according to our geek experts. Just like the code Amira wrote. And this signature was detected in the ruins of one of the trucks that bombed Wembley, again in the US, and finally, in the navigation system we pulled out of the Venice canal."

"So, in point of fact, you are saying every attack except the airborne ones were mounted by the same terrorist group, but with sophisticated technology provided by these women?"

"No, not necessarily supplied by. But certainly designed and built by."

"What about the oil and gas lines?"

"Same story. Women provide the technology—in this case, we know Amira created the nano bugs, or at least developed them to the stage where someone— probably her girlfriend, Michele—could finish the design off, but the terrorists delivered the bugs to the well heads and pumps. Just like they delivered the Strontium-90."

"What about the witnesses to the truck bomb at the mosque?"

"Ever got an actual, real, provable witness identification in your career so far?" The Boss smiled; it was a truism in law enforcement that three people seeing the same accident reported five different versions of the event! "But that's not the point. Look at the pattern—even the internet hack—which we know Amira wrote the baseline code for—was improved on, sat on. Remember, she developed this over six years ago, and I'm prepared to bet my not-so-illustrious salary that our Chinese refugee improved on the code over the years she had it—or people working with her did the work, to her design.

"But the hack affected every linked computer, router, and device connected at the time of the hack, worldwide, simultaneously. The geeks tell me that is impossible unless you have multiple points of entry for the virus—and Luigi ran a simulation for us showing that a minimum of three thousand upload points would be needed to achieve the damage they did in the time frame. Three thousand. As far as we know, we only have a handful of women working in the trenches on these attacks. Who were the three thousand people who uploaded the virus? And how did they do it?"

"Do our geeks have any idea of how they did that?" the Boss asked, impressed, and not for the first time, by his deputy's analytical abilities.

"Yes," I answered, standing up to stretch, "according to Amira, one of the things she worked on with Michele was an email program that carried a silent virus, with an automated pass-on ability, and the modeling which she had a copy of shows that you only need to send out less than two hundred targeted emails to achieve the three thousand required to crash the internet. And I'm willing to bet that the two hundred original targets were members or supporters of the terrorist group who acted for and on behalf of Al bar al Shirak as active participants in the terrorist event. One they never took credit for, and in retrospect, that is perhaps the most troubling aspect of this whole terrorist plan from the get-go."

"Why?"

"Terrorism one oh one—build on an attack with the promise of more, random, more terrifying, and publish the photos, dead bodies, strike fear into the heart of your targets. You know the playbook backwards. But there hasn't been a single byte of data on the attackers, other than the public broadcasting of the events captured before the net crash. That and personal videos were shot on location by the unlucky bystanders. Why?" The Boss stood up alongside me, scratching his chin.

It wasn't often he was lost for words, but this time he genuinely didn't seem to have an answer.

"Look at the prime motivations for any terrorist—identity, religion, ethnicity, disputed territory, and long-held memories—same as the reason why people go to war, I suppose. We know religion plays a role in this—more than likely a strong Muslim bias and a hatred which could go all the way back to the Ten Tribes; identity probably plays, given the priest's story about the refugee children—I don't see ethnicity playing much of a role, they seem to be ambivalent about who they kill and where they live; disputed territory not so much, more displaced persons shoved out of their heart lands for all sorts of reason—famine, war, politics, greed, all the usual suspects; and long held memories might play, given that we have a thirty-year-plus timeline, but I don't think it is germane to their real cause. No, I think this is really all about the refugee children, their condition thirty years ago, and their plight over the ensuing years until the attacks started. At least, that's what started this crusade, but I suspect it's now been hijacked." I took a deep breath, then started in again.

"The death of the Pope was undoubtedly the trigger, providing the perfect call-to-arms and a target-rich environment. They took out ninety-eight percent of the heads of the Roman Catholic Church in one attack and destroyed the Vatican and its archives, perhaps the most serious damage done to the church in centuries. The attack on the Dome of the Rock was precise, with major damage to the Jewish side and minimal to the Muslim side. As for the attack on the Grand Mosque, it was a targeted attack to make it look like the Muslims were the objective, but when you look at the evidence, minimal damage was done to anything of importance. It was blind.

"West Point was more pointed, aimed at our youth, and a clear message to the Great Satan. All the attacks on the sports arenas were, I think, window dressing, terrorists being terrorists, scaring the general population, and making them afraid to leave their homes. Very low collateral damage, part of the major attack, I think, was designed to increase the pressure on us to respond favorably to whatever their demands turned out to be.

"Avignon was just terrorists being terrorists; the only importance I can see was that one of the surviving elders of the Catholic Church lived there, but as he had passed away a day before, there seems to be no real reason for that attack.

"The space station was the women again, high technology quotient, minimal collateral damage, message clear—we can hit you anywhere and anytime we choose.

"Then we have the attacks on the oil and gas infrastructure. Have you wondered why two such totally different approaches were used in those attacks?" The Boss asked, looking at me with an intensity that warmed my heart. I put my feelings aside and rolled my shoulders. The stress was getting to me. I could feel my back literally knotting up, layer by layer. But the Boss seemed to be getting his groove back.

"Yes, I have. I even discussed it with Indigo. He had an interesting slant on it."

"Which was?"

"The money man or master planner, this Al Hemish al-bin Mohammad Karesish, had a hard-on for the Arabs. If it is true that he is one of the royals, he probably sees all the oil wealth as the source of corruption that has crippled his country, in the loosening of Shia Law, the freedom given to women, and the move towards capitalism and commercialism. Hence the use of Strontium-90 reduced the supply of those vast resources for twenty years or so. Or until someone like Amira invents a nano bug that eats radioactivity—which, by the way, Amira says is entirely possible but might take some time."

"And the lesser attacks—if you can call them that—using the nano bugs?"

"Something that maybe can be reversed, at some point in time, and Amira thinks there may be a solution somewhere in her design, but as you know, they haven't been able to open those folders. Yet."

"So, a Jihadi with a hard-on for his own country and a passion for little children who happen to be refugees. Did Stefarino give you anything else of value?" the Boss asked, tiredness lacing through his voice like a boa constrictor eating a grasshopper.

"Yes. We have the name of the leader of the terrorists—'Shetani'—translated, it literally means 'devil'—we'll call them traditional terrorists just to maintain our focus—and half a dozen locations where they may be, and an interesting conversation with Helen and two of her troops, just last week. The monks—and don't ask me how, I haven't got a clue—tracked the Helen conversation to a building in Libya, near the town where Jalo-alkufrah and Airport Road intersect—if you can believe that. Three hundred meters from an airport and, would you also believe, less than two kilometers from our famous crop circles in Libya."

"You're kidding me. We had a team on the dark fiber less than five clicks from where one of our key terrorists has set up house?"

"Yes. Small world." The Boss suddenly looked energized, went into deep thinking mode, smiled his crocodile smile, then relaxed.

"Anything else I should know?" he asked, the weariness no longer in his face or in his eyes.

"Probably a million things, but for now, my sense is we have got something tangible to prosecute. Three physical locations where our girls might be hiding or just biding their time: half a dozen locations for the traditional—I hate using that word, by the way—terrorists and the name of their leader. My advice, if that's what you are asking for, is we should concentrate on these opportunities first, then worry about the rest. Whatever that turns out to be." He nodded in agreement, the light in his eyes a joy to behold. He might be weary, he might even be tired, but the energy he was starting to radiate was infections. I waved Pete and Tom over for a chat, then remembered I had nearly forgotten someone.

"Anna," I said, pointing to our little gathering, "can you spare a minute or two, please?" She looked up from the computer she was working on, looked a little vague for a moment or two, then nodded, again, with an inbuilt weariness I was starting to see in many of the team. We would have to eradicate that before we started any serious operation. "Okay," I said, taking control of the conversation, "chip in at any time, open questions, ideas, thoughts, but here's where we are at." And I ran to conclusions for everybody and noticed not a single person interrupted me.

I sincerely hoped they weren't just too tired to register the importance of what I had just told them.

CHAPTER 69

The camouflaged truck sported every type of antenna imaginable and a few that defied the imagination. Like a specter, it moved slowly until it was positioned on the blind side of the underground bunker, around five kilometers away. It ground to a halt, bouncing on its suspension, seemed to think for a minute, then six sturdy legs dropped down and sank into the dirt floor. Nothing happened for a minute or two, then far overhead in the "doomsday" KC-135, a series of flashes were received, indicating that the beast was ready. The young operator, a sergeant by the stripes on his flight suit, adjusted his headset.

"Karma one, contact, ready." The air filled with the moan of the four turbine engines, now set for a slow cruise, as the airborne control center orbited around the target at thirty-six thousand feet, cutting through the chilled night air as easily as a hot knife through butter. The only proof of her presence was the four thin contrails she left in her wake, which streamed out for a while and then broke up into little puffs of cloud-like gas. Eight hundred nautical miles away, over the shallow edge of the Atlantic Ocean, another doomsday aircraft orbited, mirroring the flight path of ten other aircraft that, between them, formed a secured six and a half thousand-mile electronic communication link that covered the prime target areas from Montana to Libya.

In a move that was duplicated in Libya and Egypt, but initiated in Montana, a massive EDRSD—or Electronic Disruptor Radio Signals

Destroyer—fired up its arrays and promptly killed any radiated signal on every and any wavelength, including dark fiber, effectively preventing anyone within fifty kilometers of the EDRSD from communicating with anything more sophisticated than a pen, pencil, or carrier pigeon. Exactly twelve seconds later, a twenty-kilometer line of ground penetrators dug for their lives until they reached the hidden dark fiber cables, then exploded, achieving in Montana a secondary set of explosions from the escape tunnel that had been mined by the terrorists. These explosions effectively cut off the building that had been used earlier in the terrorist attacks from the underground hideaway that now supposedly held the female terrorists.

One full minute after the last echo of the underground explosions died, the special forces troops who had surrounded both the old farmhouse and the sunken command center moved cautiously into killing range. Their orders were specific— take the terrorists alive—or at least one of them, and be as patient as you had to be without getting killed yourself. The team at the old farmhouse had a bonus find in that they had unearthed the hidden helicopter on their way in.

The silent alarm that the special forces troops had tripped in their earlier foray tracking the dark fiber, fired off again but, as for the previous occasion, to no avail. When they breached the farmhouse, the reason became apparent. No one was home. But there was a veritable treasure trove of evidence in the form of photos, papers, and even a computer conveniently left out on a broken table. The invaders did not get into the subterranean control center; it had self-destructed when the ground penetrators had taken out the tunnel.

The story was much the same in Libya, up to a point. One special forces team had surrounded the large buildings from where the conversation with "Helen" was thought to have eventuated, while a second team leapfrogged the Egyptian border straight to the semi-destroyed buildings in the fallen cliff. Thanks to the signal-bouncing off the airborne relay aircraft, each team was aware of the status of the other—allowing them to move with caution but also optimism. Of course, this was normal practice for the special forces back in the day—just a week or two ago in reality—when they had access to worldwide real-time satellite communication at the push of a button.

So, the teams moved forward, breached the buildings in concert, swarmed the floors one by one to clear them, and found so much evidence left behind that trucks had to be requisitioned to carry it all away.

No women terrorists, no human presence, but deliberately stage-managed mountains of documents, files, photos, and handwritten notes. It took a few hours, but as the last of the special forces walked away, bitterly disappointed that they hadn't been in a firefight, hadn't been threatened in the slightest other than the risk of a paper cut or by the weather, which was freezing in Montana, but hot and humid in Libya, the various team leaders made the necessary arrangements to get all the evidence back to Washington.

As the reports came in, the Boss looked more and more bemused, quickly scanning the reports we were receiving from Roger and Julius. He flicked open his little computer and dialed up the head of the FBI.

"Roger, just summarize it for us, please; we haven't got the manpower to work through all this. What's your feeling?"

"We were anticipated, by a long margin, and while we have evidence up the wazoo, not a single piece of it will point to our terrorists. What it looks like is that they have complied dossiers on thousands of child refugees, some fifteen years' worth by the date stamps, but that might change as we get through it. We also have a computer from each site, all with the same prerecorded video message. It runs just thirteen seconds, and the old man, who we assume is Al Hemish al-bin Mohammad Karesish, aka Mohammad bin Azaria, delivers it personally. Watch this." And a high-quality video flicked onto the small screen, where an Arab male bowed with his head on the ground, slowly unbent, and, after the usual greetings to his God, hands waving and being kissed before retracting to his lap, spoke slowly هللالفطأبظنعأ. مكترفغملأسأالومكيلعهتلعفا، معرذتعأالdignity—" great and with كماثآرفغتستناأو." Underneath, in italics, the English translation unfolded as he spoke. *"I do not apologize for what I have wrought on you, and I do not ask your forgiveness. Look after the Children of God, and you will be forgiven your sins."*

"We have matched the video image to earlier photos from our files, with a ninety-nine percent probability that this is our man. He appears to be in his mid-seventies to early eighties; no way to really know; his history has been wiped from every database we have access to and a few we officially don't. But the interesting thing is our geospatial experts believe they can give us a location, plus or minus one hundred klicks."

"Let me guess. Somewhere in Libya, north of the location where we thought Helen was located."

"Yes, about a thousand klicks to the north, slightly east, around the Baladiyat Ajdabiya area. Nothing there but low hills, little if no vegetation, and we have no way of looking down unless we arrange a flyover, something we're not prepared to do politically at this time."

"Understood. Maybe we can help. I'll get back to you." And the Boss snapped the computer closed with a finality that surprised me.

"You're pissed off," I said, glancing at him in a non-threatening manner. I knew the Boss, knew all his moods, and I was surprised by his current reaction to the video.

"Big time. This bastard has been playing with us for weeks and has anticipated our every move. Okay, I'll allow that he had access to our electronic communications networks for years, probably still has, and I was going to prove that one way or the other, but that seems moot now. But the reason I'm pissed off is that chasing him serves no purpose at this time. We didn't find the women, but we now have absolute proof—as if we needed it—that the refugee children are at the heart of this whole chaotic exercise. But by what happened to us in Venice, I'm starting to think that this fucker—and I won't apologize for my French—has lost control or maybe even interest in his mercenary terrorists and their agenda. Somehow I think we now have more to fear from them than the women." I thought about that for a minute, watching the Boss move from hot to cold, the focused determination on his face now unmistakable.

"You're basing this on the fact that there have been no direct attacks on us nor any other government agency of any country during the major attacks – other than the ineffectual swipe they made at us back in Venice."

"Yes. Planned to the inch—implemented with ruthless and technological precision and, with the exceptions I mentioned earlier, minimal collateral damage. Totally cause-related if you accept the refugee story. Which I do. But I can't for the life of me see a way out of this without escalating our agenda to deal with these 'traditional' terrorists. We need leverage, and for Christ's sake, we're policemen and women, even though we have a pseudo-military mandate and order of battle with Pete and his friends. Our mandate is to prosecute the people who launched these attacks—we've been commissioned by Italy, Israel, and the US. None of our member countries other than these have asked for our help. I can't just launch attacks or arrests in any country that does not give us permission to cross their borders and act on their behalf. That's the law, and that's our biggest headache. For example, let's just say this 'Devil' fellow is in Arabia. Has taken over the government. Has control of the country. The facts are that the king's Secret Service and intelligence services killed the king and overthrew the government. Then this Devil overthrew the overthrowers. No matter that he is a terrorist. He now controls the government of that country. Add to that that the Pan Arabian Sovereign Wealth Fund is the paymaster for the terrorists, is based in Arabia, and Mohammad bin Azaria is the mastermind behind all the chaos, and you have a particularly convoluted political situation. Let me ask you a question." I looked at the Boss, who hadn't raised his voice, which just added a more deadly accent to his words.

"Go," I responded, my voice also held low. I had learned the hard way that when the Boss was in the zone, the best way to work with him was to hold up a behavioral mirror and mimic his tonality. I had seen him verbally destroy others who had lacked this insight.

"If we marched in and ousted 'Shetani,' on whose behalf would we be acting? And on what basis? Ridding the world of a first-class arsehole terrorist is okay, but I suggest taking over a country might not be so well received in the halls of power." I thought for a minute, then matched his frown with my smile.

"There are princes, and therefore a succession to the throne has to be; the king's family was legion. Our key terrorist Mohammad bin Azaria is supposedly seventh in line, now possibly sixth, so all we need to do is find the second and perhaps the third and get them to commission us to rid their country of the terrorist infection." I meant my words lightheartedly, but the Boss still had a massive frown creasing his face.

"Number two is a playboy in London, known for his drug and gambling habits, not to mention his other addictions; number three is somewhere in South America doing God knows what. And we haven't yet worked out what role the French played in all this. So, what's your answer?" I thought for a minute and ran the major rules and regulations we worked under through my mind, looking for inspiration.

"Well, we're an independent agency of Interpol-Section Five; we have our own charter, and it's a little vague on the subject of terrorism, child trafficking, things like that, so perhaps we can just focus on the terrorist side and ignore the politics?" I suggested, knowing full well that this was exactly what we had done in the past two years, chasing an international web of child traffickers. No one had complained after the fact; everyone was too focused to see that their political arses were covered. While Interpol had no powers of arrest unto itself, relying on the different jurisdictions in the different countries we worked with, our section had been specifically created to provide a sharp end to Interpol's relatively soft underbelly—that's why we had so many ex-military members on staff. We all carried weapons and were happy to use them.

"Red notice on the Devil and his cadre, however big it is, list different countries of interest, forewarn them diplomatically through Lyon of our intentions but without a timetable, then turn our phones off?" I asked, looking at him with the faintest of smiles. He still reminded me of a crocodile looking for its next meal, but it was a far better look than his scrunched-up frown.

"That would work. Keep it vague, move on them with in-country assistance, negotiated through Lyon, but keep the head of the snake in our personal sights. I wonder how the French will take this?" he mused, standing up again. "Let's talk to Arie." He handed me the computer, walked over to the bustling and whistling expresso beast, poured two mugs, and walked back.

"Hi Arie, how goes it?" I asked as his face swam into focus.

"Much better, thank you, Captain. We have not had a shell or missile attack for nearly fifteen hours. The silence is wonderful!" He smiled, once again reminding me of a kindly grandfather. "Hello Colonel, I was hoping you would call. Look what we found in the wreckage of the shopping mall." He held up a molten mass of black material, which looked very much like the control box we had pulled out of the desert floor from the crashed F-4 that had shot down the space station.

"Proves the link, that's good, but I have a question for you. If we issued a Red Notice for 'Shetani' and his terrorist friends, non-specific locations but a wide range of possibilities, one of which is almost on your doorstep—you know who I mean—could you lend us a squad or two of your very best of the best to help eradicate a pest infestation in your neck of the woods?" At the other end of the call, Arie looked thoughtful, sitting back in his chair until his head was almost out of shot.

"Given what we have just endured, even though none of it came from that direction, other than the shopping mall, if we had some formal cover from you, maybe one of your people on attachment, we could run it as a pure terrorist prevention operation with high-level support. I would have to ask upstairs, of course, but I think you know what the reaction would be. However, we might just have a better solution. Some information has come into our hands that might give us a window of opportunity to correct the situation in Arabia without any political risk to us."

"Thanks, Arie. We'll come back to you." The Boss snapped the screen shut and handed me the computer. "Get busy, contact Lyon, get the paperwork started, get the protocols lined up, then get some sleep. I'll bring Pete and his gang up to speed, and I'll brief Indigo and Anna. I expect she will want to talk to Washington, and I'll ask her if she can get us some assets. We'll go devil hunting in the morning." As it turned out, we didn't, having received a short note from Arie outlying a plan to engage the French in the removal of the terrorists who now had control of Arabia. It was a masterpiece of strategy, something that was as elegant as it was deadly, and sheeted home the responsibility for some of the chaos exactly where it was needed.

PARLEZ - VOUS FRANÇOIS

The DGSE—*Direction générale de la sécurité extérieure*—the *sécurit* force which reports direct to the French Ministry of Defense—is the equivalent of MI6 in Britain, and the CIA in the US. To say that it holds secrets close to its chest is to understate the paranoia with which the department covers its tracks.

In this case, the DGSE had run a closed and very secret operation in a major Arab State, with the end goal of securing precious oil in plentiful and affordable quantities to fuel the French industrial machine. The plan had been simple—replace the king with a trio of security chiefs who would be directly controlled from Paris due to the fact that they would owe their allegiance and their very lives to the Republic. It was hoped that the natural competition and tension between the three would keep them off balance while the French solidified their political hold. Then the oil wells had been poisoned and effectively put out of operation for twenty-five years or so. Then the French delegation that had been sent at the king's request had been framed for the attack on the Grand Mosque and then assassinated. To further confuse the issue, the French had proof that the attack on their operatives had been masterminded by the three security heads who had then carried out the overthrow of the king almost as an afterthought, leaving the French in the lurch.

Six highly trained specialists had been embedded in the security forces to protect French interests and had had the pleasure of seeing their coup succeed, if only for a minute or two before the terrorist "Shetani" had derailed the plan with his own. Only one of the specialists had survived, going underground for three days before being able to work her way back to France on a small and dirty dowel carrying sheep carcasses along the Mediterranean Sea. She now sat, exhausted, in front of her commander and a range of executive officers whom she had never met before.

The silence in the room was deafening, and the operative had the feeling that the entire clusterfuck was soon to land in her lap, with only one possible outcome. As she mulled over this gloomy thought, the old-style Bakelite phone on the commandant's desk rang shrilly, causing the group of executives to flinch. The commandant picked up the handset with a suspicious look on his face.

"*Oui*?"

"Director, thank you for taking my call, Colonel Anthony, Interpol." The commandant pressed a little button on the side of the phone, enabling an old-style speaker to broadcast the call around the room.

"Colonel, to what do I owe the pleasure of your call?" the commandant's English was slightly accented, something he affected when dealing with the Americans and something everyone in the room knew was false.

"Director, we are aware of your little adventure in a certain Arab country and have no quarrel with you over it. But we are very interested in getting to the new occupant of the king's office and his supporters. We would normally ask for your help to remedy the situation, but under the circumstances, all we are asking for is a little advice." The commandant looked puzzled; the call in itself was unusual enough, but the subject matter begged disbelief. How could Interpol know of their plan, something that had been shared with fewer than six people in the Republic and, to his knowledge, absolutely no one outside it. He looked around at the faces of the executive and only saw confusion, fear, and insult.

"We know nothing of any adventure, and I am not sure how we can help you," he said with some finality. He was about to put the phone down with some force but was interrupted.

"General, don't fuck with me. We don't care about your attempted coup; we're chasing the terrorists that have caused most of your pain, and all we want is a little information." The tone in the Boss's voice left no doubt in anyone's mind that he was serious and wouldn't be put off. The commandant looked at his operative, and smiled inwardly, thinking he could solve two problems with one master stroke.

"Colonel, I will transfer this call to someone who may be able to help you, and I would remind you that France is a strong supporter of Interpol and that a Frenchman currently sits as the chairman of your board, and you can be sure that I will report your rudeness to him at the first opportunity." He pressed another button on the phone, which both cut off the speaker and transferred the call to a desk out in the hallway. He motioned to the operative and fired off a harsh instruction to her as she stood and then moved out of the room. She picked up the phone, uncertain how to respond. She had just been told in no uncertain terms not to divulge anything that would tarnish the French government but to answer any question she could fall within those strict parameters.

"Captain Gaston here, Colonel. How may I help you?" she asked in perfect English. As an operative of the DGSE, she had attended numerous language schools, in which she excelled.

"Captain, good morning. Interpol has issued a Red Notice for a gentleman called 'Shetani,' who we believe is the head of, or at least associated with, a terrorist organization called Al Bar al Shirak. Further, we believe this group has been responsible for the ground attacks in Avignon, the UK and Europe, and the United States. We also believe that they provided the manpower to mine the oil wells and the oil and gas pipelines, and more recently, the fracking sites. Do you have any information you can share with us?" The line crackled, reminding both that landlines still suffered from atmospherics and electrical interference, one of the advantages of using digital devices, which, of course, they couldn't do now.

"Colonel is this the same terrorist group that overthrew the king?" she asked, mindful that the call was being recorded both by the directorate and possibly the Americans, if not Interpol itself, and who else around the world she didn't know. "You, of all people, should know the answer to that. We have your voice print, we have you at the palace during the insurrection, we have photos of you on the boat going across the Mediterranean, and we followed you all the way to the room where you have just left. I ask again, do you have any information you will share with us regarding this terrorist?" The Boss held firm; he was telling the absolute truth because the Israelis had two operatives inside the palace, had witnessed the double coupe and the subsequent massacre of the guards and security forces, and had observed the escape of the French agent. Risking their own exposure, one of the agents had physically tracked her to the boat, then launched a micro drone, which effectively followed her until it ran out of fuel, but by then, the Israelis had persons in place in France who took up the shadowing.

They followed her all the way to the DGSE HQ. And what the Boss was not-so-subtly doing was letting the French know we knew everything about their plans but didn't really care one way or another, our target being the terrorists.

"I must seek permission to speak further to you." She placed the handset on the ancient table and walked back into the room, where the executive officers were in conference. The director looked over at her and nodded curtly, so she returned to the phone and picked up the handset.

"I am authorized to brief you on Shetani and his group as far as I am able to from my experience with them in Arabia. They had over one hundred troops, were well equipped, and were housed in the back of the palace in military barracks. It was obvious that they were there with the full knowledge of the king and his security guards, and on one occasion, the king actually entertained Shetani and his officers. The security departments also seemed to be aware of him, as they were providing both transportation and accommodation, and there seemed to be no friction. Until the night the king was assassinated."

"And then they struck without warning, killing all the security guards and, no doubt, the rest of your group?" the Boss asked, hoping to draw her into a confession. But you didn't get to be an operative of the DGSE without superior intelligence, and the Captain did not fall into the Boss's trap.

"I am unaware of what you speak. I fled the palace when the shooting got so intense that I could escape with the maximum of cover from the natural chaos that surrounds such events." The Boss smiled to himself; he expected no less.

"Okay, can you describe Shetani for me?"

"Two meters tall, one hundred thirty kilos, South African, Afrikaans, very fit, and his eyes are bright blue, his hair blond, almost white. Most unusual in someone from that continent."

"And his men?"

"Highly trained, disciplined, but many of them are on drugs and are quite open about it."

"Where is his camp?"

"At the back of the palace, he has a tent encampment guarded by specials with fifty-caliber Gatling guns and mortar tubes. He openly boasted about his 'three layers of protection.' I saw two, but I don't know what the third might be. He is well guarded but not unreachable. And he likes scotch."

"He drinks?" the Boss asked, curious.

"Yes. He is a man, after all, and he drinks to excess, then rapes the women the king provided for him, mostly young girls from the villages. However, I do not know his arrangements now that the king and the security agencies are largely depleted."

"If I asked you how to take him out, what would your answer be?" For a moment, static was the only sound on the old-fashioned phone.

"My expertise is in close quarters observation, so I cannot comment on a possible strategy. But you should be aware that the palace is full of innocents, who, while they have lost their king, are still employed as staff for their new master. Whatever you choose to do, you should be mindful of this." The Boss hung up, his shoulders sagging just a little.

"Well, from her mouth to God's ear. Quite a cheek suggesting that collateral damage should be avoided when she has just actively participated in a putsch that killed hundreds and has handed billions and a whole country over to a terrorist. Good that she has some sensibilities. What was your take?" I looked at the Boss, looked at Anna, looked at Pete, and saw the interesting looks as if they were actively waiting on me to set the pace. Which, in a sense, I supposed they were.

"She's lucky to be alive and still alive. The French have a habit of burying their mistakes. I wouldn't be surprised if we never heard from or of her again. As for her intelligence, the satellite overflight we hacked showed the tent encampment, the anti-air defenses, the specials, and the location of most of the troops. My instinct is to dial up three or four cruise missiles from the Sixth Fleet and take them all out at the same time. But I take her point about collateral damage, and we are Interpol, not a military force, supposedly, so whatever we do has to be judicious. I think as the Boss has said previously, a small tight unit of maybe twenty or thirty Israeli specialists, with Tom or Pete embedded, maybe backed up with a larger force as a secondary line of defense, is our best bet. But we have to find all their bases before we launch because we need a clean sweep to be sure that the terrorists are contained."

"I have an idea of that." Pete offered. "Actually, it's Tom's idea and claims it came from something one of the Italians said to us on our little foray here in Milan."

"And this magic suggestion is?" the Boss asked, waving his hands in the air as if shooing away flies.

"Well, Boss, you said it yourself. Set them off against each other. Paint the Al Bar al Shirak as a bunch of usurpers, put a bounty on their heads, and let the other terrorists rid the planet of them. Better still, make sure they are seen as diametrically opposed to the Muslim faith, have cursed Mohammad in twenty languages, and let the righteous take care of them. Either way that should clean out most of them."

"And how do you suppose we pay them the bounty?" the Boss asked, sarcasm dripping from his words. Pete lit up like a kid opening Christmas presents and clapped his hands. The sharp sound ricocheted around the warehouse, catching everyone's attention.

"Boss, we're Interpol! Freeze their bloody bank account—that Pan Arab thing—and pay them out of it!" he said, laughing. "Bloody poetic justice, I tell you!" I thought hard about the Boss's impassioned speech only just yesterday, when he had pointed out all the political landmines around trying to close this case out, and smiled myself. It would work. We could justify it on the basis that it was used for the funding of the terrorist attacks, and any court in the world would hold that up—especially the Hague if it came to that. And if there were to be collateral damage during an attack on the terrorist camps, we could offer to pay restitution, a process made famous by the Germans and the Japanese after World War II.

CHAPTER 70

Amira's heart sank into her boots as, once again, she failed to open her folder. She had tried repeatedly, for over an hour, using every geek trick in her book and a few thrown her way by Luigi and Shami, both of whom she held in very high regard. She remembered the conversation she had had with the Colonel and the Captain about "black holes." She decided to shift her attention there, not giving up so much as giving herself some thinking room. She had an idea she wanted to test out.

"Shami, how did you find me when I hacked into your system?" she asked, drawing the attention of the entire geek squad. Indigo had been providing snacks and coffee in what seemed to be an endless stream of hospitality, and even he pulled up in his tracks.

"As part of our standard electronic defense systems, we set digital traps that warn us when an outside agency is connected. You tripped several of our traps, and we were allowed to see how far you could get into the system, given it was the most significant attack we had ever experienced." And Amira did see, clearly, in her mind's eye how that would work. Many institutions had electronic warning systems, but not many had layers, as it took time, resources, and money to really protect anything electronic from a true hacker. So, usually, the standard was just one layer of protection and a firewall or two, but the Israelis had developed multiple ones, going down many levels in their coding. She visualized the different pathways of her digital attack, able to bring up from her excellent memory the base code she had used in the attack, then bent them into different shapes and purposes, then pounced on her keyboard with a vengeance.

"Shami, look here, turn this into a mirror. Would that work for you?" she asked, creating lines of code at a phenomenal rate. Luigi was looking over Shami's shoulder and started nodding. Then leaned forward and started keying in code almost as fast as Amira. Indigo looked on amused, always surprised by his geeks and the speed with which they could pound a keyboard into submission, and while he understood some of what they were creating, the sheer pace they were working at left him in awe.

"Heya, guys, whata are you alla doing herea?" he asked, in his perfectly accented English. He leaned even more forward until his head was between Amira's and Luigi's. Three screens were now filled with code, and a picture started to draw itself off in one corner. As the flow diagram developed, Indigo traced several lines with his finger, marveling at the simplicity of the solution. He nodded, recognizing exactly what the geeks were doing.

Amira was attacking a mythical system she had created, and the boys were defending it in real-time, and every time they deflected Amira's attack, she created a new one. It was a real-time example of how advanced artificial intelligence worked. At such a high level, he looked on in wonder. He leaned back, looking at the three geeks working furiously as if it was the only thing on their minds. Which, at this moment, it probably was.

"Okay, I see what you are doing. You've taken Shami's tripwire, siphoned off the incoming data into a different stream, and replaced the original with—what— are all those zeros' blanks?" he asked, his English improving dramatically.

"Yes, Indigo, it's brilliant, but when you look at it this way," Luigi said, pointing to the expanding picture, which now had multiple colors highlighting different streams of data, all being shunted off and replaced with the white space, "Amira has cracked it, I think, the Colonel's 'black hole' theory. And, Amira," he asked, pointing to a section of the flow diagram, "wouldn't this be a possible solution to where your code is verses the location of your folders?" Amira looked at the flow, nodded to herself, then spun on her chair to look directly at Indigo. Behind her, the screens ran the code in continuous streams, with the odd bit hiving off onto another screen and the flow diagram changing to reflect the outcome. Standing off to one side, Pete and Tom looked on in amazement. They had worked with geeks for the better part of their careers, understood the raw basics of coding, but had never seen such a rapid and masterful display of it before. This is what genius-level digital technology looked like, and they both felt a little old watching it unfold. And both wondered how they could possibly impact physically on any outcome that utilized this amazing thinking.

"So, we need to find where my folder data was redirected. Perhaps you could help me do this?" she asked, dragging a section of the flow diagram onto her screen into the middle of the flowing lines of code. "Perhaps if we use this section, develop a mirror, link it to Luigi's trip wire, then attack the folder from this direction, we could get a clue, no?" Both the geeks looked at her screen and nodded to themselves.

"Nothing is ever completely wiped. There is always a shadow, the first rule of computing," Luigi said, adding his own section to the diagram on Amira's screen. "And I think we have a way of shining some light on Amira's folder." A few minutes later, the Boss and I walked over to see the geeks high-fiving and Indigo clapping. Pete and Tom looked as if they had been blinded by a flash bang.

"What's up, guys?" I asked, sipping yet another masterfully constructed cappuccino, a habit I decided I liked very much. The three geeks turned to look at us, huge smiles splitting their faces. Indigo straightened up, pulled his shoulders back, and saluted us formally.

"Colonel, I wish to report that these amazing people have uncovered your 'black hole.' We now have satellite and overflight coverage of any area you may wish to see; we are rebuilding the data streams from Amira's folders, and we can now backtrack as far as three years ago, and that's growing every minute or so. And I can confidentially predict that any data previously hidden from us will become as easy to obtain as a book from the library."

"Hey, name the nearest library to us. Go on, ten euros if you can do it!" Pete quipped, letting the tension in the room out like a pricked balloon. I smiled at his tension breaker; my thinking was simple—for the last few weeks, we had been under incredible pressure trying to solve a worldwide series of terrorist attacks without our normal tools. The net hack had blinded us and made us virtually voice-less, relying on old-style telephony and copper cables well past their use-by date. Further, the enemy had been inside our most secured intelligence services for years, learning how we worked and what we relied on. Add in mass panic, a worldwide lack of petroleum products, a shortage of transportation, food, and, in some places, even clean water, and you had a pressure-cooker environment where it was not only hard to think but hard to act. Then add in civil insurrection and the chaos created when the leadership of the Catholic Church was all but wiped out, followed by the Jewish and Muslim religions being eviscerated and thousands of people dying from radiation poisoning simply because they filled up their cars and scooters at the local fuel station, and what you had was the stuff of nightmares and horror stories.

"Bibliotheca Sormani, Corso di Porta, Vittoria Six," said Tom, holding his hand out to Pete. "Pay up, you black bastard. It's the first time I've taken money off you in years!" Pete reached into one of his deep pockets in his combat pants and reluctantly pulled out his wallet. With a look of regret on his creased face, he pulled a ten euro note out and handed it over.

"How the bloody hell did you know that?" he asked. Tom just laughed. "You know I like to read, and we had time to spare waiting for you to show up, so I made a visit." Pete shook his head in wonder. His friend would never stop surprising him with his incredible thirst for knowledge. The last book Pete had read—well, truth be told, it was more than likely a weapons manual, but he guessed that might not count.

"If you soldiers of fortune are finished, Jessica and I would like to brief you on what we would like to do next. But first," the Boss said, turning to face Indigo again, who was relentlessly filling coffee mugs for the geeks, "Indigo, can you please get your geek squad to track back the Hercules, the UAV, the Warthog, and follow up with, say, one month surveillance of every well head that was attacked? See if we can identify anyone. I assume facial recognition is back up?"

"Colonel, we haven't linked into that yet, but we can, and we will. We have just penetrated the NSA, and we are letting them know we are doing so."

"Stop!" The Boss yelled, his voice like the edge of an axe. Luigi looked up in shock and stopped what he was doing. "The bastards more than likely are still in our systems; this could tip them off." Luigi pulled back from his keyboard and, looking a little ashamed, nodded.

"Apologies, Colonel, I wasn't thinking." The Boss nodded and walked over to pat the Italian geek on the shoulder.

"Not to worry, no harm done. But everyone, please, maintain the highest level of digital security; we still don't know if they are still inside our systems, and I don't want to give them any warning that we are back up." The three geeks nodded, and I reached out and took the laptop off the Boss.

"Hello, Frank," I said as the screen opened up to my command. "Just a heads-up, your people will see some fingerprints in your system, and we are sending you the code you need to unravel the hacks that have blinded you. Don't know what form but stand very by." And I snapped the lid closed before he could respond, mindful of the fact that I had just casually addressed the head of the NSA by his first name and would likely get a kick for it. But to be honest, I was tired of all the dancing on eggshells we had to do because of the multi-country politics that stank everything up. I just really wanted to get out and take down some terrorists, and I was getting to the point where I may not be too ladylike about it!

"That was cryptic. But thanks, saved me the trouble. Are you ready to brief?" the Boss asked, taking the computer back off me. I took a deep breath, mindful that around me were some of the most talented people in their craft, and being bitchy would not help my case. I moved over to the small conference area that had been set up for us, took a chair, and placed my coffee carefully on a small table as if it were a live hand grenade. Took another deep breath, shrugged my shoulders, and closed my eyes for a minute. When I opened them again, the team was all sitting around the table, drinking their coffees or just sitting still. I looked at all of them, wondering what they were thinking.

I would soon find out.

"Let's take this country by country. Anna, we have—or will have very shortly—the code the NSA needs to unlock their systems and attach themselves to the monks' network. They will not be told about the monks; we will let it slip that this is an Interpol operation, maybe with a little help from the Israelis, and let it ride at that. Any problems with that? Anyone?" Indigo nodded his head in agreement, as did Shami and Luigi. Amira looked pensive. She half put her hand up before I waved her down. "Hands down, Amira, you're one of us now, at least for the foreseeable future, and we value your contribution. What do you want to say?" I asked, my voice softening as I remembered her recent history.

The loss and betrayal of her lover, four years in the wilderness picking fruit, then a month in jail, solitary confinement, and the inquisition by some of the world's toughest intelligence officers, a fast and rough boat ride to Venice, constant picking and probing by our team, an attempt to blow her up and eliminate everyone around her with lethal force, another fast boat ride, a car trip in the middle of the night, then a helicopter to our present headquarters, which were sparsely furnished, even by my shoddy naval standards. A security bracelet on her ankle monitoring her every movement. Then everyone expected her to be the genius she was and unpick the treachery of the terrorist's digital hack. Which she had eventually done, with a little help from her geek friends.

"We can easily disguise the network, in fact, can mimic an Israeli one. If Shami agrees?" He nodded in agreement, then rolled his head to one side.

"I think it would be best to let Arie know what we planned?"

"I agree. Why don't you do that at the end of the briefing? Amira, do you have anything else?"

"Yes. Now that we know how they stole all the data, we can protect from that, so I can say with confidence that they will not be able to copy any data or transmissions from your friends or us if that's what you want to do." The Boss looked thoughtful,

Then looked at me. "Going to hijack your briefing for five." He turned to Amira and smiled to let her know he was on her side. "Amira, can you put into plain language how the black hole stuff works, please? I have trouble making my smartphone work, which, of course, it no longer does!" The team joined in laughing at the idea the Boss was a technological troglodyte but understood what the Boss was doing. He involved Amira as one of his team, not as an outsider nor even as a prisoner, giving her comfort she was no longer under suspicion and her past sins no longer counted except as learnings that we could leverage off in the planning of our counterattacks.

"Well," she said a little tentatively, "data moves around the internet in a series of packets that bounce from node to node, computer to computer until they arrive at their destination, where they reassemble into the original data set. Every data packet has an ID header, so they can find each other. Do you need more on that?" she asked, reminding me of a student asking a teacher if the paper she had submitted was okay.

"No, that's fine. I'm more interested in how the black hole works," the Boss replied, sitting back in a relaxed posture, creating an air of confidence. Amira shook her shoulders, her long blond hair flicked over her pretty face, and she automatically brushed it out of her eyes. She leaned forward slightly, her hands locked in front of her, resting on the table. You couldn't see the shake unless you really looked for it.

"Okay, then, imagine a rail line with a train carrying people on it coming to a fork in the track. The locomotive is the ID data packet; the train splits off one way, and then a new train appears and continues on it in the original direction. The train with the people in it gets stopped in a bypass, then spun off into a tunnel. The phantom train keeps going, gets to its destination, and the system thinks it has done what it was supposed to do, that is, deliver the train and its contents from A to B, but the train is empty. The sender gets a normal receipt, but the receiver never knows the contents never arrived, as the train is a phantom. For this picture to be true, you have to imagine that the engine is the header—the digital description of what the contents of the message are—if that gets detoured, the receiver has no way of knowing that the package didn't arrive. Now, if you are siphoning off data that is non-reflective—as in it does not have to be acknowledged at the receiver's end—then only the sender knows a package has left—and they have no indication it didn't get to where it was going—like a cloud store, a backup hard drive, that sort of thing."

"What happens when there are two parties involved sending and receiving simultaneously, as in a video conference or digital phone call?"

"Good question. The shunt needs to be placed at both ends but only collected after the data has passed through. There would be no image or shadow as both the sender and receiver would have gotten the message or video, with the data only being side-tracked after it had been viewed or downloaded. If the data was stored locally by each user, then a local record would still be available. That's why the net crash left the data stores intact and only destroyed the chips connected to the net at the time of the attack. My original idea was that there would be an auditable record of any data that was switched out, but looking at the code we have recovered, another coder removed that section and fundamentally changed the objective of the original design. But if you look here," she said, pointing up to the middle screen where the flow diagram was getting bigger and bigger every minute, "you can see we are recovering a lot of data that was just sitting still, as it were, at the time of the attack. Consider it still on the tracks, but between the start and the detour." The Boss nodded, getting a fair idea of what was involved without understanding ninety percent of what Amira had said. I probably got another thirty percent, and it was obvious that Indigo had even more than that because he was literally bouncing in his seat.

"Indigo, what have you got?" I asked.

"Colonel, Captain, with what Amira has shown us, we can backtrack the terrorists' movements location by location, now that we are on my brothers' secret network. Remember, it has been functioning all the time, even during the internet hack. And we can use the same digital ferrets that he used to backtrack as he used to discover the Secretary's conversations with the terrorist. We can find and track them in real-time."

"Indigo, wait for one, please. Amira, back to your earlier statement—how do we blind the terrorists to our use of the monks' net?" the Boss asked, turning serious in a heartbeat. Amira took the change in his demeanor in her stride and sat back straight up in her chair, flicking her hair out of her eyes almost as an automatic reflex.

"Colonel, we simply utilize the black hole code to lead our transmissions, as a super packet, to clean the transmission lines of any hack or interference. They will know we are using digital technology again, but they will not be able to get at the contents."

"Like an old-style engine with a snow plough on the front leading the passenger train."

"Yes." She smiled and looked very young but exhausted. Once again, I was reminded that we were all running on fumes.

"Okay, back to your briefing, Captain, then let's all get some rack time, a hot meal, take an hour to decompress, then get back at it. We've got a world to save!" Everyone laughed at the Boss's quip, but no one had mirth in their eyes. The seriousness of what we were up against created its own tension and was hard to dispel just with table humor. I planned to change that dynamic.

"Okay, Anna, expanding on what I was saying, the geek squad using the methodology Amira has described, track and trace the movement of the terrorist in Montana, priority one. We're looking for where they are now and how they got there. When you get that data Anna, let Roger know. Priority two, Shami, we need the same information on the terrorists that bedded down in Egypt. And while you are at it, try to find where this 'Helen' person went. Luigi, priority three, where is this 'Shetani' character, and how do we get to him? Number four, where are his terrorist cells located, and how do we identify them for others to deal with? Make that a worldwide search; they have attacked us in Alaska, Canada, Australia, the EU, England, possibly Italy, and certainly the Middle East. I think you are looking for small cells, maybe hiding in plain sight. They are all mercenaries; check out the normal websites, and see how they were recruited; maybe we get someone into their organization that way. Start with each attack, and work backwards, see if you can get their point of entry. Amira, and Indigo, set up our network so we could talk to our friends and keep our conversations between ourselves. Also, we need a data pack ready to send to Arie and Frank, and we have to work out how to send it to them."

"Once we set up our private network, a VPN if you like, we can connect anyone we like via invitation, which we can send on the monks' computers. Once we are linked, we can send anything we like digitally." Amira seemed to have freed up during the latter part of the briefing because I sensed new energy in her. Exactly what I was trying to achieve in the whole team, so her response was a good start. I looked around the room, seeing a focus that was missing before in the faces that stared back at me, with a hint of energy lurking just behind their eyes.

Amazing how motivating an almost impossible and seriously difficult task could be!

PERSONAL SACRIFICE

The head of the GIGN—*d'Intervention de la Gendarmerie Nationale*—one of France's elite security organizations, was a little man that just stretched one meter fifty, was as thin as a rake and owed his fame and fortune to his brother-in-law, who was currently the president of France. And while the GIGN had a world-class reputation for action when it counted, such as saving innocent civilians from an aircraft hijacking or terrorist hijack, François Alban did not. In fact, in the dark and upholstered corridors of the palace, he was currently regarded as a liability, having failed so totally to deliver to France what was so absolutely hers—cheap fuel for tens of years, at the expense of the rest of the EU. And while the sycophants that roamed those hallowed halls muttered and cursed his incompetence—he was not necessarily responsible for the attack on the oil fields, although, given his scope as a supposedly superior intelligence agency, perhaps he should have known about it in advance and then prevented it? *Non*?

But *absolument*, he should have succeeded in replacing the king with the directors of Al Mabaahith Al Jena'eyah, Al Mukhabarat Al A'amah, and the Lightning Force as long planned and supported by the *Gouvernement de la République française*—at the *Ministériel levé*, and at the heads of state. What could have been simpler? But *non*, once again, the prize had slipped through France's fingers by allowing a *terroristico*—a white mercenary!—to step in and wipe out their new partners and effectively take over the country. Was there no end to the man's incompetence?

By a strange twist of fate, that question was about to be answered, for the target of all this well-founded but ill-directed ire was now sitting down in his overstuffed chair, behind an impossibly large desk, pondering how to respond to a telex he had just received from Tel Aviv. It was from Arie Rosenberg, who had officially retired three years ago as the head of

Shin Bet (Shabak). He knew Arie, and as far as he could trust anyone, especially a Jew, he looked at Arie as a possible ally in his most dire time of need. He had heard the whispers in the palace and had inwardly flinched as the repeated insults turned more and more viral every day. Arie had an offer for him, no doubt now known to the palace, as he had discovered recently that his secretary was visiting the president five nights a week and not to play cards!

The offer was simple—at least on paper—if the GIGN could repeat their earlier performance and help rid Arabia of her newest government, which by all accounts was still celebrating with the king's harem, and as many underaged boys and girls, as they could scoop up every day while killing any civilian, they came across, without fear or favor.

They (the French) would have to turn up to the party with either the second or third in line to the throne and support either or both in their quest to take back the country. If they were successful, and the world saw a clean "France to the rescue" effort that played well on the media, whenever that was restored, then there may be a technological solution to de-clogging the Kingdom's gas lines. The radioactive oil could not be saved, at least in the foreseeable future, but the telex hinted at a new technology that could be applied to freeing up the gas supply from the silver clag created by the nano bug. That would give the French a huge advantage, given the Russians and the Chinese had lost their oil and gas pipelines to the same nano bug. He started to inwardly vibrate at the thought. What a coupe! Then he puzzled over the bottom section of the telex that set out a suggested timeline. The terrorists were to be completely taken out within a week from today. The new king or kings were to be throned within two days after that. The Kingdom would then entertain a guest list made up of all the world's great leaders and personalities, where the possibility of France being able to turn the gas flows back on to an energy-starved EU would be announced. Was this too good to be true? Did he have a choice? But he had not got to where he was by nepotism alone, and he did what he had always done wherever a hard decision landed on his desk.

He called his secretary, canceled all meetings and calls for the next two hours, and summoned his personal trainer. She arrived minutes later with two rolled-up exercise mats under her well-formed arms. Dressed in a black skinsuit with a bright red loose-fitting blouse, she virtually radiated sexuality from her bobbed blond hair, chiseled face, remarkable curvy figure, and intelligent green eyes. She smiled at François and walked straight into the attached bedroom and bathroom facilities. He followed in quick order, stripping off his perfectly cut suit as he did so. In less than one minute, he was buck naked, pawing at his trainer.

One hour and forty-six minutes later, he lay exhausted across the bed, the naked body of his trainer sprawled across him sideways, a thin cigar propped in his free hand. The other was engaged in a less than delicate exploration of the trainer's shapely arse as if he had more energy to spill. He didn't think he did, so in a soft voice, ran the problem through for her comment. She, also, had not got her current position as the bedmate for the head of the GIGN by just lying around fucking everyone, she, too, had her contacts, and as she commented softly on François's story, gave him the reassurance he so desperately needed, she reveled in the fact that here was her chance to cash in big time. She just had to work out who to tell first and what to ask for in return. She reached down between their sweaty bodies, grasped his flaccid penis, stroked it gently, and, sensing she would get a rise out of him, replaced her hand with her mouth.

Merdé! The things a girl had to do in the modern age just to make ends meet!

CHAPTER 71

The house was nothing to write home about, sitting on a half-acre block next to twenty similar houses, all sharing the land as if they were a commune. No fences, just neat driveways and trimmed edges, and the occasional tree bent slightly to the west, away from the prevailing winds which in this little town on the outskirts of Helena barreled in from the north and the east. Helena Regional Airport (HLN) was just a mile or two away, just down Canyon Ferry Road. All in all, an inauspicious location for a world-changing terrorist cell to hide in, and, in many ways, perfect for its purpose.

One of the terrorists was an ex-military test pilot, considered by her peers (who only knew of her from her excellent service and performance on behalf of the United States Government and other vested interests) to be the best of the best, so being close to an airport where a private hangar housed a polished mid-sized jet with an intercontinental range made total sense. As did the beefy four-wheel drive SUV parked in a garage that abutted the house. The neighbors often saw the occupants of the house streaming out early in the morning, with canoes and paddle boards strapped to the roof, apparently heading off to one of the many lakes that congregated within the Helena and Lewis and Clark National Forest, a pastime that was enjoyed by many of the townsfolk.

Another of the terrorists was a scientist who worked at the local Helena College, an outshoot of the University of Montana, as a math teacher part-time. Her classes were the best attended in the college, and the board of governors had been trying for two years to recruit her full-time. The university had also been very interested in her and had offered a full professorship with an annual stipend in the six figures. But she had just smiled and demurely claimed to be "just a teacher" and remained in her part-time role.

A third member of this elite group was an engineer and turned her hand to working at a local garage, fixing anything that came her way. Her workmates often commented on how good she was, and a number of the male staff had made passes at her, only to be gently rebuffed. Of course, the rumors flew thick and fast when it was learned that she lived with two other women, both exotic in their dress and stature, and while Helena was in a small town with small town values, because it had a college, the acceptance of behavior "outside the lines," as it was politely referred to, was tolerated, albeit with smirks and smiles behind hands hiding sneering mouths.

Occasionally, neighbors noticed that the women had visitors, but nothing was ever made of it as they arrived late at night and left early in the morning and usually drove a chunky dark SUV with blacked-out windows. They, too, had canoes and paddle boards on the roof, so it was assumed they were friends from upstate.

Sitting around a small outdoor table, the three looked as if they were spending a lazy Sunday afternoon in the sun, relaxing as their neighbors were undoubtedly doing. Dressed in casual outdoor gear, except for the scientist and the mechanic being of Eurasian origin, no one would have given them a second look. But they were all young, beautiful, articulate, obviously highly educated, and with figures that little boys' wet dreams were made of. On the table, next to a jug of chilled orange juice, a satellite phone rested next to a small laptop. Both were closed, but both were silently tracking a French weather satellite as it transitioned from west to east as a function of the normal rotation of the earth. While the satellite was some twenty-three thousand miles above the table, it was in direct line of sight for some three minutes, plenty long enough for a heavily encoded and compressed burst transmission to be sent or received.

Which it was.

The women chose to ignore the little red flashing LED on the side of the computer, preferring to take in the sun, which two of them had not had the privilege of doing for some days. They had, in point of fact, only just cleared the dust out of their lungs from being underground for so long. With a sigh, the mechanic reached out a tanned and firm arm, stroked the top of the laptop, looked over at her companions, and sighed.

"Suppose we should get that?" she asked in slightly accented English. Originally born in Afghanistan, and like many of her playmates at that time, she had been orphaned at the age of three by a furious battle that achieved absolutely nothing strategically important except for creating yet another batch of shattered and broken bodies and parentless children. She was eventually collected like so much garbage and moved to a refugee camp on the border between Afghanistan and Pakistan. There she had come under the protection of a young girl who acted as a surrogate mother and suddenly found she had many "brothers" and "sisters." When she was five—or thought she was—as she was not really aware of her true birth date—an elder, whose providence was never established, took the children six days a week and, using bamboo canes, instilled in them a hatred for learning, visceral fear and hatred for adults, and above all, the realization that they were well and truly on their own, and the best they had to look forward to was being sold off to the slave traders who swept through the camp every three months or so, as they grew older and budded.

She had run away multiple times, sometimes with friends, sometimes alone, but had never got very far. The camp was surrounded by hills that shot up like jagged spires, the ground open and covered only by scruffy dying screed; there was no water, and every route in and out of the camp was well known and well-trodden. In fact, the first three times she had run, she had been brought back by horsemen who moved between the villages and the camps' trading supplies. Then, on what turned out to be her last attempt, she was intercepted by an Afghani woman, well dressed and carrying a khaki-colored rucksack with a Red Crescent logo. She paused when she saw the little girl, her dirty, tattered, and torn burka that barely covered her slim, bruised body, and her hijab, so ragged and torn, it served no real purpose and had slipped almost to her shoulder, revealing dirty, tangled hair. She sat down cross-legged on the dirt and gestured to the girl to join her. Reached into her rucksack, and pulled out a Nân-iAfğânī and offered it to her. Initially, the girl refused the bread, looking suspiciously at the woman. In her world, adults ate everything first and only threw their scraps away for the children to fight over once they were finished.

The woman was patient, broke off a small piece, and offered it again. "؟كمسا ام ،ايليسوجانأ."

The child looked at her, her eyes wide with wonder. This strange woman was speaking to her, and she thought she had just told her her name. And offered bread!

Instinctively, she did the only thing her little body would let her do—she wolfed down the bread, then looked back up at the woman, who by this time was smiling. She stuttered out some words, so badly mangled that the woman was unable to interpret them. But she could interpret the look of shame on the little girl's grubby face. She had no given name. Not unexpected in a refugee camp, where this poor soul had obviously run from. She made a decision there and then, handed the rest of the nan to the girl, stood up, took one of her grimy hands in hers, and while the child eagerly devoured the bread, as if she hadn't eaten in days, which was, sadly, probably the truth, she started walking back the way she had come.

They reached the Red Crescent van in an hour, the small village of Chaman six hours later, and the semi-professionally run Red Crescent shelter for displaced persons an hour after that. And in the space of just a few hours, the little refugee's life was turned completely around, something she still thought back on from time to time. The next major milestone in her life occurred just three years later when she was approached by an Imam and offered a real home, a family, an education, and a life outside the limits of a refugee camp, no matter how well set up.

She had taken that huge step and had ended up with a family of seven, excluding the dogs and the cats in Faisalabad, had been schooled right through to university, where she had excelled and where her natural inclination for anything mechanical had taken root, and with the help of her adopted father, she had worked part-time in a small vehicle factory in which machinery broke down more times than it ran properly, creating an absolute haven for someone who loved the tools and the technological challenge of making cantankerous things work. She majored in robotics and engineering, designed machinery still used in manufacturing today, and earned sufficient from her royalties to support her family and travel the world. She had ended up back at her home to celebrate her twenty-sixth birthday when she ran into the woman who had made her excellent life possible all those years before. This time she had a name, and this time she was understood perfectly. After ensuring that her family would be looked after no matter what happened to her, she accepted the airline tickets, said her goodbyes, and flew to a little town in Montana, where she got a job at the local garage and settled into a lovely house where she was soon joined by two other women with similar backgrounds but vastly different skills.

They had settled into an easy rhythm, focused on the task of secretly refurbishing the abandoned military missile bunker and attendant tunnels while publicly rebuilding the farmhouse as a supposed summer vacation destination. They had excavated what had been formally identified as a swimming pool, only to turn it into an underground hangar for their helicopter, something that was missed when the state building inspector signed off on the "renovations" Of course, he had only seen what they had wanted him to see. As the work was completed nearly a full year before they needed to occupy the sites, the whole matter was soon lost in poorly stored records and then disappeared completely by a mysterious computer bug that had attacked all the city hall computers. This, of course, was first blamed on errant university students playing a prank, then on the Chinese, the Russians, then on anyone else that lacked the energy or the ability to defend themselves.

It was not the shared backgrounds that necessarily linked the women but the vision that had been explained to them by the very people who had essentially set them free. Taking them out of the camps and giving them families, education, hope, and a future, which now seemed to be the most important part of their journey so far. No matter how many baths she took, how many perfumes she used, the filth and grime of the refugee camp were still in her skin, the stink and stench in her nostrils, and scars from the beatings on her arms and legs for all to see.

She did not bemoan her early childhood, for it was what had led her and her friends to this place and this time. And now, they had done their absolute best to see that every child in every refugee camp would share a similar fate—and be given the warmth, love, and support they needed to rise and become what they were meant to be.

And if their God was paying attention when the world moved to accord the new order of things, they would, all three of them, be able to participate in the next step out in the open, free and unbound by either politics, their pasts, or fear. She reached for the phone, engaged the replay function, flicked the "broadcast" button, then lay the phone back on the table. All three sat up in their recliners, eyes focused on the phone.

"This is Helen. We have completed all tasks successfully and can confirm that you are all in the clear. There is an issue with the hired help; they are now running their own agenda. You may care to be a little careful if you have any physical contact with any of their teams. Our tracking indicates that the team that managed our northern tasks has retreated into Canada, so contact is unlikely. The teams that are moving through your mid and eastern states do not know of your existence. However, please be on your guard, just in case. This channel will close in ninety minutes, so if you have any questions, please send them before that mark. You have all done extremely well. We are proud of you. Helen out."

The three looked at each other, inwardly calm, outwardly smooth, but mentally vibrating at the information that all the scheduled tasks had been completed without loss on their side, and in less than an hour and a half, they would be free to pursue their own lives, their own way. World news was a little hard to come by without the WWW, and the local radio station tended to focus on issues germane to their area and the rest of the US.

The women had been a precious few at the start, less than fifteen specialists, spread across the major continents in groups of three. They all had friends in other parts of the world, women they had trained with, worked with, gone to school and university with, and developed the attack plan with. Helen had been the linchpin, pulling them altogether from their disparate backgrounds and locations some five years ago, and then had finally allocated the tasks to each team just some three years ago. And at that time, they had briefly met the two very young girls who had developed the gaming platform on which their battle strategy had been created.

And since that time, Helen had been the only outside voice that had provided updates and data necessary for their work. This was the first time that they had been informed that all the other tasks had been completed, and a swelling of pride threatened to bring tears to their eyes. Now the next step, perhaps the most important in all the planning, could be taken, and the future for thousands of refugee children could be changed forever.

"We did it," the engineer said in a throaty voice. "Now we wait until we can start phase two – and bring hope to the world."

"And it could be a long one because if you just look at the US, the chaos and public panic are so great it could take months before the politicians get their act together. The local station is saying that there is rioting and live shooting, and the military is in a hand-to-hand fight with members of different militias. And this just down the road, as it were, in Denver." The scientist, a beefy brunette who swallowed massive weights the way most people carried a wallet, stood up and stretched. "I'm off to the gym; anyone wants to come?" Her partners shook their heads; neither had a thirst for heavy lifting, preferring to run and exercise more gently, as suited their natures.

"Anything you want to ask Helen?" the engineer asked. The scientist shook her head, her rugged face framed with her fringe, which bobbed from side to side.

"No, thanks. All good. I hate to wait, but as you both know, think I'll go and lift a few hundred pounds just for fun!" As she walked off, her huge thighs rippling with toned muscle, she looked anything but a world-class scientist responsible for some of the most devastating damage and chaos ever inflicted on the modern human race. Sure, the world wars had been tragic, with millions killed, whole generations wiped out, and the geopolitical scene changed forever. Yes, the two atomic bombs dropped on Japan had a marked and detrimental effect on many of the world's population. As had the random acts of terrorism that had plagued the modern world for the last sixty years. But these recent terrorist attacks had hit where it hurt the most—at the cornerstone of human belief and comfort, the ability to move and travel as and when a person chose to, and the basic rights to economic stability and personal freedom that had been so enshrined in the psyche of the average person over the last one hundred and fifty years.

The world's religions were in an uproar. The Catholic Church was still trying to sort out how to create a conclave of cardinals to elect a new Pope. And where to locate the Vatican, given that both their previous seats of power had been destroyed. The Jewish and Muslim prophets, mullahs, and rabbis were being mobbed by believers seeking the truth, vengeance, and someone to yell at. Or point the finger at it. Each side righteously shouted for anyone listening that "their" Dome of the Rock had been attacked, the very foundation of their religion. Although calmer heads on the Jewish side pointed out that the Ten Lost Tribes were at the base of the Jewish faith and not necessarily a now-destroyed piece of rock that had sat on the site of the first Jewish temple, destroyed circa 70 AD. It really didn't matter because other rocks and bullets kept finding soft targets until both sides managed to impose a hard-edged martial law, which sadly involved members of both sides being killed by their own troops.

In every country of the world, cars lay abandoned along streets and roadsides, and those countries lucky enough to have electric vehicles now approach something close to normalcy. On the Asian and African continents, horse-drawn carts and bicycles were the new order of the day. A man with a donkey or a horse was king, able to trade many essential things for a simple ride from A to B. The world economy that had been built on the back of petroleum had collapsed, and the gas-fueled sector was in danger of following, given that nearly sixty percent of the gas flow around the world had effectively been stalled. The pipes remained, but the silver clag clogging both the inlets and outlets had resisted everything the engineers had thrown at it. In fact, in some cases, the remedial attempts had made the situation worse—causing the clag to freeze and harden to the point where it could not even be chipped away.

What had gone unnoticed due to the seriousness of the major attacks was that over six hundred and fifty fracking sites in the US, Australia, Canada, Africa, and across the old Soviet block of countries, all the way into China, had also been attacked, and now were clogged up with the same silvery material. China was on the point of launching a nuclear attack—but did not have a provable target. Russia was shaking its fists but, again, could not isolate a target for its wrath. The civil war in the United States was calming somewhat, but it was still unsafe to go out in public unless you had a tank and plenty of ammunition. The strategy of sending all the elected representatives back to their respective electorates had proved to be initially successful until, one by one, many of them had been picked off by snipers who basically rejected any form of governmental authority. The military had responded in kind, and the twenty-hour-per-day curfew was slowly helping to bring order back to the streets. Food and water were at a premium, and it seemed that even as quickly as the United States had gone from the greatest migrant nation in the world to a superpower, it had descended into chaos at the speed of a bullet, undoing hundreds of years of dominating capitalism.

The rural and remote areas seemed to have been mostly left out of the chaotic response to the world crisis, and as far as the women could tell, except for the lack of fuel, business was almost as usual in Helena. Of course, Helena enjoyed the benefits of the largest solar power farm in the United States, and better than ninety percent of the houses had "batteries in the basement and panels on the roof." And better than sixty percent of the population either had an electric vehicle, scooter, or bike, and horses were in plentiful supply. So, getting around was not the issue. And being rural, food supplies were plentiful. No, the only real issue was the flood of urban migrants from the north and the south, towing caravans, floats, and trailers stacked as high as their center of gravities allowed.

The city fathers had responded with a firm but polite hand—they pointed to flat areas to the west that had been prepared in advance three years ago by a billionaire who had grand plans for the area. It was rumored that he intended to build one hundred thousand houses there, plus all the infrastructure required to support that number of people. Once the word had gotten out that the whole town and cities were on the move, the city fathers had no compunction about using this area for the inbound refugees, so overnight, hundreds and hundreds of displaced families were welcomed to their new homes. It had taken only a week or two for the early settlers to stake their claim, and while people were still pouring in from towns and states where the chaos was more virile, a sort of calm descended over the small town of Helena, population 33,525 and growing, where the biggest issue seemed to be how to manage the sewerage and waste removal as the population threatened to double every three weeks!

And then, it was discovered that this had also been anticipated, and waste remedial and sewerage recycling ponds were uncovered, bringing an air of modernity to the new civilization growing on the outskirts of the town. And it had been pre-wired to the solar and wind farm grid.

If you stopped to think about it for a minute, you might wonder why a billionaire would want to build one hundred thousand houses in a city where the population hovered around thirty-three thousand three hundred on average, year to year. But under the current circumstances, with the pressure from the incoming immigrants, it was not a question that ever occurred to anyone.

And no one thought to question their good luck either, as the steady flow of people to the area slowed to a trickle, and job ads began to appear for electricians and laborer's to build an additional massive solar farm. The town was already used to solar power, which was possibly the best example of renewable energy use on the American continent, so even this strange activity (for the times) passed with few comments.

Then job ads began to appear for builders, carpenters, and day laborers, and in short order, on the outskirts of the temporary mobile village, specific style housing started to spring up, creating the look of a massive college. Seeing that Helena was already recognized as a college town, the design seemed appropriate. The migrants from the north and the south relaxed, thinking that no matter how uncomfortable their temporary mobile accommodation was, at least their children would be able to continue their schooling at some time in the future. The fact that the school and every building that followed was being constructed out of a colorful prefabricated material that seemed to be alive and actually proved to be an excellent solar panel surprised many but was quickly accepted when it was discovered that the panels were being transported from the airport, and were being handed out free of charge to the builders.

CHAPTER 72

The Boss looked on in frustration. The geeks looked exhausted. Even Indigo had lost his swagger and collapsed in an ugly wooden fold-up chair. Amira had her head in her arms, her hair spread out like an umbrella, the screen array flickering with fast-running lines of code above her head. Surreal was one word I thought of, then I adjusted my assessment. Frustrated and exhausted beyond belief fit better. I turned to Anna and, in the softest voice I could manage, asked her what the problem was. Unlike Pete and Tom, who had worked with me for the last six hours or so over in a corner away from the geek fest, Anna had perched on the corner of the table, working on her little laptop, with an intensity that mirrored mild insanity. Her personal pain shone through her hazel eyes, and her face looked like she had aged twenty years in the past few days.

"You look like hell," I said, hoping to get a smile, "and what's up with the geeks?" I got a look that would have frozen a lesser person, which slowly dissolved into a grimace, then a wan smile. The transformation was amazing; she suddenly looked ten years younger!

"The geeks have hit a brick wall—or though they would call it just missing data—and the news from back home is unbelievable. We have over six hundred thousand deaths due to people being killed while looting, civil unrest in every major city, rioting, and outright insurrection in some states. Armed militias have tried to take over several towns and cities, only to be repulsed by a better trained, and at the end of the day, better equipped National Guard, but the reports of soldiers surrendering their arms and walking away from the fray is very frightening."

"They don't want to kill civilians—possibly people they know, from their own neighborhood, went to school with, work with. I can understand that. How's your president faring?" Anna looked sick, and for the first time in a very long time, I was glad I had become a citizen of the EU. I hadn't renounced my US citizenship, just attached myself to the continent that I mostly worked on and for as an Interpol agent. Besides, an EU diplomatic passport got me places where a US one would have had me thrown in jail or shot on sight!

"Frank says she's holding up, but most of her cabinet have deserted her; politically, she is becoming isolated, but for the moment, she is still in control. Although, from the intelligence reports I've been reading, in control of what is the real issue. The US is burning; civil unrest is so widespread, the army has been called in to backfill the reserve, and while the attrition on the vigilante side is just horrible to comprehend, the civilian side is a little better. Her strategy to send back the members of Congress and the senate has worked partially, particularly in those towns and cities where the population was low.

"But some eighty members of the House have been killed, and the estimate was twenty to thirty from Congress. The army has the remainder under guard, and some are working the local radio nets to the best of their ability, but it is going to be a very slow grind. No one ever expected this level of civil insurgency. It seems that all the pent-up frustration from the recent pandemic has just exploded out all at once, and anyone in authority, in uniform or thought to be in authority, is a target. And, of course, in the poorer areas, looting and rioting have become endemic, and the number of hate crimes is so large that literally, no one is able to contain them. It seems the very worst of us is on display for all the world to see, although Europe is not doing much better in some areas."

"But we're not seeing civil insurrection, rioting, militias, just very unhappy civilians protesting outside parliament houses," I said, trying to reach Anna's center. The FBI agent inside her skin was boiling over at the injustice and unlawful behavior of her fellow Americans, and the woman she was, was hurting for every victim. I knew the feeling; as an Interpol agent, you all too often personally felt the dichotomy between victim and persecutor, and over half the time, the guilty were only trying to survive. Rules were rules only when the majority of the people affected by them agreed to abide by them. And too often in the modern age, groups of predators, politicians, or just really greedy people after power and control created their own environments, using social media in the main, creating their own skewed rules of behavior, then bitched and bellyached when someone threw them back in their face and carted them off to jail.

But what we had here was far worse. The world, literally, had gone mad. The combination of losing their ability to get around, the immediate shortage of food and water,and the fear of being killed by an unknown drone strike or poisoned by radioactive oil, or bombed by children's toys had ripped into the psyche of everyone over the age of three, and the resulting fear was palpable. What added to it, of course, was the loss of the World Wide Web. People had become so invested in the ability to talk to anyone anywhere in the world, for pennies, and then have access to any information they ever wanted at the click of a button they had not been able to reconnect with the real, physical world fast enough to get their balance. Where just weeks ago there had been worldwide news instantly available and all the social gossip and connectivity one could ever hope for, albeit filtered through commercially vested interests who took advantage of every name, phone number, address, and password for marketing purposes, now all they had access to was a static-filled void and blank screens.

No social media. No smartphones. No electronic tablets or laptops. No electronic navigation, although the number of vehicles that could take advantage of GPS even if it was online was dramatically reduced by the worldwide shortage of oil, petrol, and gas.

I looked back over at the geeks and saw a lack of hope matching their lack of energy. I pointed to Amira collapsed over her keyboard. "What happened?" As I asked the question, the Boss sauntered over to us and sat on the corner of the same table Anna had been using.

"Amira and Luigi cracked the folder problem, and they opened it up and rebuilt the code. Then they sent a patch to Frank to enable the NSA to look back in time at the satellite data to develop a track and trace around the three sites we had identified as used by the terrorists in

Montana, Libya, and Egypt. They started back three years ago, just to be safe, and then hit a roadblock."

"Roadblock?" I looked at Anna closely as I asked the question, and the weariness came through loud and clear.

"Well, whatever geeks call a digital block. For the last thirty months, there is not a single byte of evidence of anything or anyone moving around for a thousand kilometers in any direction of the targeted area; it's as if someone got an eraser and scrubbed the images until all they showed looked like a standard electronic map. All the geospatial data is there—everything is correct as far as roads, towns, villages, and even people movement, but once you cross the invisible one-thousand-kilometer boundary, nothing. No movement of any type."

"Can you see vehicles moving in and out of those areas?"

"Only until they reach the boundary. Then nada." I shook my head in amazement. The terrorists had not only been in our electronic systems for tens of years; they had effectively controlled what we did and did not see using our best technology—or what we had considered was the best, against us. But the timeline belted me in the back of my brain again, and I asked the obvious question.

"We assume the terrorists originally got into our systems back in the early two-thousands. We have found and closed backdoors that were part of the Y2K scam. We know how the military hardware was obtained and roughly when. If the women they recruited from the refugee camps weren't old enough to do the early work, then who did? This is as classy as their work, perhaps not quite as sophisticated, but this was set up years ago, and if we use Amira as an example, she only was approached to join the terrorists five years ago."

"Yes, but five years is a long time for a highly trained group of experts to refine their strategy, planning, and tactics. This work could easily be the women, and I'll grant you that the earlier work was by others. But look at what they did. Stole bombs. Aircraft. Hacked into our systems. Nothing a competent state sponsored terrorist couldn't manage. The really sexy stuff only came to light a month ago, with the first attacks on Rome, Jerusalem, and Washington. Even the theft of the Strontium-90 was recent, as in the last year, so maybe the work of the women. And look how easy that exercise turned out to be. Shami didn't even work up a sweat."

"No, he didn't," I answered, thinking back to the time when we were all back in the Monk's hidden cavern. "But what is it you are really worried about?" I asked Anna. She looked at me, turned her head to look at the Boss, still relaxed on the edge of the table, then shrugged her shoulders.

"I'm used to being able to track an unsub using all the modern technology we usually employ. Satellite tracking, UAVs, drones, street cams, CCTV, phone tracking, GPS, numberplate recognition, and facial recognition are all stored on computers everywhere, all accessible to law enforcement, and all able to be linked to give us a visual and time-located road map of what an unsub has been doing—and hopefully, where they might be at the time, we want to take them down. These women are turning out to be ghosts. Literally and metaphorically. It's as if they disappeared off the face of the Earth five years ago, never to be seen in public again. We have high-resolution imaging of the three sites we sent the ninjas to; we have wonderful pictures of all three takedowns as they progressed. But nothing, and I do mean nothing, before three years prior and the time we went in."

"Are you saying that we have real-time imaging available now of all three sites but nothing before we launched our attack?" the Boss asked, a keen edge in his voice. Anna looked at him with a quizzical frown on her face and brushed her hair out of her eyes automatically.

"The first images we have are night-vision enhanced satellite photos of the original track and trace of the dark fiber in Montana and Libya. From that time on, it's business as normal. But before that, it's as if, as I said earlier, someone used an eraser to scrub the data and remove all moving objects. For around three years."

"They used a version of the black hole code to protect their people. So, to sum up, we have no data on who went in and out of our target areas, no ID on our women, other than our A-10 Pilot, the name 'Helen,' and the name 'Michele'— supposedly of Chinese origin."

"And Amira." I looked at them both as I added the most obvious piece of intelligence which we routinely had subconsciously chosen to ignore. Amira had been relocated by the terrorist organization when she was very young, grew up in a Jewish family, went to college where she starred in her studies and was moved by the terrorists to an American university where she developed the nano bug that killed the oil, gas, and fracking fields but had not gone to Turkey with the terrorists when asked to five years ago. She had fled to the Southern Hemisphere, only coming back to Israel in the last six months. She knew some of the terrorists—she had met with Helen at least three times by her own admission and had been Michele's lover for at least two years. I suddenly realized that in our haste to try and track the terrorists, we had been blinded to the obvious.

"Did we have any success getting data off the university databases?" the Boss asked. But before anyone could answer the question, I butted in.

"Stop. Wait. We've ignored something under our noses for at least two weeks."

"And what would that be?" the Boss asked, standing up and getting in my face. I just stood my ground and pointed at Amira slumped over her workstation. "Amira knows the faces of at least two of the terrorists, probably more. Get a sketch artist, and I bet we can get some faces." The Boss looked at me for a full minute, then backed off, shaking his head.

"You're right. We never stopped to think about what she knew—just what she had done. And I've just had another epiphany—somehow, the net crashing did not affect any hospitals, medical equipment, fire services, aircraft, and who knows what else, and we never stopped to ask. How did they manage that?"

"Good question and I suspect the answer will involve geofencing and the selection of specific chipsets, but for the moment, I think we should stay focused on the primary issue. Anna, how did tracking the mercenary terrorists go?" I asked because that was the one area we could farm out to our supporting countries who we knew would strike at them with relish.

"Well, contrary to our expectations, given we can't find a single female terrorist anywhere on the planet, extremely well. We have twenty-seven groups identified in sixteen countries, and we have them on camera from start to finish. We even know that the bombers of the Grand Mosque didn't exist. The data is solid. I am confident that we could dispatch teams to engage with the terrorist groups with some degree of accuracy."

“Good news at last. What about this ‘Shetani’ character?”

“We have him sitting in front of a tent pitched out the back of the Royal Palace, surrounded by his men, tanks, specials, antiaircraft guns, and further out more military hardware he obviously has commandeered from the Arabians. We estimate his force at three to four thousand, all told; it may well be a strategic problem getting to him.”

“Have we frozen that bank account?” I asked, referring to the Pan Arabian Sovereign Wealth Fund, which we believed had funded the terrorist attacks and probably the development of the women from day one. The Boss nodded but looked unhappy.

“Yes, the main fund is frozen, and we are now trying to trace the distribution of hundreds of billions of euros and US dollars around the world, to multiple banks, over the past five years. We may be able to shut those funds down by showing the terrorist link. However, that Fund was seen as legitimate right up until the king was assassinated, and a number of Arab countries fed into it at different times. We are walking on eggshells politically, so we need to be very careful about what we say, and to whom we say it. But we will shut down every account we identify and wait to see who protests the most.”

“Back to the mercenary terrorists then. Do we have enough to put a package together to send to interested parties to start the eradication process?” I asked, not necessarily seeing a quick solution to the banking issue. Both the Boss and Anna nodded, neither commenting on my use of metaphorical language. It was always wise to moderate a ‘kill on sight’ order, in my experience.

“I’m sending Pete and Tom with packages for the EU, Russia, and the US. Tom will also offer to act as an observer with secure contact to us for those countries that want it. It means we won’t have any real security here, but I’m counting on Aire’s help in that regard because we have a package for him and his Hezbollah counterpart, and after what the terrorists did to that shopping center, I would think that there would be plenty of interest in hitting back. Then there’s the added incentive of the bounty we have put on every head—one hundred and fifty thousand euros, or two hundred thousand US dollars—but they have to provide photographic and forensic evidence to collect. It will be very interesting to see how that goes.”

“We could end up accidentally financing the next wave of terrorist attacks,” I said, voicing what we were all thinking.

“Yes, we could. But the money will have trackers attached, and we now have access to imaging around the world, which no one else has other than our closest friends. Let’s prepare the packages, get Tom and Pete on the way, then we can have a quiet chat with Amira. I want to find out everything she knows about the women’s network, behavior, communication channels, everything, right down to whom she worked with at each university.” The Boss strode away, purpose in every step. Anna and I looked at each other, thinking that the rubber was about to hit the road.

“I suppose you’ll go back to the States?” I asked, thinking that I would miss her company and her sharp mind. Anna nodded.

“Yes, I’ll take the package for Roger and for the Canadians, who, I have no doubt, will be willing to play.” I nodded; the moment they knew they had terrorist cells that could be tracked wandering around their tundra, they would respond.

“Okay, I guess that leaves Arie for the Boss and me.” She nodded, her mind on other things as she was mentally prepared for a continent-wide terrorist hunt. I walked over to the Boss and Amira and saw she had made a slight recovery in that she now seemed to have some focus and energy. The Boss gestured towards me. Amira nodded and stood up. One minute later, the three of us were sitting comfortably in front of the burbling and hissing espresso machine, which occasionally let fly with pointed puffs of boiling steam like an angry dragon.

“Hi, Amira, you’re looking a little tired?” I asked to break the ice. She looked at me with red eyes and disheveled hair, and if I didn’t know better, I could easily think of her as a teenager, not an adult. She swiped her hair back and rolled her shoulders.

“They bastardized my code. Stole my work and used it to wreak havoc on the world, kill millions, and you ask why I’m a little tired?” she asked, with an edge to her voice and venom that was unexpected. Once again, I mentally chastised myself for having ignored Amira’s role in all of this, preferring to just deal with the “now.”

“That may be, but you are here now, helping us to unravel what was done. We need your help identifying all those who studied and worked with you both in Israel and at Harvey Mudd." She looked at me wide-eyed, then it was as if a switch had been thrown in her brain because I promise you, a gleam came into her eyes that could light up a room.

"It will be my pleasure. Lots of photos and special stuff were on my laptop, but I guess Helen wiped all that data when she and I last met. However, I did send all my social stuff up into the cloud; it was an automatic backup from my phone and laptop, so maybe we can find it?" she asked, looking at the Boss for permission. He nodded, handed her one of our secure little laptops, which she opened, tapped a few keys, nodded, then tapped a few more, then turned the screen around so we could both see it. "How far back do you want to go?" she asked. I held up ten fingers, reasoning that as she had quit the terrorists five years ago, the previous five years would be the most telling—university in Israel, university in the US. She turned the screen back, tapped again, frowned, tapped, frowned, tapped, then, with a sigh, turned the screen back to us. "I was so young then," she said, looking at the back of the screen as if it were telling us her very innermost secrets.

"Boss, let me give this to Luigi or Shami; they can compile all this data for us in a fraction of the time it would take us to sort through it." The Boss nodded, and I stood and walked over to the geeks who had their heads together at the main control station. Which was probably a little grand as statements go because the screens all stood on top of packing crates, the computers joined by millions of blue, yellow, and black cables stood humped in one corner and hastily prepared workstations littered the floor so haphazardly you would be hard pressed to generate a sensible flow diagram from them.

"Shami, can you and Luigi put all this into some sort of formalized timeline, please, with a summary of key points against each data event? We specifically want to be able to identify all the various people," I asked, noting that as I spoke, they both looked over at where Amira and the Boss sat.

"*Sì, Capatino*," Luigi replied, looking engaged but a little distant. I put it down to his weariness and left them to the data.

CHAPTER 73

By any standard, Mohammad bin Maysoon bin Nasrin was a wastrel. He currently sat at a roulette table with a very small pile of chips stacked in front of him, a very large scotch on ice in one hand, and an aggravated frown on his young and unmarked face sitting under a checked red-and-white keffiyeh, held in place by a luxurious gold and silver headband. While he proudly flourished his heritage, lineage, and royal expectations, he just as seriously defied the customs of his country and religion. He flicked a finger at a passing steward, leaned into their face, and spoke quietly, in perfect English, something he had perfected at Oxford just the past year. Not that he had passed any subject or even threatened to in the fifteen months he had lasted at the college before being politely asked to continue his studies somewhere else.

"Have the cage release another two hundred thousand, please, against my marker and a thousand for yourself." The steward, highly trained and professional to the end, gave no visual sign at the size of the tip, merely nodded, and moved on. He returned just a few minutes later, minutes in which the prince had managed to lose the rest of his chips and bent to whisper in the prince's ear. While the aggravated frown on the prince's face got deeper, if that was possible, his eyes literally bulged in his head. He looked to his left, back to the right, at the croupier, then around the table at the other players. Making sure he was not the focus of attention, he stood up, adjusted his robes with a flourish, and left his drink as he strode towards the cashier's cage, the steward in his wake.

Before he could unleash his wrath on the hapless cashier, two members of the casino's security staff flanked him and, holding his elbows to force compliance, politely asked him to accompany them to an anteroom. The steward peeled off, thinking his chance for a grateful tip was gone and was replaced by two of the prince's retinue, who had seen the prince marched out of the casino. They kept their distance from the security guards, not at all sure of what was happening. While it was unusual for the prince to be escorted by casino security guards, it was not unusual for him to be involved in something way out of normal scope. The prince entered at anteroom with the guards, and the door closed shut with a thud, effectively isolating the retinue.

Sitting on a couch, looking very much at ease, a uniformed officer of the GIGN raised his glass to the prince and nodded to the guards, who released the prince to stand back on either side of him. The prince visibly shook in anger, rolling his shoulders to flounce and ruffle his robes, which he then gathered in front with his hands crossed.

"Who are you, and what is this all about?" the prince demanded, more annoyed at having his game interrupted than being fronted by who he saw as a military flunky.

"*Monsieur*, Your Highness, I have news for you of the highest importance. Please sit and join me in a drink while I bring you up to date." One of the guards stepped forward with a large scotch on the rocks in a beautiful square-cut Waterford crystal glass that caught the light and sparkled and handed it to the prince, who, with a ruffle of his robes, sat on the engraved chair opposite the couch. He took a very large gulp of the scotch, suddenly feeling just a little off balance. Who was this military fool? He looked like a peacock in his blue, red, and black formal uniform, with medals and ribbons over one side of his chest. A gold-rimmed rigid kepi sat on a small table with enough intricate braid to indicate a very high rank. He did not have long to wait.

"Your Highness, as you may have heard, your father was assassinated last week, and his place taken by the directors of your three security services—Al Mabaahith Al Jena'eyah, Al Mukhabarat Al A'amah, and the Lightning Force. They were, in turn, assassinated by a South African mercenary who calls himself 'Shetani,' who has effectively taken over your country. This is a terrible state of affairs, one which we French have determined out of respect for your family and your country, must go on no longer. As you are aware, we have a long-standing relationship with your country and with your family. I have been sent here as the personal emissary of General François Alban to inform your majesty that we will support you in regaining your throne immediately." While the soldier had been laying out the background, the prince's face had turned sheet white at the thought of going back to Arabia in any capacity.

His role was to spread his seed and the good word here, in London, a civilized society where one could experience the finer things of life and not feel necessarily threatened every hour of every day. He shook his head with some force.

"No. I will not go back. Take me back to the casino immediately, or I'll have you arrested." The emissary put his drink down and smoothed the creases of his uniform trousers, which were sharp enough to slice open his fingers.

"Your Highness, I apologize if you thought of this chat as a negotiation. You will come to France with me tonight from this room; your retinue can gather your belongings from the hotel and join us at the terminal. There is one other thing I have to tell you, which might make your decision a little easier. Should you have been successful in speaking to the cashier, she would have had to inform you, sadly, that your credit line has been cut off. Not only that, but once your debit to the casino has been paid, which we are arranging as we speak, you will have no further access to funds in any form until you take the throne as was meant."

The prince looked absolutely astonished. In all his twenty-six years, he had never been so harshly treated, not even by his father, and he simply had no prior frame of reference he could relate to. He looked lost, and his shoulders slumped, and the Frenchman looked on with derision. If this was the best the Kingdom could do by way of a successor, he was sure that yet another assassination and takeover was in the prince's not-to-distant future!

Aire was in the middle of briefing us on his offer to François Alban when a sidebar opened up on the small screen. He paused, looking at his own view, and, for a brief moment, silence flowed energetically from Italy to Israel and back again at the speed of light.

"The French have taken charge of the heir to the throne. So that part of our strategy is in play." He nodded to himself, obviously having some sort of internal dialogue. "Now, where were we?"

"You were giving us the details of your offer to the French. Seems like that is now mute; let's talk about the elephant in the room." The Boss was neutral in his tonality, but I could see a little tension bubbling under the surface. It was in his nature to want to hit out, and so far, all we had managed to do was chase our tail and follow in the terrorists' footsteps. Arie smiled into the screen, no doubt as aware as I was of the Boss's predilection for action over planning.

"All right, Colonel, let's talk about the elephant. Do you trust the work Amira is doing with your geeks?"

"Yes. I read her as contrite, ashamed, and more than a little angry at her work being taken and bent to the will of the terrorists. She obviously takes great pride in her work, which we know to be world-class, and she seems royally pissed at what the terrorists have done with her code. She's just given us chapter and verse on all the people she met from the time she went to your university, so at least we now have some faces which we are slowly matching to new data."

"Is this Chinese person Michele on that list?" Arie asked, and both the Boss and I sensed at the same moment that Arie had information about this mysterious "Michele" that we didn't.

"Yes, she is. What do you know that we don't?" Arie smiled, sitting back a little from the camera.

"Not much more. But we have evidence that she is well known in the hacking world, is still very active, and Shami has sent us some recent data in the package you sent over. I showed her photo to a few of my friends and got a hit. It seems we used her in an operation seven years ago when we were trying to neutralize some serious hacking we traced back to Palestine.

"She mounted a denial-of-service attack on the hackers and crashed their mainframe, closed them down for over a month. She was contracted through the hacker underground, located in Russia, did the work for us under a blind, was paid in Switzerland, then as they do, she simply disappeared. The name she was using at that time was Michelob. If you look at the timeline of when Amira attended Harvey Mudd, it ties in nicely."

"So, she may not be part of the terrorist organization?" I asked, running this new information through my bullshit detector.

"No, she may not be. She was probably under contract when she was working with Amira and the others at Harvey Mudd, but again, through our contacts with the Russians, she apparently has been around free-lancing out her services over the last three years. Not the actions of a deep-cover terrorist." I thought I detected something in Arie's eyes, but the small screen didn't give me a lot to look at. So I took a punt, tapping the Boss twice on his knee to warn him I was about to go off the reservation. He looked sideways at me and nodded silently.

"Aire, would you or your people be able to contact this 'Michelob'?" I asked. The bright smile that greeted my words said my intuition had been correct. Arie had a plan for the "Michelob."

"Yes, we can. But I was going to ask you if you could get Amira to write the note, just to add the personal touch, and perhaps even manage the contact, for obvious reasons." I nodded.

"We can do that—but what's your plan?" I asked, mindful that this little intelligence genius who had been around twice as long as I had been alive always kept things close to his chest.

"Well, before we were interrupted with the news from the French, I was going to mention that part of my promise to them is that we might—and I underscore might—be able to reverse the nano bug's work on the gas lines. As Amira and Michele seemed to have developed the bug, it was only logical to suppose they could, working together again, reverse the process." Arie might have been around the block a few dozen times, but he had not lost his ability to think outside the dots. Using the very people who had created the nano bug to unravel its crippling effectiveness made total sense, but if one of the cohorts was a master Blackhat hacker, what new digital danger might we be opening ourselves up to? My mind was boggled at the sheer scale of the possibilities. But the Word Wide Web had crashed. Everything connected to it with a chip had been fried—except for select elements of the emergency services network.

How much worse could the digital world get?

CHAPTER 74

The Canadians acted promptly, their country one of the least affected by the worldwide chaos due to its sheer size, weather, and the way the population was spread outside the main cities. Yes, their fuel was depleted, and yes, so were their natural gas supplies, but largely because so much of the country was under three feet of snow, the civil unrest that plagued the Americas was all but contained to just a few small spot fires in the cities of Montreal and Quebec. Besides, the Canadians were used to looking after their own, and those houses that depended on gas or oil soon converted back to wood stoves and heating, something most houses outside of the major cities were already set up for two hundred years ago.

The Third Division of the Canadian Armed Forces was an elite unit, trained for cold, wet, and soggy terrains, the use of dog sleds, motorized scooters, and, above all else, parachuting into remote areas with no immediate support from any quarter. When the commandant of the First Remote Area Patrol Group got the call, she first thought it was a hoax. With the worldwide net down, the barracks relied on two very old copper-wire linked landlines and clunky old-style handsets, neither of which had rung for over three days. Instead, her pocket phone, a satellite-linked communicator which had been passively silent for the past two and a half weeks but she carried nevertheless out of habit, vibrated in her pocket.

She flicked it open, almost annoyed at its intrusion. She stared at the screen, punched in a code which she hoped was still current, and was rewarded with the shaggy and dark brown face of her direct superior, a general with a long history of driving his patrol group commanders insane.

"Sir," she answered, automatically straightening to the "attention" position.

Old habits die hard, even for a modern skeptic like herself.

"Commander, you can verify this call using your code book; please do so and call me back." And the screen went black, the phone now lifeless in her hands. "Chief, front and center!" she yelled in her best parade ground voice. A tall and impeccably dressed chief master sergeant came through the door, a smile on his face. His commandant was one of the best he had ever served with, young for the rank but ballsy enough to command a thousand men and women under the harshest of climatic conditions imaginable and maintain their respect and trust.

"Sir, you yelled for me?" he asked, the smile never leaving his face. The look on the face of his commandant should have warned him something was up but used to the relative quiet of the barracks at this time of the year, he missed the subtle tells from her facial expression.

"Chief, get our daily code book on the double." No please, just a straight order, with a tonality that suggested something was up.

"Sir!" The chief saluted, turned on his heel, and marched out of the office. In less than a minute, he was back, stood to attention in front of her desk, and held out a red hardbound manual. "Sir, the code book, as instructed."

"At ease, Chief, I need you on your toes. In fact, close the door and move that chair over here so you can see the phone." The chief, a puzzled look on his face, closed the door, moved the chair, then sat, mentally trying to decode what was happening in the office. The phones didn't work. Computers didn't work. In fact, bugger-all worked at the moment; they were still rewiring and fixing everything that had been fried by the WWW crash.

The commandant opened the massive book, flicked through to today's date, and ran her calloused finger along the lines of type until she found what she was looking for. She dialed the code into the phone keyboard and was rewarded with the general's face again. She sat straight in her chair, the chief mimicking her move.

"At ease, both of you. Good call, Gretchen; it saves us some time. Paper and pen, please. You are about to get an interesting brief; we will not use the fax, and you will have to do your own planning from the latitude and longitude I give you to locate the target. Once this brief is concluded, I'll take questions, then until the mission is completed, I expect you to maintain total radio and communications silence. Is that understood?"

"Yes, sir, understood."

"Good. Now I want you to select around one hundred troops, cross-trained in air, sea, and land operations, able to live off the land for extended periods of time, and used to low-tech weaponry. They will be in soft clothes, and your cover is 'hunting parties,' so I suggest teams of no more than six to eight. You will be operating in semi-rural areas but may be engaged in firefights in or around populated spaces. Collateral civilian casualties are to be avoided at all costs, but you must achieve the objective, even if it means you countermand this restriction. If that happens, you will have to provide chapter and verse to an independent government inquiry, which I have been informed will be biased against us. For this reason, I want everyone wearing bodycams and armor under their furs." The commandant looked at the chief, a question in her eyes. The chief shook his head.

"Yes, I know that will be difficult to manage, but work it out. You are to be absolutely discrete in setting this mission up; it must be contained within your barracks, and you will have a timeline to meet, so look at these coordinates, get yourselves a good map, and call me back in ten minutes." And the phone went dead again.

The chief looked at the coordinates the commandant had scribbled on a scratch pad, her handwriting obviously suffering from lack of practice. He stood up and marched out of the room. The commandant called for coffee and swiped the brica-brac off her desk, leaving a nice, clean space. She wondered if the mission they were to be briefed on would end up being as clean at the end of the day.

The chief spread a Mercator projection map scaled at 1:250,000 on the desk, primarily used by hikers and hunters, using a pencil sharpener and a small book to hold the edges of the map flat. He pointed to an area along the Cedar River, south of the tiny village of Ear Falls.

"Here is the location—Lat 50.5303/Long -93.2576—notated as Kenora, Unorganized ON. Just north of Windfall Road, the only reliable access at this time, although snow chains will be required at a minimum. This part of the country has a few small lakes dotted around, mostly frozen, and the surrounding countryside is heavy forest and undulating. There are a few tracks crisscrossing the area, but the main point of entry is the river, which is still flowing sluggishly at this time of year. Ear Falls has a single Mountie, who is relieved every two months, and if we need a local guide, I suggest we use that asset from the get-go. It's going to depend on the target. Are we ready to speak to the general?" the chief asked, looking at the commandant. She reached out and punched the daily code into the handset again.

"Got your map, excellent, and have you located the target?" he asked, looking through the satellite phone to try and see the body language of his troops. Being slightly old school, he still preferred to brief missions face to face, which, of course, was not possible under the circumstances. He needed this mission mounted long before he could get to the barracks physically, and with any luck, it would be over and done with quickly. "Okay, you work out the details. I'm now going to show you a series of images we can't send to you by any secure means we know of. My suggestion is that you photograph each image we show you, and then we can talk some more. Ready?" The chief pulled his own satellite phone out and set it on the table opposite the commandant's, lined the two screens up, then looked at the commandant.

"Yes, sir, ready." One by one, the critical images provided by Interpol clicked across the screens until the general's face replaced them.

"Okay, get those printed off, mount them on a mission briefing board, and call me back when you're ready, but don't be longer than five minutes. I want you on your way before last light tonight." The chief walked out to get the photos printed. The commandant scanned the map as closely as she could, trying to visualize the countryside from the contours.

She measured the distance from the pin position they had been given to where the river intersected the road. Twenty-six clicks. She looked up the weather report for that area and saw a temperature of minus twenty-six degrees Fahrenheit, wind chill minus eleven, overcast, snowing, and more forecast in the next twenty-four. About what she would expect for this time of the year. The chief returned with a peg board on which he had mounted the ten-by-eight color prints in the order they had been sent. He rested it on a trestle holding a large, framed photo of the barracks taken one hundred years ago. As he covered up the aging and yellowing black-and-white photo, he couldn't help but feel a premonition. Good or bad? He couldn't decide. The Commandant and the Chief Master Sergeant looked at the pictures, and as they scanned from one to the other, it felt as if the temperature in the room had dropped by several degrees.

"This must be the terrorist group that attacked the Alaskan pipeline as well as several fracking fields. Mercenaries, mixed race, around a dozen, but we'll test that. Light armor, snow vehicles, well equipped, posing as a hunting party but not so much by the looks of their equipment. Three canoes, motorized, and that looks like a mobile UAV control point. So, air, water, land capability, assume good coverage, and forward contact alarms of some sort, probably laser and/or motion sensors, maybe area coverage by microwave." The chief pointed to each photo in turn, then hovered over the low-angle oblique that showed more of the terrorist camp. "This is interesting; it looks like they have light squad weapons mounted on those snow bikes and scooters. Three-person rigs. So, four bikes equals twelve terrorists, at the least. Nice to know."

"Chief, select five of your best and brightest NCOs, back here in twenty minutes for a formal briefing, have them prepare their squads to leave in four hours from now. I'll brief transportation and support details at that time. Soft clothes, body armor, as the general requested, plus anything you believe will help us sell hunters on the move. You do the primary briefing; I'll do the wrap up."

"Sir, just one question—ground communication—this intelligence suggests they may have sophisticated electronic detection capability—could I suggest low-powered point to point and line of sight where appropriate?"

"Good call. Set it up." The chief turned on his heel, his mind working at a million miles an hour. The weather didn't worry him. His people were trained for the conditions. In fact, they lived and worked for twelve months of the year. Putting the enemy in their sights didn't worry him; they had some very good non-radiating optical systems, but he was giving hard consideration to the actual weapons—pistols and knives, not an issue, but automatic military style long guns would not readily pass for normal hunting equipment.

Except for their sniper rifles. He mulled that over all the way to the barracks. Then he had an idea, and a genuine smile broke out on his craggy face, a face that had seen frostbite and burning fire in the service of his country.

"Gentlemen, listen up. I want five squads to volunteer for a mission, and every squad is to have a top cover sniper and spotter, rocket man and loader, four shooters, and four spotters; within that, we need a medic or two, comms, trackers, crawlers, and count on being away for a week. Soft clothes, you are going in as hunters, body armor under, and cameras external on clothes and weapons. No radiating devices—phones, radios, toys, watches, swap them all out for mechanical. The NCOs whose squads volunteered, meet at my office in ten. Now, for those few of you who can count, the number of specialists exceeds the normal formation of a squad. But I want six to eight-person teams, so work it out! Questions?" He looked around at the one hundred-and-fifty-odd men and women who made up this elite unit, who had been lounging around on their day off and wondered how the volunteers would be selected and how bloody those that missed out would be. Or how many bruises the winners might have. He smiled inwardly; the terrorists didn't have a chance!

CHAPTER 75

The battle planning by the French, whose single objective was taking out Shetani and all his mercenaries, machine guns, specials, tanks, and anti-air weapons, lacked subtlety and had one distinct point of difference that was absolute. The incurring of collateral damage was simply not a factor because, in that most gallic of mannerisms, they assumed that anyone in the kill zone was the enemy or a friend of the enemy, or servicing the enemy, and therefore due the respect of a warrior's death. At least as the French described it.

Plus, they had all been instructed not to take any prisoners.

No less than three members of the general staff overlooked the battle plan, the order of battle, and the equipment list. It would be a Legion-led attack on the ground, followed up by Marines, with the Armée de l'Air et de l'Espace Française—the French Air and Space Force—setting the timing of the ground offensive with an air-to-ground attack by Rafael and Mirage jets, armed with SAR-113 missiles, each capable of taking out the biggest tank on the planet. A "see and forget" missile that was networked and talked to each other in flight to prevent two missiles from locking onto the same target, the smart weapon, was something every armored warrior feared. Typically fired in batches of twelve, and with four canisters loaded under the wings of ten aircraft, there were more than enough missiles to take out the entire terrorist fleet of specials and light armor twice over.

Just like the French preferred. They had learned from the Americans back in Desert Storm the effectiveness of "shock and awe." They liked shock and awe. In point of fact, they loved shock and awe!

A swarm of SA-30 helicopters would then disgorge troops at strategic locations, backed up by AS-555 helicopter gunships that would rake the ground out of habit with twenty-millimeter machine gun fire creating a clear path for the ground pounders. François Alban, the head of GIGN, who had been entrusted with masterminding the attack, was leaving nothing to chance. If the attack was not immediately successful, his headless, lifeless body would join those on the battlefield, a sad casualty of the intense fighting for the righteous sovereignty of Arabia—or so it would be reported. He did not intend to lend his head—or his body—to the cause; he fully intended to profit from the attack by regaining his stature within the walls of the French palace.

And then share in lording it over the rest of the cursed EU as the only reliable supplier of precious gas!

The three general officers argued over minor points, then, happy that each had made their mark for the history books yet to be written and had effectively set each other up to take the fall should things not go as planned, called their staff to attention over the planning board.

"*Messieurs, cetteattaquecommencera à zéro plus quarante-cinq, vousavezvo-sordres, vive la France*!"

CHAPTER 76

"Gentlemen and ladies, although no one in their right mind would call either of you ladies, pay attention. Make notes, take it all in, because we are relying on you converting this brief into squad-speak, and we move out in three hours, so there's not much time to bugger things up." The chief used his laser pointer to point to the briefing board he had set up next to the intelligence photos.

"The situation is as follows; a group of terrorists is located here, posing as hunters in a heavily fortified camp. You can see the squad weapons mounted on the snow skis, and in this photo, you can see the electronic trip barriers around the camp. They also have microwave air protection, so that means a generator somewhere. These images are hours old; we will get a new set just before departure, one for each team. These are hard-trained mercenaries, and they are the ones we believe who took out the Alaskan pipeline and our fracking fields between the pipeline terminal and their camp. It's just a few clicks to the other fracking fields to the east, and we would like to prevent them from getting there." He pointed to three blue circles on the map projection that filled a screen next to the briefing board.

"Our mission is to take these terrorists out, no collateral casualties, and to get as much intelligence material from them as possible. If they have samples of the nano bug, which has been identified as the means by which they killed our oil and gas infrastructure, we want them. Whatever communication devices they are using, we want them. This is the hard part—we need to eliminate them while preserving their intelligence. Now let's talk method." As he paused, one of the female NCOs raised her hand.

"Yes, Kalama?"

"Sir, from the satellite shot, the camp looks compressed. If we go for the snow skis, we could take out all their intel and personnel in the one hit."

"Yes, good call. And that is exactly what we are not going to do. Rumor has it that you and Tilly can crawl up to the arse of a guard in snow for hours at a time, unseen, and we will be counting on your ability to achieve that, so start thinking small, thin, invisible, and warm!" The NCOs laughed, breaking the tension, and everyone relaxed just a little, reassuring the chief that he had their undivided attention.

"Okay, here's what we plan to do. We will chopper into these points on the Cedar River and again here to the north, from a westerly approach. The choppers will release three teams at two click intervals and two boat teams on the river, one north, one south. We will be using line-of-sight battery-powered communications, so one of your squad will have to move into a relay position one click on either side of your advance and plant relays. You'll have to plant every kilometer all the way in.

"I want to have long-gun coverage from all eight angles by time mark plus ninety, MANPAD coverage by time mark plus one hundred, and Kalama and Tilly ready to crawl in from the west and the east starting at time mark plus one twenty. Questions?"

"Sir, what's to stop us from getting the shit blown out of us if it all goes south?" Tilly asked to hoot and call calls from the other NCOs. The chief smiled an evil smile and pointed to a small mark on the map almost inside the perimeter of the electronic defense system the terrorists were thought to be using.

"Well, Tilly, my love, if you keep your ugly shaved head down and don't go in further than this position, all the shrapnel from the MANPADS and sniper fire should go over your head and fine arse and won't that be lovely to watch up close?" Again, the room laughed, then slowly died away as the seriousness of the briefing took hold. The chief paused, letting the room get settled.

"I want at least one long gun covering the crawlers every millimeter of the way; this is the riskiest part of the mission, but the only way we can see is to get close enough to the camp to collect whatever is left after the attack. We don't know anything about backup support for them, if any, but we will take no chances. We will assume a force is available, but as they are not in any of the photos, we'll put them at mark plus zero, five plus ten. So, in, out, home. We want those nano bugs, we want their comms, and we don't want any of these fuckers to live long enough to cause us any further problems. One last point—hunting parties, don't normally carry automatic weapons—so tool up as appropriate. Now, any ideas on how we do this?" he asked, having set the stage for a healthy discussion. An NCO, black as the ace of spades, dreads proudly swinging all over his head, put his hand up.

"Chief, we can take out the snow skis with an LPD-12; that will kill their electrical circuits and fry the arses or anyone around for five meters. It'll also take out any generator. It's silent. You can't see it unless its foggy or snowing heavily, and the bang and sparkle of the batteries blowing up could be used as a signal for the attack," he said, to the muttering and "yes,"

"Good one, Alfredo,"

"Love that one" from various parts of the room. "And then the MANPADS can be used for MOP after the crawlers get in and out."

"The LPD-12 weighs in at eighty kilos; the battery pack at sixty-five kilos— which one of you apes will carry it five clicks in heavy snow?" the chief asked, having planned on the use of the personal laser destroyer from the outset. But it was a big, clunky, heavy son of a bitch, so he wanted the teams to provide the solution as to how they would get it to the target.

"Chief, we'll sled it in, three men towing, no issues; we've been practicing this for a month since Robbie broke her back in that exercise." The chief suddenly looked somber, remembering the day when one of his best NCOs had fallen under the load of the LPD-12 and fractured her back. She was recovering back in Montréal, but her chances of returning to the unit were slim to non-existent.

He was aware of the sledding technique that had been developed in the barracks based on what they did with their dogs and was very proud of his men and women for their ingenuity and their application, but he needed their total commitment to the sophisticated weapon. New weapons meant a change in strategy and tactics, and change was a soldier's worst enemy right after boredom. He did not want to lose anyone on this mission for any reason.

"What's the maximum effective range?" he asked, again knowing the answer but wanting everyone in the room to know it as well.

"Chief, we've taken the guts out of a tank at two klicks and a Humvee at three. These ski sleds should be toast at anywhere up to three klicks, given how small they are, even if they have some armor."

"All right then, here's our battle plan. Note where we will position the LPD-12, and again, I want long gun coverage over that team at all times. I want you to embed relay sticks along your inbound routes as if your lives depended on it, which they may. From the time you are wheels down to wheels up, I want you to think as if you are in enemy-held territory, behind their lines. And remember the canoes that these dudes will have somewhere; I don't want them escaping behind our backs."

"We can string one-meter cable mines across both ends of the river on the way in, once we're feet dry, maybe a click and half closer to their camp than our landing point?" The chief considered the suggestion. A one-meter mine sat under the water, linked to its cousins by an invisible wire, and would well and truly take out a canoe but not at its normal operating depth. The canoe would slide right over it unless it was set for proximity. Which they could do easily. He looked around the room, every face serious now, no doubt running the risks through and mentally working out each of their own and their teams' roles.

"Okay, start your collaboration planning; your support will only be the choppers, which will power down after drop off. They will have gunners and a two-person security detail, and you can use them for clean up if you fuck up that badly. They will wind their rotors back up at mark plus one-eighty, ready for your retrieval unless you signal otherwise. Pick your hide locations, and plan for two days at the most. I know I said seven days originally, but you can't get in and out in twenty-four hours, I'll send you all to the States for retraining with the Girl Scouts." The room erupted with laughter again, and the NCOs grouped themselves in a circle and started to plan out their coordinated but distributed attack.

One which would only have primitive communications at best, in severe weather conditions, which would limit both visibility and sight lines. The perfect cover for a covert approach.

And which would have an invisible clock counting down to the various "marks" with a fervor all of its own. But they had enough time to transition the five clicks to the target from any direction, and this is what they trained for, day after relentless day.

The chief sat down at his desk, liking what he saw and was hearing. In the modern age, you had to let your troops buy into the mission and personally own every little piece of it as well as the planning. The modern generation had proven time and time again that if they owned the plan and were motivated, nine times out of ten, they would succeed. The other ten percent could be made up by their exhaustive training and their ability to improvise under fire. He hoped. In 1880, Helmuth von Meltke, a renowned Prussian military commander, had penned "*Kriegs-gechichtliche Einzelschriften*," or "No plan survives contact with the enemy," which over the centuries had morphed into "No plan survives the first shot," and he was very mindful of this. What could go wrong would go wrong; it always did in the heat of battle and in the fog of war.

"Chief, one question," an NCO in the middle of the group asked.

"Go."

"What's the safe distance for the choppers to not be heard landing in the prevailing weather conditions?" He nodded, having expected this question at some point. His people were not only well trained, but they had also learned to think through every detail of an attack, which, when you went in with minimal communications and your force was as widely distributed as this one would be, was essential.

"Weather has the wind at ten to twenty knots from the northeast, so our flight plans will have you coming in from the southwest. Count on five clicks minimum, seven clicks maximum. My suggestion would be to have the MANPAD and LAP- 12 teams come up and down the middle, covered by long guns. The best angle on the encampment, as you can see from the photos."

"Solid, Chief. But we're thinking a MANPAD team from the rear as well."

He smiled, not an obvious strategy but very tight thinking. He looked at the satellite photos again, mentally ran through how he would plan the attack, replayed it over in his mind, then settled. It was up to his NCOs and their teams from this point in; all he could do was answer any questions and keep his fingers crossed.

He waited until he sensed that they had finished, then dialed the CO's number on his handset.

"Ready, sir."

She arrived in less than a minute, was dressed in snow camouflage, and looked like no mother any of the troops had seen or ever had. Tough was one word that came to mind, her chiseled face, square jaw, and broad shoulders gained from nearly two decades as a world-class gymnast; another might have been solid. At just under two meters, she presented a very inviting target but, happily, had never been shot in combat. Not that she hadn't really tried.

And it was ultimately her fighting spirit, courage, and leadership qualities that had won her the post of commandant of what was considered as the hardest post in the Canadian Forces. The room came to attention, every soldier bracing, which created a slightly ludicrous sight to any onlooker; given that, as it was a day off, everyone was dressed in just about anything you could imagine and a lot you couldn't.

"At ease." She scanned the faces of all her troops and liked what she saw; the grit and determination and, no surprise, pride reflected everywhere she looked. "You have been briefed on the mission at hand. The reason for the cameras is that the pointy heads are nervous about any civilian collateral damage. So am I, but let me be clear. Once you are in the zone that we have determined to be enemy territory, you are weapons-free, subject to your battle planning and your brief. If the s-h-one-t hits the fan, if your actions were righteous, and you had no options, the Chief and I will stand between you and the pointy heads." She looked around at the faces again, not for the first time realizing that the oldest might just be thirty, but more than likely only twenty-eight. The youngest is probably less than half her age. She sucked in a silent breath and squared her shoulders, hands interlocked behind her back.

"The target is believed to be one of the terrorist groups that have thrown the world into chaos and are either complicit in or directly responsible for hundreds of thousands of deaths and injuries. You will take them out. I do not need prisoners, but one or two would be nice. They don't need all their body parts, but breathing would be optimal. What I do need is their cache of nano bugs, their communications, and their battle plans, if they have any. This is what you are looking for." She paused as the chief held up a recently printed photo of a large two-person canister, mottled blue in color, about one and a half meters by one meter. "The bugs will be in sealed packages or containers inside this canister, which may be chilled or attached to a chilling device of some sort. I'm told that the bugs can't last very long if exposed to air, so take care. If you don't find one exactly like this, look for something similar. Don't be literal. These terrorists are mercenaries, and they think accordingly. Questions?"

The room held its breath, and the only sound that could be heard was the slight scratching of a chair on the floor as someone moved their feet. She nodded to the chief, who threw her a perfect salute; she returned it, turned on her heel, and walked out. The chief took one last look at his troops, then dismissed them.

From this point, it was up to their training, their instincts, their abilities, and perhaps their God.

Who knew the answer to that question?

CHAPTER 77

Shetani's tent was where the French spy said it would be. The tanks, specials, ground-to-air missile batteries where they were supposed to be, and the troops appeared to be camped out in ever-growing rings around the perimeter like an expanding ripple in a pond. But one thing the overflying mission control aircraft missed, orbiting as it was at twelve thousand meters, was how quiet it was on the ground compared to a normal day.

Yes, there were militia manning every weapons pit—and the anti-air defense system tracked the high-flying spy plane faithfully—but the normal ebb and flow of people on the ground were missing. The intelligence experts put it down to the iron-fisted control the terrorist leader had over his mercenaries, and they, in turn, had over the palace guard and the indentured soldiers that once served the Kingdom. After some ten minutes of scanning every sector of the electronic spectrum, calculating the wavelength and frequency of every ground-based radar and communications antenna, and looking for electronic traps, the airborne commander gave the all-clear.

The Armée de l'Air et de l'Espace Française led off the attack with Mirage and Rafael air-to-ground fighters laden with the SAR-113 missiles, which they fired off in salvoes from a safe five kilometers away from ground zero. In less than three minutes, everything visible above ground with wheels, tracks, armor, or heavy weapons was either burning on the desert floor or flying through the air in thousands of white hot pieces. The anti-radar missiles hit the antennas, taking out the entire command and control capacity of the terrorists in the one strike. By the time the jets roared over the attack site, there was nothing on the ground left to threaten them. A few of the surviving troops waved their fists in the air, and as soldiers who used Kalashnikovs or AK-47s all over the world tended to do, many fired their rifles at the jets thinking they could shoot one down.

This just drew the ire of the AS-555 helicopter gunships, who promptly sprayed the ground with twenty-millimeter cannon shells, at the rate of four hundred every minute, multiplied by ten gunships. The dust and sand blown up into the air by the explosive armor-piercing and anti-personal rounds screaming into the ground at supersonic speeds created its own storm, temporally obliterating the landing spots required for the SA-30 troop-laden helicopters, who were forced to hover in place waiting for the dust storm to clear. And as survivors would later comment, that was perhaps the turning point of the entire attack.

As if choreographed by the devil herself, man-portable anti-air missiles rose up from the dust storm in a perfect formation designed to kill every SA-30 helicopter—and by association, the twenty-six troopers contained within—which they did with spectacular precision. Within minutes, the burning hulks of the troop transports scattered across the battlefield created a funeral pyre that reached up into the heavens so far it could be seen three hundred kilometers away. Just ten point two kilometers overhead, the spy plane looked down in horror. The elite Foreign Legion and French marines had just lost over five hundred highly trained soldiers without ever getting sand between their toes!

Merde! Unheard of! How could it be possible?

The airborne commander rapidly brought the attack to a halt while the circling AS-555 gunships searched their instruments for the location of the MAN-PADS. Nothing registered. The dust was now joined at the hip with the foul-smelling stench and smoke from the burning helicopters and the bodies of the troops; visibility was, for all intents and purposes, zero, when from behind the slowly flying ring of attack helicopters, a massive purple-and-red bloom appeared, the airborne commander shouted out a warning, and as his frantic words registered on the pilots and gunners, a swarm of over two hundred cheap UAVs carrying high-energy impact explosives smashed into the rotor disks of the helicopters, putting the argument out of the reach of the French for some time to come.

Some of the helicopters managed to force land, saving their crews from an immediate death; most did not. And as a second and third wave of the UAVs swarmed in from seemingly everywhere and crashed into the surviving helicopters on the ground, the argument was soon moot.

France zero—Shetani Arabia.

François Alban, who had followed the attack on valve-powered shortwave radio, hung his head in despair.

His personal trainer and mistress sat at a small café on the banks of the Seine, celebrating her early retirement, her Swiss bank account now several million francs fatter. She tossed her hair, momentarily missing the close contact she had enjoyed with France's power base for so long, shrugged her shoulders, then sipped delicately at her espresso. She was sure another high-powered job would come along; it was just a question of trolling the halls of power and keeping one's eyes and ears open!

As she entertained this thought, she did not see the small Citroën swerve out of control, jump the pedestrian barrier, and as she finally turned to see what the strange grinding noise was, it struck her so forcefully she was thrown through the window of the café. The driver emerged from the wreck and, holding his hand to a bloody head, staggered off to be collected by a helmeted motorcycle rider around the corner.

Apparently, the large deposit made in her Swiss bank account had been an error, no doubt due to the technical difficulties all banks were suffering since the WWW attack, as it was reversed within one minute of the accident.

When the gendarmes arrived, witnesses could only relate a quick and inaccurate version of what they thought they had seen, and the vehicle turned out to have been stolen just hours before across the river.

CHAPTER 78

In the mid-nineteen eighties, in a rare show of collaboration, an elite Russian commando unit cross-trained with a similar unit of the Canadian Army and the American Special Forces. The purpose was to showcase all the techniques and learnings the three sides had collected over a hundred years of preparing and, in some cases, actually fighting in heavy snow-filled environments. While the Russians used tank-like nimble vehicles mounted on tracks, and the Americans used modern-looking snow scooters and bikes, the Canadians turned up with dog sleds.

Their thinking went like this—a dog consumed a kilo and a half of food daily, with around three liters of water. A trained soldier could easily carry thirty-five kilos and required only one MRE (meals ready to eat) and two liters of water a day. By sharing the load across multiple sleds, with three dogs pulling them, could each carry two hundred kilos, a small force of twelve soldiers could march across the worst snow-laden ground for over a month without the need for resupply.

And when resupply was needed, airdrops could be managed as easily as generating water from melted snow and flowing streams. Vehicles needed fuel, and fuel was both heavy and required its own infrastructure. Needless to say, neither the Russians nor the Americans necessarily learned anything from the exercise they didn't already expect to learn, while the Canadians learned a lot. Specifically, they noticed that the Russian ghillie suits that their troops used for camouflage for their snipers were mostly effective unless the shooter needed to move, which in high-density snow conditions, left a trail that could be seen from space.

They took this lesson home and, for some seven years, worked on the problem, eventually discovering that basic chemistry and physics, when applied to the opportunity, would provide them with an answer that was truly amazing. The ghillie suit worked on the principle of a mesh "suit" that fabric strips or natural brush could be fed into—and in the case of the snow version, white strips were used in place of a brush. What the Canadians discovered was that the heat from the human body wrapped up in a ghillie suit melted the snow the shooter crawled through and contributed to the trail they left behind them. No real surprise there.

They decided to experiment with a thin rubber wet suit with a cooling mechanism taken from the anti-gee flight suits of aviators. This sucked up the body heat and provided a small amount of power when the heat was converted into energy. Then they designed a material that sucked in light and, when laid over snow, became literally invisible. Then they experimented with moving and collecting snow from the crawling movement of a shooter, using arms and legs to crawl across the ground belly first.

The combined efforts of around sixty scientists and a few million Canadian dollars delivered a "slither suit," which, when worn correctly, provided a trailless ghillie suit that allowed a shooter to crawl for kilometers and leave no trail in the thickest of snow. The Canadians rightly keep this work to themselves, remembering the laughter and good-natured jokes made at their expense during the joint exercise. And they continued to use dog sleds and eschewed the more modern but technically demanding snow tractors and scooters.

This "old world" approach allowed the Canadians to initially get within three hundred meters of the terrorist camp on the Cedar River undetected, and as the clock ticked down to the various marks, the long guns providing both top and specific personnel cover were in place, the river mined at both ends some two kilometers from the camp, the MANPADS were safely located less than a kilometer from their targets, and the team with the LPD-12 was looking up the guts at the parked vehicles and snow tractors and scooters through old fashioned red-dot sights.

More importantly, the two "crawlers," using their innate skill and training, had both reached their marks on time, positioned on the east and west side of the camp less than one hundred meters from the first tent. Every team halted on their mark, waiting for the signal for them to engage. The chief had made it very clear as he saw them out to their helicopters that the American Girl Scouts were patiently waiting for anyone who f*** up, which was motivation in itself, but nowhere near as strong as the sense of pride and achievement felt by the teams as they flew off into combat. This is what they trained for, lusted after, and, in some cases, were born for. The LPD-12 fired its silent laser in a small fan-shaped force of highly excited atoms and molecules that burst every electrical connection, streaming up the wires and conduits to fry the batteries, motors, and electronic component parts at the speed of light. The LPD-12 was fired in a lull in the snowstorm, so there was no visible light train unless you were looking straight at it back up the firing axis, in which case your eyeballs would have been fried right alongside your brain, cardiovascular system, and the roots of your hair. However, while the opening attack was silent, the noise from the batteries and motors busting into superheated plasma and then spewing all over the camp was not, and while the terrorists reigned in their initial shock with a practiced calm, their camp started to seriously burn as the plasma ignited everything in its path.

As the camp came alive and people started to move, the silenced long guns, also using non-electronic red-dot sights, opened up and took out over two-thirds of the surviving terrorists before the first wild shot flew out of the camp in the super chilled air. The MANPADS, located both north and south of the camp, were held in reserve, waiting for the pull-back signal. A long gun fired one shot, effectively silencing the lone gunman who had managed to get the shot off earlier, and the two crawlers moved into the camp on their bellies, mindful of the shrapnel and supersonic bullets flying over their heads. Their mission was to retrieve the nano bugs and any intelligence they could find. But without knowing where anything was stored, they were crawling in blind.

Tilly raised her hand up high enough for her shooter, five hundred meters behind her, to see it. He promptly fired a silent shot that landed six centimeters away from her hand in reply, kicking up a little tornado of snow and ice. She shook her fist and counted down with her fingers, five, four, three, two, one, and she rose like a specter, her high-tech ghillie suit making her look like a small version of Bigfoot. She sprinted to the edge of the camp, diving for the ground as a volley of silent shots whizzed over her head like a swarm of angry wasps. With both hands locked around her close quarters combat pistol, she swept the area to her front, relying on her long-gun shooters to protect her flanks and her back.

Using only her legs, the shape of which would have impressed any Olympic weightlifter, she crawled to the edge of a tent that was slowly consuming itself by fire. She slithered under the edge, knowing she was moving out of sight of her high-powered guardian angles but risked it anyway. She wasn't here for the view. Against one side of the tent, a small table had collapsed, and on it had been a laptop computer, which had fallen onto a metallic box that looked remarkably like the picture they had been shown during the briefing. She pulled a sheet of white plastic out of her suit, put the two valuable items in the middle, then covered them with the tail of the sheet and hooked the entire package to the bottom of her suit.

She then turned around and, towing the computer, and the box behind her crawled out. She raised both fists, fingers clenched, then started a slow crawl out the way she had crawled in. In just a few minutes, three snowbanks erupted, and her shooters stood up in a crouch, ran to her as more fire flew over their heads, gathered up the booty, and ran back into the now falling snow. It took the better part of twenty minutes before they were back at their chopper, which looked like a huge blue-and-green monster bug sitting in the snow, rotors sagging down as if exhausted. The booty was loaded, and the three shooters were soon joined by others who had been positioned to the sides of Tilly's crawl and had contributed to the carnage that remained behind in the now defunct terrorist camp. The unmistakable sound of the MANPADS firing and then explosion rippled through the frozen air, signaling the end of the contact phase.

She finally stood up, hand on her hips, looking like nothing you could ever completely describe, creating a visual hole where her suit hid the falling snow. Her bald head created a strange full stop to the rise of the ghillie suit with its hood thrown back.

"Did we get it?" she asked, her voice hoarse from talking to herself for the last three hours, as two airmen started to help her out of the semirigid suit. The technician looked at the box, smiled, then pulled out a small foil-wrapped package. She wore fire gloves and an insulated padded suit. The small package seemed to radiate heat as it shimmered in the low light.

"I think so, but we won't know until we get back to the barracks." She repacked the small foil pack back into the box and closed the lid, snapping the pressure seal shut with a distinct "click." Suddenly there was a tremendous explosion somewhere on the river, and thick black smoke arched up into the snow-filled sky. "Guess someone tried to use a canoe," Tilly commented, climbing out of the suit and straight into a padded version of what looked like a giant sleeping bag.

Unlike the French attack, no terrorists were left alive, there was no counter-attack, and a second team that sled into the destroyed camp three hours later documented the bodies that were still recognizable, collected anything thought worth saving, and filmed the whole area, especially where the canoe had detonated the mines upriver. A demolition team defused the southern minefield, and within a day, the snow had covered the smoking wreckage except for one massive antenna, which stuck up in the sky like an abandoned arm. For no sensible purpose, one of the Marines had stuck a little red flicking hazard light on top, perhaps as a warning to the birds that still flew throughout the winter months up and down the river.

The chief didn't get to send anyone to the American Girl Guide Camp for retraining.

CHAPTER 79

Anna sat with the president, General Saunders, Julius Bronstein, Frank Reynolds, and a bland-dressed woman named "Jones." She wore her flaxen hair in a style that surrounded her pretty face like a mop, and her well-cut tailored suit was so innocuous as to almost be an insult to the eye. The one feature that stood out was the bright orange paint on her nails, matched by a lip gloss that defined very kissable lips. Anna's first thought had been "spook," which was kind of reinforced by the distance she kept from the others at the table. The atmosphere in the room was not overly hostile but not necessarily welcoming either. Anna was having difficulty reading the silent signals everyone she knew was sending with their body movements, so she did what she did best, took a deep breath, relaxed, and let it all play out.

"Jones, thank you for making this meeting on such short notice. We also appreciate you breaking cover at this time and assure you of our complete discretion. Would you care to share your information with us?" the president asked, sitting anything but relaxed at the head of the oval table. The woman looked up, ran her eyes over the assembled group, then slowly nodded.

"Madam President, my prime minister, has given his approval for this interaction, and the case I was carrying was confiscated by your security staff back at the gate. I gave them specific instructions on how to handle the case, which I hope will be followed to the letter."

"They will be." Short, sharp, and to the point, Julius Bronstein's comment cut through the air like a swinging blade. Anna looked at him, saw the tension in his shoulders, and wondered what might be in the case.

"It's to your advantage, Mister Director. I'm the messenger, nothing more, nothing less, and coming in at this time has cost me eighteen months of work, so I value this meeting, even if you don't." Julius looked calm, a little suave in his soft light blue suit, his starched white collar in stark contrast to the red blotches around his neck. Anna wondered how and where he had got them, then her attention was drawn back to the strange woman.

"A team of Canadian specialists used the information Interpol and your military had provided to successfully attack a terrorist camp on the Cedar River, just south of Ear Falls. Seventeen terrorists were accounted for, no Canadian casualties, and we recovered the nano bugs you briefed us on, along with intelligence on future targets in both Canada and the US. A sample of the bugs is in the case, along with a copy of the data we recovered from the camp."

"The data we shared with you came from the FBI, not the military, and Anna, whom you see here," Roger said, pointing to Anna sitting in the middle of the table, "brought the intelligence with her from Italy." Anna had a brief moment to ask herself why the director had identified her specifically to the spook, then while she was still mulling the question, the president spoke.

"Jones, we understand that at the moment, you don't trust our military. We accept that, but the FBI, in concert with Interpol, have been working on these terrorist attacks from the get-go, and their intelligence has been proven to be first class. Further, the FBI has in their custody one of the scientists who developed these nano bugs, which is why you had so much detail on them. Do you have anything else to report?"

"No, Madam President, everything is in the case." She sat back straight, shoulders squared, hands linked in front, like a schoolgirl being scolded for talking out of turn.

"Then, thank you, please pass our gratitude onto your prime minister." Frigid silence filled the room, then sensing that she had been dismissed, Jones stood up, turned her back on the president and the room, and stalked out a door that opened on her approach, then closed with a faint hiss.

"Don't know who put that stick up her arse, but that is the most disrespectful report I've ever received!" the president sat back, letting her anger flow out. The situation internally, with the chaos sweeping nearly every state, was difficult enough without having to take friendly fire at such close quarters.

"Madam President, her family was caught up in the civil insurrection in St. Paul, when American civilians took to the streets and shot up the state library.

"Some of our troops returned fire and killed numerous civilians in the process— civilians who had been out shopping, just going about their daily routine. She lost her mother and brother in the fray; her father is still in the emergency ward. She has a reason to be bitter but not perhaps to disrespect the office."

"Forget it. If she's the best the Canadians have to offer, I feel sorry for them.

What's in the case, Julius?"

"One of the nano bug bombs—their mission report says they captured six in total; as requested, the Canadian government has flown two samples to Italy for our Interpol friends; don't know what they plan to do with the rest. We have a bodycam log of the entire attack; it's being edited down to the salient points for your viewing. It should be here in ten minutes or so. We also have identification of the terrorists' future targets, two satellite phones, one portable ground satellite transceiver, and bank transfer data. The FBI is running everything to the ground, and we're providing our contacts where needed. The general here is setting traps at the noted locations as we speak."

"Why would terrorists on mission want banking data?" Anna asked.

"They were mercenaries, and I suggest they were paid by the attack. We don't know how many groups there were—or still are—but the record of this group shows nine attacks, from the Alaskan pipeline all the way across Alaska to their camp in Canada. Somewhere north, twenty-two million euros were transferred into a group of accounts, which we are tracking. However, with no payments in the last few days. I suggest that coincides with the red notice Interpol put on the Arabian bank. If this proves to be accurate, Interpol may well have shut the terrorists down simply by cutting off their funds. What happens next will be interesting."

"I gave Bridget data on seventeen terrorist groups in the US thought to be the ones who bombed the sports stadia; how have we progressed with that?" Anna asked, wanting to get back to a factual conversation rather than a speculative one. It was in her nature to push emotions and feelings aside on a case, the better to be able to examine the facts and determine what they might mean. The general looked to the president for permission and got a slight nod of approval in return.

"Anna, it turns out that the trucks were all purchased from the one dealership two years ago for cash, driven to a staging point in west Texas, were fitted out with their UAV dispensers over the course of the next year, then taken to an as yet unknown location where they were loaded with the UAV munitions. We have tracked them from a black hole located in Nevada to each location, and we now have satellite imaging of the attacks. Each truck was driven to a spot around five hundred meters from the attack point, the crew abandoned the vehicles, and they then went to their final fixes via remote or precomputed technology. Some of the trucks were parked for as long as two days before the attacks were launched."

"Why didn't the LEOs report them, or at least check them out?" Anna asked. "Every truck had the name of a major manufacturer or distributor on the sides, they were legally parked, and though many of them were reported, none were examined, as the local police didn't see any reason to. When they ran a cursory background check, the paperwork was all filed and correct. The arenas often had trucks lined up outside before an event, and no one thought to tie in the attacks in Europe and the UK until it was too late."

"We also had the small issue of the entire web going down and people rioting in the streets, so you can't blame the LEOs for not following up something that seemed, at least on the surface, to be a normal activity."

"Okay, I can see that, so you are saying two-person teams, with at least three major locations where the trucks were equipped for the attacks?"

"Yes, but the black hole prevents us from establishing where the munitions were loaded, so the number of support staff is not known."

"How did anyone think building weaponized UAV dispensers into the sides of pan-tech trucks was a normal activity?" Anna asked. Frank had the good grace to smile and shook his head.

"The paperwork was submitted to the Department of Transport in Texas, and the reason for the modifications was described as a pregame show for the NFL. The number of trucks wasn't questioned, as the NFL often does weird things to entertain the crowds, and after the shutdown of audiences during the pandemic, something as big as this was seen to be acceptable—not to mention that all the relevant documentation was sighted and approved by the NFL headquarters and provided to the workshops."

"Want to bet our favorite IT hackers rigged the whole thing in the background?" Anna asked. Then she thought for a minute, her eyes furrowed in her brow. "Wait a minute—our Israeli agent never mentioned these attacks or ever referred to anything like this. Give me a minute, please." She stood up and moved to the back of the room, snapped open her minicomputer, and dialed Jessica.

"Jessica, I'm with the president and her war cabinet; can you ask Amira a question, please?" Jessica's face was immediately replaced with Amira's. Not what she wanted, with the president, the head of the CIA, FBI, and military intelligence looking on, but she had the screen facing away from the table, so she leaned into the little screen and spoke as softly as she could. She listened intently to the answer, then snapped the screen shut with a loud click.

"Secrets, Anna?" Roger Wilson asked, not quite joking. He thought of her as one of, if not the best of his field agents and accepted that the demands of their roles often forced them to make strange bedfellows. He hoped this one would not come back to bite him on the backside.

"Yes—no—just protecting a source—who says, categorically, that none of the targets were ever discussed in her presence, and while she worked out what the nano and AI technology were used for in the attacks, she was only aware after the fact. In fact, it was the conversation with her handler where she was asked to join what was described as a private technology group to mount the prime attacks that caused her to refuse the offer and run."

"And this is important because?" asked the general sitting slightly forward in her seat. She suspected the FBI had more information than they were sharing but fundamentally trusted the director to tell them what they needed to know. She wasn't as sure about Interpol; they were a little blurry to her, seeming to sit on the one hand firmly in the legal/law side of the land and, on the other, some sort of pseudomilitary operation. Very hard to tell either side apart from each other from some of the reports she was reading lately.

"Because it solidifies a theory Interpol has developed, in that the planner/financier was working with the female terrorists at one end of the scale but only in the last five to six years; mercenaries, at the other end, no idea how long for, but the bank account might give us that data; and an as yet unknown third group or groups who have been active for the past twenty-plus years. The women did not know about the sports arena attacks. They did not participate in the original hacking back in two thousand, and they didn't steal the weaponry. Probably did steal the aircraft, UAV, and maybe the radioactive material. But we have a deeply hidden third group that's been inside our secrets for two decades, and you can't do that without leaving breadcrumbs."

"You're implying we have a major terrorist group, unknown or at least yet to be identified, working against us for two decades, and we don't know about it?" the general asked, incredulity lacing her words.

"Yes, I am. The Colonel running the Interpol team is in the process of identifying who they might be by rebuilding the connectivity between our major databases and crosschecking them against other countries. Interpol has already provided us with limited, secure communication ability. Don't ask me how. I don't speak geek. The NSA has provided resources in that area; you'll have to ask Frank about that. But what it looks like is that there has been a terrorist group working under our noses all the time and that these mercenary terrorists have been recruited into this pre-existing network only in the last few years."

"What's the difference between a mercenary terrorist and a jihadist?" the general asked. Anna paused, letting the question sink in. She made a split decision and turned to face her Boss.

"Sir, with your permission?" she asked, giving nothing away. Roger Wilson stared back at her, look for look, then, trusting his gut more than he usually did, slowly nodded.

"Madam President, if you'll forgive me, I need to make something clear; you may well be aware of it, and if so, please shut me down." The president had watched the silent exchange between the director of the FBI and his senior field agent, so now she was curious to see what all the fuss was about. She mimicked the director's facial expression and nodded her approval.

"There's a fundamental difference in the way the police and the military approach a problem, think about things, dissect evidence, decide on a strategy. The Interpol team I am working with is a hybrid unit of hardcore cops and investigators and hardcore special forcers trained military. They are 'refereed,' as it were, by a captain trained by the Navy Criminal Investigation Service with real-life battle experience. An example of what they do, they take advice from some of the most hardened intelligence professionals on the planet and feed it back to them as necessary—and, as you would know, work across international borders as part of their mandate. I have been with them as they have uncovered various elements of the terror attacks, and they were the first to recognize that the women were just a small part of the attacks; in fact, they identified Al Bar al Shirak as the terrorist group that the mercenary terrorists are embedded in. They also identified Al Hemish al-bin Mohammad Karesish, or Mohammad bin Azaria as we now know him, as the mastermind/financer using the Arabian Bank for funding. In summary, this was police work, intelligence work, and military precision at its finest. But the investigative side of the work was done physically, and that is what led us to most of what we now know."

"What's your point?" the president asked, having made a mental note to find out more about this Interpol group and how they worked.

"We need to approach this problem from a different angle. Having lost our technological edge to the terrorists has blinded us to what we were good at. Madam President, put boots on the ground, do old-style police work, knock on doors, and physically interview suspects and witnesses.

"Accept the fact that our modern technology is gone for the foreseeable future and go back to how we used to do it before the Internet. Who hacked us back in the Y2K event? There will be someone who remembers that and may give us a lead. We need people interviewing people, following leads, chasing down myths, and linking little bits and pieces together to create a picture we can do something with.

"We already know how the bombs were hijacked, from a process point of view. But who were the people involved? We know where the aircraft that was hijacked was flown to Turkey, but again, who was involved? Put boots on the ground and question anyone who worked there in the last ten years. There will be witnesses, maybe even someone who actually helped, deliberately or accidentally.

"Track the history of the F-4 that took out the space station; there had to be people involved in every step, every process. The F-4 is a very sophisticated but old-style technology, and to keep it in flying condition takes a huge, continuous, and expensive effort. That's why they were retired or used as target drones. Find out where the missile used came from-it was unique, can't be more than a handful on the entire planet.

"Madam President, in the last two decades, we have become reliant on electronic intelligence, superior real-time communications ability, and computer assistance in assessing and solving almost every problem we can imagine. We need to break that nexus and go 'old style' as fast as we can. And as to the question the general asked about the difference between a mercenary terrorist and a jihadist, think training, experience, skill, and a desire to stay alive to spend the money they are paid." The room was dead silent as everyone considered Anna's impassioned speech. Given that everyone in the room had only known high technology solutions all their working lives, had literally grown up in the lap of devices that answered any question you had, and allowed you to see your friends with the tap of a finger, they were not really sure what "old style" encompassed. The director of the FBI broke the uncomfortable silence.

"Anna, specifically, what do you suggest?" he asked, mirroring the question in everyone's mind.

"Put our oldest and most senior agents out into the field, start with the data on the Hog pilot, and physically run down her life year by year. Someone out there knows who she was and where she came from. Interpol is attempting to communicate with one of the other women who we believe might or might not be involved in the attacks but certainly was in the development of the nano bugs and software hacks. You have the details in brief, which I prepared for you earlier. We need to run these people down if we are to ever have any chance of identifying and arresting these women." The president put her hand up, preventing anyone from commenting or asking another question.

"You say Interpol has one of these women in custody who developed the high tech that they attacked us with?" she asked.

"Yes. An Israeli who is helping us untangle this mess—in point of fact, most of the gains we have made electronically with respect to communication between securitized locations and data mining are thanks to her."

"Is she considered a terrorist—or at the very least, is she a prisoner?" The president's face had taken on a hard edge, leaving no one at the table in doubt of her current feelings.

"Madam President, she is wearing a security bracelet and is under twenty-four-hour guard." Anna inwardly swallowed; while this was factually true, the reality on the ground was very different. Like herself, no one on the Interpol team thought of Amira as a terrorist but rather as a young woman who had been collected up and swept away by some very clever people who had then bent her skills and genius to their purpose, all the while posturing as environmentalists. The president took all this in, then hung her head in thought.

She looked up. "I will reserve my judgment on this for now; let's concentrate on the summary you promised me, Frank." He nodded and signaled to an aide standing near the door, who swept it open and disappeared into it all in one fluid motion. He was back in less than a minute, during which time no one spoke, lost in their own thoughts. Frank decided to choose his words carefully, mindful that the president had not yet recovered from the experience of the intelligence community offering up her lifelong friend, the secretary of state, as a potential terrorist.

CHAPTER 80

The Devil was pissed! In the hours since the failed French raid on his headquarters, he had ranted and raged around the burning wrecks of his tanks, specials, and antiaircraft guns and missiles, personally shooting every corpse he came across. At over two meters tall, his red-and-white-checked Shemagh Keltiyeh flowing out behind him, his massive frame became the ingrained memory his men would take to their graves as he vented his personal anger on the dead and dying. And when he came across the still burning wreck of a French AS-555 helicopter gunship, he literally went ballistic! Snatching a MANPAD from one of his acolytes, he fired the missile from less than ten meters, blowing what was left of the helicopter and its crew into kingdom come. The fact that the shrapnel took out some of his own men was irrelevant, as was the jiggered piece of metal that lodged in the burning sand at his feet. The mangy cat that had been trying to hide in the carnage let out a howl that would awaken the dead, waved one burnt paw at the massive specter that had invaded her space, then hissed, her mangled ears twitching like radar receptors.

His men and women, all hardened mercenaries, stood stock still, their bodies bent with the weight of equipment and guns, looking like a lost tribe from a bad "B" movie. They were all in awe of "Shetani," who had made personal fortunes with him but as yet had not collected a red cent, as he had been leading them into attack after attack so hard over the past months, none of them had the chance to spend any of their ill-gotten gains. But the killing was hot, and plenty, the after-parties long and well provided for, and they all had their choice of anyone they came across, man, boy, girl, or woman, and the condition they left them in was incidental to the amount of pleasure gained. In summary, the Devil was brutal to work with but rewarded his troops well. So, seeing him bend down to pick up a stray, smoking cat in the heat of the moment, scarred with the stains of a battle that had accounted for several hundred men and women now scattered in bits and pieces across the stinking desert floor, was a shock.

He stroked the mangy cat under the chin with one gloved finger, hugging the tangled furry body to his equipment vest, and whispered in one twitching ear. No one moved. The only sound that could be heard was the crackling and snapping of the multitude of fires created by the fragments half buried in the desert floor and the rumbling sound of the diesel engine of the huge truck Shetani used as his personal transport. Not one face registered surprise; not one face gave any indication that this show of emotion was anything but normal. Which, of course, was a testament to the iron hand with which Shetani dominated his fellow terrorists. His emotional intelligence would not even tick the very start of the scale!

"Man, we need to either make this stinking place work for us or go somewhere else, eh?" Shetani said to his offsider, a lanky mercenary with skin so white he almost shone in the sunlight. An albino from the deepest parts of Africa, he had won his position of number two to the Devil by hard work and killing off the competition, and never in a fair fight. His equals just seemed to disappear or turn up a mangled wreck eaten by birds or animals, making the determination of the cause of death impossible, even for the most talented forensic pathologist. Not that they were in plentiful supply where Shetani and his terrorists created their brand of carnage.

"We need to move on; the French might try to attack us again, and we only have one UAV truck left," the albino said, his Oxford-accented English creating a ringing sound as he spoke. For a double degree man, his work choices left a lot to be desired, but he had been picked up straight out of university by a recruiter for Al Bar al Shirak, mostly for his technical abilities, and with an offer of a million dollars down and one hundred thousand dollars a month, no other job offer could compare. Shetani gave him the gimlet eye, looking for any sign of weakness or obscuration, saw nothing to arouse his suspicions and slowly nodded.

"We trash the palace, man, take anything valuable, and then we get out of here. But I want all the guns we can carry in the trucks. Get it done." And Shetani walked off back into the smoke, still stroking the cat. The albino signaled to his team of mercenaries and moved towards the back of the palace, which had been savagely wrecked by the French attack. In a matter of minutes, shots could be heard, then sustained machine gun fire, then the explosion of hand grenades and flash bangs. Cries and screams floated across the smoke, and devastation was ignored, and once again, the old adage "guns don't kill people, people kill people" was proven correct.

But this attack was different from the others Shetani and his terrorists had mounted in the past weeks. This attack was faithfully recorded by a satellite camera, and the images were sent straight to the field headquarters, being used by Colonel Anthony and his team. The monks had struck again!

When I had been hung up on by Anna in faraway America, I got to thinking about the question she had been asked. Just as they had been blinded by the chaos created by the initial attacks, they had also just taken as read the penetration of the computer systems back in the Y2K days and been told that the backdoors the terrorists had used had been identified and closed. But they had no proof of that.

And they did not know who was responsible. I suspected that what was driving Anna's line of questioning was the desire to identify the terrorists involved in the early attacks—the web penetration, stealing the bombs, and, later, the purchase and outfitting of the L-100 Hercules and the other air assets.

We had all been very much absorbed in tracking down the major attacks from the get-go, walking the cat backwards, and had only gone down the rabbit hole of latent data when the analysis of the attack suggested a much earlier intervention by some terrorist group or vested interest.

I watched the remaining military staff reorganize the warehouse into a more comfortable environment. In this case, comfortable meant moving the boxes that had contained all the equipment into piles, repositioning the huffing espresso machine in one corner, and pushing the three worn couches someone had scrounged from a trash heap into a "U" shape with a good view of the screens running against one wall. The geeks were finishing off the tabulation of Amira's data for the last ten years, and the Boss was catching a catnap under a large equipment stacked table. One screen was dedicated to updates from Pete and Tom, another carried the data from the Canadian raid, and a third ran a summary of the French debacle in Arabia. And a fourth screen suddenly flashed to life, with perfect satellite images of the attack on the palace in Arabia.

"Boss, wake up!" I shouted, capturing everyone's attention. I rose and stood in front of the screen as the palace was razed to the ground. The Boss joined me, and we stared in horror as we saw fleeing men and women with children in their arms being mercilessly gunned down by the terrorists. As the picture captured faces, they were automatically isolated and put into a sidebar, where facial recognition compared them to every database accessible to Interpol. Which, thanks to the monks, was now literally everyone in every country.

"Get Arie on the line," the Boss said in a soft voice. I nodded, snapped my little laptop open, and dialed up the Israeli intelligence chief. His face swam into focus, and the Boss took the laptop from me none too gently. "Arie, I'm patching you into a live satellite stream," the Boss said, waving his hands wildly at the geeks. It took them a few seconds to interpret the Boss's semaphore, but they managed to get the transfer going before the Boss exploded.

"Arie, this is Shetani at work. The French attack, as you know, failed spectacularly; it looks like he might bug out, at least from the palace grounds. Do you know any of the faces?"

Arie was in Israel, standing in yet another battle-scarred smoke encrusted shell of what had been a small shopping and residential complex. The video from Interpol was disturbing but could not be his focus. He again reflected on the huge mental jumps they all had to accommodate to make any sense out of their current situation.

The chaos didn't only relate to the civilian population—the military was in just as much disarray under the calm exterior most displayed, and he sensed the added weight of absolute furious hatred for the terrorists in everyone he met.

And this passion may well be critical to Israel surviving the next few days, even weeks.

"Colonel, I'll run them through our facial recognition program. We have an agreement with the Imam who stood with me just days ago to hunt down any members of Al Bar al Shirak, and they have been partially successful in tracking the team that blew up the mall. This shopping center was destroyed by a rocket attack last evening, with the 'Enemies of the Black Hand' taking credit. The problem is, that the mercenaries are acting as the command core and then surrounding themselves with ordinary terrorists who are mostly in it for the religious fervor or the chance for payback, as they see it, and they are happy to hit out at anyone at any time.

"We are catching these miserable people, but so far, none of the Devil's mercenaries. If what you say about their banking system is true, then we may never see them in operation here again. And that would be a blessing." Aire wiped a sooty hand across his brow, leaving streaks across his thin face. Looking much older than his seventy-seven years, his somewhat frail and stopped posture was worrying in itself. The Boss wondered how they could add to his comfort, and not his pain, as he took in the furtive glances of the guards surrounding Arie.

"Arie, Shami is proving to be a first-class find, and working with Luigi and Amira here has almost given us back out technology to the point where we can now converse with you and most of our friends around the world in a tight, secure, and reliable manner. No one knows how we are doing it and, as far as I am concerned, never will." Arie straightened up, his worn face scrunching up in what passed as a smile, and he waved one hand as if brushing away flies.

"I suspect I know where this conversation is going. You want me to mount an attack somewhere."

"Yes. A couple of them, actually, if you have the time and the resources."

"Go on."

"Well, we think the leader of all this madness, the master planner, financier as it were, Al Hemish al-bin Mohammad Karesish—Mohammad bin Azaria—is in Libya, Baladiyat Ajdabiya to be precise. We would like to remove him from influence. So, we'll call that objective one."

"You haven't told me anything new," Arie said, folding his arms across his thin chest. The bulletproof vest made him look lop sided, his folded arms like a defiant schoolboy. The Boss read the body language perfectly, anticipating Arie's reaction. His country was under attack—rockets were whistling overhead of where Arie and his guards were currently standing. While the attacks were much lighter than just hours before, it was hard to imagine anyone in Israel would willingly change their focus to overseas actions of a speculative nature.

"Objective two is what you are viewing with us on relay from Arabia. We want to put a permanent stop to this Shetani, once and for all. He is obviously clever, well-equipped, and has excellent sources. There's no doubt he was tipped about the French attack. I can lend you a couple of advisers as legal observers for your attacks, but we need a separate nation-state to mount the campaigns and take credit for them. And one thing the French didn't have."

"And that is?"

"Well, thanks to the geek squad, you're looking at real-time data from the satellite, and we can continue to track him and his terrorist friends for you until you tell us to stop."

"I see. And when would this wonderous series of attacks take place, if it were at all possible for us to be able to spare the resources?" Arie asked, thinking as fast as his tired mind would allow him to. He could put two teams from Shayetet 104 Commando together and then pick three or four specialists from Unit 201 for each team. The Shayetet had been formed back in 1967 and had a long and proud history of punching above their weight in both the desert and urban areas of the Middle East.

"Who would your advisors be?" he asked.

"Pete and Tom are out and about at the minute, due back tomorrow. I can give you both of them, as well as a few of their team if that suits."

"What would their real purpose be?" Arie asked, curious because in his mind and from past experience, both Pete and Tom were heavy hitters, take-no-prisoners types of guys.

"They would be responsible for recording the actions, largely to provide proof that the terrorists have been dealt with at a satisfactory level, and they would represent Interpol." Arie thought it over for a moment; then, a question occurred to him.

"Are you any closer to finding the women who launched all these attacks on us in the first place?" he asked.

"No. We can now find and track the mercenaries; we are feeding that data to every country, as you well know. We have a bounty on their heads, and every country where they have operated is throwing everything they have at them. But women are securely hidden from us by both technology and time.

"We know where and when they attacked. We know how they attacked. We know what they attacked with, where it came from, and how they got it. But we can't trace them physically before or after any attack. I suggest that this will be a long, drawn-out effort, so I want to concentrate on the mercenaries for now and Al Hemish al-bin Mohammad KaresishMohammad bin Azaria—and get rid of all of them, once and for all, and return some balance to the world."

"Give me an hour, and I'll get back to you." And Arie closed his laptop, motioned to his guard, and moved back to his convoy. He needed forty of fifty really good soldiers, the best of the best, and he had to be prepared to lose them if things didn't turn out as planned. Well, he knew where to start, he thought to himself and smiled a smile that only he could see and feel. Perhaps, if Yahweh was good, he might have one last hurrah at the expense of a man who had created monsters out of harmless children.

CHAPTER 81

"Michele, is that you?" Amira asked, looking at the small image of her past lover with an intensity I found hard to ignore. Michele's face split with a wan smile as if she wasn't sure what her reaction should be. The background was smudged, no doubt an electronic trick to prevent us from establishing where she was. The call had been facilitated by the Israelis connected by the monks, and both parties were guaranteed privacy and no tracking. A French satellite was in the middle, acting as a high-tech switchboard. As agreed, I was watching from around three meters away and out of camera range. I could see the image on the laptop and hear both sides of the conversation, but for all intents and purposes, Amira was on her own.

"Hi Amira, how are you?"

"Fine. Confused, still a little hurt, but fine overall, I guess." Michele looked anything but guilty or sorrowful, but deep in her eyes sat something I would think about for some time. "Are you working with the terrorists?" Amira asked, almost in a sob. The code name she had been given to make this contact was "Michelob." so the chances of her lover still being on the terrorist's books were high.

"No. I quit the group not long after you did."

"Why?"

"Not my scene. Industrial espionage, yes, some slick digital work, absolutely, but not murder and mayhem. You can check with your current masters on that." Amira looked both happy and sad at the same time, a conflict or emotions flicking across her face in rapid progression.

"Were you there to steal my work then?" Amira asked, her shoulders almost collapsing to her sides.

"Yes. No. It's more complicated than that. The time we had together, that was ours, but I was working for someone else the whole time."

"Was it your country?"

"No. Other interests. And connected to Helen and her girls on the one hand, but for only one purpose at that time."

"You know about that?"

"Of course. I was one of them for a while. What I told you about my experiences in the camps was true—I was recruited just like you were. But I never had the luxury of working out who I was and what I stood for until I took off with all your work. Well, not all your work. A lot of it was mine and the others who worked with us.

"But on the plane on the way home, I started to ask myself why this environmental work was so important that someone would pay me to steal it.

"The trial we did up in Charlottetown proved the system, and I thought that would set us up for life. The speed it was shut down by the university took me by surprise, so when I got the offer to take off with the code, I did."

"How did Helen or her henchmen get the code then?" Amira asked, interested in spite of her personal feelings being in a tangle.

"While we were up running the trial, Helen was at the university copying all our work. I only found that out two years ago when I ran across the supervisor who ran our lab. He was living like there was no tomorrow, and he had no compunction telling me what he had done because he assumed I was still working with Helen. He wanted the credit for setting up the projects and the results and was pissed when he found out the university was going to clamp down on the results. He was paid over five million dollars for our work, or so he said, and he was living as if he had plenty of money on an island in Greece."

"So, you were paid to steal the code from the university, so what did you do with it?"

"I delivered it to the buyer, then, like you, went to ground. But I got itchy fingers after a while, so I set up a digital business, and I guess that's how you eventually found me. After all, before they crashed the net, you could literally work from anywhere, sell anywhere, and get paid any currency you liked in any bank you choose. Or cryptocurrency or cash, that worked as well."

"How many of the developers we worked with were on Helen's team?"

"Don't really know, but at least two others; while she put me into your team to keep an eye on you, I know she had someone there watching me as well." It was hard for me to keep my silence as I listened to all this play out, but I was getting a better picture of the process that had been used to develop the high-technology weapons that had been turned against us with such devasting effects.

"How did all these different vested interests learn of our work?" Amira asked, knowing the answer but wanting confirmation that what she had been doing was, at least from her viewpoint, legitimate research. Michele smiled, obviously relaxed by the question, and shook her head.

"Babe, we published over three hundred papers on the way through. Remember? I was already working on the code before I met you, and while the Chinese are a little more tight-lipped than the Israelis or the Americans, we published. And if you remember the seminar we both attended just before the test, we alluded to a result with the carbon three compound, and we even had a small sample on display. It was no real secret, or at least it didn't become one until after the test when everything disappeared."

"Did you do any more work on the code after?" Amira asked, shaking her head at her naivety. But deep down, she was happy because what she was hearing from someone she had once trusted and loved was that the work had been for a legitimate purpose and had only been corrupted after they had essentially finished and proved the code. Then she screwed up her face as if thinking about an unpleasant thought. "Wait a minute. Leaving aside the code for the carbon three compound for a minute, what about the code for creating the blackouts in the web? Did you do any of that?" Michele looked a little guilty, then tried to smile, failed, then set her face in a fixed neutral expression.

"Again, yes and no. If you remember, we had the very best of intentions when we developed that, and after I had been paid and scarped into my bolt hole, I was contacted by an anonymous client and asked if I could configure something for them on contract. I agreed, and the code they sent me to modify was a version of what we had created. It had already been reshaped. They were asking for a specific result, and frankly, at the time, I couldn't see any harm in it. Little did I know. But you should be aware they offered the contract to others as well and had several coders working on the problem at the same time. We were all sent updated modules to either work with or improve on."

"When was this?"

"About six months, after I settled into my new surroundings and went pirate.

"That would be, what nearly three and a half years ago now."

"Did you finish the work?" Michele smiled again, this time succeeding, and she looked for the first time both relaxed and happy.

"Yes, I did. Do you want a copy?" she asked, her brow furrowing. Amira turned toward me, raising her eyebrows. I silently nodded.

"Yes, please. And can we speak again sometime soon, maybe about other things?" Amira asked, almost wistfully. Again, I was reminded that she was just a young girl in a woman's body, with very limited life experience so far, although I had a faint suspicion she was catching up quite quickly. Michele seemed to think for a moment, then deepened her smile.

"Yes. That would be nice. Use the same codes and system as you did this time; how about in three weeks' time?" Amira nodded, waited for the transfer of the data file to complete, then cut the connection; her shoulders slumped again.

"I hope that helped," she said, her voice so flat it wouldn't raise a ripple on an ironing board. And she really looked young, her face all soft lines, her hair falling down over her ears. I felt sorry for her but had to maintain my position as both her guardian and her jailer.

"Yes, it did, thank you. I know that was hard for you, but we now have a much clearer understanding of the developmental timeline. Do you think we can reverse engineer the code? And will it help, given that we have already untangled so much from your earlier work with the geeks?" She looked a little lost for a moment, then pulled herself together.

"I won't know until I look at the code. What we have working for us now gives us back real-time accessibility to data from multiple sources. The only areas that are not resolved concern the movement of the female terrorists in and out of the attack areas and anything to do with the attacks themselves. Perhaps Michele's code will help us with that. I'll let you know as soon as Luigi and Shami play with it." I nodded, took her softly by the arm, and started to walk back into the main area that had been set up for us. Amira took the laptop and walked towards her geek partners, and I stood still for a minute and reflected on how we adults always screwed it up for the younger members of our communities by simply ignoring the differences in our standards and morals and theirs.

What seemed okay after facing down fire and brimstone as an adult made you immune and insensitive to many of the softer edges of life, like relationships and perhaps even love. Maybe that was why the Boss and I had such a tremulous relationship. I wanted something he wasn't even aware of and probably couldn't give me even if he did.

CHAPTER 82

The flyover went better than expected. Shetani's camp, now located some three hundred kilometers northeast from the burnt-out palace, was spread out over a kilometer and a half front, three roughly concentric circles, with some five hundred meters between each defended line. His heavy weapons were all in the center ring, with impressive anti-air and drone support, and to the surprise of no one, eighty percent of his troops were stationed in the classical old-style cavalry formation with foot sloggers in the front to be offered up as cannon fodder and the mobile infantry in the rear, to protect Shetani's headquarters. It was obvious he had stopped for a purpose, although from forty thousand feet up, even with the best camera lens, that purpose was not obvious.

It would take either a battalion of hardened troops supported with armor and air support to move him or perhaps a direct attack by ship-borne cruise missiles, with air support, to clean up. Either way, to the twenty-three Shayete 104 commandos and Black Pete well hidden in the desert floor, some five kilometers away, they were having some difficulty seeing exactly how they could attack the camp and survive. As they rested in their camouflaged body bags, which kept their body temperature at a consistent twenty-two degrees Celsius and covered by at least half a meter of sand, the team listened in to the command channel, watching their small personal videos strapped to their wrists. The images were in high resolution and clearly showed the layered protection Shetani had made his own. You could even tell the make of the truck he used as his mobile headquarters.

“ינודא, ואכרמחוהאוהשבשוחהתאהמל?” the intelligence officer asked the Sgen Aluf (lieutenant Colonel) in charge of the operation. Black Pete, having worked with the Israelis many times before, understood the query. He, too, wondered why Shetani had stopped where he had. In the back of his mind, he pictured the old Silk Road caravan route and realized that they were just two kilometers from a major junction on that fabled old road. And if Shetani was no longer getting funds, as Pete suspected, this could well be as simple as an issue of geography.

Where to next for a band of mercenaries whose only loyalty was to their pay-master? But what Pete deduced from the layout of Shetani's troops was the obvious disregard he had for the locals he had either recruited or press-ganged into his rag-tag army.

High overhead, the navy command and control aircraft, an ancient Boeing 707 AWACS (Airborne Warning and Control System) that had been converted three times in its long life—first as a passenger jet that changed the world, then into an aerial refueler, which extended the range attack aircraft could successfully mount their campaigns and rain death down from above, and, lastly, this iteration, a computer-filled intelligence and early warning airborne system that squashed twenty-five brave souls into the space left over from the sweating machinery and overheated electronics. Comfort was not its strong point, but it was extremely effective at collecting electronic intelligence from long range. And when Shetani dialed up his banker on his satellite phone, the call was easily intercepted and recorded.

“يفرصملاانباسحنويناطيشلادمجدقل” “؟يلامنيأ” *niemeeraanvalle.*” *geld geen*
up, fucked net is dit man, “Well, “بقاوعكانهنوكتسوأ ،كلتعفدامدقتفوس”

“*Die transaksie was toe ons die Paleisgeneem het, sou onsbetaal word vi- relkebykomendewerk.*”

“طظخموهامكرارمتساللةيفاكنمرثكأعفدمتدقل”.

“*Nee*, man. *Jy betaalonsnou, of onsgaan op onseie pad.*”

ا ن م ع د ن و د ب ة ا ي ق ى ل ع ء ا ق ب ل ا ك ن ك م ي ا ل ”.
“دهلاناطيشلااهيأةظحليفكطقسُأنأيننكمي”.

“*So wees dit.*”

،كنيديرغلككنعلأ ،كدسجنعاديعبكترشبفحزتو ،ميحجلايفكماظعنفعتت“
”!ةرفاكلاةنيعللااهيأةيدبأةاناعمبمكيلعمكحأو

The crew in the ancient AWACS 707 looked expectantly at the technician manning the screen who had recorded the call, wondering what had been said.

"Well, to sum up, the bank is closed, no more money for Shetani and his boys, and the banker has cursed him and all his men to a really ugly death."

On the ground, Pete looked at his miniature screen and watched the words scroll across, almost with a sense of anticipation. If this spat between the master planner and his mercenary terrorists meant that the attacks would stop, that could only be good news. Unless the terrorists decided on another course of action even more disruptive than what they had been up to so far, although Pete was pressed to imagine anything worse than the carnage left behind at the destroyed Palace. He passed the message onto the team commander and thought for a minute. They could take advantage of this. He just had to work out how.

In the camp, Shetani called his cadre of hard-bodied subordinates in and, passing around bottles of whisky, got down to the reason for the meeting. It didn't take long; the core group had been fighting together for over three years, and they intuitively understood what Shetani was going to do.

Within minutes, a rough plan had been worked out, and messengers sent out to the middle and outer defense rings. In less than ten minutes, over a thousand troops, who had only joined the mercenaries because death was the only other option, were on the move again, this time back the way they had just come, with instructions to retake the palace with as much force as they could muster. The promise was enticing—what they took, they could keep. Who they took, they could do with whatever they wished. Plus, the promise of fifty thousand riyals each sealed the deal.

Just under the desert floor, the Israeli commandoes watched all this movement relayed from the eye in the sky, fascinated with what they were seeing. Now they only needed half a brigade or maybe just a half-dozen cruise missiles to take out Shetani; what could be easier? The commander realized what was happening and started to plan his attack. They were currently positioned three kilometers away from the northernmost outer ring, which was now moving away rapidly in specials and personal carriers, streaming through the desert and leaving a wake of sand and diesel smoke. From overhead, they looked like a funnel collapsing in on itself and, within another ten minutes, had passed the main encampment, collected the troops in the middle ring, and headed due south.

The commander estimated where they would be in half an hour, dialed in the coordinates, and made his request. The rest of the attack would now depend on what Shetani did. If he stayed where he was for even an hour or so, that would give him the time he needed to coordinate a strike. If Shetani went on the move, he would have to wait until his direction and speed were established and work out an attack plan from there.

He had three things at his disposal—his unit had four high-frequency laser disruptors, each capable of taking out tanks and heavy armor. Working on the principle of literally cooking anything electrical or electronic, the weapon was also devastating to troops on the ground because anything they had on them that radiated energy cooked off and exploded more violently than a hand grenade. But being a portable weapon, the power supply was small, weighing in at forty kilos. Good enough for five ten-second sustained shots over three to four kilometers, or just one continuous shot lasting at least a full minute. He had the four disruptors at the four points of the compass but still at the three-kilometer mark. They had to close in a little to achieve maximum effectiveness.

The second thing he had was a fleet of cruise missiles that required a twenty-one-minute timeline and a predicted target location of five hundred meters. He had twenty missiles at his disposal, ten loaded with area denial munitions similar to the ones that had been used against the Americans at West Point, and ten with high explosives.

And then he had a fleet of F-22 fighter bombers, which had already taken off from their bases in Israel and were currently tanking just outside the border of Arabia. They were armed with air-to-ground munitions, anti-radar missiles, and fuel-air bombs and were only seven minutes away once called.

He viewed his commandos as the ace in the hole and would hold them back for the inevitable mop-up and intelligence gathering that traditionally followed such attacks. And as they were all currently watching the streaming video from the AWACS, he knew they were all up to date and their situational awareness high. He typed a message to Pete hidden on the desert floor about two kilometers away.

"r u ok to collect intel in 25?"

"y"

"any suggs on tactics?"

"n. u got it."

"ok. Stb." The commander switched his wrist comm unit to include the whole commando unit.

"team mis in 22. f22 1 after. Hflds 25, move on f22. clear?"

"clear" came back to him twenty-four times; he sighed, shook his shoulders, pulled his visor down, and tucked his head into his shoulders, opening and closing his mouth like a guppy shark. When the blast effect from the bombers and the cruise missiles rolled his way, he wanted his ears to be equalized and his lungs empty, the better to survive the high, devastating pressure waves. He pressed the signal to the AWACS, which set the clock for the attack, and thought of his family, safely back home in the Kibbutz, probably making supper by now, only knowing that their father, husband, a friend was "away" on deployment somewhere, due home later in the month, maybe.

He kept the image of his family firmly in his mind for the next half an hour as the blood and guts accumulated, and the sky turned red, yellow, and black, burning hotter than the halls of Hell, and as the molten sand and ash settled back towards the desert floor, he wondered why he ever had any expectation of making it back.

CHAPTER 83

It was coming together. Slowly, from a lot of very intense reports, a picture was evolving about the build-up and now the destruction of one of the most horrible and lethal terrorist organizations that had evolved in the last thirty years. Unlike their predecessors, the core were mercenaries, and not religious fanatics, recruited predominantly from the African continent and South American drug cartels. Al Bar al Shirak, under the brilliant leadership of the overly tall Afrikaans mercenary who called himself "Shetani"—the Devil—had taken over less than three years ago, funded seemingly by someone with bottomless pockets. Perhaps formed was the wrong word. Prior to the Devil joining the ranks with his unlimited funds, the terror organization had been led by two well-known masters-a Bedouin by the name of Malik Badawi and a rabid narcissist by the name of Amir Abbas. What had given the Devil all his power was the sheer volume of the funding he brought with him via a mystery benefactor.

We now knew that to be Al Hemish al-bin Mohammad Karesish, or Mohammad bin Azaria as he was now known, using the Pan Arabian Sovereign Wealth Fund as his source. Literally, billions of euros and USD had been siphoned off from the bank over the past twenty years to support the biggest and best-planned series of attacks on the free world in history. The irony of the bank having been funded by profits from oil and gas mining and distribution was not lost on us, as the world literally struggled to survive with over eighty percent of the oil and gas supply currently denied by the terrorist attacks. The intelligence picture that was forming had a lot of wrinkles, as the data was fragmentary and collected from multiple sources after brutal retaliation attacks, which tended to leave very little evidence behind in their wakes other than the wrecked and scattered body parts of the mercenaries.

But the data collected by the monks and geeks that Pete, Tom, and Anna had shared with multiple countries on the location and makeup of the distributed mercenary terrorist cells had been used to good effect. As of today, we estimated that only ten percent of Shetani's mercenary force still remained alive, and that number was reduced by the hour. Interpol had received over three hundred claims for the bounty we had offered, and we had a team back at Interpol HQ dedicated to auditing the claims on a full-time basis. The recent data collected by Pete and the Canadians was the most significant, and we were using it to build a solid case. We had electronic payment trails, lists of the names of people around the world who would willingly sell their countries' secrets for a few dollars, and surprisingly, Pete had brought back a hardened military laptop on which were stored all the communications between the banker and the Devil for the past three years, and from this, we were able to construct both a timeline and a resource map.

We had armed patrols on every fracking site in the known universe. We had the FBI and its in-country equivalents picking up every identified supporter, supplier, and playmate the mercenaries had been using, so over three thousand souls were either heading for or were already secured behind bars in over sixty countries. Those had been the lucky ones, as some of the lesser-developed countries had used the "shoot first and don't ask questions" method of policing and, consequently, were claiming the bounty on the heads that they had unceremoniously blown apart. Many of the photos sent in as proof were literally unrecognizable, but the Boss, on the basis of keeping faith with strange bedfellows and keeping the momentum going in tracking the mercenaries and their friends, had approved the bounties to be paid. In our hearts, we knew that this would come back to us and bite us in the ass down the road, but we had no choice. We had to help get the world back on its feet as quickly as possible—and that was as much going to rely on confidence as any other requisite disaster relief process on a global scale might require.

We also had the names of the weapons dealers who had provisioned Shetani and his mercenaries, which gave us a look into how the nano weapons had been developed and moved around the world. Surprisingly, all the nano bombs had been delivered in three batches, over twelve months, by the same female team—a pilot and a scientist—who had also instructed the mercenaries on how to most efficiently use the nano weapons. They had even produced a video on the subject, in twenty languages! The packages were dropped off around the world to staging points nominated by Shetani and stored until they had been required for use. The timing suggested that Amira's initial work had taken some three extra years to modify and then manufacture commercial quantities. I made a note to follow up on that point; where and who had the manufacturing capacity to produce that volume of nano weapons in such little time? And keep it a secret? And how did you store something that required an exact temperature range for such a long period of time? There was also the question of the manufacturing of the artificial intelligent boxes that had so successfully driven the aircraft and vehicles, and the programming of them.

"Well, what do you think our next steps should be?" the Boss asked from his small desk, which was a fruit box turned on end. He had a pile of printouts just like I did, and his laptop was busy sharing data with the Americans. Mine was doing likewise, but with Arie's people. This gave us at least another four or five pairs of eyes and shared the responsibility for developing what might happen next. Keeping our sponsors in the loop was vital because Interpol would take no further part of the terrorist hunt other than for providing the intelligence that brought them down.

"We have enough evidence to charge Mohammad bin Azaria with war crimes, terrorism, and a myriad of other cross-border crimes. I suggest we publish that and issue a formal warrant for his arrest; also, get a Red notice out on him pronto. We need the Libyan government's permission to pursue this formally, which I suggest we also do, maybe using Indigo and his boys and girls; we know he was in the Baladiyat Ajdabiya area two days ago. We could apply for overflying permission, but I suggest we rely on satellite intelligence rather than tip him off we're on the way."

"I agree with everything you've said except who should go and round up the banker." I looked at the Boss, his dark and slightly sunken eyes reflecting the tension and tiredness we all were starting to feel. I shrugged my shoulders, wondering what he had in mind. Libya was not a friend of Interpol, and while they were members and one of the countries that paid our way, they constantly played at the edges, always making it hard for us as possible to operate there.

Unless it suited their purpose.

"I think we should wait until Pete and Tom get back, rest up a day, then take our team on a little excursion." I thought about that, nodded in agreement, and smiled. The sparkle in his tired eyes told me that just the thought of getting his hands-on Mohammad bin Azaria was lightening the load on his shoulders. And we hadn't really had any fun in the last few weeks!

"You won't get out of here without Indigo, you know that?" I asked, stating the obvious. The tough little Italian head of Interpol Italy had virtually adopted us since we had arrived, and even now, as we planned a small part of what we hoped would be the end game, he buzzed around handing out cups of espresso and sandwiches.

"Yes, I know. Tom and his team, maybe minus one or two shooters to look after the warehouse while we're gone, Pete, you and I, and Indigo. Start planning the op, work out the paperwork we will need, apply for the various permissions, etc. and work out transport. Fast jet to as close as we can get, a helicopter from there; ask Arie is he wants in." I thought about that; Libya and Israel were not the best of friends, but I figured that if we had a warrant issued by the Hague, an Interpol Red notice, and a polite request from all our member countries, Libya could hardly say no. And I knew Arie had a few very large C-17 jet cargo aircraft that could easily carry a chopper in its guts, plus a few grunts, so logistically, it all made sense.

But I would have to manage the timing so that we were on site, ready to act before the Libyan government was involved because without a doubt, they knew about the banker and would inevitably tip him off we were on the way.

But first, the thing I hated the most and the thing I had spent more time on since joining Interpol than anything else—the paperwork! At least we now had electronic preformatted layouts, so I fired up my little laptop and started the grind. I must have muttered something under my breath because the Boss turned and looked at me critically, his eyebrows raised in query. I shrugged my shoulders and ignored him, putting all my concentration into interpreting the legal double-speak we needed to invoke to legally tie up our terrorist mastermind and banker once and for all.

Arie responded first; he was more than happy to lend us an aircraft and a helicopter and a few "young people," as he described them, no doubt recently close friends of Pete. He proposed setting the big C-17 down on Cofra-Jalu-Ajdabiya, a semi-sealed highway, at Latitude 29.993552, Longitude 21.545221, giving us a twenty-kilometer or so chopper ride into the terrorist camp. I worried about visibility and noise, and Arie quickly told me the prevailing winds at this time of the year were from the southwest, and the likelihood of a sandstorm was eighty-nine percent. So, I told him to keep Pete and introduce him to the "young people" and added an equipment list for the three of us.

Arie laughed, shook his head, and hung up. I went back to chasing my paperwork and was pleased to see that the Red notice from Lyons and the warrant from the international court at the Hague were stamped and issued and dispatched to all 194 member countries. The legal ball was on the move.

"Amira, can you please give me a minute?" I asked, and she turned towards me, shook her head in assent, spoke quickly to Luigi, then walked over to where the Boss had his upturned fruit box. She looked at me with curiosity in her eyes and somehow looked a little more in control of herself. I mused that it might have been the chat she had with her former lover, the Chinese woman calling herself "Michele." And the chances of that actually being her real name were zero to none. "Amira, I need you to consider these questions, please. Your answers will stay between the Boss and I; no one else on the team is to be involved at this point. Is that okay with you?" I watched carefully for any micro tells around her eyes and mouth, didn't see any, looked to the Boss for permission to carry on, and got his casual nod. "First, from the data you have recovered, do you think you could reverse the nano bug's effect on the gas lines?"

She seemed to think for a minute, looked at the Boss, then back at me, curiosity in her eyes.

"Yes, we think so, but I'll need a high-standard lab to work in and some assistance." Obviously, she had talked it over with her geek buddies, something I hadn't considered. When you worked in the intelligence field, you often stayed in a compartmentalized information bubble, as it were, and expected that everyone else around you was doing the same thing.

"We can provide that, either at Harvey Mudd or back in Israel. Extra question, sorry, but how long do you think that would take you, assuming a fully facilitated lab and trained staff?" Amira looked back over to Luigi and Shami at the computer wall, shrugged her shoulders, then turned back to us.

"Less than a year, maybe six to eight months; we can test as we go, so that should speed it up." I nodded both my assent and agreement to her statement, absolutely sure that either the Americans or the Israelis would move heaven and Earth to fast-track the recovery of the gas supply, if only in their own self-interest.

"Okay, could you do the same for the oil pipelines?" Again, she looked over at the geeks, beavering away on their consoles.

"I think so. The oil nano bug was the first one we created and tested, but the code has been so corrupted by the modifications that were made to our work that it will take some time to untangle the code and sort it out. Originally, we designed the bug to 'eat' the oil sludge from a spill and turn it into earth-compatible compounds, like carbon three. That version also dissolved in the air, making it very safe to work with, as when it was applied, there would be no toxic residue. So, the answer is yes, but much longer than the gas nano. And we would need samples of the residue at the well heads to test before we could make any determination." I looked at the Boss, saw he was, as usual, anticipating my thinking, and smiled.

"Okay, last question, could anyone either reverse engineer the nano bugs that have been recovered or use them to develop a solution from?" Amira looked critically at me, and I could see she was processing the question like she would solve a scientific puzzle. She went very still, almost to the point of not breathing. Then one hand swept up and brushed her hair away from her face; she grimaced, making a face like a small child denied candy, then smiled. And nodded. Then shook her head so fast her hair flew around her face.

"Yes and no. Michele and I could do it, given the proper facilities, but no one else that worked with us really understood what we were doing at the literal molecular, atomic level. But someone from that team would probably try and, given enough material to work with, would eventually succeed. But the number of nano bugs recovered so far would be too small a sample, plus the fact that they are stored in pressurized containers, designed to transmit into a fluid bed at pressure. Getting them open and maintaining the integrity of the contents will take skilled hands and patience, something we found was lacking back when we were developing the bugs in the first place." I nodded acceptance of what she was saying; both the Canadians and the Americans had made the same comment in the brief we had received from them after the successful Canadian attack on the terrorist camp on the Cedar River. They had both lost samples just trying to open the sealed containers.

"Thanks, Amira. We appreciate your help." I smiled a big smile and watched her go back to her geek friends.

"What's your agenda in all of this?" the Boss asked, pulling his metal chair around to face me. The screech the metal legs made on the concrete floor turned every head in our direction. "I know you; we had figured out most of what Amira said before you called her over."

"I wanted to know her feelings on the subject, get an idea of what we are really up against. We still have her under guard, wearing an electronic bracelet, but she is working very hard to help us solve this." The Boss nodded, settled into his small chair, and pushed his hands deeper into his jacket pockets.

"Okay, I get that, but what's your real agenda? I've never known you to waste an interview, and that's what that was, so give. Pretty please." I looked over at the geeks hard at work and Indigo on the phone with his troops around the country, and the remaining special forces troop sleeping untidily all over the place, holding their guns like babies cuddling a teddy bear. The Boss knew me as I knew him, so I knew I wouldn't get into any trouble for what I was about to say. Maybe a verbal dressing down, but not much more.

"I don't want to solve the oil nano bug. Gas, yes, that's both sustainable long-term and more environmentally friendly than coal or oil. But not the oil." The Boss looked very hard at me from under hooded eyelashes, giving absolutely nothing away.

"Why?"

"No oil in the Middle East, maybe they will turn to grow vegetables or something, and we won't have to keep on pretending to free this country or that from dictators whose egos are swollen with the profits from selling their countries' resources. And fracking is possibly the most environmentally destructive process right next to burning out forests or polluting the oceans. I'm not a tree hugger, but it seems to me that we are in a unique position to help the whole world solve a few very big environmental issues, and just maybe, we should use it." He looked at me with a focused attention I always felt intimidated by, but I held my ground; another thing I had learned from him—if you had a position and you gave in, you had no position at all.

"Jessica, we are Interpol. Not the UN, and not beholden to any political master. I sympathize with your thinking, and perhaps we can attack the oil nano bug last, our resources are stretched as it is, but we cannot and will not take a position of whether or not oil in the Middle East or anywhere else, for that matter, flows again. Clear?" The use of my first name indicated that this was personal, not official, but he was still my Boss, and I respected him both as a leader and as a man. I nodded, glad to have got the issue off my chest; it had been contributing to knots in my gut for a number of days.

"Yes, Boss, understood. What about Amira?" He turned to look over at the geeks, the three of them beavering away at their keyboards, screens flashing with data and symbols at warp speed.

"You made a personal commitment to Arie. I suggest you take it up with him," the Boss said, looking back at me. He slowly stood up, rolling his shoulders and twisting his neck. I joined him, thinking about the mission we were about to embark on. A mixed crew of our special services troops, Arie's commandos, and the Boss, Pete, and I, off to capture the man who had almost brought the world to its collective knees. I reached out and grabbed the Boss's arm.

"Just a thought. How about we take the priest who used to work with Al Hemish al-bin Mohammad Karesish in the camp?" I asked. The Boss thought for a minute, nodded, then moved off towards the geeks. I opened my little laptop and dialed up the director of the FBI, who I knew had the priest under guard somewhere. I hope he had been looked after and not treated like a terrorist.

"Roger, hello again. We have a favor to ask you." He looked a little frazzled, worn, and very tired, so I put on my best smile and waited for his reply.

"Hi Jessica, how are you all?" he asked, obviously sitting down from the movement in the background.

"We are all fine. Pete brought back some excellent intel. Shetani won't worry us anymore, and from the number of bounty claims Interpol is logging, a good number of his mercenary friends have been taken out of the picture as well. How are you all over there? Sorry I didn't ask first." His wan smile was forced, and that answered my question.

"We've got a large part of the US back under control; we've slowed the fighting down in all but a few major cities, and we have food and water supplies being distributed in most places, but we're still walking a tightrope between benevolent dictatorship and outright martial law. It's not comfortable for any of us, but we really don't have a choice." I nodded, understanding perfectly how he felt. When you were in control and had the power, to suddenly have it eroded and negated in the blink of an eye was unsettling at best.

"Well, we have a request for you. Can you lend us the priest who brought you the information about the children and Al Hemish al-bin Mohammad Karesish?" He looked puzzled for a second, turned to look at someone out of camera range, then looked back at the lens.

"I'd forgotten about them; we have them stashed in the VIP quarters back at Quantico being monitored but not restrained if you get the difference." I nodded.

"Who's 'them'?" I asked. We had only had the story told to us from a single perspective.

"Well, the little guy we first encountered, a Father Andretti, turned up with a local LEO, and then we found the original contract, a Brother Fernández Gómez, at Miami-Dade Airport. We interrogated all three, and the story became clearer. The brother worked in a refugee camp thirty years ago at Gouraud, in Baalbek, Lebanon, with an Imam who he knew as Fernández, and we now know as Al Hemish al-bin Mohammad Karesish.

"The Jesuits, through the Catholic Church, opened a school in the camp, and they were both teachers there. The story goes that this Fernández got really upset at the number of children who were dying in the camp and decided to take some of them away—you know the rest. Brother Gómez came to us after having the body of a dead woman dropped at his feet by a local tribe, and again, you know the rest of that story. So, we have the priest, the brother, and the cop all relaxing at Camp Quantico; which one do you want, and why?"

"We're going to collect Al Hemish al-bin Mohammad Karesish, and it might make it easier if we have someone he knows with us."

"Well, that makes sense; let me ask Bridget, and I'll get back to you."

"Thanks. Take care." We both hung up, and I stared at the blank screen for a moment, gathering my thoughts. He was wrong about us knowing about the priest and the dead woman, that part of the story hadn't made it into the intelligence brief we received, and while it was just another body to add to the thousands and thousands of dead from either the attacks or the chaos that followed, this poor woman may well have been the first casualty of whatever this gross terrorist act finally got labeled as by the media. My computer screeched at me; I opened it up to see the face of General Bridget Saunders grinning into the camera.

"Jessica, good to see you. I understand you want our priest?" she said, much happier than I expected her to be. I tried to match her mood in spite of how down I felt about the nameless woman who had been thrown at the priest's feet all those years ago.

"Hi Bridget, we have to stop meeting this way, or our bosses will start talking about us." She laughed and sat back in her chair, revealing she was in her office, or so I assumed by the crossed flags and military memorabilia I could now see at her back. "Frank tells me you would like to take one of our priests on a little trip into the desert."

"Yes. Might help us in our conversation with Al Hemish al-bin Mohammad Karesish."

"I figured that out; it's a good idea, but this infers you intend to keep him alive?" she asked, her eyebrows rising to underline her question.

"Yes, we do. In fact, we will do everything we can to keep him alive so he can explain himself to the world court."

"Do you really think that is a good idea?"

"Yes. With so much collateral damage, civilian panic, and chaos, we think an explanation will go a long way to helping people understand what this has really been about. They won't like it, but we think it will help calm things down a little. A story about abandoned children really can't be taken lightly, even by the worst of the world's dictators."

"So, you buy into the 'save the refugee children' story?" My ears pricked up at the change in tonality, and it was my turn to sit back in my seat.

"You don't?"

"There are a lot of better ways to get our attention and address the problem. You really don't have to destroy the world to solve a refugee issue." I thought about that, then shook my head.

"Take out the mercenary attacks—and by that, I mean Avignon, Shaybah, Masjid al-Haram, the oil and gas pipelines, and the UAV attacks on the sports arenas in England, Germany, and the US, and you get a different picture."

"Different how?"

"We believe that the women recruited by Al Hemish al-bin Mohammad Karesish were responsible for the drone attack on the Dome of the Rock, the bombing of the Vatican, taking out Lloyd's, West Point, the World Wide Web, and the space station. The attacks that killed people in Israel and Rome were specifically targeted to minimize collateral damage. The death tolls could have been far higher just a few hours or even days later. Yes, thousands were killed, but it could just as easily have been hundreds of thousands. And look at how essential infrastructure was protected when the web was shut down."

"And your point is?"

"Strange as it might seem under the circumstances, we believe the primary attacks were designed to minimize casualties, specifically targeted to make the most impact with the lowest death toll. We believe that the mercenaries got off their leash, as it were, and, while they performed their part as required, didn't stick to the script. This was a directed attack on the Roman Catholic Church, the Muslims, and America's war base. We can hazard a guess as to the backstory, but I would prefer to do that at another time."

"Then why the attacks on the space station and taking down the web?"

"The web hits everyone in the world, disrupts transport, communication, and anything else they do on the net. The space station simply to demonstrate that they can."

"So, let me sum it up for you—all the science-based and air attacks were the women; all the ground-based attacks were Shetani and his mercenary friends. Correct?"

"In a nutshell, yes. Provisioned, paid, and directed by Al Hemish al-bin Mohammad Karesish or one or more of his followers and synchronized to the master plan of the disruption to the two biggest religions on the planet and, of course, West Point. We believe Shetani slipped off the leash somewhere. We know he and his mercenaries got paid right up until a week ago; we have his bank accounts. He got paid first, then distributed funds to all his different groups in the different countries. We also have their bank accounts and locations, which we have passed on to everyone."

"Okay, I'm not convinced, but it's a workable theory until we can interrogate the boss-man. We'll ship you the priest ASAP; where do you want him?"

"Tel Nof airbase in Israel, please, postmarked for the attention of Arie."

"Okay, will do. Keep us posted. What do you suggest we do with the other two?"

"Treat them well, compensate them for their time, and offer to get them back to wherever they want to go. Remember the old saw about 'not shooting the messenger'?" I asked. She just smiled and hung up.

CHAPTER 84

The tarmac at Tel Nof was wet, miserable, and cold, not to mention really cold, and sitting under the wing of the monstrous camouflage-painted C-17 transport aircraft was a lesson in itself. A wet and soggy ground crew was wrestling a brace of Polaris all-wheel-drive ATVs into the huge maul of the open loading ramp, five in total, which would provide two spare vehicles just in case. Three of them would take all twelve of us and our gear, with room to spare, and had the added advantage of being able to carry two more people each, plus a large load of equipment. The ATVs were optimized for very quiet desert work and were lightly armored, but keeping you safe in transit was not their real strong point. Speed and maneuverability were. Perfect for the plan the Boss, Pete, Tom, and the Israeli Colonel had devised.

The original idea of using helicopters to fly into the camp had been ditched as too complex and potentially noisy.

Simple, really. Fly in comfort for a couple of hours, then stream out the back of the C-17 speeding along at one hundred and twenty knots three meters above the desert floor, motor over to the terrorist leader's camp, ask him to surrender peacefully, load back up, and drive back to the aircraft. What could possibly go wrong? We were dressed in street clothes; this was a capture and keep alive mission, and that had been drummed into us at least ten times by the Sgen Aluf of the Shayete 104 commandos who Pete had introduced us to. He had prior experience with the man, having survived the attack on Shetani's terrorist camp and the obvious wrath of the Colonel in the process. In contrast, my Boss, Indigo, Tom, and his Special Forces troops were demure, sitting quietly in a small huddle near the massive main wheels. They also were dressed in their version of street clothes, although every single one had light brown jeans, smudged tan combat boots, and light brown long-sleeve tees, and with what I could barely see in the dark, the giveaway bulge of lightweight body armor over the top.

The Israelis were similarly dressed, not sure about the body armor, but the slight curves that three of them presented with spoke to a well-integrated and culturally correct selection. At least I wouldn't be the only woman on the extraction. They sat by themselves also, but near enough to Tom and his team to be easily included in the briefing. It wasn't as if we were two separate teams but rather one team split into three segments. This was deliberate and part of the plan. We were waiting on the arrival of the brother, and Indigo was sitting on a grab bag that held a change of clothes for him, certain as we were that the Americans had not dressed him for our little adventure.

The pilot and the Boss were in deep discussion, and the Boss suddenly stood up, patted the young pilot, who didn't look old enough to shave, on the shoulder, and walked over to where I was standing with Indigo.

"We've modified our landing zone based on the last overflight data. We'll come in here, slightly to the south of the target, do a running dismount from three meters, and, after we stream out, move in a pincer shape towards the camp. You, Indigo, and the brother plus the shooter of your choice will lead, the Colonel's ATV will sit back about half a click from you, and I'll take the other one way round behind the camp, just in case. You will all have live video and audio, and our arc will never be more than half a click from you, so we can respond quite quickly."

"The ATVs are muffled, and the pictures show a decent sandstorm, eighty percent visibility; that should help us get really close before we are spotted."

"Yes," the Boss replied, pointing to a spot on the map he was holding. "There are no radiation signals from the camp; we know he has a satellite phone, but we can't detect anything else. There are also only three other people giving off heat signatures, which might be guards. We'll assume they are armed and dangerous, but I'll let you plan that out. Who do you want as your shooter?" I smiled. He knew my answer; there was really only one choice. He nodded his agreement.

"Okay, I'll send Pete over; have a chat and decide on your tactics. I'll go back to my team until we're ready to load." He squeezed my arm, looked me straight in the eyes, smiled, then ducked his head and walked away. A shiver ran up my spine, and I felt a little warm in the stomach. He could do that to you. Just as I was starting to enjoy the fantasy that was developing in my imagination, a helicopter stormed in, scattering debris all over the place, and settled with a heavy clunk onto the tarmac. A side door slid open, and a tall man with very dark skin wearing even darker robes crouched so his head didn't get taken off by the still roaring rotor and stumbled over towards us. Indigo ran over to him, gave him a tremendous hug, something we were all used to at Interpol Italy, waved his arms as he spoke, looked towards me, pointed, spoke rapidly, then, taking the priest by the arm, led him to an ablutions tent that had been erected near the nose of the C-17.

They disappeared, then Indigo ran back out to where I was dripping cold rain all over the tarmac.

"*Capitano*, when do you wanta us wheels up?" he asked, holding a piece of cardboard over his head to fend off the increasing rain. I looked at his makeshift hat and smiled; everyone else was toughing it out, hatless, no doubt demonstrating their manliness, myself included. I pulled him over to me and shared his temporary rain shelter.

"I want to hit them at oh-dark-thirty; it's a two-hour flight, about an eight-minute drive once we stream. Allow ten for stuff-ups and ten for take-off, so you need to be back here ready to go in three hours. Okay?" He looked at me, looked back at the small green tent, dropped his head as if thinking, then nodded.

"*Capitano*, are you okay with briefing him on the plane?" I thought about that; the priest's role was a simple one: introduce me to the mastermind who had brought the world to its knees, keep everyone from being shot, or shot at, then help us get him back to the aircraft.

In one piece. Alive. Minimal damage. I nodded to Indigo.

"Yes, that will be fine. Pete will be our shooter, and you will be our translator. I'm just along to make it official." Indigo smiled at me in a way that any alligator would be proud of.

"*Capitano*, my gooda frienda, you speaka Italian like a native, and you're Arabic is bettera thana mine! I think you are pulling my leg, young Jessica. Good joke!" And with that, he ran back to the tent to do whatever he planned to do with the priest. I checked my watch, an army issue with a black face that was designed in such a way that only I could see the digits from a specific angle. Using the timeline I had given Indigo, we had less than three hours before we were wheels up. I motioned to the Colonel and the Boss, pointed to the aircraft, and everyone stood up, shook the worst of the water off, and slowly filed into the gaping maw of the C-17.

"Listen up. Change into dry clothes. There are hot meals in the boxes in front of the ATVs. We're wheels up in less than three hours, so get some shut-eye if you can. I'll brief us all when we are on the way. Just one question. Has everyone done a hot extraction before?" I asked, looking at the expectant faces that turned to see what I was up to. No one raised their hand, and that was just bullshit because I knew all Tom's team had done them, and then I caught on.

"Sorry, I'm Captain Riley. I'll be leading the mission in ATV number one, with the master chief, Colonel Kashasini, we are all Interpol, and Brother Gómez. This is, as you have been briefed, a police action, and we're hoping the good brother, who, as we speak, is changing into someone more suitable in the ablutions tent, will introduce us peacefully to Al Hemish al-bin Mohammad Karesish, or Mohammad bin Azaria as you probably know him. The good brother knows him only as 'Fernández,' which was the name he used back in the refugee camp at Gouraud, in Baalbeck, Lebanon, when they were both teachers there some twenty-six odd years ago." At that point, I shut up, not at all sure how much the Israeli contingent knew about the backstory. The confused look on their faces told me it wasn't much, but I had always believed that when you sent people into harm's way, they had to know why, who, when, and where of it all so they understood exactly what they were risking their lives for.

So, I told them an abbreviated story of why we were here now, who the main players were, and what we hoped to achieve.

Then I asked my question again, and every hand went up. "Good, we'll extract at three meters, one hundred twenty knots. The pallets are rigged to shed on impact. The rest will be up to your drivers. Thank you."

The president, her military chief of staff, and her intelligence chiefs were sitting around a small table deep in the basement of the CIA's headquarters. The room was screened from electronic eavesdropping with a massive faraday cage built into the walls, ceiling, and floor, and the computers in the room were all air-gapped. It was as secure as AI, and humans could make it. The president had called the meeting; Julius Bronstein had volunteered the "quiet" room in his CIA headquarters. A single pot of coffee sat in the middle of the table, and a tray with cups, saucers, creamer, and cookies lay untouched next to it. A very large screen filled one wall, and at the moment, all five people were riveted to the images that flicked across its shiny surface. In one large box, Arie Rosenburg's weathered face, looking as calm as someone in church on Sunday, watched his own feed from the camera positioned on top of the Tel Nof control tower. It was raining hard; water was literally bucketing down and flowing off the sides of the huge C-17 in small floods, splashes, and waterfalls.

"They will be wheels-up in fifteen minutes, Madam President; there won't be much to see until then. And yes, we do have cameras in the cargo hold, and all three teams will be wired for video and audio, sent back to us from a satellite we have positioned over the target area. I suggest I call you back when they are airborne." Arie looked expectantly at the image of the president on his screen, saw her nod, and switched his part of the transmission to standby.

"What are their chances of success?" the president asked, rubbing both sides of her lined and gaunt face with her hands. Surviving on just two to three hours of sleep a day and mostly catnaps caught between briefings and the inevitable meetings, she looked ten years older than at the start of the week. Her light coffee colored skin showed some wear and tear, and if it hadn't been for the excellent facilities at the White House, she knew she would have looked even worse. Her military liaison didn't look a whole lot better; the only normal thing about her was her pressed and well-badged uniform.

"The intelligence is the best we have. The Israelis are our equals in that regard and, in some ways, are superior. They are constantly at war with their neighbors, so getting a good read on the opposition is critical to their survival. They have their equivalent of our SkyWatch circling at eighty thousand feet, with one-meter resolution cameras, sending back to the team and Arie in real-time. He believes the target has only two guards now; there are no electronic blocks we can detect, no signatures from mines, or tanks or any sort of air defense. It's as if he is waiting for us." The president drilled the general with a look that would have frozen a lesser person as she placed her hands flat on the table and leaned slightly forward.

"Just how good is this Anthony?" she asked, her voice barely above a whisper. She had been told before, she thought, but the pressure of keeping all the details, bits, and pieces of the attacks and the ensuing chaos in her head from day to day was proving too much for any one person to manage.

General Saunders relaxed her shoulders and moved slightly forward in her seat, matching the president. She understood her pain, the constant pressure she was under. Trying to manage the sheer magnitude of the disruption to the country and the world was like trying to carry custard in a string bag. As soon as you poked your finger in one hole, it leaked out of the others. In a flash of insight, she gathered her thoughts and put a tiny smile on her face.

"Madam President, Roger here," she said, pointing to the FBI director, "has worked with the Colonel several times, and I believe he rates him as one of the very best he has ever met. Plus, his offsider, Captain Riley, is the most talented military-trained investigator the NCIS ever graduated. Their master chief was with the Israeli Shayete 104 commando, who took out Shetani and his mercenaries and recovered the Arab palace. So far, everything they have done has been first class, and we would not be where we are today if it were not for them." She sat back, leaving her folded hands on the table, giving off the air of someone in control, and relaxed about it. The president mirrored the general and sat back in her seat, nodding to herself.

"Thank you, Bridget. That summary is appreciated. Sometimes it seems our partners are doing all the work, and we're just sitting back watching from the bleachers. Now that you mention it, what is happening in Arabia?"

"I'll answer that one, Madam President," Julius Bronstein said, shifting in his chair to look more directly at the president. "The CIA have agents in place, have had since before the first putsch, so our information is accurate and now recent, thanks to the Israelis who left behind one of the little laptops we have been using to communicate with, courtesy of Interpol. The throne has been secured, and the King's first son will be inaugurated later this week. It will be a very French affair because, as you know, they have had their hands in this up to their elbows well before the first putsch."

"They get around. Let's get down to why I called this meeting. As you are aware, the rioting in the larger cities has almost stopped, but the food queues are monstrous. The military is providing as much as they can, but our biggest problem is the internal migration from the larger cities to small towns and rural areas. We are trying to get an audit going, so we can see what will be needed and where, but we have literally half the country trying to move into the other half, with fuel running out and very little the smaller towns can do to police the newcomers or provide for them. We need a solution, and we need one fast. And the biggest single problem I can see is our communication is limited to landlines, old-style phones, and ham radio sets."

"Madam President, we have every military unit and reserve brigade setting up relay stations at the rate of five thousand a day. We will have microwave communication within the next week up and down the East Coast and as far inland as Chicago and Wisconsin. A similar system is being laid on the West Coast; it will go as far inland as Salt Lake City.

"Every army fort, military barracks, Air Force, and navy base and station will be linked; in fact, most are already. Yes, there will be a gap in the middle of the country, but only for a month or two. Anything built before twenty fifteen still has copper wire underground, so the issue is the supply of old-style phone handsets. And we have now got limited satellite communication back, and we are getting satellite phones delivered to every city and town as fast as we can."

"What about the world wide web?" the president asked. A constant question asked by her daughter at the behest of her friends was when they could get back online, considering their world had stopped as far as they were concerned. And mummy was the president, so why couldn't she just tell someone to fix it? The director of the NSA shook his head, his face a mask of uncertainty. His empire had come crashing down around his ears, and neither he nor his people could actually pinpoint a single perpetrator of the worldwide digital attack.

"No, Madam President, no web in the foreseeable future. Apologies to your daughter, we understand how hard it is for the generation who only knows digital, but we have years of work ahead of us there; we will have SciNet, DARPANet, and MilNet up and running through the month. But going beyond that is a huge task; literally, every country in the world is involved, and most have the same issues we have—rioting, food and water shortages, lack of fuel, and very unhappy constituents. Add to that the mass migration all across Europe, in every direction, and frankly, we wouldn't know who to ask for funds and resources."

"The web originally started in the universities, didn't it?"

"No, not quite. We had SciNet linking all our major science development sites, some hospitals, and some of the major universities; that was a very basic blue screen system that used slow modems hooked up to phone handsets. MilNet was its own development, parallel to SciNet, but not much better technically. Then we had ARPA; the universities got into it because they saw what we were doing and essentially created a civilian version, which, as you know, led to the Internet, which took over the world. It was driven initially by a hardware manufacturer who saw the possibility of linking every computer to one of their routers, and that's what the terrorist exploited. They effectively killed every router, then went after any computer connected at the time of the attacks, other than those areas that they geo-fenced, as you know." The president shook her head in frustration.

"I get it. Actually, I don't, but we'll let that go for now. How come these little laptops are working?" she asked, genuinely curious.

"Madam President, they are using a unique code that is encrypted and sent to a satellite. We have no idea who created this, and to be honest, we haven't had the time or mind-space to look very deeply into it. It came to us from Interpol, it works, and for now, that's all we have got for real-time intercontinental visual and aural communications other than archaic landlines."

"Next time I get hounded by my daughter, I'll send her to you." The president sat back, looked at the screen again, and noticed some movement around the tail end of the transport aircraft, but due to the poor visibility couldn't make much of it. She sighed, rubbed her face again, then shook her head.

"Sending the politicians back to their constituencies seemed like a smart move originally, but I'm not so sure now. Washington used to run on influence—industry provided the money that drove the lobbyists, the lobbyists drove Congress and the parties, and the parties drove the industry. Now we have precious few in town who can get anything done quickly; it's a mess."

"Well, we have been successful so far by concentrating on food and water supplies, and now that the major rioting has subsided, the pressure on hospitals and medical centers has lessened considerably. Thank God for the Army Reserve. Being state-based, they have the local knowledge to get things to where they are needed the most." General Saunders sat back in her seat, noticing that the president's face was losing some of its tension as she delivered her report.

"Just a tidbit of data that might amuse you. The greatest problem everyone is having is the lack of paper maps!" There were a few smiles at this news, but they were strained to say the least. After a slight pause, the general continued.

"We also have some wins on the board, Madam President; the Canadians cleaned up the terrorist cells that were shutting down the fracking plants. We haven't had an attack now for three days. Shetani and his mercenaries are completely out of action, which should calm the Middle East down a little. Interpol is about to shut down Mohammad bin Azaria, and the Chinese and the Russians, whom we were most worried about, have been consumed by their own internal difficulties the same as us." The president nodded, leaned back in her seat, and let out a huge sigh.

"I suppose we should be grateful for small mercies," she said, reflecting on that piece of news. Both the Russians and the Chinese had effectively lost around eighty percent of their oil and gas supply, which had placed a huge strain on their internal budgets. She wondered if it would last.

Indigo and Brother Gómez, who was long, lean, and gaunt as a scarecrow, skin tanned to the texture of leather, now dressed in a clean version of the traditional brown robe his order had worn for centuries, sat down inside the cavernous hold of the C-17, his trusted boots still showing considerable wear, and in spite of Indigo's best efforts to get him to take a brand-new pair of parachute jump boots, he had steadfastly but politely refused to give them up. Jessica understood his feelings on the matter; a good pair of boots, once broken in, became as much a part of her as her arms and legs.

"Brother Gómez, thank you for coming. I would like to brief everyone here on what we are going to do. Is that okay with you?" she asked in English, thinking that some of the Israelis might not speak Italian. He nodded a little uncertainly, having been rushed from the holding tank at FBI headquarters in Washington straight onto a small jet and then flown directly to Israel, his destination only made known to him just before they landed. His small bundle of personal belongings had been handed to him as he walked down the stairway onto the tarmac, where Indigo had met him and greeted him with great respect. They had enjoyed a short conversation before Indigo led him to the small tent, where he was offered a shower, a change of clothes, and a hot meal from a military warmer. He had held his silence until he had finished his meal, uncertain as to his future. No one, including Indigo, had yet told him anything other than he was in Israel. They would soon board the huge aircraft parked behind the tent for a purpose as yet unknown. He looked into the eyes of the woman who addressed him and saw both compassion and determination. She was dressed the same as all the other men and women in the aircraft but was obviously feminine, in spite of the weapon strapped to her hip, a combat knife strapped to her chest, and a close-quarter combat automatic firearm slung across her lap.

"I ama happy to listena to youa. English is not my besta language, so forgive mea if I stumble." Jessica smiled and nodded. She had introduced everyone to the brother, seeing him nod at each name, but wasn't sure how much he would retain or even understand.

"Fratello Gómez, se non sei sicuro di qualcosachedico, perfavorefammisapere, e o Indigo qui o io tradurrò." He nodded again and smiled a little at Jessica's perfect Italian and the offer to translate should it be necessary. He sensed a deep purpose here, but he felt no personal threat, so he relaxed slightly and gestured to her to continue.

"Brother Gómez, many years ago, you taught in a school in a refugee camp in Gouraud, in Baalbeck, Lebanon. You worked with a 'Father Fernández,' and you reported to the Americans that he had given you a message to take to the president, which you did."

The brother nodded solemnly, remembering the priest's words to him, *"Padre, i bambini devonoessereascoltati. Ho un piano. Fammiquestofavore, se vuoi. Quando il cadavere di una donna nonbeliever viene a voi, assicurarsiche il Presidente o il re di cui sempre sicapiscechesonoquestiultimi a bambini di Dio ha parlato! Fate questo per me, e di farlo per loro, implorote!"* The Children of God had spoken, the sign of the desecrated body of a female dropped on his doorstep, being the trigger for him to honor his promise to his friend. The promise had been made as they prepared to burn the rotted bodies of over three hundred little children, an act they were repeating day after day in the refugee camp. An act that had twisted the fate of the world.

"Brother Gómez, we are flying to a place where we believe 'Father Fernández' is camped, and we are hoping that you will introduce us to him." He looked at the heavily armed men and women sprawled around the seating area and shook his head from side to side.

"*No, non prenderòpersonearmate per vederemiofratello, il suounicopeccato era prenderei bambini daicampi, e ancheallora Dio puòperdonarlo per questo.*" Jessica looked at Indigo, who had heard the determination in the Jesuit's voice. Indigo nodded to her, stood up, removed his belt, held his pistol and knife, unslung his weapon from his chest, and laid his weapons on the floor of the aircraft. Jessica mirrored his movements, and in less than a minute, she was also unarmed, her pile of weapons at her feet. Pete sat still, not wanting to interrupt the pantomime and, as he had also understood the brother, started to think about how he could still provide protection but appear unarmed in the process!

"Fratello Gómez, rispettiamoituoidesideri. Cavalcheremo con tenel nostro veicolodisarmatoeglialtrisoldatirimarrannoconl'aereo. Èfondamentaleincontrare

il tuoamico e spiegarglicosadobbiamofare. Puoiaiutarci per favore?" In a soft voice, Indigo translated for the rest of the team as Jessica spoke, "Brother Gómez, we respect your wishes. We will ride with you in our vehicle unarmed, and the other soldiers will remain with the aircraft. It is critical we meet with your friend and explain to him what we need him to do. Can you help us, please?" The reaction of the Israeli Colonel was to be expected, but before he could utter his protest, the Boss put one hand on his thigh and squeezed. The Colonel got the message and worked his face from furious to a study in neutrality, but his eyes said it all.

No way were he and his commandos going to face down the most-wanted terrorist in the world empty-handed, a sentiment the Boss understood viscerally and agreed with.

One problem at a time, the Boss thought to himself, *let Jessica take the lead; she obviously has the Brother's trust, if not respect.* That was the reason he loved her, unrequited, this many-faceted woman who was both seriously intelligent yet soft as a marshmallow and yet could kill you in the blink of an eye. Her instinct with people was unchallenged, so he sat back and watched as she achieved their initial objective of getting the brother's willing help.

"Wea willa be traveling in thisa vehicles?" the Jesuit asked, pointing to the first ATV locked down on the cargo floor. A fifty-caliber machine gun sat on a reinforced pedestal, with its muzzle pointing down. A boxy ammunition supply was strapped to the support. Jessica looked at the Boss, who nodded; tapped Pete on the leg, who got up, wobbled forward as the aircraft hit some minor turbulence, stopped at the last ATV closest to the ramp, and in five quick movements had the machine gun and its ammunition container off the ATV and racked up on the side of the fuselage.

"Brother Gómez, that will be our vehicle, and as you can now see, its armaments are removed. We only want to talk to your brother, and we will do anything to keep him alive." The Jesuit looked at me, and I could feel his intensity all the way to my backbone. This was not a man to be taken lightly; he may be one of faith, but he was also one of steel. His survival skills and his history told the real story. He finally nodded, looked away at the other commandos, shook his head, then slumped back, closed his eyes, and gave the appearance of sleeping. Pete collected the weapons lying on the aircraft floor that Indigo and I had shed, except for the pistols and magazines, which he slipped out of their pouches and handed to us both grips first. Both Indigo and I slipped them into the back of our belts and the magazines into a side pocket. We both then slipped a desert poncho over our heads and pulled a floppy hat and sand goggles out of our pockets, and placed them on our laps. I looked at Pete as he slipped a poncho over his head and hoped it would disguise what he was carrying underneath.

"Okay, everyone, change of plan. The captain, Colonel, and master chief will escort the brother and will take ATV number one, as planned. You will all remain behind until we are needed. Everyone clear on that?" The Boss looked at the commandos, then at Tom and his crew, signaling silently the military gesture for "more to follow," then sat back in his canvas seat. It was clear to me what he meant to do. Once we had streamed out of the back of the C-17, flying at one hundred twenty knots and ten feet into the eye of a sandstorm, detecting anything else flying out of the backside of the aircraft would, for all intents and purposes, be impossible. At the very worst, our cover from ATV number two with the Israelis might be a few hundred meters further behind us than was optimal, but we could always modify our speed accordingly, and each ATV was equipped with an excellent navigation system, good enough to rival that of any aircraft, as well as a transponder so everyone would know where everyone was at all times.

Plus, thanks to the Israeli satellite that had been moved out of its normal geostationary orbit to overhead our target, we had live real-time video and audio on a wrist device for every person—except the brother, as we didn't want to alarm him unduly if things went squirrely. We also knew we would be under constant surveillance by the Israeli Intelligence Service as well as the White House. Luckily, that was going to be one-way only, as neither would be able to talk to us during the operation. Praise the Gods! There was nothing more annoying than having your every decision second-guessed or outright countermanded during a mission. And besides, I would challenge anyone to be able to make a serious decision sitting on their backsides in their air-conditioned rooms thousands of kilometers away from the flying bullets and exploding body parts.

"*Fratello Gómez, haituttociò di cui haibisogno? Possoprendertiqualcosa?*" I asked, watching the Israeli Colonel watch me. The look on his face told me he was still chewing over the Boss's revision to the battle plan and the fact that Pete, Indigo, and I appeared to have surrendered our weapons.

"Thaka you, I am fine. I will catch a little sleepa, now, *sí*? "*Si, Fratello Gómez, Con tutti imezzi.*"

I left the Jesuit to himself and stumble-stepped over to where the Boss was sprawled across the sideways-slung canvas seat. One of his enduring attributes to my way of thinking was his ability to sleep anywhere, at any time, something I had yet not learned to do. I poked him in the ribs, none too gently, and got his standard response to any interruption, one angry opened eye and his Sig Suer in my face. I batted the pistol away and sat down in front of him, slipping on a pair of headphones. He continued to look at me lopsidedly, then, almost regrettably, put his weapon away, sat up, and slipped on a headset that had been hanging on a strap near his head.

"This had better be good. I had a fantastic dream," he said, looking at me now with both eyes and an intensity that suggested he knew what I was going to say. I stared back, not giving an inch. He would take the proverbial mile and hold my stare until a small smile creased his battered face. "Okay, you win. I taught you well in the stare department. You want to know how we will cover you and still honor your promise to the brother." I nodded. It was uppermost in my mind. While I trusted the images we had been sent from the satellite, and the briefings we had received, I firmly believed that the Intelligence Corps motto was "We bet your life," and I didn't want them to bet mine, the brother's, Pete's, or Indigo's if I could avoid it.

"I'm happy with our cover being a few hundred meters behind the optimal position, but what happens if we do get in, establish a dialogue, then two heavily armed ATVs pour in behind us, proving beyond doubt that we are first-class bullshitters?" He just smiled at me, a sure sign he had thought of something I hadn't.

"We won't follow you in if all is going as we want it. We'll sit out far enough away to be invisible but close enough to bail you out of trouble if you screw up. Simple. Don't screw up." I leaned back, tilted my head towards the roof, and shut my eyes. Of course, it was simple; everything to the Boss was by his lights. But he had a point. If we didn't need the backup, there was no reason for them to come into the camp, or anywhere near it for that matter. I nodded, slipped the headset off, kept my eyes closed to shut out the world, and felt the Boss's hand on my arm. Just a small squeeze, and while it was meant to calm me and add reassurance, it set my heart racing as usual. I really didn't know what it was about this man that set me off, but it was powerful juju!

The big screen in the "quiet room" of CIA headquarters snapped to life again, this time with Arie's face in a small box down the bottom right-hand side and a clear shot of the open ramp of the C-17, a string of ATVs, with the front vehicle showing four occupants, and a kaleidoscope of sand and dust roaring away from the giant aircraft.

"Madam President, we are about to stream the ATVs. I'll hold my comments from here on and let the audio from the team inform us." The president nodded, and with a snap, the roar of the slipstream, the burbling roar of the engines of the ATVs, and the quiet countdown by the jumpmaster rippled around the room. As the countdown hit zero, the first ATV flew out of the aircraft backwards, to disappear into the chaos as the desert floor was shredded and ripped by the slipstream of the massive low flying jet. The ATV bounced once, then veered off to the right. The rapid movement inside the giant aircraft could be seen as the remaining commandos filled the remaining ATVs. At the count of ten, the second ATV streamed out, to be followed by the third ten seconds later. The ground seemed to shrink as the aircraft climbed back up to its normal operating altitude, and as the sandstorm faded to a bluey-brown haze, the rear cargo ramp slowly retracted, leaving just the two extra empty ATVs in shot.

"ATV down, nominal insertion, sending video to you now," snapped a voice that was indistinguishable due to being filtered through a sand mask, a particle filter, and a head scarf. Slowly, a picture formed of the skeleton nose of the ATV and a wall of flying sand. Superimposed over this blurry image was a heads-up display showing the compass heading, a blue line leading to a red triangle, and two pulsing blue dots representing the relative position of the other two ATVs. Individual grains of sand seemed to attack the image with a vengeance one imagined you might find in Hell. According to the readout, the vehicle was traveling at thirty-five kilometers an hour, with an ETA of just under eight minutes. The image bounced and blurred alternatively as the vehicle hit potholes in the sand, and the camera mount vibrated from the punishment it was receiving.

"Arie, will the image quality get better?" the NSA director asked, now sipping from his cup judiciously as his stomach roiled from the upsetting image on the wall. Blown up to ten times normal life-size, it was extremely challenging to watch and not feel queasy.

"Yes, Frank, once they stop, we'll have a split screen from their personal cameras as well as the ATV view. Now you know how a sailor feels in rough seas!" The joke was a good attempt to lighten the mood, but due to the president's attendance and her almost hangdog look, no one felt like laughing.

"Okay, Arie, thanks. We'll keep silent on this end as well," Frank replied, reaching forward to switch their audio off. On the screen, the two pulsing blue dots representing the support ATVs had formed up in position and now showed one four hundred meters behind the symbol marked as ATV number one, the second one off to one side about the same distance away. They seemed to be able to match their velocity to each other because now the three dots traveled in sync. The distance shrunk very quickly, and in a matter of minutes, all three symbols showed a velocity of fewer than three kilometers an hour until all thee stopped in unison.

The picture wobbled again, then steadied, giving the view from a body camera. Then, two more images appeared on the screen, obviously from the other members of ATV number one. The flapping brown robes of the brother could just be seen out of the corner of the far-right camera view, the sandstorm still obscuring parts of the video being sent back to the satellite.

"Okay, Pete, Indigo, and the brother, and I'll take it from here," I said, striding forward to grab the brother's arm. We could just see the outline of a massive red-and-white tent, and if our intelligence was right, the three remaining people would be inside. It was extremely unlikely anyone would be outside in this storm, with visibility cut to just a few meters. Indigo formed up on the other side of the brother. I took one last calming gulp of sand-filled air, mentally crossed my fingers and toes, and walked forward as unthreateningly as I could. We paused at the door. I shrugged my shoulders, then gently pushed the brother in between the folds of the door flaps.

“مالسلا alykumيخأ، اللهأانندخل؟,” the Jesuit call out in a trembling voice, bowing deeply from the waist, one hand across his heart.

“واالايكوموسلامأخي، هلوصلتكرسالتي؟,” the most-wanted terrorist on the planet replied, then, in perfectly accented Oxford English, invited Indigo and me to the party. “Please, come in out of the sandstorm. I have prepared tea.”

As Indigo and I entered, the setting reminded me of something I had seen in a video; the room was plush, lush, and covered in colorful cushions, billowing colored silks hung from the roof, with a low table in the center of a small entertaining area, the terrorist leader sitting on the far side pouring tea into small blue ceremonial cups. Definitely not the austere environment I had imagined. He suddenly looked up, smiled, then stood up and reached out for the brother, who moved forward to hug him. They held the pose for a good minute, muttering to each other but so quietly I couldn't make out the words, but the emotion in their bodies told its own story. There were two deep friends, who had suffered greatly together, one on either side of the religious divide. Here were men who had made a difference in the lives of others, giving solace and encouragement in the darkest of times. And here was a man who had declared war on the entire world and succeeded in bringing most countries to their knees.

“As-ala-amu alaikum,” I said, pulling my sand goggles off and bowing from the waist, not wanting to break up the demonstration of affection but mindful that my support team would get more and more uncomfortable the longer we took.

“Wa-Alaikum-Salaam,” Al Hemish al-bin Mohammad Karesish, or Mohammad bin Azaria as we now knew him, replied, patting his comrade on the shoulder and wiping tears from his eyes. “You must forgive me, Captain, this man and I were in the depths of Hell together, and while my religion does not embrace the concept of Hell, as such, preferring to believe in 'Jahannam,' which is a much nicer place in the afterlife, I do understand the pain and threat of such a place.”

I did the only thing I could think of, nodded my acceptance, and waited to see what happened next. Addressing me by my rank had thrown me; his calm acceptance of our presence had thrown me, and the fact that the kettle had just been boiled for the tea as we stepped into the tent had really thrown me, and only my training and my deep-seated desire to see this man in chains and incarcerated for the rest of his life keep me focused. He lowered himself to the cushions, taking the brother with him, and motioned to Indigo and me to sit opposite. Indigo had a neutral expression on his face, but as he removed his goggles, he risked a glance at me out of his eyes, saw I was not overly fussed by the events of the last few minutes, and sat beside me, softly patting me on the arm as he did so.

"My apologies, Colonel Kashasini. I did not mean to be rude. But seeing my brother again after all this time is both a revelation and a shock. When we parted, I could not be sure that he would receive my message after such a long time and then even if he would manage to deliver what I asked of him. But he did, and as amazed as I am about that feat, I am also grateful that he brought you here to sit with me over tea." Indigo nodded, giving nothing away; the fact that the terrorist had known his rank and name did not faze him in any way that showed.

"With respect, we need to ask you some questions with regard to terrorist acts that have occurred over the past few weeks around the world. We know that you provided the funds for the attacks; thanks to the brother here, we know about your message and have confirmed that you did take girls out of the camps for at least five years, starting some twenty-five years ago. We know that some of the children you supposedly saved turned their skills against the countries that had given them an identity and a home, and we know that you were paying a mercenary known as 'Shetani' to act on your behalf for at least the last eighteen months. We have proof of all these activities, and I have here a warrant issued by the world court for your immediate arrest on charges relating to terrorism, money laundering, and various other crimes. I also have an Interpol warrant for your immediate detention on behalf of Israel, Italy, the United States, Canada, and one hundred other countries that support Interpol for similar charges. You should also be aware that we have frozen your bank accounts in the Pan Arabian Sovereign Wealth

Fund and that 'Shetani' and his terrorist friends have not been paid for the last two weeks." I had been so pent up I didn't realize what a relief it was to get all this stuff off my chest. And if bin Azaria was concerned about anything I had said, he gave no indication whatsoever. Hate to face him in a poker game for meaningful stakes.

"Captain Riley, thank you, but all this is known to me, and in fact, I would like to thank you and your compatriots for ridding me and the world of this 'Shetani' fellow, as he took matters into his own hands in Arabia, as you are no doubt aware of." A lesser person would have blanched at this outrageous statement, but I was not a lesser person. I was lower than that, but I managed to hold myself in. It took all my effort and self-control not to rip into him. I grinned instead and showed my teeth.

"That's fine. Happy to help. Now, if it isn't any inconvenience, would you mind coming with us, please?" I said, my voice soft but backed with all the emotion that had built up inside me, and my hand shook just a fraction as I handed him the warrants for his arrest. He took a moment to study them, I had prepared them in both English and Arabic, and the calm look on his face gave nothing away. I hoped the same for my face, but in reality, it just didn't matter.

"Captain, before I do, might I introduce you to two of my closest advisers? They will disarm on arrival, and with your permission, I will call them in." He looked at me as if issuing a challenge. I just nodded and picked up the delicate cup of tea he had placed in front of me. Two could play the cool game. He reached into the folds of his thaub and picked out a small electronic device, tapped on its face, then, smiling as if he didn't have a care in the world, put it down on the table, where we could all see it. Indigo sat beside me as still as a church mouse, but his hands were inside his smock. No doubt in my mind that he had his weapon at the ready. Pete was still outside, and I wondered what his reaction might be.

"Traffic inbound, two on foot, three minutes out." Pete's report sang in my ear where the tiny audio bud had been lodged. I gave no indication I had heard anything; after all, I was supposed to be a professional at this game, but I watched closely as bin Azaria monitored the progress of his men on the little device. He raised his eyes to look straight at me and smiled again.

"Ask your guard to let them pass once he has cleared them, please," he said, his voice gentle and in no way that I could detect, stressed. I looked at him as I tapped my earbud twice, then put my hands on the table. I toyed with the cup until the tent flap opened, and two heavily bearded and armed people shuffled in, bent in supplication, muttered the traditional Muslim greeting, kissed their right hands, then stood tall, lowering their weapons to the ground as they did so. Pete was right behind them, his silenced Heckler & Kotch MP7 sitting comfortably in the middle of them, the barrel at waist height but hard to see due to the folds of his smock. I motioned him to stay where he was, inside the tent but still in the doorway. He relaxed his stance, lowered his weapon, but kept one hand on the pistol grip.

"Leave your weapons and sit here," bin Azaria said, in a tone that left no doubt as to who was in charge. The Arabs unwrapped, pulling head scarves and sand goggles off, revealing the tanned but silky skin of the desert Arab as Pete relieved them of their AK-47s. They moved around us to sit on one side and received a cup of steaming tea for their trouble. "These two gentlemen are with me; one is an Imam, the other a lawyer. Both speak perfect English, and both have been staying in a small camp I have nearby. Your satellites would not have picked it up; it is buried under the desert floor." In my earbud, I heard a small click, followed by a longer one, the signal that my Israeli backup was moving to within a hundred meters of us.

Silently, I hoped.

"Bin Azaria, I have served you with two warrants, both of which I intend to execute now. Please finish your tea so we can be on our way." He waggled a finger at me as if scolding a small child.

"Not so fast, Captain. I would like my lawyer to read both documents to see that they are in order." And with that, he sat back and folded his arms, the traditional way to indicate stubbornness. The Arab lawyer—if, in fact, he was one— reached across the table and took both warrants, pulled a small pair of reading glasses out of his pocket, and studied them. He blew some sand off the lenses, put the glasses on, and turned to the documents. The other Arab—supposedly an Imam—sat passively drinking his tea, the cup held in the traditional manner with both hands, one holding the side of the decorative cup, the other held underneath.

My immediate thought was that I was Alice, this was the looking glass, and at any minute, the white rabbit would run out screaming about the time.

But I had no real choice—no weapons were being brandished, I perceived no immediate threat, and apart from my Boss's blood pressure, which by now would be through the roof, everything was calm. I sincerely hoped not before the storm! I knew the video and audio from all our cameras would be streaming live to the USA and Israel, as well as our two other ATVs, and for a fleeting moment, I wondered what they might think of this amazing situation. The lawyer moved and placed the documents back in front of bin Azaria. Pete's hand moved ever so slightly, and the muzzle of his gun followed, lining up on the two Arabs.

،ةيتاذريغتاركذملاهذه ،ايرازأنبداتسوأ“

لسلااهيدلةأرملاهذهو،لوبرتنإلاوةيلودلاةمكحملانعتردصدقو

”كتقفارملعرصأانأ.يئاقولاسبحلابلإكذخألةط

This was a twist I had not anticipated, but I got in first to regain some of the power at the table. And to let bin Azaria know I spoke Arabic as well as he did.

“ايرازأنب،

ديقعلا.نآلارداغناننكل ،كلذعمةلكشميأيدلسيل ،كقفارينأنكميكيماحم .“؟كلضفنمانيلإمض،

نتشيحبةديجنوكتله

I heard the clicks in my earbuds and, within a minute, the rumble of a muffled diesel engine. The tent flap opened, and the four Israeli commandos filed in, two to each side, weapons low but their intent clear. Madam was leaving with her prisoner, and she was leaving now. The terrorist that had brought the world to its knees stood up, fired a quick instruction at his Imam, and looked at me. Nodded to himself, gathered his robes, and moved around the table to me. By the time he had done so, Indigo was behind him and cuffing his hands behind his back. Pete had wasted no time and, in the blink of an eye, had the lawyer and the Iman in plasticuffs, and one meaty hand on each of their necks.

"How do you want to play it?" he asked as Brother Gómez stood up, his face dripping with tears. Again, I exercised control by speaking directly to him to cut off any complaints about my conduct.

"Brother, I kept my word; we will keep your brother safe and secure; we will allow his lawyer to accompany us but under our control until such time as my superiors decide on how to handle the situation. You can sit next to him in our vehicle and again on the plane. Colonel, thank you, please escort the prisoner and the brother to our vehicle; the lawyer and the Imam can travel with you. He nodded, then snapped out an order to his troops.

"Captain, moving," he snapped in his best parade ground voice, causing Pete to smirk as he perp-walked the lawyer out of the tent. Indigo led the parade with bin Azaria; the commandos followed their commander, which left me with the brother and the Imam, who was still sitting at the small table. I mulled over, leaving him, then realized I was being pricky because of the way bin Azaria had tried to manipulate me. I pulled out a small knife, walked behind him, and cut his cuffs. The look he gave me would have sliced a mere mortal in two, so I just smiled, shook my head, and walked back out into the sandstorm.

I didn't get far as a muffled voice ripped through my head. "Take the Imam; wait for me. You can come back to the plane with us." I signaled to Pete to keep going; he would have heard the Boss's instruction through his earbud. I sneaked a look at my wrist monitor and noticed that the Boss's ATV was now only two hundred meters from us and stationery. Then I got it. He had tracked the emergence of the Imam and the lawyer from their underground bunker and had driven to it while we had been busy talking. Typical Boss. As I reentered the tent, the Imam sprang up with a pistol in his hand, so I did what I had been trained to do and shot him repeatedly until I perceived he was no longer a threat. He flopped down over the table, spilling blood in small gushes. It must have hit an artery. I went further into the tent and could see that he had been working on a laptop that no doubt had been hidden somewhere under all the bright cushions. It was open, alive, and words in Arabic were scrolling across the screen. Where was a geek when you most needed one?

"All good here, but the Imam needs a body bag," Pete said over the net, standing in the doorway between the flaps, looking like something out of the desert scenes from *Star Wars* with his head scarf, goggles, face mask, and poncho. He nodded to me, turned on his heel, and left me alone with the warm body of the Imam and the scrolling computer screen. I kept my weapon in my hand; we still had not formally accounted for the third man, although I suspected he had been left guarding the bunker; in which case, he was probably now toasted, just like the Imam. The fact that I felt absolutely no remorse for having taken his life spoke to the pent-up emotions I had inculcated over this whole messy investigation. I was not a big fan of machines killing people remotely, and the majority of these attacks had been executed by artificial intelligence-powered aircraft, delivering their devastating attacks without a human hand being anywhere near the controls.

I was saved from further introspection by the roar of an ATV sliding to a stop and two sand-covered special force troops bursting through the flaps of the tent.

"Hey, how are they hanging?" Tom asked, ripping his headgear off with one hand and surveying the inside of the tent with his MP-7 leading. His companion moved to the back of the tent, no doubt executing a search, which, in retrospect, I should have done right back at the start. Being short-focused tends to create operational blindness. I had seen bin Azaria; I wanted him in chains, so I only saw what I wanted. It could have got my team and I killed, and no doubt, somewhere in my future, the Boss would remind me of all my tactical mistakes.

"Hi Tom, collect the laptop, see what's it connected to, try to keep it in one piece and sweep the place for evidence. What's the story at the bunker?" I asked, my voice as smooth as silk. No need to let anyone know how churned up I was inside.

"You won't believe what we found, including another tango, sadly demised at this point. I'll fill you in back at the plane."

In faraway Washington, a more heated conversation was going on. On the big screen, Aire was looking and listening but keeping out of the conversation. He was still very much tied into the tactical visual channels on his own big screen, which showed the individual views of each Interpol officer and commando. To help make sense of the images, small data boxes below each image identified the sender and a running dialogue line whenever they spoke. Typically, the Americans had limited their viewing feed to just one camera on each of the ATVs and Captain Riley's bodycam. They had also removed Arie's face from their view. The president held up one long, manicured hand, stopping the argument between the heads of the NSA and FBI in its stride.

"Frank, Roger, can it. Bridget, what can we expect from this point?" she asked, brushing her hair away from her creased face. The two directors stopped their argument as if a button had been pressed, sitting still but still glaring at each other. For once, Julius Bronstein was glad he had remained silent. It was a righteous argument but perhaps not the one for this moment.

"Madam President, the Israelis will take control of the prisoners under the jurisdiction of Interpol. All evidence they have collected will be processed, then I expect it will be disseminated across the Intelligence community with some speed. I doubt they will release any details to the press; that's not Arie's style, nor Anthony's, if the truth be known."

"No American presence?"

"No, not unless we send Anna Bernstein or someone else back to represent us."

"Do it. Roger, are you okay with that?"

"Yes, Madam President, she has been very effective working with Interpol. Good call, General. I'll get right on it." And he stood, nodded to the president, and left the room.

CHAPTER 85

The camera feed from the cavernous hold of the C-17 had been cut, and as the ponderous jet climbed back to cruising altitude, I looked around the hold, noticing that we now had different groups formed. The brother and bin Azaria sat hunched, almost as if they were praying, far back in the aircraft, the Israelis were grouped towards the front, and Tom and his crew were sitting opposite, most with their eyes closed. That just left the Arab prisoner, who was sitting separately opposite the brother and bin Azaria, and Pete, the Boss, and me. The Israeli Colonel stutter-stepped as the aircraft flew through some turbulence and joined us in the middle of the seating.

"Colonel, I'd like a report on what happened in the bunker." Sharp, direct, and straight to the point. Pure military tonality, superior to assumed junior, only, in this case, the Boss outranked everyone on the plane all added together. He didn't show any sign that he had been bruised by the Colonel's tonality, just motioned to a seat next to me and waited for him to sit down. Pete started to get up to move away to give us privacy, but the Boss motioned him down.

"Certainly, Colonel, my pleasure. The microwave detector on our ATV registered the two Arabs when they opened their bunker door, and the infrared sensors gave us a positive position, which we drove to, timing it so that the two Arabs would get to the tent before we stopped. We cleared the bunker, then searched it for intelligence material, of which we found plenty. We have some laptops, microwave and satellite communicators, and some small arms. Once we had secured the bunker, I sent two troops to assist the captain and back you up if necessary." The Colonel looked stony-faced and slightly unhappy. I wondered why.

"What happened to the third man?" The Boss looked back to where Tom and our people sat slumped in the red webbing seats, all sleeping by the looks of it, then back at the Colonel.

"Unfortunately, we were unable to take him prisoner, as he insisted on trying to kill Tom. He tried very hard, so to speed things up, we put a bullet or two in him. That was after Tom bent the knife held at his throat back into the Arab; it was fun to watch but, as you can imagine, under the circumstances, a possible diversion." He raised his eyebrows in question; the Colonel lost some of his aggression, seemed to fight some internal battle, then looked back at the Boss.

"Did you mine the bunker?" he asked.

"Yes. Next person or persons in will get quite a surprise." The Colonel nodded, agreeing with the Boss's tactics. Once again, I had to remind myself that this Colonel lived in a country that was literally fighting for its very survival every single day. And he was usually at the very sharp end of that fight.

"What will you do with the intelligence you have collected?" he asked, his body relaxing just a fraction suggesting that he was getting more comfortable with what had transpired back at the terrorist camp. The Boss looked at him, turned to look at me, then looked over to where Tom lay sprawled. He turned his head to look at bin Azaria. "I haven't worked it all out in detail yet, but I think keeping bin Azaria and the brother together will facilitate getting what we need out of him. The other prisoner I expect Arie will handle. The Americans will want everything tomorrow, but again, we need to get what we need, not just what they want. To be honest, I'll be guided by Arie on that; his experience is far greater than mine when it comes to it. Will that be okay with you?" The Boss turned to look at the Colonel, whose green eyes flared in the sunlight that was coming in through one of the few portholes in the side of the fuselage. It made him look like a witch!

"Colonel, I am happy with you deferring to Mr. Rosenberg, but I will have to report to my commander at some stage, and she will expect hard details." The Boss nodded. He understood both the military and political hierarchies from working on both sides of the street.

"Okay, let's leave the rest until we land, and I will make sure you are included in every decision we make." He suddenly tensed, reached into a pocket, and pulled out a satellite phone.

"Colonel Anthony. Yes, general, we are on our way back. The camera feed?" he said, looking towards the bulkhead where the camera was mounted. He smiled, looked at me, then across the seats to where the Brother and bin Azaria sat. "No idea why it isn't working, general, but we have bin Azaria, one of his men, and a few bits and pieces of his technology." He listened intently over the whine of the four massive engines as they propelled the aircraft through the top of the troposphere, just below the boundary layer.

"Yes, general, that's a great idea; we'll wait for her arrival before we start the interrogations. Our Interpol geeks will work on the electronics. I'm having all three of them transported to Israel as we speak. Thank you, General. You'll be the first to know." And he snapped the handset closed, lowered the stubby aerial, and smiled. "That was the president's military liaison, General Saunders. They were concerned something had happened as we went dark on them. No idea why," he said, a smile in his eyes as he looked over at Tom sleeping like a baby. "They are sending Anna back, so they have representation at the table when we interrogate bin Azaria and his friend." I nodded. Having Anna back would be nice; as well as being smart and quick, she was also a balance for the testosterone in the room. It was looking like we would have quite a crowd, and I started to work on how to manage it. Then I had an idea.

"We have an office in Tel Aviv?" I asked the Boss. He nodded silently, trying to look through me to get at what I was thinking. We had the usual admin staff backed up with two investigators, neither of whom I had worked with. "We need a secure facility, multiple rooms, linked comms, first-class security, proper interpreters, catering, beds, all the mod cons. How about getting our office and Arie to set something up?" He nodded, hooded his eyes in thought, then reached for his satellite phone again. He stood up and, working his back from side to side, walked cautiously back towards the ramp.

"Arie, can you do me a favor? This is still a police action, and I'd like to keep it that way for as long as possible. Jessica has had a rare good thought," he said, looking back at me with a grin. "She suggests we set up a facility in Tel Aviv using the resources of our Interpol office there. Large space, several secure sections, food, beds, electronics, you know what we need; we can get all our people to you when you have a location." He listened for a minute or two, nodded twice, then turned back towards us. "Yes, I'll tell her. See you soon." He walked back and took his seat in the red webbing, which was anything but comfortable for the normal body shape, having been designed for a parachutist wearing their pack and their equipment.

"Arie says hello, well done, and yes, that is a good idea," he said as he sprawled, looking more like a vagrant than the head of a section of the world's largest and most distributed police force. I could only smile back, so I started to plan how I would manage multiple interrogations and the intelligence dump at the same time. The Boss cut into my thinking. "Jessica, there's a number of factors we have to think about. The first is Amira." I looked at him. The use of my first name suggested we were having a private, personal conversation. And I had not been thinking about Amira for some time.

"What about Amira?"

"One idea we had was for her to get to a suitable lab and start working on a retro-nano bug so we can get gas back online." I nodded; we had discussed that before launching into this current operation.

"When you look at the whole of what we have here, she might be involved in uncovering the refugee women, as well as working in the lab. And then there's this Michele character."

"Yes, it could get messy. But what are you thinking?" The fact that Amira and Michele had been lovers, as well as co-developers of both the nano bugs and the code that had brought down the Net, was a concern, especially as Michele seemed to have evolved into a gun for hire in the coding and hacking world, and we could count on some of her work has been in the black market. We were, after all, Interpol, and we had a reputation to preserve. The Boss rubbed the back of his head with his hands, still covered in dirt and smoke streaks from his encounter in the bunker.

"I think we have to view the reconstruction of the nano bugs as a high-risk, high-security exercise; it needs to be off campus, secured, and totally locked down. And we need separate teams working on the bugs and the code. What would you suggest?" He turned to face me, looking like he needed a week's sleep. But I knew this man; he would go as hard and as far as it took to get the job done, and he would continue to lead from the front.

"Well, when you put it that way, we need a security blanket over the whole operation, state-level resources, and backup, and we need to be able to isolate any communication to and from wherever we set them up. Okay, so far?"

"Yes. And if you are thinking of Arie and Israel, remember the initial work was done in the secured facility of their university, and no one detected what the work was really about until after the attacks last month. And that includes the Israelis."

"You're suggesting they have a mole or two in the lab?"

"Did have, for sure, not certain now, have to ask Arie."

"But there's a bigger issue here. We are police—we need to think about what is—and what is not—in our jurisdiction."

"I agree. And I was waiting for that penny to drop. I think we should hand Amira back over to Arie with a copy of the work the geeks have done so far; they are a nation-state that we trust to work out what to prioritize and how to go about it. They can make all the political decisions on who gets what and when leaving us right out of the decision chain. Then we take the terrorists through a proper interrogation with a view to prosecuting in the world court; then concentrate on fulfilling our mandate with respect to the attacks. With Shetani out of the equation, and the French supporting the prince they found to head up Arabia, it very much leaves us free to keep searching for the women who were used at the pointy end, as well as the people involved in the original hacks back in the two thousands. You know, the ones that got into our systems and set us up for failure."

"The monks will have the best shot at that. I vote that you and I handle the interrogations with Anna and send the geeks back with Indigo to the monks and let them work the IT side as far as they can. It was the monks, after all, who broke through the black holes and found the transmissions between bin Azaria and the secretary of state."

"If they'll have us back." He chuckled at some inner joke, but his words had sent vivid images of the attack we had experienced on the small dock outside the hidden monk's cavern rippling through my mind.

"Good point. But we have Indigo on our side, so at the very least, we should get a hearing."

"Yes. Wake me when we land." And with that, he rested his head back in the netting and closed his eyes. I looked around the hold, put the location of everyone in my mind for the last time, then closed my eyes. But I kept my hand on my pistol, just in case.

CHAPTER 86

There are over thirteen thousand FBI special agents serviced by some three thousand intelligence, administrative and legal staff spread across fifty-six field offices, just within the continental United States. Like every other government department, the advent of digitization and the Internet of Everything forced major changes to the way they traditionally carried out their investigative work. Sadly, that had led to younger and younger computer-and technology-literate agents and less and less experienced-based investigators who could easily wear the leather out on a pair of shoes in one week seeking information via person-to-person interviews and driving thousands of miles in search of the truth.

The suggestion that had been made by Anna six days ago to the director of the FBI about taking an "old school" approach had made its mark and using the information that had been gathered on the pilot of the A-10 Warthog that had bombed West Point, a hundred field agents armed only with notebooks and sharpened pencils had spread out across her history all the way back to her arrival in the United States as a refugee from Turkey.

The FBI knew her family, knew what she had done in every year of her schooling, who her teachers were, what sports she played, all the way from fourth grade through to getting her masters at Stanford, the same year she competed in a dual test pilot program with both the Air Force and the navy. That she had developed into one of the best pilots in the

Air Force and then successfully transitioned to the civilian contractor mode spoke both of her skill and temperament.

Her family had completely disappeared the year she graduated from the Air Force Academy. The whole family had traveled overseas on a celebratory holiday, but only the pilot had returned to the US. The FBI, using the resources of both Interpol and local authorities, tracked the family as they moved from country to country, doing all the things holidaymakers around the world did, sightseeing, eating at little cafes and restaurants, going on tours, and just generally chilling out until they literally disappeared one day from their hotel accommodation, all bills paid, in Northern France. The fact that it happened some nine years prior to the investigation did make some details a little vague, just like the memories of the hotel staff.

Using cables connected to laptops, the FBI was able to plug into different computers and databases and recover an amazing number of receipts and bookings, which simply illustrated a happy family of five moving from place to place at a very relaxed pace.

Then "poof!"

Two adults and two children just disappeared off the map—literally, as if sucked up by an alien spaceship.

Roger Winslow read the report summary, not only frustrated but, in a small way, amazed at how professional the disappearance had been. From a records point of view—car licenses, vehicle registrations, payment of service bills like electricity, gas, taxes, and the like had been paid out of a local bank account for over sixteen months after the family had disappeared until the funds had been expended. Then, and then only some months later, did anyone try to find where the family was. The house was owned in the name of a company that went into liquidation two weeks before the money ran out. So, it was simply left as an empty shell, which the banks and service companies fought over for the value of the unpaid bills and the interest.

The empty shell still held furniture, hundreds of dead letters, and other mail, but not a single shred of personal effects, not even fingerprints or DNA. The house had been professionally cleaned every month by a prepaid contractor on the basis that it would eventually be sold. If it struck the contractor as funny as the lack of personal belongings, what did they care? Because of the nature of the long-term contract, he had added in a sufficient puff to more than making the job profitable, and he had been paid in advance every month by the same bank that paid all the other bills.

The FBI had seen the bank as a primary source of information on the family— right up until they had been shown the documents that had set up the account and realized they had already collected all the data they were going to get because of the license, social security number, and references were all the same, genuine but now defunct, as in no longer listed on any official database.

They had collected hard copies of the report cards for the three children and numerous other documents as "proof of life," but nothing pointed to where they were now. Neighbors had been interviewed, and the pilot's professional life pulled apart day by day, and still, nothing pointed to who she really was and where she may be now.

And the really frustrating thing, from the FBI's point of view, was that they had excellent quality photos and videos of the pilot from around age fourteen in yearbooks, internet videos, and official military documents. As well as the DMV of four states, voting records (Democrat), and even military award ceremonies, where she had been awarded medals or certificates of competence. They had her name. Or at least the one she had used until she disappeared after setting the Hog off on its merry autonomous way to attack West Point.

And as for the woman identified as "Helen," whose primary data had been supplied by Amira from her recovered personal files, no face in any facial recognition database or record in any country associated with Interpol made a match. Nothing of any value had been recovered from the house she had lived in, not even her fingerprints or DNA. Another mystery woman, and at least twenty to twenty-five years older than the others—from the description given by Amira, she was at least mid-thirties when she had dropped her off in Israeli to be adopted.

Roger Winslow sat back in his seat, tapping the large report in front of him, thinking he needed another approach. Traditional policing had a simple mantra— means, method, and opportunity—but that relied on having a suspect from which to work from. In this case, they had hundreds of pages of history on the pilot, photos, and anecdotal stories about Helen, but nothing on either of them for the last five or six years. The computer hack that had shut down the internet saw to that, plus he suspected Anthony's famous digital "black holes" had been used to cover every member of the refugee team.

He had the Interpol team set up to examine all the evidence they had gathered at the desert campsite; he had agents in the field, and he had every government agency working on finding anything that might relate to the attacks.

He would be patient. He would be positive. And with that last thought, he picked up the volume of evidence and threw it across the room in frustration.

CHAPTER 87

The Boss stood; everyone else in the conference room ringed outside by Israeli soldiers in full combat gear sat, mostly uncomfortable on the small metal chairs. They formed a circle, so everyone could see everyone else without turning their heads, and for once, there wasn't a single presence of electronic equipment in evidence. On the contrary, a massive sign on one wall said, "הרהזא! םישרומםיינורטקלאםירישכמןיא, חטבואמומוטאןקתמוהז. שוע." I wondered how many years of jail time I would serve if I breached the no electronics rule, then forgot about it as the Boss started to talk.

"Firstly, thank you, Colonel, for your excellent performance in bringing down Shetani and his mercenaries and for your support in getting Mohammad bin Azaria and his henchmen." The Israeli Sgen Aluf, head of the Shayete 104 commando troop, looked anything else but happy, the stoic look on his face giving nothing away. "Colonel, Tom, I'm going to ask you both to leave at this point and pass onto your men and women our grateful thanks for excellent work." Tom, who had been forewarned by Pete that this would happen, stood, smiled, looked directly at the Boss, and saluted. He walked out behind the Israeli commando, whose body language was anything but compliant.

"We now enter a difficult phase of our investigation, and I'm going to hand over to Captain Riley to summarize where we are at and what we will do next." And he sat down in the seat vacated by Tom and looked expectantly at me. I looked around the faces I was now so familiar with, Indigo with his little smile, as if all was right with the world; Anna, a little grim-faced, probably still lagged from her flight back across the Atlantic; Pete, relaxed, although anyone who knew him would easily spot his eyes casually scanning every inch of the room. Arie, looking at all his years, the past weeks had taken a heavy toll on him personally, yet the sparkle in his grey eyes was encouragement in itself. General Bridget Saunders, now dressed in mufti, looks like someone's mother but is not really able to disguise her military bearing. She had flown over with Anna, an afterthought by the president, who was feeling distinctly not in control of her country or the events that were unraveling at such a frantic rate.

The room we were in had been organized by the local Interpol office in Tel Aviv, and in recognition of this, Senior Agent Beth Arezzo was also sitting in, and as I had had the pleasure of briefing her just an hour ago, once again I had been impressed by the caliber of agents Interpol attracted. At just thirty-two, she ran one of the busiest offices in the area and worked under the same duress as every other Israeli citizen from the constant rocket attacks on the city. She was married, had a child, and dressed like a fashion model, currently wearing a tight red sheath with a purple-and-gold scarf dropping between her arms. A lightweight cotton jacket in peach completed the ensemble, no doubt concealing her weapon and credentials. She also spoke five languages like a native. I stood up, breathed in deeply, held my hands loosely in front, and relaxed as far as I could.

"We have Mohammad bin Azaria and his lawyer secured and under guard; we have left the Jesuit priest to his own devices, but we have asked him to remain to be debriefed sometime tomorrow. The electronics and intelligence we recovered from both successful attacks are now being examined, and we expect the first summary within the next hour. The purpose of this meeting is to determine exactly what we will do from here on and who will be responsible for each activity.

"While we have used paramilitary tactics against the terrorists and the mercenaries, this is, still, essentially a police action. Interpol has been commissioned by several countries as well as those represented here to discover and bring to justice the persons responsible for the attacks that were initiated last month in Italy, Jerusalem, Abu Dhabi, the United

States, and, more recently, the international consortia that controlled the International Space Station.

"Our investigations uncovered the mercenaries led by Shetani, who was responsible for at least two mass bombings, the destruction of the Arabia oil field, and the destruction of some fifty oil and gas pipelines and fracking sites. Needless to say, every country impacted by these attacks has requested us to add their support to our mandate, which we have accepted on the condition that all political interference be withheld until a satisfactory outcome has been achieved."

"And what, exactly, do you think a 'satisfactory outcome' looks like?" asked the General in a tone more suited to the parade ground than a meeting of the minds. I turned slightly to look at her and sensed the Boss flexing his shoulders, a sure sign he was going to jump in, so I paused in my reply to let him do so.

He didn't.

I continued.

"For some days, we have been working closely with one of the refugees who was groomed to participate in the development of the technology weapons used in the attacks. She quit and ran years before the attacks were launched. Apart from helping us to uncover the internet destruction, she had records of her time with some of the other participants, who we are now identifying and tracking. When you look at the possibility of combining what the Jesuit priest can tell us, what your secretary of state can tell us, and the intelligence we are now unraveling, we may well get a better understanding of how to find the refugees who did participate in the attacks."

"You'll have to go through the president to get to the Secretary," the General barked, "and you'll have to go through me to get to the president."

"We understand the circumstances. We have been briefed by both Roger and Julius." The General seemed to be thinking about something; she nodded to herself and tilted her head to one side. She looked directly at me with an intensity I felt in my bones. She held up one manicured hand, her perfect nails showing just a hint of clear polish, and ticked off her fingers, one by one.

"So, firstly, you have identified and taken out of play a mercenary terrorist crew in Canada responsible for shutting off the oil and gas pipelines as well as destroying the fracking sites across northern America and Canada. Secondly," as another finger flicked up, "you seemed to have solved the UAV attacks on the sports arenas, at least in the US." I held her eyes, determined to hear everything she had to say before I acknowledged anything.

"Then you have masterminded an attack on Arabia, forcing the third regime change in two weeks, destroying the mercenary terrorist leader Shetani in the process." She watched me for any reaction but saw none. I played poker with people so hard to read you had to actually rely on the cards you were dealt! A wan smile crossed her eyes, her thin lips struggling to follow.

"Fourthly, you have identified, located, and captured the banker and prime suspect in the organization of all the attacks and currently have him here somewhere under guard." I held her eyes as hard as I could, not giving any sign of acknowledgement. The silence in the room was deafening. I could almost hear everyone breathing. She wasn't exactly attacking us, but her tonality suggested she was after something, but I wasn't sure what it might be. I nodded, just once, to see what she would say next. Her hand opened up so all fingers could be seen as she ticked off the last on her list.

"The problem I'm having is seeing exactly where a police action starts and stops and a military one takes over." The tension in the room ratcheted up a notch, and I saw Pete stiffen out of the corner of my eye and Indigo visibly lean forward as if to pounce on the General. Before I could answer, the Boss stood up again, rolled his shoulders as if preparing for a physical fight, and motioned for me to take my seat.

"General, as you would know, my unit within Interpol is authorized to engage and utilize military forces as and when we see fit. Our standing guard is made up of US Special Forces on loan to us from the Pentagon, as you well know. The two attacks in the desert were led by an Israeli Colonel supported by the Israeli commandos, whom you have been introduced to, and Interpol simply provided an observer in each of those two attacks. And before you point it out, yes, we had more boots on the ground when we took down bin Azaria. The situation was judged to warrant it. And don't forget the Canadians and all the other countries who have used lethal force in attacking the various arms of Shetani's network of mercenaries, including your very own, on several occasions, all without any Interpol presence." The look he gave the General was anything but contrite; the edges of his face would have cut glass. If there was one thing the Boss hated, it was Monday morning quarterbacking. The general, to her credit, immediately sat back as far as her little metal chair would allow and shook her head.

"Colonel, I apologize if it seemed I was attacking your tactics. I fully realize we would not be as far down the comeback road as we are without the excellent efforts of Interpol and your team. I was just trying to see where the line in the sand was. Please put it down to bad manners and bloody-mindedness." The Boss visibly relaxed, and with that one simple gesture, the tension drifted out of the room. Pete sat back, Indigo relaxed, and even I felt some existential crisis had been avoided. But I still did not know what was behind her verbal attack.

"General, we're all a little wound up, and I suspect if you have had as little sleep as my people, more than just a little tired. The fact remains, and I freely admit it, that we have used national troops for various parts of our investigation, with the overt approval and under the direct control of each country involved. In the case of the mercenaries, we provided the intelligence to some sixteen countries, and each country then dealt with them as they saw fit—the US being one of those countries. All within our mandate. And I took the measure of checking in with the director of your FBI, NSA, and CIA, and even yourself and the president, as warranted before we initiated any direct action." He flexed his shoulders again, looked down at his scuffed boots, raised his eyes in surprise, then looked up back at the group.

"So as for a satisfactory outcome, while we have involved the politicians at every step so far, what we do next will be determined by what evidence and data we can analyze, and which direction it suggests we move in. And to answer your unasked question, no, we may not collaborate with any one nation-state at that point. The next moves will be an Interpol police action, full stop."

"You suspect a nation-state of being the mastermind behind the attacks, or at least covert support of the banker?" she asked.

"We have from the very start. The fact that the earliest attack on the computer systems in the US and Europe took place on the back of the Y2K debacle, now over twenty-five years ago, which would make the women we are chasing just out of nappies at that time, means that someone was setting all this up well before the use of the refugees was even thought of. Or, at the very least, concurrently. We have a statement from the Jesuit priest that the discussion regarding taking the children occurred sometime around twenty years ago, we can't be definite, but we might get closer to the actual date once we have a chat with him tomorrow.

"Whatever that outcome, someone paid a lot of talented people for decades setting all this up. Look at the chronology—backdoors were set up in secure systems; tactical munitions were stolen from secured storage and transshipped around the world; aircraft and UAVs were either stolen or purchased outright and secreted in—we think, but can't prove yet—Turkey, a decommissioned nuclear missile base is taken over, refurbished, extended, all under the noses of both state and federal authorities; state-of-the-art technology weapons are developed out in the open initially in at least two world-class universities we know of, then moved underground and perfected. In fact, we have evidence that an early version of the nano bugs that took out the world's oil pipelines were trialed off the coast of Nova Scotia in full public view! The resources needed to support all this were more than just a handful of talented women. No doubt they played a part, but someone else played a much bigger one for nearly thirty years."

"How many women from the refugee camps do you think were involved?"

"Good question. In fact, a great question. Indigo?" The Boss turned, then yielded the floor to our Italian head-of-station in Italy. His thickset body was in direct contrast to the Boss's, but you couldn't miss his natural swagger or, for a change, his perfect English. He must be wanting to impress the general!

"General, Colonel, good people, our computer experts, with the help of Anna and the FBI, have run simulations working backwards from the ground zeros of the attacks, based on the real-time mirror-attacks both the colonel and the captain ran. Allowing for the Hercules and the UAV to have been housed in Turkey, adjacent to the terrorist base we discovered there, we estimate one woman pilot, one engineer, and or one technology specialist. There would have to have been a support crew at some point to keep the aircraft in flyable condition and the bombs and missiles maintained, but they could have been locally hired from the airport. That is being ascertained as we speak by local authorities."

"Two to three women for the attack on the Vatican and the Dome of the Rock!" the general exclaimed, her tonality dripping with disbelief and sarcasm.

"Yes, at a minimum, but easily doable with the right equipment and training."

"The Grand Mosque? Lloyd's of London? The nuclear attack on the Arabian oil field? The bombings in Avion? The UAV attacks in England and Germany?" Deftly, the general had held up her fingers again, counting off the attacks. She stopped at five, looking very hard at Indigo. He wasn't ruffled one bit by the intensity or harsh tone, choosing to smile and bow ever so slightly towards her.

"General, I know this is on the very edge of believable, but then, I would suggest if we had come to you a month ago with an outline that these attacks were even possible, I believe you would have laughed us out of the room as conspiracy theorists." The general latched her fingers together and shut her eyes for a minute, obviously getting herself under control. There was something behind her aggression; I wished I could divine it.

"Colonel, I apologize. I am letting all this get to me when I should be listening to your reports and helping you move forward. Please forgive me." Indigo bowed slightly again, a huge smile causing his whole face to light up.

"*Generale, per favore, capisco il tuo dolore, questo ha causato a tutti noi un po 'di dolore, e noicomprendiamo il tuo.*"

"*Colonnello, lei è troppogentile. Perfavore, continuate. Dovreicongratularmi con lei per isuoieccellentisforzi, non appendendo il mio dolore personale al collo.*" We all smiled, Italian being a second language for all of us except Indigo and were warmed by the general's words.

"So, General, to answer your questions, we believe that the order of battle at the Grand Mosque was mercenaries, Lloyd's was the women, the nuclear attack on the Arabian oil fields was the mercenaries using a weapon developed by the women, Avion was the mercenaries, and lastly, the UAV attacks were mercenaries using weapons designed by the women." She nodded, the list obviously lining up with one she had in her head.

"Just humor me for a minute. What makes you so sure Avion was the mercenaries?"

"The investigators found no bodies in the burnt-out trucks. Mercenaries are not known for self-sacrifice or becoming suicide bombers." She nodded again, then seemed to relax a little. She played the finger game again.

"How about the attack on West Point, the Alaskan pipeline, the Australian gas terminal, and the Russian/Chinese pipeline attacks?"

"West Point was the women, as was the space station. The pipelines, gas terminals, and fracking sites were mercenaries using weapons provided by the women."

"You see a distinct difference in the roles and responsibilities here?"

"Yes, we do. The women provided the weapons, the hardware, and possibly the tactical plan, although, to be frank, we can't prove that, and our best strategists have summarized that our nation-state player might eventually get the credit for that. We do not believe the women played any physical role in any bombings, truck-based UAV attacks, or oil and gas system attacks other than, and not yet proven, the design, manufacture, and fitting of the UAV bombs in the trucks and possibly communication – as in giving the 'go' order. In a sense, you have them as the planners, designers, inventors, creators, and possibly the manufacturers, although we have yet to track that down. The mercenaries were the hired hands that did all the on-the-ground dirty work.

"And at a stretch, if the women were using artificial intelligence or remote control for the aircraft attacks and never physically present, it could be very difficult to convict them." I started to see what might be lingering behind her animosity towards the way we had developed our case so far. I looked at the Boss; he saw me out of the corner of his eye, nodded minutely, then gestured to Indigo. Indigo nodded and sat down. I stood up. My next words were going to be critical if we were to keep the Americans behind us and onside.

"General, let's take the case of the Hog pilot. We have her on video doing an engineering pre-flight in the hangar, gearing up, entering the cockpit, starting the Hog, and taxiing out to the holding area. From that point on, it could be argued that she left the aircraft—maybe or maybe not under her own auspices—in ground idle and had no notion of the intended attack. She could claim that she was paid to get the Hog to the holding point and nothing more—or that she was coerced out of the cockpit and taken prisoner. When she left the aircraft, as far as we are able to prove at this time, the armaments were not live; the safety pins had not been pulled; the inflatable was not in use, and all she had done to that point was get the aircraft into position as per her filed flight plan." The general looked gob-smacked, this alternative narrative on the actions of the Hog pilot who had caused so much death and destruction at West Point obviously never having occurred to her or anyone in her orbit. But we were Interpol—and we worked to policing mandates that required absolute proof to support a conviction in the world court or the court of any civilized country on whose behalf we were operating, not a military organization that could shoot first and ask questions later. I wasn't going to let her off the hook.

"Take the case of the refugee child who was established in a home in Israel twenty-three years ago. Yes, she later developed nanotechnology that would be used by the terrorists to take out our oil and gas reserves. At the time she left the program, she had successfully demonstrated a genuine ecological solution to oil spills. She developed a system that was supposedly for environmental reasons. She left years before the final development of the nano weapons, played no part in it, and freely admits that she was a refugee who was taken out of the camps and placed in a normal home when she was but a child. It is the intel that she acquired during her time at various universities that we are now plumbing for information on some of the other players. But what, exactly, would you hold her guilty of?" The general looked like she had swallowed an apple whole; her whole body showed extreme stress, and I was afraid she would start to hyperventilate. Then the crisis passed, and she shook her head violently from side to side. Military training had its advantages.

"You cannot tell me that the woman that set up the Hog to attack West Point, killing thousands, not to mention the joint chief of staff, can get off scot-free?" She rose up to her full height, an impressive one meter eighty-eight, the look on her face enough to make a lesser person cringe.

"No, General, I'm not. I'm just putting it out there that we have a lot to do to prove beyond a shadow of a doubt the complicity and guilt of anyone involved in the attacks. And I'd like to add to what Colonel Kashasini said to us earlier. If you look at the attacks in the US critically, you really don't see a role for more than three women." I remained standing, held her icy stare, and braced myself for whatever might come. She seemed to be considering her options, but what was going on behind those icy eyes was hard to fathom.

"Captain, you graduated from our NCIS academy?" she asked, her voice frosty and hard-edged.

"Yes, General."

"And at that academy, were you exposed to the nightmare of what is now regarded as the 'Terrorist Laws'?"

"Yes, General. In fact, I helped write some of them after the attacks in Egypt on our Air Force base. If you remember, we had a medical facility there that specialized in burns and reconstruction. It was destroyed, killing all sixty of the doctors, nurses, and scientists there. The fact that it was someone else's sovereign soil, the base was not listed as a US military establishment, and the terrorists escaped initially over the border into Libya made it all the more difficult to prosecute a case."

"But you did get them and prosecute them?" she asked, knowing full well that I could not answer the question. Two reasons: I had signed a non-disclosure agreement issued by the Justice Department, the downside of that being thirty years in the stockade, no parole. The second reason was that NCIS had tracked them down using Special Forces on an illegal, unsanctioned mission that had resulted in a one hundred percent kill rate, with the small sample of proof recovered after the attack enough to justify prosecution but not lethal force. The whole sorry episode had thrown the military lawyers into turmoil, and to prevent anyone from ever uncovering anything about the retribution, it had been buried deep in the Pentagon files.

"General, as you well know, that prosecution caused a lot of debate in legal circles, and that was why we wrote the 'Terrorist Laws.' Cross border jurisdiction, arrest, and detention versus weapons-free, nation-state permissions, you know the content. And you also know I cannot answer your question." The general smiled for the first time, not much of one, but enough to crease her face somewhat.

"Well, as you know, under the 'Terrorist Laws,' it is perfectly legal to arrest someone on suspicion of aiding and abetting a terrorist act, providing comfort to identified terrorists, being suspected of arranging or planning a terrorist act, and the kicker, as far as I am concerned, physically or substantially providing materials or substances that were or could be used in a terrorist act. Now, if I am not wrong, Interpol operates under these laws, is that correct?" I looked at the Boss to see if he wanted to take this; he just stared blankly at the general, leaving me to my own devices.

"General, the laws under which we operate are those struck by the world court. And we are allowed to also act under those laws mandated by the countries who support us, providing such laws do not contravene any law of the world court. What's your point?" I asked, this time letting my voice have just a little edge. I was getting a little tired of all the legal mumbo jumbo. The Boss, Indigo, Anna, and I had discussed all the rules of engagement we would operate underway back at the start of this horror show; it should be no surprise to the Americans, or anyone else for that matter. At least she had the good grace to sit back in her chair and hold her hands out as a sign of acquiescence.

"Captain, again, my apologies. The idea of the Hog pilot getting off on a technicality riled me up somewhat. Let's get back to the main conversation. If I have heard you correctly, you are saying the total number of women used in these attacks is, what, five or six?" she couldn't disguise her lack of belief, but there was no longer a bite in her tonality.

"Yes, we are. At least in minimum terms. Your own special forces reported on their clean-up of the silo and the discovery of the helicopter in the underground hangar. The documents of the local municipality show that the restoration was done in plain view; only one woman was identified on the applications. She no longer exists, of course, but the local workers whom your FBI questioned said they only ever saw the one woman and that the work was completed over a year and a half ago. The physical records exist, but the electronic ones are gone."

"And we have no satellite footage of the data cable channel being dug or the underground hangar." I nodded; this was the real sticking point. The terrorists had used their black hole technology on the entire site and out to one hundred miles from the site to hide everything that had happened for over two plus years from any intelligence agency. Maybe.

"No, General, not at this time." And I left it at that, happy to have an ace up my sleeve. In this case, Amira's belief that she could reverse engineer the code she had been sent from Michele and reveal the actions of the terrorists.

"This 'satisfactory outcome'—what exactly is it?" she asked, folding her arms. "We view the capturing and disbandment of the mercenary terrorists and the banker as a significant phase in this case. Our next objective is to interrogate those captured and ascertain their roles in the attacks. At the same time, we will analyze all the captured data and mine all the intelligence opportunities we have now within our grasp. Then we will sit down and work out what to do and how to do it. It's that simple."

"And that would be your 'satisfactory outcome.'"

"For this phase, yes. We may have to rejig our approach to what we do next depending on the intelligence we might have. We might require different resources and engage with different technologies. We do not forget anything, just thinking through what we might need to finish the job." The general remained still, her head bowed slightly, a neutral expression on her face.

"How long before you decide on this future action?" she asked. I looked at the Boss, and he nodded.

"We are going to take an official break of twenty-four hours to rest our people and let things settle, then we expect to have the intelligence sorted within three days and a comprehensive plan in another two." The general nodded twice, stood up, looked around the room, and probably saw the same tiredness in everyone's face that I saw—at least, I hoped so. Arie stood up, nodded to the Boss, and smiled at me, making me feel warm inside.

"General," he said, "why don't you and I have a chat and let these good people do what they have to do?" and he gently took the general's arm and walked her out of the room. The bright shaft of sunlight that suddenly flooded through the open door caused me to shield my eyes with one hand. I had forgotten the time, the day, and, for that matter, the month.

Time to calm things down a little.

Look for the next exciting book in this trilogy

Tears of Hope

Tears of Wonder

Tears of Joy

The Island of Tears

CPSIA information can be obtained
at www.ICGtesting.com
Printed in the USA
JSHW030448100323
38666JS00007B/1

9 798889 450009